ROBERTA GELLIS
Romantic Times Award-winning Author

"When a novel of historical romance has Roberta Gellis' name on it . . . readers know they're getting a meticulously researched, expertly told story full of passion and adventure."
—**Waldenbooks'** *Lovenotes*

A TAPESTRY OF DREAMS

"Splendid . . . aglow with color, romance, and rich in historical detail!"
—**Jennifer Wilde,**
author of *Angel in Scarlet*

"Roberta Gellis has skillfully woven another marvelous medieval tale."
—**Beatrice Small,**
author of *All the Sweet Tomorrows*

"Intense . . . vibrant . . . alive!" —*Affaire de Coeur*

"First-rate romance in an intriguing historical setting."
—*New York Daily News*

THE ROPE DANCER

"An exquisite novel from the pen of a master storyteller."
—*Rave Reviews*

"An extremely entertaining and delightful tale."
—**Rebecca Brandewyne,**
author of *The Outlaw Hearts*

"Beautifully told . . . full of surprises . . . Roberta Gellis never disappoints!"
—*Affaire de Coeur*

FIRES OF WINTER

"Fascinating and well-written . . . a romance with substance."
—*Knoxville News-Sentinel*

"Five Stars . . . *Fires of Winter* is the best a book can be . . . I dare anyone not to be hooked!" —*Affaire de Coeur*

"A masterpiece . . . fantastic and fascinating . . . Roberta Gellis transports readers into the hearts and minds of her hero and heroine."
—*Rave Reviews*

MASQUES OF GOLD

ROBERTA GELLIS

JOVE BOOKS, NEW YORK

MASQUES OF GOLD

A Jove Book / published by arrangement with
the author

PRINTING HISTORY
Jove trade paperback edition / September 1988

ISBN: 0-515-09816-7

Jove Books are published by The Berkley Publishing Group,
200 Madison Avenue, New York, New York 10016.
The name "JOVE" and the "J" logo
are trademarks belonging to Jove Publications, Inc.

PRINTED IN CANADA

10 9 8 7 6 5 4 3 2 1

PROLOGUE

"**D**ID HE TELL YOU WHERE?"
  Robert FitzWalter gripped his henchman's tunic, shaking him in rage, for he knew from the man's terrified expression as he approached that something had gone wrong.

"He is dead, my lord," the man replied, his voice trembling, his face sallow with fear. "I never touched him. I only took him down below and showed him the instruments—and then I asked him where it was. He never spoke. His eyes rolled up and . . . and he died."

FitzWalter had released his hold on the man while he spoke. Now he struck him with such force that blood burst from his nose and he fell to the floor. He curled his body as if he expected to be kicked, but his master did not come closer; he was looking at the wooden wall of his chamber. That wall had once been stone and covered by rich tapestries, before FitzWalter had fallen foul of King John. He had been accused of treason and forced to flee the country, and out of spite and an enmity that went back many years the king had razed Baynard's Castle.

1

Then, like a miracle, his pardon had been included in the settlement of the king's quarrel with the Church, and no sooner had he arrived in London when he was told that there was a copy of John's privy seal to be had. FitzWalter ground his teeth. He was not certain what he could do with the king's seal, but it was the privy seal, the one John used for many private matters, including messages and orders he preferred to keep secret. Surely the seal could be used in some way to revenge himself on the king. Now it seemed to have slipped through his hands.

"Someone must know where it is," FitzWalter muttered. He paused, thinking, his small eyes narrowing even smaller, then said to his henchman, "Cut off his ears and some of his fingers. Break his arms and legs, and burn him here and there—whatever you would have done to make him talk. Then, tonight, drop his body by the front door of his shop. Whoever is there who knows where the seal is may take warning and bring William Bowles the answer we want."

Chapter 1

⁓⊱⊰⁓

THE HIGH, SHRILL SCREAM OF A YOUNG BOY ROSE THROUGH THE house, and Lissa leapt out the door of her chamber and down the stairs so fast that she was at the entrance before her husband's sons could come from the workroom behind the shop. The servant boy was pressed back against the door he had just opened, straining away from the body that had tumbled in when its support had been removed. Screams rose in Lissa also, but terror bound her throat too tight to free them. Not only was Peter dead, but he had been tortured.

Lissa put out her hand and clutched at the screaming boy's shoulder, more to steady herself than to silence the child, but he turned and buried his face in her skirt and was still. In the next moment she was thrust roughly aside.

"God! God!" Her eldest son-by-law's voice was thick with grief and shaking with fear, but he grasped his father's shoulders and ordered, "Edmond, help me."

The younger son bent to lift his father's feet, then uttered a muffled cry and turned aside to retch as the legs bent unnatural-

3

ly. Lissa gasped and looked away, freed by the sickness that nearly overwhelmed her from staring at her husband's mutilated body. In turn, the sickness was reduced to insignificance by a new wave of horror. Had her father committed this crime?

"Out of the way," young Peter snarled, pushing Lissa back into the shop and breaking her hold on the servant boy. "Go up to your chamber and stay there, you fool."

He turned away from Lissa then and growled something about "the guard coming before—" at his brother, but Lissa fled up the stairs without really listening. The notion that had seized her was too dreadful, too powerful, to allow room for any other problems.

Lissa had never completely understood why her father had forced her to marry Peter, a man thirty years older than herself and with two grown sons to be his heirs. Had her husband been childless, the marriage would have made some kind of sense because Peter de Flael was a skilled and successful goldsmith and very rich. Then, had she conceived a child, his wealth would have been hers and her child's when he died, which could not be many years in the future in the natural course of events. But with two young and healthy heirs already alive, the possession of Peter's wealth could not have been her father's purpose.

Lissa could almost have believed her father had arranged the marriage out of sheer spite, to punish her for periodically demanding that he find her a husband who could be a good partner for her after he died. But her father had transferred to Peter's control a far greater dowry than Lissa had ever expected to bring a husband. Of course, everything her father had would be hers eventually, since she was his only heir, but William Bowles was not the man to unloose his grasp on half a farthing while he was alive, much less the hundred marks he had paid over to Peter. Although Lissa still did not know the specific reason for the marriage, she had finally concluded that it was part of some business arrangement—and that Peter had somehow cheated her father.

It was all she could think of as she fled up the stairs and stood just inside the door of the solar with her arms crossed tightly over her breast, as if the grip could hold back her shudders of fear and revulsion. Peter had cheated William Bowles, and now Peter was dead.

Then Lissa closed her eyes and swallowed hard. I am a fool, just as young Peter said, she told herself firmly. I am building a whole castle of guilt out of two pebbles—two quarrels that I did not even hear clearly nor understand. She deliberately relaxed her arms, let her hands drop, and took a deep breath. Then she tried to fix her mind on what she must do next, but there was little to do. She could not even lay Peter out yet. Surely the alderman's officers would want to see him as he was when they found him.

She had not heard anyone go out to inform the alderman of the evil that had befallen their household, but Lissa did not doubt that young Peter would by now have sent Edmond. She thought she had been too locked into her own private horror to notice, and the question of her father's involvement rose again, but she fixed her mind on what her sons-by-marriage should be doing and what they might forget. Would Edmond have the sense to fetch a priest after he notified the alderman? But Peter was long dead. Would the priest be willing to shrive him? Would he be refused burial in consecrated ground if he was not shriven? Tears stung in Lissa's eyes. Poor Peter! Poor man, to come to such an end! No, she would not permit that. If young Peter and Edmond would not do it, she would find a priest who would say he believed Peter had been shriven and who would allow burial in holy ground.

She sobbed twice and then wiped her eyes. Lissa was sorry for Peter, grieved by the terrible death he had suffered, but she did not pretend to herself that she felt great sorrow at having lost him. She had not wanted to marry him, and they had not been man and wife for long enough to build affection. What was more, she no longer believed Peter had loved her, as she had thought when she was first told of the marriage. In fact, by now she had not the faintest idea why he had married her, although she had assumed when her father had ordered the marriage that Peter had proposed it because he desired her. The pleasant delusion had been supported at first by the exquisite betrothal gift Peter had sent—a necklet of golden dolphins with emerald eyes, leaping through a foam of tiny pearls. And the box in which the necklet had been presented was almost as beautiful as the gift itself, all carved and inset with different perfumed woods.

The gift had all but reconciled Lissa to the marriage, although she had had renewed doubts when she realized that Peter had added virtually nothing to the large dowry her father had provided. But at the wedding Lissa thought she had discovered the reason for that. It seemed that Peter had paid directly to her father what he should have added to her dowry. Lissa had been furious with William, but not with Peter, who had seemed willing to give up what he had the right to hold in trust for her and use himself until he died.

Because of Peter's seeming eagerness to have her, Lissa had thought that despite his age the marriage might be a good thing for her. It would be a pleasant change to live with a man who valued her. Her father had not. He had never forgiven her or her mother for the fact that she had been born a female. William had found her too useful to mistreat, even after her mother had died—and he was afraid of her uncles, who had beaten him nearly to death for striking her mother—but his cold distaste for her had never changed.

What would she do now that Peter was dead? She did not think she could stay in his house for more than a few days after his burial. Peter's sons hated her—and she did not know why that was so either. Perhaps they believed she would try to turn their father against them, but they must have known that was impossible. During the month she and Peter had been away at his small estate near Canterbury, she had come to realize that Peter did not love her at all.

She would have to go back to her father's house. Lissa found her hands were trembling and her whole body was ice cold. She discovered suddenly that she had not rid her mind of the fear that her father had done this dreadful thing. But the idea was ridiculous. Her father *could* not have done it. He was too fearful, too cautious, to take such measures no matter how great his rage and resentment. More likely it was that friend of his, Hubert de Bosco, who had been somehow involved in her father's relationship with Peter. Lissa shuddered again, one hand creeping up to press against her lips as she imagined the pain and terror her husband must have suffered at de Bosco's hands.

A scratch at the door made her jump and gasp. She whirled to face it, her eyes wide with fear, but when the scratch was repeated, she realized it was far too soft to herald the arrival of her sons-by-law. Neither of them would have been so gentle. It must be the maid, who had been roused and come in from the hut in the back. Peter had never permitted servants to live in the house because he feared they would steal the gold and jewels he kept. They were locked in strongboxes, but he had not considered that sufficient protection—not even against the old woman who had come with his first wife and served him for so many years.

"Come in." The words sounded in her mind, but only a faint croak passed her lips. Lissa cleared her throat and tried again. "Come in."

The door swung in, but the face that peered fearfully around it was not that of the maid. It was Witta, the little boy she had brought with her from her father's house because she was so sure her father would drive him out. She had found the child half starved and nearly frozen in a doorway. Although she knew it was foolish, that he might be a thief or an apprentice who had been dismissed by his master for bad behavior, she had taken him in. He would not tell her how he had come to be there, only his name, Witta, and he had sworn again and again that he was not a thief or a runaway but an honest boy looking for work.

The child's eyes were still enormous, and he was shaking. Instinctively, Lissa drew him in and patted his shoulder. "It is dreadful, but there is nothing for us to fear," she said, not really believing it. "Has the alderman sent his men? Am I wanted?"

"Master Peter never sent for the alderman," Witta whispered. "He and Master Edmond have harnessed the horse to the cart and carried out the strongboxes. I think they are going away."

"Going away?" Lissa repeated unbelievingly. "But their father—" She stopped because it was ridiculous to repeat what she and the boy both knew, that Peter had been cruelly murdered and it was incredible that the sons would do nothing. "Where is Master Peter—my husband?"

"They left him lying on the floor." The boy's chin trembled and he could not continue.

Lissa put both hands to her head and squeezed as if the pressure could push out what she had heard. She knew Witta could not be lying, but she could not believe what he said either. Her impulse was to rush down and see for herself what was happening, but she was afraid. And what could she do? Peter and Edmond would pay no attention to what she said and might be tempted to silence her so she could not set anyone on their trail.

"Quick," she said to the boy, "if they are in the back, go out the front. Run to Alderman Goscelin's house. I am sure he will remember that you are my servant. Tell him that Master Peter has been murdered, and—"

"And about young Master Peter and Edmond running away?" Witta asked, a malicious gleam diluting the fear in his eyes.

"N-no. No, do not say anything about them."

Lissa knew that young Peter and Edmond had relieved some of their rage over their father's marriage by tormenting the servant of their new mother-by-marriage. She kept the boy out of their way as much as possible, but, quite naturally, he disliked them. That knowledge suddenly presented Lissa with a much more rational explanation of their behavior than the one Witta had suggested and she, because she was still shaken, had accepted.

"You are a silly boy," she went on, more briskly and with a chiding note in her voice. "Master Peter and Master Edmond are not going away. I am sure they only wish to remove the strongboxes to a safe place. But I still think it wrong not to tell the alderman at once what has happened. Perhaps there was someone in the street who would remember men who passed bearing a burden, or perhaps someone heard a noise and looked out. Such memories might be lost and with them any clue to—"

Lissa stopped speaking abruptly and bit her lip. Did she want any clue to Peter's murderer discovered? What if the clue led— She did not finish the thought, just pushed the boy gently out of the room, whispering, "Go. Go."

She must put any notion of her father's or de Bosco's involvement out of her mind. Why should she blame them because of one small incident? It was true she had been surprised when her father had invited de Bosco to her wedding. Surprised, at least, until right after the ceremony when she had seen her father and his coarse and brutal friend hem Peter in, one on each side, and draw him away from the guests. That was when she guessed that her father had given her to Peter as part of some business arrangement from which he expected extraordinary profit, enough profit to compensate him for the loss of her services and her large dowry. She had also guessed that Peter was to fulfill his part immediately and that de Bosco was her timid father's threat.

It had annoyed Lissa that her father could not wait until they left the church. She felt her husband should remain beside her at that moment, and she had watched them through the group of well-wishers surrounding her and had seen Peter pass something into her father's hand. But surely that had been the money or jewels that should have been pledged to enlarge her dower portion. There must have been something missing from whatever Peter handed over, perhaps one particularly valuable jewel or some talisman that would open new trading sources or markets. Yes, that was reasonable and would explain both the arguments and that insane scene as she and Peter were on their way to Canterbury, when her father demanded they come to his house, insisted that she strip naked, and ordered his mistress to examine her clothing, even search through her hair.

Lissa's lower lip crept between her teeth again, but the grip was gentle, a sign of thought rather than fear. Considering her father's harelike nature and de Bosco's boarlike one, was it not far more likely that de Bosco had acted on his own if he had killed Peter? Doubtless he had had hopes of obtaining what Peter had promised her father and withheld. William was far more likely to lay a complaint with the king's justiciar and sue Peter than try to do him physical harm. Her eyes gleamed briefly and she released her lower lip to purse both in contemplation, but then she sighed and shook her head. No, her first idea was best: She must put both de Bosco and her father out of her mind. She was aware of William's cowardice, but others might not know how deep it ran, and any hint of de Bosco's connection to Peter's murder would lead right back to her father.

Besides, there was no necessary connection. Now that her shock had passed and she was able to think again, it was clear that if Peter had cheated her father, he had probably cheated others too. And there was the matter of usury as well. Perhaps Peter had lent money at too-high interest and some poor soul trapped by his greed had become desperate enough and bitter enough to want Peter to suffer agony as well as death. Lissa did not know for certain that Peter was a usurer, but nearly all goldsmiths lent money at interest—they called it a "fee" for their services, since usury was a sin. Cynically Lissa wondered if they thought changing the name of what they did could fool God. She hated that part of the goldsmiths' trade as much as she loved the beauty they created with their skill.

She had been dreading the day when Peter would demand that she take up her share of the burden of the business. Unable to think of any other reason for Peter to have decided on her as a bride once she realized her husband did *not* have a grand passion for her, Lissa had assumed it was for her skills as a keeper of accounts in addition to the ordinary womanly accomplishments. She had not feared the work—she had loved every part of her duties as her father's assistant, although she would have preferred a few compliments instead of constant complaints. Buying and selling she found fascinating, but she could not rid herself of the idea that charging a fee for lending money to someone already unfortunate enough to be unable to pay his expenses was a dishonest way to make a profit. She had not wanted to be responsible for keeping accounts of such transactions.

Lissa's wandering mind was recalled to the fact of her husband's death when, faintly, she heard the groan of an axle and the gritty noise of wheels on stone. She ran to the back of the chamber and loosened the shutter on the window so that she could open it a crack and peer out. Young Peter was on the two-wheel cart that was used mostly to move household goods from the London house to the one in Canterbury. The horse was just passing out of the gate into the alley that ran along the walled garden to a lane connecting Bread Street and Friday Street. Edmond was waiting by the gate, and he shut it as soon as the tail of the cart passed through.

Lissa was surprised by the sense of relief she felt as Peter and Edmond disappeared before the alderman's officers arrived. She was a little ashamed of it, but she wanted a chance to tell her side of the story first. Not that there was much to tell, she thought, if she did not wish to implicate her father. She must say— And then Lissa realized that she was in no condition to say anything to anyone. She was still wearing her bedrobe; she was unwashed, and her hair was undone. And that realization made her conscious of the absence of the maid. The old woman resented her for having replaced her original mistress, but she had performed her duties efficiently if grudgingly.

Could the woman be afraid to come past Peter's body? Witta had said the sons had left it just lying on the floor. Lissa tightened her muscles against a new spate of shivering. It was wrong. Her husband had not cared for her as she first believed, but he had not been cruel when he had taken her maidenhead, and he had been courteous, if cool, in the six weeks they had been married. It was wrong for her to leave him without dignity in his death, sprawled, all twisted . . . Her hand flew to her mouth as a memory of Peter's broken limbs sent a wave of nausea through her, but she gritted her teeth and started down the stairs.

Peter lay in the shop, on the floor, as Witta had said, but at least he had been decently covered. A shaken sigh eased out of Lissa, and she came down the rest of the stairs. She glanced quickly around the room, but the maid was not anywhere to be seen, and there was no sound from the workroom. Lissa made a wide detour around the body, almost running through the workroom and out the back door. The kitchen shed was as empty as the house, however, and Lissa stopped.

Where could the woman be, she wondered. She had not gone with Peter and Edmond. Had she run away? In blank bewilderment Lissa's eyes swept over the winter-blasted garden, pausing suddenly at the door of the hut in which Witta and the maid slept. There was a stick lodged against the door, which opened outward, locking the maid in. Furious and shivering with cold, Lissa ran through the garden and pulled away the stick.

"Come out, Binge," she called, pulling the door wide, and as the maid came forward, frowning, her lips tight with rage, over her toothless gums, Lissa added, "Something terrible has happened. Master Peter has been killed."

The maid's wrinkled mouth dropped open with shock. "Killed?" she gasped. "No! His leman could not have been so jealous. She was only a common whore. She would have been glad to see him come to her again. She would not dare—"

"There *was* no woman," Lissa cried. "I knew Peter was in

trouble when he did not come home last night." But she could not go on because her teeth were chattering. She gestured for the maid to follow her and ran back to the house. In comparison with the bitter cold of the garden, the workroom was warm, even though the fire that Witta had started from the banked embers had burned down. "Fetch me water for washing and come up and help me dress," Lissa said when she could speak.

"Where are young Peter and Edmond?" Binge asked.

Lissa shook her head. "I do not know. They took the strongboxes away. I suppose their father left very strict orders about what must be done. They—" She swallowed. "They left him lying on the floor of the shop."

"On the floor?" the maid repeated.

Lissa drew in a shaken breath. "I sent Witta to tell the alderman. He will be here or his officers will come soon. I must be dressed—"

She broke off as it occurred to her that it seemed like a very long time since she sent the boy out, and Alderman Goscelin's house was no more than a single street away. Had Witta been so frightened that he had run away instead of carrying her message? Then she took another deep breath. It was more likely that she had lost her sense of time and that it had not been as long as she thought. The alderman might not have been dressed. His servants would have made Witta wait. And then Master Goscelin would have had to send for his men. He would not come alone; he would need witnesses. Lissa repeated her order to Binge and fled, averting her head as she passed Peter's body.

In the bedchamber at the front of the house she busied herself with building up the fire and laying out a simple dark blue tunic and pale gray gown. When Binge brought up the water, she washed and then dressed, her ear cocked for any sound from the shop below, but there were only faint noises from the street, no knock on the door. Finally she opened her husband's clothes chest and began to look through the garments. But when everything was done, his best gown shaken free of wrinkles and fresh underclothing chosen, she and Binge were still alone.

"Where are they?" she whispered, not knowing whether she meant Peter's sons or the alderman and his officers.

At last, able to delay no longer, Lissa gestured to Binge and went down. She bade the maid fetch two stools from the workroom, and she herself lit two candles, carried them in, and set them on the shop counter. Somehow it seemed wrong to open the windows, so she and Binge sat down in the dim candlelight a little distance from the corpse.

Lissa's mind was an utter blank by the time the door was flung open, letting in a flood of sunlight that blinded her. Startled, she jumped to her feet, flinging up a hand to shield her dazzled eyes.

Chapter 2

"WHAT THE DEVIL IS GOING ON HERE?"

Sir Justin FitzAilwin's voice was louder and harsher than he intended, but he had not expected to be confronted with a pitch-dark room in which a pale wraith, hiding its face, seemed to leap at him out of the dark into the swath of sunlight from the doorway. His temper, which was foul to begin with from having been wakened too early after a night of unwise revels with his cousins, was not improved by feeling a fool in the next moment. When his eyes adjusted to the relative dimness, the pale wraith resolved into a slender young woman, who dropped her arm and blinked in the sudden light.

Nor did Justin feel any better when she held out her hand to him and exclaimed, "Oh, Sir Justin, I am so glad it is you."

Clearly she knew him, and now that he could see her face it had a vague familiarity, but her name would not pierce through the pounding in his head. To give himself another moment, he stepped forward and took her hand and then had to set his teeth against a groan as he bent to kiss it. He was ready to bite her

14

fingers instead of kissing them, particularly when, after his eyes cleared of the mist raised by the pang that pierced him from temple to temple, he saw she was smiling, albeit only faintly.

But she said, "You will not remember me. We met only once, and very briefly, right after the fire a year and a half ago. I was greatly impressed by your charity, Sir Justin."

Her voice was soft and musical and soothed the hammer strokes on the ringing anvil in Justin's head. Her words were equally pleasing, relieving him of the need to pretend he knew her—and, he thought somewhat ruefully, pandering to his vanity by implying that he was memorable enough to be recalled for a year after one brief meeting. But then the sense of what she had said came through the dull throbbing. Remembered for his charity, was he? By a woman whose husband had been murdered? But she was quite young. Perhaps she was Flael's daughter rather than his wife.

"You *are* Mistress de Flael?" Justin asked.

She nodded, but he realized that did not answer the question. The title *mistress* would serve for wife or daughter. He wished they were speaking French, where *demoiselle* and *madame* made the difference clear, but Mistress de Flael had addressed him in English and he had, of course, answered in the same language. Here in London, where the hand of the conqueror had touched only lightly because the skill of the artisans and the wealth and trading connections of the merchants had been necessary to the new rulers, English was not only the language of the majority but of a rich and powerful majority. However, French was Justin's native tongue, and it was not necessary to be polite to those involved in murder. Besides, if witnesses had to think carefully about *how* to say something they often became careless about *what* they were saying.

So Justin asked, "Do you speak French?"

"Yes, of course," Lissa replied with perfect fluency in the requested language, "and Danish and German also."

"And your full name and status?"

Lissa saw Justin's lips thin with irritation and the creases deepen between his brows. She had no idea what had annoyed him, but quickly answered both questions. "I am Madame Heloise de Flael, the wife of the man who was . . . killed . . . murdered."

Her voice trembled over the last two words, and she gestured with her free hand into the shadows to her left where Peter's body lay. She had been unaware until she did so that Justin was still holding the hand he had kissed. *He has the expression of an avenging angel and the harshest voice,* she thought, *but he is really the kindest person.* Thankfully she gave his hand a gentle squeeze and extracted her fingers from his grip.

Justin's eyes had followed Lissa's gesture and fixed on the cloth-covered body. He was sufficiently shocked by the careless disposition of the corpse barely to note the pressure on his hand before her fingers slipped away.

"Open the shutters," he said over his shoulder to the four men who had followed him into the shop.

Those nearest to the windows moved to obey him, the man on the right releasing Witta, whom he had been holding by the shoulder. The boy ran to Lissa. From the corner of his eye Justin noted the way the child sidled around her to remain as close as possible to her and as far as possible from the corpse. Well, that did not mean much. Everyone wished to avoid the dead; even he had no fondness for bodies, although frequent exposure to them had hardened him. Forgetting his headache in his curiosity about how Peter de Flael had died, Justin bent and pulled off the blanket.

"*Peste!*" he gasped, jerking upright.

He had taken an involuntary step back before he checked his instinctive recoil and swallowed hard. But torture was nothing new to Justin, who on occasion had ordered its application himself, and his surprise past, he moved forward and prepared to kneel down for a closer examination. A whimper drew his attention back to the wife. Her face was turned away, but he could see the glint of tear streaks on her cheek, and the boy had his face buried in her skirt. He did not know which of them had made the sound, but both were suffering and that was unnecessary.

"I beg your pardon, Madame Heloise," he said. "You may go up to your chamber. I will come to you and ask such questions as I must when I am finished here."

"Thank you, Sir Justin," Lissa whispered. "May I take Witta and Binge with me?"

Witta was the boy. Binge? Now Justin noticed for the first time the hunched figure on a second stool beyond where Madame Heloise was standing. His lips thinned with anger at himself. He had been so taken up with the effects of having drunk somewhat too deep that a great deal seemed to have escaped his observation.

"Yes, yes, take them with you," he said hurriedly as he realized he had not answered the woman, "but see that they stay with you. No sliding out the back window."

"We have not broken our fast," Lissa said. She was looking at Justin sidelong, her eyes fixed on his face so that what lay at his feet was indistinct. "Could Binge go to the kitchen, or—"

"I have not broken my fast either," Justin said sourly, and was tempted to ask spitefully if seeing her husband's body had given her a sudden appetite. Then, remembering her tears, he was ashamed of his spite and added, "I will send a man up with bread and cheese and wine."

"Ale, please," Lissa amended. "I do not think wine would be good for Witta."

Her voice had not changed much, but in those few words there was a lightness that made Justin stare at her back as she shepherded her two charges up the stair. Without removing his eyes from her, Justin gave a low order to one of the men to get whatever food he could find from the kitchen. But his mind was far from what he was saying. He was thinking about a young wife and an old, rich husband—an old, dead husband. Perhaps it was not spite but instinct that had made him wonder if Madame Heloise's appetite had been improved by the reminder that her husband was dead. Justin's eyes went back to the corpse, taking note of the injuries. A single thin trickle of blood marked the ragged stump of an ear. Where a bone protruded through the flesh in the middle of one arm, there was almost no blood at all.

Had the blood washed off, Justin wondered? He moved so that his body did not block any of the light and peered closer. No, the edges of the rivulet near the ear were clear and hard; there was no blurring or staining as there would be if water had been poured on the body—and why should there be? It had not rained the previous night either. Justin knew that for a fact; if it had rained, he might have gone home at a reasonable hour instead of roistering around with those idiots, Alan, Thomas, and Richard, until near dawn. The memory of his activities seemed to bring back his headache, and he rose with a grunt and ordered his men to bring from the workroom or the kitchen a table long enough to lay the body on, since the shop counter was clearly too short.

When his men lifted the corpse to the table and turned it so he could look for signs of a killing blow, Justin saw the unnatural bending of the broken limbs. He raised his brows. There had been no swelling or discoloration to warn of those broken bones. But any broken bone caused bruising and swelling, even a greenstick fracture, which caused no displacement of the bone.

The captain of the watch, who had been standing behind him, said, "My lord, that's queer, it is. How can all those bones be broken without a black-and-blue mark? One, mayhap, if he died suddenly, but all?"

"It *is* queer, Halsig," Justin agreed, "and so is the fact that he did not bleed when the bone went through the flesh of his arm or when his ear was cut off."

"Right you are, my lord," Halsig said with startled approval. "You cut off an ear, the blood runs real free, just like when you cut your head." Then Halsig came closer and stared at the body. "What killed him, my lord?" he asked, his voice suddenly uncertain. "I see nothing that could kill a man."

"I see nothing that could kill either," Justin agreed rather grimly, but the slight tremor in Halsig's voice warned him, and he did not mention what had leapt first into his mind . . . witchcraft. And then, because a young wife was involved, he thought of poison, but he did not mention that either, because Peter de Flael did not have the look of a man who had died of poison. What he said was "Men do die of fright, and to look at him—"

He was interrupted by the man who had gone to the kitchen, and Justin sent him up to the solar and bade him wait outside the door, where he could not be seen, and listen to what was said.

It was a real pleasure to work with Sir Justin again, Halsig thought. That fool the new mayor had appointed last year knew nothing and cared less about how a crime was committed. He never tried to find out who really did evil. All he ever did was round up the beggars and torture a confession out of one of them. That had annoyed Halsig for two reasons: The first was that the beggars no longer passed him a farthing now and then to leave them in peace; the second was that the real thieves—and what was worse, the noblemen's men-at-arms—had gotten completely out of hand.

It was the men-at-arms roaring around the town, pulling the merchants' beards, overturning their counters, and insulting their wives that brought Sir Justin back. That mewling lackwit, Roger FitzAdam, had not wanted to keep Henry FitzAilwin's nephew in a position of such power after the old mayor died, but eight months of the sloth and stupidity of the highborn jackass he had appointed had been enough. The aldermen, even those opposed to the FitzAilwin party, had come together and forced FitzAdam to reappoint Sir Justin.

Halsig smiled behind his hand as he saw Justin glance toward the stair and the rooms above. There might be trouble over this murder. The burghers were well pleased when one of the laborers or a man-at-arms was caught and punished, but they weren't going to like it if one of their own was dragged before a justice. Then the smile disappeared. It wouldn't be the woman. Plenty of wives would be overjoyed to see their husbands laid out, and this was a toothsome young one for the dried old stick lying there, but broken bones— Not a woman. A woman—

"So it was all done after he was dead, whatever he died of." Justin's voice held the incredulity he felt. He had realized that the injuries could not have been inflicted while Peter de Flael was alive as soon as he saw that single thread of dried blood from the severed ear, but he had ignored the idea because it was so ridiculous. "Why?" he asked, turning from the body to look at Halsig. "Why would anyone torture a corpse?"

"Mad?" Halsig suggested. "Or enough hate." He shrugged.

"My lord," one of the men who had fetched the table offered, "there are no strongboxes in the workroom. Maybe they were kept above in the master's chamber, but there were almost no tools on the table either."

"By God's balls," Justin roared suddenly, "didn't Flael have two sons?"

"If he had," Halsig said calmly, "they didn't make trouble and I don't know them, but—" He grimaced and made an impotent fist, his calm disturbed. "Oh, curse me! There *are* sons." He turned to the man who had spoken about the strongboxes and said, "Dunstan, go search the garden." He shrugged as he looked back at Justin. "Waste of time. They're long gone by now or they would have been the ones banging on Master Goscelin's door, not the boy. I'm sorry I didn't think of them sooner, my lord, but I never saw them that I remember."

Justin made a brushing gesture. "The fault is mine. I believe I met them at some guild function once. In any case, I should have thought at once how unlikely it was for Mistress Heloise to be alone here with a child and an old woman. Surely Flael had some menservants. He was a rich man."

Halsig frowned. "Don't know about menservants, but he once had a journeyman. That's how I know about the sons. Flael mentioned them when the journeyman was killed last year in an accident. I guess the man was drunk and fell down in the street on the way home. Anyway, he was run over by a cart. Wheel went right over his head and—ugh! Flael was half crazy when he found out. Seems the journeyman was in the middle of an important piece of work. Flael was screaming at the carter and at me—now I remember—that his sons weren't good enough to finish the piece."

"What happened to the carter?" Justin asked. He had no memory of the incident and assumed that it had taken place during the months he was out of office. If the carter had been imprisoned for what Halsig implied was not his fault, Justin intended to get him released.

"Nothing, for a wonder," Halsig said. "I thought Flael would want him hanged. You understand the carter was a little to the left of sober. Swore he never saw the man at all and that the man wasn't in the street when he went into an alehouse to get a sup. But Flael calmed down and admitted that the journeyman was a drinker and it wasn't the first time he lay down in the street to sleep. Said he could have even laid down under the cart, and the old ox could have done the job by backing up while the carter was in the alehouse."

That sounded unlikely to Justin, but the incident was nearly a year in the past and an ox-drawn cart was highly unlikely to have knocked down a man on his feet, no matter how shakily. Oxen were just too slow to cause an accident. Justin dismissed the subject from his mind as Dunstan came in to report that there was evidence that a horse had been stabled at the back of the hut in which the servants seemed to live and there were marks of a cart's wheels. Justin nodded; it was about what he had expected. He sent Dunstan off to Goscelin with a request that he send messengers to the guards at the gates to stop two-wheeled carts leaving the city, but he did not expect any results. Flael's sons would have passed the gate some time ago, he was sure, possibly before the guard changed. He would have to question both sets of guards, but that must wait until he got a description of the sons, the cart, and the horse from those above.

"Cover the man," Justin said to Halsig, gesturing at the body. "We have learned everything Master Peter de Flael is ever going to tell us. There is no one here to take prisoner, so send the men out to ask the neighbors if they saw anything. Tell them to ask about the sons leaving with the cart too."

"And me?" Halsig asked.

"You go too," Justin replied, "I will need no help with those above."

He mounted the stairs, signaled to the guard to go down, and pushed open the door without requesting permission to enter. The solar was well and luxuriously fitted out. On one side of the back wall was a hooded hearth in which a brisk fire burned. On the other side, was a large, double-lighted window covered with oiled linen. To the right of the fireplace, in the most sheltered corner, stood a handsome chair. To the left between the fire and the window was a bench with an embroidery frame before it. Just opposite the door he had flung open was a table with three stools drawn up to it on which Madame Heloise, the maid, and the boy were sitting. There were signs that they had eaten, but large pieces of bread and cheese, Justin guessed from the shapes, were covered by a cloth at one side.

"Why did you not tell me Master Peter's sons had left the house?" he asked in French as he entered the room.

"Have they not yet returned?" Lissa responded in the same language, looking surprised. "I thought they must have gone to some friend of Peter's to put the strongboxes in safekeeping, but they might have decided to take everything to Canterbury. Only that will take days if they go by road."

"Why should they take the strongboxes away?"

"I do not know." Lissa shook her head and put a hand to her lips, her forehead creased with anxiety. "I assumed that Peter had left orders for them to do so." She paused and looked appealingly up at Justin, then went on slowly. "I know very little about Peter's business. We have only been married for six weeks, and I—I was not bred to the goldsmith's trade. It seemed reasonable. I thought perhaps Peter feared that debts would be claimed against him or—or—I do not know. I think young Peter and Edmond were fond of their father. I cannot believe they would have left him as they did unless the matter was very urgent. Or unless—"

A tide of color swept up from Lissa's throat into her face and tears rose to her eyes. The fingers, which had dropped while she spoke of the reasons her sons-by-law might have had to remove the strongboxes in such haste, crept up to her lips again, making her look like a vulnerable child. And the pink in her cheeks combined with the mist of tears to wash the green out of her eyes so that they looked all soft brown. Justin had to remind himself sharply that this image of gentle timidity might easily have connived with one or both of the absent sons to murder the old man. If she and one of the sons were lovers, and if old Peter had discovered them . . .

"Unless what?" Justin asked, keeping his voice soft with spurious sympathy and suppressing the spurt of rage he felt at nearly succumbing to a glance full of appeal and admiration.

"Unless they thought I would attempt to steal their heritage from them," Lissa replied, straightening her back and dropping her hand so she could clasp both together in her lap. She looked at Justin with a touch of defiance. "I cannot imagine how they could be so silly as to believe I would have any claim to Peter's money or property. What was to be mine on Peter's death was clearly defined in our wedding contract and put into safekeeping with Hamo Finke, but Peter's sons were very much opposed to our marriage. It is possible, I suppose, that they suspected I had . . . seduced their father into making a new will while we were at Canterbury, but—"

Lissa stopped speaking abruptly and bit her lip. She had nearly blurted out the fact that Peter did not really care for her and had only married her as part of some arrangement with her father so it would have been impossible for her to influence him against his sons. She must not imply there was anything unusual about her marriage or that her father was otherwise involved than to obtain the best settlement he could for his daughter. It would be fatal to allow her feeling that Sir Justin was a strong, safe haven to induce her to tell him more than was safe for him to know. Sir Justin—she had inquired about him after meeting him—was known for truly seeking justice, and that was dangerous to her in this case.

"Then there is no new will?" he asked.

"No." Lissa brought a hint of indignation into her voice. "It would have been stupid and cruel of me to try to obtain such an advantage. I told you I know nothing of the goldsmith's trade. What good would the reversion of Peter's business have been to me? Besides, I am my father's heir—" She stopped again, troubled by the way her father kept creeping into her mind and conversation.

"And your father is . . . ?"

"William Bowles," Lissa answered shortly.

"I *do* remember you!" The words burst out before Justin thought, followed by an irrepressible smile.

The name of William Bowles, the sharp tone of her voice, and her slightly indignant expression brought back to Justin a clear memory from the past year. After the rain, which had finally quenched the terrible fire that had destroyed a third of London, many of the townsfolk who had escaped loss had come out to do what they could for their less fortunate fellow citizens. In one of the churches where the homeless and injured were being sheltered, Justin had been questioning a distraught woman, and Madame Heloise had interposed herself, telling him sharply that he would learn more if he spoke more gently.

Justin remembered being so startled by having a young woman dare take him to task with such firmness that instead of blasting her with withering scorn, he had excused himself, admitting that his temper might be short because he had not slept in two days. Then she had apologized to him and begged him to leave the woman to her. In two minutes she had obtained the information he wanted. But Justin could not see how that meeting between them would give her reason to admire him for his charity. Unless she had noticed him later when he had almost come to her assistance.

She had been tending an injured child, and his attention had been drawn to her just as hers had, no doubt, been drawn to him earlier—by a loud male voice. He had seen William Bowles standing over her and ordering her not to waste her time and *his* ointments and potions on strangers. Justin had been infuriated and had started toward them to tell Bowles that what she was doing was necessary by the mayor's will. However, before he could make his way through the injured lying on the floor and those who recognized him and plucked at his sleeves begging for help, she got to her feet and drew her father away from the child. He had not heard her first few words, but as he drew closer, he heard her bid Bowles leave her to her own devices in a voice of such cold threat and fury that the man had flinched away and, after a glance around, departed.

The smile faded from Justin's face. At the time he had been delighted with the lady's determination to continue her charitable activity and amused by the way she vanquished a man known for miserliness and driving a hard bargain. Now, however, remembering the force of will in Madame Heloise only increased his suspicion that, had she a strong enough purpose, there was little beyond her ability. But one cannot take back a smile, and she was now smiling at him, a little ruefully. The pink that had faded from her cheeks while she spoke about her sons-by-law was back.

"You cannot remember much good of me," she said. "I am afraid I bespoke you sharply, and unjustly too. That woman was a fool, and you were so good and kind to those who begged you for help."

"It was my business to bring them help," Justin said stiffly and dismissively. "I was ordered by the mayor to discover what was burnt, what was damaged, and what was whole and who was live, injured, or dead. So I did no more than my duty."

Sir Justin was one of those, Lissa thought, who could not accept praise graciously. He had done a great deal more than his duty; she knew because the very moment after she snapped at him, she had seen that what he said in excuse of his impatience was true. Not only was his skin gray and his eyes red-rimmed and sunken with exhaustion, but his face was pocked with burn marks, one hand had an angry red wheal, and his rich gown was torn and singed from fighting the fire himself instead of directing others from a safe distance. And he had also come himself to bring good news and bad so that attention from one of his high station and authority would bring what comfort it could to the afflicted. Lissa found the awkwardness with which he tried to avoid a compliment endearing in a man otherwise so assured in manner. Forgetting for a moment the dreadful circumstance that had brought him back into her life, she could not help wanting to tease him.

"You did your duty," she agreed, lowering her eyes demurely, although her smile grew a little broader. "But another would have gone home to bed first, not come when he could hardly stand to tell half-dead men that their homes were still standing and hysterical women that their husbands were alive."

"I wish more of my news had been of that kind," Justin remarked, his eyes bleak as he recalled wails of grief and faces gone dead with despair.

Lissa glanced up and saw that his embarrassment at her praise had been swallowed by the memories of those terrible days, memories that were still painful to him. "Yet to know is better than to be left in doubt."

She said the words to comfort him, but her voice faltered as she realized they were true for her at this moment. She was sorry about Peter's dreadful death and frightened about her father's possible involvement, but both emotions were far less painful than the agonies of doubt she had endured during her sleepless night.

Justin's brows rose, and Lissa sighed and added, "When the worst is known, one begins without even willing it to plan for the future. One may begin by thinking, What will become of me? but the question demands an answer and draws the mind away from grief."

Justin did not answer directly beyond a single thoughtful glance. He said, "Madame Heloise, would you please send the maid and the boy down to the workroom so that I can talk with you alone? You understand, do you not, that I must speak with all of you separately about what happened?"

Lissa felt a flood of gratitude, knowing he could have given the order himself and undermined her authority over her servants. She began to tell Binge and Witta to go down to the workroom and wait, then halted them with a raised hand and turned to Justin who had come closer to the table and taken off his cloak.

"Instead of waiting while you question me, may Witta go for a priest? I must make arrangements for Peter to be buried—or—or do you think I should wait for his sons to come back . . . or be found? Or perhaps I must wait until someone else examines Peter?"

"You may send the boy for the priest if you are sure he will come back."

"He has nowhere else to go, poor creature. At least he has never told me of any home or family. And I think he is fond of me. I am sure he will return." She told Witta what to do, and the boy ran off. Then she raised her eyes to Justin again, her lips curving upward as she said, "Now that I have nibbled on a finger of your good nature, I am about to bite off the whole hand. May Binge go to the market for food? And if she may go, should she buy sufficient for dinner for you and your men?"

Justin should have snarled at her that his presence in her house was not meant to be a social occasion. What he said was "Yes, yes, send the woman out. We all must eat."

"You may be sure she will not run away either," Lissa said, her smile broadening into a mischievous grin. "She is waiting most eagerly to tell you how much better a wife and mistress Peter's first wife was." Then a frown replaced the smile. "But she will tell everyone in the market of Peter's death, and perhaps—"

"That will not matter," Justin said. "My men are already questioning your neighbors and those who came early to the Chepe, so your husband's death is no secret."

His sense of shock at his easy agreement to all she asked had been dissipated by Lissa's grin. Either the woman was so completely innocent of ill will toward her husband that suspicion of herself was inconceivable to her or she was guilty and so good at concealing her thoughts and feelings that open attack would be useless. His reaction was most fortunate, Justin thought, watching Binge close the door as she left the room. If he wanted the truth about Madame Heloise, he would have to trick it out of her. And that could not be done at once; she would be too suspicious of him to let down her guard immediately.

Over a period of days or weeks if he allowed himself to seem seduced by her charms and sympathetic and helpful, she would relax and might easily let slip evidence he could use.

"And speaking of food," Lissa said, rising and going toward the wall that separated the bedchamber from the solar, where fine silver plates and goblets were displayed on two open shelves, "you told me you had come without breaking your fast. You must be famished by now." She smiled at him over her shoulder, took down a plate and a goblet, and brought them back to the table. "Do sit down. You may question me while you eat."

"I can indeed do so," Justin remarked, giving way and chuckling. "But I must warn you, Madame Heloise, that you are making me very suspicious with these attentions. Are you trying to seduce me away from my duty and blind me to the fact that when a man or woman is murdered it is most often the spouse who is guilty?"

He noticed that Lissa did not even blink at the warning—which he had delivered in earnest, even though his tone was light. She merely shook her head as she poured ale into the goblet. Then she laid a thick slice of bread on the plate and, while she cut eating-sized chunks from the cheese, said, "I do not think you are the kind of man who can be seduced from his purpose."

"More flattery?"

The woman did not answer his question, only shook her head again, unsmiling now. She left the plate and goblet in the center of the table too, so that Justin could choose his own position, and sat down. Justin drew a stool close to the end of the table where she was sitting rather than opposite. He would not be able to see her full face unless she turned her head toward him, but it would be interesting to see how often she looked directly at him and how often she turned away. Seated, Justin took several healthy swallows of the ale. It was soothing to a mouth dry with the aftermath of too much drink, but the worst of his other symptoms were gone, his headache no more than a faint dullness and the queasy heave of his stomach replaced by a faint appetite. He was scarcely famished, but he drew his eating knife and speared a piece of cheese with a fair pretense of eagerness. After all, he was not about to admit that the reason he had not broken his fast was not his passion for justice but because he was too sick to eat.

"You said before that knowing the worst was better than remaining in doubt," Justin said, putting down the goblet and taking a bite of the bread. "Does that mean you feared what happened?"

"No," Lissa said hesitantly, a worried frown wrinkling her brow. "At least I do not remember being afraid until last night when Peter did not come home. I do not know why—" Her voice quavered and she dropped her eyes, which were suddenly swimming with tears. "But in the past he had told me each time he expected to be out late, and yesterday he said he would be out for dinner but back for the evening meal—and he did not come back."

She does know some reason to be afraid Flael would be hurt or killed, Justin thought, but he asked mildly, "It did not occur to you that he met a friend and changed his mind, or that his business took longer than expected?"

"Oh yes, but soon after Vespers I had sent Witta to Master Hamo Finke's house—that was where Peter had dinner—with a message that Master Richard FitzReiner's servant had come to ask Peter to call on his master. Only Peter was not with Master Hamo. He had left at the same time as the others, about Nones."

"Where did he go?"

"I do not know," Lissa replied, her lips tightening with remembered fear and frustration. "Witta did not ask because I never thought to tell him to ask, and at that time I still expected Peter home soon after dark so it did not seem worthwhile to send the child out again. I did not really begin to worry until Compline, and then when I spoke to young Peter and begged him to ask Master Hamo where his father had gone, he laughed at me and said Peter had had enough of me and had gone back to the woman he kept before we were married. I did not believe him."

"Why?" Justin asked, wondering if Madame Heloise could possibly have been jealous.

It did not seem likely for a young and passably attractive woman to be jealous enough of an old man to have him tortured and killed. Then Justin remembered that Flael had not been tortured; the wounds had been inflicted after his death. He was about to dismiss jealousy as a motive until he noticed that Lissa looked astonished at the question. Justin suddenly realized a woman did not need to care for a man to hate him for wounding her pride by preferring a common whore.

Neither her reply nor her manner confirmed that theory, however. Smiling faintly and clearly puzzled at Justin's lack of comprehension of so obvious an answer, she said, "But why should he not simply say that he would be back very late or even that he did not expect to come home at all? He had done that before. Why say he would definitely be home for the evening meal?"

It was so logical and her voice was so indifferent that Justin did not know whether to accept what she said as simple truth or credit her with even more skill at hiding her emotions than he had first thought. "You were very fond of your husband," Justin stated, his voice carefully neutral.

"No, I cannot say that," Lissa replied frankly, "but I respected him. He had been kind to me from the day we were betrothed, and his manner was no different when he left the house that morning. Nor had I given him any reason to wish to hurt me."

Her color rose a little over the last few words. Justin took that to mean that she had not refused her husband's sexual advances. The idea made him slightly uncomfortable, which was ridiculous. With one out of every three women dying in childbed and older men being best able to support a wife, there were many young wives with much older husbands. Still, Justin did not like to think of Peter de Flael, with his wrinkled skin, his few wisps of gray hair straggling over a shiny skull, his swollen, flabby legs, mounting this fresh-faced girl.

That thought brought Justin's eyes up from his plate, where they had been fixed unseeing on the graceful arcs of the design. Her wholesomeness was what was so attractive about her. She was no striking beauty—a pleasant, ordinary face surrounded by soft brown hair. But her eyes were remarkable, not only for their changeable color but for an aliveness, an eagerness of spirit, that looked out of them even when they were also full of fear. Her mouth was pretty too. She shifted on her stool suddenly and dropped her eyes, her color deepening further, and Justin realized he had been staring at her without speaking for far too long. He cleared his throat.

"Nonetheless," he said, "we cannot discount the possibility that Master Peter's son might have been aware of something you were not and merely described his father's intention in the way most likely to hurt you. It is possible, for example, that your husband visited this woman to retrieve something he had given her, or money he had lent her, and that he intended to be home for his evening meal but was killed there. Do you know the woman's name, Madame Heloise?"

"I never thought of that." She looked up at him again, her eyes wide with a stronger emotion than Justin felt was reasonable, but he could not read the emotion in her face. "I am sorry," she went on. "I do not know her name or anything about her. Peter never mentioned any woman except, once or twice, his late wife. The first I knew of any leman was when young Peter spoke of her. Oh, wait! Binge mentioned her also. Binge might know."

She was now eager for him to find the woman. Because she thought he would be glad to lay the blame on someone poor and helpless? Justin reached for the goblet, more to give himself time to think than because he was thirsty, but it was empty. He put it down, and she filled it, smiling at him suddenly and adding, "Would you do me the kindness of calling me Lissa? Only my father calls me Heloise, and I have never cared for the name."

Now that was interesting, Justin thought, as he drank. Her voice was entirely different when she spoke of her husband and in that last sentence when she spoke of her father. The cold distaste with which she mentioned her father was unmistakable, while her voice was pleasant if dispassionate when she spoke of Master Peter. A strong indication that she preferred Peter to William Bowles, but not proof that she would not like best of all to be a widow with control of her own dower. Nonetheless, Justin smiled back at her as he put down the goblet, but before he could answer her request, they heard a pounding on the door.

Chapter 3

"**W**HO—" LISSA GASPED, THEN RELAXED. "IT MUST BE THE priest," she said. "I suppose he did not wish to come in the back door with Witta like a servant. Shall I go, Sir Justin, or will you?"

"I would prefer that you open the door," he said. "And if it is not the priest, please do not say anything about my being here."

"Very well," Lissa agreed, but she felt puzzled and wanted to ask why she should keep his presence a secret.

The pounding began again, however, and she ran out of the room and down the stair. The heavy bar on the door lifted easily, swinging up into the rest built to hold it. Then Lissa pulled out the metal rod that fixed the latch and raised it. The door swung in so quickly that it almost hit her, and she jumped back behind it, uttering another gasp as her father burst in shouting, "Heloise! Damn you, you bitch! Heloise, where are you?"

"Right here, father," she replied, coming out from behind the door and taking a certain amount of pleasure in his faint cry of alarm, despite expecting a blast of rage to follow.

He did seize her arm, but instead of cursing her again he asked, "Is it true? Is it true? I heard that Peter had been killed! Murdered! It was a lie! Surely it was a lie!"

There was such shock and terror in her father's face that Lissa almost embraced him in the flood of relief that washed over her. She was now certain that William had had no part in her husband's death and no knowledge of it until he had heard the news this morning. She did not wonder if he was acting a part for two reasons. First, she knew William Bowles; she had studied him with wary dislike ever since she had understanding enough to do so. She knew his every expression, and the fear he was displaying was real. Second, her father had never bothered to act a part for her; he seemed to delight in her anguish and disgust when he connived at small dishonesties. She knew he was well aware that she would never betray him no matter what he did, since any punishment visited on him would indirectly fall on her. A merchant was not put in prison for crimes; that was a punishment for the great nobility. A merchant might be put in the stocks for cheating or dragged through the town on a hurdle. He might lose a hand for a minor theft or be hanged for a major one; however, a rich merchant was usually punished by crippling fines. Fines and restrictions in the right to trade could ruin her father's business, and Lissa knew they would also ruin her, for what was his would be hers when he died.

Lissa's relief did not last very long. Although it was true that her father had neither arranged nor known of Peter's murder, his shock and terror meant he knew the reason for it. Otherwise, he would not have cared the shaving of a farthing about Peter de Flael. William Bowles cared for no one besides himself; thus he must be involved in some way even though he was not guilty of the crime. Still, the fact that he was innocent of murder lifted a great weight from Lissa's spirit, and her voice was gentler than usual when she answered him.

"It is true, father. Peter was murdered." She hesitated and then added, "He was tortured too." Perhaps it was possible for her father to disentangle himself from his involvement, and she felt it right to give the warning.

"Tortured?" William's voice squeaked with fear and horror. "But—" He looked wildly around the room, shied back almost

out of the door when he saw the covered form on the table near
the shop counter, then seemed to steady himself. "But why?"

There was a false note in that question. Lissa was sure her
father knew very well why Peter had been tortured, and what
he knew was so important that it was worth lying about to her.
But she was not going to challenge him with Sir Justin listening
upstairs. She was shocked as the thought came to her. How
could she have been so stupid as to wonder why Sir Justin had
said she should not tell anyone he was there? She felt a spurt of
anger over the trap he had laid, but she reminded herself that
Sir Justin was only doing his duty. She was really angry with
herself. She was not ordinarily a naive innocent who took
everyone at face value and trusted blindly.

Meanwhile, her father had noticed that the door to the
workshop was open. "Are you alone here?" he asked, realizing
how unusual it was for Lissa to come to the door. Then,
dismissing that question without waiting for an answer, he
asked more urgently, "Where are Peter's sons?"

Relieved that she would not have to tell a direct lie to keep her
promise to Justin, Lissa replied, "I do not know where young
Peter and Edmond are. They left as soon as the body was
found."

"They left?" her father repeated, staring at her. Then without
another word, he released her arm, which he had been holding,
and went out the door.

"Wait!" Lissa cried, stepping out of the door after him, but he
was striding swiftly away, already within the stream of people
going to the market, and she hesitated to follow him.

Lissa did not think it would be proper for so recent a widow to
go running through the West Chepe. The market was already
busy. She could hear the cries of the bakers and fishmongers,
who had stalls nearest to the west end where many of the
goldsmiths lived and had their shops. The goldsmiths did not
cry their wares, of course, nor did they as a general rule expose
them on a public stall, which would be an open invitation to
thievery. But handsome salts or platters of silver or gilt were
displayed behind stout bars in the windows, and the doors of
the shops were invitingly open. Just as Lissa shuddered slightly
and started back inside, feeling that everyone behind those
open doors must know of Peter's death and be watching eagerly
for any activity from his house, a hand was laid on her arm.

"Mistress de Flael?"

The face of the priest, who had spoken, was familiar to her, but she did not know his name. She believed she had seen him chanting the mass either in Saint Matthew's, on the nearby corner of Friday Street, or in Saint Peter's, directly across from the house. She had been to mass with Peter only once in each church since they had returned from Canterbury, and she had had no time to become familiar with any of the priests who served in either one.

She realized she must look utterly distracted for the priest squeezed her arm gently and said, "I am sorry I did not come sooner, but I did not recognize your servant and I believed at first the child was trying to make mischief."

"The fault is mine, Father," Lissa assured him diplomatically, wondering what kind of a priest feared being the butt of a boy's jest. "I should have sent Binge, whom you would have known."

He made soothing noises as he urged her gently back inside the shop, asking once they were within, "It is true, then, that Master Peter is dead?"

"Yes, quite true, Father."

Sir Justin's voice made Lissa sigh with relief and the priest start slightly with surprise. Suddenly she felt totally unable to explain how her husband had died; in fact she felt barely able to stand and found herself clinging to the frame of the door. She heard Sir Justin identify himself to the priest. Then he turned to her and gently bade her go upstairs, taking on himself, to her intense relief, the duty of explaining to the priest what had happened.

It was an infinite effort to climb the stairs, and the terrible exhaustion that had overtaken Lissa blurred her mind so that none of the words she heard made the smallest sense. She thought she would collapse in the few steps between the top of the stair and the door, and she leaned on the wall, not really listening but somehow comforted by the murmur of Justin's voice, speaking softly. Twice she heard the priest exclaim, once in surprise and once in protest, but both times he lowered his voice immediately.

Lissa sighed and shivered, then gathered enough strength to walk as far as the chair beside the fire. She sank into it, remembering it was Peter's chair and that he would never sit in it again. She knew she should feel grieved, but fatigue dulled her mild sorrow, reducing it to nothing. She would not have wished Peter dead, and most certainly not in the dreadful way he died, but she was not sorry to be free of him—and of his sons also.

A loud snap drew her attention to the fire again. It was burning brightly, the flames licking greedily at new logs. Sir Justin must have replenished it, she thought, and tears came to her eyes at the thought of his kindness. Wearily she reminded herself that, kind or not, she must not trust him too far. Had he not intended to listen slyly to what her father said? Then a tired smile curved her lips. How silly she was! Justin could not have known her father was at the door. It might have been anyone, even Peter's sons, who might have spoken unguarded words to her that they would not have said in Sir Justin's hearing.

Lissa's eyes closed, but instead of the blank, soft dark that usually preceded sleep she saw Sir Justin's face. It was not an especially handsome face, nor was it kindly. It was long and hard, with high, prominent cheekbones, a jutting chin, and a beak of a nose; the lips were thin, drawn in at the corners in a habit of severity. But Sir Justin's eyes gave away his true nature. They were gentle when he looked at her, a soft color between blue and gray, and when he smiled, his mouth was beautifully shaped. His hair was wrong for an officer of harshness and importance too; it was all unruly curls, falling over his forehead and around his ears. She smiled, only now feeling surprised and delighted by something she had been too tense to enjoy when she had first noticed it. She must tell him, she thought with sleepy pleasure, that if he really wished to cow someone, he must wear a hat.

Justin had less trouble with the priest than he had expected. When he learned the manner of Master Peter's death, Father Denis made only a few shocked exclamations and a token protest over his doubts about whether Peter could have received extreme unction. He agreed with Justin that there could be no certainty he had not, however, and agreed even more readily that there was no reason to exclude Peter from the grave he had already chosen in the churchyard of Saint Peter's. To Justin's further remark that, considering the questionable manner of

Master Peter's death, someone more skilled than his young and inexperienced wife should deal with the body, Father Denis responded by suggesting that he send for lay brothers skilled in medicine from Bartholomew's Hospital to wash and prepare the corpse for burial.

Justin nodded approval of that plan and said that the brothers should be sure to come to him if they discovered the cause of Peter's death. The priest looked startled, but asked no further questions, and Justin said no more, thinking that Peter must have made generous donations to Father Denis's church above and beyond his tithe. It was also likely that the church expected even more generous endowments to be defined in his will. Not only were goldsmiths wealthy, but most of them had tender consciences about their moneylending activities. Justin did not mention to the priest that Peter's sons had carried off most if not all of his worldly goods, and that if they were not caught it might be difficult to fulfill the provisions of the will.

After Father Denis had gone to make the promised arrangements, Justin started up the stairs to tell Lissa—his foot hesitated over the next step as the pet name, stripped of Madame or Mistress, came easily into his mind. Then he continued up with his mouth set more grimly than ever. Perhaps Flael's sons had fled with their father's wealth because they feared this woman. *She* had said she would not profit from Peter de Flael's death, but perhaps the old man had changed his will—or been about to do so—and the sons were not sure they would not be stripped of everything. Justin had dismissed that notion at first because she did not have the kind of beauty that turned men's heads. Yet she had turned his—at least enough to make him think of her as Lissa rather than Madame Heloise.

Justin entered the solar with an angry determination to place a proper distance between himself and the wife of a murdered man. In the doorway he stopped abruptly, barely preventing himself from laughing aloud. What a perfect picture of innocence and an easy conscience, Justin thought, but then he lost his smile and took a few careful steps closer. No, she was not pretending. She really was asleep, and deeply asleep. Her mouth was open, and between a snap and hiss from the fire, he heard a little snort and a soft whistle, a delicate snoring. No woman pretending sleep would expose two common features of the state that she would consider very unattractive.

For himself, Justin found neither repulsive. The open mouth exposed very pretty, sound white teeth, and the snort and whistle were rather charming. The last word of his thought sounded an alarm in his head. What the devil was it about the woman? He examined her more intently than he had while they were talking and shook his head. She was pleasant looking: Her hair was an ordinary shade of light brown and framed a face neither thin nor fat. As he remembered her eyes, they were neither brown nor green but a soft color that could be either according to the light. Her nose was short, perhaps a little too short for the long upper lip, but the curve of that lip was lovely, even with her mouth open, and Justin could recall how the full lower lip pushed the upper into a bow and pouted provocatively. Still, she was by no means beautiful. Why should he use words like "charming" when he thought of Lissa—and he had done it again, used her pet name without thinking.

He took a few more silent steps, picked up his cloak, and went out, amazed that he had stood watching the woman instead of working. The boy must have come back with the priest. This was a splendid opportunity to question him without raising fears and suspicions over the absence of his mistress. The boy would accept that Lissa—mentally, Justin shrugged and put aside the question of why she was Lissa to him—must not be wakened. But, having thought he had put aside the problem of why he called her Lissa, he found that it was solved as soon as he began to question Witta.

The boy was in the workroom, playing with a lump of clay. The activity was approved, Justin assumed, because Witta did not start guiltily or try to hide his plaything. Yet when Justin said mildly he had some questions to ask, there was uneasiness and fear in the blue eyes the child turned up to him. Justin was accustomed to the reaction and did not take it as a sign of guilt, but it came to him as he watched Witta wrap the clay in a wet cloth, that Lissa had never shown either of those emotions. In fact, she had cried out in relief when he arrived and laughed and teased while he ate. She had been worried and frightened—but not of him!

That was the source of her charm, Justin thought; her ease

made him feel comfortable. It was not a comfort Justin frequently enjoyed, and it drew him strongly. Aside from his cousins and
a few, very few, close friends, nearly everyone regarded him, if
not with active fear, with caution. The reserve made Justin stiff
and formal—he knew it but could not help his reaction—and his
formality only increased the reserve people felt. It was like a
snake swallowing its own tail.

Justin knew his problem was a natural result of his position as
master of the mayor's guard and the way his uncle and the new
mayor, Roger FitzAdam, used him to ferret out those who
committed crimes among the wealthy burghers and even the
nobles who lived in the city. And Lissa knew that, and was not
afraid at all. Did not that ease, that lack of fear of him, prove that
she had nothing to hide? Nonsense! Justin brought his thoughts
sharply to order. Lissa *was* hiding something; he had seen that
almost at once.

No hint of any answer to what she was hiding, or of any
reason she should wish to be rid of her husband, came to Justin
out of questioning Witta or Binge, who came in from the market
soon after he was done with the boy. All Justin learned was that
Witta hated Flael's sons and adored his mistress. He would
gladly have implicated young Peter and Edmond and told any
lie to clear Lissa—only he did not know what lie to tell. Binge,
on the other hand, resented Lissa and would have hurt her if
she could, but the maid's spite over having lost her preeminent
place as manager of the household was obvious, and most of
what she said only confirmed more surely, because it came from
a hostile witness, what Lissa had told him earlier. Neither
servant's account conflicted with her story in any way that
would give him an opening for further questions.

It would have been very easy for Justin to account Lissa free of
any suspicion; it would have been so easy that he trusted
himself even less than he trusted her. Binge and Witta slept
outside the house in the shed. Who could say what Lissa's
relationship to the sons had been? She *was* an apothecary's
daughter, and he believed she practiced the art herself. Perhaps
Peter de Flael had slept far better after his second marriage than
at any other time in his life. Perhaps he had slept well enough
not to notice his wife leave his bed and enter another in the
workshop. It would not be the first time a son had grown

impatient with the length of his father's life or envied his father
the young morsel of flesh in his bed.

Justin knew already that he would never prove or disprove
that notion through the servants. Had Binge had the shadow of
a hint of such a relationship or of any illness or weakness that
had come over her master since his second marriage—which
might indicate use of slow poison—she would have cried it
aloud before he asked a question. The only way was to catch the
wife and sons in some communication; then the truth could be
squeezed out of them. How much would they trust each other if
they had conspired together? Cynically Justin thought, Not
much. So they would not allow too long a time to pass before
one sent word to the other—perhaps a few days, perhaps a
week, perhaps two.

By the time Halsig and his men returned, Justin had decided
to keep his suspicions to himself until he had heard what the
brothers of Bartholomew's Hospital had to say. Halsig's report
was no help. The men had discovered nothing of value.
Unfortunately no neighbor on Goldsmith's Row had noticed
anything unusual during the night, when presumably Peter de
Flael's body had been dropped in his own doorway. One man,
who had a house along the lane that connected Bread Street to
Friday Street, reported that a cart had come out of an alley from
the direction of the market—an unusual direction at that time of
the morning—and turned right into Friday Street. The man
claimed he had only heard the cart and had no idea who was in
it, that he had not looked out because he was busy dressing and
breaking his fast.

"He's lying," Halsig said. "He knew it was Flael's sons driving
the cart." He shrugged. "No use pushing him. Once the cart
came onto Friday Street it would be lost for good."

Justin nodded without complaint, knowing it was useless to
berate Halsig or blame the men. He had had a slight hope that
Flael's sons would have believed they could best conceal where
they were going by keeping to the back lanes and alleys. In that
case, they might have been traced; however, they had not been
so ignorant and had moved as quickly as they could onto a well-
traveled way. Justin shrugged when Halsig reported that everyone his men questioned on Fish Street had laughed. Two-wheel
carts on Friday Street, at dawn, were as common as fleas on a
dog.

Still, Justin wondered, why Friday Street instead of Bread Street? Friday Street was west, farther from the bridge they would have to cross to reach Canterbury, which lay to the southeast. Unless . . . unless young Peter and Edmond intended to take a boat, which would be very easy to come by on Friday Street. Justin uttered an obscenity that made Halsig stiffen.

"Not your fault," he said to the guard captain. "Mine. I was not at my best this morning. Because the horse and cart were taken and because L— Madame Heloise said Flael's sons might be going to Canterbury, I never thought they might take a boat . . . elsewhere."

"Then we'll know for sure where they're going," Halsig said quickly, eager to soothe the only superior officer he knew who took the blame on himself instead of placing it on his men. "Any man who took a cart and horse on his boat will remember. And anyone else on the dock will remember too."

"You can send two men to ask after you have eaten your dinner," Justin said, much more calmly. It had occurred to him that if Peter and Edmond had taken a boat, they probably did not intend to return to London—and that meant they could not have conspired with Lissa. "But bear in mind," Justin went on, almost cheerfully, "that they may have abandoned the cart and even the horse. What they will surely have kept with them are the two strongboxes, so be sure your men ask about those as well as asking about the horse and cart."

Firmly suppressing an impulse to go upstairs, Justin left the men to eat the dinner Binge was preparing and walked to Goscelin's house, where he had left his horse. He intended to ride to the gates and see what had been netted, but as soon as he entered the shop, one of the journeymen excused himself from the client to whom he was speaking and asked Justin to go above, where Master Goscelin awaited him.

The solar was even more richly furnished than the one in Flael's house. There was a thick, intricately patterned carpet on the floor and hangings on the walls and two chairs on which the highly polished, elaborate carvings picked up gleams from the leaping fire. And the window—Justin hesitated for just a moment in his advance toward his host as he realized why everything in the room was so brightly lit—the window was made of clear pieces of glass like a few he had seen in rich churches.

A servant had been laying a table for dinner under the eye of the alderman's wife, but as soon as Goscelin saw Justin in the doorway, he spoke a low word to her and she dismissed the servant, coming forward herself to take Justin's cloak and make him a stiff curtsy.

"I beg you, Sir Justin, do not keep Goscelin until our dinner is all overdone. And what of that poor child down the street? What did you do to her? Goscelin would not let me go there and comfort her."

Justin bowed deeply and took Madame Adela's hand to kiss. He knew Goscelin from many meetings of the mayor's council, but he had never before spoken to his wife. She was some years younger than her husband, plump, and dressed in a plain homespun gown with her brown hair in simple plaits, and Justin found her far more attractive now than the haughty woman in brilliant, bejeweled satins he had glimpsed on Goscelin's arm at state banquets. He was sorry to see how uneasy she was in his presence, for Goscelin smiled at her fondly and Justin thought she might be clever and amusing if she could accept him more easily.

"Justin will not keep me from my dinner because he is going to join us," Goscelin said. "And as to that 'poor child'—"

"I left her fast asleep," Justin interrupted, "but I am sure it would do her good if you would visit her later in the day."

Adela nodded and murmured that Justin would be a most welcome guest. He doubted he would be, but with a glance at Goscelin, she left the room. Justin began to protest the invitation to stay, mentioning his need to discover if any carts had been stopped at the gates. Goscelin waved the protest away, saying he would send a messenger to make a round of the gates, whereupon Justin confessed that he had little hope of finding young Peter and Edmond there.

"You think them still in the city?" Goscelin asked.

"That is possible," Justin allowed, "and if they are we will find them sooner or later, but I think they might have made off by boat, in which case they could have escaped us for good, and I was too stupid to think of that."

Goscelin shook his head. "It would have done you no good,

even if the first thing you did was send a man-at-arms down to the dock. Unfortunately the boy Madame Lissa sent did not tell my servant that Flael was dead. Perhaps he was afraid or perhaps she told him to speak only to me. In any case, my servant did not tell me the boy was waiting until I had finished breaking my fast. I will admit at once, before you can think of it yourself, that by the time I sent for you, it would have been too late to catch them."

"Perhaps so," Justin said wryly, "but perhaps not. It is not so easy to get a horse and cart through those streets, and no boat would take them aboard before the catch of fish was unloaded. If I had arrived at the house with all my wits working—"

"In any case, I am sure the sons are not guilty," Goscelin insisted. "Young Peter and Edmond would not have harmed their father. In the name of God, why should you suspect them?"

"I suppose because they ran," Justin said, moving to the chair at which Goscelin gestured, and when the alderman had seated himself too, he began to tell Goscelin about Peter de Flael's death.

"He was tortured *after* he was dead!" Goscelin exclaimed. "And none of the wounds could have killed him?"

Justin shrugged and nodded. "So I believe. I hope the brothers from Bartholomew's Hospital will find some answer to how he died when they prepare the body for burial."

"Flael was an old man and not a brave one," the alderman remarked thoughtfully. "Could it be that he was not murdered at all, but died of fright?"

"That is murder to me," Justin stated, and after a moment, Goscelin sighed and nodded, and Justin gave him a summary of what Lissa had said and the servants' evidence.

"Do not let yourself be led astray by the boy Witta's feelings," Goscelin said. "Flael was a good father, and his sons truly loved him. He was not ungenerous to them. I do not know why they ran away, but I would guess—"

"You do not think they fled with the strongboxes because they feared the new wife had supplanted them in their father's affections and seduced the old man into making a will that excluded them?"

"No," Goscelin said, his shrewd eyes hard. "I did some business with Flael just before his marriage and spoke to him after he and his wife returned from Canterbury. I do not know why he married Heloise Bowles, but it was not for love. I am certain it was some business arrangement."

"A business arrangement with William Bowles?" Justin asked with raised brows.

"No," Goscelin replied, frowning, "although Bowles is rich, richer than he allows to show, and I think he has FitzWalter's ear. Still, Flael was, I am sure, too clever to want any permanent connection with Bowles himself. But the girl has uncles in the Hanse——"

Before Goscelin could finish the remark, the door opened and Madame Adela poked her head in. "Can the servant finish now?" she asked.

"In a moment," her husband said, and she withdrew her head. He said to Justin, "That is all I know anyway. I am sure Peter and Edmond did not harm their father, nor did they know who did it. If they had known, they would have stayed to demand revenge. Unless—"

"Then they ran from fear?" Justin interrupted. "Fear of whom?"

Goscelin shrugged. "I have no idea, but Flael did considerable business with the king. He made John's privy seal, and two years ago, just before the king had word of the conspiracy against him, Flael delivered a matching cup and plate of gold . . . beautiful pieces." The voice of the alderman, who was also a master goldsmith, changed on the last words, softening with admiration. Then he went on slowly, "Flael was lucky. He was given leave to go home only two days before the king had the news about the plot."

The men stared at each other in silence for a moment while similar thoughts passed through both their minds. If the king was involved in Flael's death—and death by terror as well as the seemingly spiteful and purposeless damage inflicted on the corpse were not at all unlikely results of King John's enmity—then the panicked flight of the sons was reasonable. All thought of revenge was hopeless, and it was typical of King John to hold a grudge and punish the sons for the sins of the father.

Justin looked down at his hands. "Is there a chance that Flael *was* involved in the plot against the king?"

"No," the alderman said, smiling suddenly. "I know that for a fact, and in the oddest way. Last year the September meeting of the goldsmiths' fellowship was more than usually merry for reasons with which I will not trouble you, and Flael was among the merriest of us all. We came to talking of the king's peril, for some among us think that Joan's coming with a message of warning to her father was more to benefit her husband Llewellyn, to whom we have heard she is in thrall, than to save John. Well, that is past, but Flael said a strange thing when one of the men—Finke, I think it was—said the plot had never had a chance to succeed. Flael said it would have had a much better chance if he had been a part of it. He was very drunk."

"And you think what was spoken in wine was the truth?"

"Oh yes." Goscelin nodded emphasis to his words. "Flael had no part in the plot, but I cannot help but wonder what he meant. And before anyone could ask, his journeyman—I cannot recall his name, but I remember he was killed in a stupid accident . . . a shame. It was he who made the cup and plate for the king. Ah, such beauty! Anyway, the journeyman had a much harder head for wine than Flael did, and he made a jest and soon carried his master home."

"Flael could have meant he had been approached by someone for support and refused."

"He could have meant anything," the alderman said. "But if his words were carried to the king, implying that he had known of the plot, been at court, and *not* given warning—"

"This is idle speculation." Justin shook his head, then smiled suddenly. "And if you do not open the door and tell your wife we are ready to dine, I will have an enemy I fear worse than the king."

"I too," Goscelin admitted, his shrewd eyes twinkling now. "After all, the king can only kill me. I must live with Adela."

Chapter 4

WILLIAM BOWLES HEARD HIS DAUGHTER CRY, "WAIT," BUT COULD not be bothered with her. Let the little bitch solve her own problems. His were worse. If Flael had been tortured to death and not confessed, suspicion might fall on him, William thought. FitzWalter had not blamed him originally because Hubert de Bosco had taken the box Flael had given him out of his hand immediately. He had never had any chance to open it. Thank God for that. Still, if Flael had sworn under torture that he had delivered the seal to William when William's daughter became his wife and his hostage—

William's eyes stared blindly with terror as he wove in and out of the crowd in the Chepe. At first he was so frightened he could not think at all. He could hardly keep from running, running he knew not where. Finally the desire to run formed into coherent thought. He knew his only hope was to flee before FitzWalter thought of him, and then despair made him whimper aloud. He could not flee because he had no money. He was a rich man, a very rich man, yet he could not lay his hands on more than ten shillings in silver. Much of his wealth was in the charge of three goldsmiths to be lent out at interest. All the rest was tied up in the rare and costly herbs and spices that stocked his shop and in the cargo in the ships of his brothers-by-marriage. In two days he could have money enough to live in comfort anywhere in the world, but in two days he, like Flael, might be dead by torture.

His thoughts ran round and round, panic insisting that he must escape but that, without money, escape was impossible. He was at the corner of his own street when he stopped dead in his tracks so abruptly that a man behind him ran into him and cursed him soundly.

What a fool he was! Heloise would have money. There must be gold in plenty in Flael's coffers. Flael's sons were gone and could not interfere. And if she tried to deny him . . . Despite his terror, William almost smiled. If she tried to prevent him from taking anything he wanted, he would beat her senseless. He would break her nose and her jaw, knock out her teeth, make sure no man would ever look at her again. If he fled and hid, he would have no need to fear Gamel and Gerbod, his thrice-accursed brothers-by-marriage.

William turned to walk back in the direction he had come from, so taken up with his pleasant vision that he did not notice a big man rise from a bench in front of the alehouse on the corner. He started violently when the man seized his arm and spoke his name, and he almost sank to the ground as he whispered, "What did he say?"

"Nothing," Hubert de Bosco growled. "He died before I laid a hand on him."

"Died?" William breathed, unable to believe his ears. "Of what?"

"Fear." Hubert's lips twisted in a sneer meant as much for his companion as for the dead man, but William did not notice the expression.

"By God," he snapped, his quick mind seizing the fact that he was in no danger, "why did you not leave well enough alone and drop him near the house of that woman he used to visit? Either his death would have been taken as natural or she would have been blamed. Heloise said he had been tortured. Why—"

"*He* ordered it," Hubert said. "He thought it might scare anyone who knew into bringing you news."

"He was right about making those who knew fearful," William remarked dryly. "But unfortunately it did not work the way he hoped. It frightened the sons so much that they ran away. Let us hope it also frightened them enough to make them leave behind what we seek. You had better go and tell him. I will go back to Flael's house—"

"No," Hubert said. "You come with me and tell him yourself."

William had noticed that one side of Hubert's face was bruised and swollen, but until then he had not associated the injury with Flael's death. Hubert was forever getting into brawls, but his refusal to bring his master more bad news put a new light on the bruises. Internally, William shuddered. He had no desire to bring bad news to Robert FitzWalter either, but he dared not refuse Hubert directly.

"Very well," he said, "but let us first go back to Flael's house. My daughter is alone there, and we can look for the seal without interference. Flael must have hidden it outside the house before the wedding, but he might have brought it back after he let us search for it." He saw the incipient refusal in Hubert's face and added, "We could look into Flael's strongboxes too. I suppose the sons took something, but . . ."

The suggestive drift in William's voice changed Hubert's mind. The thought of a chance to dip freely into a master goldsmith's strongbox overwhelmed even his fear of his master. His disappointment was correspondingly strong when William's blows on the door for admittance brought Halsig, still chewing but with one hand on his sword hilt. Hubert uttered a growl of frustration, but over William's shoulder he saw two more men behind Halsig and gave up hope, at least temporarily, of making free with Flael's gold. Nor did he utter any further protest when William turned to him and said, "Thank you for accompanying me. I am much recovered from my shock now and do not need to impose on your good nature any longer. There is no need for you to stay here. When I have done what I can for my daughter, we can finish our business."

Hubert had not the faintest idea what this meant, beyond the fact that William clearly wanted him to go away. Since he was accustomed to following William's suggestions without understanding them, he mumbled some meaningless response, watched the door close, and walked back toward the Chepe. On the outskirts of the market, he saw a cookshop, which reminded him that he had not eaten, and he walked across to it, ordered a meal, and sat down to eat on a stool at the end of the plank that served as a table for the shop. He had chosen the stool because it was near the brazier that kept the food hot and warmed the air around it, but the position also gave him a view of Flael's house.

Puzzlement, not suspicion, drew Hubert's eyes to Flael's door. He was far too contemptuous of William's cowardice to suspect him of any attempt to cheat. He had first been hired by Bowles to protect him after William's father-by-marriage and brothers-by-marriage had beaten him nearly to death in revenge for beating his wife. After their ship had sailed, William had paid him now and then to do to others what his wife's kin had done to him. In exchange, aside from money, William would tell him what to do when FitzWalter's orders puzzled him or when he could not understand the dangers or advantages of offers others made to him. Several times he had not followed William's advice, and he had suffered for it. That had been some years ago. Now he always did what William said—unless FitzWalter gave him orders.

Everything had worked just as William said it would this time too. When that journeyman had come to him and said he could lay his hands on a copy of the king's privy seal, William had explained just what to do, and FitzWalter had been very pleased with Hubert, *very* pleased, even though the journeyman had been killed before Hubert had a chance to tell his master about the seal. FitzWalter had been perfectly content with the way Hubert managed the business—by William's advice—until Flael died. But that wasn't William's fault. And it wasn't Hubert's either. Even his master had not guessed that Flael would drop dead.

That train of thought was unpleasant, and Hubert left it to wonder again why he had been sent away from Flael's shop. It could not be because William wanted to be alone with the strongboxes, he thought slowly; even William couldn't get anything out of those while the guards were there. And he couldn't get anything from the daughter either, the thought continued. Cold bitch. She'd see her father starve before she'd give him a farthing of what was hers—and report him to the guard for stealing too.

The food was good. Hubert cracked a bone, sucked on the marrow, and threw the pieces out into the road where two dogs, darting from a side alley promptly fell on them, snarling and snapping, until a passerby kicked them and they fled in different directions. Slowly Hubert's mind, which had been distracted by amusement as he watched the dogs fight, returned to the question of why William had been in such a hurry to be rid of him. Why could he not have joined the guards in their meal, for example, if William did not want the daughter to see him?

Hubert still had made no sense of the problem when William came out of the house some time later, but considering it had sparked enough caution in him to prevent him from calling out to his friend. He rose from the stool and followed, his longer, faster stride slowly narrowing the distance between them. They were again near William's house when he laid his hand on his friend's shoulder. This time, although William turned swiftly, he did not start or grow pale.

"The news is good and bad," he said. "Let me get a bite to eat and we will go. I had no chance to search the workshop, of course, and any hope of profit is gone. The sons loaded Flael's strongboxes in the cart and made off with them—and my idiot daughter did nothing to stop them. However, some good has come of that. The sons are being sought by Justin FitzAilwin."

Hubert grunted, being familiar with Justin, who occasionally did business with his master. But since he did not understand how he could profit in any way from the sons being found by Sir Justin, who would take good care that the strongboxes were not available to any unauthorized person, what he said was, "Why did you send me away?"

William no longer ground his teeth when Hubert asked him a question. The years had taught him patience—and that he must limit his contempt to remarks Hubert could not understand. He had once gone too far and been knocked down and kicked, like a misbehaving dog. Besides, in this case where money was involved, he had to be sure that Hubert did not, by accident, transmit any ideas to FitzWalter that could inspire even a flicker of doubt.

"Because," he murmured, stretching upward to speak directly into Hubert's ear, "if you stayed, we would have had to give your name, and once your name was known, someone would remember that you are sworn to FitzWalter. Do you think your master wishes to be connected in any way to Peter de Flael, who is suddenly and most strangely dead?"

Hubert shook his head, but he still did not understand how anyone could connect Flael's death to him or through him to FitzWalter, and he said so. William's explanations continued right through dinner, once he had made sure no one in his house could overhear Hubert's unguarded voice. Toward the middle of the meal, if he had had the courage, he would have stuck his eating knife in Hubert's eye in frustration. However, by the time he had finished eating and they were on their way to FitzWalter's house, which was perched somewhat forlornly on the mound where Baynard's Castle had once stood, he had got across the point that Hubert must not tell his master he had been near Flael's house since he dropped the corpse there, and he must not go there again, unless specifically bidden to do so by FitzWalter.

Lissa had been wakened suddenly by a voice, the most familiar and least loved in the world, making a demand she did not at once understand. For a moment the whole of the past six weeks were wiped from her mind and she was once again in her own home, fallen asleep before the fire as she sometimes did after a particularly busy day. She sat up, rubbed her aching neck, frowned crossly, and said, "Whatever do you want, father? Can it not wait—"

Her voice checked abruptly as her eyes took in a room lit by daylight and different from her own chamber in her father's house. She remembered where she was and what had happened. The frown, however, only grew more pronounced. "So you came back," she said. "Why?"

"Why? Naturally, to assist my poor bereaved daughter in any way I can."

The mockery in William's voice did not hurt her, but Lissa stared at her father. She was still somewhat bemused by sleep, and she was sickened and disappointed by the idea that Justin was below, listening slyly to their conversation. Nor could she guess from what her father said whether he was aware that

Justin was in the house. Then she saw that the door was closed, and she was so filled with joy at the idea that Justin had not insisted the door be left open, that he trusted her enough not to spy on her, that she barely prevented herself from smiling.

"I am very sorry that Peter should have died in such a horrible way," she said, "but you must know better than any other that I could not be bereaved. You forced me to marry him, and though he was kind to me, we had not been man and wife long enough for me to become fond of him. What do you want here?"

"Perhaps you should not spread the notion that I forced you to marry and that you had no affection for Flael. It is not unknown for a young wife to rid herself of an old, rich husband."

"Do not trouble your head about it, father." Lissa's soft chuckle mocked her father's sneer. "I am in no danger of being suspected on those grounds, since *you* arranged that not a penny of Peter's money nor any share in his business be added to my dower."

William licked his lips. "But his sons are fled, and if they are suspected of his murder—for why else should they run away?— you are Flael's only remaining heir. Certainly until they return and can prove themselves innocent, you must be in charge of your husband's estate."

"That may be so," Lissa agreed, considerably amused at the thought of how her father's expression of gloating greed would change when he heard the end of her sentence. "But that will profit neither you nor me, since young Peter and Edmond took both strongboxes and most of the tools with them. They have left me nothing of Peter's estate but his debts."

There was a moment's silence and then William burst out, "You fool! Idiot! You let them go with the money and the gold and jewels?"

A string of obscenities followed, but Lissa interrupted calmly, "Why should I care? It was *their* money and gold and jewels. Why should they not take them? I am sure young Peter and Edmond had nothing to do with their father's death." Her eyes, full of challenge and accusation, met his. "They ran away because they were frightened by the manner of Peter's murder—and you know it."

"I know nothing." William's voice was low, but terribly violent.

He leaned over Lissa and grasped her wrist so hard that pain lanced up her arm. She shoved herself upright, taking him by surprise, and pushed him back toward the fire so she could wrench herself around and seize the poker. William let go of her, gasping as she raised the tool like a weapon.

"She-wolf! Monster!" he hissed. "Will you accuse me of what I am totally innocent just to satisfy your hatred?"

"Do not be a fool," Lissa said, lowering the poker. "You hurt me, and I will not tolerate that from you, especially since I may be forced to leave this house and return to yours when Peter's sons are found. Sir Justin FitzAilwin and his men are seeking them in the city and beyond. As for you, I will accuse you of nothing and will do all in my power to keep any shadow of guilt from touching you. You know too much about it, but thank God I am certain you are not guilty of murdering Peter."

William stared at her and then bobbed his head in a satisfied way. "Well, then, do you want me to see to Flael's will or seek out someone to argue your case for you?"

"What case?" Lissa asked. "I have none, since I do not intend to dispute Peter's will."

"You are a fool," William said. "Every merchant in the city will be lined up outside your door insisting that Flael owed him money and insisting on immediate payment."

Lissa put a hand to her head, then dropped it and sighed with relief. "No, that will be all right. The money is gone, but Peter's records are in our bedchamber. I will be able to call in the debts owed to Peter to pay those he owed others."

"*You* will call them in? Who will be willing to pay *you*?"

"There are some honest men in the world," Lissa said with a wry smile.

"Fool," William remarked, but without much passion. He was accustomed to his daughter's stupid honesty and her insistence on giving everyone the benefit of the doubt. "You tell me what is owed by whom, and I will have Hubert collect—"

"No!" Lissa exclaimed, her eyes going wide. Then she came closer to her father to speak softly. "I think it was he who murdered Peter. I—"

"Bite your tongue!"

Her father's whisper had the intensity of a scream, and Lissa stiffened with fear, not of any attack by him but of the sudden terror in his eyes. She moistened her lips and looked down. It sickened her to be part of her father's schemes and guilt, but he *was* innocent of murder and for him to be blamed would destroy her. Justin could never— The thought ended abruptly as her father said "Heloise—" in that same tense whisper. It recalled to her the terrible panic her father had shown when he heard of Peter's torture.

Now it occurred to Lissa that though her father treated Hubert de Bosco with caution, he did not really fear him. Then there must be someone behind Hubert, someone very powerful, most likely someone more powerful than the mayor and aldermen of the city, which meant the earls and barons . . . or the king. Lissa remembered that Peter had told her he did much business with the king and the great nobles. Perhaps Peter had been involved in the troubles that had nearly turned King John's court inside out.

Lissa knew more than she wanted to know about the accusations and counteraccusations in the plot to kill the king. She also did business with the great nobles, or rather with their wives and daughters, and the ladies who came to her for perfumes and salves and powders and potions loved to gossip. But too often ladies who had carried themselves high and proudly suddenly came no more. Then another, perhaps new to the court, would whisper in Lissa's ear that the lady had been banished or ruined when King John's favor shifted. Or sometimes the whisper was that their husbands had fallen foul of the king, and a man who had thought himself too powerful to be touched by John learned that the king's slyness could sometimes outmaneuver strength. If Peter's death was part of that madness, it could go unavenged as far as Lissa was concerned. She had no intention of becoming entangled in court politics.

"Heloise!"

William's now frantic plea woke Lissa to the fact that she had been silent too long, thinking. She raised her eyes, which had been fixed on the floor, and saw that her father's face was blanched and his hands were knotted into fists.

"I will point no finger in any direction," she said, "but I will have nothing to do with that man nor any other connected to you."

"Then do not blame me if your dowry is seized to pay your husband's debts," William snarled, rage replacing fear as soon as she promised not to implicate Hubert. "And do not expect me to make good on it either."

"If I need help, Sir Justin will help me," Lissa said.

"Will he?"

William stared thoughtfully at his daughter. She was no beauty. He could never understand what it was about her that drew men. Before he needed to provide Flael with a hostage, he had refused more offers for her than he could count, which was one reason Flael thought William valued Heloise enough to make her a good hostage. Possibly she could seduce Sir Justin. If she could . . . For a moment William indulged himself with the idea of what he could accomplish if the man charged with uncovering crime dared not accuse him of anything. But he could not believe his daughter's attractions could be that powerful, and close association with a seeker of wrongdoers was dangerous.

"You would do better to stay clear of Sir Justin," William urged. "That man will see through you. I warn you that if he noses out your suspicion of Hubert, we will all—Sir Justin too— be in grave danger."

The inclusion of Justin in her father's threat startled Lissa. In view of her thoughts about the power that might be behind Hubert, she could not dismiss the threat as she usually did. In an odd way, though, what her father had said was a balm to her soul. It gave her an excellent reason to continue to conceal her suspicions from Justin. Then she had to suppress a qualm about how close she had come to telling Justin far more than it was safe for him to know. But she could not try to avoid him; that would surely make him think she had guilty knowledge.

Hiding uncertainty from her father was second nature to Lissa, and all she said was "I am not so presumptuous as to expect Sir Justin to make the time to attend to my problems himself, but I believe he will most likely be able to recommend to me someone who will collect Peter's debts without cheating either me or the debtor."

"Then I need waste no more time with you." William's voice grated with anger, and he turned to leave.

"I will accompany you down," Lissa said sweetly, but to her

surprise, for he had just warned her to avoid Sir Justin, her father only looked surprised.

When she was halfway down the stairs, Lissa saw the guard sitting near the shop door, and her amusement changed to disappointment. She should have known that her father had not seen Sir Justin when he did not argue with her about coming down. Telling herself not to be a fool, that Sir Justin had more important things to do than wait for her to finish her nap, she forced herself to say, "Farewell, father, and thank you," as she saw him out. It would be a mistake, she thought, to allow the guard to see anything he might consider unusual in her behavior. The man could not know of the long-standing antagonism between her father and herself, and any coldness she exhibited might be connected to Peter's death.

Turning from the closed door, Lissa started toward the workroom. She did not want to see Peter's body, but she could not control a single sidelong glance in that direction. He was not there! She turned to stare at the empty space before the counter where the corpse had lain.

"M-my husband," she stammered. "Wh-where—"

The guard stood up. "The brothers took the body away, mistress," he said. "Sir Justin and the priest thought it would be better for the brothers of Saint Bartholomew to make the body ready for burial. Father Denis would've told you, but Sir Justin left orders that you not be wakened. Father Denis wasn't angry. He said he'd come back later to talk to you."

Tears of relief and gratitude stung Lissa's eyes, and she had to swallow hard before she could thank the guard for the information. With a light step she passed through the shop into the workroom, but there she stopped short. Only two men were in the room, one gathering the scraps of a meal to give to his pigs or to the beggars, and the other setting aside the plank they had used as a table. After the kindness he had shown in relieving her of the dreaded duty of laying out Peter's corpse, Lissa had expected to find Justin either eating with his men or waiting to dine with her. Now, although she knew she had no right to be offended, she felt hurt and angry. Still, it was not the fault of the men who, she supposed, were waiting in the hope that Peter's sons would return, and she managed to ask pleasantly if their dinner had been satisfactory.

"Yes, mistress, thank you," the older man, who had been gathering the scraps, said with a smile. "I am Halsig, captain of the guard, and this is Dunstan. If there is anything we can do for you, just say, mistress."

"Thank you. You are very kind," Lissa replied. "If you would tell Binge to send Witta up with something for me to eat, I would be grateful."

He nodded and went out the back door, and Lissa went upstairs again. She felt lonely and lost, both emotions intensified by her idleness. Before marriage Lissa had done or overseen much of the compounding of the remedies and cosmetics her father's shop dispensed and had often served the female clients as well as keeping the accounts and accompanying her father to examine the herbs and spices they purchased. After her marriage she had been equally occupied because her husband's country estate was new to her and she wished to learn all she could about managing such a place. Even when they had returned to London, she had been busy. Now she stood looking around the room forlornly, noticing that the table where they had eaten had been cleared and that the plate and goblet Justin had used were both clean and in their proper places. There was nothing for her to do . . .

"Oh, Lord," she whispered, "what a fool I am."

There was more than enough to do. She had forgotten all about her conversation with her father in her disappointment over Justin's departure. There were the records to examine. Lissa walked quickly into the bedchamber and knelt by the chest that contained the records of Peter's business. Lifting the heavy lid, she examined the contents—tally sticks and rolls of parchment. The tally sticks no doubt were the financial records, each marked with a symbol that stood for the client and cut and notched to show the amounts owed and repaid, then split, Peter keeping one half and the client keeping the other so each had an identical record.

Lissa had little doubt that she would be able to translate the cuts and notches into pennies, shillings, and pounds or marks after a little study, but there was no way for her to determine to whom each symbol at the top of the stick referred. However, there were a large number of sticks, some bundled together. It was possible that Peter had kept a separate written record of the symbols rather than trust to his memory. Lissa scooped the parchment rolls out of the chest and discovered that there were not as many as she had first thought, because there were more tally sticks underneath. She took what she could hold and carried them into the solar where she dropped them into the basket that held her embroidery thread. Setting that on a stool to one side of Peter's chair, she went to make up the fire and then set to work.

Most of the rolls were about the same size, a few were larger. She chose one of the largest, untied the thin cord that held it into a roll, and began to examine it. At the top was an extraordinarily detailed drawing of a plate and several views around the body of a goblet. Below was a written description of the items, an agreement that the client, a Lord John, would furnish the gold, and the price to be paid for the labor.

The designs were lovely. Lissa was swept with a deep feeling of regret that the man who could create such beauty should have been so cruelly killed. She wondered, too, whether the client had appreciated what he was getting, and looked down to see if she might recognize the seal. For a moment she went rigid. Every important merchant in London knew that seal. It was the king's privy seal, the small one used for private business, which was kept in his own wardrobe rather than at the exchequer.

Lissa stared for a moment and then shivered slightly. There was no indication on the parchment as to whether Peter had been paid for his work. Had death been the coin in which his demand for payment was satisfied? No, that was silly. The king was not in London, and Peter had not had time to ride to Windsor. It did not matter anyway, Lissa thought. She had just decided that this was one debt she would be happy to ignore when Witta pranced in the open door with a tray.

The boy seemed to have recovered completely from the shock he had had and was brighter and more cheerful than at any time since he had begun serving her. Lissa was sure it was because he had not been blamed for any of the horrible events and, in addition, was free of the ill treatment of Peter's sons. She did not have the heart to reprimand him for showing he was happy despite his master's death, and simply told him to put the food down on the table.

There was no harm in Witta's being happy, but Lissa did not feel the same about idleness. She bade him wait when he was about to skip out of the room, then told him to go get his slate, for she had begun to teach him to read and cipher. He ran off with an eager smile and was soon clattering up the stairs again. The eagerness to learn was one of the things that made Lissa determined to keep the boy. He was no angel. Set him an ordinary task of sweeping or cleaning and he was as dilatory and desirous to escape as any other child his age, but show him the difference between the look and scent of varieties of herbs or the lines of a new letter, and you had Witta's full attention.

The child had been well named, Lissa thought—wise man in the English tongue. She smiled as she wrote his lesson on the slate. It was only a few words for him to copy and some simple sums and differences. Lissa had no intention of making Witta a scholar; she was not even certain she would try to teach him French or Danish. At present her aim was to have him learn enough reading and ciphering to be a trustworthy manager of her business when she was away or confined by childbirth. So far, both his devotion and his bright interest indicated she had chosen well.

Lissa smiled at the boy and told him to sit by the fire and work. Then she rolled up and retied the parchment showing the work done for the king, put it aside from the others, and took another, smaller one. She carried this to the table with her, unrolling it before she began to eat. Unfortunately, this was much the same in content as the parchment concerning the king's plate and goblet, although it was clear that this client was neither a great nor a wealthy man. The cup sketched was much simpler and was to be done in pewter with Peter providing the material as well as the labor. What disturbed Lissa was that she could find no indication on this parchment of whether the work had been completed, delivered, and paid for or whether this was just a plan for work to be done, nor did she recognize either the name of the client or the seal.

What was she to do? The disappointment drained her energy, and she felt tired and dull again. Leaving the parchment open on the table, she began to eat the stew and pick at the bread

Binge had sent up. Doubtless she could discover to whom each seal belonged, but without evidence as to whether the client had paid or not or whether the work had been delivered or not, the information on the parchment rolls was useless.

"Is that a letter too?" Witta asked in a slightly accusatory voice.

Lissa turned her head from her food to find the boy standing beside here and pointing to a symbol written below the client's seal. "Oh you naughty boy," she said. "You are not supposed to read any writing you see lying about unless you have permission to do so."

"I'm sorry, mistress," Witta said somewhat sullenly. "But how can I read if you don't teach me all the letters?"

"But I have—" Lissa began, and then looked again at where Witta had been pointing. "I *have* taught you all the letters, child," she finished, now grinning from ear to ear with delight. "That is not a letter; it is a symbol for the whole name of the client." She pointed to the name in the document. "The symbol is used to connect something with this client when there is not space enough to write the name. Now, in the chest in my bedchamber are bundles of tally sticks. Bring them out here, and bring out the other parchments, and we will match the symbols to the tally sticks."

Chapter 5

EVEN WITH WITTA'S QUICK-EYED HELP, THE PROCESS OF MATCHING parchment record to tally sticks took all afternoon. However, before the light failed all of the smaller rolls of parchment had been paired with their tallies. By then Lissa was aware that there were far more tally sticks than parchments and that she and Witta must have disarranged separate lots. The extra tally sticks, she concluded, were records of Peter's moneylending. She was of two minds about that. If she was not pressed by Peter's creditors, she was quite willing to forget the moneylending debts. She would not burn the tally sticks, but she would not try to collect the debts unless there was no other way to save her dowry—always assuming she could discover a key to the symbols on the tally sticks.

Lissa then began to laugh at herself for this "holier than thou" attitude. It was true that if the debts of usury were "forgiven" she would be losing most of Peter's fortune, but there was no reason for her to feel noble, since the money was not hers. Then the soft curve of her mouth hardened. She would wait a reasonable time; then if young Peter and Edmond did not return, she would burn the tally sticks. It was bad enough for them to have abandoned her—if she had not been brought up to understand business, she would have been in a terrible state— but to have left their father lying on the floor like a used-up rag was unforgivable.

While she thought, her fingers had untied another roll, one of the largest. She had left those for last, assuming that they were all records of work for the king or great noblemen. Despite their wealth, for the most part they were the hardest to collect from. Lissa herself usually insisted that her richest and noblest clients pay when she delivered the purchase, and it was most likely that Peter also collected his full fee on delivery. There had been no tally sticks to match the parchment showing the king's plate and goblet, so there might be none for any of the most costly projects.

The parchment she had just unrolled would be useless to confirm or deny that idea. There was no client's name, which was not surprising, because it was the design for the betrothal gift Peter had bestowed upon her. Lissa gently touched the carefully drawn waves and dolphins, regretting that she could feel no real sorrow—until her eyes moved idly to the bottom of the sheet as she was about to roll it up. There her gaze fixed, and her bottom lip thrust forward in a charming pout. No client's name above, but there was a seal at the bottom and below the seal the word "Refused." Lissa knew to whom the seal belonged too. Had she not made up dozens of doses of aphrodisiacs for him? So, the necklet had not been made for her but for one of that lecher's whores.

Lissa uttered a small resentful snort, laid that parchment aside, and briskly opened the largest roll of all. She uttered another snort, this one of contempt at herself. Here was the key to the tally records of Peter's usury. Naturally the largest of the parchments would hold the record of accounts. There were names and directions, most to clients who lived in the city but a substantial number to Canterbury and a sprinkling of other towns, too; in addition there was the symbol for the tally sticks and, most important of all, a written notation of what had been lent, at what interest, and what had been repaid. That would make it much easier for Lissa to determine what the marks on the tally sticks meant. She was certain that Peter would have used the same markings on all his records.

The question remained whether she should try to collect the loans now that she had all the information. Her instinct was to roll up that long sheet and forget it, but she had not quite decided when she heard the guard's voice and, a moment later, soft footsteps on the stair. A hope she had forgotten while she was immersed in Peter's records sprang up. Lissa quickly rolled the long parchment tight and eagerly rose to her feet. Then it took all her self-control to mask her disappointment when Father Denis, not Justin FitzAilwin, paused at the open door of the chamber.

"You seem busy, my daughter," the priest said.

"Yes, Father," Lissa replied somewhat warily. "My father came to warn me that because of the manner of his death, my husband's creditors might demand immediate payment of what he owed. Since Peter's sons went off with his strongboxes, I—"

"Went off with his strongboxes!" Father Denis repeated. "What do you mean they went off with his strongboxes? Have you any other resources? How will you honor the terms of Master Peter's will? Who will pay for his burial? For masses for his soul? Who will pay the brothers of Saint Bartholomew for fetching the body and preparing it for the grave?"

"London will pay the brothers of Saint Bartholomew."

Just as they had done earlier in the day, the priest started with surprise and Lissa sighed with relief. Both turned toward the doorway, where Sir Justin stood. He nodded curtly to Lissa but continued speaking to the priest. "Their examination of the body was at my request to determine the cause of death. That was part of my official duty. The preparation for burial was incidental, and the only cost will be for the shroud. Li—Madame Heloise can repay me for that when it is convenient for her."

"But what of Master Peter's other obligations? What of the offerings promised in his will?"

"I know nothing of his will," Lissa said. Her eyes flashed once toward Justin, but she dared not let them linger and she set them steadily on Father Denis. "I do not believe I am mentioned in my husband's will. There is no reason that I should be because my affairs were arranged by my father to be completely separate from Peter's. I am not one of Peter's heirs, you see; his sons are his heirs."

The priest's lips turned down and his eyes narrowed. "I will not refuse decent burial to Master Peter de Flael, but neither can I promise to arrange the chanting of masses for the ease of his soul without some token of sacrifice on the part of those he succored and protected in life. It is you, madam, not I who will condemn your husband to many, many years of purgatory." He turned away from her so sharply that the skirt of his habit smacked against the leg of the chair and tangled on it, aborting his stride toward the door.

"One moment, Father," Lissa said, and had to stop speaking.

Already amused by the notion that a few years in purgatory for the great sin of usury might do Peter some good and prepare him for heaven much better than prayers sung on earth would, she was nearly overset into laughter at the abruptness with which Father Denis had been stopped. The alacrity with which he turned toward her when she spoke did nothing to sober her, nor did his expression, which was again benign—benign and hopeful.

Lissa stared at her own toes for a moment, fighting for control, but her voice was still choked and quivering when she said, "I have something Peter gave to me, my betrothal gift. I am perfectly willing to part with it to ensure the ease of Peter's soul. However, I have almost nothing else, except the few coins in my purse, and I greatly fear that Peter made other promises. Thus, I will give you my necklet, if you will sign a statement that you will share the proceeds from the piece with any other church or house of religion to which Peter promised a contribution."

"Do you bargain with God, daughter?" Father Denis asked.

Lissa choked back the remark that she had better do so or she would be left without so much as a shift to cover her. What she did say instead was, "Father, what ease will my poor husband have if you bless him while those at Saint Matthew's curse him for cheating them? Not that I think he made equal promises to Saint Matthew's. I do not know what Peter promised. It may well be that he endowed only you."

Father Denis considered that, weighing his knowledge of Peter de Flael's care for his purse against the goldsmith's fear of being damned for the many sins he had committed. It was indeed possible, he thought, that in the interests of economy,

Peter had promised nothing to any other church. If he offered only small amounts, he would be accused of niggardliness; if he offered amounts equal to what he had promised Saint Peter's, there might be severe enough inroads into his fortune that his sons would have refused to pay anyone at all, leaving him to languish in purgatory perhaps forever; the best solution was to give what he wanted during his lifetime to other churches and to tell them that his death benefices were going to the place where he was to be buried.

Having come to that conclusion, Father Denis added in the fact that soon Flael's wife might begin to wonder what good masses would do a soul that was damned for lacking the final rites. He cast a sidelong glance at her and saw what he felt was a growing hardness in her expression. That decided him, and he agreed as graciously as he could to sign the statement Lissa wanted.

Lissa nodded and went to get the necklet immediately, catching up the open roll of parchment from the table. She was eager to get rid of the priest before Justin grew impatient. In the bedchamber, she quickly cut off the seal of the client, leaving only the description, price, and drawing of the necklet. Then she opened her clothing chest and picked up the beautiful box in which Peter had sent his gift. The sweet scent and satin finish of the woods made her hesitate. The box *had* been made for her; Peter had told her he had made it himself. Her lips twisted wryly. When she thought of it she realized he had never said the necklet had been made for her. She replaced the box in the chest, opened it, and removed the necklet.

Returning to the solar, Lissa picked up a quill and an inkhorn from the shelves and brought them to the table where she laid the necklet. While Father Denis feasted his eyes on the emerald-eyed dolphins leaping through the foam of pearls, she quickly wrote the statement committing Father Denis to share with other beneficiaries and freeing her from further obligation.

"Will you serve as witness, Sir Justin?" she asked.

"A witness to a priest's word, my child?" Father Denis protested mildly.

"I must ask it," Lissa said, wide-eyed. "My father would scold me terribly if I did not have a witness. I—"

The look of wide-eyed innocence, and the statement that was

literally true while implying a situation that was totally false, amused Justin but also made him uneasy. He did not like reminders of how good an actress Lissa was. They made him wonder, despite Goscelin's opinion that Lissa and Flael's sons were innocent, if he was really doing all he should to check up on them.

"Very well," he said, interrupting her sharply and preventing any further exchange.

He was still standing in the doorway and came forward rather slowly, as if he was reluctant, Lissa thought. She laid down the pen and went to take his cloak. He hesitated when she reached for it, then pulled the pin from the broach that held it and gave her the garment. When he had read the few lines, he glanced at the necklet. Meanwhile, Lissa had hung the cloak on a hook near the door and turned back toward him just in time to see him raise his brows at her in surprise. Swiftly she touched a finger to her lips, which were curved upward in a slight, reassuring smile.

Having lifted the necklet and examined it closely, Father Denis laid it down on the table and glanced at Lissa just once in a troubled way. She stared back at him blankly, and he folded his lips tightly together and signed. Justin also glanced at Lissa, but she had turned away from them and was taking from the chest below the shelves one of the napkins used for drying the hands during a formal dinner. Frowning, Justin wrote his name followed by the words "as witnessed by me" and the date below the priest's signature. While they were writing, Lissa had wrapped the necklet in the napkin.

"You can carry it more safely in that wrapping than in its box," she said. "The box is rather large and might draw eyes. It is not valuable. I believe Peter made it himself."

"Quite right, dear daughter," Father Denis replied. "You show a most proper spirit in sacrificing your worldly goods to gain the pearl of salvation for your husband." He looked a trifle uneasy as he spoke and glanced sidelong at Justin, whose thin face seemed carved, like the box Flael's wife mentioned, of wood. "You will not suffer for it," he said, shifting his eyes under Justin's cold stare.

"I am sure I will not suffer for it," Lissa agreed softly.

"Then I have troubled you long enough, daughter. Unless I

can perform some service for you? If not, I will go and leave you to eat your evening meal in peace."

"Thank you, Father, I need nothing," Lissa assured him, keeping her voice calm with some difficulty because of her urgent desire to push him out of the room. "Is there light enough to see the stair?" She turned around, looking carefully into each dark corner for Witta, who loved to make himself inconspicuous and watch and listen. When she found him, she said, "Ah, there you are, Witta. Light a candle and see that Father Denis does not trip on the stair. After that, find out what Binge has made ready for the evening meal."

There, Lissa thought, I am rid of both of them, but she had congratulated herself too quickly.

Justin stopped Father Denis before he reached the door, saying, "Just a moment, Father. Actually I came here from the church. I was seeking you, not Li—Madame Heloise. I wished to tell you that I had been to Saint Bartholomew's Hospital and spoken to the brothers there. All is ready. Flael can be encoffined and buried tomorrow. I assume"—he looked pointedly at a corner of the folded napkin that had escaped the priest's hurried effort to stuff his prize into the sleeve of his gown—"that you will make *all* the arrangements for Madame Heloise."

"Yes, yes," Father Denis said hastily. "If there is no reason for delay—"

"None at all."

A brief look of surprise passed over the priest's features. Lissa saw it but was too disappointed by the fact that Justin had not come back to see her to think what it might mean. She held her breath, silent and unmoving, understanding now why Justin had hesitated to give her his cloak and expecting him to ask for it and follow Father Denis out of the room. But he did not; he stood as still as she, with his head a little cocked, listening. By the time Father Denis had made his way down the stairs, Lissa's disappointment had changed to hope. If Justin had come only to tell Father Denis that he could go ahead with Peter's burial, why had he not simply left word at the church?

They heard a soft exchange between the priest and the man at the door and then the closing of the door. As if the sound released them, both moved at once. Lissa took a thin spill of wood from a bundle propped near the hearth, lit it at the fire, and began to light the candles around the room. Justin went and closed the door to the stair.

"Was that necklet real?" he asked.

"I believe so," Lissa replied, setting the last taper alight and turning to face him.

"Do you know what it is worth?"

She smiled at him. "Unless prices have changed greatly from last year, the worth was written on the parchment Father Denis signed. Surely it is enough to free me of all importunity over masses for Peter's soul."

"Are you mad?" Justin's face lost its rigid calm and crumpled into exasperation.

Lissa laughed softly. "Not at all. The necklet was Peter's and surely should be used to ease his soul. And I did not want it. I would never have worn it again. I suppose I could have bought a different trinket with the money if I sold it, but . . ." She hesitated and half turned away, feeling ashamed somehow, although she knew it was silly. "But I would always have felt it was tainted," she went on, now looking defiantly at Justin. "Wait," she added, "I will show you."

As she handed Justin the cut-off portion of the parchment, which she had fetched from the bedchamber, she said, "I do not know whether you know Lord Norville?"

Justin's eyes flicked from the seal to her face, and then he threw the strip of parchment into the fire with controlled violence. "I know him." He paused, and then said irritably, "But it was still a stupid thing to do. Here you are without money to buy food, as far as I know, and for a—a pet of pride you have given away what could have supported you for a year."

This time Lissa's laugh was a merry peal. "I am not as destitute as that, and to prove it, I will send Witta out to buy the most delectable meal the cookshops can provide—if you will share it with me."

She was delighted that Justin understood her distaste at being given the leavings of a lecher's refusal to pay—and had even sympathized with it before his sense of practicality interfered—but she felt a little anxious when she did not see an echo of her laughter in his eyes. She had noticed earlier in the day that even when his mouth kept its thin, severe line, she could tell when Justin was sharing her amusement. But he did not look severe now, he looked worried.

"I should not—"

"Is there someone waiting for you at home?" Lissa interrupted quickly. She did not want him to say "waste my time" or some other irremediable words.

"Do you often take the words out of a person's mouth?" Justin asked, and Lissa had to hold back a sigh of relief because he was smiling. "I was about to say that I should not impose—and possibly should not be so friendly with a suspect."

Lissa's smile broadened to a grin, but she was able to conceal it from Justin and avoid any direct reply, since she heard Witta at the door. To call her a suspect was a most excellent excuse, she thought, to watch her and talk to her—if Justin needed a reason for the time and energy he was giving to easing her difficulties over Peter's murder. She was not certain, however, whether she was free to make jokes about his finding excuses to be with her. If he had not realized what he was doing, it would be dangerous to point it out to him. She might destroy any chance she had of binding him to her.

Witta's long face recalled Lissa from delightful speculation to immediate practicality. "There is nothing but soup," he said. "Binge says she has better things to do than prepare feasts for a roomful of strangers twice a day."

"Good." Lissa laughed at Witta's shocked expression. "I will deal with Binge's sauciness later, but I cannot say I am overfond of her cooking, so we will forget it for now. I will give you five pennies. Go to the cookshop on Milk Street by Honey Lane and bring back a roast chicken, a pork pasty—hot, not cold—and some of that milk soup they make with oysters. And fill a jack with wine from the smaller cask in the back of the workroom when you come back." As she spoke and took the coins from the purse on her belt, she turned her head to Justin and asked, "What of the men? Will the soup be enough or should I order some food for them also?"

"Nothing for them. I was about to send them home. There is no more to do here."

Lissa was surprised at the nervous qualm that passed through her at the idea of being alone in the house. She was ashamed to ask openly for someone to stay, but she said, "What shall I do if Peter and Edmond return? I do not believe I can pretend no one asked about them, and I cannot see how I could keep them here for you to question."

"If they are not ready to be questioned and do not intend to stay, they will not come back at all," Justin told her. "In any case, you are not responsible for them beyond sending word to me of their coming, if they should come. I must admit, I am very puzzled about why they ran away. Master Goscelin does not believe they could have had a hand in their father's death."

"Nor do I believe it," Lissa assured him, letting go of Witta and gesturing to the boy to be off. She closed the door and walked slowly toward Justin, frowning. "They did not like me, but I think that was partly jealousy for their mother's memory. There was real affection between Peter and his sons. They would not have hurt him for any reason."

"Then why did they run?"

Lissa shook her head. "It must have been fear because Peter was tortured, but the more I think about it, the more confused I become. I believed at first, as I told you, that they had decided to take the strongboxes away to put them into safekeeping. But I have been going over Peter's records all afternoon, and truly there could be no purpose to taking the money and jewels and raw metals away. What debts he had were very small. Of course, if what was in the strongboxes did not match the records—but I cannot believe that. Peter was a fine craftsman, even a great one. I did not yet know him very well, but he seemed to have a good reputation. There was only one thing . . . He—he did lend money at interest."

To Justin's surprise, Lissa looked down and blushed over those last words. Before he thought, he had taken a long step forward and put his arm around her. "They all do," he said. "You need not be ashamed. It was not *your* fault."

Even as he embraced Lissa, Justin was appalled. From the first look of gratitude she had flashed him when he stopped Father Denis's diatribe, he had felt totally welcome, more welcome than he was to his own servants in his own home. There had been a kind of amused conspiracy between him and Lissa over the priest's greed. Even the quarrel, if it could be called that, over Lissa's too-great generosity had added to the feeling of intimacy, of comfort, of belonging. All had conspired to make him forget who he was and who Lissa was and how short a time he had known her.

Lissa looked up at him and saw that there was more than natural color in his face. He was embarrassed by what he had done, she thought, and did not know how to escape from the situation.

"Thank you," she murmured, squeezing his hand as she gently disengaged herself. She continued to hold the hand she had slipped from her shoulder for a little time and even when she slid her fingers slowly away, she remained close, her sleeve brushing Justin's. Then she said thoughtfully, "But if young Peter and Edmond suspected one of the debtors, surely they would have waited to tell you and ask for your protection. And to torture Peter . . . Why would a debtor do that? Still, I am sure that his sons ran from fear, not from guilt. To speak the truth, I am a little frightened myself." She bit her lip. "It was such a horrible way to die." Tears came into her eyes and her voice faltered over that last sentence.

Justin had just been thanking God that he had escaped his foolishness with so little damage to his pride when he found, to his horror, that he had not learned anything. His immediate response to Lissa's tears and shaking voice was a desperate desire to take her in his arms again. He had barely enough will to resist that impulse, but he could not bear her distress. He burst out, "Peter de Flael did not die horribly. At least, he was dead before any injuries were inflicted on him."

Lissa stood staring at him, one hand pressed to her lips. "But—but that—that is mad," she whispered. "Of what did he die then? Who would do such a thing?"

"The brothers are not sure of what he died," Justin replied. "They think he was afraid, and his heart was weak so it just stopped. There was no wound that could have killed him. As to who could have done such a thing, or why—"

"His sons knew," Lissa breathed. Then her voice grew louder and the horror began to be replaced with indignation. "That was why Peter and Edmond ran. They knew the mutilation of their father was a warning. How disgusting! What foul mind would so use a helpless corpse?"

"A warning," Justin repeated, rather amused by Lissa's indignation and then interested. He and Goscelin had assumed the mutilations were a kind of senseless vengeance, like a man kicking a chair over which he has tripped. But Lissa's idea fit the facts better, especially the fact that the body had been brought home, which he had not previously considered. "Yes." He nodded. "I had not thought of that, but it makes good sense."

Then he sighed. In a way it did make sense, but it brought him no closer to whoever had done it.

"You are tired," Lissa said. "Come, sit here and warm yourself."

She led him to the chair, shaking her head when he began to protest that she should sit there, and pulled the footstool forward to accommodate his long legs. "I have been sitting all day," she said, "and unless I am sleepy I am more accustomed to a stool."

She went to fetch her stool and brought her embroidery frame too, which she set where he could see her without turning his head. Lissa had discovered that men found a woman engaged in embroidery very soothing. They could stare without offense, believing the woman did not realize she was being watched. And embroidery gave her a wonderful excuse to look down, concealing any expression except those she wished to expose by deliberately raising her head.

"No," Lissa said when she had settled herself, voicing the end of an argument that had been going on in her head while she mechanically performed the physical tasks. "I cannot believe that any of Peter's debtors would have felt such a thing to be necessary. I did not study the records carefully, but none of the amounts seemed large enough to cause such a desperate measure. And Peter was not an unreasonable man."

"I did not know him well," Justin remarked, "but Goscelin could not think of any enemy who hated him enough to murder him, much less commit such an outrage on his body after his death."

Lissa leaned forward to draw the basket of embroidery thread closer to her stool and pulled out a thin hank of silver thread. With her eyes on the length she was unwinding, she said, "There is one more thing I must tell you. Among Peter's records I found drawings and a description of a goblet and plate Peter made for the king. Those were delivered two years ago in July, but there are no tally sticks and no notation that the work was paid for."

She cut the thread with a small, sharp knife from the basket and took the needle from the cloth on which she was working, turning toward the fire to see the eye of the needle better.

"I had heard of that from Goscelin," Justin said. His voice was low, almost drowsy as he watched Lissa align thread and needle. He had a sudden vision of his father sitting by the fire talking idly with his mother of estate matters while she sewed. What was he thinking of! "Your husband," he went on, using those words deliberately to remind himself that Lissa was a widow of one day. "Your husband actually presented the goblet and plate at the court where the plot against King John was exposed, but Flael left before that happened, and it seems certain that he was not involved in any way."

"Good God!" Lissa exclaimed, dropping the needle and thread into her lap and turning back to Justin with wide eyes. She was far too shocked by the implications of what Justin had said to notice his reminder that she was a very recent widow. "I never thought of that for a moment. I was only afraid that Peter had asked payment for his labor—the gold was the king's—and had been . . . taught his place with an added warning to his heirs not to presume."

Justin's lips twisted wryly. "There would hardly be a merchant alive if the king killed every one who demanded payment." He frowned thoughtfully. "I would guess your husband *was* paid, especially since the sum was not large. Because so many of his barons hate him, John needs his burghers more than most kings and treats us better. Besides, Goscelin said Flael did considerable work for him. He made the king's privy seal when John first came to the throne. I cannot believe he would set a foot so badly amiss with the king after dealing with him well all these years."

"But from what I have heard," Lissa remarked, "knowing King John well can be a double-edged sword. I hope Master Goscelin was right when he said Peter was not in that plot." She looked into her lap to find the needle and thread and lifted them again. "The king . . . I have heard the king can be . . . very cruel."

"He can be," Justin agreed, but there was a brisk matter-of-factness in his voice that took any horror from the words. "And I admit that John was like a madman just after the plot was revealed. He suspected everyone. If your husband had been killed and mutilated right after the summer court of 1212, or even in July or August last year—after John was forced to pardon FitzWalter and Vesci and the others—I would have considered seriously whether the king might be behind what was done. At that time, a deadly warning might have had some point, but now there could be no sense to it."

"There cannot be any new trouble brewing, can there?" Lissa asked. She thrust the thread through the needle quickly and drew it down, ready to take a stitch, but looked up at Justin instead of at her work.

"We do not need any new trouble," Justin replied. "The old is still with us. The enmity between the barons and the king is like an ill-healed wound, a pus-filled sore under a thin covering of skin applied by Archbishop Langton. But just now the skin with Langton's dressing atop *is* covering the sore, and John is too busy with his preparations for war in France to be troubled about the actions of any one man—oh, except perhaps Eustace de Vesci or Robert FitzWalter." Justin sighed. "I wish FitzWalter had not been included in the pardon."

"Why? Do you hate him too?"

Justin had been looking into the fire, but at the questions he turned his head sharply, suddenly alert. "Hate him *too*?" he repeated. "Did Flael hate FitzWalter?"

"Oh no," Lissa said, startled. "I do not remember that Peter ever mentioned Lord Robert, and I do not believe I saw his name among either clients or debtors. I cannot imagine why Lord Robert should have anything to do with Peter's death. I was only wondering why you said you were sorry he had been pardoned."

"That is nothing to do with my feelings about FitzWalter. In fact, I think in some ways FitzWalter's reputation is undeserved. He is certainly brutal but not, I believe, indiscriminately vicious, and he is certainly not a coward. However, he has a hatred for King John that is, in my opinion, not entirely sane."

Lissa pushed the needle she had been holding through the sleeve cuff, caught a tiny stitch to hold the thread, and then began to stitch and backstitch to create a small branch bearing a few graceful leaves. She did not look up but murmured encouragingly. She could feel that Justin was looking at her; that gave her pleasure, but she showed no sign of it beyond the single soft words that marked her interest.

"I am a little sorry for FitzWalter," Justin went on, "because I think he is driven to more aggressive action than he might really like by that label of cowardice that was affixed to him in 1203. And that need to prove himself more a man than any other, added to his hatred for John, may cause our city great trouble. You know, do you not, that FitzWalter is London's Standard Bearer? That means he leads the troops the city provides for the king in times of war. Right now the king is gathering troops for war in France again, and FitzWalter is going. I could hardly believe it when I heard."

Lissa knew that the mayor's watches were in Justin's charge. They were the major armed force in the city, aside from the men-at-arms who were based in the Tower, and it seemed inevitable that many of those men would be chosen to go with the king. "And you?" she asked. "Are you going?" Her head had come up, her eyes wide and her lips parted with anxiety.

"Are you so eager to be rid of me that you wish me in France?" Justin teased.

Color stained Lissa's cheeks, but she did not drop her eyes. "You know that is not true. I do not know how I would have survived this day without your kindness."

"Do not trust me. I am winning your confidence so that you will forget my purpose and position and confess all your crimes to me."

But Lissa was not to be diverted. "Are you going?" she repeated.

The little lines around Justin's eyes that marked amusement disappeared. The insistent question was like a caress, stating suddenly and openly Lissa's interest in him, not as a benefactor but as a man. In that moment, a last, dangerous spice—desire— was added to the strange mix of emotions that Lissa generated in him. She stared, her color high with embarrassment, which told Justin that she knew what she had exposed but did not lessen her determination. She had to know because she cared for him. Justin stared back, losing the thread of what had been said, aware only of how fine were the delicate curves of Lissa's lip and nostril and that her deep blush and the golden light of the candles had turned her eyes all green.

Chapter 6

A VOICE CALLING FROM THE DOOR STARTLED THEM BOTH. LISSA pushed away her embroidery frame and got up. Justin rose also and followed her to the door. She turned before she opened it and laid a hand on his arm.

"Please do not go."

"I must give the men leave to go home," he said, and added deliberately, "You made me forget all about them."

Then he reached around her and opened the door, which swung in to admit Witta and a miasma of mouth-watering smells. The odors rose from Witta's burden, two covered earthenware pots on which was balanced a large platter. The leather jack of wine hung over his shoulder.

Justin sniffed and said, "I will be back in a moment. I am far too hungry to go home to an icy house where I will have to wait an hour for unwilling servants to contrive an inedible meal."

Lissa chuckled at the obviously false self-pity in Justin's voice. "Poor man," she said, "I promise you will be kept warm and well fed, but you will have to pay a price." And then as his head turned, to reveal a genuinely shocked expression at the double meaning that could be read into her words, she laughed aloud. "I want my questions answered."

However warmly he might feel for Lissa, Justin was resolved not to fail in any precaution that might solve Flael's murder. He did tell Halsig and the men that they were free of duty, but he bade Halsig send two fresh men, who were not fools, to watch Flael's shop and house front and back in case one or both of Flael's sons should return. Then he mounted the stairs with a clear conscience, aware of the pleasant tension in his body. He wondered if he should test Lissa by trying to seduce her this very night. If she agreed, the same day her husband had died, would that not prove her a whore?

The question hung in his mind as he entered the room and found everything ready and extraordinarily inviting. He took a step toward the table, only to be asked whether he was preparing for a sojourn in an armed camp by sitting down to eat without washing his hands. And there was something in Lissa's voice, in the warmth of the smile she turned on him, even in the asperity with which she pointed to the bowl of water on a stand near the door, that made the question irrelevant. Her trust and admiration precluded traps on a personal level. She cared for him; it seemed very strange—and then he remembered what she had said earlier in the day and wondered if it was possible that she had cherished a regard for him ever since the fire.

He washed his hands obediently, moved the large chair to the table at Lissa's request, and sat down, noticing with wry amusement that the boy was crouched in a corner eating from a wooden bowl, with a good-sized wedge of the pork pasty awaiting his attention. Justin wondered whether Lissa had been stirred by the same strong urge as he and had kept Witta there to provide herself with a hedge against seduction. But from her first words, as she ladled soup from one earthenware pot into a fine pewter bowl, he was forced to realize that seduction had never even interrupted her train of thought.

"You will not go to France with the king, will you?" she asked, serving herself and sitting down.

"Not unless I am ordered to go," Justin replied, and after swallowing several spoonfuls of the soup, he added, "I am sorry for it. The king has the right in this quarrel. Whatever John's real reasons and despite the barons grumbling about a foreign war, curbing King Philip will be good for London and good for trade. I would gladly go if FitzWalter were not the leader."

"Then I thank God he is," Lissa said sharply, and then more thoughtfully, "Why do men always seem to look eagerly for war? When my uncles come back from their voyages, they seem happier about the pirates they fought than about a quiet voyage."

"I am not so eager for war," Justin protested indignantly. "Did I not just say that we must protect Gascony against Philip's desire to swallow it? What I am willing to fight for is my source of wine from Bordeaux. Do you know what would happen to trade if the French overran that province?"

"Yes, I do know." Lissa sighed. "I know how the prices of pepper and other herbs and other spices vary in accordance with the struggles in the east. And I buy wine for my infusions too. Is there really a danger of Louis taking Gascony?"

"I do not know. I do not think so, unless there is great treachery . . ."

Lissa paused with a spoon halfway to her mouth as Justin's voice died away uncertainly. "You do not think FitzWalter will try to turn London's troops against the king in battle!"

"FitzWalter?" Justin frowned. "I was not thinking of him. There are those in Gascony who hate King John as much as FitzWalter does, and they have more power there."

"I do not care about that," Lissa said. "I will be sorry if the price of wine should rise, but if FitzWalter's act makes it seem that London has turned against the king, we will all suffer. Whatever happens in France, sooner or later King John will return to England, and I have heard that he does not forget an injury, no matter how long a time has passed."

Justin shook his head. "There is no danger to the king, or to London either, from FitzWalter. I would not be sitting here calmly stuffing my mouth if I thought there was. I would be ahorse on my way to Windsor to warn John. If I *must* choose between FitzWalter and the king, I will choose John. I know FitzWalter. He has no object other than his own gratification. Sometimes the causes he espouses in that purpose happen to be good, but that is by accident. On the other hand, although John has his faults, his main object is the good of the realm." Justin

raised his brows and added, "Of course, his view of the good of
the realm does not always coincide with that of others, but I
would rather deal with John's reasoned greed for power than
with FitzWalter's blind hate. However, I would infinitely prefer
to avoid being caught between them. It seems to me that in this
case I can best serve my city by remaining here."

"That is most certainly true," Lissa agreed heartily, but she
was not completely satisfied, and after they had eaten in silence
for a while she asked, "Why should you be caught between
FitzWalter and the king?"

Justin pushed aside his empty bowl and made a gesture of
helplessness. "Simply because FitzWalter likes me—God knows
why—and has already asked me to be his chief captain. But I do
not know how far FitzWalter's madness of hate will drive him,
and I want no connection at all with any threat against the king.
FitzWalter swore to me that he goes to France to regain John's
favor. I hope that is the truth because I wish FitzWalter no ill,
although I cannot say I return his regard. And he will come to
ill, he will fail—and die—if he tries treachery. John has been
forewarned by what happened in 1212. FitzWalter will be
watched and separated from the London troops if necessary.
John will not permit him to make any move that is not overseen
by his own friends."

"But why does FitzWalter hate the king so?" Lissa asked,
laying most of the chicken and a slice of the pasty on the platter
she had set ready. Justin looked at it with surprise, wondering at
the substitution of a silver platter for the round of stale bread
that usually served as a plate, but before he could ask the reason
for the excessive elegance, she said, "I heard from one of the
great ladies who buy their lotions and powders from me that
Vesci, the other man who was pardoned with FitzWalter, hated
the king for tampering with his wife. Of course, that might be
only a wild rumor, but none of the ladies ever mentioned Fitz-
Walter."

"Perhaps because his is not a quarrel that is interesting to
ladies."

Lissa raised her eyes. "Perhaps not to *ladies*, but I am a
merchant's daughter and the well-doing of my city is dear to my
heart, so FitzWalter's quarrel with the king is very interesting to
me."

"Well said, merchant's daughter, well said." Justin smiled at her and took a bite of the chicken, waving a leg while his mouth was full to show that he had more to say. "The trouble goes back a long way, back to the time Normandy was lost to King Philip of France in 1203. FitzWalter and another man, Saer de Quincy, were then among King John's favorites and were given charge of Vaudreuil Castle. When Philip attacked Normandy, those who held the border keeps sent to the king for help, but he would not, or could not, come to their assistance. Many resisted as long as they could, but all were overwhelmed one after another, in some cases with great loss of life. Some say the king rushed up and down the land but by ill fortune or bad judgment accomplished nothing. Others say he sat still and would not be moved, though his advisers pleaded with him to act. What is said about FitzWalter and Quincy is that they decided King John had violated his pledge to support them and they were thus freed from their oath of fealty. So when Philip's army arrived they yielded without even a token resistance."

While Justin was speaking, Lissa had finished the small portion of chicken she had served herself and started to pick at her slice of the pasty. Then she laid down her eating knife and looked at Justin. "That sounds sensible to me."

Justin laughed aloud. "A truly feminine judgment, but if that kind of sense was allowed to rule men's behavior, the world would fall into chaos. When fealty is given, it may not be abandoned simply because it seems, or even is, more sensible to do so. It is our swearing to our lords and holding by our oaths that keeps order in the land."

"Even if your lord tells you to jump off a cliff?" Lissa asked as she lifted the jack of wine and refilled their goblets.

"There might be a necessary purpose that he saw and I did not."

Lissa turned her head to look at Justin, and her expression made him chuckle.

"Oh very well," he continued, grinning, "we will take it as said that my lord has fallen off his horse on his head and is not as sensible as he might be—a condition I sometimes face with our present mayor. In that case, one might take council with one's fellow vassals and bring a complaint to the king, who could mediate between us and our overlord. Or I could decide to cry defiance, which is an open and public breaking of one's homage. That, however, usually entails the loss of any lands one holds of that lord, unless one can keep them by force." Then the amusement passed from his voice. "Since in this case the king was the overlord, FitzWalter and Quincy had no one to whom to complain, and they did not send a defiance to John before they offered Vaudreuil Castle to Philip. I heard it said they thought the king so far gone in sloth and lustful satisfaction with his new wife that he would not distinguish, among all the other losses, between yielding from necessity and yielding from choice."

"I cannot believe the king would give up a duchy to futter his own wife," Lissa remarked dryly. "And she was not so new a wife by 1203. If I remember aright what I was told, Isabella and John were married the year after the king came to the throne— that would be 1200—so they had been married three years. I have served Isabella, and she is very, very beautiful, but it is not as if she were going to disappear."

"I must agree," Justin said. "But *something* was wrong with the king, and rumor blamed Isabella. Those who wish to find excuses for FitzWalter and Quincy say it was that rumor that enraged them enough to yield a fully stocked and manned keep, and one that was very important to the defense of all of Normandy, without a blow being struck."

"You do not believe that, yet you also said FitzWalter is not a coward."

"There is a strange puzzle concerning that yielding. I have told you what I have heard of it, but there is much that rings false to me. Why did FitzWalter and Quincy yield that keep without asking terms for themselves? King Philip might have looked down his nose at them, but he would surely have given them their freedom and perhaps even more in exchange for so great a prize. Instead, they simply laid down their arms and opened the gates. Not only were they branded cowards, which would have happened in any case, but they were branded without recompense, because Philip threw them into prison. They were chained like dogs in Compiègne instead of being treated like honorable enemies and set free on their parole until their ransom of five thousand marks was paid."

"That is very strange indeed," Lissa said, pushing aside the remains of her food and clasping her hands idly on the table.

"Still stranger is that John sent out letters patent saying that he had ordered the yielding of Vaudreuil—yet he refused to help pay their ransoms, and both went deep into debt to get free."

"I am only a merchant's daughter, but that smells of long-dead fish to me. Surely there was treachery, but I cannot tell who betrayed whom."

"Nor I," Justin said, leaning back with his goblet of wine in hand. "Nor any other man. All I know is that the only one who profited on all sides was King Philip, and it is well known that he hates the Angevins root, stock, and branch—but I cannot see how he could have done it."

Lissa laughed. "If King Philip could have been blamed, you may be sure John or one of his clever friends would have cried that blame aloud, and it was ten years ago."

"You are right." Justin drank off the last of his wine and put the goblet back on the table. "No one will ever discover the truth now, but I wish there were a cure for FitzWalter's hatred for the king and John's for him."

They were companionably silent for a few minutes, during which Lissa gestured at the remaining food and Justin signed that he was finished but nodded to another filling of his goblet. He sipped thoughtfully as Lissa called the boy to help her clear, and when he saw that he was in their way, he moved the chair to its original place by the fireside. When Witta had gone to store the remains of the meal, Lissa sat down and pulled her embroidery frame close.

"Now," Justin said, looking as severe as he could, "will you explain to me how you seduced me into talking about FitzWalter and the king—a matter that surely can have little pertinence to you—when we should have been talking of more practical matters?"

Lissa smiled at him. "That has an easy answer. The only practical matters I can think of are so unpleasant that I would favor listening to a sermon on my sins over needing to talk about them. And pertinent or not, I found the tale of the yielding of Vaudreuil most interesting."

"Do you realize," Justin remarked, "that the look I bent on you has made strong men confess, and all you do is smile."

"Perhaps those strong men had something to confess," Lissa suggested pertly, and then more seriously, "I think I have told

you everything I have to tell. If there is something you think I
might know that I have not mentioned, you must ask."

While Lissa was speaking, her eyes were fixed on Justin's face
and her manner was earnest and easy. For the moment she
really believed that she had concealed nothing. It was not until
she had taken the needle from where she had left it in the cloth
and begun to finish the spray of leaves she had started that she
remembered it was very likely that her father knew a good deal
about Peter's death that Justin would like to know also. She
thanked God that her head was already bent, and prayed that
Justin would not notice that her hand was trembling slightly.

"What I really wish to know," he said, "is where to find Flael's
sons. We have not discovered a hint of them either passing any
gate or for several miles out along the roads. They could not
have got farther with that horse and cart than my riders
searched. And they did not take ship, as I thought they might
have either. Now I believe it is possible that they are hiding in
the city."

Lissa was so relieved by this subject that she looked up wide-
eyed and asked, "But why is it so important to find them? You
admitted you did not think them guilty of anything."

"Do not talk like a fool," Justin snapped, the good humor
gone from his face. "If Flael's sons fled from fear, that implies
they knew something about why their father died or who
caused his death."

Could they have known about Hubert, Lissa wondered? She
shook her head and let her eyes drop to her work. "I would help
you if I could," she said, not at all sure she was speaking the
truth. "But as I have told you, young Peter and Edmond did not
like me. In the short time that Peter and I were here, they often
went out when their work was done. They may have told their
father about their companions or where they were going; they
never told me, nor did Peter tell me."

"That is not much help in our search for them."

Lissa hesitated, then looked up again, hoping that her guilt
would not show on her face but afraid that if she did not look
up, Justin would guess she did not wish to meet his eyes.
"Perhaps if the journeymen along the street were questioned, or
any of our neighbors who have sons eighteen or twenty years of
age, they might know who Peter and Edmond's friends were. I

cannot help. Peter and I left for Canterbury the very day we were married, and we have been in London less than three weeks. How could I know the sons' friends?" Her voice began to grow unsteady, and she bit her lip and looked down.

"I beg your pardon," Justin said softly, leaning forward and touching her hand. "I am angry with myself, not with you. I was making rather merry last night with my cousins and I came here with an aching skull and muddled wits, so I was slow to act. I will set some men to asking questions tomorrow."

"Oh, was that why you frowned so horribly at me?" Lissa uttered a little giggle. "I could not imagine what I had done to make you so cross, especially when we were talking about Peter's woman." She looked questioningly at Justin. "Did someone speak to her?"

"Yes, and you were quite right. She swore she had not seen Flael since you married him. And others confirmed that Flael had not been in the area for some time, a month or more was the estimate. She was quite bitter about it, for seemingly he paid her well and gave her pretty trinkets. She showed us two pieces. I think they were base-metal models to be shown to clients before the real piece was cast."

"Peter's clients!" Lissa exclaimed, sitting upright. "Not those for whom he made plate and jewelry, the—the clients to whom he lent money. I know I said none of the debts seemed large enough to make a man desperate and that Goscelin said he could think of no one who hated Peter, but perhaps your better knowledge of the men who are mentioned will give some meaning to the records that I could not detect."

With the words she rose and went into the bedchamber, coming out with the very thick roll of parchment that seemed to list all Peter's debtors. Handing it to Justin, she pulled her stool around to the side of the chair so she could look at the parchment too. They pored over it for some time, Justin remarking on some of the names and shaking his head or shrugging at others. Like Lissa, he could not see that any debt was monstrously burdensome, and he was about to say so when a little gasp drew his eyes and he saw her struggling to suppress a yawn.

"Good Lord, you must be half dead," he said. "I forgot that you told me you hardly slept last night."

"No, no," Lissa protested. "I slept half the morning away."

Justin laughed and then yawned himself. "Well, I did not," he pointed out. "And it is very possible that the reason I cannot think is that what is inside my head is abed at home, even though my stupid body is still sitting here. May I take this record home with me? I promise faithfully I will return it as soon as I can."

"I do not care if you do not return it at all," Lissa said. "I do not intend to collect those debts, not unless I am forced to do so."

"Do not be a little fool." Justin turned and lifted her head with a finger under her chin. "I do not mean that you should not show mercy to those who need it, but some of the names on this list are fellow goldsmiths who may have borrowed to lend at still higher interest. Should they have not only their profit but a reward for being more greedy than Flael? And other names are those of merchants who most probably borrowed to enlarge their business or to make some purchase that would bring much greater than normal profit."

"Yes, but how can I know?" Lissa said uncertainly. "I have such a fear that I will bring someone to grief or ruin—"

"You *are* a goose!"

The words were murmured almost against Lissa's lips. She moved her head, hardly knowing whether she was stretching upward to bring her mouth against Justin's or trying to withdraw. The result was the merest brush of contact. Justin jerked his head back and Lissa almost fell off the stool. Both cried some kind of confused apology and jumped up. Lissa simply stared at Justin, looking dumbfound.

"I am sorry," he said stiffly. "It was an accident."

Mutely, she shook her head, still staring, one hand pressed to her breast. Then she dropped her eyes and murmured, "No, no, the fault was mine. Forgive me."

"There is no fault," Justin said more easily. "We are both so tired that we are reeling. I will take this list, make inquiries, and let you know from whom you may demand payment safely. Will that content you?"

"Yes, yes," Lissa replied, but her breathlessness and the way she kept glancing at Justin and then away made quite plain that she had no idea to what she was agreeing.

Justin took a step toward her and she gasped, her eyes remaining fixed on him until it became clear he was not going to come closer—but she did not back away. "I will go, then," he said.

"If you must," she breathed.

Again Justin was sure she had not the least idea what she was saying, that she was merely repeating a formula she had used for many years when guests said they must go. He took his cloak and swung it over his shoulders, resisting the temptation to turn and look at Lissa. He was sure she was staring at him, and when he moved to open the door he thought he caught a flicker of motion and turned fully toward her. She had only dropped the hand she had been holding against her breast, but her eyes were on him. She lowered them and bit her lips when he faced her.

"God be with you," he said. "Sleep well, Lissa."

"God keep you." Her voice faded on the last word; then her eyes flicked up at him again and she said faintly but with a kind of determination, "And bring you to a swift returning."

Justin went down the stairs into the shop, where night candles were burning. He checked automatically that the door was barred and bolted for the night, and turned toward the workroom where he heard voices. They stopped as he entered the room, and he would have passed through without even seeing the speakers, since his mind was fully occupied, had Witta not flung himself across Justin's path.

"She wants me to sleep out in the hut and her in here in the warm," Witta said.

With his mouth already open to order Witta to do as he was told, for he had a feeling that Lissa spoiled the boy, Justin hesitated. He realized that there would be less chance that his men would be noticed or warning given to Flael's sons if both servants were in the house.

"There is no reason for that," Justin said. "In fact, after what happened to your master, I want you both inside the house with both doors well barred after dark. Go get your pallet and what else you need from the hut."

He went out with Witta but remained near the door because he had seen how furious the old woman looked and thought it not beyond her to shut the boy out despite what he had said.

When he had seen Witta safely inside, he went to the shed to saddle his horse and then grinned. Good deeds, he thought, are their own reward, and went to the back gate where he called softly for the watcher Halsig had stationed there. He bade the man saddle up for him and, when he was finished, told him that the servants were locked in the house. The guard could use the hut to warm himself now and again, but if he was found asleep in it, Justin warned, he would not think the rest and comfort worth the punishment.

If Justin had realized how indifferent he sounded when he issued that warning, he would have been appalled. Voice and expression were almost an invitation to violate the words. However, by the time the guard had finished saddling the horse, Justin's thoughts had traveled very far away from the guard himself and even the reason the man was there. More than half his mind was already given to recalling that almost-kiss and Lissa's reactions.

The guard said something as Justin mounted, to which Justin responded only with a raised hand. He was puzzling over what he had done, realizing as he thought it over that his behavior all afternoon was not only outrageous but totally unnatural for him. Never in his life, or at least not since he was a stupid, callow boy, had he thought of seducing a decent woman. He had long since accepted, not without some chagrin, that he was not a great lover whom women found irresistible. In fact, well-bred women shied away from him in general; one of the reasons he was still unmarried years after he could well afford a wife was that the girls offered to him by fathers or brothers were unwilling, some openly, some fearfully hiding terror or distaste.

Despite assurances that a few weeks of marriage would change that attitude, Justin preferred bought women, who seemed to like him very well indeed. He frowned as he mechanically directed his horse eastward along the Chepe to his own house on the Mercery. His problem with the two women he had kept in the past was that they had grown *too* fond of him and had begun behaving like wives. That might have been desirable had he felt anything more for them than the mild liking that made them acceptable as bed partners. As it was, Justin had made haste to find them other willing keepers—one was now married—and separate himself from them. Since then, he had patronized the most elegant house in Southwark. Justin grinned into the dark. He had helped build that house, or rebuild it, after it was burned in the fire of 1212.

Thought of the fire brought his mind instantly back to Lissa. Could so brief a meeting have remained in her mind and made him desirable to her? When he leaned so close and called her a goose, had she been tempted to kiss him and then thought better of it because of guilt or modesty? And if she had been tempted, could he blame her? It was his behavior that had been improper from the beginning. In any case, she had resisted the temptation, withdrawn; but her expression and actions gave no sign of fear or disgust. Shock, he told himself; she had been terribly shocked when their lips met—but he had long experience in reading expressions, and what had shown on Lissa's face was not shock; it was astonishment, which was a very different thing.

It was also virtually inexplicable. Justin could have understood shock: She might have been shocked that she had come so close to yielding to temptation, or shocked that a man she plainly respected and admired had been so cruel and so crude as to try to tempt her. But what could have astonished her? Surely that moth-wing brush of their lips could not have taught her anything new about love. Justin dismissed that slightly wishful thought as he saw, with some relief, that there were still lights on in his house. He dismounted, beat briefly on the door, and when it opened transferred his rein to his servant's hand and went in and up the stairs without a word.

A little while later he was astonished himself. He had still been puzzling over Lissa's reaction, and when he got into bed, he felt not only a definite longing to see her there but a strong stirring of desire. He would have thought, after the tumblings of the previous night, that he would be drained dry for a week. Justin settled into the furs on his cot and stared up into the shadows created by the flickering of the night candle. Lissa was nowhere near as physically desirable as any of the girls he usually lay with, but none of them could have such an effect on him when nearly a mile distant.

Justin would have been further astonished if he had known how closely parallel Lissa's thoughts were to his as she stripped off her clothing and climbed wearily into bed. She thought she had put Justin out of her mind after he left the house. She had suppressed the urges of her treacherous body and shouted for Binge to come up and make her bed ready. For a while, her attention had been fixed on the sullen old woman. She explained to Binge that she intended to remain in Peter's house until his sons returned and that if Binge would not obey her, she would find another maid and drive Binge out. She did not mean it; to put the old woman out in the street would have been the same as murder. But Lissa was tired and a little frightened by what had happened to her. She did not realize how cold her voice was or how remote her expression, but her blank and icy regard brought home to Binge that her master was gone forever and, for all she knew, his sons too. For the moment fear suppressed hatred, and Binge whined an apology that Lissa dismissed with a sharp order to show her repentance by warming the bed without any more words.

She turned away from the maid as she spoke, which deepened Binge's fear and resentment. Lissa was no more aware of that than she had been of her earlier coldness. The moment she entered the bedroom, images of Justin filled her mind. She could see him leaning toward her, feel the touch of his mouth on hers. What would have happened if she had not leapt away but had pressed her body against his? She shuddered as she slid into the bed, which Binge had left half clammy. At least she would have been warm in Justin's arms . . . and more than warm.

Although Lissa knew what had astonished her when her mouth met Justin's, she could not understand *why* it had happened. Justin was not the first man to kiss her. Some of those who had been proposed by their fathers as husbands or had asked for her in marriage on their own had desired more than her dowry and the inheritance that would be hers on her father's death. A few of those, misunderstanding the relationship between her and William, had courted her, thinking she could influence her father's decision about giving her in marriage. So there had been hand holdings and whisperings in the ear and kisses. In most cases Lissa had liked the men and had found their attentions pleasant, but she had never felt any stronger reaction than liking.

Certainly she had felt no desire of the flesh for Peter. She had found her marital duty endurable partly because she had been taught that sex was inevitable and necessary to have children and partly because Peter's attentions were infrequent and brief. In addition, she had suffered little discomfort from coupling because Oliva, her father's slave leman, who had served as her maid, had told her to smear herself well, inside and out, with a slick salve. But there had been no pleasure for her, no liking for the act.

It was astonishing, then, that the feel of Justin's breath on her face, the brushing of his lips against hers, should set up a silent clamor in her body, a feeling that her nipples were of themselves swelling and thrusting forward and, more astonishing still, that her nether lips were becoming full and moist and parting eagerly to welcome an invader. As her body warmed the bedclothes, Lissa considered the act of coupling, only replacing Peter with Justin. She was astonished all over again, not only at her own response but at how vividly her imagination painted what she had never seen—a virile young lover, naked and ready.

Chapter 7

WILLIAM'S INTERVIEW WITH ROBERT FITZWALTER WAS NOT PLEAS-
ant, but it was not as bad as it could have been. Lord
Robert was not pleased, but once his first violent spurt of temper
had cooled, he acknowledged that Peter's death was beyond
anyone's control. He himself had not realized how timorous the
goldsmith was, FitzWalter remarked to William; if he had, he
would have handled the matter differently.

"I assumed," Lord Robert went on, "that any man who would
dare so bold a violation of an agreement would need a little
strong persuasion before he confessed, or at least not die of
fright before he was even threatened."

"I wonder now," William said, "if Flael did not tell the truth to
us—that he believed the seal was in the box he handed me at the
wedding."

If he could convince FitzWalter of that, William thought,
FitzWalter would never begin to wonder whether he could have
got the seal before the box was handed to Hubert. Since
FitzWalter was aware that his henchman was not overclever, the

idea might otherwise occur to him. As if thinking of him stirred him to life, Hubert moved out of the dim area behind Lord Robert's chair.

"The journeyman did not take it," Hubert put in. "I remember what the journeyman said. He said he dared not touch the seal before he had his price because his master checked to see that it was still locked in the box. And he could not open and reseal the box because his master wore his own seal always on his person."

"That was not what I meant," William said. "It seems to me, my lord, since the sons have fled, that Flael must have taken them into his confidence. They were very angry about the marriage. Could not the sons have taken the seal? They would have had access to their father's private chamber and, perhaps, to a way to empty the box without his knowing."

"And taken the seal with them when they fled?" FitzWalter stood up angrily. "If so, they must not be seized by Sir Justin's men."

"I do not think they would have taken it, my lord," William soothed. "They could have no use for it, and it would be a grave danger to them. As matters stand, they have committed no crime. It is no crime to move one's own property—and they could say they were placing the chests in safekeeping. They know they could not be held, once they proved they had no guilty knowledge of their father's death. But if the seal were found among their possessions . . . I cannot be sure they would have left it hidden; they are young and might not have thought the matter through, but I think there is a good chance the seal is still in Flael's house."

"It must be searched," FitzWalter said. "Thoroughly. More thoroughly than your last search. As for Flael's sons, I have eyes and ears among the guards, and if they are taken, I will hear of it sooner than Sir Justin but I would greatly prefer that we find them first."

"I will speak to my daughter in the morning," William offered. "She may have some idea of where young Peter and Edmond might have gone or of friends who might have taken them in. I will also try to induce her to move back to my house so Flael's will be empty—but she may refuse. She is stubborn, and I dare not press her too hard to move lest she begin to wonder why I want the house empty."

"If you beat her well, she will be more agreeable," FitzWalter remarked disdainfully.

"And have her run to Sir Justin and tell him I want the house empty? I know her. That is just what she would do, and I cannot keep her prisoner because Sir Justin may still have questions he wishes to ask her."

FitzWalter said nothing for a moment and then smiled. "I am sure you will find a way to search that house whether it is empty or not. But do not come here again to give me news. I will have a talk with Sir Justin on my own."

It was fortunate for William that FitzWalter was not relying on him for news because he found it impossible to pry anything of importance out of Lissa when he questioned her in the hope of satisfying his own curiosity. Oddly, even William realized that she was not deliberately spiting him; what he could not decide was whether she knew nothing more than she told him or was thinking too hard about something else to hear his questions properly. Also, he had little time to question her. William had come at first light, expecting to find Lissa still abed and have some time to talk to her alone.

His first check was that he found Lissa wide awake, already dressed in the sad-colored gown she had worn after her mother's death, conferring with the priest about the burial. Ordinarily, a public crier would have been hired to call out the time and place where mass would be said, but because England was still under interdict, which meant no service could be held in a church, there were complications. The priest did not want to chance being reported for having violated the pope's order, and Lissa did not want it said that she had taken advantage of the interdict to be niggardly about her husband's interment. The matter was settled by compromise: A full mass was forbidden; Lissa accepted that, but she insisted on some ceremony. Since the king had made his peace with the pope and it was expected that the interdict would be lifted very soon, the priest agreed to say the Office for the dead at the church door.

As soon as Father Denis left, William asked Lissa about Flael's sons. She had greeted him with polite indifference when he came into the solar. Now she looked at him as if she was not sure that she had ever met him before and said there had been no news. William then changed his tack and told her she looked terrible and that she had been a fool to remain in a house where a murder had been committed. She replied woodenly that the murder had not been committed in the house. William continued to urge her to leave, but he was certain she did not hear him. Before he could decide whether to strike her to draw her attention and ease his irritation, there were footsteps on the stairs. To William's surprise, Lissa stiffened and her vague glance changed, fixing on the doorway with a sudden alert intensity.

For the third time that morning, the knock that heralded a visitor set Lissa's insides churning. Please God, she thought, not him! Not now while my father is alone with me. William was the very last person in the world to whom Lissa wished to display any weakness, and she had never felt so incapable of controlling her expression and voice.

Despite the emotional upheaval she had felt when she went to bed, Lissa had slept well and dreamlessly; however, when she woke, all the confusion and desire of the previous night renewed themselves. In vain she reminded herself that she was a widow of one day, that her husband was to be buried in a few hours. The moment she relaxed in an attempt to sleep again, Justin slipped into her mind and visions of him slipped into her bed.

In desperation, Lissa had got up and begun to go through her clothes chest. She found what she sought at the bottom—the dark, drab gown she had made when she knew her mother was dying. As she shook out the creases and made the gown ready to put on, sad memories cooled her heated imagination. Still, after she had called down to wake Binge and Witta, washed, dressed, and eaten, the sound of knocking on the door made her tremble. She told herself angrily that Justin was not a fool. He would not come so early and expose himself, and her too, to malicious gossip. Nonetheless, she found herself weak with mingled disappointment and relief when she saw Father Denis.

Her conversation with the priest had calmed her, but when the sound of knocking came again a few minutes later, Lissa was still afraid she would not be able to face Justin without betraying herself. Thus, she was almost glad to see her father when he came into her solar; not that she was surprised that he had come. She had expected him, although not quite so early; William was always punctilious about public duties. Lissa knew he would not care to start talk by failing to support his daughter at her husband's burial.

Nor was Lissa surprised when the first thing William asked about when they were alone was Peter's sons. Plainly he still hoped to get his fingers on some of the contents of Peter's strongboxes. And when he began to urge her to come home, Lissa hardly listened because she had expected that too and knew in advance all the arguments he would use. He did not want her company; having lost, when Peter died, whatever business advantage he expected from their marriage, William wanted her back at work in the apothecary shop. Lissa did not mind that; she enjoyed her part in her father's business, but she had no intention of going back to William's house unless Peter's sons returned and drove her out of this one.

The strength of the determination she felt surprised Lissa and diverted her from a simple refusal that should have cut off her father's argument. She let him talk while she considered why she did not want to go home even now, when she was certain William had not been responsible for Peter's murder. Actually, she liked her father's house better than this one. Her chamber, though smaller, was no less luxurious than Peter's solar, and it smelled sweetly of the herbs in the shop below instead of being tainted with the odor of burning and hot metal and wax. Why cling to this empty house?

As the question came into Lissa's mind, the sound of knocking came again and, with the emotions that shook her, she knew the answer. She wanted to remain because the house *was* empty, because it would be much more difficult, perhaps even impossible, for Justin to come to her without notice in her father's house. The revelation, naked and blatant as it appeared in her mind, was such a shock to her that she could not react in any way when, instead of Justin, a plump woman entered, wearing a worried expression on a kindly face.

"I am Adela, Master Goscelin's wife," she said, coming forward and taking Lissa's hand. "I was at your wedding, but I am sure you will not remember me." She chuckled when a faint consternation added itself to the blankness in Lissa's face.

"Now, now, that was not a hint that I expect you to remember me. I saw when I wished you good fortune and happiness that you did not really see or hear me—and I do not blame you at all. I have been married many years, but I remember well how confused and frightened and sad I was when I was married to my dear Goscelin. Girls have fancies . . . but that is neither here nor there. I assure you I did not thrust myself on you for the purpose of telling you about my wedding. I stopped by yesterday to ask if there was anything I could do for you, but Sir Justin's man told me your father was with you and I did not wish to intrude. I hope I am not intruding now, but I thought I had better come and tell you that Peter's brethren in the guild will wish to pay their respects."

"You are not intruding at all," Lissa said, summoning up a smile. "I am very grateful to you." Neither the smile nor the statement was false; she was truly grateful to Mistress Adela both for talking long enough to enable her to suppress the idea that had shocked her and for warning her about the visits of Peter's brother guildsmen. "I hope you will be able to advise me," she went on. "In view of the—the manner of Peter's death and also the interdict, which I was afraid would prevent the guild brothers from saying masses for Peter's soul, I did not know whether I should try to provide a—a feast for many or few—and worst of all, I—I have very little money."

"Do not trouble your head about that at all, except to have some tables set up," Adela replied. "The brethren of Goldsmiths will take care of the food and drink. The single men will bring bread and wine, and the married men, or rather their wives, will bring suitable dishes."

"I am most grateful," Lissa repeated with heartfelt sincerity, "and I will do whatever you think is best as well as I can, but I must tell you that I do not inherit any part of Peter's business and therefore have no right to know of the mysteries of the guild."

"Is that the truth?" Adela seemed very much surprised. "Goscelin told me that young Peter and Edmond had run off with the strongboxes, and I imagined— What in the world could have made them behave like that?"

"Well, it was not that they needed to hide Peter's wealth from me," Lissa said, but she guessed from Adela's remarks that her husband did not confide much of his business to her, and she hesitated to say any more.

"It is just as well," Adela said, but she looked a little disappointed. "I was wondering what the guild would do if Peter had made you his heir. They have no women members at all."

"Too bad the Pepperers have not the same rule," William remarked caustically.

He spoke softly, but Adela had sharp ears and flicked a glance at him that raked him up and down as she said, "The Goldsmiths have no rule against women. It is only that in the cases where wives and daughters have inherited among the brethren of Goldsmiths, they knew nothing of business and preferred to remarry or sell. I heard Master Peter praising Mistress Heloise's abilities in reading and keeping accounts, and I wondered whether she would wish to apply for Peter's place in the guild."

Lissa's eyes met Adela's and she smiled. Apparently the lady had a fine sense of mischief and perhaps a little resentment of her husband's practice of keeping her in the dark. "Will you call me Lissa?" she asked. "It is what my friends and my mother called me."

Before Adela could answer with more than a smile, William said, "It would not have surprised me if Heloise expected to be given her husband's place in the guild."

"Now, father, you know I would not have wanted that," Lissa retorted swiftly, her voice dripping honey. "I know I am too ignorant of the craft." Then she turned to Adela and went on in a natural, pleasant tone, "It would have been most unfair. The place belongs rightfully to young Peter. I do not believe any craft can benefit by accepting those who have not been raised in it. I will have my father's place among the Pepperers, if I survive him, and that will be right and just because he has taught me the craft of an apothecary from childhood, and I can be a credit to the Pepperers Guild, which I could not be among the goldsmiths."

"Perhaps that is why most guildsmen marry within their craft," Adela said. "And now I think of it, of course it must be best. When I look back on all the years my dear Goscelin and I have been married and how little I still understand of business, I see it is better if a wife is bred to her husband's trade. But there are so few goldsmiths that you can see such marriages are not always possible. My father was Sir Sefrith of Poges. Goscelin made a chalice for our church and I suppose took a fancy for me when we met twice, but I never suspected and no one could have been more surprised than I when my father told me I was to marry a burgher. Still, it worked out well. Goscelin has always been so kind, and our eldest son now holds papa's manor—" She stopped abruptly and said, "Oh, my dear, I am so sorry. My tongue does run on so."

"There is no need for apology," Lissa said. "We had not had time, Peter and I, to come to a true bonding. But Peter was kind to me, as Master Goscelin was to you, and I am grieved at his death—"

"I am sure you are," William interrupted impatiently. "I am also sure you have many duties that you must be about immediately. It was very kind of Mistress Adela to come to you, but—"

"I cannot imagine what you are talking about, father," Lissa said, as both women turned to stare at him. "Mistress Adela has come to help me with those duties. She knows far better than I what should be done."

For a moment William was so angry that he could not speak. He knew it would be far more difficult to get his daughter out of Flael's house if she made a friend who lived close by. He was seeking wildly for something to say when there was another knock on the door and a young man's voice asking for "Madame Lissa," followed by the sound of boots taking the stairs two or three at a time.

An instant later a young man, richly but soberly dressed, appeared in the doorway and made his way straight to Lissa, to whom he bowed. "I am Thomas FitzAilwin, Justin's cousin," he said in French. "Some matters of importance have made it impossible for Justin to attend your husband's burial, and he asked me to come here in his stead and support you in any way that is necessary."

Thomas was telling the truth in that he was repeating exactly what Justin had said to him; however, it was not the whole truth. Thomas, the handsomest and most charming of the FitzAilwins, had one assigned task he had been told to keep to

himself. Beyond that, he did not know the whole truth. There
was a second task he did not even know he was performing.

The assigned task was simply to keep his eyes and ears open,
first for any surreptitious appearance of either of Flael's sons,
who were known to Thomas, and second to watch in general for
any remark or incident that was in any way, no matter how
slight or seemingly unrelated to Flael's death, out of the
ordinary. Thomas had performed similar tasks for Justin a
number of times, and he was very good at them. His open
friendliness was very disarming and, aside from inducing most
people to like him at once, led them to discount the keen
businesslike mind he had inherited from his father.

The task Thomas did not know he was performing was to
determine whether Lissa was a flirt who threw out lures to every
man. Justin had taken considerable pains to hide from his
cousin what he felt was a ridiculous and incomprehensible
infatuation. He had not been perfectly successful; Thomas had
sensed a special interest in Lissa, but he had connected it with
the crime he was helping his cousin investigate rather than with
any emotional entanglement. Certainly he saw nothing in Flael's
widow as he bowed over her hand that could arouse a suspicion
of Justin's motives. She had been pale as chalk, her eyes dull and
her voice flat as she thanked him for being willing to come in his
cousin's stead.

It had taken considerable will for Justin to remain in his chair
after Thomas left his house. He felt guilty about setting a spy,
even if an unknowing one, on Lissa. Still, he had to know
whether her manner to him had any meaning. If she behaved in
the same way to Thomas . . . The thought woke in him an
unexpected quiver of anger and disappointment. He should
have sent Richard, who, despite being the youngest FitzAilwin,
had the ponderous manner and gravity of a king's justice during
a trial. It was unfair to test her with Thomas, who could elicit
flirtatious behavior from a matron of sixty. Justin half rose and
then sank back into his chair. Richard was useless for general
investigation, and Justin had no idea whether Richard knew
Flael's sons. Thomas had to be the one to go. Justin told himself
he simply would not blame Lissa for her response to Thomas—
every woman responded to Thomas—but when he broke his

fast, he felt as if he were eating cold pebbles, and when his servant came up the stairs and told him there was a messenger from Robert FitzWalter at the door, Justin bade him send the man in with a definite sense of relief.

He was, therefore, in a mood to agree to anything that would occupy him and prevent him from thinking about Thomas's effect on Lissa—and hers on Thomas—when he learned that FitzWalter wished to see him on a matter of business that might be profitable to them both. The messenger said his master would be glad to receive Sir Justin as soon as he could ride over or, if Sir Justin was unable to come, would be glad to set a time to come to him. Without pausing to wonder about the remarkable courtesy of FitzWalter's invitation, Justin told the messenger to assure his master that he would come as soon as his horse was saddled. When the man had bowed himself out, Justin rose to exchange his sober merchant's tunic for a more elaborate one better suited to a gentleman's dress and to belt on his sword.

Since he was only half befuddled by his jealousy and confusion over Lissa, Justin began to wonder, when he was about midway between his house and the partially reconstructed Baynard's Castle, what made FitzWalter so polite. If the business he was about to propose was equally profitable and no more risky to one than to the other, he was doing Justin a favor and could afford to suit himself as to the time and place of making the offer. Thus, Justin entered Lord Robert's presence with a smile but with a certain wariness, which was not lessened when FitzWalter rose from the bench where he was sitting near the lively fire and gestured him to a second bench set at an angle to his own.

In general Justin had no complaint about FitzWalter's courtesy to him. They were of different ranks—FitzWalter among the greatest in the land and Justin's father barely within the barony—and Justin did not resent Lord Robert's looking down at him from a chair of state on the dais when they were in council on the affairs of the city. FitzWalter was not only of high lineage but was the Standard Bearer of the city of London. Nor did Justin feel specially honored when FitzWalter greeted him as an equal in social company; they were both gently born and Justin knew himself to be as strong as Lord Robert and probably more skilled with weapons. But this fraternal warmth was something out of the ordinary.

Before Justin's doubts could show on his face, FitzWalter said, "I have a favor to ask of you."

Justin sat down, openly sighed with relief, and then grinned. "If I can do you a service, I will be glad, my lord. And I am glad you come so quickly to the point. To speak the truth, I was wondering why I was being gentled."

FitzWalter laughed aloud. "You too will profit from this favor—within reason. But I am far too clever to hold out honeyed bait if I wished *you* ill or intended trickery. That would be like calling out 'This is a feint' in battle. And before you begin to wonder if I am doing just that so you will be sure it is *not* a feint, let me tell you what I desire of you."

Justin echoed Lord Robert's laugh and raised a brow in wordless query.

"You have not changed your mind about remaining here when the king goes to France, have you?"

"No, I have not," Justin replied, feeling wary again but keeping his expression mildly questioning.

"Well," FitzWalter said, "if you will not serve me in one way, perhaps you will serve me in another. I have heard from an agent who came from France last week that two of my ships loaded with wine, cloth, and blades of Damascus steel are beating their way up the coast from the south. It is ever thus. When you desire a thing swiftly, it is laggard; and when a delay would better suit your will, the devil adds wings. I had hoped the ships would arrive before it was necessary for me to join the king, but even if they came tomorrow I would not have time to dispose of the cargoes now. I would like to leave that task in your hands."

"I will be happy to serve you in this," Justin said heartily, enormously relieved, for he had feared FitzWalter intended to order him to accompany the London forces to France. "All I need know is what you wish to reserve for your own use, how you want payment for the cargo—in gold or in kind—whether you desire a quick return or you would prefer me to hold the goods to get the greatest return, and whether I should send the return to you, keep it for you, use it to begin a new trading venture, or pass it to the goldsmiths for profit."

Lord Robert's lips twisted. "Should you not first ask how you will keep the king's appointed regents, Peter des Roches and

Nicholas of Tusculum, from swallowing the cargo whole in the name of some fine or tax John has levied against me?"

Justin frowned. "I thought all such debts were canceled when you were pardoned by the king."

"That was when the king was still the enemy of the pope. Now that John has yielded the kingdom into the hands of Innocent and made his legate a regent, any abomination the king wishes to perpetrate is readily sanctioned by the pope's legate. Do you not know how Nicholas of Tusculum agreed in every matter with the king, even against the bishops, not only about the reparations that the king promised to pay the Church and others who were injured—" FitzWalter waved a hand around at the rough timber hall, which was all that had yet been erected to replace the keep the king had had destroyed. "But the legate has appointed to Church offices every candidate, no matter how unsuitable, that the king has suggested."

Justin had to repress a spark of amusement at the self-righteous rage with which FitzWalter uttered that last sentence. Lord Robert was ordinarily far from a champion of the rights of churchmen and had been known in his own territory to press for the election of his favorites without much regard to their holiness or scholarship. However, Justin was grateful that he had not been pressed to make any response about reparations for the destruction of Baynard's Castle. He was quite certain John would never pay a single silver penny for that, no matter what promises he had made or to whom. Moreover, Justin was not certain John *should* pay reparation for Baynard's Castle. There was very little doubt that FitzWalter had been involved in a plot to kill or overthrow John. Surely a king must have the right to punish rebellious barons and protect himself from plots. But what about those cases in which a king saw plots where there were none?

Since Justin had no intention of discussing that particular question with Lord Robert, he nodded a vague agreement and said, "The cargoes—"

"Yes, my cargoes," FitzWalter snarled. "Now that we cannot even look to the Church to protect us, we can no longer be at the mercy of the vagaries of the king's will. We must have some charter, some bond, from the king other than spoken words, which each man remembers differently. You were at the meeting of the council in August of last year, and I could swear I saw you among the men Archbishop Langton called aside when he spoke of a charter from the reign of the first King Henry. Is it not right that we should have such a charter so that my cargoes could not be seized for a whim but only for a cause of law judged by my peers?"

"I have no quarrel with that," Justin replied gravely. "I said so then and say so now, and say also that I will do all that is lawfully in my power to forward such a purpose." Then he shrugged and smiled wryly. "However, that is for the long tomorrow. We will have no such protection when your ships arrive. Is there already a fine or a judgment against you?"

"No, but there will be as soon as the king hears that rich cargoes of mine have come into England."

Justin chewed his lower lip thoughtfully. It was true that King John was malicious enough to make up some crime or slight that would justify a fine to injure an enemy; however, in Justin's opinion the king was too busy to look for trouble now, involved as he was with his plans to get an army to the Continent to fight King Philip. And since John was not expected to come to London before he sailed from Portsmouth, there was a fair chance he would never hear about FitzWalter's ships.

"Besides the agent that told you of them, who knows the ships are coming?" Justin asked. "And is the agent likely to speak of the matter widely?"

"You know the ships are coming," FitzWalter replied with a grim smile. "I know, and Hamo Finke knows, and I assure you the agent will not speak about my business to anyone without leave."

"Excellent!" Justin smiled. "Let us leave matters just as they are. I will take possession of the cargoes in the presence of Master Hamo Finke, pay the captains what is owing to them, and sell under my own name, taking back any cost to me. Do you desire that I have the ships refitted?"

"I had not thought of you doing the business in your own name. Thank you."

FitzWalter sounded not only surprised but somewhat less pleased than Justin expected. Then he realized that Lord Robert was torn between his natural desire to profit from his trading venture and his need to have a new injury from the king to display as an example of John's irrational injustice. In another moment, however, FitzWalter's smile became warmer. Justin assumed that he had realized that even the most punitive and unreasonable fine levied by the king's justiciar, probably after the king had left the country, would not rouse much resentment against John in those who did not already hate him. Peter des Roches was thoroughly detested by many for his own sake, and the blame would fall on him rather than on the king.

"Yes," FitzWalter went on after the brief pause, confirming Justin's thought. "That will almost ensure the safety of the cargo, unless there is a special effort to determine that it is mine." He nodded, then added, "And if it will not be burdening you too greatly, I would be glad if you gave the captains permission to refit the ships and kept at least one eye on them to be sure they do not arrange for the charges to be doubled so that they can put half in their own pockets."

Justin nodded acknowledgment of that common practice and promised to speak to several shipwrights himself, after which FitzWalter went on to answer specifically all the questions Justin had asked about the disposal of the cargoes, ending with a question of his own about what share Justin desired as payment.

"You asked a favor," Justin said, "let us leave it at that—or if you wish to be generous, I would be glad of, say, five casks of that same wine you bade me reserve for you."

"It is good wine," FitzWalter remarked, shrugging, "but not a fair return for the trouble my business may give you. I said a favor, and you bestow that by your willingness to take my affairs in hand at all. I did not intend that you lose time from your own affairs without some recompense."

Justin sincerely hoped that Lord Robert's remark about trouble was only a result of his constant conviction, since the yielding of Vaudreuil, that he was being persecuted and did not imply any future intention of overt treason. However, he was not much worried about being stained by the pitch FitzWalter might pour over himself. Justin had not been willing to serve as FitzWalter's captain in France, but the sale of cargoes was a far cry from treasonable acts while under arms during a war, and he was confident that his reputation and the strong determination of the merchants of London to protect their own would keep him safe. Still, it could do no harm to make the arrangement appear more like business and less like a personal favor, Justin thought.

"If the matter of a favor owing troubles you," he said, "I would be glad of a share in some future venture either in fine cloth—silks and velvets—or in wine, or if you would allow me some limited shipping space, say, a tenth, for a cargo of my own."

"Gladly on either or both," FitzWalter replied, "but I thought you had your own partners and shipping arrangements within your family."

"I have and I have not," Justin said. "Even before my uncle's death, my cousins were expanding their trade in wool. It is profitable and growing more so, especially since the risk of loss is much reduced by trading only across the narrow sea. I have my share in their ventures and in the profit, but they do the real trading. I make no complaint of that. It is, in fact, fortunate because much of my time, as you know, is given to keeping the peace in London and also because I find the wool trade very dull. I would like to add a little of the spice of the East to my business, and I can afford the risk."

FitzWalter laughed and extended his hand to grip Justin's wrist. "Done! The shipment of supplies to La Rochelle, which will be the next voyage for my ships, will not serve your purpose, although you are more than welcome to add any cargo you desire to send to that port, but when I return to England, we will plan something more interesting. And speaking of interesting and your peacekeeping duties, whatever happened to the goldsmith Flael? Was he murdered as I heard?"

"Yes and no," Justin answered, stifling a sigh of relief at having escaped from further talk about a partnership that Lord Robert would soon discover he welcomed more warmly than its proposer. "The whole matter of Flael's death is most peculiar," he went on quickly.

Then, intent on keeping Lord Robert's mind on that subject and away from any extended discussion of joint trading ventures, Justin described the entire case. Lord Robert listened with a slight smile, and when Justin was finished, he shrugged.

"You have a strange puzzle there," he remarked.

"I have, indeed," Justin agreed. "Did you know Flael at all?"

"I suppose I must have met him," FitzWalter replied, "but I did not *know* him. He was too much a king's man for me to do any business with him. It is strange that the sons fled, but if Master Goscelin says they had no reason to hate their father and would not have harmed him, he must be right. Likely it is a waste of time to seek them. No doubt they feared Flael had written a new will leaving all to the young wife. Bowles's daughter . . . I know of Bowles, and any child raised by him should know how to make a penny into two or even five. And any woman, even if she does not have the sense of a hen, somehow always seems to know how to cozen an old man into settling his sons' birthright on her."

"Do you know Madame Heloise?" Justin asked, his voice totally without expression.

FitzWalter shook his head. "Not at all. I do not believe I have ever laid eyes on her, but women are all the same—witless and greedy." He laughed and added, "I suppose she was frightened to death when she saw Flael all broken to bits."

The coarse pleasure in that laugh, which showed the amusement FitzWalter plainly felt at the idea of an innocent woman's fear, was one of the reasons Justin could never like the man. In addition, he suddenly felt there was something besides amusement in the quick glance FitzWalter had given him when he spoke of Lissa, a kind of curiosity that belied his remark that all women were alike. It was fortunate that Justin was always wary and guarded when dealing with FitzWalter; it made it easier to clamp down on the rage that leapt to life in the wake of that notion. But to ask why FitzWalter was curious about Lissa would be useless; Lord Robert would only deny his interest— and, worse, his attention would be drawn to her if Justin had read him wrong and he had not previously been curious. Lord Robert might be coarse and brutal, but he was not stupid. All Justin could do was swallow his rage and turn down one side of his mouth while he lifted a shoulder with pretended indifference.

"She was shocked, of course, but I would say she was more bewildered than frightened. She said over and over that she could imagine no reason why Flael should be tortured—that was before we knew the wounds were inflicted after his death."

FitzWalter sneered. "You mean she did not at once take her

husband's injury to herself and shriek with terror and demand a guard to watch her every step?"

"I do not think it ever came into her mind that Flael's death had anything at all to do with her," Justin said. "She seems to think that the cause stemmed from his moneylending activities, and for all I know her guess is as good as any other."

Justin had answered FitzWalter's tone with a denial before he really considered what FitzWalter had said. After he spoke, he remembered that Lissa had been frightened, not only by Flael's death and the manner of it but by something she was hiding. But that was none of FitzWalter's business, he thought, keeping his hands open and relaxed on his knees with a deliberate effort when the man responded to his reply with a brief bray of cynical laughter.

"Was she not even curious about who killed her husband or why?" FitzWalter asked. "Was she that glad to be rid of him?"

"She did not pretend to be bereaved," Justin said, struggling to keep his voice even and indifferent.

Now Justin was more eager to leave the subject of Flael's death than he had been to divert FitzWalter from the idea of offering him a partnership in a trading venture. He was very much afraid that his control would crack if Lord Robert made another remark about Lissa, and he forced a smile and stood up.

"I am beginning to wonder whether this is not likely to remain a mystery," Justin said rather mendaciously, and then to kill the topic completely once and for all, he went on, "Nor am I sure it is worth my time to pursue the answer because it cannot be proven that any harm was done Flael while he was alive. So, even if I find out who broke his bones—with what can he be charged?"

FitzWalter laughed loudly again. "With what indeed?"

He also stood and clapped Justin on the shoulder in a blow that was friendly but at the same time was hard enough to hurt, hard enough to have knocked down a slighter man or one who was unprepared. Had Justin fallen, FitzWalter would have laughed even louder; it was the kind of jest he loved. However, when the buffet produced nothing but a faint smile on Justin's face, a flicker of approval showed in FitzWalter's expression, and he took the trouble to accompany Justin out to the courtyard and wait while his horse was brought. He mentioned then that he intended to leave London before the week was out and, when the groom led Justin's horse to them, put his hand on Justin's arm to hold him while he gave him a few more details that had come to his mind about the expected arrival of the ships and how to deal with the captains.

Justin assured FitzWalter of his attention to all the details of the business as he swung into the saddle and lifted his hand in a farewell gesture, but he was really thinking about Lord Robert's inexplicable interest in Lissa. Then he began to wonder whether that interest had been anything more than natural curiosity about a person involved in a murder. After all, most of FitzWalter's repetitions of what was said by rote of all women— that they were stupid and greedy but sly as serpents and that they were always eager to be rid of a husband and inherit his goods. Was it not because *he* felt a special interest in Lissa that he even noticed FitzWalter's remarks? If it had been some other woman, would he not have answered without thought or anger and with the same scornful laughter that Lord Robert uttered?

That must be so, he told himself. FitzWalter was not the type to let go of any subject in which he was interested before he had all the answers he wanted. If he had been truly curious about Lissa, he would not have permitted Justin to cut short the conversation and, when he walked out with him, would have asked more questions about her rather than returning to the topic of the ships.

And now that Justin thought about it, that was a far stranger thing than any curiosity FitzWalter showed about Lissa. Why had Lord Robert asked him to deal with the cargoes? Surely Hamo Finke could have handled the whole matter. Not that Finke would have sold the cargoes himself, but the services of a factor would have been easy to obtain. Was it possible that, being unable to involve him in his treasonous plans in one way, FitzWalter was seeking to drag him in in another? Justin considered the notion and then heaved a sigh. He was making goblins out of shadows in the corner. Perhaps FitzWalter might have some intention, in a business sense, of binding him closer and, through him, his uncle's family and friends; however, it was far more likely that he had been, so to speak, present in FitzWalter's mind because they had had recent dealings over the muster of men for the king's army. It was natural, then, for

FitzWalter to decide to choose a man he knew to handle his business rather than to leave the burden on Master Hamo, who was a goldsmith, not a merchant.

Suddenly, becoming aware of a strong odor of fish, Justin looked around and discovered that he was riding north on Friday Street. Why in the world had he turned off Knight's Bridge Road onto Friday Street into the stink of bad fish when he could have ridden up Cordwainers Row or Soper Lane? And then his hand tightened on his rein so abruptly and so hard that the quiet palfrey he used for riding about the city slid to a halt and began to rear.

Justin brought the gelding down and soothed it with absentminded skill. Then, with his long jaw jutting forward and an expression on his face that made apprentices and fishmongers scurry out of his way, he turned his horse back the way he had come. There was only one possible reason to ride up Friday Street, and that was to pass Peter Flael's house when he turned east toward his own. Master Peter's house was only a few doors from the corner of Friday Street. Any other route north from Knight's Bridge Road would bring him to the West Chepe beyond Lissa's home.

It was ridiculous that while he was thinking of FitzWalter his treacherous body had set him on a path that led directly to her. The woman had ensorcelled him! As he thought the word a faint chill passed over Justin. She was an apothecary's daughter, and a sly dog of an apothecary at that. Could she have put some potion in the food he ate or in the ale or wine? Nonsense! There were potions that could stir the loins, but without witchcraft that effect was brief and only physical, and whatever was said of William Bowles, no one had ever accused his daughter of being a witch.

Still, it was strange how heavy and sad he felt as he turned away from her. He had fancied himself in love in the past and was familiar with the warmth in his loins that started up at the thought of a beautiful woman, the images of a soft bed in a firelit chamber that enticed him in an idle moment to think of visiting the object of his lust. Never before, however, had thoughts of a woman unbalanced his judgment, as had his desire to defend Lissa while he was talking to FitzWalter, nor had he found himself wandering toward any other woman when he believed himself occupied with more serious matters.

It was not something he needed to worry about, Justin decided as he rode east along Knight's Bridge Road. The urge to see Lissa remained, but it certainly had no power to move him toward her against his will. All he need do, he told himself, was ignore the impulse and it would fade until he was entirely free of his desire for her.

Chapter 8

⧫

THE ONE AND ONLY GOOD THING ABOUT THE MESSAGE THOMAS FitzAilwin brought, Lissa thought four days after her husband had been buried, was that she could hardly remember that day at all. She had been numbed to everything by the shock of grief and disappointment that struck her when she realized that Justin was not coming at all, that he did not feel the urgent need to be with her that she felt to be with him, that he probably had felt nothing for her but pity, which she had misread into caring. It was almost as if the Justin she had obviously created out of her own imagination and desire was the man who had died. She could think of nothing at first but her loss, and she felt dizzy, as if the solid floor she stood upon were melting away and letting her slip into an endless void.

For the rest of the day, everything that happened was vague, only a few events standing out as shocking vignettes in a gray mist of misery. She recalled coming down the stairs from the solar into the shop—she supposed she had been summoned— and seeing a coffin draped in a black pall. The surprise of seeing it there, for she had no idea when or how it had come, must have drawn some sound from her, because both her father and Justin's cousin reached out to support her; she had shrunk from both of them, stepping back to cling to Mistress Adela. She also remembered being surprised at the number of people who had followed her down the stairs. They must all have been in the solar; she must have spoken to them, but for her life she could not remember doing so.

Six men, richly but soberly dressed, came forward and lifted the coffin onto a bier made of two strong poles with wooden crosspieces. They carried it to the church, where Father Denis was waiting. In normal times, the coffin would have been carried to the chancel gate. There the Mourning Office would have been said, the body censed and sprinkled with holy water. Then all the mourners would have joined in the Lord's Prayer, and the priest would have pronounced the absolution before the coffin was carried to the burial ground. Because the interdict was still in effect, however, the cortege moved directly to the burial ground and a much truncated mass was said, although Father Denis faithfully celebrated as much of the service as was permitted.

Seeing Peter lowered into the open grave was the last clear memory Lissa had of that day. She knew that all the mourners returned to the house, that somehow tables laden with food and casks of ale and wine had appeared. Perhaps they had been there all the time and her eyes had fastened only on Peter's coffin, or perhaps the servants of Peter's guild brothers had arranged the feast while their masters attended the burial service. She was also dimly aware that men and women came and spoke to her and that she must have answered them in some reasonable manner because her father, who stood close beside her, did not interfere in any way. All she really remembered, however, was going over and over Justin's every word and gesture the previous day and trying to discover how she had misunderstood him so completely.

Although she was unaware of it at the time, she was exhausted by the effort of disguising her true thoughts and responding properly to the condolences of Peter's friends and fellow goldsmiths and to questions about the absence of Peter's sons. At some time she found herself alone, except for Mistress

Adela, who looked pale and exhausted and who said she must go, that Goscelin was waiting below for her. She also asked, with a troubled frown, whether Lissa would be all right, alone in the house, and whether—since she would not go home with her father—she wished instead to sleep in Goscelin's house.

Gratitude had brought a touch of brightness into the black blanket of misery Lissa had wrapped around herself. She managed a smile and hugged and kissed Adela, swearing that she did not fear being alone in the house at all, that she had been recalling her mother's death and burial, which had seemed like the end of the world to her. She was glad to see the anxiety fade from Adela's face and was able to listen to her comforting words, which were cut short by a bellow from belowstairs. The two women smiled at each other; then Adela fled to her husband and Lissa kicked off her shoes and tumbled into bed, clothes and all.

Lissa slept, as far as she knew, without stirring or dreaming; however, when she woke it was with the conviction that she had *not* misunderstood Justin. She had seen in other men the symptoms he exhibited; in fact, he had gone farther than several who had offered for her. Justin had shown every sign of a man delighted with a woman and desirous of her, a man who needed only a few more meetings to convince him to make an offer to that woman's father to have her as his wife.

Tears filled Lissa's eyes and coursed slowly down her cheeks. That was all. Clearly, as soon as Justin thought of making an offer for her he had remembered that he would become not only Lissa's husband but also William Bowles's son-by-marriage. Justin, of all men, could not afford to be associated with a man of Bowles's dubious reputation.

Under the circumstances, Lissa was even less willing than she might otherwise have been to listen later in the day to her father's reasons why it would be more sensible and convenient for her to return to his house. The fact that those reasons were perfectly sound only made her more furious, and she would not even discuss whether she would come each day to his shop to take up again her part in his business. She hardly noticed when her father yielded her a prize she had desired for years and said he had missed her and that her absence was a great loss to the business.

Worse yet, the knowledge that she was being unreasonable, that she really wanted to get back to the work she loved, rubbed her temper even more raw. Thus, when Binge and Witta appeared just as her father was leaving, each accusing the other of laziness and malicious mischief, Lissa scolded Binge with an unnatural ferocity and again threatened to cast her out if she did not mend her sullen manners. Binge fled from the room weeping, and Witta grinned smugly, whereupon Lissa slapped him so hard she knocked him down. Her father's mouth twisted in disgust and frustration, and he snarled at her that she was impossible to talk to that day and that he would return on the morrow, hoping to find her more sensible.

Guilt was added to guilt when she walked idly to the window for no better reason than a restless craving for movement and saw her father near the back door apparently trying to soothe the maid before he left. Because her emotions were raw, what seemed like a total reversal in her father's behavior toward her shook the foundation of her entire life. Was it possible that her mother's attitude to her father had so colored her own that she had built a monster out of an ordinary man who was hurt and angry—as she had built a lover-hero out of an ordinary man who only felt kindness and pity? This notion was so devastating that instead of telling Binge she was sorry for her threats, which she had meant to do, she found fault with dinner and also with the evening meal Binge had provided.

By the next day, resignation had taken the place of bad temper. Instead of screaming at her father to get out and leave her alone, she listened to him; however, she would not agree to move back into his house.

"I will return to work for you after another fortnight," Lissa said. "I cannot come sooner because there is the matter of Peter's debts to settle and the debts owing to him to collect."

"That is ridiculous," William snapped. "You are not responsible for that business. I told you before that if you meddle you will find your own fortune eaten up—and I will not replace it. It is Peter's son's fault that all is left in confusion. Let them come back and mend matters."

"I do not think they will come back, father. At first I believed that they feared I had seduced Peter into making a will in my favor, but they knew their father better than that. I now think they fled from fear when they saw how Peter's body was cut and broken and burned."

"I tell you I need you now. Why will you not be reasonable and come home? You could at least oversee the young fools in the shop, and perhaps make up a few of your special drugs and lotions while you try to collect the debts owed Flael—and you would be protected from those who wish to collect from you also."

"I do not *wish* to be protected from them," Lissa said wearily. "I have every intention of paying all of Peter's debts as soon as possible. Besides, it would be very wrong to leave Peter's house empty. You know an empty house draws thieves the way bad meat draws flies."

"Leave the old woman. Nothing could give her greater pleasure than to have the house to herself."

"No," Lissa said, her lips a thin line in her set face. "When I am ready, I will ride or walk to our shop each morning, but I will finish Peter's business first."

William knew that look. In the past he had tried every device he dared try but had never found any threat or reason that could alter Lissa's mind when she spoke it with that expression on her face. He stood up so abruptly that the stool he was sitting on overturned. "I am done trying to save you from yourself. Remember! All the pain and grief that come to you, you have brought upon yourself."

Lissa shrugged when he stormed out. In fact, had her father reasoned rather than argued, he might have won his point, because Lissa had a guilty secret. Her real reason for remaining in Flael's house was a thin thread of hope that Justin might have withdrawn less because of his reluctance to be associated with her father than because he felt that the day of her husband's burial and even the following week or two were too soon to be courting a widow. She was ashamed of that silly hope, knowing that Justin could have sent a written message or found some other way to make the reason for his absence clear. Still, she could not bear to leave the place where they had really met. And what if Justin's absence was owing to some totally unknown cause? If he sought her in the future, she did not wish either to remind him of who her father was or expose him to her father's company, which would happen if he came to her at her father's house.

Lissa's misery was only deepened and confirmed in the afternoon when Thomas FitzAilwin again presented himself at the house. This time he came to return to her the list of debtors that Justin had taken. A single glance told her that the list was not being returned because more important matters had crowded it out of Justin's schedule; Justin had fulfilled his promise. Either written beside the record of the debtor or on a separate sheet of parchment rolled into the list, Justin had indicated the circumstances of nearly all of Peter's clients and even suggested how she should request payment. But Lissa could barely restrain tears and make civil conversation. To send Thomas with the list instead of bringing it himself amounted to a clear statement that Justin had no intention of meeting her again if he could avoid it.

Although Lissa was tempted to do so, she did not actually suggest that Thomas leave. She felt so reluctant to invite him to warm himself by the fire and have a cup of hot spiced wine, however, that she was ashamed. Shame drove her to mend her manners, and in response to his polite question about her health, she made herself smile and reply that she was feeling better. She managed to smile again when she refused his equally polite offer of his services if he could help her in any way. She did not remember what they talked about after that, but he did not stay long and when he was gone she could weep in peace.

Thomas had other business to finish that day, a shipment of wool to be delivered to traders from the Hanse in the Steelyard. Stepping into the Hanseatic enclave was like voyaging into a foreign country. Neither the king's sheriff nor the mayor's guardsmen had power in the Steelyard. If a merchant of the Hanse desired your business enough, he might come to you, placing himself under English law. Most often, however, the outsider was asked to come to the Steelyard, where he was in the power of the Hanse. Rarely did worse than frustration befall a merchant who visited the Hanseatic enclave, but Thomas like most others who dealt with the Hanse found that in full measure and overflowing.

So long had Thomas's argument with the Hanseatic wool dealer taken, that it was quite dark when he reached Justin's house. He found his cousin had just come in himself, after chasing several false rumors concerning Flael's sons. The upper chamber, lit by the golden light of a dozen candles—for Justin did not stint himself in comforts—was a welcome haven. Two chairs stood at a table covered by a white cloth and set before the leaping fire. As Thomas took off his cloak, Justin bellowed down the stairs to hurry the meal. Then both men stood before the fire, roasting the chill of January from their bones.

"They have slipped away, I think," Justin said, continuing his remarks about Flael's sons, "and I no longer believe we will find them. We have found the cart and we have found the chests— separate and empty. Both have changed hands more than once already, and each step back leads to blind paths, no one being willing to say he knew the seller. Thus, I would guess both cart and chests were abandoned in different places in the town. Young Peter and Edmond must have realized soon after they fled that the cart and chests would mark them. And I had a thick head and gave them time to recover from their panic and become clever."

"Nonsense. They had time enough to plan before the servant boy was brought to Master Goscelin, before you even knew Flael was dead, and you would be no closer to catching them, except by chance, if you had sent your men after them immediately. You do not even think them guilty," Thomas said, glancing sidelong at his cousin, but Justin's face revealed nothing and he did not turn his eyes from their contemplation of the bright flames. "In the name of God, you do not even have a murder you can prove. Why do you *want* Flael's accursed sons?"

"Because I think they know why their father died, and to me it is murder to frighten a man to death."

"Not unless it was done apurpose," Thomas protested.

Justin sighed. "Perhaps not, but the whole thing makes me uneasy. One might believe that Flael was involved in some secret matter and was threatened for some reason—perhaps to make sure he would remain silent. Flael, being weak and timid, was more affected than whoever took him intended, and he died. In case others knew the secret, his body was mutilated as a warning. The sons took heed and fled. If that is the true case, the secret must be powerful and dangerous. Should we not know what it is? But there is another way to look at Flael's death.

That he was deliberately shocked for private reasons by someone who knew of his weakness and then mutilated so that we would think the purpose of his death more complex."

"I think your reasoning has more bends and coils than a crazy snake," Thomas said. "And to answer your first question—no, we should not try to discover the secret. We would be wiser and safer to know nothing at all about a secret so important that one who knew it died of fright when threatened or questioned."

He was about to say more, but the sound of heavy steps on the stairs silenced him. In his mother's household, Thomas would have paid no attention at all to the coming and going of servants. Several of his mother's people had belonged to the family before Thomas was born, and the younger servants were their children. However, Justin's old manservant had died, and he had taken on, rather hastily, the husband of the woman who had nursed his servant through his last days. He liked the woman, who kept his house and clothing decently clean and provided such food as she could, considering his irregular hours. The man, however, he did not like or trust; Hervi mistreated his wife and was mealymouthed and whining.

Both men watched the servant lay thick trenchers of bread on the table and then place between them a wooden platter of broken meats, half a cheese, a fresh loaf of manchet bread, and a large flagon of hot spiced wine. With simultaneous sighs of pleasure, both reached for the horn cups still on the tray. Thomas seized the flagon with his other hand, and Justin waved the servant away, saying they would serve themselves. Thomas poured wine, and both men drank silently while the servant went down the stairs. Justin raised his cup in warning, then went and shut the door.

"I forgot him," he said as he returned and sat down at the table. "He listens—and talks too, I think, but I do not yet know to whom."

"Get rid of him then," Thomas said, sitting down at the opposite side of the table.

"I am sorry for his woman." Justin shrugged. "And I would like to know whether he is a hired spy or just sells what he hears for an extra penny to whoever will pay."

"It would not be on account of the business," Thomas said reflectively. "Alan might have that problem or Richard, but not you. If he is a spy for one man, that man must be our dearly beloved mayor, Roger FitzAdam."

"More the fool he," Justin remarked with a shrug. "He is wasting good money. I tell him the truth and all the truth of what I do." He laughed as he drew his eating knife and began to pick pieces of meat from the platter. "It is safe to tell Roger everything because he does not understand half I say and forgets the other half."

Thomas also speared meat on the platter, rather harder than was necessary, and he looked up at Justin before he moved the selection to his own trencher. "The less he understands, the less he trusts you. And he remembers what he can use against you, Justin. Why did you not refuse him when he asked you to lead the guard again?"

Justin's mouth hardened. "Because I do not like to see justice bought and sold so stupidly that the burghers would soon cry to be back in the king's hand, from which we only escaped a few years past. I am reasonable enough to take account of the man and the reason as well as the crime itself, but to blame the beggars and the players for every crime and let the lords run riot in the city—"

Thomas held up a hand. "I have heard this lesson before. There was no need for you to answer me as if the subject were new to us. I just wished to remind you that a man may be dangerous even though he is stupid."

"Oh, I am not likely to forget that." Justin laughed and tore a portion from the loaf of bread, which he handed to Thomas. Then he frowned. "But to tell the truth, I have made no report to Roger about Flael's death. I have spoken fully to Goscelin, and since he summoned me directly I do not see how I can be blamed, especially since the man was not murdered by blow or rope. Now I know I should have gone to Roger at once to see the look on his face when I described Flael's corpse, but by the time I knew there was something strange about Flael's death, Roger would have been warned. At first, of course, I thought it was the woman—young wife, old rich husband—but she does not profit. I have seen Flael's will."

"Ah, I thought you might have had some suspicions of her," Thomas mumbled around a mouthful of meat and bread. "But I felt neither guilt nor fear in her today or on the day Flael was

buried. And I will tell you right now that Madame Heloise is not
driven by greed. There is a look one cannot miss in those who
love money. She was not indifferent to the debts, but it was as if
she were witnessing a business arrangement of which she was
not partaking. And as to murdering Flael for passion—"

Justin went on chewing when Thomas stopped, grateful to
have a reason to grind his teeth together, but he knew his cousin
was not deliberately teasing him and managed to keep quiet.

Thomas had cleared his mouth, but he paused to take a deep
drink and then to laugh. "It is ridiculous. Madame Heloise is
clever, I grant you—she barely glanced at your notes, but when I
later asked a question or two, she had the answers already in
mind—but passion? She has none, or at least none that relates to
her husband in any way. I think she has a good nature; she is
gentle and thoughtful, but she is as flat of disposition and as
passionless as a cold oat cake."

Is Thomas mad or am I, Justin wondered, remembering the
intense liveliness of Lissa's glance and repartee, the quick
snapping answers when he annoyed her, and most of all, with a
physical reaction that was driving him to the edge of despair, the
warmth of her response to him. He picked up his cup, which
would partially shield his face, and said, "Passionless? You
mean she did not flirt with you?"

Thomas paused to chew another mouthful. He had not
expected that question. He would not have been surprised if his
cousin had waved away the whole topic of Madame Heloise's
involvement in her husband's death, satisfied once Thomas's
opinion confirmed his own. He would have been equally
unsurprised if Justin had questioned him minutely on every
word and gesture of the suspect. Sometimes Justin could obtain
hints and information Thomas did not know he held. But the
question regarding the quality of Madame Heloise's nature had
not been asked within the context of Flael's death. And the tone
of Justin's voice—the mixture of smugness and uncertainty
when he asked if Madame Heloise had flirted—would in any
case have put a new light on Justin's interest in Flael's widow.

Having spent as long as he reasonably could on chewing and
swallowing, Thomas looked up and shook his head. "Not fair,"
he said. "I was judging the woman as heart-free because I
trusted you when you told me that she did not pretend any

particular attachment to her husband. If I had known that she was sealed to someone, I would not, I think, have judged her as passionless. No wonder she grew white with pain when I said you would not come to Flael's burial, and again today when I handed her the list."

"You did not tell me that," Justin said, putting down his cup without drinking.

"I did not tell you that she stirred my spiced wine three times with a silver spoon either," Thomas retorted. "I was taking account only of what might pertain to the crime. I marked her disappointment when you did not come to the burial as a sign of her innocence, of which there were many other marks. By Mary's bright eyes, Justin, I thought you suspected the woman of a hand in her husband's death—"

"She could have been involved with one of the sons," Justin said defensively. "She was more the younger Peter's age than the elder's."

"Such things happen," Thomas agreed, "but I would say not with Madame Heloise—"

"Call her Lissa. Her father calls her Heloise and she does not like the name." The words were out before Justin thought, and he could feel his ears grow hot when he realized how he had betrayed himself. Although he had spoken of far more intimate matters to his cousin without embarrassment, he found he could not mention Lissa without awkwardness.

Thomas's reply was delayed by no more than an eyeblink, yet that brief silence was painfully apparent before he went on smoothly, "But I would say that Mistress Lissa is far too experienced and far too clever a woman to be much interested in a boy younger than she, even if not by much."

"Unless she thought such a one would be easily ruled," Justin said, staring straight ahead but not meeting Thomas's eyes.

Thomas frowned, and his voice sharpened. "What the devil ails you, Justin? You do not believe the woman to be guilty of her husband's death, I know that. Then why do you seek this reason and that—and one more unlikely than the next—to involve her?"

"Because I find myself too much drawn to her," Justin replied savagely, "and because, guilty or not, she is hiding something from me. And I could not pry it out because I sank deeper into pleasure with each exchange between us. She made me desire to be with her—not only to lie with her but to *be* with her—as I have not desired a woman's company since I was a green boy. But she *is* hiding something, and I will not be easy about her part in this until I discover what it is, no matter how small."

"You sound as if you were considering a wife." Thomas's voice was somewhat higher than normal, and he laid his eating knife down by the side of his trencher.

"Why not?" Justin asked, laughing suddenly. "I desire her and she, you say, desires me, which is a better beginning than many marriages that start in antipathy. Moreover, there are even the usual enticements to taking a wife. She is well dowered; she will be heiress to a very good business when her father dies—"

"Yes, but until he does die you will have William Bowles as a father-by-marriage," Thomas remarked and picked up his eating knife again.

He had been startled, even alarmed by Justin's earlier intensity, but his cousin's voice had lightened and he was smiling as he spoke of marriage. This, Thomas judged, was a jest, even if a painful one; clearly Justin *did* have a strong desire for this Lissa. But the reminder about her father might deaden the desire somewhat.

"He can do me little harm if I do not keep my position as the mayor's watchdog," Justin replied thoughtfully. "And I fear I will not keep my position long in any case. I am being careful, but sooner more likely than later I will step on our mayor's toes, and enough of his friends will support him to enable him to dismiss me again. I will not repine. Remember what I told you of FitzWalter's offer to me? I will instead extend my trading into spices and silks. Lissa may have William Bowles for a father, but she also has two uncles in the Hanse."

"What?" Thomas dropped his eating knife again and stared. "That might make even a father-by-marriage like Bowles worthwhile."

But Justin burst into a harsh roar of laughter. "Oh Thomas, my Thomas, I did not think I could draw you like that any longer."

Although Thomas was not certain Justin was perfectly sure himself whether he was jesting or not, he took the words as a warning off dangerous ground. "Well, let me tell you what I suffered from the Hanse today, and you may yet reconsider," he said, and launched into a description of his business at the Steelyard.

Justin was deeply interested in the Hanse for many reasons, and the discussion lasted through the meal. When Justin got up to call Hervi to clear, Thomas rose also and asked his cousin to bid the servant get his horse first. Justin protested that he expected Thomas to stay and would never have suggested he come for the evening meal if he had suspected he would ride home after it. Thomas laughed, protesting that he was not likely to get lost on the way to Candlewick Street, no matter how dark the night.

After seeing his cousin out, Justin hurried back up the stairs and shoved his chair closer to the fire, telling Hervi over his shoulder to fill his cup with wine. With the drink in hand, he thought back over his conversation with Thomas, and slowly began to relax.

So Lissa had been disappointed when he did not come— bitterly disappointed, her face grown white with pain, Thomas had said. It made an enormous difference; there was no question of her amusing herself with other men while he was tormented by some spell or potion and could not even think of another woman. But Thomas had also judged her passionless— no, he had said that judgment was unfair, made while he believed Lissa loved no one, was heart-whole. Later he had said her heart was sealed to someone, as if the heart, having been wounded, was now covered with a plaster to protect it from other attempts on it.

The notion made Justin smile, but a moment later his lips twisted and the creases between his brows deepened into a frown. There had been times in the past few days when his chest ached enough to need a plaster, if one could reach inside to place one. How cruel of him to inflict such pain on Lissa! He almost stood up to go to her that minute, but controlled the ridiculous impulse. She would be abed and asleep by now, the house locked and barred. What excuse could he give for hammering at the door? What excuse would he need? If she loved him, would she not receive him with open arms at any time? Perhaps and perhaps not, for the maid, who hated her, would surely carry the news . . . and his own guards would ruin *his* reputation too. Justin laughed aloud. Tomorrow would be soon enough.

He drained the cup, rose to set it on the table, which now stood against the wall, and went about the room pinching out the flames on the candles. As always on such a bitterly cold night, he looked with disfavor on the furnishings of his bedchamber. The hearth, though it vented to the street and did not fill the room with smoke, was too small to warm the room thoroughly. Worse, he was still sleeping on the cot he had brought when he moved in, mostly because he could not make up his mind what sort of bed he wanted.

At the time he had taken the house he had been negotiating a marriage, and knew the girl had already chosen and ordered her own bed. But the marriage had fallen through when he discovered the girl was terrified of him. He might not have dropped the negotiations on that account, expecting that he could teach her he was no monster, but fortunately he had overheard her talking to a young man whom she favored and did not fear at all and discovered that her blank looks and nonsensical remarks were not owing to terror but to lack of wit; in fact, he had almost been trapped with a woman stupider than he could bear.

After disentangling himself from the family, Justin had never got around to ordering a bed, partly because he never thought of it when he had the time and partly because a bed was often a substantial part of a wife's dowry. To have two beds would be ridiculous; it was rare even for great noble families to have more than one bed. On the other hand, two chairs, Justin thought, his mind going back to his dinner with Thomas as he stripped off his clothes, were a reasonable extravagance. His uncle, while he was alive, used to visit him often; Justin had many older, important visitors, and he did not relish sitting on a lowly stool in his own house.

Still, on cold winter nights like this one, as he slid his shivering body into the cold cot, he swore he would have a bed made for him at once so that he could sleep warm and soft in featherbeds. A slow smile parted his lips. He did not need to order a bed for that, only dismiss the guards who were watching

Lissa's house and find a way in that would not wake the old woman. A deeper warmth pervaded him than that normally reflected by his own body from the furs on which he slept and drew over him, and Justin allowed his eyes to close. Tomorrow.

Chapter 9

LISSA'S MOTHER HAD TOLD HER, WHEN SHE WAS A CHILD AND WEPT because nothing she did could ever please her father, that the only use for tears was to clear the eyes. Over the years she had found that to be true; God knew the bitter tears she wept over her mother's death did not bring her mother back. And now the bitter tears did not soften the blow Thomas had dealt her.

At least she was sure now, she told herself. She need no longer sit at home waiting in hope that Justin would come. Whatever his reasons for deciding that their mutual delight was a mistake, he had made it plain that he did not wish to see her again. Lissa wiped the tears from her cheeks with the heel of her hand and unrolled the list of Peter's clients again. Tomorrow early, she would go to Master Hamo Finke and ask him to find a trustworthy agent for her. And meanwhile, she told herself firmly, she had better decide whom the agent should see and for what he should ask.

Although there had as yet been no rush of creditors beating

on the door, despite the inevitable spread of the news that
Peter's son had fled with his strongboxes, two merchants had
asked to speak to her. Witta had turned them away without
difficulty, simply saying his mistress could see no one yet but
promised to attend to them on the first Monday coming. Peter's
position and the open support of Goscelin and the other
goldsmiths had quieted anxiety and permitted her a little time to
gather her wits, but Monday was only three days hence, and
she must be ready.

The thought repeated itself, and Lissa looked down at the
parchment in her lap, only then realizing, because it was
growing too dark to read, that she must have been sitting for
some time utterly blank of mind. She shivered, not only cold but
shocked at how much she had allowed her disappointment over
Justin to affect her. That was stupid. She was a widow now, in
control of her own dowry and independent of her father. She
could marry any man to whom she took a fancy; some of those
who had wanted her were still unwed and sought her eyes
hopefully. Lissa nearly burst into tears again, and decided that
was not the best way to cheer herself. Well, she was free of any
master, within reason; she need not marry at all.

The dim, empty room mocked that thought. She did not want
to live alone. Hastily Lissa got up to throw more wood on the
fire and, when the flames began to dance again, went around
the room lighting candles. When that was done she felt better
for the brightness and went to close the shutter. As she took
hold of it, to her surprise, Lissa thought she heard her father's
voice. She hesitated, tempted to unloosen a corner of the oiled
parchment that let in some light and kept out the cold, but the
voice had stopped by then and she did not bother, certain she
had been mistaken. There was no reason for her father to come
back after their quarrel in the morning. His habit was to give her
a day or two to "forget" and then broach in a new way the
demand they had argued over.

Below the solar window, Binge retained her scowl as the
bitch's father said fare well and gave a nod that was almost a
bow. A courtesy like that made her suspicious, as did the second
silver penny she clutched tight under the cloth that protected
her gown while she was cooking. When Bowles's dark cloak had
disappeared out of the gate, Binge sidled into the kitchen shed

near to the fire, lifted her gown and shift, and slid the penny into the purse she wore against her flesh.

As she pulled down her skirts, Binge considered her source of new wealth. She had promised to open the back door to the new wife's father tonight. That was what he asked her to do when he gave her the first penny the day after the master had been buried. She had not answered him yea or nay then, even when he promised another penny after the door was open. And today, he had given her a second penny and promised three more when the door was open. So his need to get into the house was very great, far greater than could be caused by his ill will toward the bitch.

Absently Binge stirred the soup she had made for the evening meal. Bowles had said he needed his daughter at home, but Heloise was lazy and stubborn and did not want to return to her duty of keeping his house and attending to his business. She wished to live in idle luxury, and he did not dare force her because she might, to spite him, mix poison instead of medicine. She must be frightened into leaving Flael's house and believe her father was doing her a favor to take her in. Thus, Bowles had said, he would pretend to be a thief and beat her because there was nothing to steal in the house. After that, she would be afraid to stay, and Binge would be left to care for the place until Flael's sons came home from Canterbury.

The whole idea was very appealing to Binge. The thought of Lissa getting a good beating and then leaving the house so that Binge would have it all to herself was delightful. The only trouble was that she did not believe a word the bitch's father said. Could this be planned between the two of them to be rid of her? No, that was silly. With all the true family gone, the bitch could be rid of her without needing any excuse. Still, perhaps she should not open the door? But then she would have to give back the pennies, and she might be beaten and thrown into the street anyway. That was the bitch's threat, and for all she hated her father she would believe him above a servant's word.

Binge looked at the wall between the kitchen shed and the house. She would never have done it, never have let a thief into the house, if the mistress were alive, not for ten silver pennies, not even for thirty. It was different now, with even the master dead and the boys run away. Canterbury, he said. That was a lie.

Binge knew the boys had not gone to Canterbury, although they had told her nothing. They must have done something wrong after the mistress died and there was no one to keep them straight.

Maybe the bitch had led the master wrong, tempted him into some evil act. Surely it was her fault he was killed. That lord with the hard face, who made Binge shiver when he questioned her, was plainly seeking evidence of the bitch's guilt, so it would be right to get that one in trouble. Maybe I can, too, Binge thought. No one knew that young Peter had given her all his keys, so the fact that all the inside doors were open would be blamed on the bitch's carelessness. It was true too. The bitch never locked the doors the way the real mistress always had. But Binge knew the first one accused by the wardens was always the servant. She would have to take care that if it all went wrong, she would not be blamed and no one would know she had let the bitch's father into the house. If the silver pennies were found, would they betray her? On the thought she nervously pressed her left hand against the hardness of the purse under her clothes.

"Got a pain, I hope," Witta sang out as he dashed from the house and into the kitchen.

Binge shrieked with shock and dropped the spoon into the soup pot, splashing herself with the hot liquid so that she shrieked again.

Witta laughed and danced around her, grabbing the heel of a bread and an irregular piece of cheese that had been left lying on one of the tables used for cutting.

"Thief," Binge screamed, snatching up the spoon and throwing the hot liquid from it at the boy.

"Am not!" Witta exclaimed impudently, stopping dead, but well away so the shower from the spoon missed him. "Mistress Lissa never holds back on food. Boys got to eat. She said so. I'll tell—"

"Tell!"

Binge's voice rose hysterically and her face changed, twisting, the toothless mouth open, panting, the eyes showing white all around in a way that both frightened Witta and wrenched at his heart because he could remember a terror that was beyond screams. He had been playing with the old woman, teasing, not realizing until it happened that he had gone too far.

"No, no, I won't tell," he promised. "I know you're scared mistress will put you out, but she won't. She gets mad sometimes and says bad things, but she's good, really good. She never hurts anyone, never."

It was fortunate that all Binge had in her hand was a wooden spoon. She threw it with intent to kill, and it flew truer than the liquid that had been in it and struck Witta on the side of the head as he turned to run. He gasped, but did not cry out, as he fled into the house. Binge took a few steps after him, then stopped, picked up the spoon, which she wiped absently on her gown, and turned back. The bitch's father would have to kill Witta because the boy had seen where Binge's money was hidden. She would not let Bowles in until he promised that, and she would threaten to confess that he forced her to admit him if he did not keep that promise.

As she came to that decision, Binge suddenly realized that it might be impossible to let Bowles in at all if Witta was sleeping in the workroom with her. The boy usually slept deeply, but she had noticed that he always woke, sometimes with a cry of fear, when she lifted the bar of the door. If he woke he would interfere, cry out, warn the bitch; the whole plan would fail and Binge knew who would be punished. She hissed with irritation, realizing she should have locked Witta in the hut while she had him outside, but then she shook her head. Better she had not tried. She might not have been strong enough to handle that little devil, and even if she got him in, he would not have sat still and waited; he might have forced his way out. But maybe she could get the mistress herself to banish him. There was one thing she could say that might get him driven out of the house and would certainly stop his mouth about where she kept her money, because to admit he knew that would prove her complaint.

Lissa dismissed from her mind the silly notion that she had heard her father's voice. She must be desperate indeed, she thought, if she started imagining her father had come rather than be alone. Idleness was her fault; sitting and dreaming like a fool about what existed only in her own mind. When she was busy, she did not have foolish fancies.

She then walked briskly into her bedchamber, took the list of creditors from the chest, and carried it back with her into the warm, bright solar where she began to compare it with the list of debtors. Lissa had remembered that one goldsmith often borrowed from another to lend to a third party, outside the guild, at a higher rate. If she found such cases, she decided, she would simply sign over the debt to the creditor, splitting the difference between what Peter owed the creditor and the debtor owed Peter. This arrangement would give the creditor a greater profit than he would have collected from Peter and the debtor a lesser payment. Everyone would be very happy, Lissa thought—and when her father discovered what she was doing he would have a fit. That made a wan smile curve her lips, until Binge's and Witta's voices in mingled outrage, floated up the stairway.

"Filthy animal," Binge was shrieking, "I won't let you sleep in the workroom. I won't!"

"She's crazy, mistress," Witta cried, bursting into the room. "Why would I want to look at her dried up old dugs and behind? I never did! I never did!"

"You did! You did!" Binge panted, following hard on the boy's heels. "I saw your eye at the door!"

"You can't even see to cut meat for the pot—"

"Be quiet!" Lissa shouted, getting to her feet and facing the pair.

"He's a dirty beast," Binge wailed. "He picks up the blanket at night and looks at me. I feel the cold. I know. I won't have him in the workroom with me."

The stunned disbelief on Witta's face, the way his eyes popped and his mouth hung open, working but producing nothing, was a good indication to Lissa that Binge's accusation was without foundation. Still, it was not beyond belief that a boy of Witta's age might, out of curiosity, peep at any woman, even one as old as Binge, and Lissa credited his denial no more than she credited Binge's first accusation—apparently that Witta watched her on the pot. Binge's complaint was pure madness. Whatever Witta's curiosity, it was not possible that he had managed to perform what amounted to a miracle for the poor reward of peering at the old woman's body in the dim light of the night-candle. He would have had to unwind her blankets and lift or even remove her clothes—for on these cold nights no one who slept on a straw pallet on a stone floor would think of taking off any clothing—and then restore everything, all without waking her.

Lissa, who had opened her mouth to tell Binge not to be an idiot, closed it again as the word "idiot" echoed in her head. To say what she had said, Binge must be beyond reason, so it would be useless to argue with her.

"Mistress," Witta cried, finding his voice, "I—"

"Be quiet, I said," Lissa snapped at him.

"He's to go out to the hut," Binge yelled. "He's—"

"One word more from you, and *you* will go out to the hut," Lissa cried, turning on her.

"I'll freeze," the old woman wailed. "You want to kill me. You told him to look at me, to spy on me. I won't go out! I won't! I won't! You'll have to drag me. I'll scream. I'll—"

"Be still!" Lissa commanded at the top of her voice. "No one will put you out in the cold tonight. I am not a murderer. But I will not put Witta out either."

She hesitated because Binge looked utterly stricken, but a moment later the old woman cackled with laughter and said, "Just as you say, mistress. Just as you say."

Lissa found that she had gone cold all through. God knew what the crazy old woman would do. She might kill the boy in his sleep. Repressing a shudder, Lissa said, "Very well, Binge, you may sleep alone in the workroom tonight and try to calm yourself. Witta, go down and get your pallet and blankets. You may sleep in this room for tonight." She followed the boy to the stair landing outside the door and said softly, "Look to see if there is a key in the door between the workroom and the shop. I do not think so, but if there is, take it out."

She turned quickly, but Binge had not moved and was not even looking toward her. The old woman had a thoughtful expression that changed to satisfaction while Lissa was watching. What Binge could find satisfying in the fact that Witta would have more comfortable quarters than she herself Lissa did not want to attempt to guess, but she took a position near the door to prevent Binge from rushing out and pushing Witta over the rail or down the stair when his arms were full. In fact, Binge did nothing but mutter a few words to herself when Witta came in and dumped his pallet and blanket near the hearth. Lissa felt rather foolish, but not so foolish that she failed to send Witta out—through the front door—to buy a simple evening meal for them at a cookshop rather than eat the soup Binge had prepared. And when she went down to check that the bars had been set into the front and back doors, Lissa turned the key that had been Peter's in the lock of the door that closed off the workroom from the shop.

Later Lissa began to feel rather guilty about Binge, although she had not the faintest idea what else she should have, or could have, done. The old woman had been of great help, whether she meant to be or not; Binge's fancies had provided Lissa with a companion when she sorely needed one and would not have acknowledged it. Witta served this purpose admirably; he was not a man who would hurt her and enrage her by not being Justin, and he could be set a task connected with settling Peter's accounts. Moreover, he was quick witted and interested enough to keep her attention on those accounts also. So the evening passed more pleasantly and profitably than Lissa had expected, and she went to bed with the satisfied feeling of work well begun.

That calming influence carried Lissa into sleep, but in that unguarded state the bonds she had set on her grief, her desire, and her imagination were loosened. The pleasant images she had dwelt on of happy debtors relieved of part of their burden dissipated into visions of herself wildly searching through an empty house, a huge place like the White Tower, which had many towers and halls and endless dark chambers within the thick walls. She had been in the White Tower a number of times, most frequently since the last year of her mother's life when Sigurth had found attendance at great state dinners too tiring. Lissa had not feared the Tower when she visited it, not even when a young courtier had taken it upon himself to show her some of the less frequented parts of the keep. But after her mother's death she had the searching dream many times, and now that she felt she had again lost something precious she ran once more through the dark keep, first into an echoing chamber and then into a small dark one, which muffled her voice, calling . . . calling . . .

Lissa sat up in bed. Her voice? Had she been calling out? But her throat was not sore, as it often was when the dream lasted a long time, and she had not wakened Witta. Through the open door she could see his pallet and the hump of his body against the dull glow of the banked fire. She listened but could hear nothing and was just about to lie down when she wondered if Binge had called out to her. Uneasily she told herself not to be a fool. She could not hear Binge. The workroom was at the back of the house, her bedchamber at the front, and the sound would not come up the stairs because of the door between the workroom and the shop.

Then there was another sound, a dull thump. That must be something fallen on the roof, or the house settling, Lissa told herself, but her conscience already had its knife into her. What if the madness was only a symptom of another disorder and Binge was really sick? What if the maid had screamed in pain and tried to get upstairs for help but had found the door locked and banged on it or had fallen against it? It was not a very thick door, only meant to keep the apprentices out of the shop and away from the valuables at night. Lissa thought she might hear a loud scream through it; certainly she would hear if anyone beat on the door. She hesitated a moment longer. Then it seemed to her that she heard a faint scratching. Instantly an image of the poor old woman lying on the floor and clawing at the door with her last strength wiped all rational doubts from Lissa's mind. She snatched the household keys from beneath her pillow and jumped from the bed.

The shock of icy night air on her body reminded her to throw on her bedrobe before she wrenched the thick night-candle from its heavy, worked iron stick and ran out of the bedchamber. She did not pause to wake Witta. Her guilt at having locked away an old woman when she should have known from her unusual behavior that she must be sick, even dying, permitted no delay or assistance in correcting her cruelty.

There had never been a lock or a bar on the door at the top of the stairs. It was open, no hindrance to check her and give her time to think, but when she stepped on the top stair, a draft made her candle flicker. Lissa thrust the keys into the sleeve of her nightrobe so she could guard the flame with her free hand. She was watching that, after a single glance at the stair to safeguard her feet, fearing to be left in darkness and be delayed in finding the door and getting to poor Binge, when she realized what a draft must mean.

Then it was too late. A huge shadow was already halfway up the stairs. Eyes gleamed out of blackness. Lissa opened her mouth to scream, but something burst with a roar and a light like the worst of the great fire, and her voice was drowned.

"Just drop her on the floor," William said to Hubert, who had knocked Lissa unconscious with a single blow to the head. "I will gag her and tie her."

Hubert dropped the girl down the bottom third of the stair and went on up into the solar. A moment later a bundle of what seemed like old rags, except that it fell with a solid thud, landed beside William. "There is the boy." Hubert's voice was somewhat muffled by the cloth that was wrapped around his head. "Tie them and gag them as you will, they might still see or hear something that will be dangerous. The old woman is already dead. Why should we not kill them both and be done with it?"

William ground his teeth briefly, then said, "No, it would be more dangerous to kill them. Believe me."

Days before, he had finally convinced Hubert that it would be dangerous both to himself and to his master if he was discovered to be involved in Flael's death. Unfortunately once an idea was fixed in Hubert's head it was there for good, and there was no way to shade it. Hubert's response was simple and direct—kill everyone who knew or might know of any connection between him and Flael. William had given up trying to explain why that was likely to create more problems than it solved. He simply insisted that Hubert allow him to judge what was a necessary risk and what, by drawing too much attention from Sir Justin and others, would anger FitzWalter.

William had chosen this path as the lesser of the evil choices facing him in dealing with Hubert. He could not leave Hubert out of the search of Flael's house for two reasons: First, FitzWalter would surely become suspicious of the exclusion of his simple but faithful henchman; also William wanted a witness FitzWalter would trust to say he had not kept the seal if he could not produce it after the search. Second, William knew he was incapable of searching the house adequately himself and certainly preferred Hubert to any hired stranger.

The trouble with using Hubert was that he was totally

indifferent to William's needs and desires unless they affected him directly. Thus William could not simply tell Hubert that the maid had to be killed because she could clearly and convincingly identify William as the man who bribed her to open the house, but that Lissa and the boy, who also knew them both, must not be seriously harmed because Lissa was necessary to his business.

To Hubert the maid and Lissa seemed equally dangerous and equally worthless. William knew that was partly his own fault. In the excess of his panic on the day he learned of Flael's death and seeming torture, William had found Lissa worthless too and had foolishly confided to Hubert his intention of wreaking vengeance on her for all his own fears and petty spites; however, now that he no longer feared he would be FitzWalter's next victim, his panic had abated. With that, the desire to destroy his daughter had also abated. Heloise had regained her normal place in his regard—an intensely disliked but also intensely useful pawn.

In fact, the tale William had told Binge had not been all lies. One purpose of the invasion of Flael's house was to seek the king's seal, but a secondary purpose, and not far secondary to William, was to make the house uninhabitable and force his daughter to return home. Heloise had gained considerable importance in her father's opinion since she had been married. Her absence from buying trips and from the shop itself had been an expensive lesson to William.

The need to have Heloise at home had led to the preservation of the boy's life—partly because William knew Heloise might suspect he was involved in this "robbery" and if the boy was hurt she would find a thoroughly nasty way to be revenged, and partly so that she would not be openly singled out, the only living witness. With two of the three people in the house alive, the maid's death might be taken as an accident, a quieting that had gone too far. That would be greatly preferable to any serious investigation of Binge's death. William had been as careful as he could, but it was almost certain that he had been noticed talking to the old woman, and innocent as his conversations might have been, suspicions might still be aroused.

William heard the stair creak and looked up hastily, realizing that he had not given Hubert any further instructions. "Never mind these two," he said. "I will make sure they see and hear nothing. You begin the search of the bedchamber, but do not touch the writings. I will examine those. Take everything apart—the pillows, the featherbeds, even the bed itself. We must open the posts to be sure there is nothing inside them. And by Christ's hangars," he called after Hubert's retreating back, "I will poison you if you tear Heloise's clothes. She will make me pay for new ones."

Chapter 10

❦

"**M**Y LORD." Justin turned, pulling his shoulder away from the hand that touched it before he came up out of sleep enough to recognize the voice was not the one he expected. Then he was sitting up, asking, "What is wrong?" as Halsig began to repeat, "My lord."

"Flael's house has been torn apart, my lord," Halsig said, his face set.

"Flael's—" Justin swallowed the rest of the senseless repetition and stared at Halsig, but the man's face told him nothing, and something had him by the throat so hard that he could not speak. All he could think was that he had delayed; for a foolish reason, his pride's fear that scandal should touch him, that there would be gossip binding him to a suspect, he had not gone to Lissa last night to cure the hurt he had done her. His heart was a cold leaden weight in his throat, blocking his voice and making it hard to breathe. There would be no gossip now. Now it might be too late ever to heal her pain.

Fortunately Justin was not also paralyzed. He thrust Halsig back, jumped out of bed, and began to pull on his clothes, first his chausses, then the shirt and tunic. By the time his head emerged from the tunic, the icy, leaden block of fear had settled down from his throat to his belly and freed his voice. He was able to roar down the stairs for his horse to be saddled, but when he turned back to Halsig, he still could not say Lissa's name.

"What happened?"

"I do not know, my lord," Halsig replied, his eyes dropping like those of a scolded dog.

"There were two guards on that house, front and back, and you do not know how the house was entered and damaged and those within—"

"The mistress and the boy were only bruised," Halsig said hastily, adding more slowly, "The old woman is dead, but by accident, I think."

Justin, bent over the stool on which he was resting his foot to tie his cross garter, flattened the long ribbon with exquisite care. "And your men?" he asked, as he wound the garter and tied it below his knee.

His voice was steady, belying the tears that had started to his eyes. Lissa was safe! Justin fought back the tears of relief and the insane desire to throw his arms around Halsig and dance him around the room. Then he suddenly wondered why Halsig rather than his own servant, Hervi, had wakened him. Halsig, with a broad hunting knife in his belt and a long sword at his side, was loyal . . . but did Hervi know that? The first rule in any gentleman's household was that no armed man should be allowed to come upon him sleeping. Very likely Hervi's refusal to wake his master himself was only a result of laziness and cowardice, an unwillingness to commit the double sin of depriving Justin of sleep *and* giving him bad news. But whose messenger would he send up next?

"Also stunned and bound, but alive."

Justin had no trouble connecting Halsig's reply with the question he had asked earlier about the guards, and Halsig, who had paused but not finished all he had to say, then added grimly, "They may be sorry for that before I am done with them."

Halsig's grim promise struck Justin funny in the lightness generated by his relief; he suddenly felt rather sorry for the men, who already had sore heads and might suffer worse harm from being bound hand and foot on such a cold night.

"I suppose they grew careless after four nights with no alarms," he said, tying his second cross garter and looking up. "Did they tell you how they came to be taken by surprise?"

"I did not stop to ask. When Dunstan, who was the change of watch, found John trussed like a roasting fowl, he came running to me. I went into the house, finding the back door unlocked and unbarred. I suppose, since the word about Flael's sons taking the strongboxes was common knowledge, that some thieves had paid the maid, who spoke much ill of the mistress, to make a quick snatch of the silver and gilt plate in the lady's solar. My lord, I could not believe my eyes. The workbench was ripped from the wall and all pulled apart, the heavy beams split open. Then I saw the old woman dead, under the shelves torn out of the wall. I tell you my heart all but failed me. I thought they were all murdered, but Mistress Heloise heard us and had sense enough to kick something over. She could not call out; she was gagged."

Justin had belted on his sword, swung his cloak over his shoulders, and started for the stair, but he stopped and turned. "You left her in Flael's house?"

"No, my lord. She is with Master Goscelin. She is a great lady, with no doubt. For all her bruising she wasted not a wail or a gasp but knew just what must be done: Leave one man to guard the house and let no one in, she told me, and send another to fetch help."

"Did she send you for me?" Justin asked.

"That wouldn't be her place," Halsig answered stoutly, troubled by the novel idea of being told to fetch the correct person by someone who did not have the right to give him that order. He shook off his discomfort and said approvingly, "She bade us inform Master Goscelin, which was right, and ask Mistress Adela for shelter, which was granted at once."

She could not have been badly hurt, Justin thought, lingering to listen just to hear Lissa praised, though he knew he was being foolish. Then, making up for wasted time, he walked away from Halsig so fast that he took the man by surprise. "I will meet you at Goscelin's," Justin said over his shoulder as he ran down the stairs and opened the door.

His horse was not yet there, however, and Halsig caught up. "But the house—"

Justin bellowed his servant's name and what he would do if the man did not appear that instant and, when the sound of hooves followed at once, turned to Halsig. "The house will not forget. Anything it can tell me will be there for me to see if I wait an hour or ten days before I look. But people forget. Most easily do they put out of their minds what frightened or hurt them—or else they add horrors. I must speak to the boy and Mistress Lissa while what befell them is still clear and not diminished or blown out of its true form."

His servant having arrived, Justin grasped his palfry's rein in one hand and fetched Hervi a sharp blow on the side of the head with the other, cursing him for sheltering in the warmth of the stable instead of having the horse ready at the door. Once in the saddle, he looked down at Halsig and shook his head.

"I need to take my own advice," he said. "Do not follow me to Goscelin's house but discover instead what you can from the guards who were overpowered. You can use the servants' hut in the yard to question them. When I have learned what I can, I will join you. Then we will both go to look over the house."

He rode away on the words, concerned for Lissa but overjoyed at the way all his problems seemed to have resolved themselves. Still, Justin was afraid he was twisting truth into the shape he wanted. Surely if Lissa missed him and desired him she would have asked for him when she was hurt and frightened. But had he not hurt her worse than a physical bruise by seeming to reject her? She was a strong and clever woman. He knew that from the way she had withstood the situation of her husband's death and from what Halsig had said of her reaction to the invasion and damage to her house. No wonder she had not asked for him. Her pride would hold her back from crying for what he had himself shown her she could not have. If he rushed into Goscelin's house with fond words and cries of joy for her escape, Lissa would probably break his head sooner than she would embrace him.

No, he could express his joy for her escape, and apologize for the danger to which she had been exposed. That was only normal courtesy, together with an explanation of why he had not expected her to be in any danger—and, if he was fortunate enough to be left alone with her, he could say a word about his fear of embarrassing so new a widow by too great attentions. That was a safe excuse for having stayed away. Later, when they were more certain in their loving, he would tell her the truth, that he had so feared her power over him that he could only flee her and hide himself, and she would laugh and preen herself as a beloved woman does.

The pleasant imaginings were laid aside, perhaps to be renewed by mingling with reality, Justin hoped, as he drew his horse to a halt before Master Goscelin's house. There was a groom waiting, and every crack in every shutter shone with light. The door opened before Justin touched it, exposing Master Goscelin himself in furred slippers and bedrobe.

"Come in, come in," he said. "I am glad you stopped here before you went to the house. Mistress Lissa is a most determined young person. As soon as she heard me tell Halsig to report this to you, she insisted on staying awake until she had spoken to you. I am not certain why. She had little enough to tell me."

Justin blinked at the master goldsmith, who seemed a trifle offended by Lissa's preference. He smiled self-deprecatingly. "She has a great confidence in me, owing, I fear, to a mistaken impression of my kindness." He chuckled at Goscelin's unbelieving expression. "If we ever find the time and I do not forget, I will explain how that came about, but now I think I had better go to her at once."

Goscelin nodded and gestured for Justin to precede him up the stairs. At the entrance to the solar, he guided Justin to the right and, without saying a word, pointed around a sharp corner. Then he walked very deliberately back across the solar and withdrew into his bedchamber. Justin watched with a troubled frown. Were Goscelin's feathers simply ruffled because Lissa had not chosen to trust him in a moment of crisis, or did Goscelin sense, as Justin had when he questioned her after Flael's death, that she was hiding something?

Two steps took Justin to the corner, into a small extension of the solar, which he realized took up the width of the stairwell. The space was almost filled by a cot piled high with pillows.

There was just room enough for a large brazier, the air around it shimmering with heat, at its foot. Justin saw that much before Lissa—who had been half sitting against the pillows, facing away from the light in the solar—turned her head toward him.

"Who?" Justin choked, forgetting everything he had intended to say, barely getting the one word out in his rage. Her face was all swollen on one side, black and blue, with one eye shut. "Who?" he croaked again, stepping forward and going down on his knees beside the cot. "I will kill him. I will kill him over many years, an inch of flesh at a time. Who did this to you?"

"I do not know," Lissa whispered. "He was just a—a black shadow and—and the head—the head was all black too with gleaming eyes."

She shuddered and Justin reached out. She came into his arms, wincing, but clinging when he murmured he was sorry he had hurt her and would have let her go.

Then she sniffed and lifted her head so she could see his face. "But it was no evil spirit," she said. "His fist was solid enough."

"I will kill him," Justin muttered.

"I will not hinder you," Lissa agreed with a watery chuckle, "but your knees will soon hurt. Take the stool."

Justin bent and kissed her hair. "I never meant for you to be in any danger, beloved. I would not have let you stay alone in the house if I dreamt you might be hurt. There were guards, Lissa, front and back. I do not know how they could have been taken by surprise—"

There was only one word in all that speech that had real meaning for Lissa, and she repeated that. "Beloved?"

"Is that name displeasing to you?"

"No, oh no. Only . . . if you could not come yourself because of business, why did you not send with Thomas a word of—"

Lissa hesitated and Justin chuckled. "Yes? A word of what? What could I tell my cousin to say to a day-old widow whom I did not dare face myself for fear of blackening both our names?"

He pulled the stool nearer and sat, and she leaned against him so that he could not see her face. That was as well, because the sight wakened such senseless rage in him that he could not think clearly about anything. Still, in the little pause that followed his explanation, he wished he could guess what her response would be so he could plan an additional defense. But he did not need one. Lissa gave a little sigh.

"What a fool I am," she murmured. "I did think of that, but I would not allow myself to hope it was true. So I deserve my punishment; if I had had greater faith in you I would not have suffered at all."

"I did not entirely enjoy our separation myself," Justin remarked dryly. "In fact, I was quite out of charity with you most of the time. I went so far as to wonder if you had put something into my food or wine to bind me to you—" He heard Lissa laugh. "It is not at all funny."

"Yes, it is," she said. "You have no idea how many times I have refused to mix love potions, because I am so sure they will not work and then it might be said that *all* my remedies were faulty. Also, such things are elaborate formulae and can take hours or days to mix. Did you imagine I kept one by me at all times to use on any man who came along? And worse, do you think I am so poor a thing that I cannot draw a man without? Then you should be ashamed to yield, even to a potion."

Justin kissed her hair again, chuckling himself. "I am glad to know that you used no artificial means to enchant me. Still, you have done so."

He was more enchanted with her than ever, and for perfectly sensible reasons—for the musical voice that was a delight to his ears, for the warm, lithe body he held in his arms, for the sweet nature that blamed itself first without self-pity.

She put up a hand and touched his face. "Does enchanting the mayor's warden deserve punishment?"

Instinctively Justin tightened his grip, and Lissa cried out softly. "Dearling, forgive me," he said. "Let me lay you down."

His voice was trembling, and when he had propped her carefully against the pillows, Lissa took his hand. "Do not look so tragic. You have done me no harm."

"I am angry," he said, but Lissa had turned her face half away so that he could see only the unhurt side and that helped him realize one part of what was troubling him. "Also, I want to stay here with you at the same time I want to go to the house to discover from it any hint of whom I should pursue for this outrage."

Lissa sighed. "I wish I could be more help in finding him."

Those words reminded Justin of his earlier suspicion that Goscelin was affronted because Lissa was hiding something from him. The idea only stirred up the roiling mix of conflicting emotions in him. "Can you tell me nothing?" he asked almost bitterly.

"I will gladly tell you everything I remember and any idea that has come into my mind. And I will answer any question you wish to ask. Only the whole thing, from the beginning, is completely beyond my understanding."

There was a difference in the way the eye she could see him from met his. She looked honestly puzzled, not afraid, but nonetheless Justin asked, "Then why did you not want to tell Goscelin what happened? Was it not because you knew I was so bedazzled by you that I would believe anything you said and he might not?"

She laughed aloud, not a chuckle of satisfaction but a peal of joy at this further confession of love. "How can you be so silly?" she asked, turning her hand in his so that she could fold it between both of her own. "I wanted a chance to see you and talk to you again." Then all the laughter disappeared from her voice and expression, and she clutched his hand. "I wanted to plead with you, to tell you that if you could not love me I would not ask more if you would only be my friend."

Justin did not answer that in words, only bent forward and kissed her mouth.

Lissa laughed again, more softly. "I am not saying that I would have been telling the truth, you understand. While you were being friendly, I would have been trying my best to incite you to a more passionate frame of mind."

It was Justin's turn to laugh. "You would not be so cruel. I am ill enough with wanting, and you in no case even to listen to my pleading, all bruised—" He stopped abruptly as anger flooded him again, and then he said, "I should let you rest now, but if you can bear to tell in short form and without questions whatever you remember, there might be some hint therein that will work with what I see in the house to show me a direction in which to seek."

Because she had to explain what she was doing on the stair in the middle of the night, Lissa began with the quarrel between Binge and Witta and her growing concern for the old woman.

"So when I started down to unlock the door and see what was wrong, I had the night-candle," she said. "I should have been able to see the man's face, even in the single moment that I looked at him, but it was all black. Now I think he had wrapped a cloth around his head—and, Justin, does that not mean I should have been able to recognize his face? But there is more than a face to knowing a person, and I swear I did not know the body either."

She spoke with the sincerity of a clear conscience. Lissa was perfectly certain that the man who had hit her was neither her father nor his disgusting friend Hubert. When she had first regained consciousness, she had been in pain from the blow and totally disoriented, unable at first to remember what had happened to her, where she was, or anything else. The crashing noises, total darkness, and difficulty in breathing caused by the gag and the blanket her father had wrapped around her, including her head, had added to her confusion. She had drifted in and out of reality, hearing strange distorted voices and seeing lights and images she knew could not exist because her eyes were closed. She thought she might have slept for a while, too; later she wondered about that, but decided that the pain, the suffocation, the cold, and the confusion had induced a kind of exhaustion.

What Lissa was certain about was that the man was gone by the time her head had cleared. Then, although her physical discomfort had become worse and distracted her so that her thinking was fragmentary, she had pieced together the event, returning again and again to that horrific vision she had seen on the stair. At first all she wanted was to convince herself that the creature was altogether human, but persistent review of what she had seen had fixed the image strongly in her mind. Later, when good sense had conquered superstition, she had plenty of time to wonder who had attacked her and why.

From her position two or three steps above him, the man seemed about her father's height, but twice as broad. To Lissa's mind, the foreshortened stature also eliminated Hubert, who was broad enough but much taller than her father. She was so convinced of these facts that neither man even crossed her mind when she described the events to Justin and stated so positively that she had not recognized the body shape of the man on the stair.

"I have thought and thought," she went on, frowning and then smoothing her brow as the expression hurt her swollen eye, "but I cannot think who it might have been. I have seen many men like that, but none with whose face I am so familiar he would need to hide it."

"The shape, was he like Goscelin?" Justin asked.

Lissa giggled. "Please! I have insulted Master Goscelin enough. One of us will have to give some reason for my reluctance to confide in him. Do not use him for a model for my man on the stair."

"What about young Peter or Edmond?"

"Not close, although the height is near right. Both are too slender, and they have the thin shoulders of boys. Goscelin is closer to what I remember, but he is round and that man was flat, like a wall."

"A powerful man, then, more likely to be a fighting man than a simple thief."

"Yes, yes," Lissa agreed eagerly, her impression of the man suddenly coming together with something that had been at the back of her mind. "Oh, Justin, would any thief clever enough to break into a goldsmith's house bother with Peter's? Even if he knew that there were only two women and a child there, surely as your men sought young Peter and Edmond the word would have spread that they had taken with them Peter's strong-boxes."

Justin nodded slowly. "By now I am sure that fact is well known. If the robbery had taken place earlier, I would be less certain. Still, all goldsmiths are believed to be rich. There would be clothing, personal jewelry, and the plate—"

"But clothing and jewelry and plate can be found in any merchant's house," Lissa said. "Why attempt a goldsmith's house, which is always doubly and triply protected, when the real wealth is gone? Besides, there was no plate. I asked Master Goscelin to take everything but the pewter. He was kind enough to ask if he could help in any way, and I begged him to sell the pieces for me to give me some ready money to pay small merchant's bills—a mercer and Peter's baker had already been to the house. I thought that if I tried to sell the pieces myself I would be offered less because many would think me desperate."

"A clever piece of business." Justin chuckled and then shook his head. "Yes, but surely Goscelin would not have spoken of the matter, nor would you, so a thief might expect to find the plate."

Lissa put a hand to her head. "Merciful Christus," she whispered, "can it be because a thief found nothing that such damage was done?"

"Damage?" Justin repeated, and then remembered Halsig's first words, that Flael's house had been torn apart.

Before he could say more, common sense had reasserted itself and Lissa said more calmly, "No, it cannot have been a thief. I am not thinking straight, and you have not seen the house. No thief would do what was done. You must go and look to see what I mean."

Suddenly the eye Justin could see dropped half shut and the color drained from her skin. He jumped to his feet, frightened. "I have tired you too much and made you ill. I will call Mistress Adela to you—"

"No," Lissa murmured, clinging to his hand. "She thinks the maid is with me, but I sent her down after I heard Goscelin go to the door. I told her to mix a poultice for me—a long, complicated poultice with much grinding." She smiled, still carefully keeping her head half turned from him, so the curl of her lip looked natural. "I am tired, but I will be better after I sleep. And you, after you look at the house, should also go back to bed."

"I will," he promised. "Unless I find some sign of who did this thing. I have your leave to pursue at once, I hope?"

"You have my blessing, and I hope you hang him by the thumbs while you question him," Lissa responded with as much enthusiasm as her exhaustion would permit.

"Sleep now," he said, and she squeezed his hand once, then released it and shut her eye.

Justin walked toward the stair, then placed his feet most softly and carefully as he crossed the door to Goscelin's bedchamber. It was open a little way, and he scratched softly, hoping the goldsmith would not call out or that Lissa was already so deeply asleep that she would not hear. His luck was good. There were steps on the stairs, and the maid entered the solar just as Goscelin came to the door.

"Can you come down with me?" he asked softly. "I do not wish her to hear."

Goscelin nodded at once and followed him down into the shop. There was a brazier with ash-covered charcoal by the counter, and they stood near it for the little heat that remained.

"All she told me that she would not say to you, though I cannot guess why," Justin said somewhat mendaciously after repeating Lissa's description of the invader, "was that she did not believe the man was a thief. At least, she did not believe that his first purpose was to steal. She said no thief would do such damage. Halsig also spoke of the house being torn apart. Do you wish to come with me to look?"

"No, it would take too long for me to dress and keep you from your work and then from your bed unnecessarily," Goscelin replied. "I doubt there will be more to see by night than by day tomorrow."

Justin nodded, then asked, "Did you feel that Mistress Lissa did not wish to explain what happened to you for fear you would see she was hiding something?"

The goldsmith looked surprised. "I did not think of that. Why should she? No, all I felt was that she was the stubbornest young woman I had come across in a long time. She looked half dead, but would not agree to rest until she saw you. But I hardly spoke to Mistress Lissa myself. When she was carried in she was like a stick of ice and had to be put to bed and warmed at once. Adela was attending to her while I spoke to the men who brought her and the boy—good Lord, I had forgotten the boy. I had him put in with my apprentices and bade them warm him. But he told me he had seen and heard nothing, that he had gone to sleep by the fire in his mistress's solar and woken freezing, bound and gagged, with an aching head. Do you want to speak to him?"

After a moment's thought, Justin shook his head. "It does not sound as if it is worthwhile waking him if he is sleeping. In any case, I will be back in the morning to look at the house again, and we can talk to the boy and to Mistress Lissa together, if you have time."

"Good enough," Goscelin agreed, his good humor restored. "But do not arrive here at first light. We have all had a disturbed night and will benefit from sleep."

Chapter 11

THE KNOCKING ON THE DOOR WILLIAM BOWLES HAD BEEN FEARING since he had parted from Hubert not long before dawn came just after the sun peeped over the horizon. He shivered with terror. It was too soon. The idiot Hubert must have awakened FitzWalter to tell him the bad news instead of waiting, and FitzWalter must have been furious. William now bitterly regretted that he had acted so confident that the seal would be in the house. It had seemed best at the time, a way to get Heloise back and to provide FitzWalter with the expectation of obtaining what he wanted until he was almost ready to leave for France. By then William hoped Lord Robert would be so busy that the failure to find the seal would shrink into insignificance.

He heard the door of the shop open, and rose from the curtained bed near the door to the stair on the inner wall of the solar. He had slept in that bed from the time he had abandoned hope that his wife would bear him another child. There were advantages to leaving the bedchamber to her and Heloise; not only could he now have a woman who would give him some pleasure whenever he desired but he could also listen in secret to what went on in the shop below. At this moment, he blessed himself again for the foresight that had prevented him from moving back into the bedchamber as he heard an excited voice asking his journeyman for leeches and unguents and explaining that Flael's house had been broken into and Mistress Lissa injured.

Wiping a broad grin off his face with an effort, William pulled on his bedrobe and rushed down the stairs to ask what had happened. He did not wait for a full explanation, ordering his journeyman to provide everything while he dressed himself. Like a good, anxious father, he told Goscelin's servant not to wait but to hurry back with the medicines, saying he would follow as soon as he could.

When he arrived, William found the same servant waiting for him with polite apologies. Master Goscelin and Mistress Adela were still abed, and Mistress Lissa begged him—that, William thought caustically, was the servant's way of putting it, not Heloise's—not to trouble her yet but to let her rest and treat herself until the next day. This was exactly what William had expected and, indeed, hoped for. He could think of nothing duller or more exasperating than needing to sound shocked and sympathetic over his daughter's injuries, so he was able to say with good grace that, of course, he would do whatever she wished. He then spent some time questioning the servant about how those injuries had been received, which the man considered perfectly natural in a concerned father and willingly told him everything he knew about the robbery.

The servant's tale was more good news for William. Hubert had sworn that neither guard had seen him or suspected any attack before he was felled, but William never completely trusted Hubert's judgment. In this case, however, the servant told the same tale. The guards had been brought to Goscelin's house to be warmed and revived, and they could give no information.

Having thanked the man and dropped into his hand a packet of spices, William asked the servant to send a message when his daughter or Master Goscelin was ready to speak to him and returned home in better spirits than he had left. He grew even happier and more confident when he found there had been no messages or visitors, except some customers on ordinary business, while he had been away. By now Hubert must have seen FitzWalter. Had Lord Robert been really angry about their inability to find the seal, either Hubert or a messenger or, at the very worst, four or five men-at-arms would have been waiting for him.

Good humored with relief, William walked back to the workroom and called to Oliva, the woman who had been his maid and occasional bed partner for some years, to bring him something to eat. Then, without finding fault or striking the apprentice just for pleasure, he retired to the solar, where he broke his fast and savored his triumph. Heloise had got the beating she deserved for not obeying him and coming home when he bade her do so. Had she done so, she could have acted as if she were doing him a favor; now she was the one being helped. Should he refuse to take her in at first and make her beg? No, that devil would just as likely find another place to live and tell the world how he had denied her in her need. Besides, to refuse her would fit ill with his "concern" over her hurt, and William wanted no questions on that subject.

When he was pleasantly replete and had dozed a bit to ensure good digestion, William went down to cast an eye over what his journeyman was doing. He was halfway down the stair when the sound of horses' hooves made him tense and hesitate between running up again or dashing out to the back where he could escape. His hesitation saved him from looking a fool; he saw a woman's riding skirt through the open door as the horses stopped. The garment was a rich, dark but brilliant blue that William knew must be a most costly dye, and he hurried down the rest of the stairs in time to hear an imperious voice ask for a pound of the rose-damask cream and a quarter-pound of the cherry cream for the mouth. Mistress Lissa was to bring them herself, the woman said, because she wanted a word with her.

Before he could reach the door, his journeyman had bowed deeply and uttered a profound apology. "The creams are not ready-made, my lady. Mistress Lissa was married and went on a journey thinking there was stock enough—"

"My lady."

William had reached the back of the wood planks set on

trestles, which made the counter that stood just outside the shop. It was laden with heaps of dried herbs of the common sort—basil, bay, rosemary, thyme, majoram, sage, mint, parsley. At the ends of the table, to weight the boards and keep the lighter, untied bundles from blowing or rolling off, were covered crocks—most small, some larger—filled with seeds of anise, coriander, fennel, caraway, and cumin, or with the dried flowers of marigold, chamomile, rose, and lavender. Where the counter ended were baskets of pepper, black and white, and peony seeds set into weighted barrels. These were conveniently placed to keep a customer from blocking the front of the counter while the condiments were weighed by an apprentice. The barrels also helped to discourage unnoticed entry into the shop itself, where more precious and some more dangerous substances as well as expensive creams, lotions, potions, and philters were kept.

Pushing past these obstructions, William hurried to the front of the counter to bow and repeat, "My lady," adding quickly, "I beg you only to allow me to say that my daughter will be back in the shop on Monday. If it is inconvenient for you to come here again, my lady, I am sure Heloise would most gladly bring to you the creams you desire."

The woman, who had lifted her rein and was about to urge her mare forward with a tap of her heel, paused. "I am not sure I will be still in London on Monday." Her face was set, cold and indifferent. "However, if your daughter wishes to take the chance of coming"—there was another pause, then a shrug—"tell her Lady Margaret de Vesci might have work for her."

She moved away before William could make any reply, and he took a step or two after her, wishing to ask where Heloise should bring the creams. He was cut off from Lady Margaret, however, by two mounted men-at-arms who fell in behind her as others forced pedestrians ahead of her to scatter out of her way by driving their horses into the street. She was going north on Soper Lane, but that told William nothing. She might as well be going toward the Chepe as toward her house. As he went back behind the counter, under his breath he cursed the stupid sluts who, because they were noble born, were so proud they thought the whole world knew where they shit and believed the place would shine like gold to the common folk. Now, no doubt, she would take him in spite because Lissa did not know where she lived and would not take the trouble to find out.

"Is it true?"

William turned to see that his journeyman's face, which had not lost its frown since Heloise's marriage, had lit up as if a torch had been kindled behind his eyes. "What?" William snarled. "Is what true, Paul?"

"That Mistress Lissa will be coming home on Monday?" Paul was too eager for a confirmation to fear the blow William might give him for asking a question he did not want to hear or for knowing too much.

But William only nodded. He had said Heloise would bring the creams on Monday, but even if Heloise did know where to find Lady Margaret and he could force her to go, the journeyman had said there was no stock of the creams the idiot woman desired. William had not dealt in creams or lotions beyond the most crude and common sort before Heloise took an active part in the business, but he knew the compounding of fine products took several days.

"Yes," William said, "she will be back here, possibly even before Monday, but she is all bruised and might not feel ready to work. If she is to take those creams to Lady Margaret, you had better get that useless Ninias to mix up a batch of them."

"He cannot," Paul answered, stepping back out of William's reach. "We do not know the proportions nor all of the ingredients. The mistress herself mixed the special creams for the great ladies."

"Surely the receipts are in her book," William began and then uttered a violent obscenity and snarled, "but the book is—" He stopped abruptly. He had remembered seeing Heloise's book crumpled under a pile of splintered bedposts and torn bedding in Flael's house and had nearly spoken of it. Fearing he had exposed knowledge he should not have, he raised his hand and took a step toward the journeyman, his face threatening.

"The book is not in the workshop," Paul gasped nervously, backing up still farther.

William dropped the hand he had raised to strike the journeyman. Clearly Paul had sensed nothing unusual in his angry remark. To explain his fury, he muttered something about losing Lady Margaret's custom, and then raised his fist again as he thought of the possibility of gaining her enmity and having her warn her friends against his shop. Before he could blame Paul or strike him, however, two more customers approached, one lifting a bunch of sage and sniffing at it while the other asked the price of pepper. William recognized both and wasted no more than a curt nod of the head on them, as neither was rich or powerful. On the other hand, he was not a man to forgo a profit for the pleasure of beating his servants—he could have that pleasure any time—so he turned his back and went into the shop.

Behind him he heard one woman say to the other, "I would not buy here from that sour churl but for the quality of his goods." And Paul's voice following quickly, saying, "The pepper is ten pence the pound, and Mistress Lissa chose all we have from her own uncle's ship."

"You are four pence higher than Master Bartholomew down the road," the woman countered.

Paul laughed. "Now mistress, you know and I do too that that price is for last spring's shipment, not for what came before the last storms in the autumn. Master Bartholomew would not sell that pepper as new-come any more than I. I can give you a farthing on the quarter-pound, or I can ask Ninias to see if we have some spring-shipped pepper left, but you cannot have our best—and we have none but the best—for last year's price."

"You will do no better," the other woman said. "Cheaper may be come by, but what is chosen by Mistress Lissa has a most excellent savor."

William continued into the shop and on up the stairs. He was irritated by the fact that such folk dared express a low opinion of him, but that was unimportant compared with his renewed satisfaction in having made Flael's house unlivable for his daughter. The realization that Heloise had taken her book of receipts with her had made him wonder whether she might have thought of beginning a rival business. That would have meant certain ruin for William, for her uncles might well have refused to sell to him and far too many of his clients would certainly have abandoned his shop for hers. Of course the brothers of the Pepperers Guild might have rejected her and forbidden her to sell on her own, but William was not very sure of that. Heloise was a great favorite with the brethren of his guild.

Just within the door of the solar, William paused and stared thoughtfully at the floor by his bed. Did it matter what Heloise did? Perhaps now was the time. A nasty grin split William's face. Heloise had always believed she would be his heiress, inherit his business; William, however, had always intended one day to sell everything—house, furniture, stock, business—convert everything to silver and gold, and simply ride away, leaving her behind. Yes, with Flael's house destroyed, perhaps now was the time.

William took two steps to the right, bent, and drew a flat box from under his bed. He carried it to the hearth, where he sat down in his chair beside the fire, pulling to him a stool, on which he set the box. From it he took a single sheet of parchment. Several small sacks slid off it with soft metallic clinks. William frowned at them. On the one hand, he hated to see money lying idle when it could be making a profit at usury. On the other hand, he had determined never again to be without funds to escape his "friends" if escape became necessary.

As he examined the listings of probable worth, William's frown deepened. It was not enough. Oh, he could eke out an existence with what he would have, but he could not buy a rich property and be indifferent to pennies. And it was Heloise's fault, that dowry he had been forced to settle on her. He had thought then that he would make it back in a day or two out of the favors he would obtain from FitzWalter. But the seal was gone, and so was the money, and there was no way to get it back. Ungrateful bitch, she would not leave the money with his goldsmith but insisted it be placed with Hamo Finke, who was hard as stone and rigid as steel. With the money in her own hands, there was no way he could control her properly. She could marry again without his permission, marry another Pepperer and gain a home and begin a rival business that way.

He considered the problem for some time, even wondering if he should arrange to have his daughter disfigured or maimed, but he could not see that crippling her would solve the problem. First, unless she was damaged so badly that she could not work or serve in the shop, she would still be able to marry or to live alone. Second, she might die, which would ruin him just as surely as if she started her own business. And third, even if it worked right, he would end up in the power of whoever did the work for him.

That made him think of Hubert, and he remembered that he had convinced the man not to come to his house unless he was specially bidden to do so by FitzWalter. Instead, he had arranged to meet Hubert, "as friends will," to dine together at the cookshop in the Strand. With a sigh, William put aside his thoughts of selling out. He closed his box and replaced it under the bed. His luck had been good that morning, he thought. Perhaps it would continue good and Hubert would not be at the cookshop. That would mean he was engaged in other tasks or errands that FitzWalter thought more important than any message to him. It would also mean that FitzWalter now assigned a low importance to the counterfeit seal and, if matters went well for him in France, might forget it entirely. However, William had not walked the length of the lane before he saw Hubert coming toward him.

"You are late," the big man said. "I have not forgotten what you said about coming to your house, but I have no time to waste. My lord leaves tomorrow, and I with him, and I have a message from him. You must find Flael's sons before Sir Justin does, and get the seal from them."

William gaped at Hubert, unable to find his voice for a moment. "But how can I do that?" he cried.

"I do not know, and I do not care," Hubert answered, seeming astonished at the question. "But it must be done," he added. "My lord is determined to have the seal. And my lord says: 'Do not think of being too clever. Hubert goes with me, but others do not.'" He frowned at William. "I have said his words just as he said them. Did he mean me when he said Hubert? And what does the rest of it mean?"

William stared blankly, then shook his head. "I am not certain, and I do not wish to guess about Lord Robert's words. I cannot have dinner with you—"

"I cannot either," Hubert said. "That was why I decided to come to the house instead of waiting at the cookshop. I will be a rich man from French loot when I return. Do you not wish you were coming with us?"

"Almost," William said faintly. "Yes, almost."

Hubert clapped him on the shoulder so hard that William staggered forward out of control and stepped into the central gutter, spattering himself with a heap of filth that had not been carried away to the river by the last rain. He uttered a choked, "Curse you—" which was drowned in Hubert's roar of laughter.

"Well, you have a taste of it then," Hubert shouted back over his shoulder as he walked away. "That is much like a battlefield—mud and blood and shit."

William stood staring after him. "And may the blood and shit be yours," he muttered.

Then he stepped out of the gutter and made his way back to the house, where he entered by the rear gate and shouted for Ninias to bring him clean shoes and hose. He changed, told the boy curtly to have Oliva clean the soiled articles, and walked out again, north toward the Chepe this time, where he entered a familiar alehouse. The hearth on the back wall was flanked by two trestle tables with rough benches on each side. William stalked down the left-hand table, which was about half full. Two men, who were talking to each other, drew closer together, leaving a large space free, and William stepped over the bench and sat.

The potboy, seeing William, ran out without being told to fetch him a pasty. Since Heloise's marriage he had eaten in this place often, indifferent to his own food because of the satisfaction of depriving his household of theirs. When no meal was prepared for him, none was prepared for anyone else either. They could find scraps of past meals or beg or buy food. He and Heloise had quarreled often and bitterly on that subject. She, like her mother, ordered large meals, simple in content but generous in proportions, whether she intended to be at home to eat them or not, and neither of them had ever chided maid or cook for giving the apprentices this and that between meals. It was only a few shillings' difference in a year, Heloise claimed; the thought flashed through his mind as it always did when he entered this place, and it angered him more than usual today. Those few shillings over the years Heloise and her mother had managed his household would have added to several more pounds in his purse now when he needed them.

Too late to do anything about that, William knew; nonetheless, an added flicker of rage passed through him when he remembered Paul's joy at the news of Heloise's return. He should fix that young man so that food would be only torment to him, but he had more important problems. When the boy brought his pasty, he ate it, washing down each mouthful with a swallow of ale. He could not really concentrate on the important subject of how he could avoid FitzWalter's vengeance if he could not fulfill his unreasonable demand, however. He kept seeing himself staggering into the gutter, after which a second image recurred in his mind—that of finding Hubert and administering to him a slow-acting and very painful poison.

By the time William's fury over being pushed into the gutter dimmed, he was able to think clearly about FitzWalter's demand that he find and obtain the seal. The order had seemed utterly impossible when Hubert delivered it, and his first response had been that he would do what he had planned—sell everything and run. Calm now, he knew that if he tried to sell out quickly, he might have to take a great loss, and worse, news of his attempt to escape might reach FitzWalter through his connections in the merchant community.

Once he had recognized the folly of any immediate flight, William also saw there was no need for it. He raised a hand and snapped his fingers, and the boy filled his cup with ale again. He drank slowly, thinking that FitzWalter might be a devil, but he was not a fool. He would not expect Flael's sons to be discovered within the next few days. In fact, before FitzWalter could begin to feel dissatisfied, in less than two weeks, he would be aboard ship; and since the king was making for La Rochelle they would be at sea for another two weeks or so. A month—a month of complete safety, which, with a little plausible playacting might be stretched to many months, perhaps as long as FitzWalter was abroad.

William set down his cup and smiled into it. A little playacting of looking for Flael's sons . . . Perhaps he had the answer to all his problems at once. He would leave London and travel about. FitzWalter would believe that he was looking for Flael's sons— and, indeed, he would inquire for two young goldsmiths either selling metal or seeking work. He might even find them or find news of them—which would be best for him because it would not only solve his problem most directly but make him rich and give him a real hold on FitzWalter. William licked his lips, then lifted the cup and drained it. When he set it down, he had pulled himself out of his delightful dream.

Whatever happened, he would be safe, at ease, free of his cursed business. He could do what he wanted when he wanted, like a nobleman. And FitzWalter would not be able to touch him if he did not discover the seal, because there would no longer be a William Bowles in London or anywhere else. From the time his father- and brothers-by-marriage had almost killed him for beating his wife, William had known that sooner or later he would need to escape from himself.

A year after the beating, William had gone north to buy herbs. He had returned, some ten days later than he should, with a fair supply and a tale of having fallen ill in Lincoln. His wife did not care that he was late and would have preferred if he had not come back at all; Heloise was too young to remember. In those ten days, a young gentleman called Amias FitzStephen had introduced himself to the minor gentry in the area around Bristol asking about small manors for sale. There was not much for him to look at and he did not like what little he saw, but over the years he had returned now and again and had by now a circle of acquaintances who would swear to the identity and good character of Amias FitzStephen.

Just in case he did not find Flael's sons, William would also enquire for a buyer for his business among the merchants in the places where he traveled. If he saw his search was hopeless or became afraid that FitzWalter was growing impatient, in swift strokes he could sell out, ride away, and disappear as neatly as— William uttered a bark of laughter—as Flael's sons. Then, recalling how much diminished his hoard was by Heloise's dowry, William resolved truly to search for the boys. He could buy a small place and exist—if the crops were good—on what he had, but if he could find the seal and hand it over, he could make FitzWalter himself turn courteous. Not that he cared for that, but he could make himself rich, rich enough for Amias to buy a fine manor and live as he pleased.

William rose to his feet and turned toward the door, the alewife coming to meet him. He dropped two farthings into her hand and pushed past her. Her lower lip made a gesture at him, but she said nothing and turned to speak to another customer.

William did not even notice her. He was thinking that he must hold off selling as long as he could; perhaps he could yet take his full revenge on Heloise. Meanwhile, he would have to wait until he got her back in the house before he left. No harm in that; he had a list of Flael's clients and debtors from the parchments he had seen when he emptied the contents of the chest in Flael's chamber. He could ask those in London about Flael's connections in other cities and ask there about the sons.

At least the journey would cost him nothing, because he would take with him some stock—luxuries like saffron and cumin and fennel—and sell or barter for food and lodging. More important, he would take every penny of coin and tell his goldsmith to give Heloise nothing. Let her draw on her dowry to buy. William snarled at Paul as he pushed past the pepper barrels and went on into his house. That would not hurt the bitch; she would restore what she spent and make a profit on her money in no time. Then William paused with his foot on the stair. No doubt Heloise would credit the profit to the business, so that much would come into his pocket in the end. Fool of a girl!

Chapter 12

❦

"FOOL OF A GIRL!" JUSTIN EXCLAIMED. "SHE SHOULD BE ABED. What does she think she is doing?"

"Nothing of which you would disapprove." Mistress Adela laid a hand gently on Justin's arm.

"I said she was the most stubborn young woman I had ever come across," Goscelin remarked with a chuckle.

"She was too troubled to rest," Adela said, casting a disapproving glance at her husband. "She was so worried about whether Peter's accounts had been destroyed—and she was not ill. She had no fever."

"She was half dead when I left her, too sick to lift her head."

"Mistress Lissa has more will when half dead than most people fully alive." Goscelin laughed outright that time. "She did me the courtesy to wait until I woke before dragging me over to Flael's house—"

"She did not go alone?"

"No, and she did not *drag* Goscelin either." Adela was the one who replied, studying Justin's face as she spoke. "Lissa woke earlier than we and sent one of our servants to her father—"

"Her father," Justin repeated thoughtfully. "Well, I suppose that is natural."

"She needed supplies with which to treat herself," Adela said with a touch of asperity. "The servant told us that she would not see Bowles when he came. Poor Dick was quite shocked at what Lissa said."

Justin blinked and Goscelin put in, "I would not place any special weight on her sharpness. She must have been buried under leeches and poultices. I think she would have refused to see anyone."

"I cannot imagine how Bowles could be connected with this—"

"Assault," Goscelin interrupted, all amusement gone from his face. "It may be strange to speak of assault on a burgher's house, but that is what it was, an assault—a deliberate effort to break and destroy. I swear the only reason the rooftree was not torn down was that there were not the means to do it."

"You think the destruction utterly wanton?" Justin asked.

"Utterly?" Goscelin considered, then continued with a shrug. "I do not know. To speak the truth, I did not stay long, only long enough to be sure that Lissa had a place to sit and to make her promise not to overtire herself. The feeling of hatred in that house made me sick. And no, she will not destroy or conceal important evidence—though how you can suspect that girl of hiding anything now is beyond me—because Halsig is right beside her and I instructed him, in her hearing, that she was not to take away anything until you came."

"I do not suspect Lissa of anything," Justin protested. "I lo— like her."

"You ask strange questions about her for one without suspicion," Goscelin retorted.

Justin shrugged. "I cannot allow my likes and dislikes to color the facts surrounding a crime. If I did, a third of the city, at the least, would be decorating gibbets. Like it or not, Master Goscelin, I must take into account that wives are the most frequent purveyors of their husbands' deaths. I admit Lissa does not fit the usual pattern in all respects, even in the most important—that is, she inherits nothing at all in his will.

However, she does gain in many other ways, and I cannot ignore her."

"But what has the robbery to do with Peter's death?" Mistress Adela cried.

The two men looked at each other. "Is it possible that Flael's death and the destruction of his house are separate matters?" Justin asked.

"You saw the house," Goscelin replied. "Does that look like an ordinary robbery?"

"No. But I have seen houses damaged out of spite when a troop was sent to search out an enemy, and this goes beyond that too. One does not splinter a workbench when looking for a man."

"And what of Lissa?" Adela put in. "Do you think she arranged to have herself beaten black and blue?"

"And for what?" Goscelin asked, his voice rising. "What purpose could she have? She herself gave me the plate and other valuables to keep, so she would not have hired a thief to raid Flael's house. What purpose could anyone have had? As you said about searching for a man, one does not splinter furniture when one comes to steal plate. The effort needed goes beyond anything that would satisfy spite."

Justin was relieved to be able to avoid Adela's question. He had not meant to wake this passionate defense of Lissa by his excuse for his fury when he heard she had already gone to Flael's house. He shrugged.

"There is always a reason that makes sense to the doer," he said. "You mentioned hatred."

As he said the words, Justin looked curiously at the portly goldsmith, remembering also that Goscelin had said the intensity of hate made him sick. But it was not surprising really that Goscelin should be so sensitive, Justin thought, recalling the beauty of Goscelin's own work and the deep appreciation he had for beauty in the work of others.

Goscelin nodded and Justin went on, "Then that brings us back to some connection between the murder and the damaged house, with Flael's body being mutilated out of hate. Yet you say he was not the sort of man who inspired hatred, and his wife agrees. They were not married long, but six weeks is long enough for a man to make a bitter enemy of a wife, and I must say that Mistress Lissa spoke of her husband always with . . ."

"An indifferent respect?" Adela suggested as Justin hesitated.

"Despite what was done to the house, I have not changed my opinion," Goscelin said, ignoring his wife's intrusion into the conversation. "I have given the matter some thought, as you can imagine." He threw up his hands in a gesture of despair. "I have even considered whether witchcraft or possession . . . or true madness might be at work here. But no one could hide that kind of madness or possession, and the use of witchcraft brings us back to hate. I cannot think of anyone in whom Peter could have aroused such hatred . . . unless . . . Was there anything in his accounts, anyone close to ruin?"

"A few who borrowed from him might be hard pressed to pay, but there is no way to tell about real desperation. A man would hide that from all. And even if such a person killed Flael, why pull the house to pieces? The parchments were not stolen. I saw them."

Goscelin shook his head, looking troubled. "I do not know. I can see that there is little sense to it, but I know that desolation was made by hate."

Justin put his hand on the goldsmith's shoulder. "Sense or no sense, I agree with you. There was hate in the destruction, I think, but I do not think it was wanton. I must go back and look again before I decide, but I felt there was a kind of pattern to what was broken."

A quarter of an hour later, Justin rushed up the ladder that had replaced the stairs in Flael's house and advanced on Lissa. He had been distracted from his anger by the conversation with Goscelin, but the closer he came to her, although he could not explain or justify his rage, the more furious he became. She looked at him, one eye wider than the other, unsmiling. From her cheekbone to her temple, the left side of her face was terribly discolored, but most of the swelling was gone.

"You should be abed," Justin said, his voice grating on the words. "What are you doing here?"

Lissa's eyes moved to Halsig and back, questioningly, to Justin. "I look worse than I feel," she said with a faint smile, and then, sober again, "I had to look for Peter's accounts. I was afraid whoever did this would have carried them off."

"You should have waited for me," Justin snapped and turned away sharply, as though to examine the room.

He hoped he had moved quickly enough so that neither Lissa nor Halsig had seen his color rise. The remark rang with the petulance of an excluded child, and he suddenly realized his rage was not caused by any fear for Lissa's physical well-being but because she did not need him.

"I am so sorry," she said, "but I swear I touched nothing except my receipt book and the parchments, and I did no more than lift them from the floor."

"That is true, my lord," Halsig agreed. "Mistress Lissa has only been here for a little while and has touched nothing but what she said."

"I do not care about what she has touched," Justin said with a sigh, gratefully aware that both Lissa and Halsig believed he feared she might have altered or hidden some clue. He shook his head at Halsig, but his voice was lighter, almost teasing. "Bruised as she is, all purple and green, how could you let her climb a ladder and crawl about on the floor lifting wood and dragging out books and parchments?"

Lissa began to laugh. "How could he stop me, Sir Justin, when Master Goscelin said I could?"

Justin laughed too. "I am sure he could not if Master Goscelin could not. You are cleared of guilt, Halsig, and also relieved of duty. Just be sure that the guards who usually watch the house are now within to help me if I need them, and you and the other men can go home. I do not think I will need you again today, but stay by your lodging or leave word where a messenger can find you. If I do not send for you, you can begin normal watch duty again on the morrow."

"Yes, my lord."

The voice was expressionless and the face a mask, but Lissa watched Halsig disappear down the ladder with a most uncomfortable feeling. She was sure that Halsig was deeply disappointed at being sent away, and that she should have said something or done something to change Justin's almost curt dismissal. Halsig had been very helpful to her; he could have refused to allow her into the solar and bedchamber, but had not been the least obstructive. She owed him a favor, but she felt no need to repay it now, and it was not so great a favor as to deprive her of this chance to be alone with Justin, a pleasure that she had planned for and achieved.

When Halsig's head disappeared, Justin came and knelt beside her to kiss the hands she had folded over the parchments. "You are a fool," he said very softly. "You will make yourself ill."

Lissa bent her head over his and kissed his hair. "I could think of no other way to have a little time alone with you," she murmured as he lifted his head. "And I was not sure how much you wanted Goscelin and Adela to know."

"Goscelin and Adela—so soon? I am not surprised. Adela defended you as if you were a daughter."

"They are wonderful people, so good and so kind, but I suspect they would be troubled if they knew we had come to terms so soon."

"Have we come to terms?" Justin asked. "What terms?"

"Any you name," Lissa whispered, grinning at him. "I am utterly shameless."

Her remark took Justin completely by surprise, for he had been a little hurt by what she had said about coming to terms, and he wrapped his arms around her and kissed her. She responded, his grip tightened, and she whimpered with pain. Justin released her instantly, growling, "Oh, curse it, I am sorry. You see, I would not have hurt you if you were abed where you should be."

That made Lissa giggle. "You have not hurt me, just squeezed a bruise. No, and I have not hurt myself either. The only thing that was under a pile of wood was my receipt book, and Halsig was kind enough to take it out for me. I hope that was not wrong. I could see it because the wall between the solar and the bedchamber was almost torn away." She gestured, and Justin glanced behind and nodded.

"The accounts were not buried?"

"Oh, heaven." Lissa's hand stole up to touch her lips. "Have I indeed interfered with your work? Goscelin told me you came here last night, so I thought you had seen everything. I am so sorry. I will try to put everything back—"

"No, that is not necessary." Justin got to his feet and began to look around the room, pausing here and there. Then he nodded. "Yes, now that I think back, I can see the parchments scattered about all untied but, as you said, not under anything except . . . dark wood, and some panels that were carved . . ."

"Pieces of the chest they were kept in, I think."

"Two men, then, at least two," Justin said.

"I saw only one."

"The other could have been still in the workroom or even outside. There must have been one who came up here and broke the bed apart with an ax or a pick, broke the walls, tore the bedclothes but did not touch the accounts or the chest. Later the other came and went through the accounts . . . but why was the chest broken? For that matter why hack up a bed?"

"To look for something," Lissa said, "something perhaps a quarter- or half-inch thick and I would guess not more than three inches across, or something that could be rolled or folded to that size."

"What?" Justin roared, turning on her. "How do you know?"

"I do not *know*," Lissa replied, not flinching a bit and looking back at him steadily. "I am guessing from what was broken to pieces and what was not." She pointed to the beautiful casket that had held the necklet Flael had given her. The box was lying open on its side, but it was intact. "The cloth lining was torn out," she said, "but I suppose whoever it was felt the panels were not thick enough to hide what they sought. And look at the chair. The seat was broken, but the back and legs were left— I think because there is no part of the back or legs an inch thick and three inches wide."

"Are you sure the men were looking for something, not just taking vengeance?"

"Vengeance on whom?" Lissa asked. "Peter is dead and cannot be hurt; his sons are gone and cannot be hurt; and the vengeance is certainly not meant to hurt me. It is true that a few of my silver trinkets were stolen from Peter's box, but the box itself, which I swear is more valuable, was not broken. And look there," she gestured, "my gowns are all neatly laid out—"

She paused, staring at him, and Justin realized that he had picked up the box and closed it, gently brushing away the bits of wood and dust that clung to it. It was very strange indeed to care so much for a woman that even the inanimate things that belonged to her became precious to him. He almost flung the box away, but he could not and he held it out to her.

"You picked up my clothes and folded them," Lissa whispered, and dropped all the parchments on the floor and ran to kiss him.

He felt absurdly pleased, as irrationally delighted by her emotional response as he had been irrationally enraged when he heard that she had gone to face the destruction of her home without him. "I could not bear to see them crushed and crumpled," he said when their lips parted, his voice growing husky with remembered rage. "I kept seeing your poor swollen face. When I find the man who did that to you, I will kill him. Do you think a blow like that was not dealt in hate?"

"Probably not," Lissa said, frowning thoughtfully. She took the box from him and after an exasperated glance around, set it down atop a pile of rubbish. "Not that I wish to dissuade you from your purpose," she went on, her voice sharpening and her hand coming up to touch her bruised cheek. "I will help you all I can, but I do not think he struck me out of hate. I told you last night; I believe he did it to deprive me of my senses, to render me blind and deaf, and the only reason for that would be that if I saw him or heard his voice I would know him. But Justin, surely a common thief would not need to fear that, and I have thought and thought and I cannot call to mind any person who is like the man on the stair."

"But if this was, as you think, a search, the men likely were not common thieves," Justin pointed out. "Also there were two men, at least two. Aside from what I noted about the wood on the parchment, there was too much done here for one man to have managed alone. Perhaps it was the second man or some other you never saw who was afraid you would know him."

"But if I did not know the man who hit me, why did he hide his face?"

"So if he was seen in company with the man you did know, you would not recognize him."

That was a most uncomfortable thought. Lissa closed her eyes for a moment and shuddered. If what Justin said was true, one of the men who had invaded and destroyed Peter's house could have been her father. If he sometimes hired Hubert to do dirty or dangerous things for him, could he not have hired another man to do this? No, that was silly. He would not take a chance on a second henchman having power over him. Besides, suspicion was nothing. There was no evidence that her father was involved, and no love or loyalty to Justin required her to ruin herself.

"It might be so," she admitted, "but I do not see how that gets us any closer to whoever did it."

"Nor do I. And if you are right and this was a search, I fear we will never find those guilty. Most often it is through recognition of what was stolen that thieves are caught, but if their purpose was search, these men will be in no haste to dispose of your trinkets. Moreover, I am almost certain that they did not find what they sought."

"Why do you say that?" Lissa asked. "I am sure they left some time before Halsig found me. I am not certain how much time, but they could have searched longer."

"No," Justin said. "They had come to an end of what to search, if not to an end of their allotted time. I say they did not find what they sought because the trail of destruction goes right through the workshop. They covered the whole house, and they would not have done that if they had found—" He stopped and looked down at her with lifted brows. "What?"

"I wish I knew," Lissa snapped. "If I had found it, I would have sent out the crier to say I would give it to the rightful owner if he would then leave me in peace."

"But I doubt the searchers are the rightful owners," Justin remarked, and then, as Lissa's chuckle caught on a sob, he put his arm around her again and said, "You are tired, my love. Let me take you home."

"Home?" She drew a deep breath and then sighed. "Where is that? Is there any hope of clearing this house and making it livable in a few days? I could bring my own furniture from my father's house."

"No," Justin said. "The house could be cleared and even repaired, but I will not have you living here alone. Beloved, do you not understand that if what you think is true, if you were not struck in hate but to prevent you from seeing and hearing what you should not, that may prey on the minds of the men who were here. He who struck you might wonder whether you will recognize him when he is with the person known to you, even though his face was hidden. He who is known to you may wonder whether perhaps you came to yourself and heard his voice, recalled the sound of the way he walks. God knows what other fears they might dream of, but if you are living alone, there must be a strong temptation to silence you. I can set guards, but not forever, my love, and guards will only increase the fear that you *do* hold information. Your greatest safety will be to live in a busy household among those who care for you."

"Then I must go back to my father's house," Lissa said, her words barely audible.

"Is he cruel to you?" Justin asked. His voice was soft, but there was such threat in it that Lissa turned cold and could not speak. "I will speak to him," Justin went on, equally softly, "and you may be sure that he will not even look coldly in your direction after that."

"No!" Lissa exclaimed, finding her voice.

The last thing she wanted was any contact at all between Justin and her father. She did not know whether she feared more that Justin might discover her father's possible involvement in Peter's death or the search of the house or that her father might discover that Justin was in love with her. She knew that William would try to use that knowledge to put pressure on Justin and that, no matter what Justin's reaction was, disaster for her would follow.

"No," she repeated more calmly. "My father is not pleasant company, but he does me no harm. That was settled years ago when he beat my mother very harshly. Her father and brothers nearly killed him when they heard of it and told him that any injury done to mama or me would bring worse upon him. Grandfather is dead, but my uncles, Gamel and Gerbod, still come to the Steelyard. And even if father did not fear that they would break his bones, he would not dare cross them. Half our wealth comes from the herbs and spices they permit me to buy at special prices, and they will not sell to him."

"The uncles from the Hanse!" Justin's voice went flat. "I had forgotten them. Of course, you would not want my interference. But I do not understand then why you are so reluctant to return to your father's house."

"Justin, do not be an idiot." Lissa burst out laughing. "As long as I lived alone in this house, you could come to me whenever you liked. How am I to get you past my father, whose bed is in the solar between my bedchamber and the stair?"

For a moment Justin just stared at her with his mouth half open. Then he shut his mouth and swallowed hard. "Oh," he said. "Ah . . . well . . ."

"Yes? Well?" Lissa managed not to laugh aloud, but her eyes sparkled and her voice quivered with amusement as she delivered the challenge.

"Well, there is no need to consider that subject just at present," Justin retorted with enormous dignity. "You are all bruised and in no condition . . ." His voice wavered. "There is always my house," he muttered, looking at the floor.

"Will that be safe?" There was no amusement in that question, and Lissa took Justin's hand in both of hers and clasped it tight. "Not for me, my love. The worst that can happen to me is that tongues will wag about the widow taking her pleasure. It will not hurt my business. But my father . . ." Her voice faltered. "If he discovered I was your leman, he would hold it over you—"

"I have a nearer problem," Justin interrupted, wishing to spare Lissa the pain of describing her father's character. "I had forgot when I said that . . . I had almost forgot my name . . . that my servant is not trustworthy. And you must think me a monster to say it anyway, to act as if I would expect . . . Only . . . I am so hungry for you."

"I find that no fault in you," she said, lowering her head to his breast above the hand she held and resting her whole body against his.

Justin stood quite still, then gently freed himself and stepped back a pace. "I find it a fault. I am not a green boy. I have known women before."

"I said I would accept your terms."

"Why?"

Lissa lowered her eyes, then lifted them again and they were full of laughter even though her face was sober. "I will not lie to you, Justin. I will accept your terms because I think I can change them into my terms as we go along together."

A choked sound made its way up Justin's chest. He struggled with it, glaring balefully, but Lissa continued to regard him with a nearly perfect bland astonishment, seemingly nowise intimidated by the glare, until Justin erupted into laughter. "Go."

He pointed to the ladder. "Ask Goscelin as a favor to me if he will keep you one more night."

"Adela will not like it if you fetch me out and—"

"Woman!" Justin roared, and then as Lissa frantically pointed below and he remembered the men, he lowered his voice to ask, "What the devil gave you the idea that I intended to fetch you out of Goscelin's house?"

"Forgive me," Lissa murmured. "It was my own indelicate thoughts and your indelicate . . . er . . . member, which was rather . . . ah . . . pressing in its attentions during our embrace."

There was a brief silence, in which Lissa heard Justin draw breath, but when he spoke, his voice was gentle and wondering, almost as if he were musing over some interesting question to himself. "It is true," he remarked, "that I have a growing wish to be in a dark and secret place alone with you. I am curious whether my head's desire to strangle you would triumph or my rod's desire to . . . for something else. Now, if you will go back to Goscelin's house and wait until I come, so that I can quiet this war between my body and my head, perhaps I will be able to think of some solution to our problem. Go. Now."

Defiantly Lissa flung one arm around his waist, caught his head with the other hand and pulled it down, and kissed him hard. She felt a surge, an increased stiffening in the "indelicate member," and stroked his cheek as she let him go and turned to flee to the ladder. Lissa was a little troubled about what he would think of her, but she did not fear that he would account her a whore so much as she feared he would ask her to marry him. If he did, she had come to the conclusion that she must refuse him. A proposal to marry would be flattering, but she would only have the choice of hurting him by refusing without reason or exposing her shame beyond the brief reminder she had given him about her father. It would be far better if Justin did not, at least for the present, think of marriage.

The decision that she must refuse marriage had not come easily to her, but it had come swiftly because much of the reasoning behind it had been done during the days when she believed Justin had decided to avoid her because she was William Bowles's daughter. She had chewed the bitter cud of that knowledge over and over until it was well digested and she understood how terrible it would be for a man like Justin to be bound to her father. Justin would then have the choice of concealing her father's crimes and thus being party to them or exposing William's wrongdoing and having the smut cling to him too. So it would not matter which he did; either path would ruin him, blackening his own name, his wife's, and when they came, his children's blood. Thus the great joy of their mutually declared love had lasted no longer for Lissa than her restless sleep.

At least she had hardly felt the pain of her bruises when she woke and remembered that Justin had named her beloved. The pain of knowing that, far from avoiding her because of what her father was, Justin had not yet wakened to that problem overwhelmed all physical discomfort. Lissa knew that she should point out the difficulties that would make any relationship between them impossible and send him away—but she could not. Justin was her dream, her vision of the ultimate perfection that a human man could achieve. In his kindness, his integrity, his sacrifice of self to duty, he was the absolute opposite of her father.

That would have been enough, but Justin offered more. He offered stability, a love that would always be present, not warm and protecting for a few weeks and then gone for many months. Her grandfather and uncles were good men and they did the best they could, but they were bound to their will-o'-the-wisp lives. It had been their need to set sail on a new voyage that had pushed them into accepting William Bowles as a husband for Sigurth, for her mother had died and they had nowhere to leave her. And, even after they knew what William was, they could not provide a refuge for her and Lissa.

Lissa walked slowly back to Goscelin's house, thinking about the urgency in Justin's body. It had awakened something in her, a kind of uneasy restlessness quite different from the mild distaste she had felt when Peter indicated he intended to exert his marital privileges. What she felt did not matter, she thought, smiling at Goscelin's journeyman as he made way for her at the door of the shop; she could pretend to be whatever Justin wanted—and Justin himself would show her that. He would not be at all sorry to know that Peter had not given her any pleasure; he would be delighted to teach her the joys of coupling.

Justin did not turn to watch Lissa go down the ladder. He stared straight ahead at the hearth, where the dead ashes of the fire lay, not knowing whether to laugh or to weep. Slowly, the tumult in his body died, but it made no difference. Already he desired nothing so much as to follow her, just to be with her, to speak to her, to have her infuriate him—and make him laugh. That was much worse, much more serious than any desire to lie with her, no matter how urgent his lust. The lust could be satisfied somehow, the other need had only one solution— marriage.

Clearly Lissa did not intend to ask that of him before coming to his bed. She understood that it would be impossible for them to marry until the noise about Flael's death died away. To have the seeker of justice announce his intention of marrying the widow of a man only four days dead, mysteriously dead, was asking for scandal. And Lissa had said she only feared the scandal for his sake; she must know the mayor was seeking an excuse to be rid of him, and she had said the scandal could do her little harm. That was true enough. Hints of a lover could only increase her business in women's lotions and—

The half-amused thought vanished as Justin remembered what else Lissa had said. She was not talking of only a few weeks' waiting until the noise about Flael's death quieted. She expected them to be lovers for some long time . . . or perhaps she expected that when he had supped of her and was able to think with his head instead of with his staff that he would not wish to marry her at all. All that talk of "terms." Justin's lips twitched. Lissa was more a fool than he if she did not know the power she held. Coupling could only spice, not sate, the appetite she raised. But she had warned him about her father. What had she said? If my father discovers . . . he will hold it over you. There was a real threat in that, considering the position he held, but all that Lissa's warning accomplished was to make him want her more.

Did he want her enough to marry William Bowles's daughter? Justin walked to the hearth at which he had been staring and kicked at the seeming structure in it, an ashy formation that showed how the fire had been banked for the night. It was true that William Bowles did not have the best reputation. A man who dealt with him, it was said, had better be sure of good witnesses with sound memories or he might discover that he had sworn to much more and would receive much less than he intended. That was unpleasant, but was it so terrible? The man was dishonest in small ways. Was it not Lissa's own determined honesty that made her father seem so black to her? No, he would certainly not have chosen a father-by-marriage like William Bowles, but there was no way but marriage to slake the thirst for Lissa's presence in his everyday life.

Justin stared at the untidy heap of ash into which the formation had collapsed after his kick. It had been a well-banked fire, showing still, after all these hours, a tiny red spark at its heart. Lissa was a good housewife as well as a good apothecary, he thought, recalling the way the coals had been heaped and at the same time feeling irritable at being fatuous. And then he smiled broadly as the real reason came to him why the undisturbed condition of the banked fire stuck in his mind. It had nothing to do with Lissa, had only got confused into his thoughts about her. What had been trying to get into his thick skull was that no one had burned anything to destroy it.

That was not an earthshaking observation, but it did at least close one avenue of investigation. Justin shouted for the men waiting below to come up. While they picked their way to the ladder, Justin cast a glance around to decide how to begin sifting through the debris for some sign of the men who had created it. He was briefly distracted when he saw the parchments strewn just as they had fallen when Lissa jumped up to kiss him for pulling her gowns out of the debris. She really had used them only as an excuse to speak to him alone. He gathered them up, placed her receipt book atop, and tied them into a thick packet with pieces of the torn bedding, then said to the first man up the ladder, "Take the gowns that are lying in what was the other chamber, these parchments, and the wooden box atop that pile of scrap to Master Goscelin's house and ask that they be given to Mistress Lissa."

He turned to the other man, but as the first came toward him with his arms full of gowns, he realized that what he asked would take some doing and laughed. "Go down first with the box," Justin said, unwilling to take a chance that the beautiful casket would be broken. "I will throw down the parchments and the gowns. Meanwhile, John, pick up some of the splintered wood and make good fires in both chambers. We need not freeze while we work. But John, be careful to look at each piece. If you find anything at all caught in the wood or stuck to it, bring the whole to me."

Chapter 13

‿‿‿⤳‿⤳‿‿

SCARCELY TEN MINUTES AFTER JUSTIN LEFT GOSCELIN'S UPPER chamber, William Bowles came into the shop and asked for his daughter. Mistress Adela, who had followed Justin down to reinforce the idea that Lissa was a sweet child and must be treated with gentleness, was still in the shop. Once belowstairs, she had noticed that one of the apprentices had a dripping nose and a thick voice, and she began to question him. Her first impulse when William entered the shop was to step into a dark corner and pretend she was not there, but she knew if she did not prevent it, William would follow his daughter. Although she had no real reason at all, Adela felt strongly that she must prevent William from interrupting Justin's meeting with Lissa.

"God be with you, Master Bowles," she said, coming forward. "I suppose you have come to inquire about your daughter. I must confess I have not kept so strict a watch on her as you might desire, but do come above with me. You must not scold me here where my husband's folk will hear."

"I have indeed come to ask about Heloise," William said. "She did not wish to see me this morning, and I had not thought to disturb her again today, but a matter of our craft has arisen which makes it necessary for me to speak to her as soon as possible. I hope she has her senses?"

"Good heaven, yes," Adela exclaimed, shepherding him up the stair and into the solar. "Dear Goscelin," she cried, shutting the door behind her as she entered the room, "here is Master Bowles so much concerned for Lissa's health that I was afraid to tell him I could not stop her from going out soon after dinner."

Goscelin rose from his chair, his face perfectly blank. He had no idea why Adela had brought Bowles up here instead of sending him to Flael's house, but he had learned over their twenty years of marriage to trust her, and he said, "You need not worry about your daughter's health. Her injuries looked worse than they were—no bones broken or cords torn, just bruises. She will be back in a little while, I dare say. If you are in a hurry, I will be glad to give her any message you wish to leave for her."

"I am not in any hurry," William replied blandly, although he was furious with Goscelin's none too subtle attempt to be rid of him. "I will wait, since it is a matter I must discuss with Heloise herself, and in private, as soon as possible."

"I see." Goscelin's face now wore, if possible, even less expression than it had before. He had become quite fond of Lissa during his dealings with her over the four days since Peter de Flael's death, but he was not prepared to become familiar with William Bowles for her sake. Still, it was not in the goldsmith's nature to offend any man who had given him no personal insult, and he turned to his wife and said, "Pour a glass of wine for Master Bowles, Adela. And you, Master Bowles, come to the fire and warm yourself."

"Thank you," William said, one corner of his mouth curling in acknowledgment of the grudging hospitality.

There was a silence and then, feeling the need to make small talk, Goscelin said, "It seems that the king will not come to London at all before he goes to France."

"And just as well," William replied. "Each time he comes, he has another demand."

"But he has balanced what he asks of us with great favors and great liberties," Goscelin pointed out.

William shrugged. "So all say, and yet I have seen little benefit of those words and seals on parchment. One could come to terms with a king's sheriff or bailiff who held office for years. Now—" He sipped at the wine Adela had handed to him, angry because he knew how the goldsmith would interpret those words and angrier because the interpretation would not be so wrong. "Well," he went on briskly, "it is all the same to me. I have little to do with such men. Still, I will be glad if King John stays in France and even gladder if he keeps with him all his great nobles."

Goscelin laughed, covering a certain interest. He had heard that William Bowles could ask a favor of Lord Robert FitzWalter and be reasonably sure of having that favor granted. What Bowles had done to earn such consideration Goscelin did not wish to guess because he had no desire for his conscience to urge him to go against Lord Robert, but now it sounded as if FitzWalter either had withdrawn his goodwill or was asking payment in return.

"I cannot agree with you," Goscelin said easily, still smiling as if he spoke in jest. "It is easy enough for you, whose business is mostly with the ladies who will remain here in England, but not so good for those of us who depend on the lords' custom to make our profits. But," he went on smoothly, "you sound as if you have been pinched. Let me see, who is in London who could have—"

"No, no!" William cut him off sharply and tossed off the remainder of his wine. "There is no special case. I am only afraid that the quarrel between the king and the barons will break out into open war. If so, let them fight in France. You know who will suffer the worst if they come to marching armies here in England."

"Alas, I do," Goscelin said in total if unwilling agreement.

He was aware from William's barely concealed alarm that there must indeed be some reason for him to wish FitzWalter would go far away. There was no use in pursuing the question directly, however, and Goscelin drew his wife into the discussion, easily inducing her with a hint here and there to turn the talk to illness, medications, and the problems even the best compounders had in predicting the strength of certain most valuable but dangerous drugs, like hemlock and foxglove.

Goscelin missed his purpose, which was to discover if William would avoid the topic or look in any way uneasy while discussing it, implying that he might have provided a fatal dose of something or other to someone.

Quite the contrary was true. William leapt on the subject, and he spoke with a peevish sincerity, which Goscelin could not mistake, about his own ignorance of all such matters. It was Heloise who had initiated and carried out that end of the business, and if disaster struck, it would be on her head. He never did more than sell the herbs themselves, and he added, at considerable length, that he preferred to deal in condiments, which brought a better profit. He had not quite finished all he had to say on the subject when a brief scratch heralded the opening of the door and Lissa came into the room.

"Oh, my dear," Adela cried, "where have you been? You look so tired. There, I blame myself. I should not have allowed you to go out. And here is your father, quite out of patience with us for being careless with you, for he is in a great hurry to tell you something."

Lissa was tired and in no mood to deal with her father, but before she could protest, he said, "That is quite true. Also, I must talk to you privately, Heloise. I am sorry to be rude, but the matter is of importance and of some urgency."

"Very well." Lissa knew it was useless to try to escape her father in this mood. In any case, since she no longer had the refuge of living in Peter's house, it would be better to pacify him and listen to what he had to say. "I suppose, we could go—" she began vaguely.

"You need go nowhere," Adela interrupted. "You may talk here in the solar. Goscelin must come down to the shop with me anyway. One of the apprentices has a running nose, and I must know whether this boy can be spared and may be sent to bed."

Lissa walked quickly across the chamber, limping slightly for, with the stimulus of Justin's presence gone, her whole left side ached and throbbed, and kissed Adela's cheek. "My most heartfelt thanks," she murmured. "I am tired and ache in every limb. I am very grateful not to need to go out in the cold again."

"Poor child." Adela loosened Lissa's cloak pin but did not pull off the garment, urging the girl silently into the smaller of the

two chairs by the fire and only then opening the cloak to allow
the heat easier access. "I should not have allowed . . ."

Adela's body hid Lissa from her father, and the small satisfied
smile Lissa allowed to appear communicated enough that Adela
did not finish her remark. Instead she said briskly, "No use
bemoaning a cracked cast. Better to melt it down at once and
begin again—so, off to bed with you, Mistress Lissa, as soon as
your father has his say and is gone. And that—pardon *my*
rudeness, Master Bowles—should take no long time. Come,
Goscelin."

"And what was that all about?" the goldsmith asked his wife
softly as soon as the door was closed behind them.

Adela looked confused, as she often did when he asked the
reason behind some seemingly purposeless action. "Oh, I am
not sure," she admitted. "I just felt . . . I knew Lissa wished to
be alone with Sir Justin. I do not know why, for he is not at all
the kind of man most girls would wish to be alone with. I
mean . . . he is so *hard*. If I did not know you had more power
than he, I would be afraid of him."

"There is no reason for anyone who has done no wrong to
fear Justin," Goscelin assured his wife somewhat absently while
he considered what she had said. "He may be hard, but he is
also perfectly just."

"But sometimes justice is not at all appropriate," Adela
protested.

Goscelin looked startled. "Whatever do you mean, Adela?"
he asked. "*Justice* is *always* appropriate."

She put her arm around her husband's portly waist and
squeezed. "You know I am never quite sure what I mean," she
admitted, "but I am very glad you are a goldsmith and not a
hunter of men. I think Lissa has a . . . a hunger for Justin.
How does one lie abed with a man who has caused the hanging
and maiming of hundreds?"

Goscelin laughed and hugged his wife back without answering as he led her down the stairs.

Upstairs in the solar, William had come forward and now
stood directly before Lissa, looming over her. "Good," he said
with a satisfied chuckle. "You have got a sound beating, and
well deserved too. Did I not tell you to leave that house and
come home?"

Lissa did not answer the remark, except by a single flashing glance, but she was now sick with the near certainty that her father had been involved in the robbery and destruction of Peter's house. All she said, however, was "Oh, step back, father. By now you should have come to understand that you cannot frighten me, and you only annoy me by making me twist my neck to see you. Say what you must say to me and go."

"I have no intention and no need of frightening you, you stupid slut," William said, "but I would be glad to buy a drink for the man who gave you a lessoning you need."

"And that you are too afraid to give me?" Lissa's mouth curled with contempt. She pulled the pin from her cloak and held it up so William could see it. "Stand away from me, I said."

"Fool! I simply do not wish to shout at you so that overcurious goldsmith and his prying wife hear every word I say."

"More the fool you," Lissa snapped. "Do you think because you listen at doors a man like Goscelin would do so? Besides, they have been so kind to me. If they want to know what your business with me was, I will tell them."

"They will not ask and you will not tell them." William laughed, and then laughed again when he saw Lissa drop her head with shame and swallow. "There *are* advantages to being the one wise man among a great many fools. Never mind that. I did not come here for the pleasure of having you lecture me on honor. Do you know that the king is going to France to—he says—win back Normandy?"

Startled, Lissa looked up. "Of course I know. What has that to do with us?"

"Not with us, with me. Lord Robert FitzWalter, who is accompanying King John to France, has asked me to oversee some business in the north for him."

"You?" Lissa's amazement and disbelief were too quick and sincere to have been designed as a deliberate insult and thus displayed her contempt all the more, as did her next incredulous question. "Why should he ask you?"

Her voice wavered on the last few words because the answer had come to her. If a man wanted a deputy who would not worry about right and wrong, he might well ask William Bowles to play that role. Then, while her father sputtered over her disregard of his worth and importance and called her several obscene names, she remembered her conversation with Justin, remembered that what he had said implied that FitzWalter was ordinarily honest in business matters, remembered too that FitzWalter was an inveterate enemy of the king. So another, more dangerous, reason occurred to her for FitzWalter to employ her father, someone little known to him and of bad reputation. If he wanted treason done and wished to be able to throw away the soiled tool he had used to do it, her father would be ideal.

"Father," she said desperately. "I am sorry for what I said. Please listen to me, truly you *must* listen. You must not involve yourself with Lord Robert. He hates the king, and John hates him. If what he has asked you to do can be accounted as treason . . ."

William looked at his daughter as if she had turned into an adder and bitten him. Finally, his voice high and his eyes staring fixedly into hers, he told her, "If there were even a smell of treason, I would have nothing to do with it, you fool. I am not such an idiot as to let myself be crushed between two great ones. The matter has to do with trade, nothing more, and the king will never hear my name."

Lissa did not believe him. That fixed stare, eye meeting eye, which so many felt was a sign of sincerity, always meant William Bowles was lying. Common sense also protested. Surely Lord Robert had his own servants to deal with simple matters of trade. "Listen, please listen," she begged. "What might look as innocent as washed wool to you might be goat hair. How did Lord Robert come to know you? What do you know of his business?"

Then, to Lissa's amazement, the fear she had seen under her father's words about trade disappeared. He laughed. "It is none of your affair how I know Lord Robert," he remarked, almost good-humoredly. "If you are so concerned about my doing business for him, all you need do is keep your mouth shut and there will be only three in the world who ever know of it. Why do you think I wished to speak to you in private?"

"You will ruin us," Lissa said, but she sounded and felt uncertain.

Perhaps there was no danger in what her father was doing. One of Lissa's hands crept up to touch her lips. He was not the kind of man to expose himself to danger, if his greed did not blind him to it. And he had been afraid when she first spoke of treason; but when she asked how he knew FitzWalter, he had recovered immediately. Could that not mean that, by being reminded of the person who had introduced him, he had been reassured that his business for Lord Robert was not treasonous? Lissa, who had been frowning into nothing, now glanced upward quickly. Her father's expression confirmed her opinion that there was nothing more she could do to change his mind now. She would have to raise the subject again once she was in the house. If she pricked his pride, he might let slip more information so she could judge whether what he had agreed to do was truly innocent.

William had been watching her while she sat with one hand to her lips and a worried frown wrinkling her brow; he was thinking sourly that Heloise was looking for a way to cause trouble. But when he caught the flicker of her eyes to him and then away, a look he thought of as sly, it occurred to him that she might be worried because she feared she had already talked too much, and he asked sharply, "How do you know so much about Lord Robert?"

Tears stung in Lissa's eyes as a vivid memory rose of that evening when Justin had talked about FitzWalter. She might never have the joy of that kind of companionship of mind and body again because the first aim of her life must be to keep her father from gaining a hold on Justin. His question had startled her, and she had no ready answer, but she was determined never to mention Justin's name to him again.

William came closer and seized her arm. "I asked you how you knew so much about Lord Robert," he repeated.

She bit back a cry—he had grabbed her bruised left arm and hurt her, but she would not give him the satisfaction of admitting it—and pushed him away hard. He released her, knowing the limits she would allow before defending herself so violently and viciously that she frightened him. It was a game he often played, taking pleasure in the small but constant pain he inflicted on her, knowing she was too proud to complain to her uncles over a minor misery. This time, however, her eyes were strange when she looked at him, and he backed away farther than he intended.

"I have to know," William said, turned half away from her, his voice defensive now. "Where you learned so much about Lord Robert might be important. Have you been asking questions about him? Did Peter speak of him?"

"Women talk," Lissa said, looking down at the fire.

"Oh, court gossip." William was relieved. "And speaking of court ladies, you have just reminded me that Lady Margaret de Vesci came by the shop this very morning asking for the creams you make for her, and we had none to sell her. You must come back at once and begin to prepare a new batch. I said you would bring them to her on Monday."

"I cannot come today," Lissa said, barely keeping herself from sobbing, knowing that she could not dare let Justin come to her father's house at all and that she would somehow have to explain that to him. "I am too hurt and too weary. I will come tomorrow."

"If the creams are not done in time, on your head be the blame," William said lightly. "You will have to carry your own explanation and excuses to Lady Margaret. I will not be home on Monday. By then I should be far north as York."

Lissa, who had been staring dully down at her fingers in her lap, looked up, eyes wide. "York?" she repeated.

"What the devil ails you?" William snarled. "And do not begin to warn me against Lord Robert. You accursed idiot, once he had singled me out, do you think I could have refused him even if I had wished to do so? I told you I had to go north."

"It had gone out of my head," Lissa admitted. "I will come home tomorrow without fail." She hesitated then, unwilling to take the chance that she would miss seeing Justin, whose rigid sense of duty might keep him in Peter's house long past a reasonable time to visit in the evening. "But not until after dinner, I am afraid," she went on. "If you are to be in York by . . . No, York by Monday is impossible. Even if you were to ride like the devil—"

"No, no," William said hastily. Since he had never intended to go as far north as York, he had not considered traveling time to that place. "I am going to York, but I do not have to be there on any particular day."

"Thank God for that," Lissa said, not wishing to seem eager to be rid of him for fear he would stay at home two weeks just to spite her. "We will have to settle the accounts and see about trade goods and coin for your journey. And there must be a way to keep your name and FitzWalter's separate. There is money enough? You have not done any heavy buying since I have been gone, have you?"

"Do not be stupid," William snapped. "What is there to buy in winter?"

Lissa detected the uneasy tone in William's voice, but she associated that with her remark about FitzWalter, and she was too absorbed in her own happy visions of the immedate future to look further for a reason. And when her father growled that he had better go before her protectors came back and drove him out, she was too glad to be rid of him to find his behavior different from normal. His quick departure was not out of character. From his point of view, he had got his way. She had agreed to come back to live in his house and take care of the business. Lissa uttered a soft, choked laugh that was half sob. If only he had told her honestly in the beginning that he had to leave London and she had known she would be alone in the house and could invite Justin, she might have agreed at once— or would she?

The exhilaration that had lent her strength when she realized her father was going away had disappeared and left her more exhausted than ever. She levered herself out of the chair and tottered across the room to where the cot she had slept in stood. Carefully, because her left side throbbed and felt swollen, as if it would burst and bleed if she struck it, she eased herself down on the cot. Once she closed her eyes, even pain could not keep her awake.

Twice Lissa was aware of a disturbance, of a kind voice urging her gently to wake, but she shrank away from physical pain and from nagging worry and sank back into the warm dark of rest. The third time she heard the voice she was near waking, recognized that it was Adela speaking to her, and opened her eyes. The room was bright with sunlight, and she was terribly hungry.

"Oh dear," she said, "I am afraid I have slept the whole day away."

"Very nearly," Adela agreed, smiling at her. "All of yesterday anyway. We were beginning to worry about you."

"I am very sorry. I have been a dreadful guest."

Adela laughed. "Not at all. You have been very quiet, not demanding at all." The sharp lines of merriment in her face changed to softer ones of pleasure and relief. "But to speak the truth, I am very glad to see you so alert. I had a cousin who was struck on the head while tilting. He fell unconscious, but when he came to himself he seemed quite well. Yet later, at the evening meal, he fell down suddenly—and he never could be waked. Some said he was ensorcelled, but there was no one who had a spite for him and no witch nearby." She sighed. "I could not help thinking of it when we could not wake you and I had let you persuade me to allow you to go out."

"Perhaps I should not have done that," Lissa admitted, taking Adela's hand. "It did make me very tired. But I really had to speak to Sir Justin. You see, Goscelin believes the damage done to Peter's house was done out of hate. I cannot say there was no hate behind it, but I felt whoever did it was searching for something. I did not wish to contradict Goscelin in his own house and—and going out has done me no lasting harm, I am sure, because I am starving, and one is never hungry when one is really ill."

"True enough," Adela said briskly, squeezing Lissa's hand and then removing her own. "Now, shall I bring you something to eat in bed?"

"I would rather get up, please," Lissa answered. It was true, but she also thought it would make less trouble for Adela's maid. She was well aware that her reason for wanting to speak to Justin was not the most convincing excuse ever offered and, feeling uneasy, babbled on. "I am glad I fell asleep in my clothes and do not need to dress. I seem to have slept away my tiredness, but I am so stiff I am sure dressing would have taken a long time. And I promised my father that I would be home soon after dinner."

She saw the flash of curiosity in Adela's eyes, but she dared not tell Adela about her father's employment by FitzWalter. Simultaneously, Lissa could not bear to seem coldly unresponsive in exchange for the warm support she had been given. What she must do, she knew, was offer as a diversion a subject that Adela would find much more interesting than William Bowles's reasons for wanting to speak privately to his daughter.

"I must go home," Lissa said. "I could have Peter's house repaired, but Justin said I must not live alone there." She used Justin's name without his title deliberately. Adela did not acknowledge this "slip" by so much as a flicker of an eyelid, but Lissa was sure her hostess was too practiced in her woman's skill to miss the use. "He thinks," she went on smoothly, "that the men who stunned me and let me live will begin to have second thoughts and fear I will recognize them in some way. I do not want to go, but I cannot act the fool. But it will be very hard for Justin to come to the house of William Bowles."

"Aha!" Adela exclaimed triumphantly. "I *thought* there was something very strange about the way Sir Justin kept asking Goscelin questions about you." She looked eagerly into Lissa's face and dropped her voice confidentially. "Does he know he desires you yet?"

"Yes, but I am afraid he does not like it yet," Lissa replied just as softly but with a much merrier expression. "I do not think he has any plans to marry."

Adela nodded slowly, giving no indication that she echoed Lissa's amusement. Marriage was a serious matter to her and had only marginal relevance to the feelings of the man and woman involved.

"There is no real reason why Justin should marry," she said thoughtfully.

"Hush!" Lissa hissed. "I do not think we should talk about this."

"Whyever not?" Adela asked. "I am sure you are eager to know his situation, and it is right that you should. He is a hard man. Goscelin says he is just, and he may be just among men, but that does not mean he would be just to a woman. He might use you—" She saw then the way Lissa was looking over her shoulder into the solar and smiled. "Oh, we are quite alone. Goscelin has finished breaking his fast and has gone down to the shop. I thought I would let you sleep." Then she patted Lissa's cheek. "No, the truth is I wanted to have a free hand for a little while if I could not wake you easily, and I did not want Goscelin to know if you woke up muddled in the head."

"I am sorry I caused you so much worry."

Adela gestured that away as unimportant and said, with considerable relish, "Never mind that. You want to know about

Sir Justin. Well, his elder brother, who inherited the father's lands and the title of baron has, I believe, three sons and two daughters. And I have heard that Justin is much attached to his cousins, the late mayor's sons. So he does not lack a choice of heirs." She paused and her lips quirked. "How interesting. That does not trouble you at all, my dear, does it?"

"Why should it?" Lissa asked. "I do not care about Justin's estate. I am well able to provide for myself and even for any children I might have."

There was a moment's silence while Adela considered that. "I am not sure whether to be horrified or to envy you," she said. "Even if I had not married into a craft and come to live in a city where most of my training is useless, it is almost impossible for a woman to hold her own land. A craft, however . . . Still, that is not to the point except to make me wonder all the more why you want Sir Justin of all men."

"Because you are wrong about him," Lissa said, smiling. "He is not hard, at least, not as you mean it. He will do his duty at any cost to himself, that is true, but he is really very good. Have you not noticed that he looks blackest and most grim when he is praised or offered a kindness?" She chuckled. "He cannot bear it! Poor man. He becomes embarrassed and has not the slightest notion of how to accept a compliment, so he growls to warn away such dreadful threats to his peace."

"Hmmm." Adela still did not wish to encourage Lissa to attach herself to a man she thought of as covered in blood, but what the girl had said rang surprisingly true. Still, in Adela's opinion, men got what they could for as little as they could. If Lissa was set on the man—and perhaps he would be a good husband—then the girl should not be deceived and done out of her rights as a wife with a tale of starving relatives.

"Of course," Adela went on, "there is no reason why Sir Justin should *not* marry. I do not know how the brother plans to provide for his children, but I never heard there was any lack among the FitzAilwins. Moreover the children are young and may be thinned by time. As for the cousins, I know they need no legacy. They are well-to-do and growing richer. So if Justin did take it in his head to have a wife and a family, he would not be spoiling any expectations."

"He is a long way from desiring me for a wife," Lissa said, more hopefully than truthfully.

"I am not so sure."

Adela suddenly remembered that she had not been much worried about Lissa until Justin had appeared the previous evening. When she said Lissa was still sleeping and she did not think the girl should be wakened to answer questions that could be answered just as well the next day, Justin had insisted on seeing her anyway. It was he who remarked on how pale she was, that she lay too quietly. At the time Adela had been very angry, thinking that he was making excuses so that she would wake Lissa to be questioned. But he had stood looking down for so long, his face without expression but his hands clasped together so tight that the knuckles showed white, that Adela had begun to think of her cousin who fell into a swoon and never awoke, and whose temple had also been deeply discolored. Now, suddenly, she began giggle.

"He was here yesterday, after the evening meal. He said he came to tell Goscelin that they had found nothing that could hint at who had forced a way into Peter's house, but I think he came to see you." And she repeated aloud to Lissa her thoughts, summing up with, "So you see, it was not your fault at all that I was worried and kept thinking of my cousin's long death. It was Justin's fault. Now I mind on it, you were not pale at all and your temple did not have that strange hollow that his had."

While she spoke, Adela had helped Lissa out of bed, gently straightened her gown as well as she could, and led her out into the solar to the fireside, where a small table had been set between the two chairs. Lissa glanced around for a stool, but was told to sit in the smaller chair.

"I have eaten already with Goscelin." Adela brushed the cloth and drew bread and cheese and a cold meat pasty within easy reach. As she poured ale into a horn goblet set into an exquisite tracery of silver wire, she paused. "Ah," she said, recalling suddenly what was to her the ultimate sign of physical or mental distress, "I have just remembered. Sir Justin would not take a bite to eat, although he admitted he had had nothing since dinner."

"Poor Justin," Lissa murmured, sorry now that she had not

forced herself awake enough to say at least a few words to him. But he had not made a sound, most likely because he knew she would respond to his call from beyond the grave and he would not wake her when she needed rest, despite his own fear.

"My dear," Adela said, her voice sharp, "you should think twice before you take a man like Sir Justin into your heart. Even if everything you say about him is true and he would be the gentlest and kindest of husbands, I am afraid you do not understand honor and what dedication to duty really means." And then, seeing the color rise into Lissa's face and remembering William Bowles's reputation, she cried, "Oh, no, I did not mean *you* in any special way. I only—"

Lissa found a smile, certain that Adela had not meant her in particular and was only speaking the general opinion of a member of the landed nobility about the common born. It was a ridiculous opinion, Lissa thought. She had heard enough from Peter to realize that honor was about as common among the nobility as it was among burghers. The king himself was known far and wide for his lies and deceptions, whereas she would trust Goscelin and Hamo Finke with anything, just as she would trust Justin. And then she realized that Adela was still talking, trying to soothe her.

"—think you have him already, if you want him. So he may be closer to asking for marriage than you believe."

"Not for long if he believes my wits to be addled," Lissa said merrily.

She intended only to show that she had taken no offense but realized as she said the words that she had provided herself with an opportunity to speak to Justin before she had to go home. She did not want him to follow her there before she was rid of her father.

"So," she went on before Adela could protest, "if Witta is still too sore to run an errand, will you lend me a messenger to find Justin and tell him I am well, wide awake, and eager to speak to him any time before dinner?"

Adela sighed. "Yes, if it is what you want."

Lissa touched her hand. "I assure you I am not going to snap at Justin's offer—although, truly, I do not expect any offer from him. Before he comes to it, I will have time enough to consider and reconsider. Peter is not dead a week. I would not shame him by pretending what I do not feel, but he was kind to me and I will wait a decent few months at least before I act."

"You are a good girl," Adela said, bending and kissing Lissa's sound cheek, "so sensible. And there, I have been talking away when you said you were starving. The best thing is for me to go attend to my business and leave you in peace. I will look at Witta and, if he is not well enough, send up one of our men."

Chapter 14

Lissa had almost forgotten her hunger during her conversation with Adela, but as soon as the goldsmith's wife was gone, she attacked the food with an enthusiasm only moderated by the aches and pains any movement cost her. The first cautious motions, accompanied by grimaces, became more free as her muscles warmed out of their morning stiffness, and Lissa soon managed to put away a large piece of bread and an equally large piece of the soft, crumbly, and high-flavored cheese.

As she ate it, Lissa resolved to extract the source of the cheese somehow from Adela—such delicacies often being a tight-kept secret of a housekeeper. But everything was good, and Lissa ate a good half of what had been left of the pasty, too. Having washed down the food with draughts of ale, she found that the goblet was empty. Lissa was just considering whether it would be worth the pang of reaching for the pitcher to have more ale when she heard steps. That would be the messenger for whom she had asked, and whether Witta or another, he could pour the ale. She busied herself with tearing another piece from the loaf and, taking up her knife, looked from the cheese to the pasty.

"I am glad to see you with so good an appetite." Justin's voice was very dry. "Mine suffered somewhat from seeing you lying like a corpse yesterday."

Lissa squeaked as she turned too quickly and her body protested, but the smile she gave him dismissed his cold voice and angry expression and set his words at their true value, an expression of relief so intense that it manifested itself as anger. Just so will a mother who has saved a child from near death caused by carelessness embrace the child with one arm while beating it with the other.

"Then my well-doing must have restored your taste for food," Lissa said, her false gravity a fine match for his false anger. "So take off your cloak and sit down and eat. I am sure Goscelin will not begrudge you the crumbs from his table, and I know Adela will not because she complained to me only this morning that you would not take an evening meal with them."

"I would have choked. I was frightened out of my wits. I could neither eat nor sleep."

"Well, I offered to cure one of the ills," Lissa said, laughing and holding out her hand to him. "Come here and eat. As to sleeping, you can go home and do that as soon as you are fed. Meanwhile, pour another goblet of ale for me, please."

"You are very indifferent to my sufferings," he said, but softly, bending so that he spoke almost in her ear.

She grasped at him, pulled him still closer, her lips moving against his as she murmured, "You know I am not. Had you called me, I would have answered. I did not know you were there."

They kissed, but Justin pulled away quickly. "Not too much silence," he said. "They cannot hear words. I know because I was listening while Mistress Adela was with you, but some sound does come down if the door is not closed." He poured the ale into her goblet, drank about half, refilled it, and handed the vessel to her.

"You will have to serve yourself," Lissa remarked, gesturing to the food. "I am too stiff today to be a proper hostess."

"And a proper wife?"

"Here?" Lissa whispered. "You are mad!"

"Not completely, but very nearly," he said.

But Lissa noticed that as he was speaking he had cut substantial portions of the food. Her heart lurched inside her, not because of the teasing words Justin had said but because he really was hungry. His tone might have been light, but his eyelids were dark and bruised looking, as was the skin below his eyes. He had not been exaggerating when he had said he was so worried about her that he could not eat or sleep. Lissa dared not let her feelings show, not in Goscelin's solar with the door open and—she would have staked her life on it—Adela standing as near the stairs as she could get and straining her ears for every sound, or lack of sound. And even if they had been in private, Lissa thought, she hurt too much to give their first coupling the attention it must have to be an outstanding success. The only path was the one Justin had started on already.

"Ah, I am glad to hear that you retain some of your wits," she said, picking up the teasing note his voice had held when he told her he was not completely mad. "You kept enough, I hope, to listen to some good news. If you can be patient for only a few days more, you can test my qualities—and I can test yours. My father told me yesterday he has business in the north and will be gone from the house very soon. For that reason and others, I must go home as soon as dinner is over today. I am not sure when he will leave, but I will send Witta to you with a note when he does, and we can arrange to meet."

"Go home today?" Justin's voice was choked, and his glare forbade her to refer again to the blatant invitation she had offered. "Cannot you wait until tomorrow? I cannot escort you home today, not after dinner. The reason I was not here at first light to see how you did was that I had a message from FitzWalter to say his ships were in on the night tide and I should come with him to meet the captains. I could not refuse. I had promised him to deal with the cargoes, and I must go to see Hamo Finke after dinner to arrange exactly what part of the business he will do, if any, or if he will only hold the money. I have had time for very little else while attending to your affairs."

"You are acting as factor for FitzWalter?" Lissa asked, hardly believing her ears and dismissing everything else Justin said as irrelevant. "Does he not have his own servants to do such work?"

"Yes and no," Justin said. "I suppose he uses an agent who bargains with the merchants, but it is FitzWalter himself who decides that the price is right or not enough according to the conditions that prevail at that time and what he can guess or foresee about conditions in the future. It is his work, not his agent's, that he desires me to do, although it may be that I will do both tasks and save myself a fee, since I am not so high and mighty as FitzWalter, and to speak the truth, I like to deal directly with the merchants myself."

"I also—I mean I like to deal with the trader if I cannot buy directly from the captain. Often both you and the trader are saved a shaving on the price that the agent puts in his own purse atop his wage." Lissa answered easily, having said the same thing many times before, but only half her mind was on her words.

She was tremendously relieved. If FitzWalter had asked Justin to dispose of the cargoes of his trading ships for him, it was not at all impossible that he would ask her father to perform some smaller task peculiarly fitted to his abilities. Nor did that necessarily mean a dishonest task, Lissa reminded herself. Her father's acquaintance with Lord Robert must be recent. It was possible that his lordship knew only that William Bowles was a Pepperer and had not heard, being out of the way of guild gossip, that Bowles was a sharp and not overly honest man. So her father had most likely told her the truth after all, and she deserved the anxiety she had suffered for always thinking the worst of him. The busy thoughts and the easing of her anxiety did not interfere in the least with Lissa's ability to hear Justin.

"Do you often go to the ships yourself?" he asked.

"Only to my uncles' ships," Lissa replied, smiling. "There my uncles make the price and I pay whatever they ask. They are too kind. I fear they lose on what they sell me. As to the other ships, I go with my father. I do the choosing, but he likes to do the chaffering himself, and I admit he is much better at it than I."

"But you said your father would be away for a time, did you not?"

Lissa's smile broadened. "Yes. For some weeks, perhaps even several months. He will not tell me exactly what he intends to do, only that he must travel north."

Justin did not respond to her smile. "That means he will be away during the first dockings of spring."

"It does not matter," Lissa assured him, somewhat puzzled by what seemed an excessive concern for her profits. "I know most of the captains. I suppose I will be charged an extra shilling here or there, but I can talk price well enough not to be badly cheated."

"Who cares about your being cheated?" Justin snapped. "You little ninny, worse might befall you than paying an extra penny on a pound of pepper."

"Worse?" Lissa repeated blankly, and then her eyes opened wide. "Oh, Justin!" She shook her head. "I have known most of those men since I was three years old and went to the docks holding my mother's hand."

"Yes, and when you were three you were perfectly safe. Unfortunately, you are not three years old any longer. You will send for me when you wish to go to a ship, and I will escort you until your father returns."

Lissa's mouth opened, then closed. She was not sure whether Justin was joking or serious. She was not sure, if he was serious, whether she should be flattered because he thought her so irresistible that old friends would suddenly run mad with desire and attack her or whether she should be furious at his overbearing attitude. She opened her mouth again to say that her father's journeyman could escort her, and Justin forestalled her.

"No, I do not really suspect men who trade regularly in London, but there are others. Also, until I lay my hands on whoever was in your house, or until a long enough time passes, I do not want you to go alone, or even with the escort of an apprentice or journeyman, to places like the dock. Stop and think, Lissa. Men who will sail away in a few days and be safe from pursuit and from our law can be easily and cheaply hired to do murder."

"Oh, I see. Yes, I will take care."

The words were soothing and promised nothing. Lissa did not really think anyone could be hired to do murder on the busy docks of London in the middle of the day, but she could see no point in arguing.

"And you will stay here until tomorrow, so I can see you home?"

Lissa now remembered that was the question he had started. There might be, she thought regretfully, something in Adela's warning against loving a man like Justin. He had a mind that never lost the trail. No matter how many diversions he came up against along the way, in the end he would return to his original point. Adela was quite right; that could make life difficult for a wife. She saw too that somehow only the heel of the loaf of bread remained, the cheese was gone, and so was the pasty. Justin reached across the table, finished the ale she had left in the goblet, refilled it, and drank that down. Then he sighed. He was full of food and contentment. This was a good moment, Lissa thought—or as good as there ever would be with this man—to say no.

"I cannot stay here another day, Justin, truly, I cannot. It is not only that my father is leaving. I do not suppose that a few hours would matter in making our arrangements, but I must prepare two creams that my father promised I would deliver on Monday to Lady Margaret de Vesci."

"Who?"

Justin's roar made Lissa jump with surprise. "Lady Margaret de Vesci," she repeated. "What is wrong with that? She has been buying from me for several years."

"Do you know how long she has been in London? Did she come down from Scotland or did she come from Windsor?"

Lissa saw the anxiety that tensed Justin's body and understood that his questions concerned larger affairs than those of her shop. "I do not know, Justin. I did not see her at all. She spoke to my father about the creams yesterday, and he told me nothing else. I can go to her now, if you desire. I can say I wished to explain why she could not buy the creams she wanted. I could then tell her about Peter's death, and by that path I could try to get answers to your questions."

"You say she is a longtime client. Are you friends? Do you trust her?"

"I am not certain how to answer you, Justin. Are we friends? Certainly not. Lady Margaret is the sister of the king of Scotland—"

"Natural sister," Justin put in.

Lissa shook her head. "She is still a king's daughter. She is recognized and accepted and was married to a man of wealth and power to help keep peace in the north."

"That sounds"—Justin lifted his brow—"either as if you were curious enough to seek facts about her or as if she said more to you than how much of which cream she desired."

"Lady Margaret cannot be the friend of an apothecary's daughter, but sometimes she does talk to me of women's matters. I will not repeat—"

"No," Justin said at once. "I would not ask that of you. In fact, I will ask you no questions at all."

"But I cannot see how it could hurt Lady Margaret if I tell you whether she came directly to London from the north or went first to—"

Lissa stopped abruptly. She had just remembered Lady Christina de Mandeville's sidelong glance and titter when she passed Lady Margaret leaving the shop one day, and then the vicious voice in which Lady Christina recounted Eustace de Vesci's excuse for plotting to kill King John—that the king had meddled with his wife.

"I still do not think it could hurt Lady Margaret to know from where she came," Lissa now said slowly. "That she is here virtually proves her innocence. Had she been forced by John, no power on earth, I think, could have driven her here, and her husband would not permit her to come within a hundred miles of the king."

Justin laughed harshly and Lissa said, "I am not an innocent. I know the pressure that can be applied to a woman to do what she does not wish to do."

"There can be none applied to you from this day forward," Justin said softly. "Not by any man who wishes to go on living."

"I thank you, my love," Lissa responded, stretching a hand to him across the table and repressing a shudder.

She was both thrilled and repelled by the cold ferocity that needed neither shouting nor violent gestures to carry conviction. He meant to reassure her, but such a promise could only add complications to her life. His lips touched the hand she had offered him, and she withdrew it gently, wondering whether he included himself among the men who must not apply pressure to her and hoping she would never need to discover the answer.

Partly to avoid thinking about a conflict of wills with Justin, Lissa returned to her original point. "But what I meant to say was that none would believe Vesci's excuse a second time."

"Not unless he said the king sent for her and Lady Margaret went willingly," Justin remarked, his lips making a thin line with downturned corners. "Many women go willingly to John's bed, not only because they hope to gain his favor but for pleasure."

"But Justin, who would believe that the king had summoned her?" Lissa protested. "King John may be accused of doing foolish things, but it would take a drooling idiot to summon Vesci's wife at this particular time."

"I said Vesci could use it as an excuse for rebellion. I did not say anyone would need to believe it." Justin's eyes were cold and gray as dirty ice. "Those who wish to be rid of the king and those who will be loyal to him do not need to be convinced. Their minds are already set. Of course, if a letter could be produced—"

"How could such a thing be done?"

Justin shrugged. "When many orders or summonses are written, sometimes the signatures or the seals are set on the parchment first. Then if the scribe leaves a little too much space the true letter can be cut away and something else written there. Seals can be forged also, or used without the owner's knowledge, although I have never known anything like that to happen with the king's seals. They are carefully guarded, made by, and entrusted only to those above suspicion. But John is more hated by his nobles than any king in my memory."

They were both silent for a little while; then Lissa said, "I think I will go to see Lady Margaret. I cannot help her, but perhaps she needs someone to listen." She saw Justin about to protest and added, "Not about the king and her husband. She never speaks to me of such things or of matters of state. She is too proud for that. But small things that trouble her—of pain in her teeth, or that her skin is too dry. There is a comfort in talking of little sorrows and finding some help for them."

"There is no harm in what you offer, if that is all, and there might be good in Lady Margaret thinking well of you. But do not let her confide too much in you, even matters of a purely

personal nature, unless you are sure y⌐
turn on you."

Lissa nodded. "It makes for an uneas⌐
secrets of the soul have been bared. You ar⌐
her go too far."

Only after she said that did Lissa wond⌐
Margaret would be in the house she and her hu⌐ ⌐ ⌐each
time he had come to attend the king's court i⌐ ⌐ne past. She
mentioned this to Justin, who said at once that it was not far out
of his way and that he would escort her there. If Lady Margaret
was not living there, he would go on, leaving two men to see
her to whatever other places she wished to try. Lissa objected
only mildly, pointing out that he was mounted and she had no
horse, which Justin solved by saying he would borrow Adela's
riding mule.

Lissa did not think she needed an escort, but she did not feel
much like walking and she saw no reason to quarrel with Justin
about borrowing the mule and escorting her when accepting
would allow them to be together longer. She also felt that if the
men who had invaded Peter's house grew to regret having
allowed her to survive, they would take action soon or not at all.
She was not much afraid, just enough to be glad of the guard
Justin offered.

Her interview with Lady Margaret did not answer any of the
questions Justin had asked, mostly because Lady Margaret
exclaimed quite kindly at her first sight of Lissa that she hoped it
had not been her request that had caused Lissa's bruises. The
sympathy, accompanied by an unexpected warmth that had
replaced the lady's usual haughty manner, increased Lissa's
reluctance to pry. Moreover, in her haste to assure Lady
Margaret that she did not permit herself to be misused in such a
way, Lissa told the tale of the thieves who had wrecked her late
husband's house.

To Lissa's surprise, because she imagined so high a noble-
woman must live a life more exciting than her own, Lady
Margaret was quite thrilled by the "adventure," and asked a
great many questions. So, although Lissa could not find an
opening to discover whether the lady had come from Windsor,
for which she did not have much heart by then anyway, she did
have the satisfaction of knowing that she had pleased her client.

most forgot the creams in the comfortable give-and-take their talk, and it was Lady Margaret who called Lissa back and reminded her, this time with a pleasant smile so that the words lost any sting, that she was a businesswoman with a living to make. She asked for two more pots of each cream then, and when Lissa protested that she might be using too much, her eyes grew sad and she shook her head.

"I use them as you told me, but it may be . . . a long time before I come to London again," she said.

Lissa did not answer that, only saying that she would send the creams as soon as they were ready and, if Lady Margaret was no longer in residence, would see that the pots followed her if she would leave a message to say where they should be sent. Her eyes dull, the lady nodded and then waved a dismissal. It was only as she left the room that Lissa realized it was strangely bare. There were no tapestries on the walls, only the one chair in which the lady sat, and two stools. And when she went down she saw that all the litter of a nobleman's existence was missing from the hall. There was no extra armor, no squires working over men's or horses' harness with one ear cocked for a bellow from above—well, the lord and his squires might be out, but there were no hawks or empty perches, no racks of boar spears—only a small fire burned in the large hearth, the dais was empty, and everything that was in the hall clearly belonged to the five rather elderly men-at-arms.

Vesci was not with his wife, Lissa concluded, and Lady Margaret's movements were somehow tied to those of the king. Lissa did not know the whole story and did not want to know it. She wished now that she could go home at once to begin preparing her creams and settle matters with her father. However, she had to return the mule and collect Witta, and as soon as she showed her face at Goscelin's house, Adela was there, insisting she stay to eat with them and tell her all that had happened.

Adela had been too kind for Lissa to refuse, so she did her best to content the goldsmith's wife without saying anything of note. There was no way to escape admitting how bare Lady Margaret's house was when Adela pressed for descriptions, but that did no great harm, since Lady Margaret might well be only passing through London. Still, Lissa was glad when, as soon as they were done eating, she was able to plead much work to be done in starting the creams, beg the loan of a little handcart that Witta could draw loaded with the parchments, Peter's box, her receipt book, and her clothes—all she had left—and leave for her father's house.

Chapter 15

THERE WAS NOTHING OUT OF THE ORDINARY ABOUT THE HOUSE OR shop that could be seen as Lissa came down Soper Lane from the Cordwainery. The plank with its bundles of herbs was athwart the door of the shop, the barrels of pepper in their accustomed places, and Paul was behind the counter holding up a bundle of dried mint for a woman, his head turned slightly to Ninias, who was talking to another. Lissa was prepared for a warm, excited welcome because she knew her father tended to mistreat his servants and she took their part; however, she did not expect that when he saw her Paul would drop the mint or that an expression of terror would come onto his face.

"I am not really hurt," Lissa said, as soon as she was close enough, thinking that it was her bruised face that had frightened Paul, but he only looked more terrified, and then she saw that he was looking beyond her at the two men-at-arms. "Paul!" she exclaimed. "Whatever is wrong?"

"N-nothing," he stammered. "N-nothing." And turning to the woman at the counter, fumbled for the mint again, asking, "Do you like this bunch?"

Unsettled by the nervousness of the journeyman, the customer glanced over her shoulder, saw the waiting men-at-arms, mumbled something about returning later, and walked away. A second woman, who had been sniffing at a peppercorn that she had crushed between her fingers, also walked away after a sidelong glance at Lissa's guards. After a distracted glance at Paul, who was pretending to rearrange the wares with hands that shook so hard the dry leaves were shaken loose from the stems, Lissa turned and smiled at Justin's men.

"I do not know what your orders are," she said, "but as you can see, you will not do my business any good if you stand here. I am sure I am safe now, so you may leave, if that will not cause trouble for you. Otherwise, you had better come inside the shop where the customers will not see you."

After a brief consultation, the men-at-arms decided that their duty was done, smiled in acknowledgment of Lissa's thanks, and walked away. Lissa turned around and caught Paul staring in open-mouthed amazement at their retreating backs.

"Ninias, stay here. As soon as more than one customer arrives, call us. If you are asked, you tell exactly what you saw—and not one word more or I will tweak your ears until you wish you had held your tongue. Paul, come inside, there are two creams I must start at once."

Lissa slipped past the barrels and gestured for Paul to enter the shop. She turned back to Ninias to bid him tell Witta, who was just in sight at the end of the street, to come in through the back alley and wait by the garden gate until someone could let him in. By the time she entered the shop, Paul was grinning at her with every evidence of the joy she had expected in the beginning. Exasperated, she grasped Paul's arm and shook it. "What the devil is wrong with you?" she asked, her voice too low to carry but the irritation in it like a scream.

"Nothing now," he replied eagerly, still smiling, and holding out to her a heavy bunch of keys. "It was only . . . I found these keys on the counter when I woke this morning. I swear it was just dawn, but your father was already gone. I went up to give him the keys—well, you know he sometimes takes more wine than he should—and he wasn't there. His clothing was gone too, all of it, and nearly all of the rare spices. All the saffron is gone, all the cumin, and the flask with the sleeping potion too. When I saw the men-at-arms behind you, I was sure he had been caught in some bad crime and that they had come to arrest him. And I thought they would blame me for not holding him and account me an accomplice—"

"Do not be so silly," Lissa snapped. "How could you hold your master? And as for being his accomplice, your face would protect you. No one who looks so much like a hooked cod could be other than a dupe."

Paul looked so shocked—for he was accustomed to support, not blame, from Lissa—that she laughed. The situation was not humorous, however. She was sure, as she hurried up the stairs, that she would find empty money boxes. What she did not expect was that the chest below the shelf for the money box would also be empty—not a scrap of parchment or a tally stick remaining. All the rare spices gone and not a farthing to put down on account to buy replacements. All records of the debts owed to the shop, gone. All proof of payment of debts owed to others, gone. Lissa stood staring into the empty records chest and cursing her father with every vile disease she had ever seen or heard of.

Lissa was not really surprised that her father had taken all the money. Now that she thought back on the conversation they had had, she knew she should have read the signs of nervousness, felt suspicious of his easy agreement to her suggestions, and realized that he never intended to wait for her to return to the house. The sleeping potion . . . Lissa shrugged; her father used that often. But why had he taken the records? Out of pure hatred, because he wanted to make keeping the business alive as difficult as possible?

That was mad! The business was his living as well as hers—or was it? Perhaps her father no longer cared whether she came home to run the shop. Because he had found what he was looking for in Peter's house? No, if he found it, why did he bother to come to Goscelin's house to talk to her at all? He had wanted to make sure that she knew he was leaving and would come back. Taking the records was pure spite. Lissa recalled William's real pleasure when he saw her discolored face. Perhaps he had not seen the marks before. Perhaps he had not been involved in that search.

Her heart lifted, then sank again. Perhaps the whole tale he had told about FitzWalter was a lie, and he was fleeing the law. No, he could not have fallen afoul of the law; if he had done so, Justin would have known about it and told her. Then her lower lip slid between her teeth and she stared at the empty chest with fixed attention. She had found what she felt must come closest to the truth: Her father had got some kind of windfall, perhaps some legal but distasteful business that he had kept secret from her, like buying out some young fool's inheritance, and it had suddenly brought him either an estate or enough gold to buy property. With that, he had simply gone away.

Lissa closed the box that had held the records. He had not taken them out of pure spite. He had taken them as proof that the house and business were his, in case he lost what he now had and needed to return to London. When she had got that far, Lissa sat down rather suddenly on the chest she had just closed. Could her reasoning be sound? Could it be true that her father had gone for good? That he did not intend to return and would do so only if he had no other choice? She took back her curses. If he would only stay away, she would wish him the best health, the longest life, the greatest happiness any man could have. She would even send him half, even three quarters, of the profits. She—

"Mistress Lissa," Ninias's treble voice floated up the stairs. "Can you come help at the counter, mistress? There are people asking for you."

"Yes, coming," Lissa called, and ran down to the shop, snatching at a smock that hung near the workroom door.

She smiled like the sun on all those who had seen her arrive followed by two men-at-arms—or had heard about it from others—and had come to discover what scandal was brewing. Lissa was glad to serve them up a fine dish of attack and robbery and threat of future harm, with her bruised face as evidence, just so long as each bought something. And buy they did, for it was only when the coins came into her hands after Paul and Ninias served them, that she told a part of her story to each. The larger the sale the more of the story was told.

After the first rush of those who had actually seen Lissa's return or heard of it immediately, the number of customers diminished and she was able to slip away into the back room to begin preparation of the creams for Lady Margaret and a replacement for the sleeping potion her father had taken with him.

Oliva was standing at the door of the workshop, her eyes down, her shoulders slumped in despair. She expected, Lissa knew, to be punished because she had been William's leman, but she was a good maid and Lissa suspected she had gained little pleasure from her special services, and not much profit either.

"Oliva," Lissa said, "do let Witta in at the garden gate and help him carry my clothing up to my chamber. You will have to look over the clothes. They were treated roughly by those who robbed my husband's house. They will need to be sponged and brushed and checked for tears."

"Yes, mistress," Oliva said huskily. "Thank you, mistress. And—and I am sorry, very sorry for all your hurts."

Lissa could not help laughing at that cautious remark, which committed Oliva to nothing. "I am sorry my husband had to die," she said, wanting matters clear, "but I am not at all sorry to be a widow. Do you understand, Oliva? Peter was kind to me. I had no reason to wish him harm, but there was nothing between us to make me feel great grief either. Now that my father has gone away, I am very glad to be home attending to my own business."

"And I am very glad to have you home, mistress." Oliva hesitated a moment and then said, "There is no food in the house, not even stale bread. Shall I go to the market?"

"Monster!" Lissa muttered, then laughed. "I have not a farthing, Oliva, not a single farthing. My dear father took every coin and shaving of a coin that was in the house, but do not despair. We have already profited from my adventures, and I promise you a rich evening meal to make up for your lack of a dinner." The promise made Lissa think of Justin and the evening meal they had shared the day her husband's body had been discovered. If he had no duty and she could get a message to him, there was no reason they should not share the evening meal again. "Go up and tend to my clothes," she said to Oliva, damping down a somewhat tremulous feeling of expectation. "I have a potion and some creams to make."

As she entered the workroom an old pleasure pushed Justin

to the back of her mind and Lissa stood for a moment looking around with a rich sense of homecoming and contentment. Everything was in its proper place, clean and tidy. There were little differences that told her the workroom had been used. On the broad shelf that served as a workbench, the largest mortar now stood on the right; she always placed it to the left. Also, the large containers of goose grease and tallow were on the counter instead of her own favorite smaller covered pots for each substance.

None of that bothered Lissa; it only showed that Paul stood in a different place than she did to work and that he was taller than she and had no trouble scooping portions from the big crocks. Why then should he bother to fill and refill the smaller ones? She was jealous neither of her tools nor of the place, for this was her kingdom and in it she ruled, no matter how many shared it with her.

Smiling with pleasure, Lissa took from one of the shelves below the workbench a smooth, heavily glazed earthenware bowl with a lip for pouring. From the shelves opposite, she took quart-sized crocks, tightly stoppered with cloth-wrapped, carved wooden tops, each marked with a symbol that matched the one on the belly of the crock. One showed a stylized onion, the other a comb of honey above a teardrop form. With a bronze measuring spoon and a thin, flexible steel spatula, Lissa prepared a base of equal parts of honey and onion jelly, the taste and odor of which were disguised with mint and lemon balm. To this she added juice of aloe and decoction of betony—the betony on general principles, as betony was good for everything.

Then she walked to a part of the wall where the shelves held light woven containers of rare spices. Behind one basket was a keyhole into which Lissa thrust a large black iron key that served as latch as well as lock. The door swung open displaying flasks of varying sizes, and on the bottom some flat leather containers. Lissa did not look at those; they held various roots and seeds, some of which she had not yet even tried to use, from lands whose names she had never even heard. As gifts, her uncles bought for her not only velvets and fine silk veils, but everything any man told them was a drug. Descriptions of each and what her uncles had heard about them were carefully inscribed in her receipt book. Someday she would know them all.

The flasks on the shelves at eye level held powders and decoctions whose uses Lissa knew. In the center a small horn flask was scribed with the stick figure of a man with leaves growing from his head. Mandrake, more precious than gold; that would certainly give anyone sleep, but Lissa did not want to use it. It was too costly. She could add it later to a small quantity of the potion for anyone who could afford the fee.

Farther along the same shelf was a much larger horn, which she took down after a moment's thought. This—poison hemlock—was good in small quantities for inducing sleep. Stronger doses might easily make the sleep permanent, and without much blame to the giver of the dose because each plant steeped produced a different strength. Lissa always made as large a quantity as she thought would not spoil, then tested it on a pig or two. If the dose was too strong, it was a peaceful way for the pig to die, and the flesh was still good to eat.

Lissa measured the proper amount of hemlock juice into the preparation in the bowl and added sweet wine, a few drops at a time, until the consistency was that of a thin syrup. She poured the finished draught into an empty earthenware jug, which she covered with a small piece of oiled parchment tied around the neck with a string. When that was done Lissa set dried roses to steep and, simmering on a hook above the fire, a pot half full of dried chopped mossberries covered with water. The rose water would provide a sweet scent for the hand cream, and the mossberries the red color for the cream for the lips. Witta, who was fascinated by any operation in the workroom, was delighted to attend to stirring the roses and the mossberries and to watch that the latter did not begin to boil over.

That done, Lissa came out to serve behind the counter again, to Paul's great relief. People had heard from others that murder had been done in William Bowles's house and that the mayor's guard had arrested Mistress Lissa. Out of curiosity they were now passing by the shop. Many just went on their way when they saw only Paul, seeming calm and undisturbed, but business picked up as soon as Lissa came out and remained brisk all afternoon. These were mostly farthing sales, but Lissa did not scorn them a bit. Four farthings made a penny, and she would need at least three pennies to get a decent evening meal at the cookshop and another four to provide breakfast and dinner the next day.

It was after she had anxiously counted the coins for the third time, having suddenly remembered that she would need an extra dish and more of each dish if Justin was able to come for the evening meal—and then almost begun to weep when she realized how late it was and that she had forgotten to send any message to Justin's house—that she closed her eyes in disgust. What an idiot she was, counting farthings when all she had to do was go to Hamo Finke and ask for money. It did not matter at all that her father had taken his money; she now had her own!

Paul served a final customer, this one quite genuine, who glanced at Lissa without interest or recognition and snapped at Paul to hurry in weighing out the caraway seed. As soon as he walked away, Lissa put the coins in the purse at her belt and said, "Close up. I will call Oliva down to help you carry in the counter and barrels."

"We have almost an hour to sundown," Paul said, considerably surprised, "and business is still good."

Lissa grinned. "It will be even better tomorrow if we close early today. Can you not imagine how rumor will spread? And I may give more substance for those long tongues tomorrow. I must draw on my dowry so I can pay to replace our spices, which means a visit to Hamo Finke and to the Hanse, and Sir Justin has ordered that for the next week or two I do not go abroad without a guard."

Lissa did not hesitate over Justin's name. While she was mixing potions and measuring out dried roses and chopped mossberries, she had considered at length what to do about Justin and her household. She had concluded that it would be embarrassing and useless to try to keep their relationship a total secret from Paul, Oliva, and the boys. Thus she said Justin's name as she would have spoken that of any other friend and went on to tell Paul that as soon as the stock and counter were safe inside, she would ask him to carry a message to Sir Justin.

"I would not want you to faint with terror if he should decide to come here or send his men for me. We have become friends, and Sir Justin fears I am in danger from those who caused Peter's death and destroyed his house. No, never mind why, I will explain later if I have time. Serve this woman who is coming. If she asks for me, tell her I am tired and in pain and have gone to bed. Come up when you are done and I will give you the note."

When she entered the solar, Lissa was somewhat startled, wondering whether Oliva had somehow divined that she hoped for a very special guest that evening. The room had been cleaned and polished until it looked as if no one had ever set a foot in it before. Even the bed was stripped down to its leather straps; pads, feather beds, and pillows were all gone, the curtains looped back to show the gaunt skeleton. Color flared in Lissa's cheeks with the suspicion that the maid had somehow been privy to her thoughts about Justin and had stripped the bed to remove temptation—as if she would use her father's bed—and that idea brought the realization that the removal of all traces of use in the room had also removed all traces of her father.

Lissa remained still for a moment longer, savoring the thought and then called out. Oliva came from the bedchamber, looking a trifle apprehensive, but Lissa smiled at her and said she had done right to clean the room before she cleaned the gowns. "Whatever still needs to be done with them can wait for the morrow," Lissa said. "Go down now and help Paul close up the shop. I want an accounting of the barter. Out of that, put aside a dozen eggs, a pound or two of barley, and the small hank of thread I saw. Tomorrow I will decide what to do with what else we have."

Oliva ran down to help Paul readily, and Lissa went into her bedchamber where her writing desk stood ready. It was odd, she thought, how reluctant she had been to take anything with her to Peter's house, almost as if she had known the marriage would not last long and it was not worth the trouble to move her furniture when she would only have to bring it back. A chill passed over her, and she told herself firmly not to be a fool. There had been no room in Peter's lavishly furnished house for anything of hers. In the next moment she was suddenly filled with delight by the memory of Justin admitting that he had never furnished his bedchamber and would be ashamed to bring her into it. I will bring it all to him, she thought, and our marriage will last very long.

In that mood writing to Justin was surprisingly easy. Lissa had thought of this excuse and that for inviting him while she worked at her compounding, and wondered whether Justin might think her coarse or bold. But as she pulled a sheet of parchment from the desk and cut a slip off it, she only wondered why she had been so silly and was relieved to discover that the ink in her little horn was still liquid enough to use and her quill did not need trimming. She did not need any excuses for asking Justin to come to her. If she did, he was not what she believed him to be and she would be better off without him.

"My dearest Justin," she wrote, "I am well if you are, and I will be better still if you have no plans or duties this evening and can come to share my evening meal once again, this time in my father's house, south of the Needlers on Soper Lane. You will know the house for that it is all of stone and with a slate roof and there is a ship scribed in the capstone of the door. If you are not home, my journeyman will tell me. Come if you can. If not, we will meet tomorrow when you have time."

Then, of course, worry began to mix with eagerness. She could say he was not the man she thought, but would that cure her feeling for him? Turning her mind from the note she had just rolled and tied with a thread of wool, she remembered her need for money. There was more than enough for tonight's meal, but it would be only mannerly to warn Master Hamo that she would draw on him for twenty shillings, and the goldsmith's house was on Lombard Street, so Paul could just turn north into the Poultry Market and east into Lombard and take that message at the same time.

The journeyman came up just as she finished the note to Hamo Finke, and she gave him both, directing him to Justin's house, which was just past the Mercery, where it turned southward to become Bucklersbury. Master Hamo's place he knew well, for he had carried both messages and coin there while arrangements were being made for her marriage to Peter.

When he was gone, however, there was little left to do but worry. Lissa built up the fires both in her room and in the solar, and sat down in her chair. She knew she should try to think about Peter's affairs. There were the parchments, lying atop her clothes chest, but those debts and payments seemed to be almost part of another life. She could not make herself think about the past when her life might be about to take an entirely new path. She wanted Justin to come, yet she knew that if he did they would almost certainly become lovers. And suddenly her hands were clammy, her mouth dry with fear. Not that Lissa feared the act itself but because she might—naked and silenced—be found wanting.

Nonsense, she told herself; Justin is kind. He will not cast me off if I am not perfect but teach me what he desires—which brought to her the image that called forth such strange feelings in her flesh: a male body, tall and broad-shouldered with a hollow belly and strong, firm thighs (all she had ever seen was a sagging paunch and mottled, swollen legs) and . . . And what, she asked herself, afraid to paint a picture that Justin would not match, what if he takes great pleasure in me? What if he chooses to stay all night?

Being lovers was not the problem. Once their meal was carried up to them, no one would intrude. Although Oliva slept in the solar, she would not come up until any guest was gone. Thus, if Justin did not stay too long, it would be easy. She could simply say that she and Justin had come to know each other over Peter's death and admit, as she had to Adela, that she was considering marriage but that neither he nor she was certain it would be wise. Problems would arise only if Justin wished to remain with her past any reasonable time for a guest to leave. Then Paul and Oliva would guess they were lovers. They would not tell her father—she was almost sure. And she could make it clear that Justin would not like talk linking him and a woman, especially one whose husband was newly dead, before a betrothal took place. Both Paul and Oliva knew there were forces more dangerous than William Bowles—like Justin—and they would hold their tongues.

The boys would be told nothing, except—if they had to carry a message now and again—not to gossip about Sir Justin, who was the mayor's chief thief taker and had methods of dealing with loose-lipped boys. As Witta and Ninias would be closed into the workroom to eat their meal before Justin came and, no doubt, fast asleep before he left, they would not see or hear much while winter lasted. And by summer . . . well, if her father had not sent any message or returned . . . She sat dreaming by the fire until the slam of the door and the sound of male voices made her start from her chair.

Chapter 16

LISSA'S FIRST SHOCK AT HEARING MALE VOICES IN THE SHOP BELOW after trading hours, which brought with it an instinctive and unreasoning sense of fear, was dissipated by recognition. Paul's voice, soft and deferential, was overridden by Justin's harsher tones. She made out what they were discussing as she came to the door of the solar and heard Paul telling Oliva to go up and see if the mistress was sleeping.

"No, indeed I am not," Lissa called down. "When did you know me to sleep in the middle of the day, Paul?"

"When did he know you beaten half to death and still not completely recovered?" Justin said, looking up at her and laughing. "And I have found you unwakable two out of the three times I called on you in the afternoon."

"Monster!" Lissa cried, laughing too. "That is manifestly unfair. Both times I had been awake nearly all the night before."

"You expect fairness, do you?" he asked as he began to climb the stairs.

Lissa watched him, a provocative smile replacing her frank

laughter. "I expect favor," she said, but softly enough so that only he heard her as he closed the distance between them. Then she turned and went back into the solar quickly so that he had room to follow her a little way in, where she turned back and embraced him. "Thank you for coming so quickly," she whispered.

"Why? What has happened? Where are my men?"

"Oh, Justin, nothing has happened." Lissa took his worried face between her hands. The man was so accustomed to being used, she thought, welcome only for his ability to bring peace where there had been riot or protection where there had been fear, that he did not believe his coming alone could be precious to her. "Cannot I be glad you are come only because I so desire your company? And because I am afraid when you are away from me that I have dreamed all this, that we do not fit together like ashlar? Then you come and say something utterly outrageous and make me laugh, and my heart is like a—like a fountain of too-strong ale."

The simile made Justin smile, bringing a vivid picture to mind of the bung being shot from a cask and the ale fountaining up for a few moments and then continuing to bubble out frothily. It was an image of light spirits, and most of him was humbled in grateful wonder that so charming and clever a woman could set aside the fear most felt in his presence and desire him so ardently. One little part, bitter and ugly, remembering others who had insisted he was a delight to them, recalled Lissa's pointed and provocative "I expect favor." What sort of favor? When?

"I am not so sure about that ashlar bit, though," he said very gravely. "As I remember, the stones are fitted so that half of two top stones meet in the middle of each bottom stone. Now, if you are planning to get another woman to share me, I wish to point out that neither of you would be settled in a suitable position to—ouch!"

The complaint was very mild and meek, even though Lissa had bitten him quite sharply on the neck. He knew he had been shocking, but he had wondered how far Lissa would go to get or keep his favor. The painful result was a good sign. He had almost been afraid that she would signify her willingness to share the debauchery he had implied. She lifted her head now to where she could see him and raised her brows.

"Do not allow your lecherous mind to run away with you," she remarked without heat. "I am not at all a generous or a sharing person, and if another woman came into our lives, you might find that no position at all was suitable."

"Are you threatening me?" Justin asked, amused and shocked all at once.

Lissa's eyes widened. It was the only language her coward of a father understood, but it was all wrong for Justin. She put out her hand and said softly, "I suppose I was. Do forgive me, my love. I was not thinking, and it was all a jest. If you want to know why I said ashlar, it is because you are so tall. I had to rise on my toes to place my arms around your neck, and the stone formation in which the top stone overlaps the bottom by a handspan or so at each end came into my mind."

Justin began to laugh again, pulled her tight against him for a moment, and then said, "I will have to take care not to smother you."

"Do you do that often?" Lissa asked.

"That is between me and my priest, or me and God," Justin said warningly, thinking she was about to protest his use of whores.

"I am glad to know you confess, but what do you do with all the bodies?"

Lissa's look of bright-eyed interest was irresistibly comical when coupled with her statement. Justin groaned horribly and squeezed his eyes shut. "If you do not stop teasing me," he said, putting his hands around her neck, "you are going to find out."

She turned her head and kissed one of his hands. "I am so glad to laugh again. It has been a long time—I did not realize how long—since I have truly enjoyed a jest. But we do have more serious matters to discuss." And on those words, she went and closed the door.

"Your visit to Lady Margaret?" Justin asked.

"You are too duty-ridden," Lissa said. "I meant personal matters, but I can say what little I have to say about Lady Margaret first. I learned nothing from her, but I can tell you what I saw myself. Vesci is not with her, and she is very ill attended—I saw only five rather old men-at-arms and two maids—and the house is nearly unfurnished."

"So it seems my first guess was right. She was sent south alone so Vesci could again cry out of being cuckolded by John. But as you said, no one would believe it, not now, unless there were proof. I wonder if there *is* a sheet with the king's privy seal on it and no message." Justin chewed his lower lip thoughtfully, then shrugged. "It is too late to worry about that. John will be leaving Windsor for Portsmouth tomorrow . . . hmmm. I think I will just set a man to watch that lady and see which direction she takes when she also leaves."

"Send Halsig, unless you need him for something more important," Lissa said.

Justin stared at her as if she had turned green. "What did you say?"

"I asked you to give the special duty to Halsig," Lissa repeated, cocking her head questioningly. "Have I done wrong? I meant no offense, and I have no private reason to praise him. It is just that I have spoken to the man several times. He seemed to me to be interested in why and how Peter died, rather than just taking orders dully. He was cleverer than the others. Also, I thought he seemed somewhat disappointed when you dismissed him to his regular duty that morning in Peter's house. Surely such a man could be used for better things than bashing heads."

"But he is the captain of a troop . . ." Justin's voice drifted into silence, and he frowned. "Still, I could speak to him."

"I am sorry if I should not have made a suggestion about one of your men," Lissa said, thinking that she had paid her debt to Halsig and would do him damage if she said more. She was not really sorry she had introduced the subject, however. It was a relief and a delight to learn that Justin was able to reconsider a fixed idea he had, even though he was not accustomed to having women intrude into his business.

And then he gave her more pleasure by smiling at her, although he still seemed mildly surprised, and saying, "No reason why you should not make suggestions about the men. I was only surprised that you should be able to tell Halsig from any of the others. Women tend to avoid my guards."

"I have not had much choice," Lissa pointed out. "And it was

Halsig with whom I discussed meals for the men and such matters. He was very civil and thoughtful of my problems, even polite—"

Justin laughed, then took her by the shoulders and kissed her. "Only you, my love, would worry about whether the watchmen ate or not! Of course Halsig was polite and thoughtful. Often the poor devils must get their own food or go hungry, and are not offered even the simplest meal of bread and cheese, and there you were concerned lest soup and cold meat and ale were not sufficient."

"But that is wrong." Lissa's brow wrinkled. "My mother and my grandfather taught me that fair work deserved fair pay. The men were in a sense working for me—guarding my house and seeking my husband's killer. I owed them—" She stopped and laughed. "What a silly subject. I promise I will make no more suggestions about your men."

"There is no need for that," Justin assured her again. "I will be glad to hear anything you have to say."

"You cannot really mean that!" Lissa exclaimed, her small face gleaming with suppressed mischief. "No man in his right mind would extend such an offer to a woman."

Justin did not make any verbal answer, merely raised his hands and put them gently around her neck. She laughed and then grew sober and exclaimed contritely because they were still standing not far from the door and Justin had not even been invited to take off his cloak.

"Although I would think, my love," Lissa said on a note of gentle reproach, "that you would not need a special invitation in my house."

"I assure you I do not." Justin lifted her chin and kissed her lips. "You gave me such delight that I forgot not only my cloak but how tired I was." With which words he pulled the pin from the cloak, laid the garment in Lissa's outstretched arms, and— without invitation—walked over and sat down in her father's chair, pushing the footstool away with a booted foot to a suitable distance for his long legs. It occurred to him then that Lissa had not moved, and he looked at her and grinned. "What is it? Is it right to take off my cloak without asking but wrong to sit in this— Oh, Lord, there is only one chair. Have I taken your seat?"

"No, do not be foolish," Lissa said, her voice shaking only a little. "But why are you all in mail? Have you been fighting?"

"No, nor do I expect a battle. I was summoned by the mayor to attend the ceremony of appointing a deputy Standard Bearer to take FitzWalter's place, which means, of course, that I never even began, much less concluded, my business with Hamo Finke."

"Who was named deputy Standard Bearer?" Lissa asked and then, before Justin could answer, said, "No, do not tell me yet. We can talk of that at leisure over our meal." She laid his cloak carefully on the stripped bed, placed a stool right beside the chair, and sat down but did not lean against him. "Let us get practical business out of the way before we begin on politics," she said. "I must go to Hamo tomorrow also, and I was going to ask you if I could just take Paul—"

"Unless your business is so private that you do not want me in Hamo's place at the same time, I will escort you myself."

"It is not private at all," Lissa said. "I must draw money to buy certain spices, since my father took some of our stock with him on his journey to use as barter goods. So after I see Hamo, I must visit the Hanse. My uncles are not there, but they have instructed one of the factors, who is always there, to attend to my affairs as if I were one of the brotherhood. I suppose in a sense I am; I have daughter's share from my mother."

"Daughter's share in a Hanse shipping business?" Justin laughed and shook his head. "Let us marry at once, dear heart. I had no idea you were so valuable a prize." Then he looked puzzled. "Why did your father marry you to a goldsmith? That craft is the least likely to profit from or care for your link with the Hanse. A wool merchant would have paid the full value of your dower for you in gold. Even a mercer would have bid high. Why of all men a goldsmith?"

Lissa's lips twisted wryly. "I have no idea, but I assure you that he had his reasons and made his profit. I had expected, since I am a daughter, that he would have married me young to a second or third son of a fellow Pepperer who also would have paid well to have his boy settled into a good business. Many offered and I was very angry when he always found an excuse to turn the offers away." She stopped, blinked, grinned broadly, then jumped up from the stool, leaned down, kissed Justin hard, full on the lips, pulled free before he could grasp her, and said, "Never mind. I am glad now. If he had done what he should, I would be a sour wife with a large nursery instead of a widow dame with free choice."

"I cannot imagine you sour."

"Ah, just wait until you see my face when you tell me you cannot take off that steel shirt and stay to eat with me." Lissa turned her lips down and Justin laughed.

"I do not dare—and do not wish to, but perhaps you do not realize this hauberk is your best protection. Had I been free of it, you might not have escaped me after a kiss like that. I am neither celibate nor saint. Take warning."

"Tell me how to take it off you."

Justin stood up. "It might be better to call your man. It is heavy."

Lissa shook her head, and though she felt herself blushing, she met his eyes. "There may be a time or a reason for not wanting another person. Let me try."

Justin's own color rose, the implication of Lissa's remark being unmistakable, but he made no overt response. He was aware of the care she had taken not to give an open invitation. She was not teasing him now, and apparently she *had* taken warning.

Since Justin had had enough occasions to practice methods of being rid of his mail without much assistance as his old trusted servant grew older and more feeble and, recently, because of his reluctance to use Hervi, the procedure was not difficult. Bending from the waist, he instructed Lissa to pull the hood over his head and the sleeves forward over his hands. As he bent farther forward and backed away, the weight of the mail was added to the force Lissa was exerting, and the whole garment slid off into her arms. She very nearly dropped it, but she had been warned of its weight and had some practice shifting heavy bales in emergencies, so she curled her forearms upward and clutched the hauberk to her chest, letting her shoulders take most of the strain.

A moment later Justin had straightened up and taken the burden from her. He held the hauberk in his left arm as if it were nothing, using his right hand to cup Lissa's chin so he could kiss her as well as thank her gravely for her expert assistance. She laughed at him, but there was something different in the touch of his lips, and as he went to lay the hauberk on the bed beside his cloak, Lissa's courage broke. She fled from the solar and down to the workroom. Just outside the door, she stopped and caught her breath, letting the familiarity of the scene calm her.

The boys were playing some game at one side of the hearth while Paul and Oliva sat talking at the other side. Even the abrupt way the conversation terminated when they heard her footstep was familiar, for she had often seen that happen when she was in the workroom already and her father came to the door. That she was the "intruder" this time was evidence enough to Lissa that the subject of the conversation was Justin or herself or both, since Paul and Oliva had never before felt the need to curtail their talk in her presence.

Lissa had no objection to talk between Paul and Oliva so long as it spread nowhere else, so she did her best to seem unaware of the sudden silence, merely beckoning Oliva to her and stepping into the shop. There she unfastened her purse from her belt and put it into the maid's hands.

"Go to Joseph's cookshop," Lissa said, "and buy the best he has—roast, stew, soup, and enough for all, for six. Sir Justin will eat his evening meal with me. If you think you will need help in carrying the food—remember, you must buy bread and cheese also—take Paul along. Oh, and if Joseph should be curious about the reason for the feast, tell him only that it is a celebration of my father's departure and my homecoming to oversee the business in his absence; Joseph will believe that. Sir Justin, who has high responsibilities, does not like to be the subject of gossip. I would not like it either. Do you understand?"

To Lissa's surprise, Oliva shuddered visibly. "Never you fear, mistress. It would take red hot pincers to drag his name from my lips." She swallowed. "Don't go back up, mistress, stay here. I'll say—I'll say you went out."

"I am not afraid of Sir Justin," Lissa said rather sharply. "He has always been very kind to me, and he is a good man. There is nothing for you to fear either"—she stopped; in her desire to defend Justin and reassure Oliva, she was losing the point, which was that it would be far better for the woman, and for Paul too, to fear Justin—"unless your tongue wags too freely. Gossip can do great harm to a man in Sir Justin's position. Make sure that Paul understands that also. I want no talk of being favored by the mayor's officer among the apprentices and journeymen."

"No, mistress."

"Good. When you return, bring up some of everything for us. After that, you are free to do as you like."

Having stated her lack of fear so firmly, Lissa did not dare linger and display any reluctance to return to the solar. And in a sense she did not wish to delay; certainly she did not fear Justin in the way Oliva meant. Only that last touch of the lips had set off a turmoil in her—not desire, and yet it was desire . . .

Lissa turned away from Oliva briskly and mounted the stairs at a steady, sensible rate. It was fortunate, she thought, that the maid could not see inside her chest where the beat of her heart was neither sensible nor steady. That made her utter a tremulous chuckle, which caught in her throat as she opened the door. Habit had turned her head to the right, for her father was often lying in wait at the foot or side of his bed. William Bowles was not there, of course, but Justin had laid out his mail shirt, with the two hind tails folded back away from the central split and the arms upthrust. Even to a woman as ignorant of fighting as Lissa it was apparent that in an emergency Justin had only to push his head and shoulders under the turned up tails with his arms extended, stand up, and his hauberk would slide down his body into position.

"Why—" she cried, turning her gaze from the ready fighting garment toward the chair by the fire, and then had to catch her breath again.

Justin had removed his arming tunic too, and now wore only a loose shirt over chausses and braies. In sitting down, the shirt and loose pants had been pushed up and Lissa's eyes were caught by the powerful thighs outlined by the chausses.

"Why?" Justin repeated. "Why what?"

Lissa raised her eyes to his face, fear momentarily driving out all other emotions. "Why is your hauberk laid out to be donned at any moment?"

"It always is," Justin said, watching Lissa's face. "That is part of my life, Lissa, and something you must think about. It is not often I am called out, but when I am, it is my way to lead my men, not stand back and call out orders from behind."

"I know that," she said. "I remember how you were scraped and burned from working with your own hands at the fire. There were not many knights and burghers so marked."

"There were more than you think, my love, but that is not the point. The fire was every man's work and every woman's too. Keeping the peace in London is *my* work and it does mean that sometimes I must put on that shirt and wield a sword. I have killed"—he shrugged—"many times. It is no pleasure, but it is no horror to me either."

"I do not care whom *you* kill!" Lissa exclaimed. "What I fear is that someone else will kill you."

Justin shrugged again, but he was smiling as he said, "I am nearly thirty years of age and I am still alive. I am skilled in my profession. I have tourney prizes to prove my prowess in arms."

"That is horrible," Lissa snapped. "Not content with killing those who deserve it, you must take to murdering total strangers?"

Justin laughed aloud at that and held out his hand, and she came to him and took it. But when he spoke his face and voice were very sober. "You prefer to turn all ugly things to jest, but you cannot put this question aside that way. I am a merchant, but I am also a knight. If you cannot accept my position, if you see me spotted and splotched with blood or followed by grinning ghosts, your love will sicken and a canker will grow between us."

She was shaking her head even while he was speaking. "What I said about killing and being killed was no jest. I have no silly notions about such matters. My grandfather died in a fight aboard his ship, and my uncles wear harness and bear swords. One does not sail the world without meeting those with evil intent. I am afraid for you, that is all. I love you. I fear to lose you."

"That is better than feeling I am a leper, but—" He hesitated and then said quickly and harshly, "If this fear will grow and poison your life, Lissa, it is better that we part friends and do not again meet. I wish I could offer, as you once asked, to come to you as a friend only or as a brother, but I cannot. You are too much a desirable woman to me. I must have you in all ways or not have you at all."

"So I feel also, Justin, but you are unreasonable to ask that I predict the future. How can I say whether the sight of your mail laid ready will grow more and more hateful, and I more fearful, or whether I will grow hardened and see it no more than I would see a pair of slippers by the bed?"

"Then what should we do?"

She leaned forward and kissed his brow. "Eat the meal I have ordered my maid to fetch from the cookshop—"

He pulled her forward roughly so that the fronts of her thighs were pressed against the side of his right leg and her hip collided painfully with the arm of the chair. "Lissa—" was all he said.

"And go to bed," she finished.

"Lissa—"

"Whatever comes after," she said, "I wish to know you in every way. If it be only for a little while and then my fear for you grows too great to let us be happy, then we will part and I will endure afterward what I must."

"And I?"

"Are you afraid?" she asked wonderingly.

"Yes."

"You face wounds and death and fear love?"

"I know the pain of wounds, and in death there is no pain. I trust the mercy of my Lord and His Mother. But love . . . To have it, and then have it torn away . . ."

She put a hand on his shoulder and pushed herself back so that her position was less uncomfortable. "You will not suffer, I promise," she said, chuckling. "I will follow the true path I have heard of lovers parting, and by the time we have trod it to the end, you will be delighted to be rid of me. I will take to nagging you to give up your work, and you will tell me to mind my own business, and I will say my lover's life *is* my business, and you will say you are a man and well able to guard your own life, and I will say—"

"Lissa!" he roared, letting go of her so he could gesture more freely. "Is nothing sacred to you?"

"Nothing silly," she said, stepping just out of reach. "And you are being silly. You must know that no matter how great my fear, I could never part from you because of it. How could parting reduce the fear? Instead of being afraid for you only when you were away from me, I would be afraid all the time. You might grow tired of my tears or fearful looks, though I promise I will try to hide them, and decide to end our—"

"Decide? How could I decide to end a marriage? I am not poor, but I am not rich enough to buy an annulment from the pope—"

"Especially when I will be so unreasonable that I would give you no cause—although, of course, I might prove to be barren so that—"

"What are you talking about?"

"I have no idea," Lissa said. "You have not even asked me to marry you, and you are already annulling your marriage to me. I do not take it kindly."

First Justin made a "grrr-ing" noise in his throat; then he folded his hands together and tapped the fingers of one on the fist of the other. Finally he said, "I am very sorry I made you no formal offer. Actually, I thought I had that night in Goscelin's house, but perhaps I did not."

"No. It is something a woman tends to remember."

"Well, you were very shocked and hurt, but I will take your word for it." Justin's voice remained soft, but the tapping fingers moved faster. "But I did believe as I did, and also that you had accepted me. What sort of a man do you think I am to come into your home in the company of one of your servants, speak to another of them, come up here, and remove my clothing uninvited?"

"You were invited to take off your hauberk."

There was a brief pause and Lissa swallowed. That last remark had been unwise.

"Lissa, what sort of a man would expose a woman in that way without intending marriage?"

"Justin, I did not misunderstand you. Truly I never thought you one to use a woman and cast her aside. But you must believe that you have not exposed or endangered me in any way. My servants will not speak of your visit to me, nor will they speak if you make many more visits."

He stared up at her, all emotion gone out of his face. "You bedazzle me, Lissa. You wrap me round and round in a cloud of glittering words and laughter so that I am dazed with a kind of joy I have never known—but I am lost also. Have I asked you to be my wife and been refused? Or is this another of your mad conversations where one annuls before one marries?"

"It is the usual way," she said, unable to resist, "if one desires a second marriage." And then she stepped forward and bent over him and kissed him. "You have not been refused, my dearest, most beloved. I cannot think of anything, except your long life and good health, that I desire more fervently than to be your wife. And yet I will not accept either lest you feel bound in some future time. No"—she put her fingers over his lips—"do not swear you will love me forever; I think it very likely you will because you are as single-minded and stubborn a person as I have ever seen."

Justin was suddenly light and warm and extraordinarily happy. He might not always be able to match Lissa's verbal acrobatics, but he was no fool. He knew Lissa had a secret and it still troubled him that she would not tell him, but now he thought that she was trying to protect him, not herself. She cared for him too much to want him tarred with whatever black brush was poised over her, but she also wanted him too much to send him away to safety. He grinned up at her.

"You mean you dress your hair without looking in a mirror?" he asked.

Lissa laughed, but her voice was sober when she said, "My caution about acceptance is nothing to do with you or with me, Justin." She hesitated and then went on with a rush. "You know my father's reputation is not—not without stain."

So it was fear for him that made her cautious. "That is nothing to do with you," Justin said forcibly, recalling with real shame as he said it that he himself had thought it would not be wise to marry William Bowles's daughter.

"Perhaps, my love," she said, sighing because she knew her father would make it something to do with her. "But that you might be smirched with that reputation troubles me deeply." Again she put her hand over his lips. "No, do not, I beg you, quarrel with me over this now and spoil what we have. Let us put it aside. My father will be away for some time. I have, as you know, an agile mind. Let me try to think of some way to keep him and his doings utterly separate from us. And Justin, you simply *cannot* announce to the world that you are going to marry the chief suspect five days after the latest important murder."

"According to the mayor, there was no murder. Flael did not

die of a blow or a cut, and Roger FitzAdam does not see why his death should be further investigated."

"And the attack on Peter's house did not change the mayor's mind?" Lissa asked caustically. "Well, it has not changed mine either. Someone killed Peter, whether with a knife or a threat makes no difference. Peter was a decent man, and I would like to see that person caught and punished." She turned and sank down on Justin's lap. "That is nothing to do with us, except that I could not accept a formal offer of marriage for a few months anyway, to show respect for Peter, so let us just enjoy being together for a little while without thought of tomorrow."

"But that is not fair to you—" Justin began, only to be interrupted by a voice craving admittance at the door.

"Get the table, Justin," Lissa cried, jumping from his lap to go to the door and pulling it open to find, as she expected, Paul with both hands so full that he could not scratch or lift the latch.

For a little while, all were busy, Lissa fetching a cloth and exclaiming when she saw the silver salt and cups were also gone with her father. But there was a plain pewter dish into which she could empty some salt from the box, and there were pewter and wooden bowls and horn cups and extra wooden platters on which to lay some of the slices of meat Paul had carried from the cookshop. A single glance at the quantity had told Lissa that he had brought everything to her to be apportioned. She did that swiftly, remembering to take half again as much as her father would eat of each dish for Justin, who was bigger and more active.

When their table was laden, she dismissed Paul with what food remained, drew a stool to the table to sit on, and began to serve. As she poured wine, laid meat on the thick round of bread before Justin, and spooned stew into his bowl, something at the back of her mind kept niggling at her. She knew it was a little thing of no importance, and if Justin had not been so passionately devoted to what she had served him and had begun a conversation, she would have forgotten the uneasiness altogether. Justin did mumble an excuse for his voracious attack on the food, that he had had no proper dinner because of arriving late to the mayor's ceremony, but beyond that he made no effort at polite talk.

Lissa let him eat, confining her attentions to refilling his bowl and cup and piling more meat on his trencher, while she consumed her own meal more slowly. The feeling that she had forgotten something remained, however, and she began to feel a spark of concern, wondering if she had left something undone in the workshop below that would spoil her preparations. She let her eyes wander around the room until they returned to the table, and she suddenly remembered that she had told Oliva to divide the meal and send up enough for herself and Justin.

Well, now, that *was* a matter of huge importance to be nagging and niggling at her, Lissa thought, smiling as she piled what remained of the gravy-soaked trencher into her bowl and pushed it away. Why on earth had the matter even come into her mind, she wondered; but she had the answer almost as the question rose, and Lissa's amusement disappeared. The fact that Paul had brought up all the food had troubled her because it was a sign of Oliva's terror of Justin. Lissa caught herself and began to reexamine that wild-leap conclusion, but slower thought processes only made it more certain. There was no chance that Oliva had forgotten an unusual order. It was customary for her not only to divide the meal but to serve it, and she was in general a resigned and obedient creature, not sullen or rebellious. Some extraordinary pressure had caused her to disobey both custom and a plain order, just as the need to be rid of every reminder of her master had driven her to clear all sign of him from the solar before she cleaned Lissa's gowns.

A mingling of ideas sprang into Lissa's mind—first, that she had not realized how much Oliva disliked her father; that was a good mark for the woman. Second, that Justin was as opposite to William Bowles as it was possible to be, yet both Oliva and Adela feared him for no reason at all. Or was there a reason? Lissa sat, turning her cup of wine round and round in her hand and glancing from Justin to the fire. His face was very hard; she could see that the mouth in particular, with its thin, cruel line, promised no mercy. But she had felt the lips full and soft, and she had heard of many harsh acts but never one of wanton cruelty, cruelty without purpose.

At first Justin continued eating, but he was just picking a tidbit from his bowl now and again, and he soon became aware of those repeated glances. He pinched off and popped into his mouth a last, particularly succulent gravy-soaked piece from his trencher, tore off a piece of fresh bread on which to wipe his greasy hands, then lifted his cup of wine and leaned back in the chair. When Lissa's eyes came to his face again, he smiled and asked if he had turned green.

"No," Lissa replied, gazing at him contemplatively. "Truly, you are, if not a great beauty, at least a good-looking man. I know you have a good reputation. I can see nothing about you that should induce fear, yet my maid, who is ordinarily sensible and obedient, sent up the whole dinner rather than dividing it belowstairs as I bade her."

Justin lifted his wine cup and drank. "If you mean she sent it up because she was afraid I would be displeased with the portions she chose for us, that must be nonsense," Justin said. "She is your maid; she must fear you, not me. Likely she just forgot your order."

"I suppose you are right," Lissa agreed, smiling at him; but she did not really agree, she only wanted to soothe the hurt that had flickered across his face and been swiftly masked with the lifted cup. She got up and piled the dishes together, then looked around and said, "Stupid woman, she forgot to send up water for washing our hands. I will just run down and fetch it."

"Do not bother," Justin said. "I should go now. My arming tunic will come to no hurt from a little grease and it will do my mail good."

"Justin!" Lissa exclaimed. "Do not you dare say to me that I invited you to share my evening meal as if that were all I meant. All you want is to force me to ask in crude and blatant words for your body in my bed."

He smiled, but somewhat uncertainly. "That was not my intention. I only wished to give you time for second thoughts."

"Because I said Oliva was afraid—and you thought I was naming what I felt under a new name." She came around the table and leaned against his shoulder. "I swear that is not true. It is exactly the opposite. I cannot see in you anything to fear—"

"And have begun to wonder if you are in some way blinded and whether I am a monster? I do not think so, but I am ready to give you all the time—"

"Justin, stop." Lissa laughed at him. "You *are* a monster. You look so innocent and prate of giving me a choice, but you will not leave me a shred of decency or pride if I must—"

He pushed the table away, nearly knocking it off its supports, and stood up holding Lissa by the shoulders. "You say you are not afraid, but you are. Twice we have come close to loving; the first time you ran away, and just now you tried to run away again. I do not want any sacrifice. Whatever you want of me—"

"Oh, you fool," she sighed, pressing forward against his grip so that she could rest her head on his breast. "Of course I am afraid. I fear you will find me wanting. I am no beauty. I am not the best-formed of women. I have no skill in coupling—to speak the truth, I do not look forward much to it. I found it distasteful, but—"

"Did he hurt you?" Justin asked softly of the bowed head.

"Very little. I told you he was kind. But he was—" she swallowed and then shuddered.

"Old and soft, like a used, dirty cloth?" Justin suggested. "You will find me different."

Lissa looked up and smiled. "Of course. I never doubted that." She hesitated and then went on very softly, "I was sure it would be better with you because I love you and wish to please you. I would not be only doing my duty with set teeth. But what if you find me like—"

She could not bring herself to say it, and Justin burst out laughing. "More likely I will find you like a new shoe that pinches and must be worn soft." He caught at her chin as she began to look down again. "Dearling, I am not the handsomest of men nor the greatest lover either, you know. Women do not tie their sleeves or stockings to my tourney lance—and that is not because they fear I will be beaten and shame them. Perhaps I am not such a novice as you, but only because I am some years older and men do not wait for marriage. We will have to learn together."

"Learn, yes. That I can do. But what if looking on me displeases you?"

"Oh, it will," Justin said gravely.

Lissa gasped in shock. "Why?" she cried. "I am not crooked or clubfooted."

"No, but I prefer my women in the ordinary colors for skin— pink or white or sort of tan. I am sure you will be all purple and blue and green and yellow—"

"Oh!" Lissa seized his ears, pulled his head down, and kissed him, whispering "Monster" against his mouth.

"You see, I am not the only one who can be befuddled by the perfect truth."

He put one arm around her waist as he spoke and turned her toward the door to the bedchamber. Lissa had been about to make a smart rejoinder, but the words died in her throat. However, Justin hesitated again, and it was Lissa who took the first step. She freed herself from his grip as they passed through the door so she could pull it shut behind her, then stood facing him.

"If you will tell me what to do . . ."

"Come to the fire," he said, and bent to replenish the fuel when they stood near the hearth. He straightened up and turned to face her. "Now give me your hand."

She offered her right hand, somewhat puzzled when he lifted it to his lips and kissed the palm; then she gasped when he tickled it with his tongue, but she did not pull away. The next thing she knew, her sleeve was hanging loose, the tie undone. Without further instruction, she offered her other hand. It took quite a long time before Lissa stood only in her shift, but she had been so distracted by Justin's kisses and tickles that she did not give a thought to how the body she was baring compared with others. He ran his mouth up her arm. That bent him forward enough to reach the hem of the shift, which he pulled quite suddenly over her head and flung aside, turning his head to take her nipple in his mouth in a swift, drawing kiss. Lissa uttered a little cry and started back, then stopped and held her ground.

Justin looked her up and down, stepped to the side for an all-around view, smiled at her, and said, "Very neat. I have seen some larger and more curved, but I have no complaint—except about the colors. That shade of puce on your hip . . . I do not favor that at all."

She had lifted one arm across her breast, but she lowered it deliberately. "I will promise willingly to avoid such skin colors if I can, but it seems to me you have an unfair advantage. Perhaps I might find this and that to complain of if our conditions were equal."

"By all means," Justin said with enthusiasm, pulling loose the ties on neck and sleeves and tossing his shirt to the floor.

Lissa said nothing; no smart words would come because he was so beautiful to her. His skin was very fair below the tanned neck, lined with thin blue veins that fed the swelling muscles of chest and upper arm. Across the chest below the collarbone and pointing down to a neat navel, which Lissa could see peeping over the tie of his braies, was a mat of tightly curled light-brown hair. Her eyes ate the strong body, and she felt her skin prickle. Without realizing what she was about to do, she came closer as Justin twisted to pull off a boot; then she knelt and removed it for him. She took off the other and untied his cross garters.

Meanwhile, Justin had untied the waist cords, and as soon as he felt the garters loose, he pushed off all his nether garments in two powerful shoves, presenting a very shocking sight to Lissa, who was kneeling before him. She uttered a choked cry, but before she could leap to her feet, he had knelt beside her.

"I did not mean to frighten you," he said, putting one hand on her shoulder and cupping her face with the other. "Surely you have seen a man ready—"

"Not so ready as you," she said, then giggled softly and shook her head. "No, I never saw a man ready before. Peter tired more easily than I did and always went to bed before me. And if he looked at me, I did not know of it. I—I turned my back."

Justin bent his head so that their foreheads came together. "I did not know," he said softly. "We cannot begin again, but we can study each lesson more slowly."

"Slowly?" Lissa blinked and looked uncertain. "But will not your—your readiness . . . ah . . . depart if we do not hurry?"

Her speech ended uncertainly as Justin let out a roar of laughter and clutched her close. "Oh, no," he assured her. "Master Cockrobin here will not soon tire of standing to arms, especially while he has hope of a soft, warm bed if he remains upright."

Lissa blushed but did not presume to offer any more advice, since Justin's "readiness" was pressed against her belly by his grip on her and certainly gave no evidence of departing. Her awareness had been mostly fixed on that, and she did not notice that the hand that had been on her shoulder had slipped down until it began gently to stroke her breast. Lissa shivered, but this time she did not draw away.

"It does not seem to me that you need any lessons," she said, her voice breathless and trembling.

"I need to know what pleases you," he said.

"*You* please me," she whispered.

He bent his head and kissed the shoulder he had released, then let go of her face and slipped his hand under her arm, pulling her up with him as he rose. "The floor is too hard. Come to bed."

"It—I forgot to have it warmed."

Justin grinned. "We will warm it soon enough, and I will show you a way that you will never know at all the sheets are damp." On the words, he flung back the covers, lay down, and pulled her atop him. "There. Are you not warm and comfortable?"

"Warm, yes," Lissa replied, startled out of her nervousness into merriment. "Comfort is another matter. You are all lumpy—"

She was about to complain about his hipbones and knees, but a smile of such delight and relief greeted her pert words that two revelations came to her simultaneously: Justin thought she meant his shaft when she said "lumpy" and was delighted that she could joke about it, and more important, he was as uncertain about pleasing her as she was about pleasing him.

"Move up," he said, pulling at her, sliding her body along his until her mound of Venus had overpassed his shaft, which was moved against her nether mouth by the motion. A thrill of soft pleasure passed through Lissa. She uttered a sigh and, desiring to keep that warm pressure against her, could not control a small gesture of resistance to further movement. Justin stopped pulling at her immediately and whispered, "Open your legs."

The words were familiar enough to bring a flicker of recalled disgust into her mind, but Justin flexed his body, slid her down against him again, and closed his powerful thighs against hers, imprisoning his shaft between her legs. Instinctively, remembering the pleasant sensation, she moved herself against him. Justin groaned softly. To Lissa's surprise the sound, which could not be mistaken for anything but an expression of intense pleasure, and the fact that he closed his eyes, increased the thrill she generated by her movement. She moved again, and again, felt Justin tip her sideways so he could take her breast in his hand and rub the nipple. That drove her harder and faster against him, bending and twisting until she was, it seemed, rent apart by pangs of sensation radiating from where his shaft touched her and encompassing her whole body. She cried out, and he drew her head down and dammed her mouth with his.

Chapter 17

⌒∽⟲⟳∽⌒

EVEN DAZED AS SHE WAS BY ASTONISHMENT AT A PLEASURE SHE HAD heard hinted at often enough but had come nowhere near imagining, Lissa realized her satisfaction could not be the end of the matter. She knew Justin had not been satisfied; he was caressing her breast with even more fervor, his lips clung hungrily to her mouth, and Master Cockrobin was larger and harder than ever. Her body still ringing like a bell with the echoes of her climax, Lissa understood the torment she would inflict by ending, or even delaying, further love play. Still gasping, she rolled over on her back, determined to complete Justin's satisfaction, even though she felt some trepidation about a rod that seemed four times the size of Peter's.

The bread of kindness cast upon the waters does not always provide an immediate return. In this case, Lissa's pure desire to please Justin yielded rich rewards at once—a proof, in the renewal of her own physical delight when Justin entered her smoothly and easily, that she had no need to fear Master Cockrobin, no matter how tall he stood; and, much to her amazement, after Justin worked awhile, a repetition of her full climactic pleasure, even deeper and richer now that she was filled.

When the lassitude and trembling of that second convulsion of joy eased, she sat up and looked down at Justin. "Thank you," she said.

He opened one eye. "I am not sure yet."

But Lissa, although wrapped in her own sensations, had not been at all unaware of Justin's soft cries of supplication and praise, of his moans of pleasure, and of the final ecstasy that drove him so hard against her that she felt bruised in places she did not think could be bruised. She knew quite well she had not been found wanting. Thus, his enigmatic remark did not disconcert her at all, and she laughed softly and kissed his lips and said, "Of what?"

"Of whether I will live or not." He allowed the open eye to shut. "I have never been drained so dry in my life. I thought my blood would leap out after my seed, but you drew me so, I could not stop."

She laughed again. "I wonder how many times you have said that."

Justin opened both eyes. "Do not be a fool. Since I came to London, more than ten years ago, I have lain with no woman about whose feelings I cared—nor one to whom I was willing to show what I felt."

"Forgive me," Lissa murmured, lying down again close against him. "I warned you that I would be jealous."

"I do not mind that." Justin chuckled softly. "I am not so much desired that I do not take it as flattery, but why should you not believe me when I tell you that you gave me more joy than I have had in any other coupling?"

"Because you gave me so much pleasure. How could you know what to do if you had not long practice with women?"

"I did not say I was celibate." He shrugged. "I am no better or worse than any other man, except that I have never thought it safe to have a mistress or repeat too often my visits to any one woman. Familiarity can breed a kind of dependence and a kind of looseness of the tongue, and neither is safe for me. But I did not learn what I did with you from the women I use, or not much of it. I only did what gave me pleasure."

"I hope my urges have as successful an outcome," Lissa said thoughtfully, looking down the length of Justin's body, which was outlined under the covers.

"Now?" Justin asked, then his color rose and he added apologetically, "I am sorry. I am not sure I am ready yet."

Lissa drew her head back to see his face better. "Of course not now! You are not jesting? People begin again? Well, you need not say you are sorry to me. I am sure I am not yet ready. I am just trying to gather strength to get dressed and—"

"Not so soon," he pleaded, sliding an arm around her and pulling her closer. "Lie here with me in comfort for a little while—or is it not safe? You said your people would not talk."

"It is safe." Lissa relaxed against him. "I do not think they will have finished eating below. And even if they are done, no one will come until I call or you go out. Nor will they talk, no matter what they see, hear, or guess. Getting up has nothing to do with them. I was thinking of gathering up the scraps for the beggars—a stupid task that can wait. I have the bad habit of always being busy with something."

"Then be busy with this," Justin said, settling Lissa's head comfortably in the hollow of his shoulder. "Why did the mayor insist on appointing a deputy Standard Bearer when the troops London is required to send the king are gone already with FitzWalter?"

After only the briefest hesitation, Lissa replied, "Because the mayor desires more troops to be trained. Plainly a Standard Bearer, deputy or no, must have troops to follow the standard."

"So I thought myself," Justin agreed, but his voice was sour.

"You do not like it," Lissa stated; that was clear enough, but she was not willing to guess further. "Why?"

"Why?" he echoed in surprise. "Do you not smell rotten fish? The city is not as a rule so generous as to prepare troops before the king sends an order, and to have the men trained under FitzWalter's son-by-marriage—"

"Ah, I did not know that," Lissa interrupted. "If you remember, I stopped you before you told me who was invested as deputy. So it was William de Mandeville, Lady Christina's husband." She hesitated and then said, "I do smell bad fish. From this and that remark made by Lady Christina in my hearing, I understand Mandeville is married more to FitzWalter than to his daughter. You say FitzWalter's spite against the king is undiminished. The troops will learn to obey orders from Mandeville. Will they know whether those orders support or defy the king?" She hesitated again and then asked, "Justin, is it a safe thing to hold office under this mayor?"

He was silent for a time, then said, "You must not ask me that." There was another silence, after which he added slowly, "I do not love Roger FitzAdam. He is weak and sometimes surprisingly foolish for a man who has done so well as a merchant. He bends too easily to pressure. I do not know whether he does not understand the result of a large troop in the city that calls Mandeville master or whether there is something else in his mind. In truth, I think it more dangerous to be ignorant than to be close and able to watch what goes forward. But even if that were not so, I do love London and I can see no other way to help protect my city than to hold my place as long as it is possible. If you are fearful, perhaps—"

"Not for myself." Lissa put her arm over his chest and hugged him. "At least, not more than for any other person in the city if general ill comes of London being set against the king. That is what you fear, is it not?"

"Yes. As I have said before, King John is not a good man, but he has not been a bad master to London." Justin shrugged suddenly and said briskly, "It is certainly not a problem we must face tomorrow. Raw troops do not train in a day, and I do not believe Mandeville has the money to pay them. If the mayor and his party withdraw their support, the scheme will die a quiet death."

"Are those who support FitzAdam so powerful now that your uncle's old party has no influence?"

"We all supported FitzAdam for lack of being able to agree on anyone stronger," Justin said, lips twisted wryly. "And this is another case where it was more indecision than lack of strength that held us back from protest." He stared past Lissa and sighed. "No one trusts the king. I said John had not been a bad master, but much of what London has gained from him has been yielded grudgingly because he was always in trouble and London always had something he wanted or needed. Now that he has made his peace with the pope—he has indeed become the apple of Innocent's eye—and has raised a powerful army, many fear he might be less accommodating. He might even wish to take back the rights and privileges he has granted the city. Think, Lissa, if the king is successful in his war in France, and if he and his German allies do succeed in catching Philip and Louis between them and crushing them so that they cannot be a danger to anyone for many years, what will be left to check John? What favors would he need? We might then be glad of trained troops in the city."

"If he were that powerful, would troops protect us?" Uneasy, Lissa freed herself from Justin's grip and sat up, frowning down at him.

"Not if he were really determined, of course," Justin admitted. "But to break the city if the walls were well defended, John would need to spend a fortune in gold and thousands and thousands of lives. Even then it might take years. Why should he pay such a price when he need only be reasonable in what he asks? The troops ensure that the city *can* resist too-great pressure and thus make the demands on us more moderate."

"And if the king's war is not a success?" She lowered her voice and asked softly, "Did you not tell me that you feared FitzWalter might have chosen to lead the troops of London just to fail at a crucial moment and ensure the king's defeat?"

"It might be his intention, but he will not succeed in that. He is being watched. I am not privy to everything, but I believe he was even allowed to know he was being watched. However, if FitzWalter is more subtle than to preach open rebellion, he has ways enough to do damage. He can in private remind the barons of John's laxity or bad luck in 1204 when Normandy slipped from his hands, and he can point out that John could at any time go back to England, leaving them to face Philip and Louis."

"But if the king is defeated, would that not endanger FitzWalter himself?"

"I never thought FitzWalter a coward, although that has been said of him. I doubt he would worry about the danger. More likely he would think it a chance to wipe out that old stain on his honor. FitzWalter could even protect himself from being again accused of treason by fighting bravely for John, covering himself with glory and a cloak of loyalty—and still obtain the king's defeat." He made an irritable sound. "I was angry yesterday at my cousin and two of my uncle's friends because they bade me hold my tongue over Mandeville's appointment. I had no right. I do not know *what* I want." He levered himself up so he could lean forward and kiss her. "It is time for me to go, I think."

"Stay a little longer," Lissa begged, sliding an arm around his neck and twisting to press her body against his.

"Once more, then." He began to kiss her throat and let himself slide flat, carrying her with him. "I am a little curious about the way you looked at me before we began to talk of the new troops and what you desired to do to me."

"No hurt, I assure you," Lissa murmured.

She let her hand run down along the hard muscles of his shoulder, and from his strong upper arm to the broad pectoral, which she outlined with her fingers. From there, reaching the hollow of the breastbone, she followed that to his navel, and so down. Justin twitched and sighed, lifting his hips slightly in a sensuous invitation that Lissa accepted with an eager excitement she tried to conceal by casting doubting glances at him. His encouragement, not only to touch freely but to allow her lips to follow her hands, was so enthusiastic that the covers slid to the floor; however, both enjoyed the exploration so fervently that neither felt cold until some time after they had subsided into exhausted satiety.

Eventually the chill of sweat on her naked body drove Lissa to reach a languid hand down for the covers, but Justin caught her arm and pulled it back. "We must get up," he said. "You can straighten the bed after we are dressed."

"We have time to rest." Lissa shivered slightly and, not really thinking, only desiring warmth, turned so that more of her body was touching his.

Justin held her against him and chuckled. "Yes, there will be time to rest, but after we get our clothing on. If I lie here"—he nuzzled her neck and stroked her buttock—"I will be at you again as soon as Cockrobin can lift his head, and then I will not have strength enough to crawl home after."

"Do you wish to stay?" Lissa asked softly, not knowing what answer she wanted.

"Yes," Justin said promptly, and in the next breath, "No—at least, not unless you will marry me at once."

"Justin, you know that is impossible—"

"It is not. I can walk out of this house, go down to Saint Anthony's, bring back a priest, and we can be married. How is that impossible?"

Lissa extricated herself from his arms, slid out of the bed, and began to straighten the tangle of clothing that lay on the floor by the hearth. She had just drawn out her shift when Justin came up behind her and pulled her upright against him. She could feel that his shaft was beginning to harden again. Lissa turned around in his arms and said, "My people will be silent, I promise you. If you wish to stay, no word of it will come out of this house. You know why I say marriage is impossible."

He stepped back and bent, first to kiss her lightly and then to pick up the shift she had dropped. He pulled that over her head, then kissed her again. "I do not distrust your people. Unfortunately, my man, whom I do *not* trust, was there when your journeyman brought your message and like a fool, instead of looking at the note I asked who Paul was. Then I should have written you an answer or told Paul I would stop to see you 'on my way,' but I—I—"

The light was only that cast by the fire, but Lissa saw Justin's complexion darken and knew he had colored strongly. She could not tell, however, whether he had blushed with embarrassment or with rage. "What did you do?"

"Like a lovesick moonling, I gave my helm and shield to Hervi and said I would walk back with Paul at once. So my man knows who you are and that I was not going to your house on business."

"He cannot know that," Lissa said soothingly, "only that you did not expect to fight a battle here. In any case, what does it matter?"

Justin said nothing until he had lit a splinter and from that the two tapers that flanked the hearth. Then he turned to look at Lissa. "You fear the talk that would rise if we married so soon but do not fear gossip that could name me your lover?"

"What gossip?" Lissa put more wood on the fire and then picked up Justin's shirt but did not hold it out to him. "Say you stay with me. Say your man does have a loose tongue. All he knows is that my journeyman came for you, you went with him in haste, and you did not come home. Surely you have done that before in response to summonses from others—solved their problems, listened to their troubles, and then gone on to your pleasures. I promise there will be voices enough to swear you left this house at a reasonable hour."

He took the shirt from her hand. "Not this night, dearling. You make a good case, but I do not like to ask people to lie for me, especially not serfs and journeymen who may be tortured without a second thought for revenge that might be taken. Not that where I sleep is likely to become a matter of great enough importance to torture anyone for an answer, but it makes me uneasy to know a lie may be needed. I will go home and lie in my cold, hard bed—" Justin had been mocking his reluctance to leave in tones of drawling self-pity, when a pleasant idea occurred to him and he said much more briskly, "Which reminds me, I must now order a bed, and how are we to arrange your choosing of it? We should not delay—"

"Why should you order a bed?" Lissa asked. "Do you have some complaint about the bed in which we lay?"

"Of course not, but—"

"This was my mother's chamber, and the furnishings are of her choosing. It is now mine, part of my dowry. I did not take it with me to Peter's house because"—Lissa's voice grew fainter and slightly uncertain—"because Peter had a fully furnished house and . . ."

"And you did not wish him to sleep in your bed," Justin finished. "We will talk no more about a new bed. I will be honored to have our bedchamber so furnished."

The reason Justin gave had never entered Lissa's mind, and she was both surprised and a trifle amused by the hidden jealousy that was its cause and the self-satisfaction of his tone. However, it was true enough; had she thought of it, Lissa knew she would not have wanted to lie with Peter in her own bed.

Justin had put on his shirt while he spoke and pulled on chausses and braies. Lissa tied his sleeves and neck ties and picked up his cross garters, but he took them from her hands and told her to dress herself because she was shivering. Lissa did as she was told, grateful for what she believed was Justin's steady consideration for her, and he was ready to lace her tunic and sleeves when she needed help. He had just come back into the bedchamber from the solar where he had gone to build up the fire—which they would have done if they had not left that room—and helped her restore the bed to at least outward order.

Even after all was ready, however, they could not bear to part, and Justin pushed the table aside so that Lissa could sit beside him on the stool. Their fingers twined together, hand stroked hand, as they talked quietly of when they would meet on the morrow and what business should be done first.

There were some words that were not completely loverlike; Lissa first thought Justin too protective for her taste when he said he would come and escort her to the goldsmith's shop, and she asked him if he planned to be her gaoler. To which he retorted that she was a ninny. If she asked her journeyman to escort her to Hamo Finke's house, in whose hands did she plan to leave her shop while they were both gone? The maid's? The apprentices'?

Lissa had forgotten momentarily that no one but Paul or she could serve in the shop; however, even if Paul could not escort her, she did not really want Justin to be seen too often by neighbors who might mention him to her father. Since she could not admit that to him, she suggested tentatively that she would be riding. Justin acknowledged that was safer than being afoot but reminded her that if the men who had searched Peter's house wanted to harm her, they would lie in wait at her doorway to follow her and do their work as soon and swiftly as they could; they would not wander around London hoping to catch sight of her.

They compromised at last. Justin would send a man to escort her to Hamo's and from there would take her care into his own hands. To the latter she agreed readily, since she intended to introduce him to her uncles' factor and see whether some favors—on both sides—could be arranged. If the factor would see to it that Justin's trading affairs with merchants of the Hanse were attended to fairly and courteously, Justin would see that Gamel and Gerbod were not beaten unnecessarily by the watch nor detained longer than it took to get a message to him.

"I will even promise that the watch will not lay a hand on your uncles," Justin added.

"Oh, do not promise that!" Lissa exclaimed, laughing. "You do not know Gamel and Gerbod. It is often not possible to stop their merrymaking without applying a cudgel firmly to their heads. What I am most anxious about is that they be let go as soon as they are sober and have paid their fines, or if they are without funds that I be summoned and told what to pay. Several times each has been held so long that cargoes promised to them were lost. Perhaps that was the purpose of holding them, but such delays are costly to me also, and I hope they can be avoided."

"Your uncles must 'play' with considerable spirit," Justin remarked mildly. "I am looking forward to meeting them."

Not before I get to them and explain this and that, Lissa thought, but all she said was that she expected Gamel sometime in May.

"We will marry then," Justin said, getting to his feet suddenly. "You will have a man of your own blood to look over the contract and to support you. I will not wait longer than that, Lissa."

She stood up too, and he held her against him and kissed her hard. He was aroused again, which surprised her because, to her mind, there was nothing in what they had been saying that was exciting. All she could do was ask again if he wished to stay, but he put her aside almost roughly and went to the bed where, his back to her, he donned his arming tunic.

"Shall I—" Lissa began.

"Stay where you are and leave me alone," he said.

With his back still to her, Justin bent forward and slid his arms up inside the hauberk, opening it and lifting it so his head and shoulders could follow. The bed was too low for him to slide into the garment easily, and Lissa twitched to help him, biting her lip. He pulled back and wriggled forward twice before he forced his body far enough into the limp mail to stand up and let it slide down him. Finally he belted on his sword, pulled his cloak around him, and turned back to face her.

"I still have FitzWalter's business to do tomorrow after we are finished at the Steelyard. Will you want me to bring you home?"

"No, I am going there to look at what stock is held by my uncles' factor, if any. Then I will go on to see what others have. Master Wilhelm will escort me himself if he can. If he cannot, as it is such short notice and he may have other business, he will send one of his servants. I will promise, if you like, not to go unescorted, but I doubt anyone would follow me once I am seen with you, so—"

"Am I to come here later or not?" he interrupted, his voice almost metallically harsh.

Lissa ran forward and took his face in her hands. "Justin . . ." She shook her head sharply, let go of him, and stepped back. "We will only quarrel we talk any more tonight. Do not be a fool. Of course I expect you tomorrow—as soon as it is dark. I will wait so we can eat together. I do not care about dinner; I can eat with my people or eat alone—dinner is business. But the joy of sharing the evening meal . . . I will wait, Justin, until you come, whenever it is."

"I will do my best not to be late, but I cannot always be sure—"

"I understand," she said, and went back to the fireside to take a candle and lead him down the stairs.

The door to the workroom was open, and Lissa could see two dark silhouettes seated before the fire as she held the candle up so Justin could lift the bar on the door. Justin had apparently seen them also and suspected, as she did, that they were listening intently. He said a polite good-night and then, one corner of his mouth twitching, thanked Lissa gravely for her kind entertainment. Gazing straight into his eyes, Lissa said, with equal gravity, that she had never had a guest it was less trouble to entertain—and stamped heavily on Justin's foot. There was an odd, gasping noise as he passed through the door, but Lissa did not try to discover the exact cause of the sound, only closed the door and called out to Oliva to set the bar again and make ready for bed.

The next evening it was both harder and easier to part. The anxiety was less because each was more trusting, more sure of the partner's steady affection—and sexual enthusiasm. The pain was greater because they were even more eager to remain together, whether for simply talking over the events of the day or for exercising newfound ways of making each other half mad with lust.

By the time Justin finally staggered to the hearth and pulled on his clothes, it was very late, and Lissa did not bother to dress. She only drew on a bedrobe so she would not freeze when she walked downstairs with Justin to have a few more moments with him. Paul and Oliva would not talk. Justin was not worried about how late it was either, although he refused to stay the whole night because he never did so in the houses in Southwark where he went to buy his pleasure with women. That was where he had arranged that Hervi be told he had gone. It was simple enough.

Justin took a breath preparatory to pulling the door open and stepping out into the freezing air. Then he remembered something he had been meaning to tell Lissa all day, and he turned back to her. "You were right about Halsig," he said, giving in and leaning on the door. "He was very pleased to be set to watching Lady Margaret. He had a few excellent ideas on how to approach her men-at-arms. And, from some things he said, I think he would like to take service with me directly."

"Is that possible?" Lissa asked, showing her knees were as shaky as his by leaning on him.

She seemed to be keeping her mind on the subject better than he, Justin thought, because she went on, "I think Halsig is a man you could trust, and you said you did not like your present servant."

Not to be outdone, although warmth was spreading insidiously from his loins throughout his body, Justin said calmly, "True enough, but I like Hervi's woman, and I think life would be hard for her if I dismissed them."

"Will you let me know where Lady Margaret goes?" Lissa asked, then lifted her head and kissed him under the chin, whereupon Justin said "Traitress!" pushed her away, and went out.

Lissa laughed softly as she pulled the door shut and dropped the bar in place. Then she looked toward the workroom. That door was open, as it had been the night before, but the fire had been banked and there were no seated silhouettes. Lissa hoped Oliva had come up softly to the solar and taken her bedding while she and Justin were in the bedchamber. Something about the maid's behavior had been tickling Lissa's mind these past few days, but she was too tired just now to worry about it. She had no intention of calling Oliva when she did not need her help either to undress or to warm the bedclothes, and the last thing Lissa wanted was to talk to anyone; she had barely strength enough to crawl up the stairs and into bed.

The next day she was almost too busy to think about Justin. It was long after dark—not until she bade Oliva take food up to her chamber while she covered and put away the last of the medicines she had been preparing for sick customers—when she realized how very late he was. It did not trouble her; she never doubted he would come. And to make sure he would not doubt she waited, she set a taper where it would shine through the half-open shutter of her bedchamber window. Then she allowed herself to doze in her chair, smiling as she drifted off to sleep because she was simultaneously thanking God that Justin had not arrived and she could rest and also thanking God that she would be in his arms again very soon. She thought she would hear his knock and be down the stairs in time to let him in, but Paul or Oliva would admit him if she slept too soundly. It was useless after last night to pretend he was not her lover.

A grumbling belly woke her. Lissa nibbled on bread and cheese, taking care not to eat her fill so that whenever Justin came, if he was hungry, she would be able to eat with him. Even when she heard the bells for Compline her only concern was that Justin would be terribly cold and tired—and in no mood for interruptions, whether he wanted to eat, sleep, or love. She thought a moment about the wisdom of what she wished to do, then shrugged and called down to Oliva.

The maid seemed frightened when she came up, which puzzled Lissa until she guessed, after Oliva had helped her to undress and put on a warm bedrobe and slippers, that she had expected to bear the brunt of Lissa's disappointment in her lover. That amused Lissa very much, but she did not try to disabuse the maid of her notion, only told Oliva to take her pallet and blankets down to the workroom because she would be sleeping there in the future.

The woman's lips parted as if she were about to protest, but Lissa's ears, keen with expectation, caught the sound of a horse's hooves on the hard frozen street. "Go!" she ordered scooping up the bedding, thrusting it into the maid's arms, and shooing Oliva before her down the stairs. She shut the workroom door firmly behind the maid, and ran to unbar the front door. There had been no knock, but she thought she heard a horse stamp, and Justin might be waiting to see if he would be let in without knocking.

Lissa's first sight and smell of him taught her that the hesitation was less consideration on his part than a difficulty first in dismounting (he was somewhat muddied along one side) and second in finding the door (as she opened it, his shoulder struck her nose and he fell in on her). He made a wordless sound to which Lissa replied sharply, "If you are going to vomit, do it in the street."

"Certainly," Justin replied, with enormous dignity. "There can be no chance of my doing otherwise, since I do not intend to come in."

"You are in already," Lissa pointed out, wrestling him upright with some effort. "And you are bringing in the horse too." She pushed him back against the frame of the door. "Stand there. Can you stand there?"

Hoping for the best, she ran to the workroom door, flung it open, and shouted for Paul to take the horse to the stable. She then wrested the reins from Justin, tied them to the metal U that held the bar, perforce leaving the door open, and led Justin toward the stair. The horse's nose quivered and it advanced into the shop, drawn by the herbal odors. It was just lipping up a bunch of something when Paul came running.

Justin sat down on the stair. "This is not a sensible arrangement," he said thickly. "I should not be here, but I knew you would wait all night if I did not come. It was those accursed ship captains—"

Lissa could not help laughing. "I know all about ship captains, but you could have sent me a message. I understand that business must come first. I would not have been angry."

He hung his head. "It was not business," he muttered. "They insisted I celebrate their successful voyage with them, as FitzWalter does. I know I should have sent a message, but I hoped I could get free of them. I wanted . . . I wanted you."

Lissa was resigned to the fact that men would drink too much, but she had still been shocked and annoyed when she first realized that Justin was drunk. The fact that he was so apologetic and showed no tendency to violence reassured her— the only time her father had more courage than a rabbit and became dangerous was when he was drunk. Amusement had soon become her predominant feeling, and when he hung his head like a scolded child, she could not resist the mixture of guilt and desire he displayed.

"Can you get up the stairs without falling, or do you want to

wait for Paul to help you?" she asked, pushing back his hood
and then his tumbled hair. "You are too heavy for me."

"I should go home."

"I doubt you would get there."

"The horse knows the way—I think."

Lissa shook her head and gave him a quick hug. "Let us not
make the experiment. I value you too much to take the chance
that you would freeze, and I do not wish to send Paul out with
you. Come up and sleep for an hour or two."

Chapter 18

JUSTIN WAS IN NO LAUGHING MOOD WHEN LISSA WAKENED HIM before full dawn the next morning, yet he managed to summon up a twisted smile at the haste with which she offered him the pot. He promised he would not vomit on the lovely carpet by her bed, and though he first resisted the cup she held out to him in her other hand, he drank when she insisted. By the time she had retied his cross garters and pulled on his boots, he had used the pot for its usual purpose and said, in a much more cheerful voice, that there were hidden benefits he had not considered to marrying an apothecary's daughter.

"There are," Lissa agreed, and bade him sit while she wrapped a cloth around his head. "You can take this off on the way home. But for now, you are an early client who has broken his head. Paul has your horse at the door."

"That means you will not let me to take you to mass."

Lissa shook her head. "It is too dangerous. My neighbors know by now that I have come home, and I will be expected at Saint Anthony's. I am well known there. To come escorted by a

251

strange man so soon after my widowing would give rise to too much talk. Go home and finish your sleep."

He looked at her anxiously. "But it is Sunday. Can we not be together?"

The look was more troubled than the subject merited. Justin had surely filled many Sundays before he met her—but so had she, and suddenly the day stretched before her, endlessly empty. She smiled, took the hand he had reached toward her, and held it to her breast.

"I am half dead for sleep, beloved," she said, grinning. "My nights with you are not peaceful ones—not that I would have it any other way. We will both be better for a little rest, but I could meet you after dinner." She hesitated, not sure where to set their meeting, going on half to herself, "I am in no mood for bearbaiting or cockfighting . . ." Then she nodded. "I know. I will meet you by Aldgate—Paul can bring me there—and we can go to the marsh. We can look at the fools gliding about on the ice, or perhaps be fools too and join them."

"If you intend that, I think I will not take off my bandage," Justin said, lifting the hand that held his and kissing it. "I will surely need it before we are done."

Justin's broad smile and shining eyes were again too strong a reaction, and it suddenly occurred to Lissa that he had thought she was still angry about his drunkenness and was punishing him by withdrawing herself. She almost told him she would never do such a thing, but before she could speak, Justin had pointed out that on her way to Aldgate she would pass right by his house. He began to enlarge on her plan, suggesting that if she was willing, he would invite Thomas to accompany them to the marsh; then on the way back, they could take an evening meal together, all three, at his house. They would also leave his house together; then Thomas would go his way, and he would escort her home after dark. By the time he asked if she would allow him to come in with her and she had laughed in his face and admitted she would drag him in by force if he seemed unwilling, she had also reconsidered reassuring him about her reaction to drunkenness. Justin's own habit of silence with regard to future behavior was far wiser.

The subject did not arise again, but the incident and its resolution marked a new measure of confidence in the relationship. From the first they had been so comfortable together that it was a shock to be reminded, as both had been because Lissa had never seen Justin drunk before, how short a time they had really known each other. But the shock had been absorbed and passed, and one more surety had been added to the basis of their affection. Justin in particular needed reasons to love. He had responded to Lissa immediately with such eagerness that he still could not help looking for flaws in her that would free him—and rejoicing like a soul liberated from hell when no flaw could be found.

Another hurdle was passed at the end of the next week when the onset of Lissa's flux made coupling impossible for five nights. The staining of her shift that Lissa noticed when she was about to dress in the morning brought both relief and apprehension, relief because she did not want to be carrying Peter's child—or even Justin's at the present time—and a slight anxiety about how Justin would receive the news. That was wasted. He wrinkled his nose in disappointment; he voiced indignant protests at the vagaries of women who deliberately withdrew from their natural duties for a week of every month, just to frustrate their male partners; he complained of his deprivation— and drew her down on his lap and kissed her soundly and laughed at her, mentioning in no less serious a tone that it was just as well he was to have a few days' reprieve or Cockrobin's head would be worn away by overuse.

More important to Lissa, he never sent an excuse and failed to come that week, and to her surprise he also insisted on sharing her bed each night, confessing that the comfort he derived from simply embracing and being embraced was as important or more important to him than coupling. She found that hard to believe when he said it, but later she knew that her agreement that they rest together was one of the most important decisions she had ever made. Justin told her things in the warm dark that she did not think he could ever have said in the solar. Most were little nothings, of note only because they troubled him or had a place in his heart, but she needed all her iron will to keep from weeping when she heard the echo of his loneliness, untouched by the love and company of his cousins. She lay silent, holding him warm in her arms, knowing any word no matter how soft or kind from her would silence him. And she could not weep anyway because of the joy she felt at being acknowledged the cure of his hurt.

Lissa was relieved when the end of her flux permitted Justin's enthusiastic, indeed almost violent, resumption of lovemaking to replace pillow talk in bed. His revelations called for similar confessions from her, and she had had to bite her tongue to keep from telling him her fears about her father. Instead she had told him some things about her past, but she was much afraid that if the murmurs in the dark continued long, he would become suspicious of her reluctance wholly to open her soul to him.

That first coupling was too quick and wild a release for anything but a gross physical response, but in the second Lissa finished first and, seized by a demon of mischief, teased Justin to a pitch of excitement he had not previously reached. As she looked down at him while he was catching his breath—she having ridden him to extinction and being still perched astride his thighs—the contrast between quiet talk and active bodies struck Lissa anew. She marveled aloud that she did not feel Justin's eagerness to couple cast any doubt on his assertion that he was happy to lie abed with her even when they could not make love. Justin opened his eyes to stare at her unbelievingly for a moment, then shut them again.

Lissa recognized the unspoken protest against conversation, but she was caught up in her idea. "But Justin," she mused as she let herself down to lie atop him, "do you not feel that the physical pleasure we take in each other is worth more now when it is not the only tie that binds us?" She wriggled absently to settle herself more comfortably into the curves and hollows of her lover's body. "It is an interesting case," Lissa went on, "of a part being greater than the whole, so that must be possible in the spiritual if not in the real world."

Normally Justin found the kind of discussion Lissa had proposed fascinating, but at the moment the only sound he uttered was a groan, followed after another intake of breath by a threat to roll over so that she would fall out of bed if she planned to keep him awake with philosophy at such a time. Lissa laughed then and kissed his ear, promising to offend it no more.

She certainly meant to keep that promise. Lissa had frightened herself with her talk of what love meant, and she intended to think and speak no more about so dangerous a topic. She now knew that what she had felt for Justin in the beginning was nothing to what she presently felt, and as the bond between them grew more and more stable, so, if they had to part, would the agony of separation increase. The subject was better out of mind if she intended to keep her sanity while she expected any day—or never—to hear from her father.

I will have to remain barren too, Lissa thought. She wanted very much to bear Justin's child, but a child would only be another weapon for her father. There were receipts in her book for keeping a woman barren and for clearing her womb if it became full by error. Some of the formulae had been told to her by her mother, others by birthing women, by herb women, and by others less savory to whom she sold scents and lotions. She had been very foolish until now, and sorry as she was for it, she would take care not to conceive.

Another week passed; Justin arrived every evening as soon as it was dark, and except that they did not dine together, they lived as a married pair, sharing their daily experience. In the first week in March Justin's business kept him out of London for several days, but the absence did not disturb their easy bond, and when he came into Lissa's solar, it was as if he had never been away, except perhaps that they were a little gladder to see each other. Even then their talk probed no great depths, for which Lissa was grateful. She was in daily terror that Justin would ask why FitzWalter's business was taking her father so long, and the thought of other questions he might ask in the quiet hours in the dark during her next flux brought cold sweat out on her body.

Fortuitous circumstances saved her. A day before she needed to say she could not receive him, there was news from the king's justiciar, Peter des Roches, bishop of Winchester, regarding the king. It was all very favorable. Despite the winter voyage there had been few losses; the vassals from Aquitaine were obeying the king's summons to swear their fealty and bring with them the forces they owed by oath; a few very minor actions mounted against barons who were more outlaws than landlords had been successful—and then, of course, came the sting in the scorpion's tail: Money was disappearing at a rate far higher than expected. A scutage was owed by those who had not gone with the king, and Peter des Roches was ordered to levy the tax.

The scutage was not a surprise; it was one of the ordinary ways for a king to replenish his treasury in time of war, but the news that John was in need of money so soon was most unwelcome. It was certain, Justin told Lissa, the barons would find endless excuses not to pay, and there was nothing at all the justiciar could do about their delinquency; nor would Peter des Roches, who was clever, try to force them, so why did he send the news now? Lissa would not ordinarily have been terribly interested in the question or the answer because London, having sent a force to which her father, like all other guild members had contributed, was not liable for scutage and she did not see how Winchester's news could affect her. The next night when her bleeding had begun, however, she raised the question herself, most grateful for any subject that would occupy Justin's mind and keep him away from personal topics.

He was clearly pleased with her interest, praising her for having a mind alive to matters outside her own narrow sphere. The praise came somewhat closer to the truth after her interest was truly aroused by learning that Justin, although not a tenant in chief, might himself have to pay the scutage. But Justin was less interested in the personal cost than in the public effect. He believed the scutage had been levied early so that the barons could become accustomed to what would be demanded of them, make their complaints to the justiciar, and be soothed. That would avoid conflict when the king either returned or ordered William Marshal to collect the scutage by force. Aside from saying she thought it a clever move, Lissa could think of no way to extend the discussion, but should have saved her effort because the question of payment of the scutage brought up the whole relationship of the baronage to the king.

The subject was well to the fore in Justin's mind because the mayor was not the only one who had received news. William de Mandeville, Robert FitzWalter's deputy, had summoned Justin to receive a special message of thanks from his father-by-marriage for the profitable dispatch of his business. One of the ship's captains had carried supplies to La Rochelle. He had given FitzWalter Hamo's accounting and also told FitzWalter of his personal satisfaction with Justin's dealings.

"That was very kind of Mandeville," Lissa commented

neutrally when Justin related the matter to her, as they lay abed in the dark.

"So you are as ungrateful as I." Justin sounded amused. "Now, the message might or might not be real, but Mandeville certainly delivered it in person only as an excuse to talk. Does that stink as high to you as it did to me?"

"I would not say it stank of bad fish," Lissa said, "unless he had something very particular to say to you."

Justin laughed. "He did indeed. First Mandeville told me that FitzWalter made much less of the king's successes than Peter des Roches did, and FitzWalter also warned Mandeville not to expect any easy victory over the French because the Poitevin barons were not to be trusted. They would follow the king into such actions as corrected outlawry and injustices in their own lands, but would not fight against King Philip."

"Is that not possible?" Lissa asked.

"More than possible. It is likely. They and others have done it before, when Normandy was lost, for example. I cannot condone such behavior. An oath is an oath and cannot be set aside for profit or convenience. But I do see that there is a problem: King John will go home with his troops after the war, leaving those barons cheek-by-jowl with King Philip. Moreover, Philip is old. If he dies, his son Louis might easily find a way to violate any treaty his father made as a result of defeat."

"And FitzWalter encourages the Poitevins' fears, I suppose," Lissa said. "I can see why you told me it might not need open treachery to harm the king."

"True, but that is not the point. What Mandeville came to in the end was that he would pay no scutage to a defeated king. I mind me"—Justin's voice grew sour—"that he said nothing of how he would serve a victorious king." Lissa felt him shrug, dismissing that problem before he went on, "He raised the old argument—the same the barons used when they refused to follow John to France last year—that their oaths do not require them to fight in foreign wars, only to support the king here in England where their own lands lie. This is not new, so why make a special meeting to tell me now, and why tell *me*."

"You said FitzWalter likes you," Lissa said, her voice sharpening slightly with anxiety. "Could he be giving you a warning?"

"There is a possibility that FitzWalter would do me a favor if it was no trouble to him, but what is it to me if some of the barons refuse to pay the scutage? I cannot see—" Justin stopped and stared into the dark at the foot of the bed. "No, wait. You have set my mind on a new path. Bless you, Lissa. I think I see where Mandeville was trying to lead me, but do I want to tread that path? And would it lead to good or ill?"

"What path?"

"I think it was Mandeville's intention that I carry to Stephen Langton FitzWalter's warning of the Poitevin barons' disaffection and the English barons' defiance."

"Good God, what have you to do with the archbishop of Canterbury?" Lissa cried.

"I served him last year after he returned to England. Stephen Langton is no coward, but he had the example of Becket and Henry the Second. He wished to accomplish his purpose before he took any chance of being martyred by the son as Becket was by the father. I do not know how Langton's need came to Roger FitzAdam's ears, but the mayor had been seeking a way to be rid of me along with others my uncle had appointed." Justin chuckled softly. "However, neither did he wish to offend my uncle's party, which had supported him as a compromise, so he offered me to Langton. I liked the archbishop and he me, but it was dull work leading his guardsmen. And before the end of the year he was certain there was no personal threat to him.

"So Roger FitzAdam had you back again."

Justin laughed aloud at that. "Ah, but by then he was glad to get me back. Even those who hated my uncle had had their fill of the man FitzAdam had put in my place. He let the lords' men-at-arms run riot more than once, not only in Southwark but in the Chepes as well, and once among the goldsmiths' shops. There were broken heads and looting. Yes, the mayor was glad to get me back, but he may be regretting it again now. I have refused him a favor or two and brought to public disgrace two of his supporters who were charging tolls for the use of a public well." He laughed again suddenly. "Worse yet, it was not only FitzAdam I offended. Soon all will be glad to be rid of me. I sent three to the pillory: two were FitzAdam's men, but one belonged to our party."

Though Justin himself scoffed, there no longer seemed anything strange to Lissa in an earl's brother seeking to use him as an intermediary with the highest churchman in England. Justin had fallen asleep, but she lay awake bitterly aware that all the great men turned to him because he was truly unstained by any selfish motive in his desire to serve London—not one party or the other, although he did not pretend to be above party, but the city itself came first of all to Justin. That he was involved with the mighty made her afraid as well as proud, and it was another reason her father must not be allowed to smirch Justin's honor. One rumor of weakness on his part, and they would all try to buy him. Then, likely as not, they would hate him and try to destroy him when they found he was not for sale.

Lissa spent half her time hoping and praying that she had seen the last of her father. After dreaming for weeks, however, she forced herself to face reality with the sick knowledge that he would never go off for good, leaving the profit from the business behind him. Sooner or later she would hear from him, and if she married Justin or allowed her affair with him to become public knowledge, her father would think he could commit any crime without fear of retribution. He would not believe her when she told him Justin would pursue him and expose him without regard for personal considerations.

But Lissa knew that being her father would not reduce by a hair the charges Justin would bring; it might increase them because of Justin's fear of showing favor. Likely as not their business would be ruined by the restrictions and fines levied; her father might even be cast out of the guild and she with him. And how would Justin bear such shame, he whose family had never endured whispers behind their backs and sidelong glances, especially if he was tied to her for life. Surely he would come to hate her sooner or later. She must avoid marriage or find a way to control her father. Lissa shuddered.

As March ended and April began, Lissa spent more and more of her time desperately seeking without success for some threat, some hold, she could use on her father. She had hoped to have Justin until William's return forced them apart, but now it seemed that she might lose her lover sooner. Justin was growing impatient with her reluctance to name a date for their wedding and more and more suspicious of her insistence that they conceal any relationship between them. Suitors had begun to appear; she had put them off with the excuse that she would consider no man until her father returned, but Justin had heard speculation about whom she might choose, and he was very angry and hurt that she would not name him as her chosen.

At the end of April he came very late one night, drunk again but on battle not on wine. His hauberk was splashed with dark stains, he stank of sweat and blood, and his eyes were glazed. Lissa caught her breath and asked if he was hurt and he said no. But he looked strangely at her as she held her candle high and close to examine him, and finally said, "Well?"

"You stink," she replied, "and it is too late to get a bath for you. Come above with me and I will help you get that armor off. Then I will wash you as well as I can."

"No," he said, "this time I will go home. Halsig is waiting outside, and Hervi must clean my armor before the blood dries hard. I came because I—I wanted you to know, to see with your own eyes. First I thought I would clean myself before I came, but"—he licked his lips and went on in a rush as if afraid she might interrupt him—"when we are married I will have nowhere to go but my own house when I am stained with battle." He took a deep, shaken breath. "Thank God you did not turn away."

He reached out and touched her face, then uttered an oath and withdrew his hand. It was too late; Lissa's cheek was marked with blood. She did not flinch, just wrinkled her nose with distaste and asked if the fighting was over.

"Yes."

"You are sure?"

Justin laughed tiredly. "Yes, at least my responsibility for it is ended. It started at Smithfield at dusk, just as the market was about to close, with two gentlemen claiming the same horse. It progressed to blows, to each fool calling his guardsmen, and spread as such things will, growing worse and worse in the dark until the Smithfield guards were overwhelmed and the entire watch was called out. The two gentlemen have been escorted out of London by different gates. If they wish to meet and kill each other elsewhere, I have not the smallest objection. As long as their quarrel takes place outside of London it is not my affair."

Lissa sighed with relief. This was not a rising of the apprentices or journeymen, which could continue for days before they were all subdued. There would be no more fighting, so she would not insist he stay so that she could be with him every minute until the chance of losing him rose again.

"Come back in the morning," she said. "I will have a bath ready for you by then, and I will be able to see to your bruises."

"I am not hurt."

She shook her head at him. "You will be black-and-blue by tomorrow. I will forfeit any prize you desire if you are not."

"Will you—"

Justin stopped and laughed. He *would* be black-and-blue in the morning; he always was and was always surprised. And the forfeit he had been about to ask was stupid. Lissa would have agreed; she always agreed to marry him, but no date was ever set. He thought perhaps he was being unreasonable. He himself had said they should wait for her uncle Gamel, and his return could not be more than a week or two away—unless some ill had befallen ship or man—but Justin had expected that Lissa would begin to press for marriage long before Gamel came. And she had not. That made him uneasy. Except by them, Flael's death was long forgotten by now. Justin knew he was good value as a husband, and Lissa was too shrewd a businesswoman to overlook that. Why should she hesitate?

"You mean you will let me walk into your house in broad daylight?" he asked caustically.

"You will be a customer with bruises to be salved. Of course you will come in daylight. You know I do not take a client at night unless blood is flowing or it is death to wait."

"Do you often salve your clients' bruises in a bath in your solar?"

Lissa smiled and shook her head. "You are very tired, my love, and hurt and sad. Were there some innocents who came to harm and lie heavy on your heart? I am very sorry, but I cannot let you quarrel with me now. Take off your armor and come to bed—just to sleep, or to rest if you cannot sleep. Tomorrow you can shout at me, and I will shout back, to your heart's content."

He had to laugh at that, but said, "No, I cannot stay. I told you Halsig is waiting for me, and this armor must be cleaned." He turned and opened the door and then turned back. "Lissa, I am very glad you did not shrink from me, bloody and stinking as I am. I thought perhaps for all your brave words you did not want a husband who did the work I do. But if that is not your reason for delay, I am lost. I will tell you true, I am growing tired of this hiding and I do not understand it. The days are growing longer, Lissa, the nights shorter. Think about that."

Poor Lissa had been thinking about little else. Justin grew more irritable by the day as his time with her grew shorter and shorter. Just now he was still very busy as the town seemed to grumble and groan while it stretched to take in larger and larger numbers of merchants, some from other parts of the country, some foreign. It was as if the people of London forgot over each quiet sleepy winter where their profit came from and that in the spring they would have to accommodate the odd accents and odd manners of the outlanders.

As the first ships arrived and the earliest comers streamed in from river and road, there were endless fights. Most solved themselves so quickly the watch never saw, or quieted when the watch appeared; a number were serious enough for the watch to hustle the combatants to Justin's house, where tempers usually cooled rapidly under his frigid questioning and icy glare; a few became so dangerous Justin had to be summoned to the scene, where he appeared in mail on his destrier, followed by a well-armed troop.

At present Justin's days were filled, but Lissa knew that as the season wore on into summer some process always made the Londoners more hospitable. She never could fathom whether it was because their ability to be shocked by strangeness grew numb, whether the mounting profits in their strongboxes pacified them, whether the growing heat made them dull, or whether they simply began to enjoy the excitement of the overcrowded city. In any case, as the spring advanced, quarrels would grow fewer and less virulent so as the days grew longer Justin would find himself with little to do. Lissa trembled at the thought of him idling away long afternoons and evenings, imagining how his temper would be tried, especially if his ordinary amusements with his cousins were cut off so he could be at Lissa's house as soon as it was dark. And, to add worst to worse, Justin would be shorter and shorter of sleep as dark came long after Compline and the sky grew light by Lauds. For those who lay with beloved spouses, the long hours of half-light brought delight; for those who had to creep secretly in and out of a lover's house, the time was a torment.

Although he was angry and resentful, Justin had long practice in controlling his temper. He managed to avoid a really bitter quarrel, largely because he could see Lissa was truly worried about her uncle, until Gamel came finally, at the very end of May. No harm had befallen Gamel, however; he had heard of the war in France and had taken the opportunity of stopping at several ports along the coast to sell to merchants who had a new market in the massed nobility of the English army.

So far one success had followed another for the vassals of King John, and they were rich with loot. The king and his men had taken Miervant in a single assault on the sixteenth of May and had besieged Novent with such ferocity that it was yielded by the twenty-first. Thus Gamel succeeded so well in ridding himself of his cargo that he would not have come to England at all had he not wished to see his niece and deliver to her some special packets he had carried all the way from Egypt and the Arab cities of the Holy Land.

Justin outsmarted himself in dealing with Gamel. He succeeded too well in gaining the captain as an ally. Instead of getting Lissa to marry him, she accused him of treachery and nearly denied him entrance to her house. His ruse began innocently: Justin had arranged to have the arrival of Gamel's ship reported to him with the simple intention of rejoicing Lissa with this good news. But the report came just after Justin had dragged himself from her bed to his own, and a kind of fury at being held off from the settled life he so desperately desired made him throw on his clothes, rush down to the dock, and demand to speak to Master Gamel in person. Not that this led to a quarrel with Lissa's uncle; Gamel and Justin took a great liking to each other at once, despite Justin's high-bred Norman manners not being usually to Gamel's taste.

Justin liked Gamel both because Lissa loved him and because manner meant very little to him. His own behavior was the habit of his training, but he had long since given up judging men by the fact that their manners were different from his. Gamel's liking came partly because Justin's first words were such a pleasant surprise and relief—he had said in his simplest French, "Master Gamel, I am mad with love for your niece, Lissa Bowles. I have reason to believe she returns that love, and I would like your permission to marry her and your voice to support her in the making of the marriage settlements."

Gamel, on first hearing that cold, authoritative voice asking to speak to him, had expected that he had fallen afoul of some new regulation, and he was delighted to discover instead a gentleman who valued Lissa almost as highly as he felt she deserved. He had invited Justin to sit and offered him a drink, apologizing for the condition of the ship after a long voyage, also in simple French, before he realized that Justin's asking *him* for permission to marry Lissa was most peculiar. His face then turned a very strange color, and he spoke in English in a roar that made even Justin wince, characterizing "that William," in terms that were both startling and original, for having refused his permission.

At that point Justin, also speaking English, admitted that he had set the cart before the horse and asked if Master Gamel could come to his house where he would explain the whole matter, which was a long story.

Justin's house also impressed the sea captain, who understood the use of authority. The large chamber on the lower floor, usually a shop, was arranged as a kind of court. Although Justin did not try to pretend to higher status than he had or to overawe those brought before him with a thronelike canopied chair of state, he did have a high-backed seat behind a table that was set at the very edge of a dais. Those who stood before that table were subtly made to feel small, and as many arguments were diminished by that implication of their insignificance as by Justin's reasoning or threats.

Benches lined the walls, and more benches and stools were piled under the stair behind the dais. Gamel was puzzled by so much seating but had a good laugh when Justin explained his own innovation some time later. Since he could not have a whole crowd kneeling to him without raising unhealthy ideas about his ambitions and intentions, the stools and benches were his method of dealing with large groups, usually subdued rioters, who were easier to control by standing guards when they were sitting.

Candelabra stood at each end of the table and brackets holding torches were fixed along the walls and beside the door. Sir Justin did not like to miss anything, Gamel thought. The place would be bright as day no matter what the time or weather. At present the candles and torches were not lit, as there were no felons to examine, and the windows, open to the morning, gave light enough.

One grizzled man-at-arms stood up as they entered, and Justin smiled suddenly and said, "Halsig, this is Lissa's uncle, Master Gamel, a sea captain—" And then he became aware that both men were looking aside self-consciously. "Ah, I see you have met already," he went on, his smile broadening. "I hope the wounds are healed."

"I bear no malice," Gamel said. "At least not against Halsig here, who only did as he was ordered."

"I had no choice, master," Halsig agreed, nodding. "It was the order of that one who was my lord then. I tried to send you on your way, but you would not listen."

Gamel laughed and admitted to being unreasonable at times when he was drunk, and Halsig muttered something under his breath and also laughed. Justin then recalled what Lissa had told him when she had introduced him to her factor at the Hanse, that her uncles had been taken up for fighting and then imprisoned so long that promised cargoes were shipped on other ships.

"Yes," Justin said, "I heard from Lissa that you were held overlong for no more than breaking a few heads. I am sorry. I will not say that you will be allowed to break heads while I am master of the watch—at least, not beyond reason—but I can promise that you will lose no business by being restrained." He looked at Halsig. "You hear? Take him in charge if you must, but bring me word of it."

The man-at-arms grinned from ear to ear. "Aye, my lord. I hear."

Once he had escorted his guest up the stair and seen to his comfort, Justin began his story by reporting Flael's murder, only to discover from a few choice expletives that Gamel had not known about Lissa's marriage. If William had made the arrangements before Gamel's last visit in the autumn, he had kept them secret until after Gerbod and Gamel had left. The brothers generally did meet both in the spring and the autumn in the Steelyard.

"We try to make it so he comes a few days before I leave in spring and the other way in the autumn. But he will not come at all this spring. We met in Rochelle and he gave me all he had for Lissa. He will come, likely in July, and I again in August. Mostly we come, turn about, every month in the summer—we are mixed up this year because of the war and the extra trade in France—but I will swear Lissa knew nothing of any marriage before I left the first week in November, and she was married in December." Gamel shook his head. "So fast. Why? It stinks of one of William's games."

"Goscelin—he is master of the Goldsmiths' Guild and knew Flael well—said it was a business arrangement. Yet what business a pepperer could have with a goldsmith I cannot imagine, nor has a goldsmith any real use for Lissa's ties with you and your brother. I do not know why Lissa agreed, but she told me that Flael was kind to her. She also said she did not wish him dead, but she did not pretend any great grief when he was killed."

"Lissa did not kill him," Gamel said seriously. "Unless he was terribly cruel or frightened her very, very much, she would have waited for me or Gerbod to deal with him for her." He looked at Justin. "That would be true for any husband."

Justin made no direct reply to that. He understood the unspoken threat, but he was almost amused. Whatever quarrels he had with Lissa, he was confident they would settle between themselves. It did not occur to him even after he had explained the whole matter and his whole relationship with Lissa—it took them right through dinner time—that he had committed an offense he knew she would not condone—he had drawn a third party into their affairs. No matter what his anguish, Justin would never for a moment have thought of complaining about Lissa's behavior to his own relatives. Somehow, it did not seem to be the same thing to tell her uncle, who loved her dearly, how she hurt and puzzled him by refusing to marry him or even to acknowledge him as a suitor. Without thinking what he was doing, Justin poured out all his anxiety and frustration. He did, of course, hope that Gamel would take up the cudgels in his defense, but he had overlooked the sea captain's direct methods of dealing with problems.

Gamel went from Justin's house to Lissa's, where he was greeted with nearly hysterical delight and relief—Justin having forgotten to pass along the news of Gamel's safe arrival. After he had calmed her and followed her up to the solar, Gamel warned Lissa that Gerbod would not come until July and that she should not expect either of them at regular intervals this year owing to the opportunities for unexpected and profitable trading that the war was creating. Then, having looked about with satisfaction, for he had rarely come to the house to avoid having to meet William, he remarked that she was fortunate to be rid of her father.

"Rid of him!" Lissa exclaimed. "Is he dead?"

She felt in the instant before Gamel replied a vast, whirling confusion in which were mixed a hope that the answer would be yes, a terrible shame for desiring her father's death, an equally sickening fear that Gamel or Gerbod might have been responsible for his death, and an utter inability to find a response to a confession of responsibility amid gratitude, revulsion, joy, and shame. And Gamel's answer made all the riot in her heart foolish.

"No," he said, "but Justin told me that he is gone."

Lissa sat down suddenly on the stool nearest her. "Justin?" she gasped, so surprised that she had no time to feel relief that her uncles had not murdered her father.

"He seems a fine man," Gamel said approvingly. "Of course, I must speak to a few people to be sure that he is what he says he is, but I have little doubt of his honor. You are a clever girl to wait until I could make sure. God knows our haste to make what seemed a good marriage brought great grief upon your poor mother, and I will be sure not to make such a mistake again, but—"

"But uncle, I cannot marry Justin."

"What?" Gamel roared. "Did he lie?"

He half turned toward the door, and Lissa leapt to her feet and caught at him, crying, "No, I am at fault. I lied to him."

"You lied?" That had stopped Gamel in his tracks. "I have never known you to tell a lie."

"Not in business, uncle, but I love Justin so much. I could not let him slip away without knowing him." She began to cry softly. "I know I have wronged him."

Gamel patted Lissa awkwardly, begging her not to cry, offering to fetch her wine, ale, water, anything, until she drew her sleeves over her eyes and cheeks and begged him to sit

down while she explained. She then retold much the same story
Justin had related, but Gamel was not bored because Lissa filled
in her father's part.

"So he knew why Peter was killed," she ended, "and if he
was not one of the men who destroyed Peter's house, I am sure
he was involved in that too."

"It is not at all certain he was as closely involved as you say,
child," Gamel said slowly, "but even if he was, he is gone and
does not intend to return. Why else would he have taken
everything of value with him?"

"Uncle, he will come back, and soon, for he will want to drain
off whatever profit I have made since he left. And how can you
say he was not involved after what I have told you and with all
you know of him? Cannot you see that taking the money proves
he has guilty knowledge of some sort? He is hiding it, I suppose,
so that if he is accused, he can flee, leaving his bondsmen to be
fined on his account, and he will have the wherewithal to live."

"Very well, if you will have it so," Gamel said impatiently,
"but he is such a coward. If he ran because he suspected he
would be accused, I do not think even the money would draw
him back. And, more important, I cannot see what all this has to
do with your marrying Justin. I should think you would take
him in haste, before he gets a real smell of your father."

"You would have me cheat him on the quality of the goods?"

"No!" That came out as a roar. "*You* are the goods, and the
quality is perfect."

"But there is a bond that goes with me. I am tied to William
Bowles and will never be free of him." Lissa shook her head and
laid her hand gently over Gamel's mouth. "Let me talk." And
she did, trying to explain the disaster that must sooner or later
follow her father's return if she were married or betrothed, and
that the ultimate outcome would be that Justin must come to
hate her.

"You are quite mad," Gamel said. "Your father might, indeed,
be stupid enough and dishonest enough to do what you say, but
what has that to do with you?"

Then Lissa explained Justin's political position with regard to
the parties that jostled for power in London and how easily he
could lose his place if scandal touched him. Gamel laughed and
said Justin seemed to expect to lose his place anyway and

certainly would not be fool enough to blame it on her if he did. To this, Lissa could not agree, and when her uncle told her to ask Justin, she burst into tears again and said it was no use asking. He would tell her just what her uncle told her—that he loved her, that nothing would change that love, that he would find other work if he lost his present place—but Lissa knew it was all dreams. When the shame struck him, his feelings would change. It would not be by his will, and the fact that he had promised to be constant would swell his guilt and double and redouble his resentment.

"Stop that weeping," Gamel said. "I am ashamed of you. Do I love you less for your father's faults?"

Lissa thought that was a stupid thing to say. She was growing angry at her uncle's persistent blindness, and she dashed the tears from her eyes and pointed out, "You are here a few weeks a year. You do not need to live with people who sneer or laugh behind your back."

"Lissa, this is womanish nonsense—or it is worse." Gamel's voice lost its warmth and sounded more like that in which he spoke to her father. He stood up and looked down at her. "Is this all some woman's game you are playing, using your father as a crown piece? Are you laying a good man on the rack to show your power? You have led him on, have you not? He said you had agreed to marry him, told him that it is the dearest wish of your heart. Did he lie?"

"Uncle, it is not true!" Appalled at her uncle's idea that she had wantonly hurt Justin to amuse herself, Lissa also jumped to her feet.

"Justin is a liar then?" Gamel challenged.

"No, no. And I *do* wish to marry him, but I will not see him smeared with—"

"Enough! I will test the truth of what he told me about his business and what is thought of him among the merchants. If he is as good a man as I think he is and you will not keep your word to him, then you have been dishonest, and I will be very angry with you, Lissa."

Chapter 19

LISSA WAS PERFECTLY CORRECT ABOUT HER FATHER, HAVING A MUCH clearer understanding of his nature than her uncle did. At the time Gamel was leaving the house in Soper Lane, William Bowles was entering one on Wine Street in Bristol. He was at once shown upstairs to where a very old man nodded at him. William broached his business at once, telling the aged vintner that he was confirmed in his desire to buy the manor of Red Cliff but that he still had some business to complete before he could pay the full price. Master Henry nodded again, and they bargained politely for a little while, the discussion ending with an agreement that William, who was known as Amias Fitz-Stephen, would pay another quarter's rent to hold the manor.

They agreed on a price, touching hands to seal the bargain. In Bristol Amias FitzStephen had an excellent reputation, and the vintner did not feel more than a handclasp was necessary. William smiled with satisfaction. The old man, he thought, could be no more than days or weeks away from death, and the nephew who now ran his business and would inherit everything else would take a much lower price. He would believe Master Amias's word and, since the money was to be Master Henry's death gift to the Church and would not come into the nephew's purse in any case, would care little.

Meanwhile William knew he would have to stay away from Red Cliff until the old man died. He might as well go back to London and sell the business there. He would get a better price if he was not in a hurry. There would be more chance that Lissa would find out what he was planning too, but what could she do? He had paid her dower; that was daughter's share, and she had no right to son's share. Of course, she could tell her cursed uncles, who were in and out of the Steelyard at this time of year. William shuddered. Maybe he would not rush home. Perhaps he should first travel to the north and return to London from there, just in case someone became curious about where he had been.

Partly because William was not much more eager to see Lissa than she was to see him, partly because the weather was unusually dry and pleasant, and partly because he had felt the need to be circumspect in his behavior while he was Amias FitzStephen, he retraced his route northward. There were places he had stayed on other journeys where, if he was not much liked, his coin was known to be good and his needs were supplied. At one of these places, to his enormous surprise, a message was waiting for Master William Bowles. A fellow Pepperer of Peterborough had written to say that two young men had sold a pair of goblets to a goldsmith of the town at a suspiciously low price.

Peterborough was hardly out of William's way, and he rode over to speak to the goldsmith who showed him the goblets, which he still had. William recognized them and asked about the seller; the pepperer had written no details and he wanted to hear firsthand what the goldsmith had to say. There were two sellers, the goldsmith told him at once, and of two different minds. The price the older of the two young men was willing to accept was very good, so good that the goldsmith had been hesitant, thinking that the pieces might have been stolen. The younger man had then snatched the goblets up in anger and made some observations that proved he had done much of the work. The older had then drawn the younger aside and spoken to him earnestly, several times mentioning how close was King's Lynn and the need to have money for passage before they arrived there.

William did not doubt for a moment that the two young men were Flael's sons and that they intended to take ship at King's Lynn for the Low Countries; however, there were several questions in his mind as he rode back to his lodging. Should he merely collect whatever more information he could and send it off to FitzWalter? Should he perhaps forget he had received any information, sell his business as quickly as he could, and disappear? Should he invest a little more time and some money and follow Flael's sons, if he could discover where they had gone in a reasonable time? The latter course had some attractive features. Since he already had a bolt hole and a new life selected, could he make a profit on the seal? Even when he sold his business, Master Amias would have to live carefully, not uncomfortably but carefully. If he could actually lay hands on the seal and bring it to FitzWalter, William thought, he should be able to wring a very nice reward for his service and his silence from Lord Robert.

There were also dangers in that path. There was the war with France being waged by King John's allies. So far, both the king and his allies had been successful, and the French had been driven back, but if Philip mounted a counterattack and flooded over the Low Countries while he was there, an Englishman might be ill-treated because of the sins of his master. And the cost? His passage would have to be paid, and food and lodging he had not counted on because he expected to be at his own house in London. However, he might rightfully ask Lord Robert to repay those costs, and so rich a lord would never even notice if he added a few shillings here and there or took only the most luxurious quarters, as a lord would. Perhaps he could say payment would be made by Lord Robert? That was very tempting. FitzWalter had many contacts in the Low Countries.

William was still not sure the next morning, but he could not resist riding to King's Lynn and asking questions around the docks, using FitzWalter's name freely. Like a beckoning finger, an alewife in the second place he visited recognized the names Peter and Edmond and the descriptions William gave of Flael's sons. The young men had spent the night at that alehouse where they had met the ship master who took them down the coast and across the narrow sea. That ship master was not there, but the alewife knew him well because he often stayed with her and made regular trips. She even knew his home city, which was Haarlem.

The temptation to follow young Peter and Edmond became too great for William when the alewife brought to him another ship's captain who sailed a similar route. That man listened willingly to William's smooth story about the young men as soon as he understood that FitzWalter was not seeking them for vengeance and did not attach any guilt to anyone who had helped them. William claimed that neither he nor his master had any idea why they left London after their father's sudden death but assumed it might be because the old man had married a young wife of whom they did not approve. All FitzWalter wanted, William said, was the design for some plate their father was to have done for him. It was not very important—as the captain could see by his neglecting to pursue the matter since February—but if Peter and Edmond could be found easily, William knew FitzWalter would be pleased.

The ship master, who was eager to please FitzWalter's servant because he wished to do business with FitzWalter if he could, admitted he had no way of knowing where Flael's sons had gone but offered to carry William to Haarlem for a very reasonable fee. William was so well treated during the voyage, owing to his supposed influence with FitzWalter, that he almost regretted the arrangements he had made to become Amias. The eager attention and help he received from the captain who had carried Peter and Edmond—who also sailed along the Essex coast and would be delighted to carry cargo for FitzWalter— made him resolve to reconsider selling his business in London if he could find Flael's sons and recover the seal. If the sons had it, he would have to rethink all of his plans, he told himself.

Through various merchant connections of the sailing masters, the young men were traced with little trouble. Feeling safe once they were outside of England, they had resumed their name and openly approached guilds of goldsmiths in various towns. They had settled at last in Reims.

Despite the best efforts on everyone's part, this final information did not drift back to William until the end of July. The ship masters were growing a trifle less eager to please by then. When William had first come to Haarlem, his influence had been on the increase. William of Salisbury and a substantial army of English had landed in Flanders at the invitation of the count. To the count of Flanders's great pleasure, Salisbury had brought even more money than men and had bought mercenaries with it. A little to everyone's surprise, Salisbury had honored to the letter the agreement between his brother and the count of Flanders and was protecting the country vigorously.

In the west, it seemed as if the English king would defeat the French and rule all the ports along the coast, gaining great power over trade. John appeared to be about to subdue all of Anjou. After bringing the Lusignans to their knees, he had taken Nantes, where he captured King Philip's cousin, Peter of Dreux, who was count of Brittany. Angers promptly opened its gates, but there was a great keep at La Roche-au-Maine whose seneschal held from King Philip and remained faithful to his oath. John promptly marched north to lay siege to the place.

La Roche-au-Maine did not fall, however. King Philip sent his son Louis to break the siege. He did not succeed through battle, but King John's campaign was damaged almost as badly as it would have been by a major defeat. First whispers and then reliable information reported that John had been unable to attack Louis's army, which was greatly outnumbered by his force, because the Poitevin nobles refused to fight.

This news brought the first chill to William's relationship with the ship masters and guild masters of Haarlem. Not that they turned their backs on him; there was still Salisbury's army in Flanders and Otto of Brunswick, the Holy Roman Emperor, was marching from the southeast to join Salisbury in France. John could not be considered defeated while King Philip still had to face a major battle with his allies. After all, no matter what the political situation, there would always be trade between the Low Countries and England; no matter which king ruled what territory, fleeces and other goods would be carried from the ports in the east to those in the Low Countries, and fine cloth, Damascus steel, exotic spices, and other cargoes would be carried back. Still, the favors a defeated king could grant his nobles and, through his nobles, others, were less valuable than the favors a victorious king could grant. The defection of John's vassals made William a less reliable investment.

William was furious. Desire for it made possession of the seal seem so close. He could not imagine why Flael's sons had taken it with them, since the seal was useless to Peter and Edmond in France, and William was sure he could induce them to relinquish it. However, if King Philip defeated King John's allies, William wanted to be safe in England. It would be better to accept the lesser reward he would be able to claim from finding Flael's sons than to be caught by the French.

Once he had resigned himself to being deprived of his chance to have the seal himself and exact what price he liked for it, William approached the captain who had brought him to Haarlem. The captain willingly agreed to take him home as soon as his cargo of metal came upriver from Strasbourg, but with the cargo came the news that King Philip had marched into Flanders with the whole feudal host in an attempt to cut Emperor Otto off from his English allies. Otto had been slow in gathering the German forces, but he had moved swiftly enough to foil Philip's advance and the king of France had turned back from Tournai. William brought his bags down and put them and himself on the ship. It would take some time to load the cargo, but he thought grimly that the captain would rather sail without some of it than be caught with an Englishman aboard his ship.

The captain never gave him a thought. His thoughts and energy were all given to loading his cargo as fast as human flesh could accomplish it. William was no problem at all compared with the fact that if the French did sweep through Flanders into Holland, they would surely confiscate his cargo and perhaps his ship too. He was as prepared as William could wish to abandon some of the cargo if it was necessary, but he would drive himself and the men he hired to dropping to get it all aboard if he could.

On 29 July, two days after the battle, the bad news came. The French had won. Salisbury and most of the other leaders had been captured; Otto had fled. There was no chance of the allied army reforming to fight again. The single saving grace in the news was that the battle had been so fierce and so bloody that there was little chance of Philip pursuing the tattered remnants of his enemies into Flanders and that Holland was certainly safe from any immediate threat. William came out from behind his barricade, but he did not leave the ship. He was finished with adventuring. He had found Flael's sons. Let FitzWalter extend his long arm into France and pluck the seal out.

On the day her father began his adventure, leaving Bristol and his new role as Amias FitzStephen, Lissa came near ending hers by telling Justin she would not marry him as long as her father was alive. She had not intended to go so far; she had intended to introduce the subject gently, but guilt and a resentment that grew bitterer because of her guilt, caused her to say much more than she intended to Justin when he came that night.

The guilt had lain uneasily under all her joy from the very beginning of her affair with Justin. The resentment was new, sparked by her uncle's attitude toward what she felt was an utter sacrifice of her own happiness to another's good. Lissa had been shocked into immobility by the scorn and disappointment in her uncle's voice and expression when he called her cruel and accused her of toying with Justin's affections for amusement. Even after she explained, he had been adamant and told her she had wronged Justin by promising to marry him if she would not fulfill that promise.

The shock had been severe. Never in her life had Gamel shown Lissa anything but love and support. She had run after him down the stairs after a moment but had caught only a glimpse of his back as he thrust past the pepper barrels, shaking one so hard it would have spilled if it had not been almost empty. It was too late to catch him—and what would she have said? All she could do was to repeat what she had already told him. She stood halfway down the stair with a hand pressed to her cheek, staring through the open doorway, reviewing once again her fears and wondering if Gamel could be right.

Slowly Lissa had gone down the rest of the stairs. She had stood indecisively in the shop for a few minutes, then finally stepped to the door and told Paul that she did not want to be troubled with customers unless death would follow her neglect. Then she went into the workroom, where a heap of celandine lay on the worktable together with a flask of very strong wine, a copper measuring cup, and a tablet of wax on which Witta, who was sitting cross-legged on the floor scrubbing the plant press, would record the mixture and the date. She sent him out to gather cowslips—it was too late in the season for cowslips and they both knew it, but Witta was glad to run off. Cleaning the press was a nuisance and pressing for juice was hard work. Lissa heard him in the back, asking Oliva for bread and cheese to take with him.

She moved around the workroom, not accomplishing any-thing but too restless to be quiet while she struggled with an unpleasant truth about herself. How appalling. If Justin did not resent her for the damage her father did, she would resent him. But she had no right to hurt him to save herself discomfort. Must she then agree to marry? That was mad! If she grew to hate him, would he not feel it? Would that not hurt him? Then clearly her original plan was best, not to allow her father any hold on Justin . . . unless Justin would not care, in which case . . .

With a muffled cry of frustration, Lissa looked about until she saw a crock of lilies of the valley, which had been steeping in wine for a month. She rushed to find a cloth for straining and a proper crock for the liquor. And when that was done she cleaned the press, but she could not forget her uncle's expres-sion. Grief at having disappointed him had not outlasted the careful wringing of the cloth that held the solid remains of the lilies of the valley. Shrewd Gamel might be, Lissa told herself as she put the cloth to soak clean, but he did not understand this situation and he certainly did not understand the problems of a man and woman who had to live together day in, day out, year after year, within a circumscribed group of people.

Of course, Gamel cared little or nothing about what was thought of him—except that he was honest in business. Sudden silences among those who had been his friends could not rub his temper; contemptuous snickers behind the hand could not add shame to shame. His cargo unloaded and sold, he would be gone in a week or two. By the time the press was cleaner than it had been in years, fury against her uncle burgeoned in Lissa.

The rage lent strength to her arms as she pressed the celandine, but did not last long. The misunderstanding was not Gamel's fault. He would never have blamed her and called her cruel and dishonest if Justin had not thrust himself between them. The trouble was Justin's fault, Justin's not Gamel's!

At last there was no more to do. Lissa had cleared the workroom, heard Witta return, seen Paul and Ninias drawing in the counter and shutting the shop door. Grim-faced, Lissa climbed the stairs to the solar and got her accounts, but she could not bring herself to think about them and put them away. For a while she sat staring into the empty hearth, then paced the floor, cursing the long, long evenings of late spring. Eventually she dragged her chair to the front window and sat staring out into the street, praying that Gamel would return and say he was sorry he had been angry with her and that he forgave her. But it was Justin she saw, striding toward the house.

In the dark Justin was no more than a blacker shadow. Still, Lissa could not mistake him, and her heart first leapt and then sank. She rose to her feet when she first saw him, but when he passed the house she stood still, leaning on the chair, shaking with fear and guilt and renewed anger. When he was late he came to the front door, knowing she would be on the watch for him no matter the hour. Other times he would go around into Budge Row, where the alley that led to the back garden opened, and enter by the back door. She had time before she must face him.

When her breath came evenly, Lissa moved into the solar. She knew she should consider what to say, but her mind refused to bring a single clear thought out of the chaos inside it. Then she heard his voice faintly from the kitchen, making some remark to her servants followed by a laugh, and a burst of rage so strong overcame her that she gasped for breath. She had no awareness of the next few moments. If he talked longer to the servants, she did not know it, nor did she hear him on the stairs. He could have appeared by magic for all she knew, but suddenly he was there.

"What have you done to me, you fool!" Lissa cried. "Why did you turn my uncle against me?"

Justin stopped just inside the door and stared, then walked two steps farther into the room so he could shut the door behind him.

"If you think that I, or any man, or even God, could turn your uncle against you, you are the fool, not I," Justin replied, but he found it difficult to meet Lissa's eyes. The full enormity of what he had done had just come to him, but then the sense of what she had said totally overwhelmed the shame he felt at having drawn a third party into their affairs, and he echoed, "Turned your uncle against you? What are you talking about? If there is one thing your uncle and I agree upon, it is that you are the most beautiful, most perfect woman in the world."

"You convinced him that I had promised to marry you without conditions," Lissa said, stony-faced.

"I did not tell your uncle you had agreed to marry me. Far the contrary. I told him that I wished to marry you but that I could not bring you to set a date. I told him also that I loved you and that I felt I would be a good husband for you, and I made him acquainted with my birth and with my ability to support and protect a wife."

"Oh, innocent man," Lissa's voice dripped poisoned honey. "I am sure you told a tale without bias—"

"No I did not." Justin was growing angry and his voice sharpened. "I desire you for my wife. I told the tale so that he would feel your greatest happiness and well-being would be served by becoming my wife. It so happens that I believe this to be the truth."

"You did not care what your sad tale of woe would make him think of me. He called me cruel and dishonest. He accused me of . . . of toying with you for amusement. He was angry with me! He has never before been angry with me in my whole life."

"You are being ridiculous, Lissa. Nothing could make your uncle think ill of you. Angry . . . well, a man might feel for another man."

That statement reignited into a blazing fury what had been diminishing to a tearful resentment. Suddenly Lissa stood on the edge of a vast gulf with all of womankind, all scorned, all bearing bruises and scars and burdens while distantly, across the gulf, came the voices and laughter of men blaming them for all of mankind's sorrow, calling them lecherous and the fount of original sin.

"Out!" she gasped, barely able to croak out the word. "Out! Go enjoy my uncle's company. Go revile the light-minded, lighthearted whore who has wronged you so much by loving you when she should have had more sense. Out!"

"Lissa! What did I say?" Justin was startled, almost frightened, by the distortion of her face, the barely restrained violence he could sense in her.

"The truth," she spat. "You have spoken nothing but the truth. Men, no matter how different, will always bond together to constrain a woman to their will. Now go, and do not bother to return."

Justin stood staring and then said softly, "Lissa, you cannot mean that. I am sorry I drew Gamel into this business. Perhaps it was a mistake—"

"You do not know how great a mistake," she said. "But I will not be forced by you and my uncle to do what I know is wrong and will only bring me—and you—more grief than we have ever known. Now get out of my house. And you can suck on this sweet comfit to take away the sour taste of not having your own way: You have taken from me the one protection I had against my father; you have left me naked to his cruelty."

"Listen to me—" Justin began, but the look on her face stopped him, and before he could begin again she simply walked away into the bedchamber, and he heard the bar on the door go down into the slot.

Justin had taken two angry steps after her before the sound froze him in his tracks. He stopped not only because the bar made it impossible for him to force his way into the bedchamber but also because its presence, not common in a private house, recalled to him what Lissa had told him of how her mother and father lived together. One blow on that door and he would lose her forever, Justin thought, and wondered in his fury if he should do it and be done with her. The ninny, he raged, staring at the wood with eyes so hot they should have bored holes in it. If she is afraid of her father, all she need do is marry me and I will protect her. Instead she mopes and mows about my making her uncle angry—as if that will stop him from caring for her.

But the rage was only a cover for anguish and guilt. He knew that he should not have confided in Gamel or tried to win his sympathy. He should have given Lissa a chance to speak to her uncle first. However wrong she was, he had hurt and frightened her terribly and she did not deserve it. She might be silly, but she was trying to protect him—God alone knew from what. He swallowed hard and drew a deep breath. He would have to find and talk to Gamel, who would have to convince her that he would love and protect her no matter what she decided about marriage.

Chapter 20

JUSTIN HAD NO TROUBLE AT ALL FINDING GAMEL SINCE HE PRESENTED himself at the Steelyard at first light. That was easy enough; he had not closed his eyes all night. Still, having learned that Gamel had slept in the quarters kept for him, he waited politely until he was told that Gamel had finished breaking his fast. Then he sent in his name, and unlike certain unpleasant episodes in the past, he was taken at once to the hall and brought to the table where the ship master was toying with some ale. He was hailed with pleasure; a second alehorn was brought and filled. All went well until Justin tried to explain the mistake he had made and what he felt Gamel should do to correct it. At first Lissa's uncle was simply incredulous. He could not believe Lissa had taken his remonstrance so much to heart or that she would believe he would try to push her into a marriage that she herself did not desire.

"She told me she loved you, that she *did* wish to marry you," he protested, slamming his alehorn down so hard half the liquid spouted out.

"She has told me the same," Justin agreed dully, his head in his hands. "Yet she thinks she has some reason to wait—"

"Some stupidity about that snake William," Gamel said, pouring more ale into the horn.

"Yes. She seems very much afraid of her father."

"Afraid of William? Lissa?" Gamel laughed heartily. "He is more afraid of her than she of him. And until you began this tale, I would swear that Gerbod and I were more ruled by her than she by us. Not that we were afraid of Lissa, but she is so clever . . ."

He began to laugh again and spent considerable time recounting the occasions on which he had scolded Lissa for this or that and she had laughed at him and danced his words around until he seemed to be approving her. He began to think Justin's concern quite humorous and that Lissa might be playing a trick on her too-serious suitor.

"It is true enough that she does not like to be told what to do," Gamel said, still chuckling, "and she may have decided to punish you for bringing me in to settle the matter before she was ready. But she will be sorry when she realizes that she has gone too far and hurt you. She is most tenderhearted. She was only jesting."

Justin reached for his own ale, but his hand was shaking and he clasped both together and let the horn stand. "Gamel, I know Lissa's humor. She often teases me and never goes too far. I do not know why, but she was truly frightened by your telling her that she had been unkind and dishonest in her treatment of me."

The sea captain was silent for a little while, and then he nodded. "She said I had called her dishonest, did she? Hmmm. If I did, I had forgotten that. Yes, she might take that to heart. We were afraid, all of us, that her father might twist her to his way of thinking. It might be that we marked her a little too deeply with a fear that we would not love her if she was not always honest."

"God knows you have done your work well."

"I cannot be sorry for it." But Gamel's voice did not have its usual ring, and if Justin had known him better or even been less consumed by his own misery, he would have sensed something amiss when Gamel spoke again. "She told me the same farradiddle about William as she told you," he said uncomfortably because he did not like to speak half-truths and Lissa had told him much more than she had told Justin. "But that cannot be the real problem."

With the worst over, Gamel leaned forward over the table and his bass rumble became easy and as confidential as its natural volume would allow. "You have only to give William a few bruises and tell him you will break both his legs if he steps out of the straight and narrow path of virtue, and he will cause you no trouble. But Lissa knows this . . ."

Gamel refilled his drinking horn and looked at Justin's, which was untouched. Then he looked at Justin, who was sitting with his head in his hands again, and he was moved to pity for the younger man's misery. Why had Lissa been playing this woman's game? Was it because she had tasted the joys of being a widow, of having complete power over her own life and money? His niece might not wish to yield that up even to a man she loved. Gamel shook his head. She was too young to seize the bit between her teeth. She might be the best a woman could be, but she was still a woman and needed a man to rule her.

"Perhaps I am not sorry she was frightened," he said. "I am sure she loves you but not so sure she was not testing her power over you, which is not a good thing for a woman. We have spoiled her, Gerbod and I, and my father was even worse while he was alive. She may need a little lessoning. Let her think I will withdraw my affection. She will the sooner come to heel. You can be married before I go—"

"No!" Justin exclaimed, looking up. "That would turn love to hate. It is half hate already. You did not see her face when she bade me leave. I beg you, just assure her that you will love her and protect her, no matter what she decides about our marriage. If you cannot do that, do not speak to her of it at all. Forget it. Pretend that I do not exist. Gamel," he said desperately, "I will not marry Lissa by force."

"Force! Do not be ridiculous! She said she wishes to marry you. She gave her word, which must be her bond."

"Marriage is not a business contract."

Gamel looked at Justin in blank surprise. "What are you talking about? Of course marriage is a contract, and sanctioned by the Church and the law."

"Gamel!" Justin cried. "Do you know your niece at all? You will destroy us. She will hate me until she dies if you make her choose between losing you and marrying me. I tell you she is playing no games with me. She is mistaken, but she thinks she is holding off our marriage for *my* sake, to protect me."

That statement made Gamel look thoughtful. The truth was that he did not know his niece very well. He was in her company a few hours a day, a week or two at a time, four or five times a year. That might not be a good way to develop an intimate knowledge of a person, but some things had impressed themselves on Gamel—and the persistence of Lissa's opinions, particularly of her dislike, was one. He began to doubt the wisdom of pushing Lissa into something she did not want to do, and it crossed his mind briefly that if Justin was right, she would in the end come to hate him too.

A chasm of loss so deep he could not bear to consider it opened before Gamel's feet, and he asked, "Then what do you want me to do?"

"Only tell her you love her, that you will always love her, no matter what she does."

"Well, that is the truth," Gamel said and set down his alehorn. "Come, we can go now."

Paul's face, frightened instead of welcoming, when he saw them was warning enough that the storm had not blown over. Before Gamel could make any suggestion, Justin said he would go up the street to the alehouse.

"If I am wanted, one of the boys can fetch me," he said. "If I am not, you will know where to find me."

"Surely you can wait in the shop," Gamel rumbled.

Justin glanced sidelong at Paul and his lips twisted wryly. "I am not welcome where clients can see me. No one loves a thief taker. I drive away trade."

He turned and walked away and Gamel, who was now beginning to feel ill-used, did not try to stop him. He pushed behind the counter and through the shop to the stairs. When he flung open the door of the solar, Lissa stood up.

"I was just making ready to come to you, uncle," she said. Her voice shook. "I have done wrong, I confess it. I can only beg you to forgive me. I will amend it in any way I can, except that I will not marry Justin, not until my father is dead. If he still wants me then, I will marry him on any terms he names."

"Girl . . ." Gamel said, but he could say no more and only opened his arms to her. She flung herself forward into them, sobbing and trembling, and he held her for a time while he mastered his voice. Then he shook her gently. "Lissa, I cannot imagine how you can be such a fool. You are all the blood that is left to Gerbod and me. How could you think I would stop caring for you for any reason? You little idiot. Did you stop caring for me when you heard things I had done that you did not like?"

She did not answer that, only asked, "What am I to do?"

"About what?" Gamel asked. "And why ask me?" he went on, half jesting and half irritated. "You will do what you like no matter what I say. You always have done."

"Not this time, uncle," she said. "Can you sit with me for a few minutes?"

"All day, if you like." He went and sat in the chair, adding as Lissa carried a stool to his side and sat beside him, "I only came to see you. My cargo is mostly gone already, except what I carried for you."

"I must ask what you think I should do about Justin." Tears began to roll down her cheeks. "I have done so much harm already that I cannot trust myself—"

"Oh, no," Gamel said. "I am not fool enough to pick up the same hot coal twice. If you have something to settle with Justin, you settle it with him. I like the man. I think he would make a good husband for you, but I am not going to stand between you and get kicked by both." He drew her to him and wiped her face roughly, then kissed her cheeks and forehead. "You are a very foolish girl, but I love you nonetheless and always will."

On the words he stood up and went out, leaving Lissa on the stool with her head on her knees. Perhaps she had been frightened by his anger at first, Gamel thought, but she was no longer shedding those hopeless tears from any fear that he would abandon her. "Sir Justin will be coming back to see your mistress in a few minutes," he said to Paul as he went out. "She is expecting him."

Lissa, however, was not expecting Justin nearly as soon as he arrived. She knew she would have to face him, since Gamel had refused to be her intermediary, but she was stupid with exhaustion from a long night of regret and remorse and tears. Had she been capable of thinking, she would have realized that Justin must have spoken with Gamel to tell him what had happened. She also could have guessed that if Gamel and Justin had been together, they might come to the house together. And it was just like Gamel to leave with Paul an order she had never given.

As it was, she was still sitting with her head on her knees, wearily trying to decide whether a letter could serve her purpose or whether it would be better to go to Justin's house, when she heard a choked voice say her name.

She lifted her head. "I am so sorry, Justin."

Her voice was raw with weeping, faint and cracked. Justin winced. In his work he had heard that kind of voice far too often from other women, women who had been misused beyond bearing one way or another. He had never thought to hear it from his own woman.

"In God's name do not beg my pardon," he said, going down on his knees and taking her in his arms. "I swear I would have cut off my right hand rather than cause you such pain."

"But it was my fault." She rested her head on his shoulder. "I fell in love with you. I think I loved you from that first time I saw you after the fire, but I did not know it until you came to the house that day we found Peter. That day . . . you were so fine and fair, and yet so kind to me. I knew I could not really have you because of my father, but I wanted you so much . . . so much."

Justin could feel the little catches in her breath, the remnants of sobs that the body was too exhausted to produce. He got up, lifting her with him, and sat in the chair, holding her on his lap. "Lissa," he said, "I am very glad you love me. Nothing else matters. We will live just as you like. Do not weep anymore, beloved. We will do just what you wish to do. But, dear heart, I do not understand . . ."

He did not finish the sentence. Suddenly he was afraid he did understand. He remembered his strong feeling, on the day he had been summoned to investigate Flael's death, that she was hiding something. The juxtaposition of that memory with her saying she could never really have him because of her father, together with all the other oddities—the unlikely marriage to

Flael, the sudden departure of William Bowles the morning after Flael's house was ransacked, the fact that he had taken every asset he could carry and had not returned—raised a suspicion that had never entered his mind before: Had Bowles caused Flael's death?

Without conscious thought, he continued to comfort Lissa, striving to put aside his shock and horror. Nothing Bowles had done was Lissa's fault; nonetheless, if he was found to be a murderer, his property would be stripped from him and—and that of his family might be attached also. So *there* was the danger Lissa saw in marriage and from which she wished to protect him. But he would have taken her penniless, and gladly, and she must know it, so that was ridiculous—or was it? From the first Lissa had been aware that he had political enemies. If it became known that his wife's father was a murderer, that knowledge could be a nasty weapon.

Only that question was dead now. By the crown officer's decision Flael had not been murdered, so there was no longer any danger of confiscation of property. And Lissa still resisted marriage . . . of course, because that news would reach her father sooner or later and he would come home. Yet Gamel said she was not afraid of Bowles; Gamel had been utterly contemptuous of Bowles's physical courage and indicated that Lissa was too. In any case, Justin thought, she must know he could protect her physically, so there was something about Bowles he had not yet penetrated. Justin bent his head and kissed Lissa's hair.

If Bowles was a murderer, whether or not the crime could be fixed on him, he needed more consideration as a father-by-marriage than Justin had been willing to give him in the past. Perhaps Lissa was not the fool he had called her over and over, and it was better they should not be indissolubly bound before Bowles showed his face in London again. Then, Justin thought, he would be able to see for himself whether marriage was wise or not. As he made that decision, Justin could not help feeling a flicker of relief, which was immediately followed by a stab of shame. His hands tensed as fury touched him because he had been tempted by Bowles's evil to go back on a promise, but that too was not Lissa's fault. Justin buried both shame and relief in the darkest corner of his soul and turned his full attention to soothing her.

Justin never remembered what he and Lissa said to each other that morning beyond the fact that a peace was patched up between them. They agreed to resume the life they had led before he had tried to make their relationship open to the world, but it was not the same. The perfect comfort they had felt in each other's company was gone. Shame tinged the pleasure of Justin's lovemaking too often when he remembered that temptation to avoid marriage and wondered whether he was using a fine woman as a whore. And grief threaded all of Lissa's days, no matter how firmly she tried to forget that sooner or later she must lose Justin entirely. She tried desperately to recapture joy, but often she wept instead of laughing as she used to when her culmination came. Neither blamed the other; each took all the fault alone, but that bred quarrels about stupid little things— because they were afraid to talk about the important ones.

Gamel took on cargo, largely provided by Justin's cousins, and sailed on 12 June, and Lissa received offers of marriage from Thomas (who was joking) and Richard (who was not), solely for the sake of her ties with the Hanse. Lissa thought it was funny, although she did not show that to Richard. She teased Thomas with high-flown nonsense and rejected Richard with gravity, pointing out that although Gamel had taken wool at this time of year because he intended to cross the narrow sea, he seldom did so later in the season when he set off on longer voyages thus having Gamel and Gerbod as uncles-by-marriage could not be much advantage to a wool merchant like Richard. Justin did not think his cousin's suit was humorous and had a blazing fight with Lissa because she had not refused it with truth, that she was already sworn to him.

After that quarrel, Justin stayed away from the house on Soper Lane for a week. Lissa wept a little, but she was so exhausted from fearing the next word either of them would say wrong that she was not altogether sorry to miss him. They met quite by accident in the Chepe. Lissa had gone to the Cutlery to buy a new chopper and literally bumped into Justin, who was walking home. The accident occurred because she was looking toward his house instead of at Soper Lane, and he was looking back toward Soper Lane instead of toward home. Both laughed so much over this mutual silliness when each confessed, and such a shock of longing passed between them, that Lissa waited up for the first time in a week, and Justin came when it was hardly dark.

She did not scold him for coming too early, and they went along better for a few weeks after the separation, just long enough to present a relatively contented image when Gerbod arrived. He had the full story from Gamel, whom he had met in Hamburg, and he went out of his way to meet Justin and spend time with him. Gerbod said nothing of marriage, but was driven to ask whether Lissa had any news yet of her accursed father. His burst of rage, expressed against William but actually in response to his inability to help his niece, was accepted calmly at the time, for Justin and Lissa were in heartfelt agreement with him; nonetheless, it was unfortunate because it broke the tenuous peace they had achieved, and only a week after Gerbod sailed they quarreled bitterly and parted again.

Not all the tension that contributed to their quarrels came from Lissa's conviction that her father would bring them trouble. The entire merchant community in London was tense and braced for trouble. The tale of the treachery of the Poitevin barons was widely known. Justin had been one of the first to hear the story as William de Mandeville, with a kind of grim satisfaction, passed on the news he had had in FitzWalter's letter the day it arrived. Not long after, a kind of confirmation came in a letter from the king addressed broadly to all his earls, barons, and knights in England. This, under the guise of confidence, was an appeal for men, but very few responded. In general, the merchants who came from the countryside reported that anxiety and dissatisfaction with the king's foreign war were widespread, although the discontent was muted by better news from the earl of Salisbury in Flanders.

Lissa heard more than she wanted about these matters, although she did not see Justin. Her second parting with Justin had been less painful because she had been less happy while they were together, and by avoiding the Chepe, she made sure that they would not again fall into each other's arms. She was much busier than usual too, because she was doing all the purchasing from the many vessels that arrived in the good weather.

She had an entirely different kind of trouble during the bartering with merchants who came from outside London.

Dealing with major purchases and sales herself naturally generated questions, particularly as to why she was using Hamo
Finke as the goldsmith to whom payment should be made. Not
wishing to malign her father's goldsmith, Lissa mentioned that
she had been married and widowed and said that she had
placed her accounts with Master Hamo simply to avoid confusion.

What Lissa did not expect was that this news would bring
offers of marriage from her fellow merchants, including those
from within London who had been waiting for Lissa to signal
her willingness to remarry but who did not want to be behind
with their proposals. Lissa's constant activity dulled her sense of
loss, and the first few men who presented themselves with
proposals were a support for her wounded spirit. But soon Lissa
was crying herself to sleep every night because of a proposal of
absolute and ultimate suitability. A fellow Pepperer, Edward
Chigwell, offered his eldest son, Edward, a young man who,
only two years before, had courted Lissa on his own and on
whose account, because she liked him very well indeed, she had
fought bitterly with her father. To further sweeten the offer,
Master Chigwell suggested that Lissa should have the choice of
which business, his own or her father's, she and her husband
would handle directly. The other shop would not be given to the
second son but only be managed by him or by some other
member of Chigwell's large family, again according to Lissa's
choice.

Such an offer was not one Lissa could refuse and forget or
laugh about in privacy. She forced herself to say that although it
was true her choice was her own now, her father must still be
considered. William could create so much unpleasantness when
he returned that she would not come to any agreement until her
husband and his family had talked to him and decided whether
they still wanted the marriage. Lissa hoped that being reminded
that her father was alive and might reappear any day would
discourage this particular suitor, who knew William Bowles
well. On the contrary, her "fairness and honesty" caused both
father and son to become even more enamored of her, and the
younger Edward began to present himself to escort her to any
function of the guild that she attended.

Under the circumstances, Lissa could not avoid considering

the young man as a husband. He was certainly kind, thoughtful, and attentive, if somewhat more reserved and patriarchal than she remembered. He had a tendency to reprove her—most gently, it was true, but reprove her nonetheless—when she whispered jests about the long, pompous speeches made by some masters at the formal guild dinners. Worse yet, he did not understand her when she teased him. She would ache with longing for Justin when Edward answered one of her fanciful flights either with literal instruction, as if she were feebleminded, or with shocked incredulity followed by indignation at her levity. In two words, Edward was incredibly dull, and Lissa could not understand how she had overlooked that shortcoming when he first courted her—except that she had not then known Justin.

On the other hand, it was plain from Edward's manner and the way he looked at her that he was more experienced with women than he had been two years earlier. That idea set Lissa's mind along a different path, and involuntarily she considered him as a man. He was handsome—much better looking than Justin, if one were to tell the truth. His eyes were a clearer blue, his nose, though straight, did not look so much like a knife blade, and his mouth did not make a hard and bitter line above a cruelly determined chin. And if Edward's body did not have the strength and grace of Justin's . . . well, he was still well made. Then Lissa thought of that body in her bed and nearly vomited.

That was when she began to cry bitterly over what she had lost, but she checked her tears and reprimanded herself harshly. She could not embroil Justin with her father just to satisfy her lechery. If she had endured Peter without worse than mild distaste, she told herself, she would soon grow accustomed to a younger and more virile partner. But scolding herself was little help, and she found the company of her eager swain harder and harder to endure.

Matters came to a head between Lissa and Edward on the first day of August with the arrival of the news of the defeat of the king's allies at Bouvines. Lissa heard of it at the Steelyard, where she had gone to examine some fine cloth her uncle's factor had set aside for her. As a courtesy—and to discipline herself because the thought of seeing Edward was so distasteful—she stopped at the Chigwell shop to pass along the news if they had not yet heard. Master Chigwell was not in, so she told Edward of the disaster. She then began to speculate on the probable results of France's victory, whereupon her suitor told her, somewhat loftily, that it was not a subject on which a woman was qualified to comment.

Lissa responded with some heat that it was a subject any merchant had better consider very seriously indeed, but Edward did not take warning. He answered with a superior smile, patting her shoulder as he said he was sure they would suffer no harm from King John's foolishness, and if trouble should come, he would do the worrying for both of them. At that point, Lissa lost her temper in earnest and told him that unless he did his thinking with his rod, which she was beginning to believe must be the case, she had as good equipment for worrying as he did and that if he did not agree it was plain he was not the husband for her. She left the house before he could reply, chuckling all the way home over the expression on his face and feeling, she thought, as a bird must when its cage is opened and it is set free.

She had rejoiced too soon, however; Master Chigwell appeared at her shop barely two hours later to apologize for his son. Mistress Lissa must pardon a young man's pride, the elder Edward pleaded. It was not that his son failed to appreciate her business acumen but that he wished to appear strong and protective to her. This was so likely that there was little she could say, but she persisted in her opinion that she and young Edward were not suited, giving as examples the many times her light humor had offended rather than amused him. That was only a foolish young man's pretense of dignity and wisdom, Master Chigwell said, and his lips smiled but his eyes did not. A *very* foolish young man, he repeated. Lissa was smitten with pity for poor Edward, who was no longer what she wanted but who certainly did not deserve what his father would inflict on him if she could not be appeased. She temporized, promising to reconsider, but she could feel the net of the bird catcher swooping down on her and felt suffocated and frantic.

What made everything more dreadful was that Edward, after being threatened by his father, began to touch her suggestively and try to kiss her. Lissa had never found the idea of coupling with Edward pleasant, and now when he attempted to display a sexual desire she was sure he no longer felt, she was sickened.

More than once she bade him leave and then felt guilty for causing trouble between father and son. The result was that when William Bowles came and pounded on the door soon after dark in the third week of August, Lissa very nearly ran down to greet him with joy. One thing she understood was how to manage her father, and all she had to do was convince him she still craved Edward. After that she could trust him to change Master Chigwell's desire for the match into loathing and thus rid her of Edward too.

Showing William that she needed him was no way to get his help, however; so when he flung open the door of the solar, Lissa restrained her welcome to an indifferent "So you are back, are you?"

"Tell Oliva to get me something to eat," he snarled.

Lissa laughed. "Food is easy enough to get, but you will sleep on Paul's pallet on the floor tonight until I can have your mattress restuffed. Did FitzWalter's business occupy you so fully that you had not time to send a message to say you were alive?"

He turned from an angry contemplation of the bare boards and leather straps of his bed to stare at her. "Are you saying you cared whether I was alive?"

"Oh, no," Lissa replied, not very truthfully because she did care; she would have been glad to hear he was dead by any cause except her uncles' hand.

"Well then, mind your own business or I will kick you out and sleep in your bed."

That threat was mere bad temper and did not trouble Lissa at all. "I have been minding my business," she retorted. "You left me in a fine state when you ran off with every farthing. I had to use my dower to buy stock."

"I grieve for that." William grinned. "Oh, how I grieve."

"You need not," Lissa replied with the sweetest of smiles. "I lent the shop the money and took a handsome fee for it out of the profits. You did me a good turn by giving me to Peter de Flael, you see. I learned something from dealing with Peter's accounts."

"You practiced usury on your own father!" William shouted. "You bleeding bitch! I will teach you a lesson. Oh, I will teach you a lesson!"

"I can be beyond your lessoning any time I wish, *dear* father."

Lissa continued to smile good-humoredly. "That is another good your forcing me into marriage with Peter has brought me. I hold my own marriage portion—I have even added substantially to it—and I am free to choose whom I will. I have had offers from a dozen men. Consider that while I get you something to fill your belly, and mend your manner to me if you wish to keep me here to manage your shop."

Leaving William speechless with rage, Lissa ran down into the workroom. She had considered telling her father to get his own food in order to make him even more furious, but she realized that she had to prime Paul and Oliva on what to say about Edward. If she mentioned Edward herself, her father just might be clever enough to work out that she did not want him. If he did, he would certainly agree to the marriage to spite her. If, however, William got the information about Chigwell's offer from Paul or Oliva, he would probably remember that she had once wanted to marry Edward and do all he could to make Chigwell withdraw the offer.

There was a gasp when Lissa opened the door to the workroom, a sound of fear; it could not have been one of surprise because Paul had opened the front door to his master. All must have known who had come . . . Lissa paused with her hand still on the door. It had been closed. But in summer that door was always left open to take advantage of whatever breeze made its way down from the open windows on the upper floor. One could not leave windows or doors open on the ground floor at night; that would be an invitation to the thieves who roamed the dark. With the door to the shop closed, the workroom became an airless box, hotter because of the fire that was in use all day for brewing.

Paul stood up and looked at her. Even by the light of the night-candle she could see how pallid his face was. She drew him into the shop, closing the door gently behind them, and whispered, "What is it? What is wrong?"

"Oliva has run away," Paul whispered back. He swallowed hard. "She said she would not go back to—to his bed and she . . ." His voice shook so that he had to stop.

"I do not blame her at all," Lissa whispered, chuckling with delight at the thought of her father's fury before she thought of what would happen to Oliva. "Poor woman," she added, and then, "No, I will save her. Paul, go see what there is in the larder that I can give my father for an evening meal. Give me a minute to think."

By the time Paul came back with bread, cheese, part of a hard sausage, and a flagon of wine, Lissa was smiling broadly again. "Listen. I will tell my father that out of spite, because he took the money and plate and even the rare spices, I would not have his leman in the house, and I drove Oliva away. She will then be blameless and I will so testify for her if it becomes necessary. But I do not think it will come to that if you know where she is hiding."

Paul stared at Lissa for a minute and then took her hand and kissed it, which puzzled her, but she forgot about it as he whispered, "Yes, I know."

"Good," Lissa said. "Tell her to seek shelter in the hut in the garden of Flael's house on Goldsmith's Row. I will meet her there tomorrow, as early as I can. I think I can find a shelter for her for a few weeks. That will be time enough to see what my father intends to do about her. If I must, I will send her away."

"Thank you," Paul whispered and took and kissed her hand again.

Lissa, whose mind had gone back to her own problem, did not stop to wonder why Paul should thank her so fervently. At the moment it seemed reasonable that he did so in Oliva's stead. She told him that no doubt her father would question him about what she had been doing. If he so much as mentioned Justin's name, she would cut out his tongue, but he was free to tell William anything else.

"I want him to know about Chigwell's offer," she said, and "particularly about how Edward comes courting. But try to seem reluctant to tell him about Edward. Do you understand?"

A pleased grin spread slowly over Paul's face as he realized how Lissa intended to manipulate her father, and he nodded vigorously.

"And bring up your pallet for my father to sleep on," she finished. "You can use Oliva's for tonight, but you must get rid of it in the morning before he comes down, and be sure the boys tell the same story you do."

Chapter 21

FOR NEARLY A MONTH BEFORE HE RETURNED TO LONDON, WILLIAM Bowles had been constantly in a foul temper. First one thing and then another had conspired to irritate and frustrate him. First, King Philip had brought the French army east just in time to prevent him from going to Reims and getting the seal from Flael's sons. Then the stupid allies had lost the battle so that he had to flee Holland with an angry and contemptuous captain instead of a subservient and pleasant one. And when he had sent a messenger to Bristol, ostensibly to say his business was taking longer than he expected but really to find out if the old man had died so he could go back and purchase Red Cliffs, he discovered that not only had the old vintner clung to life but he had found another prospective purchaser. Amias had first claim, of course, but that meant he had to ride all the way to Bristol and pay out another quarter's rent to hold the claim. Worst of all, if the other purchaser did exist and if he was persistent, Amias would have to pay a fair price for the manor.

Now William had begun to wonder whether selling the

London business would provide enough money. He would have to get a substantial reward from FitzWalter. There was no comfort to be had in that thought, and all the way from Bristol to London William had tested this scheme and that for getting what he thought news of the seal was worth.

The disparity between what he desired and what he would dare ask from FitzWalter was great enough, William being no fool, to feed his fury until it gnawed like a worm in his belly. And that rage was little appeased when he looked at his bed, reft of mattress, feather bed, and curtains, a sure sign of how eager Lissa and Oliva were to be rid of any reminder of him. Then he suddenly remembered his plans to sell the house, which contained the shop, as well as the business. The worm in his belly lay still as he thought of how much Lissa loved the fine stone house her grandfather had had built in the expectation that his grandchildren would enjoy it for many generations. Lissa loved the business too, and William knew it was mostly her hard work that had built it to its present worth.

William smiled and the grinding in his belly eased. He sat down in his chair and smiled more broadly as he thought over what he would force Oliva to do to pay for her crime. He knew quite well that she might only have been obeying Lissa's orders when she removed the bed furnishings and that, slave that she was, she could not disobey. The knowledge added a certain fillip to his pleasure; the agonies of the helpless were more amusing somehow than those of a bitch who snarled and snapped back like Lissa. Still, when he contemplated what Lissa would feel when she discovered that *her* house and *her* business had been sold out from under her feet, that she no longer had a roof over her head nor owned a stick of the furniture that was so precious to her, a warm delight suffused him. He only regretted that he would not be there to see it himself.

These cozy plans for enjoyment suffered their first check when Lissa came up with the platter of food. William looked at her in surprise and then twisted his mouth in scorn. "If Oliva has claimed sickness to avoid coming to my bed, you are a fool to have believed her and bothered to carry up my evening meal yourself. Just shout to her to come up. If I go down to get her, it will be the worse for her."

"Oliva has not been in this house since the day I came back to it," Lissa said. "So you can get up and move the table, or I will set this on a stool if—"

"What do you mean, Oliva is gone?" William roared. "She was my slave. I bought her. You had no right—"

"Perhaps not, but I could see no reason to keep your leman in my house. You can send out to seek her, but I bade her go in February, and if she is not beyond measure stupid, she was out of London under some man's protection that very day."

William leapt to his feet, gibbering with rage, and came toward Lissa with his fist raised. She kept the tray between them so he could not reach her and said, "Gamel will be here any day, and I will hit you with this flagon if you do not let me be. You had no right to take every farthing out of the business. I was angry. By the time I thought I could have sold her instead, she was gone—and that is that."

He grabbed the platter from her, pushing her so hard she staggered back, dropping the flagon. He came at her again, having flung the tray away, and slapped her face. Lissa staggered back again, tripped over the stool, and fell. William charged at her and kicked her, but she had expected that and was already rolling away and up on her knees, grabbing the stool and holding it by the seat with the legs pointing at him. She prodded him once hard enough and near enough his genitals to make him gasp with pain and back away, giving her time to climb to her feet. But this time William had not waited. He had turned swiftly and rushed into her bedchamber and shut the door.

Lissa stood gasping for air, absently setting down the stool and rubbing the places that hurt. She had been surprised by her father's violence. Usually he threatened and screamed like a child in a tantrum, but nothing came of it. She listened intently, fearing he might damage her possessions, but then she shrugged. There was no tool with which he could break the chair or bed or chest, and he probably would not tear the bedclothes because he wanted to sleep in comfort.

A sound made her tense and brought her hand to her throat, but the gold chain and carved ivory picture of her mother that she always wore were safe, and she no longer had any other jewelry. The few other pieces had been taken from Flael's house, and she had refused to allow Justin to buy anything for her. The thought of Justin made her close her eyes in pain, but the pang of grief and longing was thrust into the back of her mind by the sound of footsteps pounding up the stair. Lissa had just time enough to realize the noise she had heard had come from below when Paul rushed into the room with a heavy pestle in his hand, his face twisted with hate. Lissa drew a deep, steadying breath as he stopped and stared around.

"Hush," she said softly before he could speak, and gestured him to go out. She followed him onto the landing of the stair and drew the door closed. "I am not hurt," she assured him. "Let us go down. I will sleep with the boys in the workroom. You put your pallet by the foot of the stair so that he cannot come down without giving us warning. It is better that he sleep in my chamber so I can go out and arrange for Oliva's safekeeping without him knowing I am gone."

At first light, Lissa slipped out of the house, taking the two boys with her. She wanted to discover what they were likely to tell her father if they were questioned. To her relief she found that they had, as she had hoped, slept soundly and remained unaware of Justin's visits, barring the few he had made during the day when Gamel and Gerbod had been in London. And, apparently by a direct special dispensation from the Merciful Mother, neither of the apprentices had been present any of the times she had driven Edward out of the house. Thanking God, Mary, and all the saints that she did not need to rehearse the boys in complicated lies, Lissa told them that Oliva had run away. This they knew, and both nodded with eyes large and round with fear.

"If my father learns that you did not stop her or run above at once to tell him," Lissa went on, "you will be punished. I do not think it fair. There was nothing you could do to stop her. For my own reasons I told my father that I sent Oliva away the day he left. I do not think my father will question you, but if he does, you are to say only that Oliva has been gone a long time and that there have been many different maids since then."

Both boys nodded again, much more happily this time, for claiming ignorance and using vague terms like "a long time" was easy for them. She then gave Ninias a penny and two farthings and told him to buy a pound of candles in the market. Witta got two farthings and instructions to get two dozen eggs—

and not to break them. Both were to go home when they had made their purchases and not to linger. If they were asked where she was, they were to say she was also at the market and had sent them home ahead; and they had better arrive before she did.

When the boys ran off, Lissa walked quickly west to Friday Street and into the alley that led to the back of Flael's house. Oliva was in the hut, pressed against the back wall and trembling with terror when Lissa opened the door. She fell to her knees as she recognized her mistress and began an incoherent plea, which Lissa cut off with assurances that she would do what she could to help. She then explained to Oliva what she had told her father and what she hoped to be able to do, but when she turned to leave, the woman clung to her skirt half fainting with fear at the thought of being taken by slave catchers. She was too frightened to take in Lissa's explanation easily, and it took Lissa some time to convince Oliva that no one was searching for her and that it would be safe to remain in the hut until she returned to get her.

Lissa was more patient than she might have been under other circumstances. She wanted Oliva to remember her flight as a time of terror and misery, lest it breed in her a tendency to escape every time she was given an unpleasant order; thus she was willing to take the time to make clear what would have happened if she had not been protected by her mistress's lies while easing her immediate fears.

The market was just coming fully awake when Lissa walked to the widest part of the Chepe where stalls were being erected. With more of an eye this once to who had goods already displayed than to the quality, Lissa chose a leg of lamb, a rump and tail of an ox, two chickens, and a variety of greens. She paid the butcher, farmer, and henwife, told them to hold her purchases, and turned back to Goldsmith's Row. She was early, which she intended, but not so early, she hoped, that she would catch Master Goscelin and Mistress Adela in bed. This hope was fulfilled; the journeyman who opened the door to her smiled and told her to go up, the master and mistress being at their morning meal.

Lissa had cemented her friendship with Goscelin and his wife over the months she had been Justin's mistress—not that she had admitted to the relationship or been with him when she visited them or when Adela came to visit her—but she had not seen Adela since Gerbod set sail. That was longer than she had ever gone without at least sending a note to explain why she could not repay the visit, but Lissa had no intention of beginning her plea for help with excuses. So, as soon as she opened the door, she said, "I have just committed a crime, and I hope you will aid me in escaping the consequences."

Goscelin burst out laughing and waved her to a stool, which she brought to the table. "Criminals," he remarked blandly, tearing off a large chunk of bread and placing it before her, "never seem to stop for breaking their fast. Will you join us?"

"Yes, indeed I will," Lissa said, reaching eagerly for the various foods Goscelin prodded toward her. "This criminal missed her evening meal as well as breaking her fast. My father came home last night."

"You did not murder him, did you?" Goscelin asked, with a thread of anxiety under his jesting manner.

"No, I was glad to see him—for about five minutes. I have been run off my feet you know, doing his share of the business as well as my own."

"I heard you were seeking a—a partner to share the work with you," Adela said.

"Oh, no I was not!" Lissa exclaimed, garbling the words and needing to catch the overflow from her mouth in her hand because she had been too eager to reply to chew and swallow properly. She licked the crumbs off her palm and explained about the sudden wave of offers of marriage. "And I could not refuse Chigwell outright," she went on more collectedly. "He made me too good an offer, and for the moment I forgot Edward went with it."

"But Edward Chigwell is a very fine young man," Adela cried. "He is kind and virtuous—"

"And so dull and pompous you would not believe it," Lissa interrupted. "If he knew what I had done, he would first faint and then run to the sheriff. I know I could not go to him with this problem."

"And you could not go to Justin with it?" Goscelin said quietly. He was surprised when Lissa did not blush and look away but turned furious eyes on him.

"Of course I could not. I could not go to any man with this crime—although I fear Justin would just laugh—so I beg you to finish breaking your fast and leave me to confess to Adela."

At that Goscelin laughed more heartily than before, finished his wine, and rose to his feet. Lissa kept her eyes on her food, feeling distressed because she had deceived him by her manner into thinking she was jesting about having committed a crime. It was for his own good, to protect him from involvement, but she did not like to manipulate her friends, even for their own good.

So when Goscelin was gone, she said quickly to Adela, "I made a jest of it, but it really is a crime. That was why I sent Goscelin away and could not ask Justin's help. How could I involve them in keeping my father's runaway slave leman?"

Adela frowned. "Do you expect me to keep her? You do not seem to be considering Goscelin's reputation. He is an alderman, after all."

"He is also well married, and you are here in the house. Also, Justin is known to have visited my house, whereas I do not believe Goscelin ever set eyes on Oliva in his life. And even if he had seen her and desired her, he would not have brought her to your house." She grinned at Adela. "No one would believe you would allow *that*."

"I did not mean that kind of reputation." The goldsmith's wife laughed. "I meant defying the law." Then she asked curiously, "Is she such a beauty?"

Lissa thought about it, frowning. "I suppose she is rather beautiful. I never thought about it before because she slides along the walls trying not to be noticed. She was just the woman my father bought to be our maid and then took to his bed. I thought it disgusting that he should use her so openly, but I did not understand how much against her will it was until my father returned and the poor woman fled the house rather than lie with him."

Adela blinked. "But surely bedding him is less dreadful than the punishment for being a runaway slave."

"I would think so myself," Lissa said, and then shuddered suddenly. "Perhaps not. My father might have peculiar tastes."

"Poor creature," Adela sighed, "but still, if a runaway slave were to be discovered in an alderman's house—"

"Oh heavens," Lissa exclaimed, interrupting her, "I have told this all backwards. Oliva does not need a place to hide from slave takers—oh, Adela, how could you believe I would ask so dangerous a favor? She is not being sought and I do not believe she ever will be. She only needs a place to live quietly until I can discover whether my father intends to go away again. If he does not, I will arrange to go to Peter's house in Canterbury in October to check the harvests and the accounts—for all I know about it, a cow could do it, but anything runs better when someone is responsible, and they know me. I will take Oliva with me and leave her there."

"But Lissa, why do you say she will not be sought? Even if your father has not missed her yet, he soon will."

Lissa laughed. "Oh he missed her. She will not be sought because I told my father I threw her out in February. It is barely possible he will lay a complaint, but I do not think he will bother. He must know how impossible it would be to find her after so long. In any case, she would not be punished, nor would anyone keeping her, because I will testify that I drove her away against her will." Her lips twisted. "If my father lays any complaint, it will be against me for depriving him of his property, and I am sure he will not do that, for fear my uncles would kill him."

"Well in that case, of course the woman will be welcome here." Adela sighed in relief. "You were perfectly right not to tell Goscelin, and as for Sir Justin—"

"There is another part of the problem," Lissa interrupted hastily. "I need to take back to the house with me a woman who is strong but both old and ugly. If she could cook, at least plain things, so much the better, and for the rest, the maid's work is simple enough. We do no spinning or weaving, so all that is left is the polishing, caring for the bedclothes, and fetching and carrying."

Adela had been studying Lissa's face while she spoke, and now she said, "Your father beat you. The bruise is faint, but I see it now. And you are thinner, Lissa, much too thin."

"As for the bruise, I gave him back better than he gave me," Lissa said with a smile, but her eyes were thoughtful and she added, "But his manner is very strange. For all his threats, he has never actually hit me before. He used to pinch me in private places or pull my hair or twist my ears so that there would be no bruises to show. He was always too much afraid my grandfather or uncles would hear I was bruised, even if I did not complain, but this time I even told him Gamel was due any day, and he did not seem to care."

"Then you must have Ebba," Adela said. "She has courage enough to brain your father with a pot if matters look dangerous to her, but she will not lose her head either. And she can cook, so perhaps you will regain some flesh."

"Oliva can cook, too," Lissa said merrily. "It was Edward Chigwell following me about that was taking away my appetite. Every time he opened his mouth and I thought about needing to listen to him for the rest of my life, I could feel my gorge rising. Really, you will find Oliva a good, obedient maid. She mends well also."

"Very well, you can bring her here. Meanwhile I will explain the situation to Ebba."

Adela watched Lissa go out and heard her run down the stairs, calling out to Goscelin that she had forgotten a parcel of fish and would be back in a few minutes. She even took the time to run down Friday Street and buy a fish from the first vendor, then back to the hut in Flael's garden. Oliva hung back in terror when Lissa prepared to lead her out of the hut, and Lissa had to stop and tell her again that it was safe, that no one was looking for her.

Despite what she had said to Adela, Lissa was not as confident of that as she sounded; however, when she got to her house after delivering Oliva safely—Ebba following her loaded with the fish and all the purchases she had made in the market—she learned it was perfectly true, at least for that morning. And it remained true, for her father seemed to have lost interest in Oliva.

William was still abed when Lissa entered the house, but he rose soon afterward. He was in so pleasent a mood that she was frightened to death, but everything came back to normal by dinner time. He attacked her when he came home, not physically this time but with words, as he had in the past, only he was nearly hysterical, not simply nasty. This disturbed Lissa also, but to her it was far more important to get him out of her chamber, so she did not stay to hear out what crimes she had committed, but snatched up some food and her work on the furnishings for his bed and locked herself in her chamber.

The little thud as the bar dropped into its slot left William feeling as if he might burst. "I will sss—" He choked on the word and then put his hand over his mouth in shock. He had almost said, "I will sell it anyway," and exposed his whole plan. For a moment the idea that Lissa had ruined her own chances of saving herself by running off into her room calmed him, but nothing could change the basic fact that without Lissa his business was worth almost nothing.

He had decided, after throwing himself into bed the previous night, that there was nothing he wanted or needed so much as to leave his daughter without a house, without furnishings, without a business, without anything at all. He planned to sell to the richest Pepperer he knew. John, called le Spicer, could give him the gold in hand that very day as soon as he made out all the deeds and transfers. He would sleep the next night in Lissa's chamber also, but he would set fire to or otherwise destroy all her clothing, all the records of the business, and if he possibly could, her receipt book. Then he would get on his horse and ride north. Somewhere along the road, William Bowles would disappear and Amias FitzStephen would be reborn.

William had known he could not get the best price for his business by selling so quickly, but it was far more important to him just then to know that Lissa would be homeless, penniless, a beggar in the street. The shock was all the greater, then, when Master John said, "I suppose you are taking your daughter with you or she is marrying? I heard that she was about to come to terms with Edward Chigwell." He shrugged. "Without her . . . I am not sure I wish to make an offer at all. Without her the business is worthless. If she stays in London, every customer will go to her, wherever she is. If she leaves, your shop is no better than the next. The house is a fine one, though. I will offer for that."

In vain did William protest how profitable his business was, how widely known were the medicines that came from his shop, and his special arrangements with the Hanse. Master John looked at him coldly, contemptuously, and replied that if he could only sell Mistress Lissa, who was well known to be the source of all the profit and cures, and who moreover had daughter's share in two Hanse ships, he would pay five hundred pounds for her and another two hundred for the shop and business. The contempt struck William like a blow across the face, for it told him that John le Spicer not only knew his daughter had carried the business on her shoulders for years but also that she was beyond his governance.

There was little William could do except ask Master John not to prejudice others against him, and this the Pepperer agreed to with faintly curled lips. All the way home William was too stunned to think or react. His hate and disappointment only boiled over when he laid eyes on Lissa, but the spate of loathing that had poured out of his mouth and the shock he felt when he almost gave the game away brought him to something approaching rationality. He did not want to remember most of his interview with John le Spicer, but the idea of selling Heloise was not at all unpleasant and opened a pathway to thought.

The first result was a new rush of fury. A man might sell a daughter. Such transactions were not well thought of, but they were certainly legal. Unfortunately, however, Heloise was now a widow, free and independent, and too many people knew it for him to try to lie about her condition. That conclusion made William physically sick so that he threw the dinner on the floor and ran out of the house. It was only after he had walked himself into exhaustion that it occurred to him that there were other ways of binding people to a kind of slavery. If he could somehow induce Heloise to sign a contract for her services, she would be more firmly bound because she was acting as a free and independent widow.

He burst into hysterical laughter and had to lean on the side of a building until he recovered. Heloise would as soon stick her hands in a fire as sign anything he presented to her. If she had only committed some crime . . . Could he say he had proof that she had poisoned a client and he would show it to all if she did not sign? William saw an alehouse and sank down on the bench outside because his knees were shaking. She would laugh at him, and so would everyone else. But poison was an idea that recurred to him. He could poison her. It would not be easy, but it was possible.

Only that would do him little good. William signed for a cup

of ale and drank it when it was brought to him. If Heloise were
dead, her skill and knowledge would be subtracted from the
value of the business, and it seemed that everyone knew that it
was she, not he, who had the ties to the Hanse. And if she were
dead, what Gamel and Gerbod would do to him was not to be
thought of; they would never believe her death was natural,
even if no one else suspected him. But Gamel and Gerbod
would never find him. William shuddered and shouted for wine
because he was suddenly cold as ice despite the warmth of a
pleasant August afternoon.

When the heat of the wine spread through him, he suddenly
realized that there was no need to get Heloise to sign anything.
Any woman, properly gowned, could appear before a justice
and swear that a particular signature was hers. Who would
suspect that the woman was not Heloise if she was with her
own father? The signed contract need not be presented until
the money was handed over. Nor was there any need for
Heloise to be present at that ceremony. William himself could be
gone . . . He imagined himself saying he wished to deposit
the buying price with his goldsmith and would meet his dupe at
his house, going a street or two away, mounting his horse,
which would be waiting with what little baggage he would need
for his journey, and riding off to Bristol, leaving the buyer to
deal with Heloise himself. William had no idea who would win
that struggle, but he almost wept to think he must miss seeing
it.

He brought himself out of this pleasant dream with some
effort, and sipped more slowly at the wine left in the cup. Dream
or not, parts could be translated into the real world. William
stared into the distance, now looking with care at each part of
this new plan, and saw there were two essential points. The first
was that Heloise must not be married or contracted to marry; the
second was that the buyer be unable or unwilling to ask Heloise
about the arrangements. William nodded with satisfaction. That
meant the purchaser must be from outside London or thoroughly unscrupulous—but that could wait, as could the details
of the contract to which he would forge Heloise's signature. His
first step must be to get Chigwell publicly to withdraw his offer
of marriage. William smiled for the first time since his meeting
with Master John. Bitch in heat that she was, Heloise had

wanted young Edward two years ago. He licked his lips over the satisfaction of frustrating that desire twice.

William's easy success in driving Chigwell to repudiate the offer he had made to Lissa had two sources he did not recognize. The first was Edward's growing distaste for her, which he had communicated to his father. The elder Chigwell had at first dismissed his son's doubts, saying a woman could be tamed after marriage in ways that could not be used by a suitor, but he was not as sure as he sounded. The most important factor, though, was that the whole merchant community was waiting with grave anxiety to learn what repercussions there would be in trade from the French victory at Bouvines.

Master Chigwell's fears were greater and his anxiety deeper than that of many others because his trade had been founded on the spices and delicacies that could be obtained more reliably from southern France rather than on those from the East. If King Philip gathered more troops in Paris, where a week-long celebration had followed the victory, ordered his son to join him—for Louis's troops had seen no action—and pursued the English, he might drive John out of France entirely. Even if Philip did not succeed in that, he might defeat King John again and impose punitive trade regulations. All English merchants, and many French ones also, would be hurt, but Chigwell, whose sources were almost exclusively French, might be ruined. His temper was very short.

Part of Master Chigwell's purpose in desiring to secure Lissa was that her sources of supply would balance his. Unfortunately he forgot this and other far more important considerations when, at a meeting of the Pepperers Guild, William accused him of fraud. Master Chigwell, he complained, had intended to marry his daughter and steal his house and his business, which did not belong to her. Chigwell denied this, of course, but William made matters look blacker and blacker. He pointed out that he had refused Chigwell's offer two years earlier, that his own business had improved and Chigwell's had not over those two years, and that Chigwell had deliberately waited to address his offer to Heloise until her father was away for a protracted time on important business.

Chigwell could have pointed out that the last accusation was utter nonsense; William had left London only five days after his daughter was widowed and Chigwell had not offered his son for a full five months after that. However, Master Chigwell had already lost his temper because the first two accusations had too much truth in them. He raved over William's "sale" of a brilliant apothecary to a goldsmith for God knew what unsavory purpose, and then gathered his wits enough to point out that Mistress Lissa was a free woman with the right to marry whomever she pleased. William admitted freely that this was true, but asked if it was fair that Chigwell had crept behind his back and sent his son to flatter and court his daughter. A father had a right and a duty, William protested, to advise and protect his daugher, even if she was a widow. It was dishonest to work on her feelings so that she would accept an ungenerous marriage contract.

Most of the men there knew that Lissa was quite capable of reading and understanding a contract on her own, but most of them also knew she was generous and impulsive. It was thus possible that if Edward seduced her, she would accept an agreement that was less favorable to her than she could obtain. Nor did any of them doubt that William could squeeze the last quarter-farthing out of any contract made on his daughter's behalf—if he wished to. So, although they liked Chigwell and did not like William, the consensus was that Chigwell must make clear that there had been no formal contract or betrothal and that he was withdrawing his son from any informal offer to the lady. As consolation they offered that Edward could explain this to Lissa, and if she desired, the agreement could be renewed.

William protested loudly that this gave Chigwell an unfair advantage, but he was told contemptuously by the master not to be such a greedy cur, that if Edward and Lissa were agreed in love they should have their way. Whereupon William cried that he would not be cheated out of his daughter's service and would see that the marriage contract was very clear on that point. To this, Chigwell responded at the top of his voice that he would not allow his son to form a blood bond with William Bowles if his daughter were the last woman on earth.

Lissa's reaction to Master Chigwell's visit the next day to withdraw his offer was disappointing from William's point of view. She showed no emotion beyond a concern that she should not lose Master Chigwell's goodwill, taking his hand and saying in a tone of regret that she was glad now she had not made a more definite arrangement or her father's behavior would have been ten times worse.

"You are a good girl, Lissa," Chigwell replied, and added, with a venomous look at William, "Surely the poison in his heart must kill him soon. Then we will see."

Lissa made no reply to that except a faint negative shake of the head, but she had to lower her eyes to hide the tears in them. She would not need to consider callow, humorless Edward if her father were dead; she would be free to fly to Justin. She had swallowed the pain by the time Chigwell left, however, and her eyes were dry when she turned eagerly to her father.

"I cannot thank you enough for getting me out of the pit I had dug for myself," she said, smiling brilliantly at William.

Her heart ached a little less when she saw her father's mouth drop open with surprise. His dismay was a little salve for her hurt, perhaps only a pinhead's worth in comparison to the pain he had caused her in separating her from Justin, but it was something.

"I like the old man very well," she went on before William could speak, "and he made me so good an offer—my own will in what business I did and where I lived and all other things—that I forgot I would have to take Edward with the contract."

"You cannot fool me," William said, sneering. "You wanted him. You fought like a cat to have him two years ago."

"Indeed I did." Lissa laughed heartily. "That was another reason for my mistake. When Edward came into my mind I remembered him as handsome and kind. I discovered to my sorrow and terror that in two years I had grown into a woman and he was still a boy. So, father, I thank you. I could not imagine how I was going to extricate myself from that agreement, until you appeared. I knew you would do it for me."

His daughter's obvious good spirits took some of the head off the ale of spoiling the marriage for William, but the ale was still there. Lissa was unmarried and through Chigwell's fury the whole merchant community knew no contract for her marriage was under negotiation. Still, William delayed beginning to seek a gullible buyer for his business. The uncertainties of the

political situation on the Continent were causing many Pepperers to draw in their horns. Few would be ready to offer him
any price, and those few would be harder to deal with than John
le Spicer.

Then, during the first week in September, Gamel sailed into
port with a cargo that had been dumped in La Rochelle by an
Italian captain. The Italian had hoped to sell to merchants
dealing with a victorious army and had found no one would buy
his goods. The loot from the early victories of King John's army
was gone, all hope of a new campaign had died with the defeat
of his allies at Bouvines, and the English lords were bitter and
destitute. Most of the merchants were equally bitter and
destitute. Many had not been paid for earlier purchases and
could not have bought even if they wished. None were ready to
take on luxury goods. Gamel had gladly taken the cargo off the
Italian captain's hands. The lords who had followed John might
be temporarily destitute, but the merchants back in England
would not be.

Gamel's presence alone would have paralyzed William. If
Lissa somehow got a hint of his intention to sell, all hell would
break loose; if Gamel heard of the matter, William would be
beaten to death, since Gamel regarded the house his father had
paid for as Lissa's. However, the news Gamel brought was an
even greater deterrent to William to loosing any rumors of
selling his business. Gamel had heard that King Philip had not
moved from Paris to attack John and that the pope had sent
Robert Cardinal Curzon, an Englishman, to help negotiate a
truce. Far more important to William was the news that, all
hostilities being at an end, Robert FitzWalter was on his way
home.

Gamel sailed at the end of the third week of September, but
William went on with his life as if he had never been away from
London. As soon as he heard FitzWalter would soon be in
England, William had devised a new plan. He knew that
without the seal in hand he could never summon up the courage
to ask Lord Robert outright for the sum of money he wanted.
But a loan—that was different. He could ask for a loan and give
the business as a surety. Sitting in his chair in the solar, with
Lissa safe in her bedchamber, William began to laugh aloud.
What a comedy! A purchaser coming to London who thought he

owned Lissa. Lissa who thought she owned the business. And FitzWalter who really owned it all and had the power to take it!

William was very glad he had not, except for his one conversation with John le Spicer, indicated that he intended any change in his way of life. Let FitzWalter believe he would be a pawn easily within his grasp for as long as he was wanted. FitzWalter would be less suspicious and more prone to grant William his loan. Accordingly when FitzWalter arrived in London two weeks later, he presented himself and asked for a private audience.

He began with the good news that he had discovered the whereabouts of Flael's sons and then with some anxiety described the frustration of his plans to reach them. He was relieved when FitzWalter nodded acceptance of that quite calmly and asked, seemingly with simple curiosity, how he had traced them. William explained the trail he had followed from the goldsmith in Peterborough to the ship master of Haarlem, carefully naming each man who had helped him in the hope of gaining FitzWalter's favor. After all, William thought, he might someday want another favor from one of those men, and if they profited from their efforts they would be willing to help him again.

"I will see what I can do for them," FitzWalter said. "But since you used my name in this matter, I hope you gave them a sensible reason for my seeking these young men."

"Oh yes, my lord," William replied, and related the tale of the design Flael was supposed to have done. "That was another reason," he added, "that I gave up trying to reach them. I did not wish to give the impression that the matter was of any great importance."

"Very wise," FitzWalter agreed. "As soon as I have word that the truce is signed, I will decide what further I wish to do."

He raised a hand as if to dismiss William, who said hastily, "My lord, I have a favor to ask."

"Yes?"

"This affair has been costly to me, in many ways. The dowry I was forced to pay Flael was very large, much larger than I would have had to give another Pepperer. Also, I expended my own money in the long chase of Flael's sons, and I was forced to neglect my business for many months. I would not ask you for any gift before the matter is concluded to your satisfaction, of course, but if you could lend me—"

"Costly to you?" FitzWalter interrupted and laughed harshly. "What do you think the king's little war cost me?" He stared at William and then waved him away.

Such a fury gripped William that he nearly screamed aloud. He would not be cheated of his prize! He would not! "You have laid a heavy burden on me, my lord," he said. "It is not easy to carry in my heart the knowledge of the whereabouts of the fruit of Flael's crime and the cause of his death and such matters. And the money would be only a loan. I will give you a bond on my house and business as surety that I will pay it back."

There was a brief silence in which William would have turned and run, except that he was too terrified by what he had done to move. FitzWalter had been staring at him with a look of astonishment, but rage did not follow, as William had expected. Lord Robert blinked and then said, quite blandly, "A surety for a loan that will lift the burden from your heart? A bond on the house and business? Well, that is not unreasonable. How much do you want?"

Chapter 22

JUSTIN FELT AS IF HE HAD HARDLY CLOSED HIS EYES WHEN AN insistent pounding on his door and a man's voice, almost as high-pitched as a woman's in near hysteria, brought him awake again. He tumbled out of bed, cursing Hervi and swearing for the hundredth time to get rid of the man. He was probably out drinking again, or dead drunk already, and his poor wife too frightened to go to the door.

Dragging on his bedrobe and boots, Justin seized his sword and went down. The figure that burst through the doorway once he had lifted the bar and the latch did so with such impetuosity that he almost spitted himself on Justin's half-raised sword. Justin jerked the weapon back, half turning away to protect the oblivious summoner. The gesture seemed to transmit a message Justin had not intended because the young man seized his arm and cried out.

"Come! You must come! You cannot be such a monster as to refuse her now. He is dead—dead. All blood. So much blood."

Justin, who had been fully occupied in trying to come

314

completely awake and prevent his visitor from inadvertently killing himself, peered more intently into the face turned up to his.

"Paul?" he gasped. "Paul?"

"Come," Paul repeated, tugging at Justin's arm. And then, as Justin resisted, "Have you not hurt her enough? Will you refuse to do your duty just to cause her harm?"

"What the devil are you talking about?" Justin shouted, the sense of Paul's first words finally penetrating. Then his breath caught and he dropped his sword and seized Paul in a grip that wrung a cry of pain from him. "Blood? Is Lissa hurt? *Who* is dead?"

He shook Paul as a terrier shakes a rat, almost producing the same broken neck, cast him aside, and took a step toward the street. He was just barely sane enough to stop when Paul croaked, "Master William is dead."

Justin's life, which had gotten badly cracked in the last few months and felt as if it had flown all to bits when he thought Lissa was dead, reassembled itself. It had not come together right. Here and there it was badly misshapen, but it was a life of a kind and he was too dazed to complain or to wonder what was wrong. He picked up his sword and put out his other hand to help Paul up.

The journeyman ignored the offer and climbed shakily to his feet on his own. "Will you come?" he cried.

"Will you tell me what is wrong?" Justin retorted, the remainder of what Paul had said about his being a monster and "refusing" Lissa having had time to be absorbed and sting him.

"Master William is dead," Paul repeated, and gulped.

"Thank God I am not called out to every death in this city," Justin remarked caustically. "If he is not dead by violence— Oh yes, all the blood—"

"All over the shop." Paul's voice almost failed, and he grasped Justin's arm again. "Come. Please come."

"He was killed then? By whom?"

"I do not know," Paul wailed. "I was asleep."

"You slept through a killing that covered your shop with blood?"

Paul's mouth shook, then firmed. "Mistress Lissa asked me to fetch you. All I know, I have told you. Master William is lying dead in the shop in a pool of blood. If you will not come, will you tell me whom to summon?"

"I will come, of course, but I must dress," Justin said. "If William Bowles is dead, he will wait for me quite patiently."

"But the mistress—" Paul called after him.

Ignoring the implied plea for reassurance that he would be quick, Justin walked swiftly up the stairs. He shut the door to the solar with a bang when he reached it, hoping the sound would discourage Paul from following him to urge him to hurry. Justin did not know what his face showed, but he would take no chance, even in the dim light, that anyone would read there the misery he felt. There was rage in him too, but even his anger was not strong enough to lift the dark weight that lay on his soul.

It had been there all the time, Justin realized, as he pulled off his bedrobe and reached for shirt and chausses. He pulled on the chausses and wrapped the cross garters around the legs to keep them from twisting. No braies under an arming tunic, and these days Justin did not stir without arms and armor. His thoughts followed their own path as his hands worked, revealing to him that he had lived under that black burden ever since he had tried to force Lissa to marry him at the end of May. He had pretended to himself that he was glad to be free of her, and perhaps there was some relief in having escaped the agony he suffered when they spat cruel words at each other and parted, and came together again. But the dark pall that wrapped him round had turned the whole world black and bitter.

The banked fire did not give much heat and Justin shivered, but not really because of the chill in the room. So William Bowles was dead. Because almost a year ago he had murdered Peter Flael? Had Lissa known that and lied about it? Was that truly why she would not marry him? And if that was true, what would she do now? How would she greet him? What would she say? Justin shivered again. What should he reply to the daughter of a murderer, who had picked him up and cast him down—and other men also—like a cheap toy. The darkness in his soul was split by a red shaft of rage. "Whore," he muttered.

"Sir Justin—"

Justin jerked and pulled the shirt over his head. Then he walked into the solar and flung the door open. Paul had carried up the night-candle from the ground-floor room to light his way. The light also gave him too good a view of the expression on Justin's face, and he backed up and almost fell down the stairs. Justin caught his arm and steadied him.

"Go down to the back room and kick my servant awake. Tell him to saddle my horse. If Hervi is not there, you will have to saddle Bête Noir yourself. Do you know how?"

"Yes," Paul breathed, and ran down the stairs much faster than he had come up.

Cursing Hervi again, Justin pulled one tie of his shirt sleeve with his teeth, made an awkward one-handed knot to hold it, then did the other sleeve. He realized he should have kept Paul to help him, but he was glad he had not. He needed more time to grind down his urge to kill anything connected with Lissa. As he struggled into the arming tunic, which was stiff and stinking of sweat, and then wearily pushed his head and shoulders into his hauberk, he recalled that his cousins had barely prevented him from attacking and killing Edward Chigwell without the slightest excuse. They had then forced Justin to leave London. He had spent the harvest season working in the fields on his father's estate and only come back to London when word of the truce reached the mayor, who had summoned him in fear of trouble from the returning men-at-arms.

Since then Justin had been too busy trying to keep the peace with his depleted forces to think of Edward Chigwell, especially since he heard that William Bowles had put an end to any prospect of marriage. Justin paused in the middle of buckling on his sword belt, then finished what he was doing and thrust the sword into its sheath in a hurry. Had Lissa feared he would abandon her as easily as Edward Chigwell had? Could that be why— But wait, Edward had not been involved directly; Justin remembered every word he had heard about that affair. Bowles had made some ugly accusations, and the elder Chigwell had withdrawn his offer. So perhaps Edward had not given Lissa up willingly. As he caught up his shield and walked back through the solar and down the stairs, Justin remembered something else. The old man had said he would never countenance the marriage while Bowles was alive—or something like that. Could it be that Bowles's death had nothing to do with Flael?

Both Paul and Hervi were standing by the horse. Justin

snorted irritably and pushed aside the stirrup to check the girth himself. He slammed Noir in the ribs and drew in the girth another inch before the big black could draw in the breath he had expelled.

"I will speak to you when I get back," he said to Hervi, and then looked at Paul and shook his head; both together could not saddle one horse properly.

He mounted and rode along the Mercery, turning south into Soper Lane. Just past Needler's Lane he was challenged, and he lifted his shield and put his hand on his sword hilt; but the men who came forward with torches were part of the watch, and he hooked the shield back on the saddle. He called his name almost at the same moment as the leader of the group recognized his horse and shield and apologized for the challenge. Justin then paused to ask if the watch had heard any disturbance down Soper Lane. There had been some men abroad earlier, he was told, but they were quiet and sober, had given their names readily, and had been allowed to pass. Did Justin want the names? He gave a negative shake of the head.

Cordwainers was a quiet area, the watchman said, there being little to attract roisterers. But less than an hour past a pair of men going west on Watling Street had hurried on instead of stopping when they were hailed. They had turned north into Soper. The watchman shrugged. He had pursued the pair, but they had disappeared by the time the watch reached the corner. They had not looked for them. Two well-dressed men could have many reasons not to want to give their names to the watch, and they were not likely to be thieves or cause a riot.

Justin agreed and rode down the street. If by any chance Bowles had been one of those men and they had been coming from the east along Watling, they could not have been coming from Chigwell's house, which was farther down Soper in the Vintry. But if the watch— Justin stopped the thought, appalled. The woman had driven him insane. He had been about to think of ways to alter the watch's evidence to involve Edward Chigwell—and for all he knew, William Bowles had never left his bed except to walk down the stairs into his shop and be killed there. And if one wanted Bowles dead, there was another who was even more eager for him to pass from the world—Lissa herself!

With his heart a lead weight in his breast, Justin drew his sword and pounded on the door of Lissa's house with the hilt. Instantly her voice came down from the window above. "Justin? Thank God. Come around by the back. The space by the front door is a sea of blood."

He looked up instinctively, just in time to see the shadow that was her head withdraw, but he did not move. The sound of her voice . . . he had forgotten her voice. In the bitter days and weeks and months he had remembered much about Lissa, little good, much bad or twisted from what had been a delight to him into badness, but he had forgotten her voice. No, he had not forgotten it. It had been different; it had lost its music after she had cried it hoarse the day Gamel "ordered" her to marry him. After that it had only been a voice, without the lilt that had made it especially Lissa's voice.

Noir shifted uneasily under him. Justin steadied his hand, which had been trembling, and touched the horse with his heel. He closed his eyes as if that could shut out memory as he turned into the back alley. How often had he come this way to the warmth of Lissa's arms? He had to stop and breathe deeply to ease the pain in his chest and throat before he could dismount. As he swung his leg over the saddle, the door opened and a golden path fell across the yard. A small figure ran out along it, stopping a few respectful feet away to quaver in Witta's voice, "I will take your horse, my lord, if he will let me."

"Yes, he will," Justin responded. "Just do not shout at him or hurt him."

Everyone was afraid of Bête Noir because he was not only very large but also all black without a single lighter hair. That made the red of his mouth and flared nostrils, the white that surrounded his eyes when he rolled them, all the more startling. But for a stallion, Noir was very steady and gentle. It would scarcely do, Justin thought as he walked down the golden path to the open door where a slender figure stood waiting for him, for a man who needed to take his destrier into crowds to have the kind of mount that was half mad to begin with and went totally mad at the smell of blood. And then he was looking down into Lissa's face, knowing he was totally mad himself to be thinking about his horse instead of about her and William Bowles and the blood on the shop floor.

She put her free arm, the one that was not holding a candle, up around his neck, pulled his head down, and kissed his lips. Justin, who had let her do it in a kind of horrified daze, jerked away, and Lissa said, "I did not kill him. I did not arrange to have him killed." She then looked very surprised, her fingers crept up to cover her lips, and through them she added, "Perhaps you will not believe me, but I never thought of hiring a man to kill him. Oh dear, I am afraid if I *had* thought of it— But perhaps I would have been too sensible to place myself in the power of the kind of person who does—"

"Lissa!" Justin bellowed.

His heart was pounding like a hammer wielded by an insane blacksmith in a great hurry. The kiss had nearly made him sick, implying as it did that she was ready to sell her favors for his service in protecting her. But before his anger could do more than drive away the sickness, there she was explaining, as only Lissa could, that she *would* have been guilty if only she had thought of hiring a murderer, unless she had happened to remember that such men could not be dismissed as easily as they were hired.

"But Justin," she protested, staring wide-eyed into his face, "there is no use not considering such suspicions. Too many people know I hated my father. And some might have thought my bitterness would be increased by his causing Chigwell to withdraw his offer of marriage—"

"And was it not?" Justin asked.

Lissa stared upward, her face as astonished as if he had struck her, and then her eyes filled with tears, which spilled slowly down her cheeks. "How can you ask that?" she whispered. And then she lowered her head and bit her lips. "No, you are quite right. I deserve your scorn. I was so lonely and miserable. I was desperate for you and I could not have you, so I wanted someone, anyone, and Master Chigwell—of whom I am very fond—made me an offer that was most flattering. I was to have either his business or mine, and the other only to be managed by his younger son or another of my choosing, and a dower surety of—" She brushed the tears from her cheeks and looked up at Justin again. "It was greed, pure, simple greed."

"You lie!" Justin's voice grated through his tight throat. "Whore!"

That time she did not flinch. Her eyes continued to meet his and she shook her head slowly. "No, not that. I thought I could endure Edward. After all, I had endured Peter, and Edward was young and handsome. It made me sick to think of bedding him, but I was sure I would grow accustomed in time. But I never wanted him, Justin. Never." She sighed then, and the flame of the candle she was holding wavered. "But all the same, I suppose your word was true enough. A whore sells herself for coin, and I was ready to sell myself for—well, for what would amount to a great deal of coin, but coin nonetheless."

Justin grasped her wrist. "Is that true?"

The bones ground together almost audibly. Lissa cried out and dropped the candle, and two small forms hurtled into Justin, staggering him for the moment. He felt a fist hammer at his arm while fingers pried at his hand, and he looked down in amazement at Witta and Ninias, who were both shouting at him to let go and struggling physically to free their mistress.

"Stop that, you naughty boys!" Lissa snapped. "Sir Justin and I are good friends. He is not hurting me. I was only surprised. Ninias, pick up that candle and light it again."

Her face was still white with pain, but she did not rub her wrist. The boys drew off, Ninias bending to pick up the candle at Lissa's feet, but despite a confusion so violent he felt physically dizzy, Justin could not help chuckling at the expressions on their faces. Although he had released Lissa when she spoke, her apprentices were plainly not convinced by her statement that she and Justin were friends. Probably the boys thought she was trying to save them from being punished. They both looked frightened now. Still, the way they had flown at him and continued to fight him to protect her, even after he looked down at them with a glare that had been known to quell more hardened souls, spoke well for Lissa. And if she had truly wanted Chigwell's business and not his son . . . Justin almost reached for Lissa again to draw her close more gently.

"Did you call, mistress?"

A large gray-haired woman appeared in the doorway between workroom and shop, her right hand hidden behind her in the folds of her skirt. Lissa drew a shaky breath. "No, Ebba, thank you."

Justin frowned. "Wait. This is not the woman who used to be your maid."

"You mean Oliva," Lissa said. "No, Oliva is serving Mistress Adela, who lent me Ebba to take her place."

"When was this change made? And why?" Justin asked.

"Ebba has been with us since my father came home in August," Lissa replied. "He misused Oliva, who, you may remember, is very timid, so I asked Adela to give her shelter and lend me a maid who is not easily overawed."

"Did you not once tell me that Oliva was a slave?" Justin asked after a moment's thought. "Is it possible that your father promised her freedom in his will?"

"It is possible that my father did anything," Lissa said, "but I doubt he would offer a slave a promise, even a false promise. If you are thinking that Oliva could have killed him—it is impossible. I do not think any woman could have done this, or even an old or weak man. Take some candles. I left the room dark . . . you will see why."

Her voice was not quite steady, and as Justin reached out for a branch of candles standing on one of the counters he realized why golden light had spilled from the open door. Almost certainly every single candle holder in the house had been filled and lit. The room was brighter than day. Only then did Justin realize that if Lissa was innocent of her father's death, she must have been frightened almost out of her wits by what had happened. He wanted to turn back and comfort her but fought down the impulse. And when he walked to the door and lifted the branch of candles, shock wiped even Lissa from his mind. Paul had talked about a shop full of blood, and Lissa had spoken of a sea of blood; Justin had dismissed the words as the sort of exaggerations to which those who had never been on a battlefield were prone. This time, however, they were closer to the truth than he liked. With an exclamation of disgust, he walked forward to examine the body.

Justin saw at once what Lissa meant when she said she did not think the crime could have been committed by a woman or even by a man who was not powerful. The stroke that had sprayed blood all over the door, wall, and floor had cleaved deeply between neck and shoulder, severing the artery, but there was a puddle of blood around the dead man's waist, and the clothing over his abdomen was soaked in blood from a deep thrust into his belly. Yes, but the blood from the belly had not made the puddle, and there was something strange about the deep gash at the neck. Justin reached down and pulled the corpse over on its face. He nodded in satisfaction as his suspicions were confirmed.

Bowles had been stabbed from behind with tremendous force. A very long, broad hunting knife or a short sword had been thrust into his back hard enough to break a few ribs. But the impact could not have broken the ribs, Justin thought, unless the body had been braced . . . Yes, and that was why Paul had slept through the attack. The murderer must have put his hand over Bowles's mouth and held him while he delivered the blow. But he had struck below the heart and not killed him instantly, so the second blow had followed. Then, to make all sure, or just for hate—Justin flipped the body over on its back again—the killer had turned Bowles over and stabbed him in the belly.

A sound of retching made Justin turn his head and say irritably, "No one asked you to watch."

The words were out before he really saw the person in the doorway; Paul, not Lissa, was backing away.

"Wait," Justin ordered. "Send in—"

He stopped abruptly, swallowed hard, and stepped out of the direct light coming from the workroom, because he knew he was darkly flushed. The woman really *had* driven him mad. He had been so eager to get to her that he had not even sent Hervi to wake a few of the watch who were quartered close by his house. Worse—far worse, he now realized—he had not *wanted* to bring any men with him. His need to be alone with Lissa had driven out of his mind all thought of extra men.

"No," Paul breathed, putting a hand on the frame of the doorway to support himself. "This shambles is no fit place for my mistress."

"What are you talking about?" Justin snarled. "Who the devil wants your mistress in here? Although it seems she is not of such fine sensibility as you, since she must have been back and forth several times already without harm coming to her." He paused again and gritted his teeth. Why in God's name was he talking about Lissa? "Never mind that," he said to Paul. "Go to the alehouse on the south Poultry—it is nearer the Mercery than the Stock Market. In the house next door you will find my man Halsig. Tell him to bring four more men and meet me here."

Paul backed farther out of the room and said, "Yes, my lord," with an eagerness that Justin found rather surprising, considering that the journeyman had just walked all that distance twice.

Lifting high the candles he was holding, Justin examined the room as carefully as he had examined the body. What he saw indicated that there had been only one large body near Bowles when he was stabbed. Another much smaller person might have been close to the victim on the side opposite where he was struck in the neck, but the dead man's own body could have blocked spattering from that side. Justin thought the murderer had probably worked alone and that his clothes had been drenched in blood.

Almost as that thought came, it had to be abandoned. Tossed aside near the outer door was a dark heap. Justin walked to it and prodded it with his foot, lowering the branch of candles to see better. He sighed philosophically. A bloodstained murderer might have made life too easy for him. As he had suspected at the first glance, what he had found was a cloak, parts already stiffening with dried blood. So the killer had covered himself. No doubt he would have an easy explanation for the few spots the cloak had not caught.

Following his general inspection, Justin made a closer examination of the premises and looked closely again at the body to confirm his first impression that the killer was most likely a tall man—as tall as himself, or taller—and probably broader and stronger. He mused on the idea, then shrugged again. He knew one or two men, hired swords, who would fit that description and who would kill willingly enough, but that was meaningless. London must harbor hundreds of the same kind whom he did not know, and any one of them could be guilty if Bowles had been caught on the street and forced into the house. But that was unlikely. The shop had not been looted; nothing seemed to be disturbed. It was more likely that one of the two men who had run from the watch had been Bowles and that the dead man had known—and trusted—the man who came in with him. Justin looked from the outer door to the body consideringly. He could take his conclusions one step farther. Either the two men knew each other well, because Bowles had preceded his guest into the house rather than gesturing the guest politely ahead of him, or the attacker was of an inferior class.

After another moment of studying the body, Justin decided he had discovered everything possible from looking. Now he must learn what he could about William Bowles, and that meant he could no longer avoid talking to Lissa. His reluctance to face her made him ashamed and angry, and he stalked into the workroom prepared to snarl, only to see Lissa perched on a high stool with her head down on the counter, fast asleep. To either side was a boy, also asleep, heads pillowed on arms supported by the rungs of the stool.

Chapter 23

A MOVEMENT ON THE OTHER SIDE OF THE WORKROOM BROUGHT Justin around, hand on sword, but it was only the woman, Ebba, who lifted her head from her pallet and then lay down again. Justin quietly put down the candlestick he was carrying and stood looking at Lissa. Ebba's presence had at least saved him from his immediate desire to fondle Lissa into simultaneous wakefulness and passion. Only the temptation to let her sleep and escape from her remained, and he knew there was no escape for him. He would only increase his torment by putting off the confrontation.

He touched her shoulder and, when she did not stir, shook her gently. She drew a deep breath and lifted her head, twisting to look at him. Justin was surprised that she had not started or cried out, and when she saw him, she did not smile. Nonetheless, as they looked at each other he was assaulted—the strength of the feeling was such that he could think of no other word—by an aura of gladness, of welcome, of gratitude. Justin swallowed.

"Come away from your protectors," he said softly. "I wish to ask them questions later, and I desire to hear what they saw, heard, and believed, not repetitions of what they think you said."

Lissa nodded at once, smiling slightly now. "You will have to help me," she whispered. "I cannot get off the stool by myself without waking them." She shook her head as she saw him about to protest and said, "Let them sleep. They are very frightened. It is my fault. I should not have screamed, but when I saw . . ." Her voice faltered and she paused, breathed deeply, and reached for him. "Lift me a little, and I can get over them."

Justin stepped carefully between the two sleeping boys and lifted her off the stool, swinging her legs well over Witta's head. The feel of her in his arms brought an avalanche of memories on him, and he was paralyzed for a minute, until fury at his weakness let him set her down. Lissa glanced at him and away. Her smile was gone and she was pale and strained, her eyes ringed by bruised-looking skin. After a moment's hesitation she gestured, and Justin followed her to the door, both taking candlesticks.

Lissa hesitated again at the door. She seemed to try to walk straight in, but if that had been her intention, her resolution failed. She slid along the edge of the shop counter, her head turned to the wall, away from the blood-clotted thing that had been her father, and fled up the stairs so fast that two of the candles in the three-candle branch guttered out despite her sheltering hand. When they reached the solar, she ran right across to the hearth, set the candlestick down, and began to lay sticks on the banked coals. As Justin came closer, he saw that she was shaking. He wanted to kneel down beside her. He wanted to take her in his arms. He wanted to take her into bed and warm her cold body. And even the least of those desires was a dereliction of duty and, far worse, the mark of a man who could be led around by his rod by any whore.

"I will see to the fire," he said. "You are doing it more harm than good. Tell me what happened."

"It is swiftly told because I know little or nothing. My father went out about an hour before Vespers. When he did not come back for the evening meal, I locked the door but left the bar off. I was abed but not asleep when he came back." She glanced up at

Justin and then lowered her eyes. "I have not been sleeping very
well of late—"

"You mean since your father drove Edward Chigwell from
your bed?"

Lissa's head came up and her eyes widened. Her mouth
looked stiff, as if she had bitten something sour and dry, but she
was only trying to hold steady lips that were on the verge of
trembling with hope. The sneering question should have cut her
to the heart; instead, it confirmed the suspicion she had that
when Justin had lifted her off the stool he had held her a little
closer and an instant longer than was necessary. Had his eyes
not had all the color and warmth of dirty ice when he set her
down, she would have been certain. But surely his violent
jealousy of Edward meant he still wanted her himself.

"Edward kissed me on the mouth four times. That was more
than enough for me," she said. "He never set foot in my bedchamber, let alone in my bed, nor has any man but you." She
dropped her eyes and sighed. "Nor, I think, will any man ever. I
have learned that I cannot bear to be touched by another."

Justin thought his heart would leap out of his chest, but he
raised his brows and retorted, "Until someone offers even more
than Chigwell, eh?"

Then her eyes filled with tears and she dropped her head. "It
was a mistake," she whispered. "I thought I could never have
you, so I grasped at wealth. With Chigwell's business and my
own together, my man could have been master of the guild,
perhaps mayor—" Her hand flew up to cover her mouth as she
heard the words that betrayed her pride and ambition.

There was no retribution for those sins. On the contrary, she
saw some of the tension lines around Justin's mouth ease.
Instead of a straight, nearly invisible crease, a slight curve of lip
appeared. Lissa lowered her eyes and bent her head as if
ashamed of having exposed herself, but in reality she was afraid
her relief would show on her face. She had known that Justin
never understood, or discounted, her reasons for refusing to
marry him, but until he had pushed her away and thrown the
word "whore" at her, she had not realized he had assumed she
had tired of him and wanted a new man. She had been in
despair after that, believing he had seized her wrist and hurt her
in anger and disgust. But she had just repeated her reason for

considering Chigwell's offer, and he was not angry now, not at all. Lissa began to hope that Justin was glad to think she wanted place and riches rather than Edward.

Lissa's guess was very close to the truth. Justin was surprised and relieved to discover that Lissa had cravings to be the wife of a mayor or an alderman. He could supply something even better, for he was a knight and a gentleman born. It was clear to him also that she had not properly considered what came with the opportunity the elder Chigwell had offered. That sour pursing of the mouth when she spoke of having kissed Edward was more eloquent than any speech.

Choking in an effort to keep from laughing aloud, Justin said, "Your entanglement with Chigwell certainly *was* a mistake. Your greed and your father's interference in the plans Chigwell had made may have caused his death."

He hardly knew what he was saying. The weight on his heart had flown away, and if not for a tiny core of uncertainty, one hot coal of doubt that everything Lissa had said and done from the beginning was a lie, Justin would have swept her into his arms—and into the bed waiting in the room beyond the inner door. He was more than ready to forgive Lissa for wanting to make a rich marriage. He would forgive her anything—except wanting another man. But the doubt was there, and he could not yet bury it deep enough or trust her enough to quench the heat completely, so he turned away and put the candles on the table against the wall. When he turned back, Lissa was shaking her head.

"Oh, I do not think Master Chigwell was *that* eager to get me. Certainly he could not have done the murder himself, and to hire a man—"

Calling to mind what he had said, Justin snapped, "I did not mean the old man."

"Edward?" Lissa's face was totally incredulous, and then she began to laugh. "You cannot suspect Edward could do—do *that* to my father. He would be more likely to faint than to finish."

Justin took a step closer. The contempt in Lissa's laughter was a balm to his soul. That kind of disregard could not live with love. Whatever she had felt in the beginning, Justin was growing convinced that she certainly did not cherish Edward Chigwell now.

"But if he was desperate enough to hire someone?"

Lissa laughed again and began, "Edward is far too proper and cautious to . . ." But her voice faded before she said any more and she frowned, suddenly remembering something far more important than Edward. "The killer was no hired man," she said. "I heard their voices through the window as my father opened the door. Although I could not understand any words, I am certain they knew each other."

Had Lissa said that to distract his attention from Edward Chigwell? Justin told himself not to let his jealousy make an ass of him. He was almost sure from what he had seen below that Bowles and his attacker were acquainted, possibly close friends. "That is possible," he said to Lissa. "What happened next? Why did you go down?"

"To lock the door. They were laughing as they came in, and then I heard a sort of cry, but not loud. I would not have heard it if I had not feared—because of the kind of laughter—that my father was drunk. He was not a pleasant drunk. I was afraid he and his friend would hurt Witta or Ninias and that Paul and Ebba might be afraid to interfere, so I was listening. Then, a few minutes later, I heard the other man go out, still laughing, and the door close. I did not hear the lock or the bar, which my father might forget if he was drunk enough, so I waited, I cannot say how long, but long enough for him to get to bed."

"You did not hear him come up," Justin pointed out sharply. "Did that not surprise you?"

"I would not hear that. I have always kept my door barred against my father. I might hear if he shouted in the solar or if the boys screamed, but not sounds like footsteps or even if he stumbled into the furniture. What I heard came from the window," she reminded him.

Justin nodded acceptance of that. He remembered being surprised by the bar on her door when he had first seen it, and being equally horrified that Lissa's mother had needed that protection against her husband and that she would have dared to defy him by using it. He wondered whether Lissa's use of the bar was habit or defense, and whether that had any bearing on Bowles's death.

"So you went down to lock the door," he said. "When did you see him?"

Lissa did not answer at once. She bit her lip and blindly held out her trembling hands to the dying flickers of the fire that Justin had forgotten to mend. "I st-st-stepped on him." Her voice was a thin, breathy thread and she began to shake. "I was half asleep, so tired, so angry because he had—I thought—got into bed without even taking off his shoes. I know the shop so well. I d-d-did not look. I stepped on his arm and fell—"

"Hush, dear heart," Justin said and pulled her into his arms. "You will forget it."

She was racked with dry sobs and was shivering convulsively. "I hated him," she whispered. "I am glad he is dead. I am sure he brought it on himself and deserved even so horrible a death. I was sorry about Peter. I am not sorry about him, but—oh, Mary help me—I cannot stop seeing it."

Justin had taken both her hands into one of his. They were very cold. He knew there was no warmth to be had from his body while he was in armor, but he could not bear to let her go and continued to hold her. Her shivering began to abate, and that told him that fear and horror might have chilled her as much as the night-cool room. He was glad to think he could relieve her of most of that with a few judicious lies.

"I hope you are not very vindictive," he said, allowing a hint of humor to come into his voice. "Because I am afraid I must disappoint you about your father's death. I doubt it was really horrible at all. I should think from the wounds and the expression on his face that all he felt was a hard blow and surprise at that before he could feel nothing at all."

Lissa began to weep aloud then, and Justin stroked her hair. After a few minutes she sniffed and wiped her face on her sleeve, then looked up at him. "If that is not like my father," she said, the words breaking between sobs and wry laughter. "Just think, he managed to make his death more horrible for everyone else than for himself."

"No doubt that will be some satisfaction for him in whatever afterlife he finds, but I hope you are not so glad to be rid of him that you wish to protect his murderer."

"God be my witness, no!" Lissa exclaimed. "I hope and pray it is not someone he cheated and drove to desperation, but rage is no excuse for hacking a man to bits." She shivered again over those words and drew a trembling breath.

"It looked worse to you than it was, my dear." Justin lied as smoothly as he had about William's expression. She would not see the body again, and he could see no reason for her to be tormented by horrors. "I expect you were shocked by all the blood and did not look closely, but a large vessel in his neck was severed, and the loss of blood is what killed him with little, if any, pain."

"I find I am glad of that after all," Lissa said in a small voice. "So many times when my mother was alive and he hurt her I thought of dreadful things I would like to do to him, but now I am glad he died without pain and without knowing. He was such a dreadful coward." She sighed and then asked, "Could I sit down? My knees are not willing to support me much longer."

Justin tried to place her in the chair, but she preferred to sit on the stool he had chosen for himself. And then, somehow, Justin was in the chair and they were arranged in the old, familiar positions.

Lissa raised her head from where she had been resting it on his knee. She examined the frozen mask of his face, and her lips quivered. "Your legs are too long for a stool," she said. "How can you ask questions and glare at me properly when your knees are touching your chin?"

Subduing a mixed impulse to laugh and choke her, Justin asked quietly, "Do you not deserve to be glared at?"

"No, I do not!" Lissa exclaimed. Then she touched his hand tentatively and spoke more softly. "I hurt you, and I am sorry. I did it to save you worse pain. You do not believe me, but it is true nonetheless."

"Let us not begin that old argument again," Justin snapped. "Finish now the tale you began. After you found your father's body, what happened?"

"I screamed." Lissa licked her lips. "I am not a screaming person, and I have seen blood before, but—"

"Never mind that," Justin said harshly. "Since I did not find you lying on the floor, I assume you got up. I do not need all the little things now. I may ask about them later."

"But I did not get up." Lissa closed her eyes and laid her head back down on Justin's knee. "I lay there shrieking like an idiot until Ebba and Paul came in, and the boys too—oh, the poor things—and this is all, really. When I saw how much I had frightened Ninias and Witta, I stopped acting like a fool and told Paul to go get you. Ebba was not as frightened as the boys and I. She lit some candles and went to get more candlesticks. None of us wanted to be in the dark. But then I thought I would see you sooner if I waited by the window, and it was not hard at all to go through the shop."

Justin heard the longing in those words, but all he said was, "So you saw nothing at all of the man who came into the house with your father?"

"Nothing."

"Did you recognize his laugh?"

"No, but I should if I heard it again. It was hoarse and deep, as if it came from the bottom of a barrel."

Justin nodded. That fit very well with his deduction of a man bigger and heavier than himself. "That may be helpful after we lay hands upon the killer, so tell me who, aside from the Chigwells, wanted William Bowles dead."

"I did." Lissa lifted her head and looked at Justin with wide, pleading eyes. "My father's death meant I could—could try to win you back. I did think of poisoning him, but I was afraid, not so much that I would be found out, because I am very clever in such substances, but I knew what I had done would give me no peace or rest and I would rot inside. I wanted him dead, but not by my hand or the hand of one I loved."

"Lissa—" Justin began, intending to stop her.

She shook her head and put a finger gently on his lips. "Listen," she said. "You may in the end decide I am lying, but it is better for me to tell you how much I wished for his death and why I did nothing. I even hid many of the little hurts he did me for fear Gamel or Gerbod would kill him. If I had thought of hiring someone I did not care about and who was already damned beyond another sin doing him harm . . ." She frowned, her face very intent. "I do not know. I might have . . . But I did not think of it, Justin. I swear I did not."

He took her chin in his hand and laughed at her earnestness. "You are quite mad, Lissa. Most people exhaust themselves in trying to convince me that they had no reason to wish ill to the victim. I have never before had anyone explain carefully that she wanted to murder the victim and had not committed the crime merely by a slight oversight."

"Well, you will go out and about asking questions, and you will soon discover what kind of man my father was." She smiled faintly, and gently touched the hand that was holding her face. "I suppose I would rather have you know I thought of killing him than have you believe I felt no shame and anger at what he did. He was a liar and a cheat. He would have done much worse, except that he was too much afraid of being caught and punished."

"Then he must have had many enemies."

"Oh, he did, but as far as I know, none who hated him enough to kill him. The ill he did was mostly little things." Color rose in her cheeks as she spoke. "He was more despised than hated, I think."

"The kind of man who might ferret out secrets and make those who had them pay for his silence?"

There were tears of shame in Lissa's eyes, but she kept them on Justin's and answered steadily. "He would do it gladly, but I cannot think who would tell him a secret."

Justin stroked her hair. "I am sorry to cause you pain, poor child, but these are things I must ask."

"And I wish to answer, Justin."

"I will need a list of—" Justin paused, realizing that there could be hundreds of names on the list of those a merchant would know, for good or ill. Perhaps it would be possible to shorten the list, he thought, and said, "If I tell you what I think I have discovered about the man who killed your father, will you try to match that to anyone he knew?"

"Yes, but what if I am mistaken?" she asked faintly.

"That you name a person will not convict him." He patted her shoulder. "Besides, there cannot be very many who will fit. The man was, I think, taller than I and broader, of great strength, and—"

"Hubert de Bosco!" Lissa burst out, and then added, "But he was one of my father's friends—or, at least, my father employed him"—she looked down, then up again—"for ugly work, like collecting debts. They drank together too. Why should Hubert kill him?"

"So?" Justin nodded. "That is most interesting. With such men it is more often a quarrel among friends that breeds violence than an attack by a petty enemy. Do you know any more about this man? Where he lives—" He broke off his questioning and laughed. Lissa's hand had flown to her mouth again, a sure sign she had suddenly realized that she had said more than she should. "It is too late for second thoughts. Out with the rest of it. You have said too much to hide anything with success."

Liss did not answer him immediately. She had remembered her father's fear when she said she thought Hubert might be involved in Peter's death and her guess that Hubert was only the tool of someone of great power. But the effect of the intensity of her father's fear had been diluted by the passing of many months, his murder removed the reason she had had for concealing his possible knowledge about the cause of Peter's death, and she was sure Justin was astute enough politically, to use, or not use, what she would tell him to the best purpose.

"Lissa," Justin urged in a minatory voice.

She had been looking past him and now turned her head to meet his eyes. "I will tell you everything I know now, and I hope you will not be very angry with me. I told you no lies when Peter died, but I did not tell all the truth either. I had reason to suspect that Hubert de Bosco was the man who killed Peter—"

"What?"

"Please, let me tell the whole tale, Justin. It is a very long story, and you may shout at me all you like at the end of it, but if you interrupt me each time I say what surprises you or you dislike, I will never be done."

He stared at her, blank with rage for a moment, certain that her only purpose was to divert him from suspicion of Edward Chigwell, and then he remembered that his own first reaction had been to link Bowles's death with that of Flael. There was something else too. The name Hubert de Bosco had a familiar ring, as if he had heard it before. Justin nodded curtly.

"As you must have realized, there was something strange about my father's decision to marry me to Flael," Lissa began, going on to point out all the anomalies about the marriage. Justin glared impatiently, having been struck by the peculiarities himself; however, when she began to describe the behavior of her father and Hubert at the wedding itself and the strange way she had been searched before she left with her husband for his estate in Canterbury, he leaned forward, listening intently.

"I had no choice but to believe that Peter had promised something to my father that he had pretended to deliver but had actually withheld—or that his sons had substituted false for true gems or something of that kind, since young Peter and Edmond were violently against the marriage from the first. You can guess then, that when Peter was found dead and, as I thought, tortured, I was frightened to death that my father had been trying to get from Peter what he was cheated of, and had gone too far."

"So *that* was what you were hiding!" Justin exclaimed. "But why? Surely you did not think we would hang the innocent daughter with the guilty father."

"Hang me, no. But I did fear that the court might confiscate my father's business or fine it so heavily for blood money that it would be ruined. That would have ruined me too, and it is my sweat this business has floated on for years." Lissa put a finger on Justin's lips when she saw he was about to protest. "I might have told you anyway, but I learned before you returned to Flael's house that my father had nothing to do with Peter's death, did not even know of it until after the body was discovered. He nearly had a fit when he heard that Peter had been tortured, and I thought he would die of fright himself when, seeing he was not guilty, I told him I thought Hubert had done it, trying to get for himself what Peter had withheld."

"Then he must have thought this Hubert guilty too. So why did you let your father's fear of the man silence you? Did you think I would have the name of my informant called aloud in the marketplace?"

"I was not concerned about that," Lissa replied. "What held me silent was that my father was not afraid of Hubert. He was cautious in dealing with him, but no more than that. When I saw my father's dreadful terror at the idea Hubert would be exposed, I realized that there must be someone beyond Hubert de Bosco, someone with great power—"

"De Bosco," Justin broke in. "By Christ's sweet ears, I remember where I heard that name. Hubert de Bosco is one of FitzWalter's men—a giant, but a stupid lout . . ."

"Perhaps—" Lissa began, but Justin was not listening and she did not continue, realizing that Justin had also made the connection among her father, Hubert de Bosco, and Lord Robert FitzWalter.

Then Justin shook his head. "No, I cannot see any reason why FitzWalter would order your father's death."

"My father told me when he left London in February that he was going north to do business for FitzWalter," Lissa offered.

Justin blinked, thought a moment, then shook his head again. "From what you have told me, William Bowles does not seem like a man who would dare cheat Lord Robert FitzWalter. Am I mistaken? Did he account himself so clever?"

"No. No, I cannot believe he would dare. He was a coward and took advantage only of the weak and those with no redress. And yet," she added slowly, thinking back to her last conversation with William before he left London, "he meant some mischief. There was a kind of gloating pleasure under his talk . . . Still, no. I cannot believe that had anything to do with Lord Robert or my father would have been afraid also."

After a moment's silence, Justin shrugged. "Even say your father did dare cheat him, FitzWalter would not have ordered him killed. Why should he take such a chance? All he need have done was to swear out a complaint over a crime committed on his estate. He could then have dragged your father off to Dunmow, where he could have tortured him at leisure and killed him at will."

"Of course, that is perfectly true," Lissa agreed heartily, not caring in the least whether it was true or not so long as Justin did not take it into his head to try to bring FitzWalter to account. "It is ridiculous to think that Lord Robert had anything to do with this. If it was Hubert with my father—they were both drunk. A quarrel could have started and Hubert struck before he thought."

Justin raised his brows and began to say that her idea did not fit at all with her account of the laughter and the very short interval between the time the men entered the house and the time the killer went out. His remark was interrupted by a heavy pounding on the door, and he got up at once, saying over his shoulder, "That will be Halsig with my men."

Lissa got up too, more slowly, and then hurried after him, crying, "Wait, Justin," as she reached the landing. He was already halfway down the stair, but turned to face her as she started to come down. "You will not charge FitzWalter with this, will you?" she pleaded, and then, before he could reply, she drew a startled breath and added, "Oh, my God, it *was* Hubert in Peter's house that night. He looked short because he was below me."

The last remark made no sense at all to Justin, and he had no intention of answering the first. He was annoyed and said, "I cannot listen now. Go back to bed. I will come tomorrow," raising his voice as the pounding on the door began again.

"Will you dine with me?"

"I do not know. Let me go."

He pulled away as if she were holding him, although she had not touched him except with her eyes and voice. Yet it was hard to go down the stair while she went up, and Justin had a vivid mental image of her taking candles and going into her bedchamber, wearily drawing off the bedrobe . . . He uttered an obscenity under his breath and ran down the remaining stairs to let the men in.

Chapter 24

LISSA LOOKED AROUND THE SHOP AS THOUGH SHE HAD NEVER SEEN it before. All signs of her father's bloody murder, except some dark stains on the floor near the door, had been removed in several days of furious and unremitting scrubbing and whitewashing. Now the light of a brilliant October morning coming through the open windows and door lit the whole small room, reflecting back from the newly whitened walls and the highly polished counter to show the bales and boxes piled against the lower walls, the many bundles of herbs hanging from the rafter pegs, and the rows and rows of shelves, each with its line of pots or sacks. It was a perfect apothecary's shop, just what she had always dreamed of; moreover, it was all hers without debt or doubt—and it was dust and ashes in her mouth.

On the night her father was killed, she had been almost certain Justin would soon be her lover again. The pain in his eyes when he looked at her, the tenderness that kept creeping through his severity, the difficulty he had in parting from her, all cried aloud of undiminished love. But he had not returned as he had promised to speak to her the next day, and the day after that, when he had come, he had been all business, interested only in specific facts. He would not let her bring up any extraneous subject that might provide an excuse for a longer conversation. Worst of all, he had been quite cheerful. The sick longing was gone from his eyes, and he left her with a casual wave when he had his answers, without a single backward glance. And he had not returned since.

Lissa had not felt much beyond a vague worry until this morning, owing to the rush of duties that had occupied her. She had grown accustomed to being alone and had been fully occupied getting her father buried, proving his will, which she was relieved (and surprised) to discover had not been changed since he had made it under pressure from her grandfather, and applying to the master of the Pepperers to be accepted into the guild in her father's place. That would take time, and she would be expected to prove herself, nor were there many other women in the Pepperers Guild, only two, but she was well liked. The only anxiety she felt about acceptance was opposition from Master Chigwell if he renewed his offer of marriage with Edward. She would have to refuse, and he might be angry.

There were also puzzles to occupy her mind in the odd moments when she was not directing the servants in removing signs of the murder from the shop, dismantling her father's bed, or giving the few garments William had brought back with him to the priest, who would pass them on to the deserving poor. For example, who was Amias FitzStephen? And why had her father been carrying, in a belt under his clothing, receipts made out to Amias for three quarters of rental of a manor called Red Cliff? Why had a message of thanks come from a ship master whose home port was Haarlem and with whom Lissa knew they had never done business? And why had Master John le Spicer asked her if she was in urgent need of money and laughed when she assured him she was not?

The questions rose in her mind again, but they echoed hollowly. All they woke in her was hurt. She had savored them at first, thinking about how she would discuss them with Justin, but it seemed that Justin was no longer interested in her or in her problems. But perhaps she was losing hope too soon. Perhaps he was simply too busy to attend personally to the details of a single murder just now. Lissa had heard that King John was already back in England and was expected to come to London in the next week or two. If so, there would be a great influx of lords and ladies and their servants, and preparations would have to be made for keeping order.

If Justin was deeply involved in those preparations, he would never think of taking the time from his duties he might believe necessary to reestablish their bond. Lissa knew it would take no more than one sentence, but if he would not come near her, how was she to let him know she desired no prolonged courtship? She had no objections to Justin doing his duty; she was busier than usual herself at this time of year because every captain who could find a cargo was bringing his ship into port before the autumn storms began. Much as she loved Justin, Lissa would not want him clinging to her. She would be glad he had his own duties to occupy most of his time. Still, a man had to eat and sleep, and there was no reason why he should eat or sleep alone.

Lissa bit her lip, knowing that she was grasping at a hope founded on nothing but her desire. Nonetheless, she could not bear not knowing. If Justin truly did not want her any longer, it would be better to know. Then she could water the dust and ashes with her tears and mold a new life from the remains of the old. But if Justin would not come to her . . . Well then, she would go to him, but she needed some excuse. She could not simply walk into his house and say she wished to marry him now that her father was dead. A murder— Wait: The receipts made out to Amias FitzStephen would be the perfect excuse.

Before she could lose her courage or have second thoughts, Lissa ran up to the solar and put the receipts into her purse. She wiped her hands nervously on her skirt after touching them. The outside of the parchment was stained with blood that had seeped through a tear in the soft oiled-leather belt her father had worn under his clothes. The stains were long dried, and wiping her hands was silly, but Lissa could not help it. Yet for all her horror of her father's murder, it was easier to think of that than of what she was about to do.

She was not the kind to shrink from a truth that, however painful, would free her from continuous misery, so she threw her cloak over her shoulders, told Paul she was going out and was not certain when she would return, and walked as quickly as she could up Soper Lane, past the Mercery, and around the curve to Justin's house. The door was open, but she stopped outside, startled by the noise within. The large room was full of men, talking and laughing. She could not push through them; it was impossible. But it was equally impossible to retreat because she feared she would never again find the courage to thrust herself into Justin's life. She hesitated, taking a step into the room, and when several of the men turned to look at her, backing away.

A burly man followed her out, and Lissa backed up two more steps, not recognizing him in her distress until he said, "Mistress Lissa? Did you want Sir Justin?"

She blinked and peered at the man, knowing him now, but wondering if the terrible accuracy of what he had said was deliberate. His face showed only friendly recognition, however, and she sighed and said, "Oh Halsig, how glad I am to see you. Yes, I did want to speak to Sir Justin. I found something that my father was carrying that was very strange, and I thought Sir Justin should know of it, but I can see he is too busy. This can wait until—"

"He isn't working with the men, mistress. There's a clerk for that, and we're only taking on men for the watch. Most of them are from the old watch who were sent to the king's war and have come back. Only a few I don't know, and Sir Justin will talk to them later. You come with me. I'll find a quiet place for you until I can go up and ask him if he can see you now."

"I can give the receipts to you," she said, her heart sinking because she knew that Justin would find it much easier to say he did not want to speak to her if he did not need to face her.

She was not allowed to escape, however. Halsig said he could not take anything pertaining to the murder without witnesses, and the clerk who could serve as witness was too busy. Even as he spoke, he beckoned her forward. She had little choice but to follow him around to the back of the house where he brushed off a stool in the kitchen and told her that Mary, gesturing to the maid, would bring her a drink or anything she wanted. Lissa shook her head mutely. She sat quietly, not thinking at all until Halsig came back with a broad smile on his face.

"Come this way, mistress," he said, leading her to the door

that opened into the main chamber, and then behind the bench on which the clerk was sitting. "I knew he'd want to see you if what you had might be to do with Master Bowles's death," Halsig went on in a friendly way. "He's been away two days, after that big man you thought might've done it. Up in Essex, I think, and only got back late last night. Just go up." He gestured at the stairs. "The door's open."

Essex, Lissa thought. Dunmow, FitzWalter's estate, was in Essex. She ran up the stairs and into the solar. "In the name of God," she cried, "you have not been asking FitzWalter about my father's death, have you?"

Justin, dressed in a handsome blue robe embroidered around the neck and sleeves with an elaborate pattern in gold thread, was coming out of his bedchamber. The blue robe lent color to his eyes, but his mouth was hard. When she spoke, he stopped in the doorway and said, "I thought we had agreed that I would never tell you how to mix a potion and you would never tell me how to find a murderer."

"But FitzWalter is—" Lissa began, and then the real meaning of what Justin had said penetrated to her and she stared at him, holding her breath with hope until he opened his arms. She ran then, flinging herself at him with such force that he grunted and staggered backward a few steps.

"There is no need to be so eager as to push me back into my bedchamber by force," he said, chuckling, "particularly since my bed is not wide enough for two. Why did you not wait for me at home?"

"I could not wait. The floor will do," Lissa said, tightening her grip on him, and then began to laugh aloud at the shocked expression on his face. "I was only jesting, my love," she murmured, and kissed his chin and then each corner of his thin mouth.

The lips began to fill immediately, but he pushed her away— not roughly and not far, just enough so that her body did not press against his. "You will find it is no jest at all, if you kiss me like that."

If Lissa had thought she could seduce him into it and that they could escape interruption, she would gladly have coupled on the floor, less because she was aroused than to seal their new bargain. But the time and place were wrong. Instead, she flung her arms around his neck, despite the hand that held them apart, and kissed him again—a great smacking buss that held joy and amusement and understanding without anything of sex.

"And what was that for?" Justin asked, as she released him and they both walked into the solar.

"For not being a stuffed-up pompous ass," she replied, then stopped and stared as Justin whooped with laughter.

"Like Edward Chigwell?" he gasped.

"Absolutely!" Lissa agreed fervently, and giggled. "I was afraid to say his name for fear you would believe I did nothing but think of him—and to speak the truth I have been giving him more thought recently than is good for my digestion."

"Why?"

"Because I am in terror that Chigwell will renew his offer and, when I refuse, that he will be angry and oppose my application to join the Pepperers Guild."

"*When* you refuse, not *if*. You have no doubts?"

"I have had no doubts since the second time I spoke to Edward," Lissa said, grinning, and then with a sly look under her lashes: "Now if the elder Chigwell had proposed himself, I might—"

"I am not as old as he, but I might have enough influence on the members of the Pepperers Guild to turn aside his spite, if he should feel any. Do you favor only old men? Or will you consider me as a husband?"

"I am finished considering husbands," Lissa said.

The mischief in Justin's eyes, which had matched that in hers, died suddenly. "What does that mean?"

She put her hand on his. "That I will marry you where and when you say, without condition, without even a contract, if you ask that of me. That is what I promised, and I will keep my word."

"I do not want a wife who comes only in fulfillment of a promise."

"You know that is not true, Justin. I love you with all my heart. I have loved you for a long time, since before I even knew you."

He looked down at her soberly. "I sometimes wonder whether

you are still dreaming of some hero of romance. I am a thief taker, for all my knightly spurs. I *like* the work. I—"

"Yes, I know," Lissa interrupted. She had heard Justin's troubled defense before. As a good burgher, she thought the hanging of thieves admirable and was slightly impatient with the gentle-born feeling that the sniffing-out of criminals, if not the pursuit and hanging, was dirty work. "And before we begin to think only of ourselves again," she continued hastily, pulling her purse from under her cloak, "let me give you what was found in a secret belt under my father's clothes when he was made ready for burial."

Having heard Lissa say what was of basic importance—that she loved him and would marry him when he wanted—Justin was ready to put aside his personal need for a little while. He took the pieces of parchment from the purse and examined them. The first was a full sheet, dated the first day of March, and stated that Amias FitzStephen had paid a quarter's rent on the manor of Red Cliff, which was then described as to its extent and buildings, with intent to buy on the part of Amias and to sell on the part of Master Henry, vintner of Bristol. The remaining two slips were receipts for two more quarters of rent, referring to the first agreement.

"Who is Amias FitzStephen?" Justin asked.

"I have no idea," Lissa replied. "I never heard the name before in my life."

"Well, the answer may be easy enough to come by. I will send a message to the vintner of Bristol asking for particulars about this Amias. Until he replies, I do not see what more I can do. Do you want these back, Lissa?"

"No." Lissa drew herself together for a moment. "There is blood on them. What if it is not my father's blood but is Amias's and is of my father's spilling?"

"Forget it." Justin tossed the receipts on a chest and put one arm around Lissa. With his other hand he pulled at the pin that held her cloak. "Will you not take off your cloak and stay?"

"I will do whatever you want me to do, Justin, but you have a room full of men below. Halsig said most of the work was for him and the clerk, but he did tell me that you would have to speak to some of them."

Justin groaned. "True, but I have not yet broken my fast, and you can sit with me while I do that."

He went to the door and shouted down the stair for his servant to bring up some food. Lissa took off her cloak and added wood to the fire, which had obviously been made up earlier in the morning and had burned down more than it should. When he saw what Lissa was doing, Justin cursed Hervi, but without much heat, and put the small table from against the wall between the two chairs near the hearth. By the time he and Lissa were seated, the little maid, breathing heavily, came into the room carrying a heavy tray. Her face was bruised, one eye swollen shut, and she looked fearfully at Justin who asked, sourly, "Where is Hervi?"

"I do not know, my lord," the woman whispered.

"You are very quick with the food," Lissa said.

A very faint smile parted Mary's lips. She had several broken teeth, but from the condition of the others Lissa realized she was younger than she seemed and the teeth had probably been broken by ill-usage. "Halsig told me to ready it," she said, her voice a little stronger.

"Thank you, Mary." Lissa smiled and nodded at her, and Mary tried to curtsy and then fled.

"It is a great shame," Lissa remarked as soon as she was sure Mary could not hear her, "that her husband cannot be hanged. She would do better with Halsig."

Justin's lips twisted. "And so would I," he said. "I wondered if you would think I had beaten her, from the look she gave me."

"I know you too well for that," Lissa said, smiling. "If she deserved a beating like that from you, she would no longer be your maid. Besides, I knew her husband should have carried up the tray. It is too heavy for her, and I doubt you like to have a woman freely in and out of your private chamber. You told me you suffered the husband for the woman's sake, but he will beat her again if you ask him why he was not here to serve you. The next time you hit him, you should hit him too hard."

"I have been tempted," Justin said, breaking off two pieces of the pasty and offering one to Lissa while he bit into the other. "Her cooking is excellent, and she keeps my clothing in good order, which is no easy task, considering how often I am called aside from pleasure to business and dirty my fine gowns."

"I will give some thought to what can be done for Mary," Lissa said, "but I cannot be sorry that her husband has made himself scarce so that Halsig was the one who greeted me. I am sure Hervi would not have known and so could not have told me that you had been to Essex. And do not scowl at me. I am not trying to tell you how to seek a murderer. I only wish to beg you, because you are *very* precious to me, not to try to bring a man like FitzWalter to justice for cracking a louse."

Justin raised a brow. "You do not mince words as to what you thought of your father. Thank God he did not die like Flael or I would need to suspect you in earnest. It is *cui bono* that solves most murders, you know, and you do not try to hide that you benefit greatly."

Lissa shrugged. "I know I am not guilty of my father's death. If it will amuse you, I give you leave, with my love and goodwill, to try to discover evidence of my guilt. What I regret bitterly is that I told you the truth about Hubert de Bosco. I never would have done so if I had known he had any connection to FitzWalter. Justin, I am sick to death with worry. Will you not tell me what you were doing in Essex?"

"Not bringing FitzWalter's wrath down on my head or yours," Justin said, laughing. "It is not very kind of you to all but tell me to my face that you think I am lack-witted and suspect me of flinging unproven accusations at one of the most powerful men in the kingdom. After all, I have my own doubts on the subject of my wits and do not need yours to make me more uneasy."

"Justin!" Lissa cried, exasperated.

"Oh, very well." He was still smiling. "I did go to Essex to talk to FitzWalter, but I made no accusations against him or against his man. I asked him about the business he had ordered your father to do for him in the north, but as if that were a matter much to the side of my real interest. I said my main purpose was to speak to Hubert de Bosco, who was known to be friendly with your father. I hoped, I said, that Hubert could tell me of William Bowles's other friends, of his amusements, and such matters, because you could tell me nothing except about business affairs."

"What did FitzWalter say?"

"First he laughed and said that I was welcome to question Hubert and if I could get him to remember what had happened ten minutes ago, much the less nearly a week past, I should leave a receipt for my method. Then he asked me to repeat what I had asked at first, and when he had heard me out, he swore— and I believe it was the truth—that he had not asked your father to do any business for him in the north. He was truly surprised when I asked about that, but what troubled me was that I felt he was . . . relieved also, as if he expected a different question."

"But what other question could you ask when you were talking about murder? Surely he did not expect you to ask if he had ordered the killing?"

"No. He seemed surprised, too, when I told him your father had been murdered, but I am not so sure that surprise was genuine. If he was involved, he had plenty of time to prepare his response. He is a clever man and, I suspect, has faced down more astute questioners than I. Nor was I trying to trap him. A fine case I would have been in if he had confessed to murder. What could I have done about it, with three men at Dunmow, the center of his power? And I am not sure FitzWalter is involved."

"Neither am I," Lissa said. "I am more inclined to believe Lord Robert than my father about the business in the north. My father would rather tell a lie than the truth, and he could easily have used FitzWalter's name so that I would ask no questions. I have no proof my father knew Lord Robert at all."

"He did. FitzWalter told me that he knew your father through Hubert, who had brought him to Baynard's Castle, and that several times your father had asked permission to use Hubert in some private enterprise. Almost certainly that was true, and even more convincing was that FitzWalter made no objection to my speaking to Hubert, nor did he insist that I question the man in his presence. But that could be thought of in several ways. I would have expected FitzWalter to be less agreeable to further- ing my investigation; and I could think of his willingness as the special desire to appear innocent that is common to the guilty. On the other hand, I had done him a favor about those cargoes, and he professes to like me, so he might be innocent and merely wish to show himself as accommodating."

"It must be that, Justin," Lissa agreed. "Really, there is no sign anywhere in the records of the business, even those my father kept private from me and left with his goldsmith, that my father was employed by Lord Robert. We never even bought wine from him, and he does not deal in spices, as far as I know. Whatever happened must have been a private quarrel between Hubert and my father."

"But it does not look as if Hubert could have killed your father. He admitted freely that he was out drinking with your father—but on Tuesday night, not on Thursday. He said he could not have been with your father on Thursday because he accompanied his master to Dunmow on Wednesday and remained there from then on. FitzWalter did ride from London to Dunmow on Wednesday with his household, and Hubert was with them when they started out. That much is certain. Several men I spoke to saw him. However, they arrived very late, and I am less certain he was still with them then or that he was at Dunmow on Thursday. I asked Bosco where he was on Thursday, and he looked at me very strangely and said, after hesitating awhile, that he had been out riding. He seemed to be as stupid as a man can be and live without a keeper, but I wonder whether that was real or a pretense."

"My father said he was a stupid lout," Lissa put in.

Justin shrugged. "Yes, but he would be likely, from what you have told me of him, to say that spitefully about anyone slower of wit than himself. In any case, if Hubert is as stupid as he seemed, he could easily have confused Tuesday and Thursday. However, he was at Dunmow Friday morning quite early. One of the grooms saw him coming into the stable."

"Justin," Lissa protested, "why are you trying to twist and turn the evidence to make Hubert guilty if it is likely he was not? You are saying that he stole away from his party on Wednesday, rode back to London, concealed himself all day Thursday, killed my father, somehow got out of the locked gates of London Thursday night, and rode all night to Dunmow, where he got into a sealed keep in time to appear in the stable on Friday morning—all because you did not manage to find anyone who clearly recalled seeing him in Dunmow on Thursday."

"That sounds unfair," Justin admitted, "but there was something in the air around me at Dunmow. Everyone seemed open and willing to talk, but a party left the keep soon after I arrived and did not return while I was there."

"I am sure parties come and go from so great a lord's household all the time, " Lissa said. "And surely the fact that I

saw Hubert with my father several times and that the laugh I
heard was deep and hoarse cannot be enough to mark him
guilty. I have seen small men with deep laughs, and I never
heard Hubert laugh the few times I saw him. I do not remember
hearing him speak."

"I do not suspect him on your evidence alone," Justin assured
her. "Remember, it was what I saw that called out your memory
of Hubert."

"But there is no proof it was Hubert," Lissa pointed out. "He
is not the only large man in London. My father was drunk. It is
possible that while he was out drinking he picked up a
companion I had never met before. I admit his purse had not
been taken, but there was very little in it, so perhaps he had
been robbed."

"If that is true, I will never find the killer," Justin said.

"I am sorry." Lissa looked down to hide the fact that her
words were not entirely true. "I know you do not like to have
unanswered questions about such crimes, but that is all I can
think of. I have told you everything else."

Lissa was surprised, when her eyes passed over the table, to
see the tray almost empty. She had not been aware of Justin
eating and drinking while he talked, but clearly he had. Then
surely enough time had passed for her to plead a need to return
to her business. She did not fear parting from him now. He
would come to her; she was sure of it, and she was afraid to
continue talking to him. His mind was too fixed on her father's
murder for her to turn it to a different subject without waking
suspicion in him. And if she urged him again to accept Hubert's
excuses, he was more likely to wonder why and begin a closer
examination of them and of the alternative she had offered.

Lissa knew quite well that, drunk or not—and she was not as
sure now that William had been so drunk—her father never
picked up strangers and brought them home. Also, since he
never carried more than a few pennies and a few farthings when
he went out for pleasure, she knew he had not been robbed.
Nonetheless, she did not want Justin to continue any line of
investigation that might lead toward FitzWalter.

A notion had slipped into her head that what connected her
father, Peter, Hubert, and FitzWalter was the thing Peter had
seemed to pass into her father's hand at her wedding but

actually withheld. If Hubert had been at the wedding as FitzWalter's man rather than her father's, the two deaths— separated by many months, but those months the time when Hubert and FitzWalter had been in France with the king—might mark FitzWalter's anger at not obtaining what was promised him. That would account for the destructive search of Peter's house too.

The whole idea was so reasonable that she was afraid it would slip out of her mouth and add to Justin's conviction that guilt lay with Hubert and his master—and that could only lead to danger, if not disaster, for Justin. Lissa needed to escape for long enough to bury her treacherous thoughts, and her inner panic intensified when she looked up and saw that Justin was staring at her.

"Perhaps Paul or Oliva could tell you some of the places my father went drinking," she said, as if she had been racking her brains on that subject, "but he is more likely to have told Paul than Oliva. Oh, I forgot to tell you. Oliva is with us again. If you need to talk to Ebba, you will find her at Goscelin's."

Justin raised his brows. "Paul will tell me nothing at all. He answers 'I do not know' to every question I have asked, even questions that have nothing to do with your father's death. If he were not your journeyman, I would have stretched him a little taller on the rack to teach him a little courtesy of manner also."

"Paul is discourteous and will not answer you!" Lissa exclaimed incredulously. "But why? Good God, he could not have— No." She sighed. "That is foolish. Paul is not strong enough."

"Are you sure?" Justin asked. It had flashed across his mind that Paul could have been Lissa's tool; he could have plunged that short sword into his master's body on her orders. He watched her face as he went on, "He lifts that heavy counter twice a day, and the barrels and bales. And while you lay waiting for your father to go up to bed, he had time enough to clean the blood off himself. Did he have reason to hate your father?"

Lissa was almost in tears at the idea of suspicion falling on Paul. "Justin," she said with a sigh, "everyone who was dependent in any way on my father had a good reason to hate him. But why should Paul kill him at that particular moment? Why not any other time?" She stood up. "This is dreadful!

Dreadful! I must go home. I must talk to Paul." She pushed her chair back and looked about for her cloak, but before she remembered where he had laid it, Justin had come from his seat and seized her by the shoulders.

"Do not you dare tell Paul you suspect him of murder. You will be next."

She shook her head. "No, oh no. Paul would not hurt me, and anyway, I do not suspect him of murder. I only want to know why he refuses to talk to you." She hesitated and then said, "Come home with me, and—"

"What? In the middle of the day? When anyone can see me? Will I not drive away your trade?"

"I do not care if you do." Lissa smiled. "That was only another excuse to keep my father from hearing that you were my lover. Now that he is dead, jewel of my heart, you are welcome to me day or night, at any hour it pleases you to come."

Justin opened his mouth, but before he could utter he knew not what exasperated exclamation about the dangers of speaking too freely of her joy in William's death, heavy footsteps pounded up the stair and Halsig stuck his head through the doorway.

"We've got all the men I think will do, my lord," Halsig said. "I turned away a few from the old watch. They were drunk, and I knew them for drinkers when they were in the watch before, but I know where they're lodging and we can get them if we need them."

"Dismiss those from the old watch who have been chosen and bid them return by Nones," Justin said. "I will assign them then. Bid the new men wait. I will come below to speak to them."

Halsig withdrew his head and went down the stairs quite silently. Justin chuckled. "All that noise was because he wished to warn me he was on his way." Then he bent and kissed Lissa. "I meant to come to you this morning and ask if you would have me as a suitor again. That is why I am so elegantly attired. I wished to tempt you."

Lissa blushed and giggled as she remembered how she had charged into his arms. "Alas, I am afraid I have betrayed myself and taught you that I do not need much tempting."

"I must deal with these men," he said, his voice suddenly husky. "I will explain why when . . . *if* I may come tonight."

"Beloved"—she stretched tiptoe and kissed his mouth— "come when you can. As soon as you can. But no matter when you come, I will be waiting."

She fled then, and he let her go, but she was aware that he was watching her all the time, following her to the door so he could see her go down the steps and behind the clerk where Halsig came to her to see her out the front door. That and the fact that Justin's eyes had been so beautifully blue and his lips so full and soft made Lissa expect him before the sun set.

He was not as early as that; he did not ride up to the front door until dusk. And when Lissa saw him from the window, armed and mounted, tears of frustration and fury rose to her eyes. She knew that was no way to begin anew, however, so she found a smile for him as she ran down the stairs to open the door. She was so quick that he had not even knocked, and her smile became more natural when she saw he had dismounted and tied the horse to one of the posts that supported the counter.

"Can you stay awhile, at least have the evening meal with me?" she asked eagerly.

"Am I invited only for a while to eat?" he countered.

"No, for all night and all day and forever, but I supposed you had some duty—"

He laughed, recognizing the cause of the misunderstanding. "No, no duty. And I would be grateful if someone would take my horse to your shed and unsaddle him. Do not look so worried, Lissa. I am not hiding any danger from you. It is just that with so many of the men dismissed from the king's army finding their way to London for one reason or another, it is better for me to be armed and ready whenever I leave the house. I told Halsig where to find me. I hope you do not mind."

"No, of course not." She looked out at Noir, who was in full war panoply. "How much of what you have hanging on that horse do you want brought inside? Paul will— Oh, Justin, it was the stupidest thing. Paul would not speak to you because he believed you had tired of me and cast me aside. He will tell you anything he knows now—not that he knows much."

Justin stepped in and pushed the door closed with his heel.

"Do you never pay *any* mind to what I say to you?" he asked. But he refused to think about that little coal of doubt that burned in him, and he did not let her answer, taking her face in both hands and covering her mouth with his. "Never mind Paul," he said thickly, his lips moving against hers. "Let us go up. I will talk to him later."

Somewhat dazed and totally unable to speak, Lissa backed toward the stairs, one arm around Justin's neck. She stopped when she had gone up three steps. This gave her a small advantage in height, which she used to kiss Justin in all the places it was usually hard to reach because of the difference in their height. He stood with his face lifted to her, his eyes closed, pressing her hard against him and moving his hips slightly. That gave him no relief, however, her body being too high, and he opened his eyes, turned her about impatiently, and pushed her up the stairs. They embraced again in the solar, Justin kissing Lissa's face and throat feverishly and applying a crushing pressure to her buttocks to bring her belly and mount of Venus hard against him.

This time it was Lissa who broke the embrace. "Why in the world did you wear that accursed mail shirt?" she complained. "My skin must look like a fishnet. Let me get it off you."

Lissa was not the only sufferer from the pressure of the linked rings that made up Justin's hauberk. Despite his padded arming tunic, a fold of the hauberk had made a cruel impression on a sensitive portion of his anatomy. He had hardly noticed the discomfort. It was far more important to rouse Lissa before she returned to a subject he did not want to touch, at least not before he had quenched the need for her that had been scalding him ever since the night of her father's death. He murmured apologies, loosening his belt with one hand, while with the other he drew apart her gown "to kiss away the bruises." She let him do it, bending her head to nibble his ear, but she felt when the belt came loose and she took it from him, pushing him gently away so she could lay it aside.

He had bent double and was struggling with the hauberk when she touched him again, and after that he did not remember every detail of how they had got into her bed. He remembered her laughter when he growled, "Let it lie," when she wanted to pick up and lay out his mail instead of coming into his arms at once, and he remembered groaning when he lifted her, the better to suck her breasts, and she closed her thighs over his standing man. Now she lay, with one hand on his hip and another on his shoulder, laughing up at him.

"I wish I were three men," he muttered, his eyes flicking from the true rose of her lips to the brown-rose of her upstanding nipples and down to the brown-gold curls on her mount of Venus. He wanted everything at once, to kiss her mouth, to suck her breast, to invade her nether mouth with his tongue. And he wanted to impale her, to thrust sword into sheath and draw and thrust again, a sweet impalement that drew cries, but not of pain. But at the same time he did not want that, because that greatest of pleasures was also an end to pleasure.

"Well I am glad you are not three men." Lissa's voice shook with laughter as the hand that had been on his hip slid swiftly inward, then down and up in a practiced caress. "See? I can barely close my hand over you. How could I accommodate three?"

Justin had no voice with which to answer. The touch drove all but one desire, that one he had tried to resist, out of him. He lurched forward, but Lissa had already twisted under him, sliding her legs up around his hips, and guiding the blind but lively Cockrobin into the empty nest. His delight in being home again created a period of violent activity, after which there were a few minutes of exhausted silence, broken only by Lissa's labored breathing. When Justin gathered enough strength to roll off her, both were still. Soon after, Justin stirred restlessly and stroked Lissa's arm.

"I cannot see how three would fit," Lissa said suddenly. "You are a large man. I might barely manage two, but three—"

"Have you no shame?" Justin sighed.

"Why should I be ashamed?" she rejoined, widening her eyes in false innocence, knowing he was ready to begin again but unsure of her willingness. "You were the one who suggested it."

"You know perfectly well that what you mean never occurred to me at all," Justin protested, and then burst out laughing. "And if you dare to ask me whether I meant the three of me should take turns, I will—I will climb back atop you and just lie there until you smother."

"Three times, one after another . . ." Lissa murmured. "Well, I do not know, but what of the two who were waiting? Might they not be overexcited by watching? And then, if the one who went first watched the others, he might desire a second turn, and that could go on forever. I really do not—"

She clapped both hands over her mouth as Justin sat up, picked up a pillow, and held it threateningly over her head. But he dropped it and pulled her hands away and covered her lips with his. Some time later, when Lissa was trying to pull him over her, he said, "When I am not in a hurry, I find that one of me is quite enough."

"I too," she whispered.

But still later when Lissa had sung aloud her bursting joy and he was nearly blind and deaf in the midst of his own release, he thought he heard her murmur within her sighing, soft as a bee's hum: "And I wonder how I did not kill my father when he first came home to get you back again."

Chapter 25

JUSTIN SLEPT VERY DEEPLY AFTER THAT SECOND COUPLING. HE had been tired before he came to bed, having ridden almost the whole previous night to get back to London from Dunmow. There was no reason why he could not have stayed at FitzWalter's keep; he had been invited to stay, pressed to do so, but he had pleaded urgent personal affairs and ridden out in the late afternoon. His excuse for leaving was perfectly genuine: He could no longer resist his need to reestablish his position with Lissa. He had been too aware of her invitation to him on the night her father was killed, but he could not accept it then. Although every instinct told him that she was innocent, he had to find some confirmation of that outside his own desire.

The next day he had questioned the Chigwells, managing to approach father and son separately. He felt their surprise upon learning of Bowles's death was genuine. The elder made no secret of his feeling that if William had not been killed by a thief in the street, the homicide was almost certainly justified. Edward Chigwell, on the other hand, had been not only surprised but appalled by the news. To Justin's well-hidden amusement, Edward unguardedly deplored the fact that William's death would mean he would probably be forced to marry a dominating and ungovernable shrew. In casual fashion Justin had tested the young man's strength, and he did not think Edward's arm could have dealt the blow that had crushed William's ribs. So far, then, everything Lissa had told him was true.

Still, Lissa gained the most by her father's death, and Justin needed a viable suspect to pacify his conscience. His journey to Essex had provided that, which was why he thanked FitzWalter both for his cooperation and his offer of hospitality with such warmth instead of displaying his increased suspicion with a cold formality. Justin was quite certain that FitzWalter's courtesy was a screen to hide guilt—his man's if not his own. He should have been furious over the clever attempt to lead him around by the nose. Instead, he felt pleased with himself for recognizing it, grateful that Hubert was exactly what he expected him to be, and generally grimly satisfied; the more certain he was that Hubert was guilty, the less he was troubled by the possibility that Lissa was offering herself to bribe him.

Despite Lissa's fears, Justin was in no great hurry to bring Hubert to justice. Eventually he would discover who were the men who had been sent out of Dunmow after he arrived and why they had been sent away. There were also those in what had been Baynard's Castle to question. If Hubert had been in London on Thursday, Justin would learn of it, although he might never learn how Hubert got out of the city after the murder. No gate guard would admit to allowing a person of Hubert's description to leave; probably, but not necessarily, that meant the guard had been bribed. Harsher measures might be used to question them, except that there was a possibility that Hubert might have left London by way of the river; it could be watched, but only so carefully, and it could not be locked at all. Nonetheless, Justin knew that time and patience were likely to bring him proof of Hubert's guilt. And that proof would tell him directly or indirectly whether FitzWalter was involved in the crime.

As to bringing FitzWalter himself to justice, Justin had no illusions. The only way he might accomplish that was to present his case to the king. And other considerations, far more serious than the murder of one unpleasant man, could develop from involving the king. Unless John was looking for a reason to attack FitzWalter, he would refuse to listen to evidence of murder against a powerful baron; and if King John was ready to listen, Justin had to think whether he was ready to precipitate a new war of king against barons—one in which London might be a battleground—just to satisfy his sense of justice.

So by the time he reached London everything was settled in his mind, and he hardly knew how to contain his joy when Lissa flung herself into his arms. He was a little annoyed when she argued against his suspicion of Hubert; her reluctance to have him follow that line of reasoning cast a small shadow on the brightness of his joy, as did Paul's sullen refusal to answer even the most innocent questions. The shadow was not dark—it was not nearly dark enough to keep him out of Lissa's bed—but it made half-heard words echo in his dreams. He did not remember the dreams when he woke, only felt uneasy, and he sat up suddenly and pulled back the curtains.

Lissa, who was already up, heard the leather straps of the bed creak and rose from the chest, which had been pulled from the wall so she could sit by the fire. "What is wrong, my love?" she asked in response to his frown. "You told me you had no duty, so I let you sleep."

For a moment he did not answer, trying to recapture the dream, but he was distracted by Lissa's appearance. She was wearing a bedrobe he had never seen before, of a soft rose color, with a small gray fur collar and wide sleeves deeply trimmed in the same fur. She looked lovely, her light brown hair loose, curling around her face and trailing down her back to her hips. As she came to the bed, a shaft of sunlight caught the fine hair near her cheek and turned it to gold.

"It is morning," Justin said.

She laughed and held out a bedrobe that she had picked up from the chest. "It often is when one has slept the night through."

He took the robe and put it on, muttering through the folds, "You are very ready to throw your reputation to the winds," realizing as he spoke that such a move could be used to trap a man into marriage. The thought confused him. It was he, not

Lissa, who had pressed for marriage. And in response to the idea, as he ran his hand over the richly embroidered soft blue wool of the robe, jealousy almost strangled him. Lissa was no member of a rich house of whores where bedrobes would be ready for men who paid well enough to stay all night.

"Where did this come from?" Justin asked almost too softly for her to hear.

But Lissa had seen his hand lie still on the fabric and his face freeze, and she laughed again. "From hopes and dreams. Smell it, Justin. No other man has worn it before you. Look at the length, dearling. How many men could wear a robe that long? I have a chest full of shirts and gowns, and every one will fit only you—you have wide shoulders, my love, and much less to sit on than most merchants or craftsmen. Jewel of my life, I sat here in this room every night after we parted and sewed—and prayed."

He stared at her for a moment, remembering that Edward Chigwell's head came about to his ear, then began to laugh himself and caught her to him and kissed her lips and throat. "Come back to bed," he said.

She played with the hair at the back of his neck. "I am willing enough," she murmured, "so long as you will not later blame me for keeping you from your duties."

Justin groaned, but left off kissing her and straightened up. "I probably have a new houseful of men," he said. "You were right about taking Halsig into my own service. I did so last week, as soon as the mayor told me to bring the watch to its original numbers. He is a very good man, steady and clever. Still, I cannot leave the final choice of men or the placing of them to him. I must go. I should not have bothered to put on this robe, as I must now take it off and dress."

"Surely you have time to break your fast," Lissa said, "and there is no need to sit in your armor while you eat. Halsig knows where you are and will send for you if any emergency arises. And you can tell me while you eat why your house is full of men applying for places on the watch. Surely each ward's watch is the business of the alderman of that ward?"

"Yes, usually—"

Justin stopped abruptly as he came to the door to the solar and smiled with pleasure at the vision of ease and comfort that struck him. The morning meal was already laid out on the table before the hearth where a small but bright fire was leaping. Two chairs flanked the table, and Justin looked over his shoulder, aware now of the change in the bedchamber that had given him an uneasy sense of strangeness before he recognized what was missing. Lissa's chair was gone. There was nothing now between the fireplace and the foot of the bed but a rug made of two bear pelts. It was a large rug. Justin smiled. Perhaps the next time they were in a hurry they *would* make love on the floor.

"Usually?" Lissa's voice recalled him from thoughts that had already started a warmth rising in his body.

Justin cast a last glance at the fur rug and then advanced purposefully on the table. "Usually it is just as you say, but the mayor suggested to the alderman that this time, with so many trained men home from the war in France, it would be quicker and easier for me to hire all."

Lissa gestured him to a chair and sat in the other. "I suppose that is reasonable."

"Reasonable enough. We do not usually take on so many at one time. The watch is much like any other kind of work. Sons or brothers or nephews follow their elders, except that the watch gets the lesser men. Those truly skilled in arms who have strong spirits usually try for a place in a nobleman's meinie. The young ones who prefer to stay in the watch are the timid and the clumsy. It is dull work, sometimes dangerous, and not well paid."

"I do not think Halsig is timid or clumsy," Lissa said, cutting a formidable wedge out of a meat pasty, setting it on a round of bread, and passing it to Justin. She added a wedge of cheese almost as large and poured ale from a flagon into a double-handled cup.

Justin watched her in some surprise and then said, "I am starving. How did you know?"

"Because you never woke to eat the lovely evening meal I had all ready for you last night." Lissa laughed as Justin took a huge bite and washed it down with the ale.

"I am glad you kept it for me," he said when he could speak, but after a few more mouthfuls the urgency of his appetite diminished and he remembered her remark about Halsig. "Halsig is old. He served for years with . . . let me see . . ."

Justin drank again, took another bite of pasty and chewed contemplatively.

"I remember," Justin went on. "Halsig was in the household of the earl of Leicester, but the earl died childless in 1204. The earl did have two brothers, but one was bishop of Saint Andrew's in Scotland and the other, poor man, was a leper, so neither could inherit. The estate was divided between the earl's two sisters. I suppose the husbands of the women had their own men and were less than welcoming to Halsig, who had only a few years of hard fighting left in him. I am not sure how he came to London or who hired him. He was captain of the watch of the Chepe when my uncle put the business of the mayor's guard into my hands."

"That is rather sad," Lissa said, "not so much that he ended up in the watch as that he should be cast out because he was old. Thank God for the guilds which, if great misfortune overtake a merchant or craftsman so that he has no haven in his old age, will care for him."

Justin nodded agreement about the benefits of guild membership, but he protested the idea that all masters were cruel and indifferent to aging retainers. He told her about the crippled and infirm who were cared for on his father's estate and on others he knew. He also pointed out that it was really the business of the Church to care for such men, which would have the added benefit of bringing them to remorse for the brutal lives they had led and thus saving many of them from hell.

"And that brings me back," Justin said, smiling and pushing away the few remains of his meal, "to the fact that my house is full of men, and the mayor and aldermen, having heard that the king is coming to London, want the watch back to full strength and perfectly trained to their duties the day before yesterday. I must go."

Lissa understood that perfectly. With King John would come his barons, some who supported and others who opposed him. Each baron brought a household, and each household espoused its master's cause, often with more fervor than the master did. Mingling freely in the city, the households—from stable boys with casually picked up sticks or horse harness to men-at-arms in full armor—too often came to blows. As long as the intentions of the lords were not behind the quarreling and the watch was capable, the fighting was usually kept to the alehouse or street where it started and was easily quelled. If the watch was not able to drive the contestants apart, however, a riot might ensue during which shops could be looted and, worst of all, a fire sparked.

She stood up at once and they went into the bedchamber where she began to help him dress, watching his face grow blacker and blacker until, at last, she asked what was wrong. He bent to pull his chausses tighter and also, Lissa was sure, to think how much he wanted to tell her. Then she could see a kind of ease come to his face, a softening of the hard lines in his brow and around his mouth, as if he had remembered suddenly that this was a person with whom he did not need to pick and choose words.

"The mayor is frightened," he said. "He does not like me and will not confide in me, and I cannot guess of what he is afraid. It may be simply because the king has made it clear that he intends to insist on collecting the scutage that the barons would not pay in May. That means serious trouble if John tries to arrest men who refuse to pay and they resist. The watch, even at its best, is not fit for such work, and the king's forces in the Tower are under the orders of FitzWalter, who hates King John."

"I remember," Lissa said. "You told me of the quarrel between them because FitzWalter yielded a keep in France and then King John destroyed Baynard's Castle. But FitzWalter obeyed the king's summons and seems to have served loyally in France, so perhaps that trouble is over."

Justin shrugged. "I can hope, but I would be a fool to believe it. One of the reasons we need so many new men is that both FitzWalter and his son-by-marriage, William de Mandeville, picked over the watch whenever they wanted men, leaving me with a set of toothless dotards and a few, like Halsig, who had had enough of noblemen's troops."

"I do not know the others," Lissa put in, "but I would say that Halsig stayed out of loyalty to you."

Justin smiled at her, clearly pleased, although he only shrugged and said, "Perhaps," before he began to frown again. "I had a devil of a time this summer. There were riots that never should have happened, but the watch simply had not the strength or skill to manage a crowd. I will say that Mandeville never failed to send any men I asked for, and they obeyed me when they came, but by then it was always a matter of breaking heads."

He fell silent for a moment, wondering whether he had waited until too late to send for help because he wanted to break heads to give an outlet to the violence that roiled in him while he and Lissa were apart. But the flicker of resentment he felt was swallowed up in the overwhelming peace that presently encompassed him. Whatever his grief had been, it was over and well worth enduring for what he now had. A brief recollection of last night's coupling blended into the warm comfort of the fire, the good food and ale filling his belly, and Lissa's quick hands tying his sleeve and neck strings. He had reason to know she never talked about what he told her, not even to her beloved uncles, unless he said she could tell them, which was more than he could swear to about his cousins.

That was worth most of all—to be able to talk out his worries to the only person in the world who placed him above every other consideration, including her own happiness. Despite his jealousy of Chigwell, he did not really doubt that when Lissa originally refused to marry him it was because she thought she was protecting him from her father. As if he could not manage a man like William Bowles! The contemptuous thought was stained with doubt, however, as Justin recalled that someone, perhaps a man as powerful as FitzWalter, had decided the only way to manage Bowles was murder. And a prick of conscience reminded him that if FitzWalter was not guilty, Lissa might have taken a man's life to get him back. But he did not want to think of that, and he walked briskly into the solar where he found his armor conveniently laid out over boards raised on two tall trestles, which had replaced William Bowles's bed.

Lissa called down into the shop for Paul to saddle Bête Noir and Oliva to come up. Justin started to wriggle into his hauberk, and Lissa came and lifted it so it slid down easily. While he settled it comfortably, she brought his belt and sword.

"I may be late tonight," Justin said. "A council is called at which I must report on the watch and other matters, and I have no idea how long everyone will talk."

"I will be waiting whenever you come," she assured him, and

then smiled. "You know I never mean to interfere with your duty. I would not have gone to your house yesterday had I known—"

"Oh? Are you sorry?"

Lissa widened her eyes. "If I say yes, will you take back what you gave me?"

Justin burst out laughing. "I deserve that. I will be more careful when I fish for compliments another time."

"Silly man," Lissa said, flinging her arms around his neck and kissing him heartily, "if I try to tell you what I feel without jesting, I will burst into tears—and men never understand weeping with joy, so you will waste time trying to soothe me and wonder, no matter what I tell you, about what I was weeping. That is no way to send a man off to his duty."

"No indeed," Justin agreed, stepping aside from the doorway and gesturing to Oliva to enter. He stepped out himself then, but grinned back at Lissa adding, "Especially when that duty is with a mayor who cannot make up his mind. Add another discontent to what he will induce in me and I will strangle him."

Lissa laughed, kissed her hand to him, and went back to her bedchamber where, with Oliva's help, she dressed. But only a few minutes later she wished she had indulged herself with tears of joy so that she would have red eyes to show to a most unwelcome visitor.

She had been thinking while dressing that if king and barons were coming to London, many would bring their wives. It was then time to look to her supply of lotions and creams, such salves as tinted the lips and cheeks, and the powders made of henna or leachings of lead by strong vinegar that brought back red and black to hair grown pale with time. The light had been fading as she dressed, and she saw that the morning sun was gone, the clouds darkening by the moment. A cloudy sky could not spoil her mood, however, and she thought it was a good day for taking stock of what she had and preparing a list of supplies she might need. She was just making ready to descend to the shop when the sound of hurried footsteps made her stop just beyond the solar door so that she was almost knocked down by Paul.

"Master Chigwell is below," he whispered urgently. "And he saw Sir Justin leaving the house. I am so sorry, mistress. I stopped Sir Justin outside to beg his pardon for how I behaved and to promise I would answer anything he asked me. I did not see Master Chigwell because I was on the other side of the horse."

For a moment Lissa was tempted to send Paul down with the message that she was not yet up or dressed. That would confirm what Master Chigwell must think anyway, after seeing a man leaving her house at this hour of the morning. Probably that would save her from further importunities to marry his son— but he would say she was a woman of bad character when her appeal to be admitted into the guild was discussed among the masters. And then she called herself a fool for panic induced by a guilty conscience. Aside from the evidence of the shared morning meal, there was no sign of Justin's overnight presence. Justin could have come for many reasons. If she had been eating when he arrived, common courtesy would demand that she offer food and drink.

"Send him up," she said, and went to the table to brush away the crumbs that marked where Justin had sat. She left his cup; it was more likely for a man who had come that morning to accept drink than food, but for what should she say he had come? Her visitor answered that question himself with the first words out of his mouth.

"Is there some news about your father's killer?" Master Chigwell asked as he entered the room. "I saw Sir Justin leaving the house."

His face wore an angry scowl. Master Chigwell had unpleasant memories of his last meeting with Sir Justin. He had hung back at the corner of Budge Row, watching Paul wringing his hands as he tried to explain something to the mayor's ferret. Chigwell had not enjoyed realizing that he was a suspect because of his unguarded remarks to William Bowles about his opposition to Lissa's marriage to Edward. In fact, he had been so shaken by the cynical regard of Justin's icy eyes and the disbelieving line of his hard mouth that he had put off for a whole week coming to renew his offer to Lissa. Even now he felt somewhat uneasy, wondering if the public announcement of his son's betrothal to her would reignite the suspicions he hoped he had laid to rest. He began to doubt his purpose altogether when he realized that Lissa looked frightened half to death.

His own anxiety made him misread her expression. It was true that his question had shocked Lissa; her eyes had widened and a hand had come up to cover parted lips, but she was struggling to control amusement, not fear. It was ridiculous, but she had forgotten that Justin was investigating her father's death and his most obvious business with her would be in connection with that.

"No," she whispered. "No news. Sir Justin had some new questions to ask me. I am afraid he has become aware that . . . that I did not . . . that I hated my father. He is . . . he is very suspicious of me. I am . . . afraid."

"That is ridiculous!" Chigwell exclaimed. "From what he told me it is impossible that you could have caused your father's death. It needed a man, and a strong one, to strike the blows that killed your father. I am certain it was a low companion William picked up in some alehouse."

"I thought so too. I told Sir Justin that a stranger must have killed him," Lissa said, looking down so that she seemed to be guiltily avoiding Chigwell's eyes. "But my father was not robbed, and that, by Sir Justin's judgment, makes his murder a personal matter."

"Personal?" Chigwell echoed. "What do you mean by personal?"

"Sir Justin does not think the murder could have been caused by any dispute over business matters," Lissa replied in a trembling voice, "because my father had been away for nearly eight months and had no time, in the few weeks he had been back, to become deeply involved in any business arrangements. He thinks the man who killed my father was hired to do so."

"Hired! Hired by whom?" Master Chigwell knew he had not arranged William Bowles's death and he was absolutely certain Edward had not. Edward had made his distaste for marriage to a strong-willed wife very clear. He had been delighted by William's intervention and had grieved aloud over William's death.

Lissa turned away, seized the poker, and stirred the fire, which did not need any attention. "What does it matter?" she cried, her voice shrill with suppressed giggles. "I did not ask him. I do not want to hear his theories." Then she dropped the poker with a clang and turned back to face her fellow Pepperer. "Master Chigwell, I fear that I must ask you not to renew your offer to me. I am sorry that we will not be able to fulfill the plans you made, but to do so even after my father's murderer is found—if he is ever found—will only arouse talk and suspicion."

The expression of relief on Master Chigwell's face almost broke Lissa's self-control. As she listened to his false regrets and grave good wishes for her future, her lips quivered and her eyes filled with tears. When he finally took his leave, she sank into her chair and gave way to laughter that was mixed with apprehension. Justin might murder her when he heard what she had said, and if she had gone too far and convinced Master Chigwell that she had been involved in her father's death, she might have stolen and strangled her own goose. Instead of opposing her entry into the guild because she had refused his son and because he could accuse her of being Justin's whore, he might oppose it because he believed her guilty of patricide.

Then Lissa laughed more easily. Justin would not mind her saying he suspected her if it permitted her to convince Chigwell that she could not accept his offer. Moreover, Chigwell would not accuse her of patricide; in fact, he would not say a word of any kind against her for fear of waking ideas of his own involvement in her father's demise.

Chapter 26

A s Lissa got up from her chair and finally went down to the shop, Justin dismounted in front of the stable in the yard behind his house, flung open the door just as the rain poured down in earnest, and stepped in—right into a pile of manure. In a way it was his own fault in that he had not looked where he set his foot, and it certainly was not the first time in his life that he had stepped in a horse's leavings. He did not even find the odor of manure particularly offensive, and aside from a brief, pungent remark he would have let the matter pass if Hervi had come in response to his shout.

There was no reply to his call, however, which did not surprise or anger him since the door and back window of the house were closed. He peered out into the downpour and judged that it could not last long. To stand idle would chill him, so Justin unhooked his shield and helmet from the saddle, hung them on pegs by the door, and began to unsaddle the horse, working more by instinct than by sight in the dim corner. His first shock came when he swung the saddle toward the trestle that should have been ready to receive it and found that it had been knocked down and not picked up. He dropped the saddle back on Noir and bent to lift the trestle, only to discover that it was lying in more manure, which had been spread into a sodden puddle by urine.

Then Justin began to look around the stable in earnest and was appalled by the filth and disorder. But worse, far worse, the animals were not being properly cared for either. When Justin went to set Noir's saddle on the trestle near the fine jennet that served as his pack animal, he saw that her legs were all clotted with mud. And when he lifted Noir's saddlecloth he found it stained with mud which, from its color, came from Essex, not London. That meant the saddlecloth had not been beaten clean since he returned from Dunmow. Justin hurriedly brought Noir to the doorway and examined his back with minute attention. There were no sores, for which he thanked God, but in two places the hair was already rubbed thin.

Because Justin was well aware that most of the fault was his own—he knew Hervi was lazy and unreliable and had not overseen him as closely as he should—and because he also knew he would kill the man if he laid eyes on him, he walked around the house and entered by the front door. Fortunately for the innocent men seeking to join the watch, the room was not as crowded as it had been the day before. Justin was able to enter without knocking anyone down, and his awareness that that infuriated him further made him realize that he was in no fit mood to interview men.

"Halsig!" he bellowed.

It was a credit to the courage of the old man-at-arms that he came forward and said, "Yes, my lord?"

Justin swallowed and took a deep breath. "Get the records from the clerk and bring them up to my chamber." The men had all turned to look at him, those nearest cautiously backing out of reach. Justin gestured at Halsig, who walked quickly toward the clerk's table, and Justin raised his voice so all could hear. "Those of you who have already given your name to the clerk, go away and come again tomorrow. The rest can tell the clerk what he wants to know and then go."

He went toward the stair then, the men moving aside to make a clear path. The clerk, who had caught a glimpse of Justin's face over the heads of the waiting men, wasted no time in arguing about which records were needed and which were not. He gathered together everything that had writing on it and thrust it into Halsig's hands, casting the older man a glance of commiseration. He was surprised when Halsig nodded casually, seeming unworried, and hastened after his master up the stairs.

"Set the parchments on the table," Justin said, as he unbelted his sword, "and help me get this armor off."

He said no more until he was dressed in a somberly gorgeous gown of black velvet with wide borders of silver leaves and flowers with pearl hearts; then he told Halsig about the condition of the stable. "Find someone among the men below who wants a day's work and set him to oversee Hervi. He is not to help. He is only to make sure that Noir is curried and polished until he shines, without being hurt, and that Jenny and the palfrey are also so treated, and that the stable is scoured and pumiced until it smells like an open window. Also, do you know of someone who would want Hervi's place? He must go when he has cleaned what he made filthy."

"That will be hard on Mary," Halsig said, eyeing Justin cautiously, but seeing only a look of regret, he added, "I could do Hervi's work."

Justin shook his head. "I need you for more important things than shoveling dung, and I do not want that man around. I would like Mary to stay, and if she is willing I will do my best to protect her. But she is his wife . . ." He shrugged. "Women are very strange. Well, I will leave you to talk to her. I have never even raised my voice to her and yet she seems almost as afraid of me as she is of her husband, who beats her."

Halsig chuckled at the aggrieved tone and said soothingly, "Not really, my lord. She does not fear you will hurt her apurpose. She is just in awe of you, as if you were a man and she an ant and you might step on her by accident."

"That is ridiculous—" Justin began, then sighed because it was even more ridiculous for him to argue with Halsig about Mary's feelings. Then he suddenly remembered the way Mary had smiled when Lissa spoke to her. Lissa could deal with the woman, Justin thought, with a feeling of warmth and relief, but he had no time to go back to Lissa's house now. "Let Hervi stay this one night more," he said to Halsig. "I will ask Mistress Lissa to come tomorrow and find out what Mary truly wants to do."

Halsig nodded. "She said she wished there was so gentle a mistress here."

Justin smiled. "That, thank God, is a wish she will get if she stays." He went to the table and picked up the sheets of parchment Halsig had put there. "Now I will do what I can about settling the men we have decided to take on within each ward, but most of that will have to wait until tomorrow. I must dine with my cousins, and from there go on to the mayor's house. I do not think I will bother to come home after the council. I will go directly to Mistress Lissa's and stay the night."

"Yes, my lord." Halsig hesitated and then said, "My lord, may I bring my pallet and blankets and—"

"No need," Justin interrupted. "Sleep in my bed. You will be more comfortable and what I have of value is in my bedchamber. I would prefer that the room not be empty until Hervi is out of the house."

"Yes, my lord."

Halsig had no intention of arguing with his master or of disobeying him—it was not every day that he got an invitation to lie soft and warm on furs and feather beds—but he also thought it would be wise for him to take some time in the afternoon and get himself scrubbed clean at a bath house. Sir Justin would not thank him for leaving lice and smells behind in the bedclothes. He ran down while Justin began to put in order the sheets the clerk had handed over and fortunately spied a man in the now nearly empty room whom he knew had been on the watch before the war. He explained what was wanted to Dick the Miller's son, got a grateful agreement—even one day's wages were worthwhile to a soldier who had gone through his pay—and, followed by Dick, went back into the kitchen where he was rendered momentarily speechless by seeing Hervi still fast asleep.

A kick brought nothing but a groan, so Halsig bent and grabbed Hervi's tunic and hauled him off the pallet and half upright. He almost let him go because of the stench of vomit and urine and feces that came with him, but he turned his head and spat and then slapped Hervi stingingly on both cheeks.

"Sir Justin's been in the stable," he said, when Hervi's eyes opened. "He was in a real temper when he got into the house. He's going out to dinner, and you'd better have that big black of his shining like jet before he goes and the saddlecloth so clean a lady would wipe her eyes on it. I'll tell you the rest later. I've got no time to talk to you now, but if you hurt that horse while you're doing him, Dick here will beat you purple, and Sir Justin will kill you when he gets back. Nor don't try to run neither, because Sir Justin's not done with you." He turned to Dick behind him. "You see he's here when wanted, or Sir Justin will have *your* guts for cross garters."

Some time later, as Halsig sat on the wooden bench in the bath house, gasping in the steam created by dumping water on hot stones, he felt warm with contentment as well as from the surroundings. Now, if he could lie abed with a woman like Mary instead of needing to buy whores at his age, he thought, he would have nothing left to desire. He had begun to chuckle at the thought of a perfect life, and the sound checked suddenly. Perhaps, he thought, he should just slip his knife between Hervi's ribs and dump him in the river or in the yard of some stew. There would be no question then that Mary would stay, which was what Sir Justin wanted. Everyone would be saved a lot of trouble once Hervi was dead. Halsig had no delusion that the man would be easy to get rid of any other way. He would hang about, trying to beg or steal, possibly catching Mary in the market and beating or terrorizing her so that she would give him food or let him in the house. It would be better for everyone if Hervi was dead.

Yes, but not by his hand. Halsig shuddered, and the attendant raised another cloud of steam, but Halsig had not been cold. If Sir Justin ever discovered what he had done, he would be hanged as high as any other felon; that was the way Sir Justin was. And there was another thing: He did not think he would be able to work for Sir Justin or lie abed with Mary in peace while hiding the knowledge that he had murdered Hervi. Halsig signaled the attendant that he was ready to be scrubbed and began to think of more practical ways to deal with their encumbrance. Perhaps if he just beat Hervi nearly to death the first time he came back to the house . . . Sir Justin wouldn't mind that; he had done it once himself.

When Halsig finally got back to Justin's house, the front door was locked and he breathed a sigh of relief. As it was, they would have to turn away quite a few of the men who wanted work, so the fewer who came, the fewer who would have to be disappointed. He went around to the back, stopping at the stable to see how Hervi was progressing with his cleaning, and Dick jumped to his feet and asked if Halsig would watch the man while he went to the privy.

"I went once before, but soon's I dropped my braies, he tried to go off. I had to chase him with my ass bare. That's why his eye's closed and he's walking a little funny. I wouldn't want you to think I hit him for fun."

"I wouldn't think that of you, Dick," Halsig said, laughing. "It's no fun to hit his kind. He's more like something you want to step on—if you can wipe your shoe without touching it afterward. Go ahead. In fact"—he had been looking around the stable as he spoke—"you can go home afterward. I'll see that he finishes. And if I have to go, I'll just hang him up on one of the hooks until Sir Justin gets home."

Halsig had no intention of doing any such thing, and Dick, who knew him well, laughed heartily at the idea. It did not occur to either of them that Hervi, who enjoyed inflicting pain, would believe Halsig seriously contemplated such an act or that Dick's laughter would strike terror into his soul. He had really worked like a madman after his abortive attempt to escape. The palfrey and jennet were clean, and all the harness had been polished. The hayrack was spotless, and the floor had been cleaned. Sir Justin had so often overlooked his "mistakes" in the past that Hervi had really expected no more to be said about the dirty stable and ill-cared-for horses after they were cleaned up. Terrified, he began to plead with Halsig not to hurt him and to tell Sir Justin how hard he had worked so he would not torture him.

Halsig roared with laughter at the idea of Sir Justin torturing Hervi for punishment or amusement. Not that Sir Justin did not apply rack and thumbscrews when necessary to obtain information, like any sensible man, but . . . He saw suddenly that his laughter was misunderstood, and that gave a new direction to his thoughts: If he frightened the man enough about what Sir Justin would do to him, would he not run? And knowing Sir Justin's power within London, would he not be likely to leave the city? So he told Hervi a few more tales and kicked him a few times while he finished making the stable clean and sweet.

The last streaks of daylight were fading and Hervi was scrubbing the trestles—it was the last thing Halsig could find for him to do—when the gate to the alley creaked open. Halsig, who was watching Hervi and had his back to the gate, had not seen the long arm that came over and lifted the latch. He stood up, thinking that Justin might have decided to come home, but the big man who entered was on foot.

He stopped when he saw Halsig and said, "The front door was locked. I—I want to speak to Sir Justin."

"Not here. Come back tomorrow," Halsig said, watching the small eyes shift from him to Hervi and back. He had been alerted by the way the man had walked in without hesitation, the surprise at seeing him there as well as Hervi, and the uncertainty with which he asked for Sir Justin. Halsig noticed the man's eyes had gone back to Hervi and, looking at the thick, sullen face, a notion took him. If it worked, Hervi would not be able to take Mary with him.

"Will you do me a favor?" Halsig asked, as if he had not noticed the exchange of glances between the visitor and Hervi and was too stupid to realize the man was lingering when he should have turned to go. "Keep an eye on this man for a few minutes, and don't let him run off. I want to get something to eat while I watch him. Sir Justin's going to have the hide off him tomorrow, and I'll be in deep trouble if he gets away."

Halsig then went into the house and closed the door behind him. He not only asked Mary for bread and meat, but told her to heat the meat over the fire so the fat would crackle and be more tasty. He wanted to give Hervi plenty of time to persuade his big, stupid friend to let him run off, and he was very disappointed when he returned to the stable to discover both men just where he had left them. It did not surprise him that the big man got up and went to the gate immediately when he came out the door or that Hervi kept his back turned and his head bent. Halsig wished for one minute that Sir Justin's reputation as a seeker out of wrongdoers were less potent. Clearly the friend had been too afraid to yield to Hervi's pleas to let him escape.

Disgusted but not really surprised—men like Hervi seldom had friends who would risk anything for them—Halsig oversaw

Hervi's final polishing of everything, then herded him to the privy and finally into the house. He told Mary to feed her husband because he was tired of watching him and intended to tie him up. Hervi whined and protested but desisted when Halsig lifted a hand in threat, and he ate greedily. Halsig was rather disappointed; he had hoped he had frightened Hervi enough to spoil his appetite. If the man was not too frightened to eat, possibly he would not try to run either. Halsig muttered imprecations as he tied him hand and foot.

When he had Hervi stretched out on the floor, he said to Mary, "You did not sweep the other room properly. Get your broom and I will show you what you missed."

Mary's eyes became pools of fear, but she ran for the broom and followed him, only beginning to whimper with terror when he shut the door.

"Hush, I'm not going to hurt you," he said to her, taking the broom from her hand, and patting her shoulder gently. "You haven't done nothing wrong. I only wanted to tell you in private that Sir Justin won't keep your husband for a servant any longer. He'll send him away tomorrow."

Mary had looked up when he said she had done nothing wrong, so Halsig saw her eyes fill with tears when he told her Justin would dismiss her husband. She did not speak—she seldom did—but her head dropped and her whole body slumped in utter hopelessness.

"Not you," Halsig said hastily. "That's why I wanted to talk to you private. Only Hervi's got to go. Maybe Sir Justin'll give him a good beating. Maybe not. Sir Justin's not one to hold grudges. But he wants you to stay and go on serving him, Mary. He really does want you to stay. He even knows he scares you, so he's going to get Mistress Lissa, that nice lady who was here yesterday, to ask you tomorrow."

Mary had lifted her head again when Halsig said Justin wanted her to stay. Now tears started to pour down her face. "I want to stay," she whispered. "It was heaven being here without Hervi when the old man was sick and I was taking care of him, but Hervi won't let me."

"He's got nothing to say about it," Halsig replied. "Sir Justin said if you stay, he'll protect you—and I will too, Mary. If you want, I'll tie Hervi loose so he can get free. If he thinks he's running away, he won't want you with him. And if he tries to make you go, just scream."

"I couldn't," she breathed. "If I scream, I'll wake Sir Justin—I couldn't!"

"Sir Justin won't be here," Halsig said. "It'll be me sleeping abovestairs tonight, and never you mind why, nor don't you say a word to anyone about that."

The council was shorter, if no less infuriating, than Justin had expected. He was not late in arriving at Lissa's house. It was still light enough, when he made the turning into Soper Lane, for him to see that the counter was gone. Since the shop was closed, he thought it would be more discreet to ride past and come through the alley, but Paul came out before he reached the door and greeted him, saying he would take Noir. Lissa was just behind her journeyman, and when she saw Justin's grand gown she dropped him a deep curtsy.

"What splendor!" she exclaimed. "It is quite awesome. Who were you trying to frighten to death?"

"Ghaah!" Justin replied, causing Lissa to burst into giggles. "I have wasted a whole afternoon. I should have gone home and changed this gown, but I am in such a temper that I would have murdered my man Hervi if I had seen him."

"Come up," Lissa said, drawing Justin in and shutting the door behind him. "I will feed you sweet comfits to take away the taste of the council. And I have a handsome new gown, fortunately not nearly so grand as this one, that you can wear tomorrow."

Justin laughed. "I think I will either have to give you up or give up my position," he said, following her up the stairs.

Lissa stopped abruptly and turned to face him, looking frightened. "Why? Who has spoken against me? Justin—"

Justin's heart lurched at her fear. Or was it her guilt? He took her hand. "I was jesting, sweeting, only jesting. I meant only that you have so soothing an effect on me that I will become too mild to punish those who commit crimes when we are married."

"Justin!" she protested. "You frightened me nearly to death." But she was smiling as she turned to go up the rest of the stairs, and she spoke again over her shoulder as she entered the solar. "I thought perhaps Master Chigwell was telling the whole city that I had murdered my father."

This time it was Justin who stopped short. "What?"

"Out of spite because I frightened him into withdrawing his offer of marriage to that dolt Edward," Lissa said hurriedly. And when she saw how the tension went out of her lover on those words, she continued, making a merry tale of her fears that Chigwell would oppose her acceptance into the Pepperers Guild and of the device she had used so that he would be glad when she asked him to withdraw his offer.

Laughing with his eyes, Justin mourned aloud at the damage done to his reputation. "You make me out a monster," he complained.

Lissa contrived to look amazed. "Well, you do not think me such a fool as to tell anyone that you are really gentle and kind. You would be snatched away from me in a minute by some beautiful woman who has nothing to do all day but coddle you—"

He caught her to him. "Coddle herself, you mean, and think herself neglected because I have other duties than to dance attendance on her." He kissed Lissa's nose and then trailed his lips across her cheek, murmuring, "And you *are* beautiful," before he began nibbling the lobe of her ear.

"Come into the other room and change your gown," Lissa whispered.

"If I take off the gown, I will not stop there," Justin warned her.

Lissa chuckled softly. "We are two busy people. I do not believe in wasted motion either."

It had grown completely dark before they finished, although they wasted neither time nor motion in the use of bodies from which the clothes had been removed. Justin had had a well of energy to expend from sitting still and holding his tongue when he wanted to bellow and pound the table. Quiet at last, he admitted to Lissa that working off his frustration in her bed was far pleasanter and probably would accomplish equal results.

Lissa lifted herself on one elbow and peered at him in the dim, flickering light that made its way from the hearth across the room to the bed. "You have lost me," she admitted. "Surely you are not the kind of man who would futter the mayor to make a point—and I know he has faults, but I did not think loving men was one of them."

Justin laughed aloud. "No, I only meant that shouting at that lot would have been utterly useless, and unfair, too. They are frightened." He was quiet for a moment and then added, "Well, so am I."

He threw back the covers and bent down to pick up the bedrobe their movements had jostled to the floor. "I am hungry," he said, and Lissa, who had risen when he did and also picked up her robe, put it on and went into the solar to call down to Oliva to bring up the evening meal.

When Justin came in, she had lit the candles. He put another log on the fire, and then, to Lissa's delight, he sat down in her father's chair as if he belonged there. But his face had set again, and Lissa asked anxiously, "Justin, of what are you afraid? Surely you are not talking about the disorder that comes with the arrival of many noblemen in London? You are accustomed to dealing with that. Yet what else threatens us? There is a truce for six years with France—"

"If none can bring them to reason, there will be open war between the king and the barons."

"That is nothing to do with us," Lissa said, but her voice had become a trifle shrill. "The burghers of London will take no part in such a war."

"It would be better indeed if the city could close its gates and lay chains across the river and call a pox on both barons and king, but this time we will not be allowed. We will be forced, I think, to show ourselves as for the king or against him. Do you not remember I told you that because FitzWalter is Standard Bearer of the city his men have duties guarding the walls? They could refuse the king entry—or open London to those the king names rebels."

"The force is not large. They can be driven off."

Justin laughed mirthlessly. "But then you have taken sides already, with the king. Besides, are you suggesting that the watch fight FitzWalter's guards? Within London?"

"Oh, God, no!" Lissa exclaimed, realizing what she had proposed without really thinking.

"Without ever saying the words, that was what all the quarreling was about at the council." Justin sighed. "They could not make up their minds to pay the price for the best men-at-arms when so strong a watch will not only cost high but may make both the king and FitzWalter suspicious. Nor could they agree to save expense by keeping the watch as it is and telling the king he is not welcome in the city."

"Telling the king he is not welcome! Justin, you cannot mean it! He would revoke London's charter and exact such retribution—"

"I heard hints from some aldermen that the barons would defend us."

"Do you believe it?" Lissa asked.

"They are not strong enough to fight the king . . . yet. But they *are* strong enough to make real trouble, so the aldermen are caught between the upper and nether millstones. They fear to refuse the king and also fear to offend the barons. But that was all the mayor found as a solution—to save money by not hiring new men and pretend we do not see what is happening, thus chancing looting and fire."

"I think I am more afraid of the fire than either the king or the barons," Lissa said.

"I too." Justin's eyes darkened with memory. "Which is why I am hiring the best men I can get. I reminded the council of what happened two years ago, and at last most agreed that above all else peace must be kept in the streets."

Oliva came in with their food at that point, and neither said any more until they had taken the edge off their appetites. Lissa would have turned the talk, but Justin could not leave the subject yet.

"What started the argument in council," he said, staring down into his cup of wine and swirling it gently, "was a letter from the king. I am beginning to think John is mad. He will not see that this is not the time for high talk and threats. He has been beaten at war, and the allies to whom he poured out our money have been utterly ruined. I understand that the money is gone and he needs more—"

"For what?" Lissa asked sharply.

Justin smiled wryly. "To live. King John must pay his servants and buy food for them, even as you and I. He must also repay the Church for what he took by force during the interdict."

"He stole the money from the Church and now wishes to steal from me to repay them?" Lissa's voice was tight with fury. "The king has lands, greater lands than the greatest noblemen. They live off their lands. Why cannot he?"

"The king must rule. All men benefit from a land at peace, and all men must pay for it, just as you are willing to pay for a strong watch to keep London at peace." Justin ran a hand through his hair. "And do not tell me that London pays for its own peace. It would do this city little good to have the countryside all around laid waste by warring barons—" He stopped suddenly and then went on, "Yet that is just what we are likely to have if King John does not very soon recognize that this is a time for quiet conciliation, not harsh demands. One of the aldermen read out the letter he sent demanding payment of the scutage levied last May and blaming the English barons for the failure of his campaign because they did not come when he summoned them in July, after the Poitevins deserted him."

"He is indeed mad if he sent such a letter to the mayor of London," Lissa remarked indignantly. "London sent every man pledged. We owe no scutage."

"No, the letter was to a baron, Eustace de Vesci."

"Eustace de Vesci?" Lissa repeated. "But how could a London alderman have his letter? Vesci is from the north."

"Ah yes, I remember, his wife buys from you, does she not?" Lissa nodded, and Justin continued, "I do not know how the letter, or a copy of it, came into the alderman's hands, but the man does business with FitzWalter."

Lissa shivered, but shook her head when Justin asked if he should rebuild the fire. "No, cover the coals for the night. I will be warmer and feel safer abed."

Justin got up at once and began to bank the fire, burying the glowing coals under a layer of ash that would slow the burning so the coals would keep some spark until morning. Lissa glanced at the remains of their meal, but there was not enough to wrap up for saving. Oliva would clear all away the next day. She got up and began to move about, snuffing the candles, then coming back to stand by Justin. He was still frowning, and Lissa felt she could no longer bear to talk about such great troubles, which no one seemed to have any power to avert. And then in the way thoughts will veer from a deep fear to a lesser one, she recalled what Justin had said when she greeted him at the door.

"What in the world has your man Hervi to do with the mayor

allowing the reading of that letter, which he should not have done? Why do you want to murder your servant? Surely he did not bring the letter."

"No." Justin straightened up and put an arm around Lissa. "I was angry at him before I started. He is lazy and left my horses and my stable filthy, and he beats his poor wife, who is honest and hardworking. He has been carrying tales of me to someone also, or stealing, because he has too much money. One anger just added to the other, and though he deserves a beating, I suppose, I would have doubled the blows if I had seen him then because I was furious with others. I could not do that, could I?"

"I have known others who could," Lissa said, rising on her toes to kiss Justin's cheek.

He smiled down at her, and they went into the bedchamber. He swung the door closed, his hand slipping down until a splinter of wood caught his finger. Then he turned to look at the uneven place. "The bar is gone," he said.

Lissa put her arms around his neck. "I had it taken off this morning. I love you, Justin. I believe you love me, and I will never need to lock myself away from you."

He held her close against him, understanding for the first time how a man could betray everything he had lived by all his life for a woman. When he thought of the hatred and fear in her past, he knew that nothing was worth more than the trust she had shown—not his life, not his honor. Desire rose in him, but it was not the hot, driving beat with which he was familiar. Instead, a suffusion of lightness and warmth spread what he could only call a physical joy throughout his entire body. He lifted her so they would not need to break their embrace to reach the bed, and though they could not undress without unwinding their arms, they continued to touch. He loved her for a long, long time, slowly, resting when they grew too quick and hot. Both came to a new, gentle ending; Lissa did not cry out and claw at him, just trembled and closed her eyes and smiled. And his seed came from him in slow pulses that for once were pure easy pleasure, not a bursting akin to pain.

Justin did not even need to wait to catch his breath, but with the last blissful pulse asked, "When will you marry me, Lissa?"

"When you say, beloved."

That easy, immediate reply gave him pleasure and troubled

him at the same time. He took the time to lift himself off her before he replied. "I am not sure what to do. I wish to bind you fast to me at once, yet that is not fair to you, dearling. You must have a man of your own blood to support you."

Lissa chuckled as she moved closer, turning her body so that she lay half atop him. "If I were a dishonest and greedy woman," she said, "I would urge you to write the marriage contract just as you wished. You would be so fearful of cheating me that you would assign me ten times what any man could wrest from you. I say again, I will marry you when and where you say, with or without contract, Justin, but for your sake, if you are willing, I think it would be best to wait a few weeks. I expect my uncles one last time before the winter storms begin. Either one can act for me, and if they do not come, then I will ask Master Goscelin. Will that content you?"

He kissed her for reply, and there was a silence in which Lissa wondered why it was more comfortable to lie against her lover's hard, angular body than on the soft mattress. She smiled in the dark and stroked his arm, thinking him asleep, and was surprised when he spoke.

"I think it would be better if we lived here in your house, if you are willing. The kind of people who are dragged into mine would not be wholesome company for you. Not to mention being wakened by shrieking nightwalkers and bellowing drunks when some inexperienced idiot on the watch feels they must be dealt with in the middle of the night."

Justin's voice was growing slurred, so Lissa only made a wordless murmur in reply, and his breathing soon slowed and deepened. She thought drowsily that though he might not welcome the disturbance, at least Justin was accustomed to night calls. Lissa did not encourage them, but she never refused to provide help for a severe injury or medicine for an illness that could not wait until morning.

Because it was the last thought in her head before she slept, Lissa felt she was dreaming and only stirred uneasily when the knocking began on the door. Justin had been dreaming, too, but of riot and fire, and he jerked upright and called out a question. His voice woke Lissa, who put a hand on his shoulder as she, too, sat up, about to say, "Go back to sleep, love. It is doubtless a neighbor with a bellyache," when Paul's voice made a lie of her thought.

"Your man is here, Sir Justin, and he is hurt."

Justin uttered an oath and leapt out of bed, pulling on his robe as he crossed the room. "Did he bring my armor?" he asked, striding past Paul, and without waiting for an answer, called back over his shoulder, "Bring down my clothes."

Lissa, who had followed him out of the room, holding her robe about her body, went back and put it on. Then she snatched up Justin's chausses, shirt, gown, and shoes and ran after him. The clothes she carried were not needed. At the door of the workroom she stopped, seeing Justin just ahead of her closing on Halsig, and Halsig struggling upright, steadying himself with one hand on the counter.

"I've killed Hervi, my lord," he said.

Chapter 27

JUSTIN STOPPED SHORT AND BLINKED. LISSA, REALIZING THERE WAS no riot, no danger to Justin, uttered a long sigh of relief and said, "Sit down, Halsig, you are bleeding. And don't look so tragic. From what I saw of his wife's face, Hervi is no great loss to anyone."

"Yes, sit down, man," Justin ordered. "Since you are hurt, it is clear enough that you did not creep up behind Hervi and strike him down—not that you would have needed to do that. What happened?"

"But in a way I'm guilty of his death, my lord," Halsig began, and told Justin how he had deliberately frightened the man to make him run.

While he told his tale, Lissa bade Paul fetch the large tapers she used when she needed good light for dressing wounds at night. She glanced around for Oliva, to tell her to renew the fire in the hearth, and saw her backed against the closed shelves, trying to drag a pallet away into the corner without being noticed. Without that secretive movement and the guilty way she hunched her body when Lissa looked at her, Lissa would never have noticed anything amiss. And it was Oliva's terrified glance that directed her own to the blankets atop the other pallet. These, although crumpled and tangled, were still noticeably double. Light dawned in Lissa's mind and illuminated the meaning of the workroom door being closed even in the summer's heat, Oliva's eagerness to help at the counter outside, no matter what the weather, and numerous other small incidents: Paul and Oliva were lovers.

Lissa opened her mouth to ask, and then closed it. This was not the time for questions or explanations—and she was not in the least sure what she wanted to say or do. She gave her orders and then got a soft leather packet that held several needles and short lengths of silk thread, which she had found caused less irritation when sewing flesh than linen. Paul had lit the tapers and placed them near Halsig, and Lissa was about to ask him to remove the man-at-arms's clothing when Halsig said, "I thought that big man-at-arms might simply take Hervi away with him. He asked for you, my lord, but I know he didn't want you. He was looking for Hervi all along."

Lissa paused. Any man Halsig called big must be more than usually outsize, and that called only one person to mind. Justin must have felt the same, because he said, "A big man-at-arms? How big? Can you describe him?"

"Taller than you, my lord, and thicker. That's big. Describe him? Big flat face. Small eyes—gray, I think. Thick lips. Nubbin nose. Reddish stubble, but his hair was brown. Thick reddish hair on his hands too—"

"Hubert de Bosco," Lissa breathed.

Justin nodded, looking satisfied. "Did Hervi know I would be out of the house tonight?"

"No, my lord, and he wouldn't have known if I let you in the front because I closed the door to the kitchen after I tied him up for the night. Mary untied him—but I told her to, my lord. Or, anyway, I told her to let him go."

Justin nodded again, looking even more pleased. "Hervi attacked you in my bed, did he not?"

"Yes, my lord. I was asleep, or he'd have never got the knife in me. And the first thing he did when Mary let him loose was to hit her so hard she couldn't move or think for a bit. Still, I'd be dead if not for Mary. As soon as she got her wits back and saw the kitchen door open instead of the outside door, she screamed her head off. And she followed him up the stairs and she—she hit him. That's how I got the knife away from him. He turned around and tried to push her away or hit her, so I was able to grab his knife hand. We were wrestling for the knife and he fell against me—"

Halsig's eyes dropped for a moment; he was pretty sure Mary had pushed her husband just as he had almost twisted the knife from Hervi's grip and it was pointing upward. Then he looked up. She couldn't have known that; she couldn't have guessed what would happen. She was only trying to help, and if any woman deserved vengeance, she surely did.

"The knife went right into his neck, and the blood gushed out so fast there was no way to stop it or help—"

"Oh, Lord," Justin complained. "All over my bed? Yes, well, it could not be helped, I suppose. I just wish you could have stabbed him somewhere else."

"Nonsense, Justin," Lissa said, coming close to Halsig and gesturing to Paul to remove the tunic the older man was wearing. "It was the best place. The furs can easily be washed clean and the bedclothes bleached. Surely, even if they must be discarded, that is better than getting blood on your fine rugs or the floorboards, and you could not reasonably expect Hervi to invite Halsig outside to be murdered."

Justin began to laugh aloud, and Halsig smiled faintly too, even though he had drawn breath sharply against pain when Paul pulled off his tunic. While they were still smiling, Lissa directed Justin to stand behind his man and hold him steady. Halsig protested faintly, but Justin told him not to be a fool just as Lissa said he was too strong for Paul. She cleaned the cut, which turned out to be not at all dangerous, although very bloody. The knife had not really entered Halsig's chest, merely cut a long gash from just under his left nipple along the curve of a rib. Having stitched him up and applied a salve, dark brown with the leachings from dried seaweed, she hooked a basket of rags from beneath the counter and began to bandage the wound. Seeing Halsig no longer needed support, Justin moved aside. For a few minutes he watched Lissa work, but clearly his mind was not on her activity.

"I do not think Hervi intended to murder Halsig at all," Justin said suddenly. "You remember I asked if Hervi knew I was not coming home, and he did not. I think he intended to murder me—"

"He would not dare!" Halsig exclaimed. "That mangy rat might think of sticking a knife in me before he ran for good, but you, my lord? He'd know he'd be found and torn to bits for that."

"Not if he was promised protection as well as gold," Justin said, smiling brightly. "I think that is what Hubert de Bosco offered. He offered Hervi the protection of Lord Robert Fitz-Walter—"

"FitzWalter wants you dead?" Lissa whispered, pale as milk even in the golden light of the tapers.

"No, no." Justin put an arm around her and laughed. "Do not be silly, Lissa. If FitzWalter wanted me dead, he would have killed me when I was in his power in Dunmow. I am certain that Lord Robert knows nothing of Hubert's plan. Apparently my questioning made that huge dolt uneasy, so he decided to have me removed in a way that would not involve him. Hubert is not a coward. He would have attacked me himself if he had not been afraid FitzWalter would hear of it. And can you imagine Lord Robert approving the use of a tool like Hervi?"

Halsig laughed and shook his head, anxiety clearing from his face, but then he frowned. "I'm doubly sorry I killed Hervi then. He would have gladly put the blame on this Hubert de Bosco, and you would have had them both cleaned away."

"No, it does not matter." Justin shrugged. "No judge in London or out of it would put the slightest credence in anything Hervi said, even under torture. You know and I know, and the judge would know too, that he would tell a new tale with every turn of the screw."

Lissa, who was still pale, interrupted with orders that Halsig must be bedded down. She bade the two boys, who had been silently listening and watching everything with eyes round as the king's golden dinner plates, to lie head to foot and give one of their pallets to the man-at-arms. The alacrity with which the pallet closest to the hearth was cleared and a blanket offered displayed the eagerness Witta and Ninias felt for a guest who had just stuck a knife in another man's throat. Ordinarily they would have squabbled about which pallet and which blanket. Despite the eager, if silent, invitation, Halsig protested that he would have to go back to Justin's house.

"I left Hervi there, on the bed. I'm sorry, my lord, but I didn't know how bad I was hurt. I had come over dizzy when I rolled him off me and stood up, and I was bleeding like a stuck pig. I didn't dare carry him down or wait before I came to tell you what happened. And Mary's alone, not knowing what will happen."

"Don't be a fool, man," Justin retorted. "Lie down and rest. I have to go home anyway. I'll stop and roust out Dunstan. He can carry Hervi out." He saw Halsig still hesitating and, recalling his last sentence, turned to Lissa. "The woman is terrified of me," he said. "Will you come with me and talk to her?"

"Yes, of course," Lissa agreed. She watched Paul and Justin help Halsig to lie down, then turned and pinched out the large tapers. "Put everything away, Oliva," she said, and then picked up Justin's clothes from the counter where she had laid them. "Come above with me to dress," she said. "Oliva is busy here, you can help me."

Lissa dressed him first, quickly and silently, not in the elaborate gown in which he had arrived but in new garments she took from her chest. Then she turned away from him, took off her robe, and pulled on her shift and undertunic. Waiting, Justin became aware that she had not said a word all the time, which was unlike Lissa, and when she came to him, he said, "I am sorry we have no time for games," and snatched a kiss as he pulled tight laces and tied ties according to Lissa's directions.

"I am not in the mood for games," Lissa snapped. "I cannot imagine what you have been grinning about all this time. Hubert is dangerous, and he is not honorable. He will try again to kill you by stealth. Even if Hervi would not be believed, Halsig would be believed. He could point Hubert out as the man who asked for you—"

Justin looked at Lissa blankly. He could not say he was happy because he considered her innocence better established with each mark of Hubert's guilt. Lissa, he was sure, assumed he took her innocence for granted or he would not be sleeping with her. To a great extent that was true. Nonetheless, he was delighted by Hubert's attempt on him because he took the man's fear as a kind of admission that he had killed William Bowles. Had Hubert been in Dunmow on Thursday as he claimed, there could be no reason for him to be afraid or try to stop any investigation with murder.

"The judge would doubtless believe Halsig saw Hubert that afternoon," Justin said, "but there can be no proof at all that Hubert ever spoke one word to Hervi or did more than watch him as Halsig asked."

"Will you do nothing to protect yourself?" Lissa cried.

He caught her in his arms and kissed her, his eyes sparkling with unholy mischief. "You silly girl, of course I will. I will go to FitzWalter and protest gently about his man's subverting my servant—"

"No!"

Justin laughed. "Yes, sweet nodcock! Lord Robert will be delighted with me. Will not my confidence in him prove I believe him to be innocent of Hubert's action? And it is quite true, too. I am certain he is innocent of so clumsy an attempt. He may well assume that I also believe him innocent of any involvement in your father's death, which is not true but may make it easier for me to determine just what part he did play. That is for the future. In the present, FitzWalter will scold or punish Hubert, which will stop any future attempts on my life far better than my going about with a guard of ten men and ringing any place I stay with soldiers."

Color came into Lissa's cheeks, betraying that she had been envisioning just such a guard and possibly locking him in the house too, and Justin laughed at her again and kissed her nose. Then they took up their cloaks and went out, Justin saddling Noir and Lissa's mare and taking them to the stable when they reached his house while Lissa called to Mary to open the door.

The woman was terrified, but Lissa soon discovered that her fear was for Halsig. As soon as Mary heard that Halsig was not badly hurt and would be back in Justin's house the next day, and that Justin was not at all angry about what had happened, she became quite cheerful. She listened intently to Lissa's instructions for getting her husband's blood out of Justin's bedclothes, nodding understanding and occasionally offering a word culled from her own personal experience. Then she shrank into herself, and Lissa thought she had finally realized about whose blood they were speaking, but before she could offer comfort, Justin spoke from behind her.

"Oh, throw the bedclothes out," he said to Mary. "I will seldom be sleeping here anyway." And then, in an entirely different voice, to Lissa, "Come, love, Dunstan has arrived and will see you safe home. Go back to bed. I will come as usual tomorrow."

Justin took her out and mounted her himself, then took a candle from the supply, lit it at the fire, and went up to his bedchamber where he lit several more. The bed was a mess, and he cursed Halsig briefly but more by habit than with anger for not having left the knife in Hervi's throat. That would have cut down the flow of blood.

A short search uncovered the knife half under the bed, and he took it out and examined it carefully, his smile growing broader and broader. The knife had certainly not come from his kitchen nor from Hervi's belt. Justin remembered Hervi's knife, a cheap, gaudy affair. This was a fine weapon, well worn but with a distinctive winding of wire on the hilt—and he had never seen the weapon before. Very likely one of FitzWalter's men would be able to identify it as Hubert's.

Justin was so happy about Hubert's indirect confession that he was almost reluctant to complain to FitzWalter and get Hubert, whose stupidity had erased his suspicion of Lissa, into trouble. That faint, if foolish, reluctance, plus the fact that he was simply too busy to take the time to ride out to Dunmow, delayed his meeting with FitzWalter for over two weeks. During that time there was no sign of Hubert, although Justin asked the men in the watch nearest Baynard's Castle and a few in other places to look for him.

Had Halsig's wound festered or his own comfort been compromised, Justin might have been more vindictive, but neither was true. Lissa had come, at first every day and then every few days, to check on Halsig, who had moved into Justin's house and insisted on carrying out his duties, using Dunstan as his arms and legs when necessary. He had easily solved the problem of a new groom, taking on one of the older men with a farm background, who was to be dismissed from the watch and was grateful for any kind of work.

On 10 November Lissa was on her way to Justin's house to take one last look at Halsig's almost-healed wound. She was accompanied by Oliva, who was going to shop for food in the Chepe, and Ninias, who was carrying a soothing hand cream to Goscelin's wife. As the three parted near the corner of the Mercery, Lissa turned to remind Ninias to tell Mistress Adela to use the cream each time she wet her hands, and saw, not ten steps behind her, Hubert de Bosco. Even his dull mind could not mistake her look of recognition and fear, the way her lips parted and her breath drew in to scream. He whirled on his heel and ran back, darting into an alley that went behind the Mercery and debouched into Bucklersbury Lane. Lissa caught back the scream, which would have been pointless, waved her servants on to their tasks, and ran toward Justin's house.

She uttered a low cry of relief when she saw Noir being held in front of Justin's house by the groom, and she ran in the open door, almost colliding with Justin, who was on his way out. "I saw him," she gasped.

"Who?"

"Hubert."

A black scowl came over Justin's face. "Why are you so frightened? Did he touch you? Speak to you?"

"No." Lissa described how she had accidentally noticed Hubert; Justin's scowl cleared, being replaced by mild interest. "But Justin, I think he was coming here," Lissa insisted, clutching his arm nervously. "He may be coming in the back gate right now."

"So what?" Justin looked down at her in some amusement. "He will not attack me in the street in the middle of the day, and if he should I do not doubt I could deal with him. Probably he wants to find out what happened to Hervi—and his knife."

However, remembering the knife also reminded Justin that Hubert might try to recover the evidence while he was away from the house, and Halsig was in no condition to contest its ownership with him. In addition, he suddenly grew concerned that the stupid clod might resent Lissa for having seen him and warned Justin. He wondered if she might have thought of it too—she looked frightened—but he did not say anything for fear of putting the idea in her head if it was not already there.

"Very well," he said, kissing her quickly. "I cannot take the chance that he will work off his anger on Halsig. I will send for some men to guard the house. You go in."

He did not tell her he would remain inside the house, although he hoped she would believe this, and left only a few minutes after he had sent her home with Dunstan and Dick as escorts. When he returned to the house for dinner, he found all had been perfectly quiet. Hubert had made no attempt, innocent or otherwise, to recover his knife or discover Hervi's fate. In fact, no one had seen him in or near Justin's house.

At that point it occurred to Justin that Lissa's fear had communicated itself senselessly to him. If FitzWalter had come back to London, it was natural for Hubert to be in the city. And the whole business about his running into the alley might have been in Lissa's mind. That alley came out into the street of the shieldmakers. Nothing could be more natural than for Hubert to be going there on an errand for his master. Justin bit his lip and thought. Even if Hubert's current errand was innocent, he really should not delay longer in letting FitzWalter know that his man had done a stupid and dangerous thing. He was able to separate the wheat from the chaff, but others might blame the master for the action of the man, and there was enough ill said of FitzWalter without adding lies. Justin pushed aside the remains of his meal and went down, beckoning Dunstan to him.

"Take the jennet and go to Baynard's Castle. If Lord Robert is there, ask if he will grant me a few minutes of his time this afternoon, or if not today as soon as is convenient to him. When you have an answer, you will find me in my cousin FitzAilwin's house—you remember, the old mayor's house, which stands on the north side of Saint Swithin's Church over against the London Stone."

Justin sincerely hoped that FitzWalter would be able to see him that afternoon because it would be the perfect excuse to break free of his aunt. He had received a message from her rather late the previous afternoon saying that she must talk to him and inviting him for the evening meal. The servant who brought the message had known of no crisis in the household, however, and Justin had not wanted to miss his pleasant, leisurely evening with Lissa. He could still hardly believe he had back all the happiness he thought lost forever, and continued to clutch at every hour with her as precious. So he told the servant he would come to his aunt the next day, after dinner, hoping by going early he could free himself early and be "home" with Lissa before the short day ended. A message from FitzWalter would solve the problem of why he would not stay for the evening with his aunt.

Justin's aunt Margaret was waiting for him when he arrived. After exclaiming in alarm about seeing him in mail and hearing it was only a precaution because of the influx of barons into the city, she brushed aside his polite enquiries about her health. Justin cocked his head, and Mistress Margaret seemed to lose the thread of what she had been about to say. She twittered around this subject and that, and then asked, "Are you not lonely in that house, all by yourself, Justin? You are very welcome to come back here to us."

With some effort, Justin refrained from laughing. He was *very* fond of his aunt, but few events had given him equal relief to moving out of her house. "But I am seldom there, Aunt Margaret," he replied solemnly. Before he could go on, she raised troubled, tear-filled eyes to him.

"Oh, Justin, it is not true, is it?" Her voice quavered. "I cannot believe it."

"What, aunt?" He came closer and took her hand. "I cannot think of anything I have done that could so much displease you."

She bit her lip. "I have heard it said that you—that you threatened to accuse William Bowles's daughter of his murder and so brought her to—to your bed."

Justin's mouth opened, but nothing came out, and his aunt stood up and stared, looking more and more frightened, until at last he shook his head.

"Oh, I am so glad!" she exclaimed. "I said you would never do such a thing, but when I mentioned the gossip to Thomas—I thought he would be angry and perhaps drop a word in the stupid woman's ear that would silence her, since I could not—but Thomas looked so strange that I just had to ask you."

Suppressing his first impulse to discover who had said so cruel a thing to his aunt and tear out her tongue, Justin gathered his wits. He could not lie to Margaret and say he had no relationship with Lissa because the lie would be exposed as soon as they married and she would be hurt, so he swallowed hard and said calmly, "No, of course I would not do such a thing. I would never take an unwilling woman to my bed. Surely you remember, aunt, that I withdrew an offer of marriage because I discovered the girl was afraid of me and unwilling."

"She was a stupid slut!" his aunt said heatedly. "I cannot understand how you could have been so silly as to let *her* opinion affect you. She would have changed her mind had you gone ahead with the marriage."

Justin's fury diminished enough for him to feel a flicker of amusement at the familiar confusion in his aunt's thinking. "Aunt," he said with mock reproof, "you cannot have wanted me to marry a stupid slut, even if she did learn to care for me as a wife should. And to tell the truth, I am afraid I used the lady's fear to crawl out of an engagement I had begun to regret bitterly, so do not speak ill of her. I will have a much better wife in Lissa, who you will see does not fear me at all and laughs at me."

Mistress Margaret was flustered by her anger at the memory of the rejection of her nephew, which she felt had hurt him despite what he said. But she had knowledge of which Justin was unaware: After his proposed marriage had come to nothing, she had approached several girls in his behalf, and every one had shuddered at his name. And truly she could not imagine any woman, even herself, laughing at Justin.

Before she thought, she burst out, "Wife? But I thought she was promised to Edward Chigwell until her father interfered."

Then she drew breath fearfully. Justin was always gentle to her, and yet she could often feel a roiling impatience in him, rigidly controlled, and half expected that one day the control would break and he would shout at her or strike her. To her surprise, he laughed.

"You will have to ask Lissa herself to explain that," he said. "She says she loves me and that Edward Chigwell is a pompous fool." He shrugged, but his eyes were sad. "Why do you not go to her shop and talk to her? I will not even speak to her of your coming so you may be sure she is free to say what she wishes."

Tears came to Margaret's eyes. Justin's face was different when he spoke of this girl. He cared for her, that was certain, but did she care for him? Did it matter? He would be good to her. She would grow accustomed to him, just as Margaret herself had grown accustomed and even learned to love her husband. She threw her arms around him, remembering the young man who had come to London, remembering that it was her husband who had laid the burdens on Justin that had drawn the hard lines on his face and changed the laughter in his eyes to ice.

"Justin, Justin, I believe you. I do."

Chapter 28

∽⤫⤬∾

THE ARRIVAL OF DUNSTAN WITH THE MESSAGE JUSTIN HAD HOPED for from FitzWalter very soon after his aunt's emotional outburst was providential. Mistress Margaret had learned many years before from her husband that business came before everything else, so she was not surprised and did not protest when Justin said he must go at once. She kissed him fondly and told him that he must come more often to see her and that he should bring Mistress Lissa. Justin agreed with a smile, glad of the invitation. He had not been sure Lissa would be welcome before they were publicly betrothed, since it was apparent his aunt knew she was his mistress. The Church frowned on bedding before wedding, but most people were more lenient to a betrothed couple, and apparently his aunt felt his word that he intended to marry Lissa was as good as a formal betrothal.

Lissa would settle any remaining doubts his aunt might have far better than he could, Justin knew, but he could think of no way to kill the ugly rumor entirely. On his way to FitzWalter's house he considered various expedients. An immediate marriage? But that might only prove he had forced marriage on Lissa. Perhaps a formal betrothal followed by a round of invitations to the merchant community and attendance at public events where Lissa could show herself to be happy? But that was the same thing, and if he was her squire to public events and celebrations, who would believe her if she claimed she was willing and happy?

Justin came to the conclusion that it was useless even to think of the subject until he could discuss it with Lissa. He saw now that her desire for secrecy, which had so infuriated him in the past, was more for his good than hers. She had told him so over and over, of course, but he had refused to accept her reasoning. That was a bitter potion to swallow; Justin hoped he had learned his lesson and would know better in the future than to argue with a woman about what damage gossip could do.

It was a pleasant relief, in comparison, to have to face FitzWalter with a complaint. It was so much of a relief to talk to someone who knew little and cared less about personal gossip in the merchant community that Justin began his story in a light voice with a half-smile on his lips. He managed to hold voice and expression steady even after tension came into Lord Robert's face when he first said Hervi's name, but he wondered briefly if FitzWalter *had* sent Hubert to kill him. By the time he mentioned Hubert's knife, however, FitzWalter's tension was all gone, and Justin realized it was Hervi alive and talking that made FitzWalter uneasy.

The smile Justin was wearing became quite genuine again. He was now fairly certain it was FitzWalter, through Hubert, who had been paying Hervi for information about him. Rather than being angry, as FitzWalter had clearly expected, Justin felt amused. He had had no idea he was important enough for a man like FitzWalter to spy on. When he finished the tale with the statement that he believed Hubert had incited Hervi to try to kill him, offering FitzWalter's protection as an inducement, Lord Robert shook his head and sighed.

"Hubert is enough of a dunce to have done it," he said. "I am sure you will be able to find someone to identify his knife. Can you imagine being stupid enough to give so recognizable a weapon to your man?" Then he frowned. "I hope you do not think this proves him guilty of Bowles's murder. He is stupid enough to panic or simply to resent your questioning him. What do you want me to do?"

Justin laughed, although he was surprised by FitzWalter's insistence that Hubert was innocent of killing Bowles. Justin had been careful not to bring up the subject directly. It was not typical of FitzWalter to be so loyal to a servant who had done wrong without his master's knowledge.

"Only tell him to stop trying to put an end to me," Justin replied easily, avoiding any remark about Hubert's guilt for Bowles's death. "I do not want to have to kill him or have him exiled. After all, he might have given Hervi that knife to cut himself free. The stabbing attempt might have been Hervi's idea. But Hubert will not be able to get into my house again, and he is the kind to hire men to help him if he decides to attack me on the street. To speak the truth, my lord, I have enough brawls to settle without needing to be the cause of one myself."

Justin did not add that having and protecting a servant like Hubert was a stain on the master. Lord Robert knew that well enough; or, if he did not, then his honor had so rotted away that being told would not help. That FitzWalter needed and used such servants was one reason, among others, that Justin could never warm into friendship for the man. He was accustomed to hiding his thoughts behind a rigid face, however, and FitzWalter read none of his disgust.

"That is very generous," FitzWalter said. "I sent Hubert back to Dunmow just today, so I cannot call him into your presence while I tell him what I think of his behavior but I will see that he does not even look at you again, not to mention make attempts on your life. And let me thank you for coming to me about the matter instead of raising a hue and cry. Do you have time for a cup of wine? Speaking of Bowles has brought a most curious incident to my mind."

Justin nodded, and FitzWalter waved him to a bench near his chair, then called to a servant for wine.

"I received a strange letter from a ship master based in Haarlem," FitzWalter continued. "He told me that he had questioned Peter and Edmond de Flael, as William Bowles, my agent, had asked him to do—and I swear to you that Bowles was never my agent in any matter of business—and that the brothers

Flael did not have the design for plate that I had commissioned
from Peter de Flael."

"Design for plate?" Justin repeated, completely bewildered.
He did not believe FitzWalter's interest in the subject of the ship
master's letter was as slight and casual as he pretended. Lord
Robert was watching him through half-lowered eyelids, but
Justin was not fooled; he was being watched most intently, too
intently. Nonetheless, whatever Bowles's involvement with
Flael had been, this tale about a design for plate for FitzWalter
was incredible.

"You can be no more surprised than I," FitzWalter said.
"Quite aside from the fact that my troubles with the king have
left me no money to throw away on plate, you must know that I
would not have gone to Peter de Flael for any work I wanted. He
did too much for King John for me to give him my custom."

That statement was plain truth, and Justin knew it. The wine
came, and both men drank in silence while the servant
withdrew. "That is a strange tale indeed," Justin agreed. "Did
the ship master say where Flael's sons were?"

"No, and I do not remember the man's name. The letter is in
Dunmow. Do you want me to send for it?"

There was no harm in Sir Justin having the letter, Lord Robert
thought, smiling faintly. There was no trail leading from the
Haarlem man to Flael's sons that could be traced back to him.
The ship master had been rewarded for his trouble, fulsomely
thanked, and told that FitzWalter had no interest in any design
for plate done by Peter de Flael and no interest in Flael's sons.
Moreover, the ship master had been assured that Bowles had
taken Lord Robert's name in vain; Bowles had never been Lord
Robert's agent. But days before that, Peter and Edmond de Flael
had told all they knew about the copy of the king's seal to men
who had falsely identified themselves as having come from the
French court—and they would talk to no one else, ever.

Justin considered, seeming to look idly at nothing but taking
in his host's manner. Although Justin was not certain that
FitzWalter had truly forgotten the name of the ship master, he
was almost certain the offer to send for his letter was genuine.
Equally important: FitzWalter was no longer watching him with
particular interest. Lord Robert had either discovered what he
wanted to know from Justin's reaction—or lack of reaction—or

he had been mistaken in his first assumption and Lord Robert really was relating a puzzling event. Under the circumstances, there was no point in his looking at the letter. He could do that any time if he later felt it was necessary.

"No," he said, "I cannot see any purpose to pursuing the sons, particularly if they have left England. They were not guilty of their father's death, and the case has been closed—although I must admit I am still most curious about why Flael was threatened so forcefully that he died of fear."

"Perhaps it is better not to know, considering for whom Flael did some very expensive pieces. Some thought the work was a method of payment for other services, which was why I had no work done by Peter de Flael." FitzWalter grimaced. "I melted down my plate to pay my debts, but our lord king simply demands more from those he has already robbed. I heard that his letter to Vesci was read in the mayor's council."

Although the subject was dangerous, Justin simply nodded. He was deeply interested in what FitzWalter would say. Despite the self-pitying tales of melted plate, Lord Robert was one of the richest men in the kingdom, and he had great influence among the barons. That influence had been increased by the recent blows to King John's power—the desertion of the king by the Poitevins and King Louis's destruction of King John's allies. If FitzWalter was about to call for war against the king without suggesting some compromise path, Justin wanted to know. Perhaps other forces could be brought to bear that could alter FitzWalter's intention or weaken his influence among the barons. Justin would hate to see it, but even wakening the old false specter of FitzWalter's cowardice and treachery in yielding Vaudreuil would be better than open war between the barons and the king.

"You did not feel that the demand was outrageous?" Fitz-Walter insisted.

"I felt the king was mistaken to take so harsh a tone, and three marks seems high to me," Justin temporized. "But it is customary to pay scutage in lieu of service."

"Scutage in lieu of service was reasonable when the king and many barons had great lands in France." FitzWalter's voice was harsh. "Now the barons of England have little reason to fight there. The king must be brought to see this."

"I cannot deny that I have often wished King John was more aware that the head suffers when by its violence the body is abused," Justin said. "But, my lord, I cannot wish for a body without a head either."

"No!"

FitzWalter's exclamation was prompt and emphatic. Justin wished that a gleam had not lit in Lord Robert's eye nor his lip quirked quite the way it did when he spoke. He had a strong suspicion that he was about to hear platitudes that would soon lead to something worse, but to his surprise what FitzWalter did next was to burst into praise of Stephen Langton, the archbishop of Canterbury.

Justin concealed a sigh of relief and remarked, "You will get no argument from me. I know his lordship moderately well. You remember— Oh, no, you had not yet come back to England. I served as chief of Archbishop Langton's guard in the first weeks he was here. I think he feared treachery—not that he is a coward; only he did not wish to die before he had accomplished his purposes. He very soon realized, however, that King John might pray in private for his early, natural death, but would do nothing to help it along. John wanted no second holy martyr. His father's creation of Saint Thomas à Becket was enough."

"Then you were present when the archbishop told us of the charter that the first King Henry gave to his barons on the event of his coronation," FitzWalter said eagerly.

"Yes." Justin did not say there was nothing in that charter about serving the king in foreign wars. "And I am certain," he added blandly, "that Archbishop Langton will do all he can to convince the king to behave with moderation."

That was true, but Justin was also sure Archbishop Langton would have no part in inciting the barons into a war against the king, which he greatly feared was FitzWalter's final purpose; he made no comment on that, however. If Lord Robert was blinded enough by his hatred of the king to believe Archbishop Langton felt the same, Justin did not wish to relieve that blindness. On the contrary, anything he could say to encourage FitzWalter to consult with the prelate, he would say gladly.

Lord Robert smiled, but he did not answer Justin's remark directly. Instead he said, "Many causes of trouble would be removed if such a charter were renewed, saying clearly what duties are owed by the barons, what rights are theirs, and what belongs to the king. You might be interested to attend the religious services on the feast of Saint Edmund at his church in Bury St. Edmunds."

"Two days' ride from London," Justin said.

Although his brief statement might have seemed as much unrelated to the topic of the quarrel between King John and his baronage as FitzWalter's remark about the religious services at Bury St. Edmunds, neither man had strayed from the subject. Justin understood that the barons would meet, ostensibly to discuss obtaining a new version of Henry I's charter, under cover of attending the religious services. The charter, Justin thought, was an excellent idea, but he was not certain what else might be discussed in secret meetings among the leaders, which might then seem to involve all who attended.

FitzWalter stared at Justin without expression for a moment, then shrugged contemptuously and nodded. "Of course," he said, "you would need to get leave, and you do not even bend the truth, do you, Sir Justin?"

"I would not say that, my lord," Justin replied with a wry twist of the lips. "I have told many women they were the most beautiful in the world and that I loved them and would love them forever." His eyes were steady on FitzWalter's face, but Lord Robert did not meet them. Justin recognized the pain of irretrievable loss under the assumed contempt in the sneer directed at him, and his voice was more gentle than usual as he added, regretfully, "But in the matter of leaving my post for a week at this time, I would need to speak the truth or lie outright. A small bend in the truth would not do."

"Then by all means speak the truth," FitzWalter snapped, clearly displeased. "There is no secret about our attendance at Saint Edmunds."

Justin uttered a soothing platitude, and FitzWalter laughed harshly, but he shifted the subject to the effect the king's war might have on the wine trade. Both men were in perfect accord on that topic and they talked for a while longer before they parted amicably. But the smile died on FitzWalter's face as Justin left the hall, and he muttered to himself, "You are just a little too cautious and clever, Sir Justin, but we will do quite well without you."

Still, dissatisfaction was mingled with admiration in FitzWalter as he stared for a moment longer at the doorway through which Justin had passed before he lifted a hand and beckoned a servant, to whom he said, "Find Hubert de Bosco and tell him to come here at once."

Although Hubert had no notion of it, the irritation Lord Robert felt over Justin's avoidance of the net he had cast saved Hubert a painful beating. The knowledge would not have diminished the rage Hubert felt when his master gave him the sharp edge of his tongue for his attempt on Justin's life, but he was far too much afraid of FitzWalter to consider disobeying him. He promised hastily never again to trouble Sir Justin in any way, but then added sullenly that he had not suggested that Hervi kill his master. He had given him the knife to protect himself.

FitzWalter cut off the excuse with a gesture. Whether what Hubert said was true or a lie was irrelevant to him. "But I will give you one more chance to redeem yourself."

"I will not fail you, my lord."

"You have already failed once," FitzWalter snapped. "Did I not tell you to fetch Bowles's daughter to me?"

"But, my lord—"

"I do not want to hear your excuses. The time for the meeting is growing close, and if she knows anything I must get it from her before then. So you will go to Bowles's house tonight near midnight and get her."

"Should I hire men to break in or—"

"Idiot!" FitzWalter exclaimed. "Do you want to rouse the whole street? All you need do is smear your tunic with blood and wrap a stained bandage around your head so that your face is hidden. Pretend you are hurt. Bang on the door and ask for help. Once in the house, you can strike down the journeyman and get the girl. And do not hurt her! I want her able to answer my questions."

Understanding dawned, and a smile spread over Hubert's coarse features. He nodded eagerly.

FitzWalter sighed, barely restraining impatience, but he knew an outburst of temper would only confuse Hubert, and he said quietly, "That is all, but keep out of sight for the rest of the day. I told Sir Justin that I had sent you to Dunmow. If you are seen by anyone outside of this household so that news of your being in

London comes to Sir Justin's ears, you will suffer for it. When you have the girl, muffle her well in a blanket and enter through the small postern gate. Bring her to the old cellar, but into my chamber there, not into the room with the instruments. I will wait for you there, so do not linger. Be sure you are back with her before Lauds."

"I will get her back in good time," Hubert assured him.

FitzWalter made a moue of distaste but said nothing more and waved a dismissal. Creatures like Hubert had their purposes, but this one, he thought, was almost at the end of his usefulness. He knew too much too. It would be a disaster if Justin marked him as Bowles's killer, seized him, and questioned him. After Hubert had brought the girl and assisted at questioning her, FitzWalter decided, would be a good time to be rid of him. Her death and Hubert's could be arranged so that it would be plain Hubert had murdered her and had been killed by those who discovered him in the act—none, naturally, having any connection with FitzWalter's own household.

He stood and stretched, pausing suddenly with his arms still out while a frown appeared between his brows. Had he heard that Sir Justin was involved with Bowles's daughter? Had not one of his factors mentioned a rumor that Justin had used Bowles's death to make the woman his mistress? There was so little chance the girl knew anything that it was not worth starting Sir Justin on a hunt with a grudge behind it. But he had no other avenue to explore. He must question Bowles's daughter or give up the idea of finding the seal. Flael's sons had not taken the seal with them; they believed their father had given it to Bowles. And Bowles was dead—by his own order!

FitzWalter dropped his arms and ground his teeth. That seal could make all the difference in the attitude of the barons at Bury St. Edmunds. It would mark as genuine, beyond any protest, false letters from the king that could be used at the meeting to push the barons, if not into rebellion, at least into immoderate language. When news of what they said came to the king, John's own actions would ensure their adherence to the party that opposed him.

Surely, FitzWalter thought, the Bowles girl could not be important to Sir Justin. He nodded, remembering that he had just heard Justin remark cynically on his casual relations with women. Possibly Sir Justin had been futtering Bowles's daughter and would be annoyed when she disappeared, but FitzWalter did not see that as any reason for Justin to pursue the criminal with more than usual intensity. Women were plentiful, particularly to those who could make trouble for them or save them trouble for the small price of a joining.

In any case, FitzWalter thought that he, who had never even met the girl, would not be connected with her disappearance and death, except through a man he had employed out of pity. Hubert was the one closely associated with her father. Probably Justin would assume that Hubert had killed the daughter in a rage because Justin himself had become forbidden prey, or he would think that Hubert was taking out on her some unfulfilled portion of his quarrel with Bowles. Since Hubert would be dead, it would not matter what Sir Justin decided was the cause of his action.

About the time Justin left Baynard's Castle, a mature lady, escorted by a maid and a sturdy manservant, came to the counter of Lissa's shop. She examined the condiments displayed with a keen eyed glance and then asked to see Mistress Lissa on private business. Paul almost turned her away, guessing from her age that she would ask either for a love potion or for something to make her fertile—both of which he knew Lissa would not attempt—but there was a timid dignity about the woman that made it impossible to lie to her. He pulled aside a barrel and bowed her in. She entered, bestowing a small smile on him, but she gestured to the maid and manservant to remain behind. Having offered her a stool, Paul went through the workshop door and told Lissa she had a customer who wished to speak to her privately.

"My name is Margaret FitzAilwin—" the woman began as soon as Paul had gone out to the counter again, shutting the door behind him.

"Oh dear," Lissa interrupted, "you are Justin's aunt. I do hope you have not come to scold me and ask me to give up Justin. I do assure you that I am not a woman of light virtue. I love Justin quite sincerely, and we intend to marry as soon as the matter of my father's murder is cleared up." She smiled tentatively and added, "In Justin's position it would be awkward for him to marry the chief suspect."

The worried look cleared from Margaret's face and she responded to Lissa's smile. "I have not come to scold you, and I would not dream of interfering in Justin's life. If Justin has given his word and you have accepted him, you are betrothed as surely as if a contract had been written. Neither of you is a child, but your agreement seemed so sudden. I—I was concerned for you—" She stopped abruptly and clasped her hands nervously. "I should not have come," she added, getting up. "It was stupid of me."

Lissa cocked her head inquisitively. "Concerned for me?" she repeated, picking up the significant phrase. Then she sighed. "There has been talk about us. I was afraid of that, but Justin claimed that I was ashamed of him when I suggested that we keep his visits secret. Are not men the most unreasonable creatures? They act as if taking the most common precaution is a personal insult. Oh, please, Mistress FitzAilwin, will you not come abovestairs with me and take some refreshment?"

Mistress Margaret protested, saying she could not stay and mentioning the maid and manservant waiting for her. Lissa did not urge her further to come up to the solar, but she was determined to learn what was being whispered about her and Justin. She put on a sad, worried face and hinted that Justin's aunt really did not approve of her, although she was too kind to say so.

In confusion and anxiety, Margaret reseated herself, and it was not long before Lissa extracted the entire tale, not only the sordid rumor that Justin had forced her into his bed but the story of the withdrawn offer of marriage and the fear and revulsion most women felt for Justin. Since Lissa had already met the reaction in Adela, she managed to control her anger and incredulity, only laughing and assuring Mistress Margaret that her relationship with Justin was not at all sudden. She had known and admired him since the great fire of 1212, Lissa pointed out, and they had come much closer when Justin had investigated her husband's death.

"He was so kind to me," Lissa said. "I know he does not *look* kind, but he helped me in so many ways that were no part of his duty and that must have been a trouble to him, although he pretended they were not. And his eyes laugh, even if his mouth does not. Justin is no pompous ass like that sucking cub Edward Chigwell. I did not know how much I loved Justin until I was almost trapped in marriage with Edward."

Margaret stood up again, smiling with brimming eyes. "I am so glad for him, Lissa, that he found you. Indeed, he is everything you say. He was so full of laughter when he came to London, but my husband needed . . ." She hesitated and then went on very softly, "I do not know why he used Justin. I hope it was not to—to spare his own sons. But Justin changed—"

"Only on the outside," Lissa said. "Inside there is still the kind, laughing boy—at least for you and for me there is. And you must not pity Justin or blame your husband. I am sure Mayor FitzAilwin chose Justin because he was best suited to hunt evildoers and keep the peace and even enjoys most of what he does."

"Please do not tell him I came," Margaret said as she walked to the door with Lissa.

"Not for the world!" Lissa assured her fervently, curving her lips into a smile with some effort.

The smile died and her lips thinned with fury as she closed the door behind Mistress Margaret. She was appalled at the hurt Justin must have felt when he heard what was being said of him and furious with his silly aunt for dealing him such a blow. Unfortunately there was nothing she could do, for it was clear that Mistress Margaret meant well. If the stupid woman were not afraid of Justin herself, she would never have believed the rumor and never brought it to his attention—and then Lissa sighed. No more than she did Justin suffer fools gladly. His aunt's silliness must rub his temper, and she must feel it. Well, that problem would solve itself once they were married and she could interpose herself between Margaret and Justin. Both would be happier and fonder, but what was to be done about the whispers?

Lissa had no answer to that question and was braced to greet a furious Justin who might propose anything from instant marriage—to which she really had no objection—to total separation. And Justin was wearing a frown when he handed his horse to Paul and stepped into the house, but it was more a frown of preoccupation than of rage or misery.

"Here, take this," he said when they had entered the solar, loosening a leather pouch from his sword belt and pouring out the contents.

A pair of intricately worked chains of gold imprisoning between them stones of a fascinating golden green color fell into her hand. "Justin," Lissa gasped, "you should not have—"

"Do not be silly. I would rather have it rumored that I bought you with gold than that I enslaved you with threats."

He undid his belt and rested the sheathed sword in the slot designed to receive it at the end of the frame on which he would lay his mail. Smiling at Lissa, who was still staring down at the broad necklet, he bent and began to wriggle out of his armor without her help. He noticed that she had not reacted to his statement about enslavement by threats, but she was clearly too lost in admiration of his gift to make much sense out of anything for a while. And it was flattering to his choice that she continued to admire it, laying it on the table and straightening the links of the chains until he came up behind her, put his arms around her, and kissed her neck.

"I ordered it before Gamel came in the spring," he murmured, "but you would never let me give you anything. The stones match your eyes . . ."

She turned in his arms and kissed him back, first passionately on the mouth and then more gently and tenderly all over his face. "I heard what you said," she whispered. "It is disgusting. How could anyone think you would shield a murderess for the sake of a little pleasure you could buy on any road? How could anyone think you such a fool as to bed a murderess?"

Justin grinned at her. "Oh, I do not think anyone believes me to be a fool. Clearly you are not suspected of your father's murder. The tale is that I threatened to put you to the question even though I knew you to be innocent."

"Justin! How can you laugh at so abominable a calumny?"

His lips twisted wryly. "I did not laugh at first. I was quite furious when my aunt first related the rumor to me, but when I had cooled down—I had a matter of greater importance to consider—I realized that there was more good than bad to be reaped from these whispers. Your reputation would be spared. You could scarcely be called a wanton if you yielded only to such pressure, and an increase in the belief in my ruthlessness could really do me no harm."

"But it is not *true*," Lissa cried. "You are the kindest of men."

"You are deluded," he said, laughing and kissing her again. "And I beg you will not go about spreading such a tale. You will ruin my ability to strike terror into those brought before me with no more than a cold glare. Then I shall have to use harsher measures to extract the truth—"

"There! You have confessed your kindness. You hate to cause pain even to those who deserve it." Lissa half turned, but without leaving the circle of his arms, and touched the glowing necklet he had brought. "I have another bone to pick with you. How could you carry that beauty in a pouch? It could have dropped from your belt, and the cost— Really, Justin—"

"The cost was nothing compared with what you have given me." He turned her back toward him so he could look her full in the face. "It is more than a little pleasure that can be bought on any road, Lissa. I do not know how to explain—"

"What is there to explain? Is it not the same for me?" Lissa asked, but dammed up any reply with her lips.

But she knew it was not. Although she and Justin were as needful to each other as foot and well-made shoe, Lissa knew that if he had not existed, other men would have courted her and she would have found another with whom she could have been content. Whether Justin could have found another woman was more doubtful; his aunt's tale marked that difference. And if she had not seen his gentleness to the bereaved after the fire—a meeting Lissa was now sure had been a special God-sent gift— she would not have read the compassion behind Justin's hard glance. Would she not have responded with fear, as she now suspected Justin had intended, when he questioned her about Peter's death?

Thinking of the goldsmith's name brought an instant solution to two problems that had been growing in Lissa's mind while she caressed her lover. The most important was a need to change the subject without being obvious before some hint of her thoughts escaped and hurt Justin. The second, minor one, was where to keep the necklet.

Lissa ended her long kiss but stood still with both arms around Justin's neck. "Well," she said, "I think you extravagant, but I cannot complain against such beauty. I will not cast your gift back at you, nor will I crumple those delicate links so carelessly into a pouch." She hesitated and then asked, "You will not be offended, beloved, if I keep it in Peter's box? I have put in a new lining."

He laughed. "I may be honest enough not to believe myself the dream of all women, but I am not such a fool as to be jealous of your memories of Peter de Flael either. By all means use the box."

Lissa went to get it from the chest in the bedchamber and spilled from it the silver chain and her mother's locket, the only jewelry left her after the robbery of Peter's house. Justin watched her arrange the necklet on the crimson velvet lining, smiling fondly at the way her fingers lingered, then bending and kissing her hair.

"It is all yours," he said, suddenly recalling her bitterness when she discovered that her first husband's betrothal gift, although very beautiful, had been a piece rejected by one of Flael's less savory clients. "Goscelin designed and made it with his own hands from raw gold and stones I had chosen myself."

Lissa turned to look at him. "You did not need to say that to me, Justin."

"Perhaps not, but since our lying together is already whispered, I think that we must announce our betrothal. Once that news is public, you will doubtless hear that I was all but betrothed once before. I did not want you to think I had given you another girl's leavings."

"Justin! You would never do such a thing."

"No, I would not." He smiled at her. "I have far too strong a sense of self-preservation to insult a woman with whom I must spend the rest of my life. Besides, I sold that girl's betrothal gift within hours of obtaining her father's agreement to the withdrawal of my offer—with, I must admit, great relief."

"Stupid slut!" Lissa exclaimed unguardedly. Then she drew in her breath sharply as she realized Justin had not told her the reason for withdrawing his offer and she was not supposed to know it.

To her relief, he burst out laughing and said, "Just what my Aunt Margaret called her, and a rare piece of discernment in my aunt, who is as good and kind as any woman can be but not, I fear, terribly clever. And by the by, my aunt has asked me to bring you to visit her."

"I will be delighted," Lissa said, "but I cannot wear your gorgeous necklet to a family meeting. You will have to take me to some grander affair. Is there not some guild celebration or mayor's dinner to which female guests will be welcome?"

"Thomas will know." Justin reached out with the hand that was not hugging Lissa and closed the box. As he pressed the top shut, he withdrew his hand with a faint exclamation.

"Oh, did you prick yourself?" Lissa exclaimed. "I am sorry. I had no pins short enough to hold the new lining to the box and the points came through. I thought I told Paul to file them down, but I suppose I forgot." She lifted the box and looked at the bottom. "No, there are none sticking out here, and I am sure the bottom piece is thinner than the lid. I suppose Paul did not see the ones on top because the wood is darker."

Justin did not answer immediately, and Lissa studied the box a moment longer, puzzled by something she could not define. The thread of curiosity was broken, however, when Justin said, "You could wear the necklet if you came with me to Bury St. Edmunds."

"To the festival of the saint?" Lissa put the box down on the table and smiled uncertainly at Justin. "But surely, my love, a display of rich jewels would be both unsuitable to the religious occasion and . . . er . . . and unwise."

"Tchk." Since the disapproving noise was followed by a chuckle, Lissa smiled more certainly and Justin began to laugh. "Are you implying that the monks are greedy and might expect a donation consonant with your ornamentation? To my sorrow, I am afraid I agree with you; nonetheless, you will be safe enough, one of the least among many more richly bedecked— that is, if the barons are bringing their wives, and I think they might well do so to cover their real purpose."

"Wait," Lissa said, realizing that there was more to Justin's suggestion then a desire to give her an opportunity to display his gift. "Let me call down for our meal, and you can explain what you are talking about while you take off your gambeson."

They were almost finished eating by the time Justin had finished describing his interview with FitzWalter and the invitation to attend the meeting at Bury St. Edmunds. He had not intended to make such a long explanation, but Lissa insisted on hearing every word and, as well as Justin could remember, every expression of Lord Robert when they had talked about Hubert de Bosco. They had nearly quarreled over that; Justin had not wanted to discuss his complaint about Hubert de Bosco. Actually, he had almost forgotten why he had gone to speak to FitzWalter in the first place and had always considered Hubert a minor nuisance rather than a serious threat.

Partly because he was flattered by her concern for him and partly because he realized she would not attend to any other subject until she was satisfied, Justin yielded and answered Lissa's questions. It was a relief to be able to assure her that Hubert was already gone from London and that FitzWalter had promised to keep his henchman under control. He was annoyed by Lissa's demand for details, but tried to soothe her, never guessing how well she gauged his rising irritation and that she had abandoned the subject long before she was satisfied that Hubert would obey his master.

Trying to bury her uneasiness, Lissa admitted to herself that there was no way Justin could assure her on such a subject. She had been convinced by what she had drawn from him that FitzWalter was not involved in what Hubert had done and would try to restrain his servant. She could not help saying "Justin, you will take care," but when she saw his mouth tighten, she laughed and shook her head. "I will say no more, but you must be more patient with those who love you."

"If you wish to fear for me, I have a better subject than that stupid lump of flesh Hubert," Justin snapped.

Then he gestured a dismissal of the dramatic statement and assured her that he would be in no more personal danger than any other man in the kingdom. He had snared Lissa's attention most firmly, however, and was able to describe without any further interruption what FitzWalter had actually said about the baronial hopes of a renewal of the charter of Henry I and what he believed to be Lord Robert's true purpose.

"You think he will deliberately spread the word that treason was spoken at the meeting, even if it was not," Lissa said, "so that those attending will fall under the king's displeasure and be forced into opposition, whatever their original intentions."

"I do not know," Justin replied, shifting uneasily in his comfortable chair and pushing forward his wine cup. Lissa refilled it, and for a long moment the gurgle of the wine as she poured was the only sound. Then Justin sighed. "I doubt it will be needful for Lord Robert to spread lies. I am sure the meeting will be plentifully seeded with the king's spies." He frowned suddenly. "I am a fool. There can be no question of your coming with me."

"You mean because it would be dangerous to me?" Lissa smiled. "That is foolish. I would be doubly protected by my insignificance and by the fact that I do not come as myself but only as your woman. A keener question than whether I should go is whether *you* should."

"I am not certain I will," Justin said. "I have spoken to the mayor, who offered me leave before the words of asking were out of my mouth. I wish I knew why he is so eager for me to attend. My cousin Richard is very suspicious and believes the mayor's purpose is to blacken the name of our whole family by connecting us with FitzWalter's cause. Thomas admits there is some danger of that, but he thinks it important enough to hear what truly passes there to take the chance—and despite Richard's fears I do not think the mayor's prime purpose is to damage my family."

"You lean toward Thomas's view then?"

Justin nodded. "I think the mayor is desperate to know the true feelings of the barons, although not so desperate he is willing to go to Bury himself. I wish Archbishop Langton were in charge of this meeting, as he was of the council in Saint Paul's last August. Then I would be sure matters would not get out of hand by accident."

"Does the archbishop even know of this gathering?" Lissa asked.

Justin stared at her as if she had slapped his face. "God help me, for a helpless lackwit is what I am," he muttered. "I swallowed that whole, and FitzWalter did not even lie to me. He never said Langton knew."

"Nor did he say Langton did not know. That is most excellent. Then it is perfectly reasonable for you to go and discuss the matter with the archbishop. Nor need you make a great song and dance about it. You can escort me to Peter's manor near Canterbury. I can look to the harvest and the house—someone must pay some mind to the estate. It is not my right, but what is to be done if young Peter and Edmond never return?"

Justin did not answer for some time. He sat sipping his wine and struggling with the unpleasant feeling that to follow Lissa's sensible plan would be a betrayal of FitzWalter's confidence. Yet if Langton did not know of the meeting, or knew of it but was not aware of the depth of FitzWalter's hatred of King John, the best hope for a peaceful solution to the problems of the realm might be lost. Once the king became convinced that the archbishop was in league with those who opposed him rather than a truly neutral mediator, whatever influence Langton had would be lost.

When Justin did not answer either her proposal to go to Canterbury or the question about Flael's estate, Lissa rose quietly and went into the bedchamber, taking with her the box holding Justin's gift. There she made up the fire, replaced her clothing with her handsome bedrobe, and moved the warming stones from the hearth to the bed. A glance through the open door showed her that Justin had not moved and probably had not noticed she was gone. A faint chill touched her, but she thrust away the fear and, to clean it from her mind, opened the box. Gold and green-gold glittered up at her, and she felt a wave of resentment against the king and the opposing barons and the archbishop—all those whose "great concerns" thrust themselves into the ordinary quiet lives of common folk and made them miserable.

Even as the thought formed she smiled wryly at her foolishness, but decided it was equally foolish for Justin to worry at whatever concerned him tonight. He would make more sense of the matter with less effort when his mind was clear. Lissa's smile broadened into mischief, and she took the necklet from the box and put it on. Then she dropped her bedrobe off her shoulders, supporting the neckline so that the long, silvery hairs of the fur would almost hide her breasts but not the wide delicate collar of gold and gems that covered her from collarbone to the first dip of her cleavage.

She came to Justin's side and gently kissed his temple. "Put it aside for now," she said. "Whatever decision you must make will seem easier in the morning."

Without lifting his eyes from his wine cup, he said, "No. I know what is right, and my decision is made. I am foolish to feel any sorrow or sympathy. Both are undeserved and would be scornfully rejected. And for a personal hatred the man may drag us all to destruction—but I cannot help it."

Lissa's heart lurched with tenderness. He truly was the kindest of men if he could grieve for FitzWalter, a man Lissa felt had no more conscience than a crow, which would peck out the eyes of a criminal or an innocent child with equal delight. All she said, however, was "Then I am doing no wrong in diverting you. Come, look up, my love and see how well your gift becomes me."

"Did you—" he began, but when he lifted his eyes and saw her, he began to chuckle and admitted, "I am more easily diverted than I thought myself to be."

Lissa never found out what he had been about to ask because he caught her around the waist and drew her close, bending her toward him over the arm of the chair so he could press his lips between the chains that suspended the stones from the top and bottom. Some places were too narrow for a kiss to fit, and Justin touched her skin with his tongue. Lissa sighed and absently put both arms around him, which permitted the unsupported robe to slip down. She exclaimed and grabbed for it, but not before Justin caught the nipple of each breast with a quick nip—teeth sheathed in lips, which made her exclaim again and let go of the robe a second time.

Justin caught her hands, leaving her naked to the waist. "It becomes you very well," he said, "but I will have to take it back to Goscelin and tell him to lengthen the chain and hook at the back. I have a great desire to see these little rosebuds"—he bent forward and nipped her once more—"peeping through the bars of a golden prison."

"You never would!" The words were garbled with laughter. "How would you explain so strange a request to Goscelin?"

"I would tell him the truth." Justin burst out laughing too at Lissa's expression of dismay, then pushed the table out of his way and got to his feet, pressing her against him so that her naked breasts were hidden and the wide sleeves of his robe covered and warmed her bare back. "Why not?" he asked huskily, his mouth against her ear.

His warm breath made Lissa's knees feel soft, and she used her arms to cling to Justin rather than attempt to cover herself. She willed him to speak again, not caring what he said; the

words themselves were nearly meaningless, but the movement
of his lips and the tickling breath were somehow reflected in her
loins, giving her a thrilling pleasure. Still, when he did speak,
the words added to her joy.

"Goscelin would envy me the sweet game of kissing such
prisoners through such bars," Justin murmured. "But I will
deny myself if you forbid me, for I am worse than a prisoner. I
am a lifelong slave."

Chapter 29

LISSA'S DIVERSION WAS VERY SUCCESSFUL IN THE SENSE THAT JUSTIN thought of nothing else at all while it lasted. But when he woke with a start and a pounding heart some hours later, he felt a flicker of resentment because it was the nature of the diversion to be temporary. Then he smiled into the dark and called himself a fool. Coupling was like fighting. No one could live at that pitch of excitement for long. And he had slept, which was more than he would have done if Lissa had not strung out her diversion, teasing him and holding back her own pleasure so that he was forced to restrain his own, until he was utterly exhausted. He had no idea how long he had been asleep, but it was not yet full morning, he thought. It was too quiet and there was not enough light, but it might be near dawn. Justin pushed back the bed curtain to see if any light was showing in the cracks of the shutters.

Just as he did so, he heard a knock on the door below, muffled and dulled by the closed shutters. He cursed under his breath and glanced at Lissa, but she had not stirred. She had exhausted herself too; it was a bad night for her to be wakened to mix up a potion for a child who would die anyway. And then a quality in the sound made him swing his legs out of bed, drop the curtain, and hurry to the shuttered window to peer through a crack. There was a saddled horse tied near the door, so he had been right. The sound was not a bare fist pounding on the door but metal against wood—a sword hilt, no doubt—and the summons was almost certainly for him. No neighbor coming to Lissa for help would ride a horse.

Justin pulled on his chausses and shirt by the light of the night-candle but did not stop to tie his laces. He rushed out, bootless, to run down to let in Halsig—or whoever else had come to summon him—so that the knocking would not wake Lissa. His arming tunic was in the solar anyway, so he closed the bedchamber door behind him, but when he stepped out on the stair landing, about to go down, he saw a gleam of light as the door of the workroom opened. Paul was coming to the door, so Justin went inside and pulled on his gambeson. He heard Paul call out and the bar of the door creak as it was lifted, and he stepped out on the landing to ask what the trouble was.

His surprise when the light of Paul's candle showed the bloody bandage and stained tunic of the man who entered kept him silent just long enough for the man to close the door behind him and strike Paul down with a powerful blow from the hilt of the sword he was carrying. Justin uttered a strangled cry of protest, and the man, who seemed about to stab down with the sword, looked up, clawing with his free hand at the bandage, which was apparently blocking his vision. He started forward then, but Justin had already stepped back into the solar to seize and draw his own sword. The action was instinctive—Justin's body told him that a blow had been dealt and a blow must be returned, even while he was still bewilderedly trying to understand why one of his men should want to kill Paul.

The puzzle did not interfere with Justin's physical response. Sword in his right hand, scabbard in his left, since his shield was in the stable with Noir, he stepped out on the landing again. The man, he saw, was not at all weakened by his injuries; he had apparently run across the shop and was more than halfway up the stairs.

"Drop your sword!" Justin bellowed, hoping that the man-at-arm's long training in obedience to a voice of command would control him despite the confusion Justin assumed must be caused by his head injury.

For half a minute Justin thought it would work. No expression could be read behind the swathing of bloody cloth, but the man cried, "No! God, no! Not you!" and the blade, which he had lifted as Justin appeared, wavered. In the next instant, however, an even worse attack of the madness seemed to seize the victim, and he screamed hoarsely and leapt up the remaining steps, slashing wildly at Justin.

Hubert's slow mind could not cope with the two absolutely contradictory orders—that he must bring Bowles's daughter to his master before Lauds and that he must not for any reason offer any threat to Sir Justin. All he knew was that FitzWalter would listen to no more excuses and that, by rushing at him with a bared sword, he had already "threatened" Sir Justin. Thus he had failed to obey one order, and unless he could pass Sir Justin, he could not seize Bowles's daughter and would fail to obey both his master's commands.

In that instant of utter terror and desperation, Hubert realized that dead men make no complaints. He sprang upward again, shouting to immobilize his victim with fright and launching a powerful blow at the still figure. Although he could see only straight ahead, Hubert did not pause to tear off the bandage. He was filled with confidence and a rushing joy. He would not be punished because his master would never know he had killed Justin. All he need do was silence the servants so they could not tell, then come back after he had taken the girl to Baynard's Castle and hide Justin's body.

Warned by the shout and his own knowledge that those with broken heads were always unreliable and sometimes danger-ous, Justin twisted away from the powerful but poorly directed blow and struck sharply at Hubert's wrist with his scabbard. He did not use his own sword or strike at his attacker's head because he hoped to disarm the "poor man" without injuring him any more. Considering the amount of blood on his clothes, Justin believed the man must soon collapse.

The bellow of rage that followed Justin's blow gave no support to that theory, nor did the answering strike, which showed no uncertainty in grip or failure in power. In fact, the parry forced on Justin sent a shock up his arm and drew a grunt of surprise from him. He remembered then tales of inhuman strength granted for a short time to dying men, and it flashed through his mind that it would be a shame for him to be injured by one in his death throes when he could end the life swiftly and be safe. But he could not do it; the man was mad, but he might not be dying.

"I am not the enemy," Justin said, trying to sound calm and sure while making his voice loud enough to bind attention. "Lay down your sword. I will do you no harm."

Cracked, crazy laughter was drawn from Hubert by the words. He did not fear that without his troop Justin could do him harm; from Justin's behavior, he believed the great thief taker was too frightened of him to fight back at all. In any case, Hubert knew himself to be too strong to fear a single puny creature like Justin. It was only his master he feared, only FitzWalter, who could send ten, a hundred, a thousand men to catch him and chain him and torment and maim him if he did not obey.

A light drew Hubert's eyes behind Justin. He was so contemptuous of his opponent that he dared lift his head, allowing the bandage to block his sight of the weapon Justin brandished so ineffectually. The candle lit the terrified face of the woman who was his rightful prey. She gasped and backed away, and Hubert bellowed wildly again with rage. If she barricaded herself inside her bedchamber—Hubert had heard of the bar she used as protection against her father—he would never get her out before Lauds. He thrust upward violently, not only with his sword but with his whole body, intending to pin Justin against the door and disembowel him.

Because Hubert had twisted his head to watch the waning of the candlelight as Lissa retreated, he gasped with surprise when a blow struck his sword arm down. Indifferent and infuriated, he struck back, expecting to push Justin's blade aside and simultaneously flinging himself forward again, reaching with his bare hand for Justin's throat. Hubert felt his sword catch against what he thought was another blade, and he heard Justin cry, "Man, beware!" He believed Justin cried out in fear because his sword was trapped, and he blessed himself for it because the light was coming back, the woman responding to her lover's

422 ROBERTA GELLIS

voice. And Hubert laughed aloud again, just as a huge pain burst in his belly.

For one instant Justin was paralyzed, hardly believing that even a madman could spit himself deliberately. In that instant, a rod came past his hip and struck the dying man in the side, toppling him off the stair. Long years of practice made Justin's hand lock with extra strength on his sword hilt when he had dealt a fatal stroke. The victim always pulled away hard, either falling down in death or trying to escape. Justin's body was prepared for the jerk even when his mind was not, so the sword, dripping blood on the stair, stayed in his hand when Hubert fell.

The poker Lissa had wielded dropped with a clatter and she cried, "Justin, are you hurt?"

"No, not at all," he said, peering down in the dim light. The man was silent, unmoving, and Justin saw that his head was twisted queerly. He felt relieved that the man's neck was broken, for death from a belly wound could be slow and painful. "Poor creature."

"Poor creature!" Lissa echoed. "He was trying to kill you."

"No, his brains were addled." Justin started down the stairs and Lissa followed, only pausing to pick up the poker, which she fully intended to use on the "poor creature" if it so much as quivered. "See how his head is bandaged," Justin went on. "Yet he could not have seemed crazed when the hurt was dealt him because he was sent, or came of himself, to tell me of the trouble—" He uttered an obscenity, then added, "He is dead. Now how am I to know where I am needed?"

"I am sorry, Justin," Lissa said, although she really was not sorry at all. "I could not know he would break his neck when he fell."

But Justin did not appear to have heard her. He stood staring down at the corpse and then said suddenly, "Something stinks here. I have been half asleep and too busy to think, but how could *any* man know where to find me? Only Halsig and possibly Dick Miller's son know I spend my nights with you, and if there were trouble, one of them would come here himself to get me, not send a badly wounded man, who might never arrive."

"The rumors—" Lissa offered tentatively.

"I doubt it. Those travel around among our own kind. In any case, what good would I be alone in a fight that dealt such wounds? It is custom to report to my house if the guard must be summoned out, whether I am home or not. Hmmm. It is too bad you have such a knack with pokers, but it is more my fault than yours. Once he had run himself onto my sword, he was dead already. And I should have known he was not what he seemed as soon as I saw him strike down Paul—"

"Paul!"

Lissa, who had been acting and speaking in a kind of frozen dream that protected her from feeling anything, was shocked back to reality. She looked wildly around, lifting up her candle and moving quickly to the huddled form on the floor near the door. She knelt beside Paul, but was afraid to touch him in so poor a light and went to the counter to light more candles, carrying two in holders back with her. She hardly noticed Justin take a third and begin to pull the bandage off the head of the corpse. Not until she had satisfied herself that Paul's head had not been crushed, and he had started to stir and groan under her gentle examination, did Lissa look over at Justin. To her surprise, he had not only removed the bandage but slit open the man's tunic; however, she was not interested in the dead man. She wanted to get Paul moved to his bed, and gave Justin no chance to speak, asking him to carry the journeyman into the other room.

She spent some time calming Oliva and showing her how to place cool cloths gently on Paul's bruised head. Beyond that, Lissa explained, all they could do was pray that Paul would come to his senses. Once he did, Oliva must keep him perfectly quiet, no matter what he said, and the more he wished to get up and claimed he was well, the stronger measures Oliva must take, if necessary, to keep him abed. If he complained of headache, she was not to worry, only keep him quiet until the worst of the headache was gone and not, under any circumstances, allow him to take any medicine to cure the pain without Lissa's express permission.

The boys were already sitting up, wide-eyed with curiosity. When they saw her turn to leave, both called that they were awake and would be glad to be useful in any way. Lissa realized she must be recovering from the shock when she felt amused

instead of furious at their ghoulishness, but Ninias, and
particularly Witta, had had enough corpses recently. She said
the way they could help her most, since they would need to
mind the shop the next day, was by going to sleep again, and
shut the door firmly behind her.

Justin lifted his head as she came in and gestured for her to
come near. He had cleaned his sword and was squatting on his
heels beside the body with the gleaming blade across his knees.

"Look," he insisted, nodding at the body.

Lissa restrained a shudder and lowered her eyes distastefully,
only to gasp aloud, "Hubert!"

"Yes, Hubert," he said in that soft voice that sent a chill
through her blood. "Hubert, perfectly whole except for the
broken neck and the wound my sword dealt him, but all
bandaged and blood-smeared so that he would be let into the
house of a kindly apothecary who is known not to turn away an
injured person, no matter the time of day or night. Tell me, my
love, could Hubert, by himself, think of such a scheme for
getting at me?"

Lissa's first reaction when she recognized the corpse had been
intense relief, but Justin's question reminded her that Hubert
was FitzWalter's servant. Her voice trembled as she said faintly,
"No. My father called him hands and feet without a head. Do
you think FitzWalter ordered—" She could not force out the rest
of the sentence and fell silent.

"No, I do not," Justin replied calmly. "It was the first thought
in my mind too, but there are too many reasons why I must
believe him innocent. First, I did not tell FitzWalter I was not in
my bed when Hervi attacked, so he must have believed I was.
Second, I do not believe he knows we are lovers, so he would be
most unlikely to send Hubert here to kill me. Third, it is my
business to read men, and I will swear that FitzWalter was
surprised and angry when I told him that Hubert had incited
Hervi to kill me. Fourth, and most important, there is no reason
for FitzWalter to want me dead. I have given considerable
thought to it, and I can think of many ways for him to make use
of me alive and not one benefit he would gain from my death."

"Can he think he told you some secret . . . Oh, he did tell
you of the meeting at Bury St. Edmunds," Lissa said.

"But that is no secret. Many men must know of that or so few would come to the meeting that it would be without purpose. Besides, if I read FitzWalter's intention right, he wants King John to know about it and to be incited to cruelty and oppression. Still, I cannot believe this creature"—he touched Hubert with his foot—"could have thought of so clever a device for getting into your house himself."

The terror that had gripped Lissa when she first thought that FitzWalter might be behind Hubert's action had been soothed by both Justin's manner and his reasoning, which she found convincing. More at ease, she remembered other things her father had said when she protested Hubert's coming to the house.

"But Hubert knew his failing," she said. "I know he came to my father to explain what puzzled him, and . . . yes, once I heard my father telling Hubert what to say and how to act to gain a purpose."

Justin stood up. "I suppose he found another to help him. Yes, he must have or he would not have killed your father. Now that *is* an interesting idea. I wonder if Hubert's new mentor convinced him apurpose that your father had done him some wrong. If so, that person is more murderer than Hubert." Justin paused, wondering if that same mentor could have deliberately frightened Hubert into his determination to kill him too, but that was not an idea he would voice to Lissa. Instead he said briskly, "Come up and help me into my armor. I must go home and get some men to pick up Hubert's body and bring it to Baynard's Castle."

"Justin"—Lissa put a hand on his arm—"could you not simply have him buried? Is it needful to draw Lord Robert's attention to the fact that you killed his man?"

"I did not really kill him, Lissa. In a way it was an accident. He thought he had thrust my sword aside, but it was the scabbard. The bandage partly blinded him, and he did not see that by holding my scabbard, he had fixed my sword arm so that the blade went right into him when he leapt at me. One thing puzzles me, though. Why did he not wear armor? Surely he knew I would try to defend myself. It was stupid—"

"But he *was* stupid, and I heard him boast that he could outfight any man. He is no loss to this world. Bury him quietly. I will even pay for masses for his soul if you think he would be deprived of that succor by not telling FitzWalter—"

Justin caught her in one arm and kissed her. "You are a sweet creature, dearling. I doubt FitzWalter will put himself to any expense or trouble over Hubert's soul." He led her to the stair and pushed her gently to make her go up. "Forget about him, love. I swear that now he is dead he will not add to the trouble he made while he was alive. And whatever happens, you and I will be well away, for I have decided that we will leave for Canterbury at dawn."

The remainder of the night was very busy for Lissa, who had to pack in a scrambling hurry without the assistance of Oliva. She had said nothing to Justin, since he too had much to arrange in addition to the removal of Hubert's body, but she was not at all sure it was right for her to go and leave Paul. Fortunately, he opened his eyes and recognized Oliva before Justin returned to the house, and he seemed to understand, although he had no memory of anything after he went to bed, when Lissa told him he had a bad blow to the head and must lie still until his headache was completely gone. She took care that Paul should have the last little hope of surviving by telling Oliva the name of a chirurgeon who might open Paul's head and remove any bone that was pushed in should Paul fall into a sleep from which they could not wake him.

Lissa tried to comfort herself that Paul's waking was a good sign and told herself there was nothing she could have done for him if she had stayed, but she still felt unhappy as she was handed aboard the FitzAilwin boat, which would take them down the Thames to Feversham. From there it was a short ride to Peter's manor, where Justin would leave her and ride on to Canterbury. Still, she managed to fall asleep in the comfortable cabin, and when she woke, very late in the morning, her mood was much lighter.

The same could not be said for Lord Robert FitzWalter, who had not gone to bed much earlier than Lissa, having waited fruitlessly for Hubert to bring her to him long past the hour of Lauds. He slept quite well, having soothed himself by going over in his mind what he would do to Hubert when he laid hands on him, but his mood was not at all improved when he woke and was told that Hubert *had* returned—his body and a letter had been delivered by Sir Justin's servant Halsig.

A violent eruption was stemmed by the terms of the letter, which were not at all what FitzWalter expected. Sir Justin was quite civil—regretting that Lord Robert had had no chance to curb Hubert's behavior and that he had been forced to kill the man when attacked by him in the house of his betrothed. FitzWalter felt considerable regret when he decided that he could not give up even the small chance of finding the seal through Lissa. It was too bad that Justin had a serious interest in her; he would have to be doubly cautious in seizing the woman—it would have to be done on the street in the daytime—and in a way so that Justin would never suspect him.

The letter crumpled in FitzWalter's hand as he considered the consequences of Justin's discovering he was connected with the abduction. He could not frighten or bribe Justin into forgetting what had been done, and Justin FitzAilwin would not be easy to kill and silence that way. Beyond that, Justin kept records of evidence and doubtless confided in his cousins. And his murder would stir those rich and powerful cousins into a frenzy. Worse yet, if they cried murder against him before the merchant community—murder of one the fat burghers regarded as their own—they would forget their quarrels with one another, turn against him, the outsider, and refuse to support him in his struggle with the king. He ground his teeth. It would be better to leave the woman alone.

That decision wavered again when FitzWalter learned that Justin had left London. He sent a trusted clerk, who whispered in the ear of another, not using FitzWalter's name; that man spoke to a third, and he to a fourth; the name of the inquirer had now become Richard FitzAilwin, who was said not to trust his cousin's betrothed. But all the effort was wasted. Bowles's shop was closed, his house locked, his daughter nowhere to be seen. FitzWalter shrugged. He did not want the woman badly enough to break into the house openly, and he doubted any ruse would get the door open, except to a well known and trusted friend, for a long time.

Two more days passed before FitzWalter heard that Lissa had left London. For a while he was angry, but her trail was cold and messages concerning the meeting at Bury St. Edmunds began to come. Most of these were exactly what FitzWalter wanted them to be. He began to gain confidence that he would achieve his purpose without the dangerous complication of the counterfeit seal, and he put Bowles's daughter out of his mind.

Had FitzWalter seen Lissa at the meeting at Bury, he would have been reminded of the information she might hold, for at first matters did not go exactly as he planned. He knew none of those who had called the meeting would bring a copy of the first Henry's charter, but to his chagrin a copy had been presented to the monks, and the abbot produced it. It was very fortunate that he did not see how Sir Justin grinned at his dismay. The terms limiting the power of the king were far vaguer and less stringent than FitzWalter had intended to suggest, and the discussion was far less fiery than he had hoped.

Still, FitzWalter was not totally dissatisfied with the results. When the discussions were over, the barons gathered in the abbey church before the high altar and swore they would renounce their allegiance to King John if he did not grant to them the laws and liberties of the charter. Then they agreed to go together to the king right after Christmas and present their demands. Most would have ended the meeting at that point, but FitzWalter made an impassioned speech about how helpless they would be should John take ill their protest. Not one voice contested this likelihood, and all agreed to use the month between their parting and their meeting again to gather men and arms and fortify their castles.

"We will use force," FitzWalter cried aloud, "if John will not listen to reason."

There were few shouts of approval but none of protest either. Content because he was so sure the king would attack rather than yield, FitzWalter went off to Dunmow to build an army.

Lissa had not accompanied Justin to Bury because Paul was still ill when she and Justin returned from Canterbury. Paul was improving slowly, but by 16 November when Justin left for Bury, the journeyman was still subject to dizzy spells and recurrences of severe headache. Lissa almost wished he were back in bed, utterly helpless, as he had been at first; she could have left him that way. As he was, half cured, she knew he would do too much if she went away, and possibly make the hurt worse than in the beginning.

No angel, Lissa resented having to stay behind and made everyone miserable for two days, but then she received her reward: Gamel and Gerbod sailed into harbor on one ship on 18 November. She rushed down to the dock to greet them, unable to wait for them to come to her as their message suggested. From their cautious manner, Lissa knew they had come together because they were unable to face her misery alone, and she laughed with joy when she told them her troubles were all over. She and Justin were not yet married, but only because they were waiting for her uncles to come and rejoice with them.

Lissa was almost crushed to death by their joyous embraces before she left them to their work, both having promised to come to her house as soon as it grew too dark to unload. When they came, she recounted the events surrounding her father's homecoming and death. It was Gerbod who suggested that Amias FitzStephen might not be a person at all but a false name her father had taken in the hope of escaping the fate that had overtaken him; Gamel nodded and said if the weather held they would sail to Bristol and speak to the vintner who owned the manor at Red Hill. Lissa shook her head, pointing out that their interest in William dead was far greater than in William alive. For herself, she admitted that Gerbod's guess sounded like truth to her, but she did not care; there was nothing her father had taken that she was truly eager to regain. But the next evening, when uncles and niece began to discuss her wedding contract, her attention was close enough to make her forget the feast of Saint Edmund and the charter of Henry I.

Justin, who had carried the copy of the charter to the monks of Saint Edmund's abbey, was less content than FitzWalter with the outcome of the meeting. On his return to London he was not sorry to find Lissa little interested in what had happened at Bury. He had already described the events and been questioned in detail by the mayor and aldermen. They were greatly alarmed but unfortunately too divided in opinion between their desire to have the charter confirmed and their fear of the king's anger to take any practical action.

The warning Justin tried to give, that FitzWalter was more intent on provoking King John than on obtaining a charter, was not well received. Some shouted their disbelief, and even the others, who felt Justin spoke the truth, bade him be still with equal energy, hoping the problem would disappear if they did not look at it. Thus there was no purpose in repeating to Lissa

events and surmises that would frighten her when he was
helpless even to take precautions. He was overjoyed to hear that
her uncles had come at last and glad to bury his own worries
about the future of the city and the realm in prospects of
personal happiness.

By the time Gerbod's and Gamel's cargo was sold, the
wedding contract was approved by all and signed. With the
profit of their venture in their purses and a dull winter looming
ahead, Lissa's uncles wanted to throw open the great hall in the
Hanse and make a wedding that would be remembered. In a
family conclave held in Margaret FitzAilwin's home, Justin's
family indicated their full agreement. The only protesters were
the bride and groom. Justin's objection, being merely a personal
disinclination to be on display, was hooted down, and he
stopped arguing when Thomas whispered in his ear that it was
the best way to stifle certain rumors.

Lissa meanwhile was pointing out that the Pepperers Guild
might find it a fault in her *gravitas*, her moral seriousness, if she
were party to so lavish a celebration less than two months after
her father's unsolved murder.

"People die all the time," Gamel roared.

"Death is one thing," Lissa responded tartly, "murder is
something else."

"Do you mean you have not yet been accepted as a member of
the Pepperers?" Justin asked lazily, turning away from his
contemplation of the flames dancing in the hearth.

"It is not something I would have forgotten to mention."
Lissa's tone in addressing Justin was no less tart than that
bestowed on her uncle.

Margaret FitzAilwin looked sidelong at her nephew, who
replied very mildly, "With all that has happened in the last
week, you might have forgotten." Margaret could see a faint
curve in the lips of that hard mouth. There was no controlled
anger or impatience in Justin at all. His remark was a simply
stated fact, but Lissa did laugh at him.

"Do not be so silly, Justin. Even the king's granting that
toothless charter or his displeasure would not be as important to
me as my membership in the guild."

"Toothless?" Richard FitzAilwin repeated with some indignation.

"Well, you must admit the charter does not say very much, especially not about *our* problems. I had a real battle yesterday with a seller of ale from York—you know they make the best brew in the north in October—but he wished to charge me for London barrels and deliver York barrels. Why cannot we have one measure throughout the kingdom?"

"A king's charter to concern itself with such small matters?" Richard was shocked.

But Thomas abandoned the comment he had been about to make to Justin and said, "Why not? It would be better than a charter that says nothing at all. When all the extra words are taken out, Henry's charter says the king should be just and the barons should support him. Worst of all, it does not say who shall judge whether or not the king *is* just. I find that I am in perfect agreement with Lissa. I cannot see why everyone is so eager to have the charter reissued by King John."

Swallowing the caustic reminder that some, like FitzWalter, would greatly prefer that the king refuse to sign anything, Justin offered a piece of news that he believed held a ray of real hope. What had been pushed out of his mind by his fury at the paralysis of the mayor and aldermen was that even the barons who would not dream of rebelling against the king might well want to control him. As word of the charter and of the meeting at Bury spread, men were not rushing to take up arms, as FitzWalter hoped, but they were expressing their grievances in specific terms.

"You are not alone in your doubts of the charter as it stands," Justin remarked. "I had a letter from my brother late last night about the meeting at Bury. It seems that word of the charter is widespread, and the gentlemen of the shire have already sent a delegation to Archbishop Langton. They want him to propose the addition of some very specific articles on rights of inheritance."

"Is that so?" Richard asked, his rather pompous voice for once unselfconscious. "I would not wish the burghers of London alone to be associated with those who threatened the use of force against the king, but if more moderate folk are joining in pressing for a charter, we of London must be sure that our rights and liberties are specially confirmed. I think, brother," he said to Thomas, "that you and I should pass this news to the aldermen.

Forgive me, Justin, but you do tend to lack a persuasive manner."

"I make the mistake of assuming grown men will recognize what is best for them without dipping it in honey."

Gamel nodded; Gerbod looked surprised; Thomas and Lissa burst out laughing; Mistress Margaret glanced from one to another in total confusion; and Richard sighed.

"Surely once they know that others are appealing to the archbishop," Richard went on, ignoring Justin's remark, "they will be willing to do so also." Suddenly he smiled warmly at Lissa. "And why should not Lissa have what she desires? We will ask not only that London's rights and privileges be recognized but that London measure be made the only one used throughout the realm."

"Why not, indeed?" Gerbod asked, nodding. "God knows I wish from the heart that there were one measure for all places in all lands. The time and the arguments that would save us! But now is not the time to change the world. Now is the time to decide on the wedding to hold for sister's daughter."

The FitzAilwins exchanged glances and returned without protest to the subject of the wedding. Lissa's uncles had little reason to be deeply interested in the attempts to wring a charter out of King John. As foreign merchants, they did not expect to be affected either by the granting of the charter or by the quarrel between the king and his barons. No king, not even Henry II, had made serious trouble for the merchants of the Hanse; fees and taxes went up or down according to conditions, but never became high enough to damage trade—despite the merchants' groans and threats of immediate ruin at any increase. Any merchant preferred that the kingdom be at peace because when war raged even neutrals could be hurt. Docks and ships caught up in a battle could be burned or looted, but even war did not pose much danger to the Hanse; the Steelyard had been built to be defended against an army, if necessary.

Later, after a compromise about the wedding had been reached—the ceremony itself would take place at Saint Anthony's Church and the celebration at the Steelyard in one week's time—Mistress Margaret served an evening meal as elaborate as any dinner. There were jests and laughter and singing and dancing, but no more talk about political subjects until Gamel and Gerbod took Lissa home. In deference to her uncles' sensibilities, Justin had moved back into his own house temporarily, and his cousins accompanied him so their mother could clear up the remains of the impromptu party.

When they were comfortably seated around the fire with goblets of wine, Richard and Thomas discussed exactly what they should propose in the special articles. Having listened to them for some time, Justin asked if they were not putting the cart before the horse.

"No," Richard said curtly. "If we come to them with real proposals, they will begin to talk about the wording and how much we can hope to get. If we ask whether we should make proposals, they will think of how much the idea of a charter will anger the king."

"And that puts me in my place," Justin said, which made both Richard and Thomas laugh, but they went back to their discussion without paying him any further attention. He was silent too, hardly thinking at all, suffused with a pleasure made up partly of the warmth of the wine in his belly and the fire at his feet, but mostly of his memory of the joy of dancing and laughing with Lissa and the comfort of knowing that they would soon be bound for life in the eyes of God and man. Next he thought lazily of the impossibility of expressing to her what she had done for him, which brought his mind to his wedding gift—armlets, earrings, and headband to match the necklet. He had better see Goscelin and make sure they were ready, or would be ready.

A slight uneasiness woke in Justin as the thought of his wedding gift passed through his mind, and he sat up straighter in his chair. But there could be no fault in the gift; Lissa had been delighted with the necklet and it looked beautiful on her when she wore it to the mayor's dinner. What, then, was niggling at his comfort? His uneasiness made him more alert, and as he sought the vagrant thought, he heard Thomas say that he did not think the charter should mention guild matters at all. That recalled his earlier anger when he had heard that Lissa had not yet been accepted into the Pepperers Guild. Why the delay? She was a better apothecary than all the rest put together, and must surely fulfill all their requirements.

Thomas interrupted his thoughts at that moment by rising

and asking Justin for his brother's letter, only as an afterthought also asking if he could make copies to show to the aldermen and guild masters. Justin handed the letter over, and suddenly realized that he might be able to give Lissa a wedding gift she would like much better than the ornaments Goscelin was making for her.

"I will speak to Goscelin, who will not mind my manner, and to Master John le Spicer, with whom I have some business," Justin said.

Richard groaned and Thomas advised him to go gently, to which he replied that he always went gently; but he remembered the advice when he was shown into the Master Pepperer's solar and introduced the matter of the charter first. Master John listened with considerable interest, and although he would not commit himself to any action without consulting the other members, agreed that this might be a good time to deal with the king.

Justin smiled but did not rise to go. "I also wish to invite you to my wedding," he said. "It would please Lissa if the master of her guild came to wish her well."

"She intends to remain a Pepperer then?" Master John asked blandly.

"Most certainly," Justin replied. "Our contract provides for her business and mine to be separate. She knows nothing of my trade, and truthfully, I do little business on my own. My cousins see to my share of the family ventures. Most of my time, as you know, is given to my duties with the watch." He lifted his brows. "Surely there can be no doubt that Lissa will be accepted into the guild?"

Master John cleared his throat uneasily. "While the matter of her father's death remains unsettled—"

"I would not let that interfere," Justin said. "I know who killed William Bowles, but unfortunately the man cannot be brought to justice because he is dead." He smiled, but his eyes were like old ice when he added, "I assure you, I would not marry a woman who had murdered her father."

"No," Master John agreed quickly, "but there is the problem of taking a woman into the guild. There are duties that no woman can perform."

"There are two women members already," Justin pointed out.

"They are old. It has been many years since a woman applied for acceptance. There has been talk of writing a new rule excluding women. After all, they cannot serve in the defense of the city, or—"

"The rule has not been written yet," Justin interrupted, "and I assure you that Lissa will provide an adequate deputy for any duty she is unfit to perform." There was a brief silence and Justin asked, "Will it be necessary for me to visit the other masters?"

"I did not think Mistress Lissa would press the issue so fiercely." Master John's voice was even, but there was anger and disappointment beneath. "She is about to be a wife and soon, with God's will, a mother. Her hopes should be set on womanly matters, not on business more fit for a man."

"Mistress Lissa is not pressing the issue," Justin said very softly. "She knows nothing of my visit to you, and if she should ever learn that I spoke to you about anything except the charter, that would be very sad."

Master John swallowed hard. "No, no. She will not learn of it from me." And then, as Justin got to his feet, he cried, "Wait."

He wiped the cold sweat from his face with his sleeve, raging at himself but unable to still the terrified pounding of his heart. It was ridiculous for a man of his wealth and power to be afraid of the mayor's ferret, but the cold fury that flowed from Sir Justin was beyond his understanding and chilled his very soul.

"What for?" Justin asked, looking down on Master John with no expression at all. At the moment he was angry enough to kill every member of the Pepperers Guild because if all felt alike they would break Lissa's heart, but he could not admit that to John le Spicer so he added coldly, "I, too, hope that God will grant children to us, but I can see no reason why I should lose the profit of a thriving business so that Lissa can nurse babes. I will speak to every member of your guild, Master John, before I forgo my wife's acceptance as a member."

"That will not be necessary." Master John had heard something he understood clearly, and he had no problem with losing a business negotiation. No longer frightened, he stood up and shrugged. "You cannot blame me for wishing to be rid of a rival in such a happy way. I thought if Lissa gave up her business for marriage I might obtain her receipt book and even an introduction to her sources of supply of special medicines and spices." He paused and eyed Justin speculatively. "I would offer a very good price for the receipt book—more than the profit to be taken in several years."

Justin stared back, balanced on a knife edge between fury and amusement. The fury had flared through him at the notion that he loved money so much he would sell Lissa's secrets for it, until he remembered that he had just virtually said his reason for marrying her was the income she would bring. "It is not mine to sell," he said. "By contract it is part of her business."

Not really having expected to win the point, Master John half smiled and showed an empty palm. "Some husbands are not so scrupulous."

Justin burst out laughing then, shaking his head. "I am less honest than fearful. No amount of gold would make my life worth living if I sold the receipt book. Have you ever heard Lissa's tongue?" Then he sobered and locked eyes with the master of the Pepperers Guild again. "I would take it as a favor, Master John, if you would come to my wedding and bring with you the gift I know would make my wife most happy—her acceptance into the guild."

Chapter 30

MASTER JOHN DID NOT FAIL TO COME TO LISSA'S WEDDING; IN FACT every master of the Pepperers Guild attended, and theirs was indeed the most welcome gift of all. The dinner and entertainments that followed when all had reassembled in the great meeting hall of the Steelyard was, most guild members thought, worth the admission of a female member. The food and drink seemed inexhaustible, especially the ale, which rivaled the wine in strength if not in variety. There was even mead for those who liked it, but after a time most could not tell the difference and filled their cups with whatever was closest. It was never farther to keg, tun, or barrel than one could reach by stretching out an arm.

Justin, who had been out with Lissa's uncles, his brother, and his cousins the previous night and had wakened swearing he had looked his last on all drink, took a cup to steady himself. Lissa began with a toast to the members of her guild. She raised her cup by demand several times more, often enough to lose track of just who and what she was toasting. At first she and

Justin had intended to leave early, but they changed their minds when a big group of guests offered to accompany them. They had wanted to avoid a procession in the streets and the shouts and advice of merrymakers surrounding the house. They did manage to avoid it, but they had forgotten by then why they had stayed and all the advice was shouted anyway. The one gain they made was by that time both of them thought the jests hilarious and did not mind a bit. No one was sober, and many slept where they were, under the tables in the hall.

Lissa and Justin did manage to get home, more because Noir and Lissa's mare knew the way than because they were directed. The house was empty, which made them very suspicious until Lissa managed to remember that they had just come from their wedding and at last sight Paul, Oliva, and the boys had been celebrating as energetically as anyone else. Lissa then found the heavy key; Justin opened the door to let her in and staggered off to the shed with the horses. He got the saddles off and the bits unhooked—he could do that in his sleep—and thrust an armful of hay into the manger, but then he eyed the beasts malevolently and said, "You are undressed. It is my wedding night; I wish to get undressed. You will have to wait for your combing and brushing."

Lissa was very glad to see Justin. She asked him whether he had avoided the trap on the sixth step, which had come to life under her and nearly tipped her off the stairs. "And the logs are ill-behaved also," she said, glaring at the hearth where one log had crushed the carefully mounded ashes and rolled away so the embers could not set it afire and the second leaned against the first, also well away from the coals.

"There is nothing wrong with the stair," Justin said. "Nor with the logs. You are drunk." He then knelt down to repair the damage Lissa had done to the fire and almost fell into the hearth.

Lissa hauled back on his shoulder, unbalancing them both so that he sat down hard and she tumbled into his lap. "That is very nice," she said, "but I do not trust the floor. It dropped away behind me. And do not tell me I have had too many cups of ale and wine and who knows what else. I know that as well as you. Nonetheless, the house is wriggling like a dancing girl." She giggled. "We will be safer abed, Justin."

With exaggerated care, each helping the other, they managed

to get to their feet and into the bedchamber. Undressing one another had always been stimulating and fun, but they achieved high comedy this time, doing battle with laces as lively and agile as young snakes and brooches that wriggled in their fingers and occasionally jumped off the garment like sportive little toads. They laughed so much that each collapsed on the rug and had to be lifted up by the other, and twice they sank down together. The second time Justin said, "I think it is meant, and since that time you invited me to take you so, I have always wanted to do it."

Even befuddled as she was, the way Justin had begun to kiss her and slide his hands under her shift made his meaning clear. She was very willing; somehow that they should couple thus on their wedding night, on the thick bear pelts on the floor, still half clothed and choking with laughter, gave an extra sensuality to the act. It was also a kind of promise that marriage would not change their delight in playfulness and decay into dullness and indifference.

Passion spent, they found their way to bed, leaning perilously on each other, laughing uproariously when the unstable pyramid of tall man, short woman, and heaving floor teetered forward and back or from side to side. Both knew the price of the release into childish merriment that drink gives; they would be sorry in the morning. But they were not. Both woke bright and cheerful with clear heads and complete, delightful memories.

Justin was sure they were spared the illness that follows too much drink because clinging together to fight the chilly dampness of the unwarmed sheets inflamed their desire for what their drink-sodden bodies could not easily give. Satisfaction came only slowly. Both worked until they sweated with effort despite the cold sheets. The exertion, he told Lissa when they woke in the morning, had driven the drink out of their blood, but Lissa smiled like the sun and shook her head. No, she insisted. God had given her a wedding gift of a minor miracle. Justin looked at the glory of joy in her face and could not find his breath for a moment. Perhaps it was a miracle. Let her be happy while she could.

For the next three weeks their lives seemed split as the household had been that wedding morning—Justin and Lissa perfectly happy and content and the rest groaning in misery. Marriage graved in stone the satisfaction the two found in each other, but there was little ease for either outside of their own home. Tension mounted in the city over the following weeks; Lissa did a greater than usual business in sleeping draughts and in small purchases made to cover anxious questions about what Justin knew of the king's intentions.

About that, she had to confess, he knew nothing, but she had his permission and gladly told them that they need not fear the whole countryside would fly to arms. The barons of the north and those tied to them in blood were arming, but most of the lords and the free burghers of the other cities, like York and Bristol and Oxford, were talking about a charter that would bring understanding and peace between the king and his people. Archbishop Langton and most of the bishops favored that charter and were prepared to plead with the king to grant it.

That knowledge was what Lissa herself clung to, but Justin was drilling his guards like an army and all the guilds had given money for new arms for the men. One personal matter was resolved. FitzWalter sent a messenger from Dunmow asking Justin to inspect the men he had left behind to make sure they were not growing slack in his absence. The message was proof enough that FitzWalter trusted Justin and felt no anger over Hubert's death, but it diminished whatever small hope Justin had that Lord Robert would actually be satisfied if King John granted the charter. Why did FitzWalter's men in the city need to be in top fighting form? Against whom would they be fighting? Did FitzWalter intend to fight off Justin's guard and close the gates against King John if he intended to hold his Christmas Court in London? Did he intend to allow the king into the city and then try to take him prisoner?

Any answer Justin gave himself was equally unwelcome, and he was particularly relieved when King John named Winchester as the site for his Christmas Court. The relief was short-lived; attendance was so thin that the king remained there only one day and then rode east and settled himself at the New Temple, the stronghold of the mighty Knights Templars outside London. His choice showed how little he trusted his own barons, one of whom held the Tower of London, or the people of the city, who

could protect him if they wished. When London closed her
gates, manned her walls, and laid chains across the river, her
great population made her nearly invincible. But John might
also have remembered that London had driven out his grand-
mother on the very eve of her coronation because her manner
did not please the burghers. John would not trust himself inside
the walls of the Tower or the city—but he did not cry treason.

On 6 January the barons presented themselves, as they had
agreed. John received the delegation and heard their demand
for a charter with seeming patience. Again he did not cry
treason, but he would not give a certain answer either, only
saying that the matter was serious and needed time for
deliberation. He would give an answer, he said, after consulting
with his advisers, on Low Sunday, 26 April.

Justin went to the meeting at the mayor's behest. He had
already been to Bury, Roger FitzAdam said, so he would be most
familiar with what was going forward. Richard again argued
against his attendance, fearing that his association with the
more bellicose barons would blacken the FitzAilwin family, and
Lissa was not happy about his going either, but a horrible kind
of fascination drove him.

"And I thought," he said to his assembled family a week later,
"that Richard and Lissa were right and I would end dead or in a
dungeon. When the king said wait, a roar of rage went up, and
the men began to close in on him. I really thought FitzWalter
would leap on the dais and have him by the throat, but Langton
intervened and said the king was right, that charters defining
rights and duties should not be written and sworn to in haste."

"True enough," Richard said. "That charter of the first Henry
is useless to us. If we want London's rights to be confirmed,
there must be time to write a new article, and others will desire
their special articles, which means a new charter must be
written."

"That was what Langton offered as a sop, but one of the
northerners—Vesci, I think—cried out that the king did not
intend to consider a charter, only to gain time to bring in foreign
mercenaries to kill honest Englishmen. It was a near thing, but
the earl of Pembroke saved us that time. Old as he is, I would
not like to meet him on a battlefield as an enemy. He let out a

roar that stilled all lesser voices, and he offered himself as pledge that King John would be where he set as a meeting place and at the proper time. God, what a man! He must hate the king more than any, for he has been more injured and insulted, but his honor holds firm."

"Still"—Thomas's lips had a wry twist—"I think the barons might trust him more to fulfill his word to them because of his hatred of his master than if he loved John."

"They would be wrong," Justin said. "He might act in gladness or he might act in grief, but the action would be the same."

"So we have until spring," Lissa said, touching the back of Justin's hand with one finger. "At least we will see the year turn in peace."

Lissa was correct; by the middle of January all the barons and their retinues had left the city and London had settled into its winter quiet. Justin was not so much at peace as others, however; he had several heated confrontations with the mayor and aldermen, who wanted to dismiss all the new members of the guard, keeping only the tiny force they felt adequate for winter peacekeeping.

"This year is not the same as other years," Justin warned. "If we dismiss men from the guard, they will go off and join the armies the barons are building—those for the king and those against him. All are crying for men, and if you will not pay them, others will. They must eat."

He came home pale with rage because economy had, as usual, won over good sense. Lissa sighed with sympathy and held her tongue, letting him talk out all the signs of trouble. She had heard before of the way the king was courting the Church, offering the bishops promises and charters by the handful so they would withhold their approval of the charter demanded by the nobles. And she thought of the news Gerbod had sent from Calais on his way south around the coast of France.

Before she could ask, Justin said, "They would not even listen when I read them your uncle's letter about the king hiring Flemings. That old snake Rochefolet kept hissing that the mercenaries were for Ireland, which they could not fail to know was what he was told to say. Can no one see that the men are being mustered into companies there and can more easily be sent to England across that water than across the narrow sea where the weather is less certain?"

"I do not understand that myself, Justin," Lissa said. "It may be easier to bring them over from Ireland than from Flanders, but I, too, feel that the best surety of using the troops in England would be to bring them here directly."

"The king is afraid to do that," Justin explained. "To bring in mercenaries when he swore he needed time to consider the charter would likely set off the war and also prove to many who still wish for compromise that there is no hope of it, thus pushing them into FitzWalter's party."

"Is there any real hope of compromise?" Lissa asked.

There was a long silence during which she rose and went to Justin to stroke his hair and kiss his brow. He pushed his chair back and took her in his lap, holding her against him more for comfort than for love.

At last he said, "I do not know. The king may well yield and offer to sign because he will believe that he can later squirm out of the agreement. But it will depend also on how much influence FitzWalter has. He wants to be rid of John; no compromise will content him. I do not think there are many as violent as he— Vesci, probably, and likely Saer de Quincy—but even in FitzWalter's party I think most only want to control the king so that he cannot rage among them like a mad dog."

Lissa shivered in his arms and said, "I have never seen a war. Will it be worse than the fire?"

"Good God!" Justin exclaimed, giving her a sudden squeeze and smiling down at her. "I did not mean to frighten you. I am only in a temper because those pinchpurses in the mayor's council will dismiss my men now, and then in the spring blame me because the watch is too small to stop riots. As for the war, thank God it seems as if it will not come near London. FitzWalter and his allies are staying where they are more sure of support."

Justin's warnings to mayor and council proved far more accurate than he hoped. Once the influx of merchants and traders began in the spring and he needed men, he was unable to hire any but grandsires and striplings. The city became nearly ungovernable. Twice because the watch was so thin a major burning was only narrowly averted—once heroic efforts by local people checked the fire and the second time God sent rain.

Roger FitzAdam spoke sharply to Justin about the inefficiency of his men, and Justin told him to do better himself with the men he had been allowed to hire and resigned his position.

Not five days later, 12 April, Stephen Langton's chief clerk came to the house and asked if Justin would be willing to serve the archbishop for a few weeks during the coming meeting between the king and his barons.

"The archbishop does me great honor," Justin said, glancing uneasily at Lissa, "but if the service must be outside of London—"

"You must go wherever it is, my lord," Lissa said. "If you are needed by Archbishop Langton, his work is more important than any other business."

She had seen the way his eyes lighted, and knew he had not been happy lately, even though he had begun to work on some trading ventures. Justin would have accepted eagerly, she thought, if he had not been afraid to leave her. The watch was disintegrating into utter helplessness without his central control—the mayor and council having decided to try letting each alderman manage the watch in his section—and the situation was getting worse. Uncontrolled merrymaking too often turned into rioting; squabbles between the retinues of rival merchants turned into bloody fights. The disorder was beginning to spill over even into such quiet areas as the Cordwainery.

"I will be safe," she went on. "The house is strong, and if you wish, though I think it unnecessary, Dick Miller's son and Halsig, and Mary, of course, can all stay here while you are away. With three men behind stone walls I will be in no danger."

"The service will not be in London," the clerk said, "but you will have a few days to make arrangements for your wife's protection. The archbishop would like you to meet him at Reading Abbey on the sixteenth. He is going to Oxford, where the king has summoned him to his Easter court."

Justin nodded, and with a smile at Lissa that was full of pride and content in her, he agreed to take service. He had been less worried about the minor disorders than he had been afraid the king might insist the barons come to London on Low Sunday to separate them as far as possible from their strongest base of support, and he had not been certain, until the clerk said so, that Stephen Langton was still involved in the negotiation about the charter.

When the king had started to hire mercenaries, the archbishop had threatened to withdraw as mediator; the king had then sent the Poitevins home and directed the Flemings to Ireland, but Justin knew how stiff-necked the archbishop could be. Apparently he had accepted John's gesture, and John had chosen Oxford for his Easter court. If John was in Oxford, Justin was sure the barons would be farther north and London would not be the center of the confrontation. Since the watch still obeyed him, even stopped him in the street sometimes to ask for orders, Justin decided he would give them orders. Despite the mayor, he would make sure that Soper Lane was adequately patrolled over the time he was away.

Although Langton was traveling with a guard of five men-at-arms, once they reached Oxford, Justin began to wonder why he had been summoned. The court was poorly attended, but the king showed no sign of temper and he was polite, even cordial, to the archbishop. News soon came of the barons; FitzWalter and his allies had come to Northampton, and a large army was gathering near the town. On 23 April, King John sent a messenger to invite the leaders to come to court under safe conduct and to leave as freely as they came. All refused to come to Oxford. They said haughtily that they could not trust themselves to the king's safe conduct.

Justin wished their answer had been more civil, although he really could not blame them. But John did not lose his temper. Justin realized with a shock that the king was pleased. Now he could claim that the barons had not fulfilled their part of the agreement. He feared he had learned why he was needed when the stubborn archbishop pointed out clearly and loudly that John had not always honored his own safe conduct and prayed the king to be patient. But even as Justin's hand twitched toward his sword and he looked warily at those who would obey the king even in such a sacrilege as laying hands on Langton, his eye caught that of William Marshal and he relaxed. And John only looked sour and agreed that he would try again for a meeting.

The arrangements for the second message to the barons taught Justin, at last, why the archbishop had been so eager for his service. He had been brought along not so much to protect Langton, who had protection enough in the presence of William Marshal and his men, as to serve as an elevated messenger

—and because he was well known to Robert FitzWalter. He went
to the barons at Northampton as Langton's man, not the king's,
but even so he did not expect any sign of reasonableness from
the rebel leaders. Had they intended to bargain about the
charter, they would not have used the terms they did to refuse
the king's first invitation and they would have suggested
another place of meeting.

Justin was rather surprised by his meeting with FitzWalter,
who was clearly the leader of the baronial group although he
had not yet been officially selected. At first it went as he
expected. FitzWalter attacked, saying with contemptuously
lifted brows and downturned mouth, "So you are a king's man,
Sir Justin. I did not think that of you."

But Justin was far too clever to rise to such a lure, and he
smiled and replied with amusement he allowed to be obvious, "I
am a London man, Lord Robert. My first and deepest loyalty is
to my city and her good. At this time, I happen to be in service
to Archbishop Langton because I believe that will best serve
London."

But then FitzWalter did not make the remarks Justin expected.
He abandoned his caustic tone and asked with considerable
interest, "You are no longer in charge of the watch?"

Justin answered that he had resigned that post, and FitzWalter only nodded. He then went on to speak of the business that
had brought them together, but his tone was now pleasant.
Justin had the oddest feeling that FitzWalter was specially
pleased by the fact that he no longer commanded the watch. He
was also troubled about so easily obtaining an agreement that
the leaders of the rebel party would come to Brackley, halfway
between Oxford and Northampton, and there receive whomever the king would send.

On his ride back to Oxford from Northampton, Justin came to
understand that FitzWalter's agreement to meet John's envoys at
Brackley had nothing to do with him. He realized that FitzWalter
dared not refuse the archbishop's plea for reason and restraint.
Most of the men who had followed him only wanted the charter
signed, not to depose or kill the king. So if FitzWalter refused
even to present the charter, which was what would happen if he
would not speak to the king or anyone else, they would see his
real purpose and might abandon him.

Still, Justin was sure he was not mistaken about FitzWalter's reaction to the news that he had left his position. He began to wonder whether Lord Robert had been involved in William Bowles's death and in ordering Hubert to kill him. The idea was on the edge of madness; if FitzWalter wanted him dead there were myriad ways to obtain that end without using the clumsy lackwit Hubert. But he could not imagine any reason Lord Robert should care about the London watch except his knowledge that Justin alone might suspect him of murder.

His uneasiness lingered, intensified by FitzWalter's pleasant smile and nod each time they met at Brackley when Justin accompanied the archbishop and the earl of Pembroke to listen to the barons' demands. Had he been more hopeful about the fate of the charter, his personal doubts would probably have been washed away by his anger and anxiety, but he had expected the negotiation to fail. He was not surprised to see that the charter had grown almost as large as the rebel army. Anyone could see that FitzWalter and the other leaders had just written in anything at all that anyone asked. There had not even been any attempt to take out articles that repeated themselves, and right in the beginning were several that were utterly outrageous.

Pembroke was disgusted. Justin thought, considering the insults and indignities John had heaped on him, that Pembroke must have had some secret hope a charter curbing John's worst excesses could be signed. But when their party was out in the open where many could hear, Pembroke said that after listening to such demands his heart was much lighter for his promise to defend the king.

"The old man is no mean tactician," Langton said in Justin's ear. "I wonder if he will not win us some changes of heart among these men."

Whether he did or not made no difference because the king had no intention of yielding anything. When they returned to Oxford, John did not really bother to examine the barons' demands before he called them unjust and said he would never agree to a charter that would make him the slave of his barons. After what he had said in Brackley, Justin was surprised when William Marshal as well as the archbishop pleaded with John to look over the charter to see if there were not some articles that were just and reasonable. The king would not listen, and Justin again accompanied the archbishop and Pembroke to Brackley to give the barons John's answer. This time FitzWalter did not smile, but Justin knew he was barely concealing his triumph. Most of the others were aghast, but they were very angry as well as frightened. John's harshness had served FitzWalter's purpose well; even the doubters' resolve had hardened.

Justin expected to be dismissed when they arrived back at Oxford, but he did not ask to go and when the archbishop said he would remain in Oxford a little longer and that Justin might be needed again, he was glad. Although he longed for Lissa, there was a feeling of incompleteness, of unfinished business, hanging in the air. First Justin thought the final stroke had come when the rebels renounced their homage to the king, appointed Robert FitzWalter their leader—with the grandiose title Marshal of the Army of God—and promptly began an active siege of Northampton.

Justin knew that the king dared not call up a baronial army; they would be too likely to march with him up to the enemy and then desert him, like the Poitevins. He expected mercenaries kept in hiding to close in on the rebels, and feared the archbishop, regardless of practical necessity, would accuse John of treachery. But nothing happened, and Justin first wondered whether Langton's presence was restraining the king. Then he assumed that John had sent for the mercenary troops and it would take time for them to come, but they did not come. Finally he wondered whether John was in the grip of the lethargy that seized him now and again. Justin had heard a long fit of that lethargy had cost the king Normandy.

In the end Justin decided John simply knew more than he did, for Northampton did not fall to the barons' siege, and their attack was inept and disorganized. Justin was shocked at what he saw when he was sent to the rebels on the tenth day of the siege with letters from John offering to put all grievances before papal arbitration. As far as he could see, the rebels were not doing anything that seriously threatened the castle. They had brought in no siege engines, and none were being built. Their efforts were so badly organized that Justin began to think he had credited FitzWalter with more ability than he possessed. He was disturbed too, when he was allowed to speak only to FitzWalter and Vesci.

The king's overture was rejected, although it actually amounted to an admission that there were grievances to be righted, but Justin heard enough while he was in the camp to learn why the attack had failed. Lord Robert and King John had similar problems. Neither could really rely on his sworn men— John because they disliked and distrusted him; FitzWalter because his aims and theirs differed. The barons wanted a charter not a war. And despite the elevated title he had been given, many were reluctant to obey him. Title or no title they knew him to be one of them, not born of royal blood and anointed by God as king, like John.

Five days later, the siege was broken. Langton waited hopefully to be asked to propose a truce, but no message came from the rebels. The day before they heard of the withdrawal of the baronial army, Justin had a letter from his cousin Richard asking that he return to London if the archbishop could now spare him. No reason was given and the letter had been carried by a merchant on business, so Justin could not believe an emergency existed. He hesitated to ask for his freedom, thinking a truce might be possible, until, a few days later, news came that the rebel army had not disbanded but had moved to Bedford keep and that its lord, William de Beauchamp, had greeted them with respect.

Justin could not see any sense in continuing his service, and Langton agreed that the defection of Beauchamp to the rebels meant that any move to negotiate must now come from them. He pressed several rich gifts on Justin and gave him leave to go, which he took quite literally, rolling hs extra clothes in his blankets and riding Noir out of the city before the situation could change and Langton think of a new use for him.

Riding along the road hour after hour left his mind free, and Justin naturally wondered why Richard wanted him to return. Until that moment he had not feared for Lissa. He had had two letters from her, sent with journeymen riding to Oxford on business, and those had given him no reason for anxiety, although they had stirred his loins to life. Now, suddenly, he became convinced that disaster had swept away his whole life. He told himself not to be a fool, that if ill had befallen Lissa, Halsig or Dick would have ridden night and day to summon him.

All he accomplished was to convince himself that the house had been attacked and burned down and all were dead. The fear was idiotic and he knew it. Richard would never conceal a catastrophe of such magnitude. Besides, Justin knew Lissa's house was all of stone and could not burn. He retained enough rationality to keep from galloping Noir to death, but he was so sick with fear that he rode through the night and arrived some hours after dinner on Saturday afternoon.

None of his fears had any substance. Lissa greeted him with tears of joy and only joy. She had no idea that Richard had asked him to return. When she heard, she was troubled, but she had no idea what might have been behind his letter.

"Goscelin has been very quiet when I have been to visit with Adela," she said. "I knew he was troubled, but I thought it was over the general disorder in the city and in the land. That is all anyone talks of these days. I am growing rich on potions to calm the spirits and on sleeping draughts."

"I had better go and find him," Justin said, but he did not release Lissa or lift his eyes from her face, and his voice was rough with desire.

"Go above," Lissa whispered huskily. "I will send Ninias. You have ridden day and night. Let Richard come here."

He kissed her then and if he had not been armed and unable to open her clothes and his without breaking the embrace, he would have had her there in the shop with Paul and Ninias just outside the door and Witta and Oliva peering from the work-shop. Common sense followed frustration. Justin went up the stairs, and Lissa bade Ninias to go tell Justin's cousin Richard that Justin was at home and ready to receive him. Lissa made all haste to strip her husband, threw her own garments anywhere at all, and they fell together to the bear pelts on the floor, unable to wait to get to the bed.

Fortunately no emergency that required instant action ex-isted, as far as Richard knew, and he had a deliberate nature. He did not leave at once but sent for Thomas. The delay saved him from arriving to find Justin still mounted. His first satisfaction came so swiftly that it left Lissa behind. She forgave him, but kisses and touches of remorse not only restored his appetite swiftly but honed it sharper so that he swelled within her and began anew. The second coupling took longer. Justin was still belting his robe when Thomas and Richard arrived, but his smile of greeting was much warmer than it would have been had they come sooner.

"I hope my letter caused no inconvenience," Richard began. "I was of two minds about sending it, but I heard a most disquieting rumor."

"You had better begin before that," Thomas said, then turned to Justin. "Did you hear that Rochefolet was caught in the street by a troop of rioters and died of it? And Lafeit left the city—to buy calves and lambs, he said, but he was well known to be the second set of ears John had on the council, Rochefolet being the first, so I wonder. Then Master White and Odo Vigil proposed inviting the rebels into the city to protect us from the king's wrath."

Justin laughed. "The king's wrath? But John said not one word about London all the time I was there."

"Did he not?" Thomas remarked. "Perhaps those closest to that one know the least about him."

"Thomas!" Richard exclaimed. "More to the point, I did not think the rest of the council were likely to nail themselves to a mast that might become a gallows, which was why I did not bother to send you that news."

He stopped as Oliva came in with a tray, followed by Witta with two flagons. Thomas jumped up to move the table, Lissa rose from the stool where she had been sitting by Justin's knee to bring cups from the tall chest for the wine or ale, and Oliva set out plates of sweet cakes, since it was some hours past dinner. Having poured each man wine or ale, as he desired, Lissa resettled herself as close to Justin as she could without actually sitting in his lap. Her body was replete, but she had had to force herself to go down to order the cakes and wine. And now she could hardly bear to release her hold on Justin to serve her guests.

Lissa marveled at her silliness. She had missed Justin, yes, but she had scarcely spent every night weeping into her pillow with loneliness. It was only now that he was back that the sensation almost overwhelmed her. He must feel the same, she thought, for his fingers gripped some part of her all the time, no matter who was talking, and she had had to strike his hand gently to make him loose her so she could get the cups. It was the sudden painful tightening of Justin's grip that drew her mind back to the conversation.

"You really believe that the gates will be opened one night and let in the rebel army?" Justin asked sharply.

"How can one be certain of such a lunacy?" Thomas asked. "I did not believe it, but you know my tongue—I spoke it to the mayor in jest. Justin, he turned yellow and gray and shivered, and bleated about having done his best and being abandoned by all. He also told me that he knew the earl of Salisbury was marching the Flemish mercenaries across England with orders to enter London and force us to the king's will. That was when I bade Richard write to you."

"Have you spoken to anyone else?"

"All of them," Richard said. "And all are worried sick. Not all trust the information Roger FitzAdam has, but fear more not to act on it. If Salisbury takes the city, they are sure they will lose every liberty squeezed out of John when they agreed to support him rather than Prince Arthur for king. Still, not one will admit the intention—"

"Richard! You did not ask them if they intended to open the gates to an army, did you?"

"I am not an idiot, Justin," Richard said stiffly. "I only asked about the rumor. All admitted to having heard it, and all said it was nonsense, but it was clear that they fear what the king will do if Salisbury comes. Half of them, at least, said that John must be forced to sign the charter so that London's rights will be confirmed."

Justin shifted uneasily and rubbed a hand over his burning eyes. Apparently the king had been cleverer than he suspected and had completely deceived Archbishop Langton. John must have sent orders to his bastard half brother while they were at Oxford. Doubtless the arrangements to bring the mercenaries to England were made before he came to hold his Easter court there. No wonder he had seemed so calm in the face of the attack on Northampton.

Hindsight revealed to Justin that John must have been waiting for two pieces of information: whether the barons truly would go to war to get their charter, and if they did, how dangerous the threat from them really was. The poor showing and disorganization of the rebel army at Northampton must have been a signal to the king to attack rather than make any further attempt at conciliation, and John had ordered Salisbury and the other leaders of the mercenaries to move. When he had crushed them, John would be merciless not only to FitzWalter and his allies but to all. And the very fact that the king had dispatched an army to "take" London clearly indicated that the greatest city in the realm was to be made helpless before John's will.

"I am not sure I do not agree with the aldermen," Justin said slowly. "I would greatly prefer to have no dealing with either party, to close the gates, draw the chains across the river, and arm ourselves to defend our walls. But if the city *cannot* resist Salisbury's mercenaries, it might be better to seem to do the barons a favor and invite them in."

"That is why we wanted you here," Thomas said. "I think we can get the council to appoint you to arrange the defense of the city—or at least to examine whether a defense is possible. Will you do it, if you are asked?"

"You know I will," Justin said, "but I fear you have left it too late."

Chapter 31

W HEN HE SPOKE OF HAVING LEFT THE QUESTION OF DEFENDING THE city too late, Justin was thinking of the time it would take to train a capable force. There were plenty of men of fighting age in London, and all even had some rudimentary skill at arms. They could wield a club, swing wildly with a sword, stab with a knife—but fighting was not their trade. They were not trained to stand firmly in place and resist when attacked by an army, although that was really all they would need to do.

Justin's remark that it was probably too late was true in an entirely different sense, however. The very next morning, while most of London was piously attending mass on Sunday, 17 May, FitzWalter and the other leaders of the baronial party marched through Aldgate, which was obligingly opened for them, with enough of their army to ensure there would be no resistance. When Lissa and Justin returned from church, Dunstan was waiting at Lissa's door with the news that a troop of soldiers had driven away his watch from Cripplegate.

"What should we do, my lord?" he asked. "We had no orders,

no warning. There were four of us and ten of them. We knew not what to do, so we obeyed the captain."

"Thank God you did," Justin said, "and that they must have been sent by a fool without proper orders. Now pass my word to the men of the watch: Go home or to any other safe place and hide your weapons, except your cudgels. Then go to whatever place your alderman has ordered as the place of meeting for your watch and wait for his orders. Obey them except for giving up your weapons. Be quiet. Do not offer any offense to the soldiers unless they attack you, in which case defend yourself as best you may, taking into consideration their numbers and yours—and the fact that there is a whole army of them near London if not in it. If you need to speak to me again, come by the back and quietly. It may be that I will be watched."

Stammering thanks, his face bright with relief, Dunstan hurried away. Lissa looked up at her husband, pallid with shock, her eyes huge. "What will happen now, Justin? Do you think the gates are now closed? Should we try to leave the city?"

He led her into the house and closed the door. After another moment he shook his head. "I have no answers yet. Send Witta to Bishopsgate. Tell him only to watch, as boys will do. After Nones he can come home and tell us what the new rules of the gate are. And Ninias must run to my house and summon Halsig, Dick, and Mary. They are to bring any small things of value here and to shut up my house as well as possible. If there is going to be violence, we are safest here and together."

Twice that day the men in the house gripped their weapons and Lissa watched with bated breath from a crack in the upstairs shutter as armed troops went by on Soper Lane. The household was not disturbed, however, and aside from isolated incidents of individual men-at-arms or small troops disobeying their orders and taking what they wanted by force, there was no violence. The punishments inflicted on those who had disobeyed were public and very brutal.

Clearly an agreement had been reached with some of the powerful men of the city that London would help tame the king, and FitzWalter and his allies were keeping that agreement most carefully. The barons were not strong enough to risk losing the burghers' help. They had, Justin learned by the end of the week, sent letters all over the realm exhorting the neutral barons to join their cause if they wished to keep their lands. The response was disappointing. Some young hotheads, with a few men, rode off to London; the lords themselves stayed at home. It was natural enough, Justin thought, that the young should be less cautious in their desire for freedom from the king's domination. Then his lips twisted cynically; the "defection" of the heirs did not really help the rebels much, but it did provide those families with a foot in each camp.

By 24 May the barons had forced Roger FitzAdam to resign and appointed Serlo the Mercer as mayor. Despite that London seemed to have returned to normal, all except the king's courts and the exchequer, which were shut tight. That would hurt the king more than taking a castle here or there, Justin thought, but it would cause little disruption in the city. Since Justin could see no serious danger of looting or riot, he sent Halsig, Dick, and Mary back to his house. Later that afternoon Dick was back with a messenger from FitzWalter, who wished to speak to Justin.

"Now?" Justin asked, having come down into the shop and wishing that Dick had come alone with the message.

The squire looked disappointed. "Not if it is inconvenient to you, Sir Justin, but as soon as it will be possible for you to come. The matter is important."

"I will come at once," Justin said. "I wished to make sure, that was all."

Justin was careful not to say what he wished to make sure about, since his question had been a discreet way of testing whether he was being invited or arrested. Apparently FitzWalter's squire had brought an invitation, but Justin remained cautious. He told Dick to saddle Noir and nodded to Lissa, who came out of the workroom and went up with him to help him into his armor.

"I will take Dick," Justin said to her. "It is possible that FitzWalter will ask me to perform some duty in great haste. If so, Dick will return and tell you. If any man other than Dick comes to you to say I will not return home by dark, send to my cousins and tell them FitzWalter has me and inquiry should be made."

Lissa had to hold on to Justin to keep from falling in her fright, but he took her by the shoulders and shook her gently. "Do not be silly," he said sharply. "If I expected harm to come to me, I would not go. This is no more than a precaution when dealing with this man in these times. I do not think he wishes me ill. I think he has a task for me."

The assumption seemed perfectly sound. FitzWalter greeted Justin in a friendly manner, perhaps a shade too heartily, but Justin thought that was because Lord Robert was a trifle embarrassed by the request he was being forced to make.

"You will be glad to hear," he said, "that William Marshal has brought a new proposal from the king."

"I am glad to hear it," Justin said, remaining carefully expressionless despite the tightening of FitzWalter's lips and the single angry glare.

"The council of barons has decided to offer our charter again as a basis for peace," FitzWalter said, his voice flat and hard. He drew a breath and then went on, lips twisted with distaste. "And we wish all to know if this negotiation fails that we are not at fault, that it is the king who is false, that John has rejected reasonable terms. Thus, we wish the charter to be reviewed and considered by those who are neutral between us. We would like you to carry our copy of the charter to the archbishop and ask him if he will mediate in this matter."

"I will serve you in this gladly," Justin said, was raked by another angry glance, and called himself a fool.

For a moment in his own enthusiasm for obtaining a charter and getting rid of the baronial army in London, Justin had forgotten that FitzWalter probably did not want peace. He asked quickly whether FitzWalter had any other instructions for him or any messages for the archbishop. There were letters for Langton, FitzWalter said, no verbal messages.

Justin blinked and raised his brows, and FitzWalter said, "You think it strange that I ask you to do what any common messenger could do, but I wished Archbishop Langton to be able to ask any question and have an answer he could trust. Also, he might desire to send back a message he did not wish to commit to writing."

Although he smiled and nodded, Justin could barely prevent his nostrils from flaring in a quest for a scent of bad fish. FitzWalter's response to his unasked question was weak as water, but he obtained no other clue to Lord Robert's real purpose in asking him to ride to Canterbury while he waited for the copy of the charter and the letters to Langton to be made into a packet and delivered to him. Just as he was about to leave, Richard Percy and Robert de Vere came in, and FitzWalter mentioned to them that Justin had agreed to be their messenger to the archbishop.

It was a minor incident and might have been mere coincidence. Still, as Justin rode home he wondered whether FitzWalter was suspected by his fellow barons of not carrying out their decisions and had chosen him to take the charter to Langton to soothe their distrust. FitzWalter's use of "the council of barons" before he was able to bring himself to use "we" implied that he had not wished to accept the king's overture—and Justin was sure of that from his own knowledge of the man and his history. FitzWalter's hatred for King John could not be assuaged by a charter that prevented royal abuses; nothing but the king's exile or death would content him. If the other barons knew that, they might have demanded a neutral messenger.

Although his explanation was better than FitzWalter's, Justin was not much happier with it. Somehow he felt that choosing him had something to do with FitzWalter's deeper purpose, which was to show that King John was not sincere in his offers of amendment. Justin was sure FitzWalter wanted to show that the king did not intend to sign the charter and was either playing for time to build a stronger army or intended to repudiate the charter as soon as the barons had dismissed their army. If the moderate barons could be convinced that dealing with John was hopeless, many would agree to FitzWalter's more radical plan to depose the king.

The reasoning was good, but Justin could not connect his carrying the charter to Canterbury with FitzWalter's need to prove King John treacherous. All sorts of mad ideas passed through his mind, including an attack on the road that could be blamed on King John. But Justin would not be traveling alone, and the chances of killing him or fooling him were too small. He dismissed that as well as a number of other silly notions, but he remained so uneasy that he ordered Halsig and Dick to move back into Lissa's house and asked her to remain indoors while he was away or to take both men with her if she had to go out.

He took Dunstan and four other men of the London guard, armed and dressed in the leather hauberks of men-at-arms. FitzWalter's seal passed them all over the bridge without question just before the gates were closed for the night. They rode west in the last of the dusk, rested until the moon rose, and then rode on until it was necessary to rest the horses. At first light they started again and reached Canterbury without the smallest interference. Nor, Justin found, was his arrival any surprise—not that Langton had expected him in particular or on that particular day, but the archbishop had been informed by the king of his offer to grant the charter and Langton had been praying that the barons would accept it. He took Justin's packet and read the letters, frowning as he gave the untidy leaves of the barons' charter into the hands of a clerk.

"I have a copy already," he said. "The king threw it at the clerk who tried to give it to him, so I took it and read it. Much in it is nonsense, but having taken the advice of my suffragan bishops and of honest and noble men, I have used what I could of it. I have a new charter that, I hope, contains just and reasonable provisions for curing the abuses of which the barons complain."

Justin bowed silently, but Langton had caught the expression on Justin's face, and he laughed. "I am aware," he went on, his lips twisting to wryness, "that what seems reasonable to me may not please those who have risked so much to bring King John to make clear their rights."

Justin's face now reflected Langton's wry smile. "True enough, but I am afraid, my lord, I was less worried about the charter than filled with a selfish concern over the distance between London and Canterbury. We both know that some adjustments will have to be made, and I have little desire to ride this distance many times." He hesitated, wanting to give warning without betraying FitzWalter, and then went on, "And, my lord, the delay in a protracted negotiation might be dangerous."

"I agree." Langton nodded. "I agree so strongly that I was already planning to come to London myself to be close by. Nor is there any need to leave the barons in suspense over my decision for even the few days I will take to make ready. Tomorrow I will give you two copies of the new charter. You can deliver one to Lord Robert and one to your mayor with letters explaining that the articles may be amended and stating my willingness to do all I can to bring peace to this land."

Justin's thanks were so fervent, particularly for providing an extra copy of the document for the new mayor, that the archbishop smiled on him more warmly than at any time since he had identified himself as Lord Robert's messenger. He then offered Justin a seat and was gracious enough to describe to him some of the more important provisions of the new charter, so Justin dared mention the desire of the burghers to have included not only a confirmation of London's privileges but the extension of those privileges to all towns chartered by the king.

"That is not unfair," Langton said. "The rights of the town descend to each free man therein, who has only the town as his lord. Yes. I will certainly speak for the towns if such an article is presented."

And Justin suddenly remembered the talk with his cousins about Henry's charter and Lissa's suggestion, so he asked, "And, my lord, would it be too small a matter to ask that some measure be decreed as the measure to be used throughout the realm? Now a merchant who buys a quarter of corn in York will not have the same amount of corn as when he buys a quarter of corn in London or Bristol. This is no great matter, such as the laws of inheritance and wardship, but more heads may have been broken over it, as I know to my sorrow whose duty it was to keep the peace."

"It is not a small matter," Langton said. "No matter that causes strife between men and might be easily amended is small. I will speak for that article also, Sir Justin. You are a mine of good advice. Have you any more for me?"

"Only to present your charter to the largest group of barons possible. There are those who cannot be contented."

The archbishop nodded and held out his hand. Justin rose, bowed to kiss Langton's ring, and went to see that his men would be given quarters for the night. He found them near the stable, taking advantage of the sun that now shone to dry cloaks and hoods dampened in the morning's drizzle, and directed them to the steward who would arrange their meals and lodging. The information was greeted with some relief; the news that they would leave for home the next morning was received more enthusiastically. The men found themselves uncomfortable in a place where authority controlled matters like eating and sleeping. They were accustomed to the freedom of city life; true, you might not eat at all and might sleep in the gutter if you had no money, but no one had the right to tell you which cookhouse to eat at or at which house to rent a bed.

Although Justin was not troubled by the workings of the archbishop's household—he had, like other males of his class, been fostered, served as page and squire, so he was accustomed to being told where to eat and sleep—he was as eager to leave as his men. He wanted to discuss what Langton had told him with his cousins and with the aldermen. Justin felt he must assure them that Langton would approve an article confirming the rights of London. He was a little afraid that FitzWalter might try to convince them the archbishop intended to exclude the towns to make them reject the charter.

One cannot hurry an archbishop's household, however. The archbishop had decided to add something to his letters after he spoke to Justin; his secretary had to oversee the scribe who wrote it, then summon the clerk responsible for copying; the packets had to be opened, the lines copied, the ink dried, the packets resealed . . . Justin and his men did not get away until after dinner. The men benefited by enjoying a good meal, at least. Justin ate it because he had trained himself to eat no matter what he felt, but he did not enjoy it. As if to rap his knuckles for not being patient, the sun, which had been shining brightly all morning, disappeared behind thick billows of clouds in the afternoon. By dusk, the rain was too hard for Justin to ignore. They stopped in Rochester, lodging at an inn in the town, and reached London the next day just before the gates closed for the night.

Justin dismissed his men and told them to hold their tongues about where they had been. He then rode to his aunt's house to speak to Thomas and Richard before anyone should know he had returned. They agreed that the more people who knew what Langton had said, the better chance they would have of getting the charter accepted and the barons out of the city.

"But not everyone is as eager as we to be rid of them," Thomas pointed out.

"Aside from Serlo, is it yet known who opened Aldgate for them?" Richard asked.

"Not *known*, no—at least not for certain," Justin said, "but Thomas is right. There must be others besides Serlo who fear what will befall them when the barons are gone. Still, little harm has yet come of opening the gates." Justin stared at the packets he held in his hands. "And if the king is brought to sign this, it may well be that good will come of what was done." He looked at Richard. "Do we need vengeance against those who have not truly hurt us?"

"There is the matter of the special charter for London signed by the king only two days before." Richard was indignant. "That was kept secret."

"I am not sorry," Justin said, and his cousins looked shocked. "A special charter for London at this time might make us hated. Certainly there would be few, or none, to support us if the king withdrew his favor as capriciously as he granted it. But if our rights are one article among other articles that give rights to others, will we not all support one another? Will not all be aware that if the king violates one article he will soon violate all? Remember, I spoke for the other towns also. The barons may or may not make alliance with us, but the other towns will."

"You have a point." Thomas raised a brow at Richard, who still seemed inclined to carry a resentment over the treacherous opening of the gate whether good or ill came of it, but after another moment he nodded.

"Then let us assure each man—no matter how likely or unlikely it be that he was of the party who invited the barons in—that in the acceptance of the charter all past differences will be forgotten."

"Very well," Richard agreed stiffly, "I will expect you at first light, and we will all go, first to my father's friends. If our party goes together to the others, they will believe we will not press the matter of the opened gate. Then all of us will accompany you to the mayor."

"I cannot hold back the letter and charter from FitzWalter," Justin said.

"Nooo." Thomas drew out the word. "But there is no law that says you must carry it to him in person, since you have no verbal message to give him."

Justin nodded grimly. "Very good. One of my men lives on the turn of the road. I will send him with the packet and bid him say no more than that it was sent by Archbishop Langton in Canterbury. When we are done with our business, I will present myself and explain that the council and even the mayor are most eager for the charter to be approved by the barons. That may give him second thoughts about opposing it too openly."

"I think," Richard said slowly, "that you should also say the united guilds will give a great dinner to welcome the archbishop and to show our support for his purpose."

"A most excellent thought!" Justin exclaimed.

"I agree," Thomas said, grinning. "It is also the perfect news to make peace with your wife. Poor Lissa obediently stayed within doors all the time you were away and will be very glad indeed to be freed from prison."

Justin had forgotten, until Thomas spoke of Lissa remaining indoors, about his feeling that FitzWalter had had some ulterior motive in sending him to Canterbury. The archbishop's discussion of the charter with him, and his approval of two articles Londoners desired, had obscured for Justin his original purpose as simple messenger. But nothing had happened on the road; the charter was safe in his hands; no one but his cousins even knew he had returned to London—and yet the moment he was reminded, he again felt uneasy. However, in the warmth of Lissa's greeting and the need to answer her eager questions about what had happened in Canterbury, the puzzle about FitzWalter's motives slipped out of his head.

Lissa had never had the faintest suspicion that Justin's orders to remain indoors had anything more to do with his trip to Canterbury than a general anxiety about his being absent when there were too many armed men in the city. The caution had seemed reasonable to her, and since Justin never interfered with her normal activities unless forced to do so, she had not asked why he gave the order. She had another reason for obedience; she was inclined for privacy while a hope was confirmed or a great disappointment endured, so it was not hard for her to stay home for four days.

Once or twice Lissa even wondered if Justin might have noticed her courses were very late and that had made him overprotective. She told herself she was silly, that men only noticed the moon times because a wife refused to couple. But in her heart of hearts Lissa believed Justin was different, more alive to her moods, more responsive to her feelings than other men to other wives. Foolish as she might be in her belief, Lissa was too wise to put it to any test; she was happy as she was, happy to

think it was Justin who sent a boy from his aunt's house to tell
her he was safe in London but had some business to finish
before he could come home.

Thomas had actually sent the message, but Justin's greeting
kisses were passionate enough so that she never discovered her
mistake, and they were soon so deep in talk about the charter
that Lissa even forgot the hope that was growing stronger each
day. She laughed aloud when Justin told her of proposing the
standard of measure to the archbishop and of Langton's
approval.

"I will see that it goes in too," she said. "Now, to whom can I
speak? Goscelin is useless. What does he care about dry or wet
measure? Well, I can speak to John le Spicer, and Master
Chigwell is quite reconciled to me since Gerbod sold him that lot
of pepper and promised another shipment in the spring."

Laughing, Justin gathered her into his arms and kissed her
again. "Do not exhaust yourself, dearling. I will make sure that
Richard proposes your article when we carry the copy of the
charter and the archbishop's letter to the mayor. And that
reminds me that we must go early to bed. I cannot put off my
riding until morning because I must be out of the house before
Lauds."

The words were lightly spoken, both the jest about riding,
which Justin's look and moving hands made plain, and the
advice not to exhaust herself, but Lissa was convinced he knew
she was with child—or hoped she was. The growing urgency of
his caresses stirred her deeply, being to her mind proof that he
desired her for her charms and skill as a lover rather than merely
as a brood mare. Lissa had few doubts on that subject because
Justin had never expressed any impatience about her seeming
barrenness. But after they were married, he had spoken about
children and Lissa was sure he wanted them. Well, so did she,
but not as her only reason for being his wife.

Grateful and excited, Lissa played harder than usual and slept
harder also. Justin was gone when she woke, but she remembered at once what he had said. She lay abed a little longer than
usual, feeling slightly unsettled—not really sick but different
enough to give added strength to her hopes, enough strength
that she was eager to confide in someone and decided to visit
Adela, who had borne several children and would hold her
tongue until Lissa was ready to tell Justin.

She went in the afternoon, when she was reasonably sure Goscelin would be busy in the shop or away from the house and Adela, shopping done, would be at home and at leisure. As she left the house, she gave a thought to Justin's admonition to stay at home or take Dick and Halsig with her, but that had been while he was away. There had been no disturbances in the city; indeed, it was quieter than before the baron's armed men had come, and when she asked Paul about Halsig and Dick, she learned that Justin had taken them with him and bade Mary go home.

Lissa was sure Justin would not have done that if he felt there was any danger. Still, she decided to take Witta with her, and when she went to get him from the workroom, Oliva asked what she should do with the extra food she had bought to feed Mary and the men.

"Pack it up," she said. "Witta can take it to Sir Justin's house on the way to Goscelin's."

That took a little time and Lissa was growing impatient to share her hope, so when she and Witta came to the turning of Soper Lane into the Mercery, she told the boy to deliver his parcel to Mary while she walked on ahead to Goscelin's house. She did not order him to make haste. Because she had been confined to the house, Witta had been kept harder at work than usual. She was walking along the Cordwainery, smiling to herself, imagining the pleasure he would have dawdling through the market and only getting to Goscelin's house when he thought she was about to leave, when she heard running footsteps and then a man took her arm and spoke her name.

She turned, her breath catching in fear for Justin. "Yes?"

"Lady Margaret de Vesci begs you to come to her," the man said.

Lissa did not recognize him. He still held her arm, but looked worried, almost frightened, and he was carrying a bundle. "Come to Lady Margaret now?" she asked.

Lissa was annoyed, both by the fright she had been given and because she wanted to visit Adela. She was about to refuse flatly, and then recalled her last meeting with Lady Margaret. She remembered the kind concern over her bruises and the frightened, bitter eyes.

"Please, mistress," the man said. "It is very important. I ran after you all the way from your house."

That could not be literally true; if he had run, he would have caught up with her long before. Lissa assumed, however, that the exaggeration meant that his mistress was in a bad mood and would punish him if she did not come.

"Very well," she said, "but Lady Margaret's house is too far for me to walk. I must first—"

"She is here, mistress." He waved toward the Chepe.

Much better. If Lady Margaret was shopping, Lissa thought, she could accept her order and still see Adela after all. "Quickly, then," she said, and followed eagerly when the man led her across the market and turned into the narrow street that led to Honey Lane. He stopped suddenly and gestured her forward. Lissa walked around him, then hesitated when she saw a tall gate and empty yard before her, but she had no time to ask a question. A hard hand came over her mouth, cutting off speech, and she was thrust hard into the yard and forced flat against the wall, the man's full weight holding her so that she could not move at all.

"Be quiet," he whispered. "You will not be hurt."

Since she had little choice anyway, Lissa stood still and made no attempt to cry out, hoping her quiescence would delude her captor into releasing her. She intended to shriek as loud as she could the minute his hand relaxed its grip, but she was not given the chance. A cloth was pushed up under the muffling hand and tied tight before she could spit it out. In another moment the man's shoulder was pressed so hard against her upper back that she would have shrieked with pain if she could, but the torture did not last long. He reached around, seized one hand and then the other, and tied them behind her. He eased his weight then, turning her toward him.

"I do not want to hurt you," he whispered, "but I will put you to sleep with this"—he held up his fist—"if you try to escape me."

Lissa would still have tried to run; she knew she need only reach the market and there would be too many witnesses for him to drag her away, but he never let go. His grip was too strong for her to break with her arms bound, even though he was holding her with only one hand while he picked up the

bundle he had dropped. She tried once to kick him, when he
bent to shake it out, but he only stood up and drew a heavy
hooded robe over her, pulling the hood so far forward that she
could see only the ground at her feet and knew her face was
hidden.

"Now walk," he said.

Hope flickered up in Lissa again. If he took her to the market,
she would hear although she could not see, and she would
struggle in his grip. Surely someone would ask why, or she
might be able to throw back the hood and show her gagged
mouth. But he did not take her that way. He held her arm
through the sleeve of the robe. They went farther up the lane,
then past a house, through a garden, and on into what seemed
open common fields. He stopped and pushed her to the ground,
tied her feet, and rolled her, not ungently, against something
hard, a fallen log, she thought. Then he passed a rope through
the sleeve, through her tied arms, and attached it somewhere
she could not see.

"I will not leave you long," he said. "I must get the horses."

Chapter 32

⤲⤳

WHEN THE HOOD WAS FINALLY LIFTED FROM LISSA'S HEAD, SHE WAS so astonished by whom she saw that she almost forgot hours of discomfort and alternating rage and fear. She was so stunned she hardly felt the gag being removed and her hands untied, and she stared speechlessly at Robert FitzWalter, not even lifting her slightly numbed hands to her lap. If she had not been seated on a bench, she might have fallen down in amazement.

"I hope you were not hurt, mistress," he said in a calm, polite voice. "I gave order that you not be harmed, and frightened as little as possible."

"If you did not wish to hurt or frighten me, why did you simply not send a message that you wished to speak to me?" Lissa said, her astonishment fortunately still superseding all other emotion.

If it had not, she would either have fallen on the ground screaming in senseless, ungovernable terror or have leapt at him to scratch out his eyes because rage, too, was roiling under her surprise. She did not recognize her own voice, faint and creaky from being gagged and thirsty.

"Unfortunately I did not wish anyone to know I needed to speak to you," FitzWalter said. He saw her breath draw in and her eyes grow blank with terror, and he shook his head and added quickly, "I do not wish to hurt you or kill you. If you tell me what I wish to know, you will not be harmed at all, but I may need to hide you until my purpose is accomplished. That is why you were taken in secret."

Lord Robert watched her face. He wanted her to be afraid but not without hope. His opinion of women was low enough that he expected her to believe the lie and not be clever enough to realize that he would not take the chance of freeing her. He also had reason to believe that too much fear only made a woman hysterical, unable to think or answer questions, no matter how much she wanted to. For the same reason, torture was useless. A woman would scream anything to save herself pain, a new lie for each pang, so fast to find one that would please him that he would never know what the truth was. Later, if this one refused to speak, he could slap her a few times, but for now he wanted her eager to please him.

"But what can I tell you?" she whispered. "I have no secrets, except those in my receipt book, and you surely cannot mean that?"

FitzWalter gestured, and the man who had captured her came into the lighted area. "Bring her some watered wine," he said, and then leaned back and waited until the cup was put into her hand and she had sipped from it.

"Please," Lissa said quickly, "may I have something to eat? I am very hungry."

She had not been fooled by FitzWalter's lie; Lissa knew that, having taken her, he would not dare let her go to accuse him. She, however, had a hope about which FitzWalter knew nothing. The man who took her might have known Witta was with her when she left the house, but he could not know the boy was to meet her at Goscelin's. When Witta got there and discovered she had never arrived, surely he would run home and tell Paul, and Paul would tell Justin—and Justin would crack London open like an egg seeking her. It was a tiny hope, perhaps, but it was a real hope. If she could only stay alive until

Justin could find her—only discover what Lord Robert really wanted and seem about to give it if only he tried a little longer.

"Get Mistress— What is your name?"

"Heloise," Lissa said, thinking the name she hated was good enough for this man.

"Get Mistress Heloise something to eat," FitzWalter said.

Lissa heard a door open and close, and FitzWalter turned to her again. "No," he said, "I am not interested in your receipt book. Your husband had a secret—"

"Justin?" Lissa caught herself as she swayed and almost fell off the bench. Liquid slopped out of the cup, staining the thick robe she was still wearing, and she put the cup down beside her and brushed distractedly at the mark.

"No," FitzWalter said. "Not Sir Justin. Peter de Flael."

Lissa's hands flew up to smother the scream that was choking her. She had closed her eyes instinctively to shut out FitzWalter's face as he spoke Peter's name, but that only brought back an image of her first husband's broken body. She groped for the cup of wine, her eyes blind, nearly spilling what was left in it when she brushed it to the edge of the bench with her fingers, allowing herself then a tiny cry of distress, finally bending over to lift the cup in both shaking hands and sip. Her mind fled the pursuing monster of fear. If she allowed it to catch her, she would scream out the truth—butcher! murderer!—and be killed at once.

"I did not kill Flael," FitzWalter said, as if he had read her mind. "I did not intend for him to die—it was the last thing I desired. I only wanted to ask him a question, and I never got to ask it. He just died."

Lissa knew suddenly that was true. Of course it was true; he had just said Peter had had a secret, and Peter had died before he could tell it. The burns and cuts and breaking—that had all been done after Peter was dead; Justin had told her that.

"My lord," Lissa began, but the door opened and he lifted a hand to silence her.

The man who had captured her came in and set a platter beside Lissa on the bench. Cheese and bread and some kind of cold pasty—a good meal. Her gorge rose and she stared down at the food, knowing she would have to eat some of it; she had said she was very hungry. To give herself another moment, she held out her empty cup mutely, and the man took it and filled it. When he handed it back, FitzWalter gestured and the door opened and closed again.

Lissa said, "I will tell you gladly anything I know about Peter or his business and about our marriage—"

"I have not quite time enough for that," FitzWalter said. "Instead, let me tell you what *I* know while you eat. Then you can tell me what might pertain to my tale."

Ice had run in Lissa's body instead of blood when FitzWalter said he had not enough time. She thought he would ask a single question and, when she could not answer, order her killed, but she fought down the fear again. If he intended that, why bother having this man bring so substantial a meal? And the last statement eased her terror by implying that he would let her search her memories at length.

He began with Flael's apprentice, bitter because the master preferred his sons even though their skills were not as great as his, who decided to sell his master's sin to the highest bidder.

"Flael's sin?" Lissa repeated, having become so interested that her fear diminished and she began to nibble at the pasty without even realizing it.

"Flael was a favorite of King John," FitzWalter said, and Lissa nodded, remembering the design for cup and plate among Peter's records. "He designed and cast the king's privy seal—but he cast *two*."

"A counterfeit seal," Lissa breathed, and then drew a sharp breath in when she remembered herself saying to Justin that whoever wrecked Peter's house had been looking for something small.

"You remember something?" FitzWalter asked eagerly, not mistaking the in-drawn breath.

"Yes," Lissa replied at once, "but I do not think it is the answer you want." And she told him what she had been thinking, glad to seem willing to please him. "I do not think they found it." She paused, fearing to suggest something that would make her useless, but could not believe he would not know already and went on to remind him about how Peter's sons had fled. "If they took it—"

"No," he said. "Your father found the sons in France, but they knew only that their father had made the seal and swore he had given it to William Bowles, as agreed. It was because they knew no more that they fled when they saw . . . I am sorry about that, but a warning was necessary."

The words were rote, spoken for propriety's sake or to soothe her. Lissa heard no real regret in them, but she pushed away the memory they evoked, fleeing terror, which could do her no good. She needed time, and to gain time she must make FitzWalter hope that something would jog a memory in her that would let him find what he desired.

"But you think Peter did not give the seal to my father at our wedding—that was the arrangement, I am sure, though I was not told."

FitzWalter nodded agreement. To his mind no one ever told a woman anything, but sometimes because they were dreadful sneaks, they saw things or their nasty, sly minds came up with thoughts no man would have.

"I know Flael did not give your father the seal then. The box that was supposed to hold it was passed directly to Hubert, and he brought it directly to me, still sealed in waxed cords. It contained a very lovely medallion—but not King John's privy seal." He paused and fixed Lissa with eyes that were suddenly alive with hate and pain, the first real emotion she had seen. "Where is it?" he roared. "I need it *now*. That accursed archbishop will persuade the others, fools that they are, to make peace with the king—as if John would ever keep a bargain. I must prove, with letters written under his own privy seal, that John intends death and ruin to every man who stood against him . . ."

Lissa dropped the piece of pasty she was holding and covered her ears, beginning to weep aloud. Whatever small hope she had of surviving was being ripped away with each word FitzWalter said. If Justin came for her, Lord Robert would kill them both now that he had spoken aloud this treason.

"You stupid bitch," he bellowed, "think!"

But thought was finally beyond Lissa. Only fear and death remained, and she tilted on the bench, putting her hands out weakly as she toppled to the floor.

Witta had not been told to hurry and knew his mistress well enough to be sure she would not punish him for being late when he reminded her of that. He thrust his bundle at Mary and rushed off to the market where he spent a most delightful afternoon, actually purchasing a farthing whistle on which he could play simple tunes. The glare of the westering sun low in his eyes warned him that he must go. Mistress Lissa was fair, but her hand was heavy when she felt advantage had been taken. He ran quickly to Goscelin's house to Ebba, who looked hard but had a soft spot for boys, and begged her not to tell Lissa how late he was in coming.

"You little devil," Ebba said, "you're going to get your hide lifted. You've forgot where Mistress Lissa said she was going. She never came here."

For a moment Witta stared blankly, searching his memory, but he was certain. "She *did* say Mistress Adela," he insisted. "Maybe you didn't see her come. Ask for me."

Ebba shrugged. It seemed an odd mistake for the boy to make, and it was possible she had been busy or out of the house. She went through the shop quietly and up to the solar, but Mistress Adela was sitting alone by the window at her embroidery frame and denied Lissa had been there at any time when Ebba asked. She patted Witta, who looked frightened when she told him, and assured him his punishment would soon be over, since Lissa was a good mistress. But all he said was that he was not wrong.

Witta ran home as quickly as he could, reaching the house just when Paul, with Oliva and Ninias to help, was taking in the counter. He asked for Lissa, and Paul looked at him in surprise. "You were with her, not me," he said.

"No, no, I wasn't," Witta cried, then lowered his voice as Paul gestured at the window above, indicating that Sir Justin was home and might be asleep. "Mistress Lissa told me to bring the food to Mary—Oliva knows about that—and said she would walk ahead to Mistress Adela's house. But she never came to Mistress Adela. Ebba went up and asked, and she hadn't been. I—I did look around in the market, but Mistress Lissa didn't say to hurry. Where is she?"

Paul stared blankly at the boy and then said in a harsh whisper, "Go in and be quiet. If there is cleaning to do in the workroom, do that. Mistress Lissa will come home when she likes. Do not ask so many questions."

The journeyman felt sick. He could have sworn that Lissa adored her husband, and they had been married only six months. Yet she was already making up visits to hide time spent elsewhere. Plainly she had expected Witta to spend more time in the market, and she would come back furious that her deceit was uncovered. Sir Justin would kill her. How could she be such a fool as to trifle with that man?

As the train of thought went through Paul's mind, he knew it was false. Mistress Lissa was no liar and no fool. She could have changed her mind and gone elsewhere, but not without leaving a message for Witta at Goscelin's. Pushing Ninias out of his way in sudden panic, Paul ran up the stairs, calling out for Sir Justin.

He came from the bedchamber with sleep-drugged eyes and tousled curls, but when he saw Paul's face his eyes swept the room, judged the time by the light, then came back to Paul filled with fear, and he cried, "Lissa?"

"I—she did not come home with Witta. I—I mean, she never came to Goscelin's house where she said—" Paul stopped, choking, terrified by the expression on Justin's face, the hand he was lifting, fearing that the man would kill him in his rage. He tried to say that Lissa would not have betrayed him, but fortunately no sound came out, for in the next minute it was plain that Justin did not suspect his wife.

"Who has her?" he muttered. "Who needs to bind me to his will?"

The hand Paul had been flinching from fell on his shoulder, but not to harm. It trembled so that Paul put out both hands, fearing Justin would collapse. He did not, and in a moment his hand steadied and he looked at Paul with clear eyes.

"Send both boys up to me," Justin said. "As soon as you have told them, go to my cousins—take the mare, you will be quicker—and bid them come to me."

Justin saw the light of relief come into Paul's face and it took all the strength he had not to burst into tears as the young man flew out of the chamber and down the stairs to do his bidding. Paul was now certain that all would be well. Justin's stern face and calm voice had solved all his problems, as they had solved the problems of many victims and convinced many criminals that all was known and confession the easiest path. Only Justin himself was lost behind the knowing face and clear eyes, uncertain of what to do, terrified, feeling as if he had been struck in the heart and the blood running from him was making him weaker every moment. He heard the thudding of feet on the stair and reached the chair to sit before his knees gave way under him.

Ninias was large-eyed with excitement, but Witta's eyes were red, his face streaked with smeared tears. "Do not weep," Justin snarled at him. "Your mistress will come to no harm, and we will have her back before morning."

The boy's face brightened and he ran forward and kissed Justin's hand. Unable to speak for a moment, Justin laid his other hand on the child's head. His chest hurt and he had to fight a cramp that threatened to bend him double, but when the pain passed he had back his voice.

"Now go back to my house," he said to Witta, "and tell Halsig and Dick to summon every member of the watch—every troop leader to gather his troop—all to be full armed and to come by ones and twos, quietly, not to be seen by the soldiers, to my house. I will be there before full dark to give further orders. Say nothing more than that."

Because he had no idea what more to say. Worse even than the pain in his chest and belly was the strange lightness, emptiness, in his head. He had no idea why he was summoning the watch, no more than he knew what he wanted with Ninias, who was waiting so eagerly, lips parted, for his task. But his mouth opened and he found himself naming five men of the watch and giving the boy direction to their lodgings. "Try the lodgings first," he said, "then the nearest alehouse, then go on to the next man. Finally go to my house and tell Halsig to send those men to me when they come in. Try for Dunstan first."

Justin did not hear or see Ninias run off. The five names had meant nothing when he reeled them off at first; they were simply five men of the watch who were trustworthy and strong, whom he had called on for special duty in the past. When he said Dunstan's name last, he realized they were the five men who had accompanied him to Canterbury. Alone in the solar, he was not ashamed to raise his hands to his head and groan as understanding burst on him.

First, Lissa had not an enemy in the entire world—even Master John and Master Chigwell were now on the best of terms with her—so it was no personal enemy who had taken her. As Justin had known without reasons from the first, he was the cause. But he was no longer the chief hunter of evildoers of London, and no man needed to hold his wife hostage to save himself from the gallows or the headsman's ax. That someone might have killed her in pure revenge, he put aside. She would have been found by now.

All his activities since leaving his position had to do with the charter, but Justin had discovered in a long day's discussion, which included nearly every man of any importance in the city, that beyond small arguments over this or that article, no one opposed the charter. Even Serlo, the mayor appointed by the rebels, wanted the charter. All were eager to welcome Archbishop Langton to London and settle their differences with the king.

Justin stared at the back wall where the open window showed the setting sun staining the clouds red and gold. West. In the west was Baynard's Castle and the one man in London who hated the king beyond reason and did not want the charter affirmed. But what, Justin asked himself, did FitzWalter think he could do to prevent the charter from being accepted? It was the archbishop who would— Justin shuddered. Stephen Langton trusted him. Would the price of Lissa's life be the archbishop's death? Then his blood ran warm again and his eyes lit. If he could get proof of that demand, FitzWalter's own kin would turn on him.

Drawing a breath and unclamping his jaws, Justin reminded himself that Lissa was safe and unhurt. *If* she was safe and unhurt, his purpose was to keep her that way, not to gain vengeance for a few hours of anxiety or to make FitzWalter his enemy for life. What he needed was a weapon against FitzWalter that could be kept secret, to be used only if he or Lissa was threatened or hurt. Hurt . . . weapon . . . knife . . . Hubert! He had the man's knife. He had witnesses to Hubert's attempts on his life. Many could testify that Hubert was FitzWalter's man. There was his weapon.

Supporting himself on the arms of the chair, Justin got to his feet. When he was steady, he lit candles; then he went into the bedchamber and got Lissa's writing desk. He wrote a complete case against FitzWalter for the murder of his agent, William

Bowles, by the hand of his servant, Hubert de Bosco. By the time Richard and Thomas, who had both been home, as tired as he, came riding up, he had added the evidence of Hubert's attempts to silence him by taking his life as well.

Justin told his cousins what had happened in as few words as possible, gave the parchment and FitzWalter's pass, which he had not returned, to Richard, and told him to go out of the city at once. Thomas he bade go into hiding until morning, and his quick-witted cousin named a whore's house that they both knew. Justin nodded. What he had written, he reminded both as he embraced them, was his safety line; he hoped it would be enough to save him. If it was not, they had no obligation to use the information, and certainly not if that use would endanger themselves or the charter.

They were out of the house before the last light had faded from the sky, and Justin breathed a sigh of relief. Richard would have time to get through the gates. Paul came in before he got out of his chair to say that Dunstan was below and to ask what more he could do.

"Help me into my armor," Justin said.

"Let me come with you," Paul begged.

Justin put a hand on his shoulder as he stood up. "I am sorry, you cannot. Someone must be here. The boys are too young and Oliva too timid. If I am mistaken in what I believe and Lissa was taken for some other reason, like ransom, someone must carry that word to me."

There was a brief silence in which Justin's hand closed a little too tight on Paul's shoulder, and Paul knew he had not said *or if her body is found*. He lifted his eyes and asked, "Where?"

"Until full dark, to my house. After that . . . to Baynard's Castle." Paul's eyes widened, but his teeth set a moment later and he nodded, and Justin continued, "Call Dunstan up. I can get into the arming tunic myself."

To the man-at-arms he said, "Put your sword into some kind of pack on your back and put a rag of a tunic over your armor. Then go idle about as close to Baynard's Castle as you can get. I will meet you at the southeast corner by the brush near the riverbank at Compline or a little after. I want to know, if you can find out, how many guards are watching the walls and whether they are on full alert, with extra torches and suchlike."

The next two men who came he gave the same orders, but he had grown too restless to wait longer and told Paul to send the two others after him. Justin went to the shed in the back to saddle Noir himself, shuddering with eagerness one minute and the next telling himself that he would bring the whole rescue to disaster if he was not cautious. He could not afford to draw the attention of the barons' men-at-arms, who had replaced the watch, and he would certainly do so if he tried to move his men through the streets like an army.

Fortunately that idea was still uppermost in his mind when he reached his house. It was so quiet, only dim light showing, that Justin's heart sank; but when he opened the door he found the room so packed with men that he could barely get in, all standing in groups, silent except for the creak of leather as they shifted and, now that he had come, a hissing of whisper. Halsig said the rest were in the kitchen and the yard, that he had ordered two clever men to repeat Justin's words exactly to those who could not hear. Then Justin almost wept because they were all faithful, and the quiet showed they knew their action would be secret and doubtless be a move against the army that held the city.

He told them the truth simply, that he believed but as yet had no proof that FitzWalter had taken his wife hostage to control him. He wished for that reason to enter Baynard's Castle quietly to prove or disprove his point. They were to remember, he told them, that they were not a conquering army; they were still the watch. They were to prevent FitzWalter's men from interfering with him, but not to start any fight, nor to loot, nor to burn. "There is a greater army outside the walls, remember. If you commit outrages, that army might be called in and loosed on the city. If we cause no damage, there will be no trouble and you will have your full day's wages from me for a few hours' work."

"I want my place back," one man muttered. "Can't we be rid of those foreign dogs?"

"God willing," Justin said, "the king and the barons will agree on the charter I brought last night from the archbishop. God willing, if it is signed, the barons will leave the city and take their army with them and you will all have your places back."

"And you to be master again, my lord?" another asked.

"That I do not know. For tonight I am master, so obey me. Halsig, get the captains of the troops in here."

He gave them orders for getting to Baynard's Castle in small groups and waiting there, out of sight, for further orders. He made sure all the group captains knew Dick, who would pass orders from him if Halsig could not, and he felt again as if blood were running out of his heart and he would faint with weakness and impatience. Hardly looking, he designated in which order the troops would leave, lifted a fisted hand in farewell, and went out. Halsig caught him just outside the door and began to talk about tactics.

"What tactics?" Justin said. "I am known to the guards there, and I doubt FitzWalter has informed all his men that he has my wife. I will ask entry for myself and my men, saying I must speak with FitzWalter. The men will be you, Dick, Dunstan, John, and Edgar. As we come in, we will seize the gate—silently if we can, but any way we can. You and Dick will go for the rest of the men and bring them in. I and the others will find Lissa. If I am refused entry will be soon enough to talk tactics."

Lissa found herself alone, crumpled on the floor just as she had fallen. She was not even blessed with a moment of confusion; as her senses returned, so did her memory of her situation. One circumstance alone changed; she had never expected to wake, and she had. Thus, no matter his final intentions toward her, FitzWalter also apparently intended to let her live until he had extracted every bit of information and every idea she had.

Lissa lay quietly on the floor, unmoving except for that first twist of the head that showed FitzWalter's chair to be empty. The other man could have been in the shadows, but he would have spoken. No, she was alone. If someone was looking in on her now and again, let him think her still out of her senses. Every few minutes was that much longer time in which Justin might learn she was missing and begin to search for her. But perhaps she was lying in discomfort for nothing. It must be night by now. Perhaps FitzWalter had gone to bed.

Tears came into her eyes with the thought because it was so lovely and so unlikely. She had heard the mad insistence in FitzWalter's voice when he demanded that she remember about

the seal. She would do her very best. She would tell him
anything and everything that might give him hope that she
would remember more, but what was she to do about the
treason he had spoken in her hearing? Could she pretend the
faint had erased it from her mind? Yes, that would be best. She
could not pretend to be so stupid as not to have understood
him. He might kill her out of hand for being that idiotic.

Lissa had no idea how long she had been lying there when
she heard the latch move, the door creak, and FitzWalter say,
"Pick her up and slap her. That will bring her back."

Since Lissa had no desire to be abused if she could avoid it, by
the time he entered she had turned around and was sitting with
her back against the bench. She was relieved when he gestured
the other man out and closed the door behind him.

"Get up," he said, but he did not shout at her. He sat down
again and waited until she levered herself up onto the bench
before he asked, "Where is the seal Peter de Flael was supposed
to give your father as your bride price?"

Lissa sat gaping with shock, eyes and mouth open, before she
got her mouth closed and swallowed hard. Because her immediate fear had diminished greatly, she had suddenly realized
where the seal might be. The words "bride price" had made
their natural connection in her mind with "bride gift"—the
dolphin necklet. And that brought with it the whole associated
train of thought—her contempt of a client's reject, which meant
Peter cared so little for her that he could not be bothered to
design and make a personal piece, and her wonder that if he
was so indifferent, he should bother to make with his own
hands so elaborate and beautiful a box to hold the gift.

If the seal existed, it must be in the box, which had been
constructed to hold it, not to please her—most likely the box
must have a false bottom and it must be there. The pins holding
the new lining had come through the top of the box—Justin had
pricked his finger on one—but they had not come through the
bottom! She knew that because now she recalled that there were
no bright places to show Paul had filed off the points. Fortunately her thoughts came swiftly and FitzWalter was making
allowance for what he believed was a weak and disordered
state. He did no more in the minute or two Lissa stared and
blinked and swallowed than shift restlessly in his chair.

"I do not know," she croaked as soon as she could find her voice, and then, lying fervently because she knew the moment after she answered his question she would die, she added, "I swear, if I knew I would tell you gladly. I will try to remember whatever I can. You said Peter did not give it to my father at the wedding and his sons did not take it. But Peter has another house near Canterbury. Could it be there?"

"No," FitzWalter said shortly. "Neither he nor his sons left the city after your father spoke to them, and we made sure of anyone else who went there."

"He had a favorite whore," Lissa said. "I do not know her name and Binge is dead, but I am sure some of Peter's friends must know who she is. It was no secret. His sons knew of her."

"Not likely, and if he chose such a keeper, the seal may have been sold and melted, but you are trying. Go on."

"There is another thing you may not know," and Lissa began to tell him about the documents she had found on her father's body concerning the rental of the manor of Red Cliff by one, Amias FitzStephen.

She hesitated when she first said her father's name and shivered, and he interrupted her tale to say, "I did not want him dead either," but she did not find that remark as convincing as when he had said the same thing about Peter. Still, she went on, spinning the tale as long as she could. She had just mentioned the vintner of Bristol when the door slammed open so hard that it crashed against the wall. Lissa leapt to her feet with a cry.

Chapter 33

"WHAT ARE YOU DOING IN LONDON?" FITZWALTER ROARED. "Lissa!"

The second bellow was the most welcome sound Lissa had ever heard in her life. She whirled and ran, was caught and thrust behind a steel-armored body and clung, weeping helplessly, to Justin's back.

"Are you hurt?" he asked.

"No," she sobbed, "no!" The naked sword in Justin's hand was a glare of light in her head, and she knew the outcome of any other answer would be FitzWalter's death.

She almost fell as Justin moved a step forward and was terribly tempted to let him go, knowing that rage had overmastered him for once and he intended to kill. But Lissa had lived too long with hate to let it blind her, and she tightened her grip on her husband and hung back. If Justin killed FitzWalter it would not be a small thing, soon forgotten, like killing Hubert. The death of so great a nobleman could not be kept secret, and though the king might pardon him gladly, Justin would be a target for all FitzWalter's kin and probably for all his friends. To say that would not stop her husband, however; only pride could control the rage that was driving Justin forward.

"Do not kill an unarmed man, Justin," she cried. "You are not so mean of spirit. Do not make yourself as vile as that creature is."

Justin had taken two more steps, seemingly unaware of the pull she was exerting on him, but at those words he stopped and stood swaying.

"In God's name," FitzWalter pleaded, lifting empty hands. "I did your wife no hurt. She is not even bruised. I did not misuse her, did not strike her. When she said she hungered and thirsted, I fed her and gave her drink. Will you kill me for asking her a question?"

"It is true, Justin," Lissa said.

Peering around Justin's back, she saw FitzWalter's pallid face suddenly gleam with sweat as he strained back in his chair. His reaction surprised her because much of the tension had gone out of Justin's body and his sword point was tipping downward. The slight relaxation gave her the courage to sidle out a bit farther, and a glance at Justin's face explained FitzWalter's panic. A smile like that could freeze hell.

"I have a hundred men on your walls and in your castle, FitzWalter," Justin said softly. "And every single man knows that you have abducted my wife. You may be sure that every single man will see her when I bring her out, so there can be no doubt she was your prisoner. There is no way you can find to silence a hundred men. And every one will stand witness to what you have done if she or I should vanish or suffer injury."

"Do not be ridiculous," FitzWalter said. "I have always been your friend."

"So I thought," Justin said and smiled again, making Fitz-Walter swallow hard and Lissa shiver. "And I hope we will continue to be friends. Indeed, I wish to be your friend, and will be—so as long as I am not troubled with arrows from blind windows or knives in the night or sudden troops of drunken brawlers who choose me to prey on. It is only that I have been a little shocked by the seizure of my wife and feel the need to make certain she will not again be troubled by your desire to have any question answered."

"I am not a dog to return to my own vomit," FitzWalter said. "I thought I could learn what I wanted quietly, that she would be at home before you returned to London. I am not such a fool as to play the same trick twice."

"No, but I do not want you to try any new ones, like outright murder—"

"I did not kill Peter de Flael," FitzWalter cried.

Justin blinked, but his ideas were too fixed to alter quickly, and he said, "No, but you did order the death of William Bowles. There is prepared, witnessed, and placed in safe charge—*not* my cousins' charge—a sealed proof of your man Hubert's attempts on my life and the reason for it: your orders for him to murder William Bowles. That will connect well with Lissa's abduction. That will be brought forward if Lissa or I come to harm. Moreover, I have already sent away the man you ordered to take my wife captive. A sworn testimony will be taken from him, and he will be kept safe to speak before a judge—alive and safe, and where you cannot reach him for a long time."

"A long time?" FitzWalter repeated, his mouth relaxing from the snarl in which it had been set. "Then you do not intend to make an accusation against me?"

"Certainly not," Justin said gently. "Would I be so ungracious as to accuse a friend of crimes that would make him a laughingstock among his peers—a great nobleman who stooped to murder an apothecary and abduct his daughter? I am only a small man, but I shudder at the thought of the whispers and laughter behind lifted hands."

Lissa made a small gasping sound, half sob, half hysterical giggle, almost smothered in the hands she had pressed against her lips. FitzWalter's eyes flicked to her, and there was a terrible bleakness in them when he looked back at Justin. She caught a shaken breath, marveling at Justin's foresight, feeling a loosening of the knot of terror that had been inside her even after he had come. FitzWalter was beaten, at least for a time. From what Justin had told her, he had too much experience of half-hidden sneers and jests at his expense. Until he could find a way to cancel Justin's threat, he would not move against them.

"No, my lord," Justin went on, catching Lissa in his left arm and drawing her close. "I do not intend, so long as there is no

threat against my wife or myself, to carry a grudge, and hope
you will not. My men and I will leave Baynard's Castle, to which
no damage has been done, as quietly as we came in, merely
locking you into this chamber. In the morning your steward,
who will accompany my men when they leave, will be released
and will, in turn, release you. If you cry attack, I will show
cause. If you do not, this will soon be forgotten."

"How did you know I had her?" FitzWalter cried.

"Hubert," Justin answered flatly, and without explaining
further or realizing that he completely misled FitzWalter, he
backed up the few steps he had taken into the room, drawing
Lissa with him, and shut the door. Halsig and Dunstan were
waiting with a wedge to jam the latch and a plank of wood to
fasten across the door.

"I will take her home now," Justin said to Halsig. "Keep to the
plan for getting the men out without trouble, and have a watch
set on my house and Lissa's. Let the steward go only after the
other man is well out of the city."

Justin had been holding Lissa all the time he spoke and now
bent his head and asked her, "Shall I carry you, dearling? There
is a long flight of steps."

Lissa remembered stumbling down them on her way in and
how it had frightened her to go under the earth. "No, I can
walk," she said, "but where are we?"

"In the bottom of the old donjon of Baynard's Castle. The
castle itself was pulled down by the king, but I guess FitzWalter
cleared this as a convenient place to ask questions and keep
prisoners."

He pulled her tighter against him, recalling what he thought
he would find when the steward had been persuaded—a little
forcibly—to tell him where FitzWalter was. His surprise and
relief at discovering that pleasant furnished chamber separated
off from a stinking, rat-infested prison with a rack and other
instruments of torture as centerpiece had been only a degree
less than that of seeing Lissa calmly sitting on a bench and
talking about the vintner of Bristol.

"Are you truly unhurt?" he asked, his voice rough, holding
her even harder.

"Oh yes, beloved, but"—Lissa giggled weakly—"you are
going to break my ribs if you squeeze me any more." But she

shivered as he dropped his arm remorsefully, and cried softly, "No, do not let me go altogether."

"Are you sure you can climb up?" Justin asked, pausing at the foot of the steps.

"That—yes. What FitzWalter said about doing me no hurt was true," Lissa assured him. "But Justin, even what you have readied against him will not hold him from us long."

"You are too much affrighted," he soothed, turning her to face him and kissing her. "Because he did not hurt you, his crime is not so great that he should fear me—"

"Yes, yes, it is," Lissa insisted. "You must listen to me, Justin. I am not bewildered with fear—or, yes, I am, but with good cause, not simple weakness. Did you not hear him deny having killed Peter de Flael? Did you not wonder why? No one ever suspected him of that."

Justin blinked at her. He had heard FitzWalter with his ears, but not with his mind. "You mean he really was questioning you," he said, then continued hurriedly, "No, do not tell me now. Take off that robe so I can show you to my men. Then we will go home. You can tell me on the way."

When they came up, Justin called for torches and cried aloud that here was his wife, safe, unharmed, not shamed or soiled, only taken as hostage—for what he did not explain. But when he said hostage, Lissa drew a sudden deep breath as the last piece of the puzzle of why Peter had married her fell into place. FitzWalter's questions had showed her a probable answer to why Peter had made the box. Now she realized that though she had not been hostage to FitzWalter, she had been to Peter. She almost laughed, but tears stung her eyes because Peter really had been a good man. He loved his sons, so when he needed a hold on her father—to be sure William Bowles would not take the seal and then betray its maker by running with it to the king—he had married her. Peter believed that William would do nothing that could hurt his daughter and thus would not betray her husband.

Lissa shuddered and Justin hastily finished what he was saying and murmured that they would soon be home. Then he mounted Noir, and Dick lifted her to be carried in his arms before him in the saddle. She could not stop shaking, and Justin asked for the robe she had shed to wrap around her. She did not bother to protest she was not cold, only clung to Justin and in a whisper told the tale of the counterfeit seal and how FitzWalter wanted to use it, ending, "With such knowledge, he cannot let us live."

"That is dangerous indeed," Justin said, but calmly. "Though not so bad as you think, my love, because FitzWalter is already so deep in treason. Do you not see that his pardon, if peace is achieved, must read most generally 'for all past acts that might be claimed offenses' or some such phrase and would excuse him for any crime at all. Still, I pray you are right and that we find the seal where you say it must be."

"You *pray* we find it?" Lissa repeated faintly. "But then we will be neck-deep in treason ourselves."

"Well, it will be a delicate balancing act," Justin admitted, "but if I can find a way to return the seal to the king publicly, we will be rid of FitzWalter. And John will remember who made the counterfeit seal, so the treason will fall on Flael, who is already dead and beyond King John's vengeance."

They came to the house then, which was blazing with light at every window, and before Justin could say more the door opened and Paul and Oliva came running out with the boys hard on their heels, all crying questions. Lissa was lifted down and hugged and cried over until, despite her exhaustion and fear, she began to laugh in the midst of her assurances that she was well and unhurt. The laughter did more to reassure her servants than all her words, and they at last made room for Justin to dismount. To be rid of them, Lissa set them tasks: Oliva to bring food and drink to the solar, Paul to take Noir to the stable, the boys to douse the torches and candles and then to go to bed.

At last she was in her bedchamber, pulling the box from her chest and watching with her breath catching as Justin pried and pried at the base. They were interrupted once when Oliva came up with the food. Justin went into the solar to take it from her. He said he would carry it in to Lissa, thanked Oliva, and told her to go to bed, that the clearing up could wait until morning. He dumped the platter on the bed and shook the box vengefully.

"I will have to break it," he said.

"Break it! Break it!" Lissa urged. "Only let us see if I am right or wrong."

With a grimace for the ruin of beauty, Justin hammered his heaviest hunting knife into the center of the base at an angle and levered up. Wood splintered, nothing but wood. He looked at Lissa and shrugged. For a moment she just stared, but then she said, "You will have to get the whole base off and break it in pieces. Peter would not put the seal in the middle; that is too obvious, once one thinks of the box as a hiding place."

"Clever, was he?" Justin remarked.

"I did not know him very well," she reminded him, "but he was successful, and he must have been angry and desperate when he decided to hide the seal—"

Lissa stopped speaking as the point of Justin's knife suddenly sank more easily into the wood he was probing. He pried and wood splintered again, but this time a cavity was exposed. No golden gleam showed though, only an ugly gray mass. "What in the world—" Lissa began.

"Wax." Justin's voice held enormous satisfaction. "Flael knew what he was doing. He half filled the hole with wax, then wrapped the seal and put it in, then poured in wax until the hole was full. Maybe he had to wait until it cooled and shrank and fill again, but the wax would stick to the wood and hold everything firm."

He probed around the sides of the gray mass, freeing the wax from the wood, and then lifted. Lissa helped him break the bulk of the wax away, but when the oiled silk wrapping was exposed, she withdrew, reluctant to touch the seal. Justin was extraordinarily careful too, she noted, trying to disturb the wax-sealed folds of the cloth as little as possible. He found an edge finally and lifted that and his breath hissed in. Lissa came and looked over his shoulder, shuddering and drawing back again as she caught a glimpse of the two lions passant. Without touching the seal at all, Justin dropped the wax-flecked cloth over it again and stood looking at his hand as if he had discovered an adder sitting in it.

"It is the king's privy seal," he said at last. "I did not really believe it." Lissa bit her lips and clasped her hands tightly together, fighting tears as Justin drew a long breath. Then he said, "Bring me a large piece of cloth, anything large enough to make into a gown."

When she took a length of fabric from the chest, he bade her unfold it to the center, laid the other cloth with its fateful burden within, and refolded it on the same creases. He nodded at her, and she put it back from where she had taken it. Without being told, she wrapped the jewelry Justin had given her in a scarf and laid that in the chest, setting Peter's box atop it. The box would no longer hold anything, but its top was intact and if Oliva should open the chest, everything would look normal. Meanwhile, Justin had gathered up all the splinters of wood and had thrown them on the fire.

"There is no way I can reach the king just now," he told Lissa, taking her in his arms, "but the archbishop will come tomorrow or the next day. I do not know what to tell him—"

"Do not think about it now," Lissa begged. "If you can eat some of that food, eat. If not, put it aside. Come to bed, Justin. I cannot bear any more."

Her voice was flat and careful and she helped her husband unarm with outward calm, but she wept hysterically when she was safe in his arms, a bursting of the dam that had held back terror until it was safe to let it overwhelm her. Justin stroked her hair and kissed her wet cheeks and murmured comfort as her mother might have done—except that after a while as the tears relieved her pent-up emotions, Lissa became aware of a pressure on her belly that no woman could have exerted. She had been aware of it for some time, but so gentle and tender were Justin's caresses that no association with desire had entered her mind.

Once the thought of coupling came to Lissa, it was like a ravening flame. Justin gasped with surprise as she pushed him onto his back and mounted him; he was more bewildered than excited, his reaction having been mostly physical, a warm pleasure below the surface of his thoughts, which were solely of comforting his wife because she was still crying hard. However, he certainly made no objection, letting her have her way in everything, continuing, in fact, to stroke her hair and arms and back rather than playing with her breasts or thighs. Oddly, Lissa found that peculiarly exciting at the moment and when he arched upward, whispering, "Careful, go slow. I cannot hold for long," she replied, "Come, then. Come with me," and let her own joy overcome her.

She slept then without even rolling off him. In the morning

when Lissa woke she remembered that and wondered how Justin had managed to dismount her without waking her. The amusement slipped away as all her memories came sharp and clear. She felt queasy again too, and swallowed hard fighting it because Justin was still in bed beside her and she could not tell him now and burden him with another worry—the fate of their unborn child if they should be accused of treason. How could they prove that she had not found the seal soon after Peter's death?

Over breakfast, which Lissa managed to eat after she made an excuse to run down to the shop and dose herself with one of her own remedies for nausea, she asked Justin the question. He smiled and said, "We can tell the truth about that." And when she riposted, "Can we? And how do I explain why I suddenly broke open Peter's box?" he shrugged and told her he would find an answer and she should dismiss "that object" from her mind.

It was unlike Justin to deny Lissa her share of any problem, and she understood at once that behind the easy smile and confident lift of shoulder there was a worry as deep and seemingly as insoluble as her own. She said no more, knowing it was stupid to nag at Justin who was doubtless already trying as hard as he could to find an answer. By midmorning she had reason to hope she could soon shed the weight that lay on her spirit because Justin was summoned to the bishop of Westminster's inn where the archbishop had taken lodging.

Lissa assumed that Justin would transfer the burden of the seal to the archbishop and waited for a message to send it or bring it herself. None came, nor did Justin, but he had taken ten armed men with him—another ten, led by Dick, guarded the house—so when he sent a message that he would not be home for dinner she did not worry. She reminded herself that the archbishop must have other business; after all, he had not known about the seal when he summoned Justin. Thus she managed to hold on to hope until Justin returned at dusk, seeming to have forgotten the matter of the seal completely in his absorption with the charter—which she had forgotten as completely, her mind going around like a millstone with worry for grain.

The barons, mayor, and council of London had spent the day in presenting to the archbishop new articles and other changes in the articles already written. "We will be at it a day or two more," Justin said, and Lissa could read the excitement and enthusiasm beneath his surface calm and tiredness. "But the barons have made no demand that is unreasonable, and messengers have already gone to William Marshal asking him to propose to the king a meeting on the fifteenth of this month in the field called Runnymede that lies midway between Staines and Windsor."

"A fortnight hence," Lissa said. "Do you think it would be better—" She was going to ask whether they should try to get rid of the seal before or after the signing of the charter, but she never got the chance.

"You need not fear for your standard of measure," Justin interrupted, laughing and stretching, then dropping into his chair. "That is already written in, and so is an article that confirms to London all its liberties and free customs by land and water; and all towns and cities are confirmed of their rights and liberties. Merchants are protected too, guaranteed safe and secure exit and entry in England, except those with whose nation we are at war. Oh, and the court of common pleas is to be fixed, so one need not chase the king for months or years while a case is pending."

"Was FitzWalter there?" Lissa asked, unwilling to spoil her husband's pleasure but seeking some reassurance.

Justin laughed aloud again. "Yes, he was. We were very polite to each other, and he looked at me very strangely when I pressed a point in his favor with my cousin, and when Thomas would not, seconded its presentation to the archbishop myself. Fair is fair, it was a most reasonable point."

He proceeded to tell Lissa all about it—something about scutage—but although she kept her eyes fixed on him and nodded from time to time when his voice rose as if in question, she heard and understood little. All that was clear to her was that the charter had taken precedence over their personal need in Justin's mind. Lissa was ready to acknowledge that the charter was of paramount importance to the realm, but private necessities must also be considered.

A battle raged in her breast between blaming Justin bitterly for leaving her lonely and frightened to bear the burden of their personal problem and the satisfied feeling that being a noble martyr brings. He talked all the while they ate their evening meal, and on into the evening, and until she got his clothes off—no easy task when he kept breaking away to walk around the room and gesticulate his hope and enthusiasm—and then he fell into bed and into sleep in the same moment.

Lissa stood looking down at her husband, strongly tempted to dig the seal out of the chest and shove it in his slightly open mouth to choke him. Then she sighed and smiled. Lips parted, hard eyes closed, curls tumbled from pulling off his clothing, he looked like a little boy who had dropped asleep after a busy day's play. Then her eyes passed over him and she turned to stare at the chest. It was not only Justin whose full attention would be fixed on the rewriting of the charter for the next fortnight. Even FitzWalter would have no time for hate or revenge.

There would be more than the articles of the charter to discuss too. If the charter was to be signed at the meeting at Runnymede, there would be much ceremony—pardons and pleas would be heard or at least presented. Certainly there could be no safer time to give back the king's seal than when he had just signed a charter guaranteeing the liberties of his subjects. And Justin would listen to her once everything was agreed. Now all she needed was a believable tale to tell.

The first part came easily; she had collected some money from the small estate near Canterbury and had decided to use it to repair Peter's house, which would bring in a good rental. That much was true too. But how could it be possible that the search, which had virtually destroyed the London house, had not uncovered the hiding place of the seal?

Lissa got into bed and lay awake a long time, moving through Peter's house in her mind from the bedchamber at the top through the solar, down the stairs, into the shop, into the workroom. For each room she tried to recall whether there could be any place left in which the seal could be hidden. The searchers had been too thorough, and how to explain the wax? With the word, an image came to her mind. She dared not get out of bed for fear of waking Justin, but she prayed softly and fervently, weeping a little in her earnestness.

When Lissa woke the next morning and found Justin gone, she forgave him everything and blessed him for being out of her way. Intent on carrying out the last thought she had had before sleeping the night before, she dressed and ate, untroubled by nausea. Accompanied by Dick and eight of the other ten men, Lissa went first to mass and gave the surprised and delighted priest a most generous donation of incense and tall scented candles. He blessed her and, still puzzled, blessed her "new endeavor" at her request.

Her next stop was Justin's house, where she thanked God for Halsig, who asked no questions and handed over the keys to Peter's house, which were stored in a chest with evidence of finished cases. There was a row of similar chests in the lower chamber of Justin's house, and Lissa's thoughts were momentarily diverted from the hope and worry that gnawed at her. The chests had been left with Justin after he resigned his place not only by Roger FitzAdam but by the new mayor also. Why? Because there was nowhere else to store them? Nonsense. Far more likely they had been left because both the old mayor and the new one and aldermen expected that Justin would soon be in office again. Another mingled hope and pain. Lissa was proud of the need and trust the great men of the city all felt for Justin and she knew how much he missed his work, but it was dangerous work and she feared for him also.

Even that idea could not divert Lissa long, however, and she hurried on to Peter's house. In the workroom, she stood frozen, hardly breathing with relief at finding scattered over the floor the large blocks of wax that had been used in making molds. Her memory had not failed her. Calm now, she picked her way through the debris into the shop.

Having looked around carefully, with no haste, she remarked to Dick that the roof and walls were sound and the house well worth repair. Then she bade him find men to clear the debris, explaining blandly that it was stupid to leave a fine London property an empty ruin. She spent some hours giving the workmen instructions and remained to watch them begin their work, choosing this and that undamaged item to take home with her—including, from the workroom, some pots, a large kettle, and several sacks filled with the blocks of wax.

At home, she told Oliva to place the wax and kettle somewhere handy. "Tomorrow or the next day, according as I have the time, we will make scented candles. There is no reason why all that good wax should go to waste."

"Such big blocks will take a long time to melt," Witta said, removing his curious nose from one of the sacks.

"We will break them up, silly," Lissa replied, grinning at him. "And since you are so wise, you can begin now. You will enjoy it. You can destroy something without a word of blame for once. Fill the kettle almost to the rim. The wax will shrink as it melts."

For the next week, she attended to her business and acted as if she had forgotten about the wax. No one reminded her. June was not the best time to make candles. In winter there was some compensation in the warmth for being burned with hot wax and having to breathe the stink. One or two scented candles alight gave a delightful savor to a chamber; a kettle full of the stuff could knock one flat on one's back.

Lissa hardly saw Justin; he was always gone before she woke in the morning and not home until after dark, but she was not really sorry. She found herself extraordinarily sleepy, dropping off if she sat down for a few minutes in the middle of the day. That had driven her to pay a visit to Adela, although between the seal in the chest and the wax waiting for the moment she felt would be right to make her "discovery," she hated to leave the house. Sleepiness was normal, Adela said, having embraced her with joy; in later months she would make up for her present lazy moments by being too eager to work and play.

On the evening of 9 June, Lissa had still not "found" the seal, but Justin had come home early. She had been reluctant at first to tell him what she planned—he was so accursedly honest— but she realized the device was unworkable without him. A tiny lingering reluctance made her hesitate when she first accompanied him up from the shop to their chamber, and as he changed into a more comfortable gown, Justin began to talk about the charter.

He said he was now certain it would be signed, and that hopeful news fixed Lissa's attention enough to let her put off what she had to say. There had been doubts at first, she knew. Messengers had come from the king with objections and caveats, but most, to the surprise of all, had been reasonable and compromises had been found. Now Justin told her the document returned to John for consideration had come back again with complaints, but fewer and milder. Those were being worked over and would not be sticking points for anyone.

"Then we will have peace?" Lissa asked.

"No," Justin said, and sighed. "The king will sign, and there are safeguards that should force him to keep his promises—but he is cleverer at slipping out of an oath than any other man alive. Worse yet, FitzWalter says much too little and his close friends, de Quincy and Vesci, are also too quiet. Mostly it is the neutral men, those who were never part of the rebellion at all, who are forming this charter. The real rebels are only waiting until the king sends away his mercenaries—that is a principal part of the agreement, and John will have to do that much or the moderates will desert him—to break out into war again."

Lissa stared at her husband, hardly knowing what to say next. He seemed only mildly disappointed at what appeared to her the foundering of all his hopes. "But then, why bother?" she asked.

"Because I do not believe the rebels can win. Once John signs the charter, the neutral barons will support him and the rebellion will die—but the charter will be there. John will try to squirm out of it, and he will escape many of the restrictions, I am sure. But King John is no longer young. And the charter will be there, and the barons will demand that the new king swear to it. As each year passes, it will become a firmer part of our law. So, it is worth having."

"Yes," Lissa agreed, thinking of the life within her that would benefit in the future. "It is surely worth having." But then her overriding worry came back, and she sighed gently and said, "And I do not wish to remind you of trouble, but there is that accursed seal—"

"I have given it some thought," Justin said quickly. "But to speak the truth, I have not found an answer. All I can offer is to bring the true tale to the archbishop and ask his help and advice."

"Ask the archbishop for help and advice, yes, but you cannot tell him the truth, Justin. Everyone will suspect that I knew all the time where it was, that I seduced the secret out of Peter—old man, young wife. Perhaps some will believe I did not ask for the knowledge and I hid the seal out of fear, but there will be those, including no doubt FitzWalter and the king, who will wonder if I used it. Suspicion might even fall onto Gamel and Gerbod. No. You must not tell the truth."

"I am not a liar," Justin said.

"Nor I," Lissa cried, "but I will lie about this!"

Justin stared at her and then nodded. "I too," he admitted, "only I am a very bad liar, and I cannot think of a lie to tell."

Then she told him about the blocks of wax and the plan for making candles and for "finding" the seal in one of the blocks. And Justin rose and came to her chair, lifted her into his arms, and kissed her. His eyes were gleaming and his mouth relaxed.

"Beloved," he said, "you have saved us. That is truly a device a goldsmith might use to hide something and one that the cleverest searcher would not think of. Best of all, it is so close to what happened that the tale is not really a lie at all."

He tugged her forward by the hand, pulling her to his chair so that he could lift her up on his lap. "I will be home all day tomorrow because the archbishop is going to Staines to meet the king. Make your discovery while I am here. You would not recognize the seal, but I would. The day after tomorrow, I will take the seal to Langton."

The archbishop did not for an eye-blink doubt the tale Justin told, but he would not touch the seal. "In heaven's name," he said to Justin, almost whispering although by Justin's request for a private audience they were alone in a small chamber above the main floor, "I am the last man on earth to bring such a thing to King John. Not even a Divine visitation could make him believe I had not first used the thing to do evil. It would be enough, I am sure, to make him repudiate the charter."

"Then what am I to do, my lord?" Justin asked. "It must be returned at once, and to tell the truth, I fear to give it back to the king in private. I was hoping it could be done at the signing—"

"That, I hope, can be arranged." Langton hesitated, then said, "My petition might be refused, but the king will not dare affront the lords who have remained faithful to him. I will write a letter to William Marshal begging him to arrange for you to speak to the king after the signing. As to what you wish to say to King John, you may tell Marshal the whole tale or not as you see fit."

Although they were by no means familiar friends, Justin felt he had come to know the great Earl Marshal well enough during the tense, angry weeks at Oxford to explain his problem in detail. "I will gladly give the seal to you," Justin ended, "if you think that would be best."

William Marshal chuckled. "It would be best for you, that is certain. For me it would be only barely less a disaster than for Archbishop Langton. I am not sure which of us the king hates and distrusts more." He sighed heavily. "However, I will arrange that your name . . . Wait. Will you take a piece of advice, Sir Justin?"

"With a most grateful heart, my lord," Justin said.

"Your wife is not a startlingly beautiful woman, is she?" Marshal asked.

Justin opened his mouth to say yes, and then shook his head, smiling. "Only in my eyes," he said, "as in hers I am the kindest of men."

William Marshal's brows rose. "If that is true, you are a fortunate man despite what your wife discovered—unless you say that to show you think her a fool?"

Justin shook his head again. "Lissa is a clever merchant in her own right. She is no fool."

"Good," Marshal said. "Then let her give the seal to the king and tell him her tale herself. I do not say King John is particularly soft to women—" The men exchanged glances, remembering how the king had locked Lady Braose and her son into a tower chamber and left them to starve to death. The whole nation knew of that. "However," Marshal went on after clearing his throat, "he is less wary of women than of men, believing them weaker. I will, if you agree, put your wife's name on the list of petitioners with yours."

That was how it came about that, on 15 June, Lissa waited with her husband and a group of other petitioners on the field called Runnymede. She, Justin, and the others with varying private petitions were gathered on the east side of the field, apart from the king and his supporters, who had massed on the north, and what looked like the most part of the baronage of England, who filled the field right to the trees on the south.

Lissa was drooping a little with weariness now, and the sun, which had been behind her, was now shining in her eyes and making her close them. For hours and hours men had been shouting at each other across the field, and riding to and fro. She had been shaking with fear when she came, having set out while the stars were still visible to ride the more than twenty miles from London. At her pleading, Justin had stopped at dawn at a wattle and daub church in a nameless village to hear mass. And she had left, again, a rich gift of incense and scented candles—candles made from the wax from Peter's house. The priest, whose rags were little better than those of his pathetic congregation, had run from the church and followed them down the road crying blessings. Lissa had felt better, even though it was very hard for her to believe that scarecrow and the mangled mass he chanted would be acceptable to God, until they had come to the field called Runnymede.

There fear had gripped her when, last of all, the king and his party had ridden onto the field, although she could see as well as anyone that John's party was outnumbered ten to one or more. She had at first been even more frightened when instead of a grand ceremonial beginning, the groups had shouted at each other. Justin had patted her hand and assured her they would be well away if the parties should come to blows, but he did not expect it. And it did not happen. After a time, when it was clear there would be no violence, Justin had dismounted and lifted Lissa down, telling Halsig to lead the horses back under the trees. Several more hours passed; Lissa sat next to Justin on the grass, but she had stopped listening to what they were saying. It seemed much the same, each party accusing the other of identical faults.

Because she had been keeping her eyes closed to avoid the sun's glare, she did not even notice when the arguments ended. There had been several periods of relative silence earlier when documents instead of curses and insults were exchanged. She did not see that a table was being set on the field and draped with a royal crimson cloth embroidered in gold, nor did she see the king—called by those who did not love him a tun on legs—dismount agilely despite his bulk. She opened her eyes with a start when a roar went up so loud that she felt as if it would lift her off the ground and push down the trees around the meadow.

"He has put his seal to it," Justin said, bending to pull her up beside him. He had leapt to his feet, as had almost everyone else who was not already standing, when the king, hearing danger in the louder growls at each demur he made, finally signed and sealed the document. "There are objections still," Justin explained. "More work will be done before it is ready to be copied and sent throughout the country—but most of the country is right here. He has signed it and sealed it. We have our charter!"

So Lissa, who could not call up the same enthusiasm for a public document when she felt herself personally in danger, began to shake again and heard very little of what was called by heralds. She did see several of the group with them depart and approach the table. There she saw richly dressed men, their tunics hung with gold chains, a few behind the king, a few more to his right, and a crowd on the left side. She heard snatches of voices also, but she could not understand any words.

Most of all she watched the king's face with the fixation of terror, but he was too far away for her to make out his expression. All she could see at first was the crown; she knew it was not the great crown because she had heard that described with its rich jewels and its alternating large and small golden leaves. This was only a golden circlet with four rising peaks— but it was daunting enough to her. Finally she was able to look away, but below the crown not much of John's face was clear, only the dark hollows of the eyes, a slash of pink surrounded by mustaches and a short dark beard shaved well away from the cheeks, and along the cheeks hair, still mostly dark, curling to the ears. Then Justin broke her concentration by removing from the leather pouch the packet of blue velvet that now held the seal and handing it to her.

"Must I go alone?" she whispered.

"No, of course not," Justin replied, smiling cheerfully. "Did I not promise to share with you and protect you when we were married? Besides, I would look much more guilty if I tried to hide."

Lissa could not tell whether the amusement he was displaying was genuine or assumed to strengthen her, and before he could say more, their names rang out. Half propelled by Justin's arm at first, Lissa soon pulled away and moved across the field, then through a path between men that opened onto the crimson-covered table. She sank down in a curtsy right to the ground, her head bent, and heard the most beautiful voice, soft and rich to the ears, like brown velvet to the fingers, ask, "Do you desire justice of me? Who has wronged you?"

Lissa felt Justin move from her right side to her left and heard a kind of strangled protest, but she could not spare any attention for that. She had lifted her head, drawn by the rich promise of the king's voice. His dark eyes were turned down to her. No promise was in his face; the eyes were glazed and unseeing, the full, sensual lips were slack, the corners drooping with fatigue and despair.

"None has wronged me, Sire," Lissa got out. "I have come to return something that is yours."

"What?" The voice was still beautiful, but it sounded different, brighter, with a sharp note of curiosity. "Stand up, woman. What is your name? What do you mean?"

Since her name had just been called aloud, Lissa knew that the king had not been listening. She rose, feeling a spurt of sympathy for the man; certainly he was as weary as she and might be as bored. Then she remembered the host of those against him and wondered if King John might not be as frightened as she also. No doubt he deserved it—Justin said so—but that spark of common feeling made it easier to speak to him.

"My name is Heloise FitzAilwin, Sire. More to the point, I am the widow of Peter de Flael, the goldsmith who, at your order, made your privy seal." She laid the blue velvet on the table and began to unfold it. While she opened the cloth, which the king watched her do with alert interest, she told of Peter's death and how his house had been searched and destroyed and then about her decision to have the house repaired and how she took the wax home to make candles. "I found this"—she moved the velvet, now exposing the wax-clotted cloth that held the seal, across the table to the king—"in one of the blocks that I broke up for easier melting."

The king unwrapped the small package and stared at the seal within it. He turned it over, then back, then laid it down. He did not speak.

"I did not touch it." Lissa's voice trembled. "I did not know what it was, only that something hidden in that way must be precious. My second husband recognized it as your seal, Sire." She was shaking again and could say no more.

"You have done well, Mistress Heloise," the rich voice intoned. "What would you have as a reward?"

"Only your mercy and your favor, Sire," Lissa whispered. "I am afraid."

"Peter de Flael would have died for this violation of my trust, but you have done no harm and need have no fear of me. You are free to go, with my thanks."

Lissa backed a step and stumbled, but a strong arm was around her, steadying her, leading her away. There were voices, other sounds, none of which made sense to her. She could hardly see or hear until she found herself sitting on the ground well back from the field, near the trees, with Justin kneeling beside her, pressing a cup of wine into her hands and urging her to drink. She sipped at it slowly, and after a while her heart stopped pounding.

"Are we safe, do you think?" she asked him.

"Oh yes," he said. "He will be too busy for a time to think about this matter, and if he inquires about us he will learn that I am Henry FitzAilwin's nephew. My uncle was a favorite with the king and always loyal. He may change his seal—I would myself—but he will hold no grudge against us."

"And FitzWalter?" she asked.

Justin began to answer but stopped as a shadow fell across them. Both looked up to see Robert FitzWalter, as if Lissa's saying his name had conjured him there. Justin got to his feet, interposing his body between Lord Robert and Lissa, and she scrambled to her feet also.

"Snakes," Lord Robert said. "All women are sly as snakes." He was not looking at Lissa but at Justin. "She fooled me completely. I would have pledged my life that she did not know where that thing was."

"I did not know," Lissa said, coming to Justin's side. "*You* told me where to look. The seal was indeed my bride price, and I have given it away to buy peace instead of melting it and using the gold. Now you know where it is and you need ask me no more questions."

FitzWalter's eyes flicked to her and back to Justin as if she no longer existed. "You have kept your word, Sir Justin," he said, suddenly thrusting out his hand, which Justin took with a rather bemused expression. "I cannot say that I am pleased to have lost such a prize, but I will have what I want anyway, and no shadow of blame can ever attach to me over this matter now. We are quits."

"I am glad, my lord," Justin said. "We are like to be near neighbors for no little time, and I prefer your liking to your hatred."

"You have that and my trust as well," FitzWalter said. "So much so that I will ask you, as a favor to me, to accept when the mayor offers you the command of the watch again." He tightened his grip on Justin's wrist, then released it and walked away.

Lissa stared after him, not knowing whether to burst with rage or sigh with relief. When she turned her eyes to her husband instead, she saw the blank, icy stare that betokened a dangerous suspicion. She bit her lips to hold back sobs.

"What does he mean?" she asked. "Why are you so wary? Is it some kind of trap?"

"Not for me," Justin said, putting his arm around her. "Lord Robert was sure that we were bringing a complaint against him when you went before King John. I had to push him away by force from thrusting himself between you and the king. Had he interrupted you, his knowledge of the seal would have been betrayed to the king. Because you did not complain of his abduction and he now sees my action as saving him—you will have noticed that no pardons were given today—he thinks I wish to be his friend."

"And me?" Lissa asked.

Justin laughed. "You are not worth consideration, my love, but he will leave you in peace, I am sure." He shrugged. "I do not know what explanation he has given himself for my coming to Baynard's Castle to release you—my pride and honor in possession, I suppose. I am sorry for him; he knows nothing of love."

"Then what troubles you?" Lissa asked, still anxious.

"Nothing to do with us, dear heart. Come, let me put you on your horse. My poor dearling, you are so tired and we have so far to go. Shall I hold you before me, beloved?"

"Not for twenty miles, Justin," she said, finding a smile for him.

When they were mounted and on the road, she said, "You never answered me, Justin. I know when you are worried, and I would rather have one thing to fear than be afraid of everything."

He sighed. "I do not think there is much for us to fear. I am not so much worried as, despite my own better knowledge, disappointed. You remember I told you neither the king nor the real rebels would be content with the charter. Fool that I am, I hoped I could be wrong—but I was not. You heard FitzWalter say he would have his way anyway, and he sounded so sure. That means the plans for war are already made. The proof of it is that he *knows* the army left in London will not be large enough to hold the walls and to serve as watch also."

Lissa was far too weary to care about a war some time in the future, a war that Justin did not seem to think would strike at London. She said no more, saving her strength for staying on her mare at the brisk pace Justin set. The rapid gait had the double advantage of occupying her mind and getting them to the city before full dark. Reaction set in fully the moment she was able to sink into her chair, and though she tried to eat the meal Oliva carried up, she was too tired and fell asleep in the chair, Justin told her later, with a cup of wine in her hand. Fortunately, he had been able to grab it before much spilled and stained the rug.

She woke very suddenly when Justin kissed her forehead and said, "Dearling, let me help you undress. You will be uncomfortable if you sleep all night in your gown."

But when she was naked and cuddled against her husband's strong body, she could not sleep again and a new aspect of FitzWalter's offer troubled her. "If the barons still rule London, will it be safe for you to hold the office the mayor offers?"

Justin squeezed her gently and drew a deep, satisfied breath. Lissa realized he had been thinking long and hard about his brief talk with FitzWalter. "Yes," he said. "I take office from the mayor, not from the barons. No greater crime may be held against me than against the mayor for accepting his office. If the war goes ill for the barons, they might at any time call away their troops, leaving London naked if someone does not see to the defense. Yes, I will take my office back, and gladly, if it is offered."

Lissa heard the deep pleasure in his voice. She would have much preferred if he could have been content to expand his work as a merchant, but she loved him enough to smile and be glad for his sake. And because he was happy it seemed a good time to answer a question he had never asked but that she knew must be troubling him, for they had been lovers a long time with seeming no result.

"Well," she said, "I must admit that I am especially eager to be sure the city will be quiet and safe in the future."

"Because of FitzWalter?" He pulled her even closer. "You need not fear him, beloved, I swear it."

"Not FitzWalter especially," Lissa said, smiling. "I am only more cautious in general just now. And I wish to warn you that you now have two to care for."

"What two?" Justin asked, looking around the bedchamber as if he expected a new dependent to pop out of the wall.

Lissa laughed aloud. "I am with child, you silly man," she said, and took him by the ears to pull his head around to kiss.

AUTHOR'S NOTE

I feel it necessary to note two historical discrepancies in this work; one was deliberate and the other was very minor and could not be resolved without more extensive research than it was worth. The minor problem was the name of the mayor of London from 1213 to 1215. One source gives this as Roger FitzAdam, another gives the name as Roger FitzAlan. To minimize the danger of confusion with the surname of several characters, FitzAilwin, I chose to use FitzAdam.

The deliberate discrepancy is my use of the word "alderman" for the important officials who helped the mayor govern London. At the beginning of the thirteenth century, at the time this book is set, the authority of the aldermen had been superseded by a group of twenty-four "substantial" citizens called echevins. The word "alderman" is Anglo-Saxon; "echevin" is French. There had been considerable unrest and many claims of corruption in the government of the city at the end of the twelfth and the beginning of the thirteenth century, and it is possible the word "echevin" replaced the word "alderman" when mayors began to be elected annually to remove the taint of that corruption from those who advised the mayor.

Certainly the echevins were advisors to the mayor; however, whether they held all the same responsibilities as the aldermen I have been unable to determine exactly. For the purpose of a work of fiction the distinction—if there was one—did not seem important to me, particularly since the term "alderman" was back in use before the end of the century. It is even possible that the word "alderman" had never fallen out of use with those important citizens whose native tongue was English, even though "echevin" was used in official records. In any case, I decided to use the more common word "alderman" in this book.

I wish I could have done a more thorough job in describing the Hanseatic League, which was an association of North German trading towns, but a novel is not the place for a study of this fascinating organization. Naturally the trading ventures of the Hanse spread all over Europe and the Middle East, but I have ignored that aspect entirely, except for a bare mention of the voyages of my heroine's uncles.

With respect to the relations of the Hanse to England, Germanic merchants known as Easterlings had traded with English counterparts during the Saxon period. A formal guild, The House or Gild of the Merchants of Almaines (also called The House of Teutonics), was formed in 1169. The guild flourished and was given many special privileges by the Crown, including the right of total independence within the physical area of its central headquarters. This area did not actually come to be known as the Steelyard until the first quarter of the fourteenth century, but I have used the name for the sake of convenience.

English merchants always resented the privileges granted the Hanse. As English merchants grew richer and more powerful, they were able to hold their own in trade. Violent confrontations occurred and strong protests were lodged with the government until the Hanse was forced to withdraw from England during the reign of Elizabeth I. For those interested, there are many excellent books on the organization.

The development of the guilds (or gilds) is another fascinating topic that could not be dealt with adequately. These organizations, which began before the Conquest as social and religious groups for the support and protection of members—for example, a guild would provide burial for a brother or sister and prayers for the soul of the deceased (a rather primitive insurance society)—had, by the thirteenth century, become the nucleus of town government.

Perhaps because of the initial purpose and because that purpose remained of primary importance for centuries—a guild looked after any member who had fallen upon hard times, it provided care for sick members, buried the dead, and supported widows and orphans—guild membership was *not* denied to women. Nor were the earliest guilds craft-connected or divided into hierarchies. Any honest tradesperson who could pay the initiation fee and perform the duties (which were nearly all religious or pecuniary in nature) was readily accepted as a member.

As society became more complex, so did the guilds, which separated into distinct craft-associated groups—the weavers, fishmongers, and bakers were among the earliest in London. The king's (or his bureaucracy's) notice was drawn to the associations. For a fee, the guilds were issued a royal charter guaranteeing them certain rights and privileges, like holding a court to settle differences between members or complaints against a member. Later it was found more profitable to fine uncharted guilds for existing without a charter. But when London won its own charter and the right to elect its mayor annually and govern itself through its own commune, the guilds were chartered by the city and were part of the mechanism of governing it.

Concurrently with the increase in public responsibility there was an increase in prejudice against female guild masters, which culminated by the middle of the fourteenth century in rules that deprived females of the right to guild membership (except in the very few guilds that were all female). The medieval reasons were as specious as those that restrict women "for their own good" today. I cannot understand why it is good and patriotic for a man to shoot and be shot in defense of his country but evil for a woman (modern weapons no longer being too large or heavy for most women to use). No reason I have ever heard makes any better sense than the medieval notion that a woman could not perform the religious duties of a guild because she was basically evil by nature. However, in medieval times, as now, women were their own worst enemies; they found it easier to hire male substitutes than to fight the guild prejudice against them until that prejudice became hallowed by time and custom into written rules.

Henry FitzAilwin was the historical mayor of London from 1191 until his death in 1212, and three sons, named Alan, Richard, and Thomas survived him. Sir Justin FitzAilwin, however, is fictional as is the "official" position he holds. My description of the watch was as close as I could come to reality from the sketchy references I found to its duties in the late twelfth and early thirteenth century.

Henry B. Wheatley in *The Story of London* (in the Medieval Cities series) says "The watch and ward arranged for the protection of the city was efficient enough in quiet times, but when the inhabitants were troublesome it was quite insufficient. The regulations were strict, but the streets were crowded, as more than half of them were used as market-places, and every moment occasions for quarrelling arose, of which the young bloods were only too ready to avail themselves.

". . . Night-walkers (male and female) were very summarily treated, but they must have been mostly connected with the dangerous classes, for we read of notorious persons with swords and bucklers and frequenters of taverns after curfew, 'contrary to peace and statutes.' We may presume that quiet, inoffensive persons, who were known to be law-abiding citizens were not necessarily hauled up for being in the streets after regulation hours."

Finally, for those who wish to ask questions (which I will try, but not promise, to answer), comment (which interests me whether or not I agree), criticize (for which I am grateful, even when I regret the error), or offer compliments (which I enjoy enormously, being all too human), my mailing address is

Roberta Gellis
Box 483
Roslyn Heights, NY 11577